WILLIAM CORDER.

As he appeared in Bury Gaol a few days previous to his Trial.

THE RED BARN,

A TALE,

FOUNDED ON FACT.

We see the ground whereon these woes do lie;
But the true cause————,———— ——— ———
We cannot, without circumstance, descry.

SHAKSPEARE.

LONDON:

PRINTED FOR KNIGHT AND LACEY,
55, PATERNOSTER ROW,
AND SOLD BY ALL BOOKSELLERS.

1828.

PREFACE.

THE following Tale is founded on a fact, so recently and so notoriously known to the public, that it is unnecessary to do more in this place than merely to allude to it; but, as works, made up of fact and fiction, are generally most approved when " Time's good mouldiness hath hallowed " the latter quality, objections may be raised against the practice of plucking the green romance from life and masking it with fiction. It may not be unnecessary, therefore, to reply to them.

Yet these objections must be so frivolous, that they scarcely require an answer. We suppose it must be granted that mere amusement is not the sole end of novel writing—that one great object of the novelist is to convey lessons of morality. If so, life in all its bearings is his province; and he may take, we think, with greater moral effect, those circumstances which pass before his eyes every day, than those which from remoteness must lose much of their vividity: the novelist may in such clearly set forth the gradations of folly, of vice, of reckless imprudence, or ungoverned passion. In this view, the circumstance on which our Tale is founded, is as legitimate a basis for a novel as any other; and the fact of its having been the subject of legal investigation and punishment can make no sort of difference in the case.

If authority be required, to second argument on this point, the highest is not wanting:—to say nothing of a host of dramatists and novelists, who have employed similar foundations for their works, we shall only mention the name of Sir Walter Scott. In some of the most interesting and affecting of his earlier productions, his plots entirely turn on cases of this kind; and one of the best stories in his last work, "The Tales of the Canongate," is that of a murderer at whose trial he was himself present:—we mean the tale of "*The Two Drovers.*" But even his high authority is not necessary to sanction what is supported by every principle of reason and common sense.

The only reply we can give to those who talk of the compromise of feelings, and the excitement of prejudice, is, "*Read our book.*" With the exception of the criminal, his victim, his crime, and those who are not within the range of painful allusion, the characters and adventures in this Novel are purely imaginary. Real names are never mentioned, except where no possible harm can result from mentioning them; and actual facts have been studiously disregarded, excepting where they were absolutely necessary to the developement of the plot.

In short, the author of the "RED BARN" is desirous that his work should not be con-

sidered as a history of individuals, or a mere
tale of horror; but what it really is—a fiction,
founded on fact, for the purpose of exhibiting
the fatal consequences of the loose principles
and dissolute habits too frequently contracted
by the young and thoughtless in this great
metropolis.

THE RED BARN.

CHAPTER I.

"Dear lovely bowers of innocence and ease!—
  Scenes of my youth, when ev'ry sport could please,—
  How often I have loitered o'er thy green,
  Where humble happiness endear'd each scene!
  How often have I paused on every charm,—
  The shelter'd cot—the cultivated farm—
  The never failing brook—the busy mill—
  The decent church that topp'd the neighbouring hill—
  The hawthorn bush, with seats beneath the shade,
  For talking age and whispering lovers made!"
GOLDSMITH.

THE place in which arose the most important events of the tale we are about to relate, is situated in Suffolk: it is one of those small but neat villages, which so frequently present themselves to the eye of the traveller in the eastern parts of this kingdom. Like most of the towns in Suffolk and Essex, it has an air of rustic antiquity about it, which produces pleasing associations of simplicity and peace in the mind of a lover of the picturesque. The latticed windows glistening beneath the brown thatch—the walls white, and squared throughout with old oak—the honeysuckle and the climbing rose tree, wandering over them in graceful clusters—the wicket of short sticks—the little garden, and the bowering branches,—are all calculated to produce pleasing sensations of tranquillity, repose, and comfort. Long may the genius of modern improvement, with its squares and parallelograms, and all its other insipid and tasteless regularities, spare these interesting relics of ancient English rural simplicity, and not convert, as it bids fair to do at last, our entire island into a vast London with its modern improvements!   Our elegant edifices of bricks and mortar—our regular and open streets—our houses, like a company of soldiers, all in uniform order, dressed in rank after one model,— are, doubtless, very fine things in their way, and very convenient; but they are not adapted to please the imagination, nor to cheer the heart. In utterly banishing country scenery, we deprive ourselves of a source not only of pleasing images to the mind, but also of the best moral affections. In substituting art for nature, even in externals, we ourselves insensibly become cold and artificial beings. A great city—its splendid buildings, the abode of pride and of luxury, on the one hand, and the striking contrast of its narrow lanes, confined courts, and wretched hovels, the refuge of profligacy, misery, and vice, on the other—is not one of the best possible schools of moral feeling, even in its exterior aspect: but the country—the view of nature—even in its least pleasing forms, harmonizes the soul, and produces a disposition to virtue.

" Can man refuse to join the general smile
Of nature? Can fierce passions vex his breast,
When every gale is peace, and every grove
Is melody ?"

No! and it is therefore we find in general so marked a contrast between the inhabitants of towns, and those of the country, and so decided a balance in the favour of the latter.

The village of Polstead, with its surrounding scenery, is a sweet relief from the sameness of the busy towns; a retired and delightful spot, breathing the true freshness of rusticity. The inhabitants are laborious, but there are no vestiges of want about them : if money be scarce among them, their necessities are but few; their industry produces competence, and perhaps, in possessing that, the inhabitants of Polstead may account themselves truly rich.

The scenery all around bears the general character of Suffolk scenery, and has few attractions for those who make *tours* in search of the bold and sublime. It has nothing of the gigantic features of primitive nature, such as we behold it in the northern parts of Scotland and Wales, or in the Alpine regions of Switzerland—none of that diversity, which ever and anon astonishes us by some unexpected spectacle. The traveller is not surprised and terrified by immense rocks, which appear to hang in ruins over his head ; nor inundated by the sparkling mists which are scattered from lofty and resounding waterfalls : not suddenly stopped at the edge of a precipice, by the view of an abyss formed by an everlasting torrent below, on the depths of which he scarcely dares to look down; nor does he suddenly escape from such astounding scenes, to lose himself in the obscurity of a tufted wood, or the labyrinths of some verdant but uncultivated wilderness.   There is nothing of all this; but there is what the lover of English scenery would delight in :—the hill and vale, picturesquely spread with fertile fields and luxuriant foliage —the rippling stream, by-road, and green lane —the farm-house and the cottage—the pointed spire, peering up from the thick bowers of beech and elm—of flowing horse-chesnut, larch, and sycamore;—while the tinkling bell of the flocks, the whistle of the passing peasant boy, and the song of the lark above, shall there be found to give life to the scene.

The village, when we saw it, contained about twenty houses which clustered together on the gentle slope of a hill, the top of which spread into a pleasant green, on which was situated a neat public house (the only one in the village) ; and here the neighbours occasionally met at fair or dance,—the old to chat of days gone by, the young for purposes more congenial to their years.   At the bottom the hill was a bright sheet of water, at one side of which passed the road; and rising from the other side, the pathway to the village church and church yard,—the walls and grave-stones of which latter mentioned, could be seen by the passenger through wide-spreading and majestic trees: waving over the water, were several willows; and the road, winding out from a thick grove at one side, passed down into a hollow covered with branches, and at the depth of which were to be seen two or three cottages, from which ascended their chimney-smoke to be lost in the clear air.

The cottage in which dwelt the heroine of our story, was situated about a quarter of a mile from the church of Polstead, on the side of a by-road which diverged from the foot of the village: a small low wicket shut it out from the pathway, over which could be seen a green plat before the door, where the inmates of the dwelling occasionally reclined. The roof was thatched; and beneath the eaves, above the door, hung a long ladder, partly covered by the branches of climbing rose-trees which clung to the wall: the gable end half fronted the road, and displayed a neat latticed window which looked out over a garden, hedged in, and bearing several well-grown apple-trees. A number of tall elms stood at the front of the cottage, and a vegetable garden (also in front) ran alongside the road about a dozen perches.

The inside of this cottage corresponded with the

outside. There were but four small rooms,—a parlour, a kitchen, and two bed-rooms. The parlour exhibited "the nicely sanded floor," the polished oak table and white deal chairs, and the few engravings on the walls from biblical subjects, more remarkable for their antiquity than the excellence of their execution. On the table was the family library, consisting of a large Bible and Prayer-book, an old book of cookery, and "THE CHILDREN OF THE ABBEY," which appeared to have felt a few thumbs in the course of its existence: in the kitchen, there was the well-scrubbed dresser, and the usual set out of shining pots and pans. You could see, from the outside, the neat white curtains of the bed-room windows; a honeysuckle growing up on the outside of one, which diffused its perfume into the apartment, and a white rose tree on that of the other.

This cottage had been, for more than twenty years, the peaceful abode of John Martin and his wife Mary. John was not much above the situation of a labouring peasant, but, by his industry and frugality, had contrived to keep himself in a state considerably above want. He lived by the labour of his hands, and was in the employ of a neighbouring farmer. He turned the little produce of his garden and his poultry yard to some advantage; and he could say,—what many who cut a more splendid figure on the theatre of life cannot affirm with truth,—that, though poor, he was out of debt, and independent. His wife was like himself, simple, industrious, and faithful: neither had any ambition beyond their humble lot; and, without having ever heard the name of philosophy, they were more contented than philosophers, and far happier than kings. While John attended his business abroad, his wife took care of the household at home. They rose at the first dawn of morning cheerfully to their respective labours; and lay down at night to that undisturbed repose, which exercise, temperance, and innocence invariably ensure.

John and his wife were blessed with an only daughter, who seemed, in all respects, calculated to complete their happiness—if, indeed, any state of life, however humble, can ensure this fleeting blessing. At the period when our story commences, Maria Martin had just entered her eighteenth year: she was rather under the middle stature of woman, but her figure was symmetry itself. Her features would, perhaps, by a connoisseur, be pronounced not strictly regular; but their amiable expression, added to a blooming complexion, a pair of brilliant sparkling eyes, and a profusion of shining brown tresses, constituted her a perfect village beauty: indeed, we may say that they would have constituted her a very attractive beauty in any sphere of life. Maria's education was rather superior to that of girls of her class in general; for the father, who was dotingly fond to keep her for a few years at a genteel school. We do not mean to say that her accomplishments were of a very high order, or that she could have acquired any such at the seminary in question: they were limited to the usual smattering acquirements of such sources of education. She gained, indeed, a very decided taste for the perusal of novels and romances,—one of the few branches of female education, that is generally most completely and successfully communicated, and most frequently kept up when every other thing is neglected.

Maria's disposition was kind, but volatile; she had all the gaiety and thoughtlessness that belong to youth and innocence; all her feelings and propensities were on the side of virtue, by nature rather than by precept,—she was virtuously inclined, from good taste and an utter ignorance of vice. Though lively and thoughtless, she was devotedly affectionate to her parents, and kind and compassionate to all. The appearance of distress would quickly melt her into tears, though her face, the instant before, had been lighted up with smiles. The effect, however, was evanescent; and, like as in an April day, the sunshine rapidly succeeded to the shower.

Of love, Maria had read much, but knew nothing. There lived, in her neighbourhood, a young man, the son of a small farmer, who, for some years, had cherished a most pure and devoted affection for her. They had known each other from children Harry Everton (this was the young man's name, having been a constant inmate at her father's from a boy. Harry was now turned of twenty years of age; his person was good; his physiognomy agreeable; and though, of course, he had no pretensions to superior refinement, his manners were neither vulgar, nor his mind wholy uninformed His demeanour was mild, modest, and sensible; and his understanding was extremely good: but what particularly distinguished Harry, was the amiable susceptibility of his heart, and the singleness and sincerity of all his feelings. He nursed in secret the most fervent attatchment to Maria; yet was he too diffident of his own merits to declare himself openly as her lover; but it appeared in his every look and action. The tone of his voice when he addressed her, the expression of his countenance, his very gesture, were intelligible enough to all observers, except the object of his passion: she, indeed, treated Harry with all the familiarity of old acquaintance, and the affection of friendship;—she looked on him more in the light of a brother than anything else, and never dreamed for an instant that they could stand in any dearer relation to each other. Their dispositions, too, were very different: Harry was serious and thoughtful; Maria, at this time, lively, fickle, and inconsiderate. She was fond of occasionally teasing his good nature in an innocent way, and of apparently undervaluing his best intentions: -her

2

volatile nature seemed incapable of feeling or understanding the passion of love. Harry had too much discrimination not to perceive the little impression he had made upon her heart, and too much sensibility not very severely to feel it: but he trusted his hopes to time and assiduity, and consoled himself with the idea that, if she did not love him, she loved nobody else; and that, at all events, her feelings towards him were favourable, though not precisely of the kind that he could have wished.

Indeed, the fact was, that Maria loved Harry better than any one—her parents excepted: his company was always agreeable to her. Her father was fond of Harry's society, and liked to have him as an evening guest at his cottage. He generally used to spend his winter nights there, and amuse the old folks by reading to them some interesting story or other; for Harry, though very plainly educated, was fond of reading, and did not read badly. Maria generally felt a sort of blank when Harry did not make one of their fire-side party: and in the summer, he usually accompanied her in her walks; when they partook together of such rural amusements as birds'-nesting, nutting, strawberry-gathering, &c. Though Harry, as I have said, made no formal declaration of his love, nor any proposal to her father, yet the neighbours were generally of opinion that it would be a match; and the young people were said, in the phrase usual in such classes, to keep each other company. The old folks, too, looked on this with a favourable eye; so Harry was, in all respects, a very suitable person for a husband to their daughter. His father was comparatively well to do in the world; as he farmed, at a moderate rent, about thirty acres of very productive land; and was generally considered, from his skill and industry, to have saved some money. Harry was his only son, understood the farming business well, and would, no doubt, succeed his father in all his possessions: they, therefore, encouraged his attentions to Maria; indeed, the mother sometimes evinced a little impatience on this score, and would say to her husband, "I wish, Jack, that Harry Everton would ask our Maria in marriage; why don't you speak to him about it?" But her husband, who had good sense and a little pride, would say, "My dear, let the young folks alone; all in good time; they are going on very well:—when Harry has made up his mind, and knows Maria's, he will not be backward I dare say; but it is not my place to speak first."

Matters were in this sort of train, when an incident took place, apparently trifling, but which exercised a decided influence on the destiny of Maria, and determined in some measure the colour of her future life. She was sitting, on a fine day in Midsummer, at the cottage door, employed in needlework, when a woman of a very peculiar appearance, rather meanly but singularly dressed, entered the yard : she might have been above seven or eight and twenty years of age ; her complexion and eyes were very dark ; her features regular, handsome, and slightly prominent : she was above the middle size ; her figure very good, and rather inclining to fullness. She wore a brown stuff gown, which, though of coarse materials, was made and put on with an evident attention to setting off the fine contour of her waist and bosom. A very short, old, black silk mantle was carelessly tied round her neck, and hung over one shoulder. Round her head was bound a red cotton handkerchief, not ungracefully, which suffered some tresses of her raven hair to escape on each side. The shortness of her petticoats displayed a well turned leg and ankle, and her small foot was set off by a shoe with a very low instep. Her arms, which were quite bare from the elbow, though not very white, were beautifully rounded ; and her fingers were covered with brass rings.

"Fair maid," said she, accosting Maria with a peculiarly expressive smile, "I am dying of thirst ; may I beg a little water?"

Her voice, as she spoke, Maria thought, was the softest and most musical she had ever heard ; yet there was an expression in her dark eye, that harmonized but little with the softness of her voice and sweetness of her smile : it was a look of the most searching penetration—of the most painful scrutiny, not unmingled with the appearance of design.

The Fortuneteller's first interview with

There is something in the expression of the human countenance that strikes the simplest persons: children, and even animals, are physiognomists in this way. Maria seemed evidently struck with the glance we have described, and looked for a moment at the woman without replying: the latter, perceiving this, instantly changed the expression of her looks, and, with an air of simplicity and languor, resumed,—"I have walked twenty miles to-day, in the hot sun —I am very tired and thirsty;—do, my dear child, let me have a little water."

Maria, whose feelings of compassion were easily excited, sprang up, and saying, "Sit down on this bench—you shall have something better than water," ran into the house, and fetched out a large bowl of milk and some nice home-baked bread. "Come," said she, "I give you the best we have got at present. My father is abroad at work; and my mother is gone to Polstead, and has taken her keys, or I should have given you some cold meat."

"Heaven bless you" replied the woman, "I desire nothing better than this."

Having refreshed herself, she continued;— "Pray, my dear," said she, "were you born here?"

Maria answered in the affirmative.

"I wonder at that!" replied the woman; "And brought up here always?"

"Yes," said Maria; "with the exception of

two years that I was at school in Colchester:
—but why do you ask?"

"Because," said the woman, "you neither look
nor speak like one bred in the country: I should
have thought you had been, at least, educated in
London."

"I never was there in my life," said Maria.

"More is the pity; but all in good time:—you
were never formed to pass your life in an obscure
spot like this. You have only to be seen, to be
admired and loved. Oh! there's many a gentleman, who holds his head high enough, that would
be glad to throw himself at your feet."

Maria, to whom, from her experience in novels,
this sort of language was by no means unintelligible, and whose vanity began to be tickled,
replied, laughing, " Oh, you flatter; I am nothing
but a simple country girl: no gentleman would
think of me."

The other, assuming a more serious look and
tone of voice, said, "You mistake; I can see
more in you, than you can see in yourself: I can
tell you that there are many gentlemen would be
proud to have you for a wife. I can tell you, too,
that the time is not far distant, when you shall
remember the words of *Hannah Woods*.

"Good God!" exclaimed Maria, "how can
you tell all this?"

"My dear," returned the siren, "I shall be plain
with you; you have treated me with kindness, and
I shall make you a return. Don't think it is not

in my power: look at me; I am poor, ill-dressed, and a woman; but I have a gift that riches cannot buy. I can see into the future; and, if you will, I can teach you your destiny."

Maria, like other girls, had heard and read a great deal about fortune-tellers, and fully believed in their skill: but to see one face to face was a novelty, and inspired her with some degree of fear. She looked undetermined, and was silent.

"You will not, then, accept my offer," rejoined the Sybil, with one of her enchanting smiles; "it is disinterested, and I have nothing but good to tell you."

Curiosity, and an undefinable mixture of vanity, ambition, and hope, prevailed over her apprehension; and Maria assented.

"Are you certain," said the fortune-teller, lowering her voice, "that we are alone? Is no one within hearing?"

"None," replied Maria.

"Then show me your hand," said the woman: "by your face I already know much; but I must see your hand."—Maria did so.

"What a delicate hand!" exclaimed the prophetess; "this hand was never made to be given to a peasant or a clown.—Ah! I thought so;—here are the lines of fortunate marriage, riches, children, and long life—no, not very long,—but long enough—" She paused.

"But," said Maria, whose curiosity began to

be thoroughly whetted, " can you tell me nothing more particular ?"

" Yes :—beneath this pretty breast you shall wear a gold watch : these white fingers shall be covered with rich rings ; and this fine hair be braided with brilliants."

" But," said Maria, " may I not know the name, or at least the condition, of my future lover ?"

" Ah !" said the fortune-teller, with a smile full of meaning, " how curious you are grown all of a sudden :—at first you hesitated to hear me at all ; now you want to know everything. Well ! I can tell you more ; but your own hand is not sufficient ; mine must be crossed with a piece of silver :—this is a form we cannot dispense with."

Maria immediately performed this operation, and the other continued ;

" Now I can tell you all I know :—in a word, your future husband is young, handsome, and rich. Moreover, you shall see him at the fair of Polstead next week. Be sure to go there. He will be mounted on a grey horse, and wear a white hat ; you will know him directly—there will be none like him at the fair. He will take a proper opportunity of speaking to you—don't treat him with shyness, or refuse to hear him : mark my words—your fortune depends upon it—you were born for great things, and you must act accordingly. Farewell : —remember the fair ;—above all, be secret."

So saying, she arose, waved her hand to Maria, and was out of sight in an instant.

CHAP II.

"Close to mine ear one call'd me forth to walk,
With gentle voice; I thought it thine: It said,
'Why sleep'st thou, Eve?'"

MILTON.

IT is easy to conceive the nature of the impression produced on Maria's mind by the interview described in the last chapter. Young, simple, and of course totally ignorant of the world—her head filled with the marvellous tales of novels and romances, where girls of low degree, by the power of their personal charms, become the wives of men of rank and fortune—and quite vain enough to suppose her own fully adequate to any conquest of the kind,—she could think of nothing but the prediction of the fortune-teller, in whose prophetic power she implicitly believed.

"So, then," said she to herself, "I am really to be a lady after all;—how delightful! How elegantly I shall dress! and go to balls and parties of all kinds. Well! I have often read of these

3

things, and wished to see them and be among them :—I can dance pretty well; but then, when I have plenty of money, I can learn to dance in the best style. Well! I wonder what kind of man he is :—but she says, young and handsome. I forgot to ask whether he was dark or fair ;—I hope he is dark—I like dark men;—I hope he is not short:—but he is rich and a gentleman—that's good. After all, perhaps, he may not like me." (On this she goes to the glass, to adjust her curls.) "Well! I wish the fair was come—I wish it was over. I am half afraid to go :—then to speak to a strange gentleman! Lord, I cannot do it;—but then I must—it is my fortune. After all, if I should not see him!—but he is sure to be there. —well! my heart beats at the thoughts of it."

Thus she ran on in her girlish way, agitated by fear, hope, and anxiety;—at one time building castles in the air, and painting scenes of future splendour and felicity,—at another, affected by misgivings that all was not right, that she might be acting wrong in going to the fair, and that the consequences might be unfortunate. Ill-fated girl! could she have really looked into the future, she would have seen it in far gloomier colours than the worst apprehensions of her fancy were at this time capable of pourtraying!

The return of her father and mother was not calculated to allay her anxious feelings. This was the first time in her life that she felt that she had any secret to keep from them: her nature was frank and open—she never had a thought before that should be concealed; disguise, there-fore, sat ill upon her: she felt that she could not reveal this affair to her parents—she had a dis-tracted, absent air—she answered questions that were put to her, quite at random—did several of the simplest things quite wrongly—when sent out of the room for something, forgot what it was, and returned without it—laughed immoderately with-out any apparent cause, and when asked the reason, felt ready to cry, she knew not wherefore.

Strange to say, all this excited no suspicion in the minds of the good old folks. Quickness of perception is not the *forte* of the English peasant He must be told everything broadly and roundly or he will not understand it. Hints and symp toms are quite thrown away upon him. To be sure, we must remark, that whims and inconsistencies of manner were by no means uncommon with Maria. The old people were accustomed to this, and notwithstanding the extreme of the present case, they did not set it down as anything very extraordinary. ·

But there was another person to be a witness of the conduct of Maria, who was a little more discriminating. Harry Everton soon made his appearance, to pay his usual evening visit; and the eye of a lover was too penetrating, not to see at once the alteration in the manners of Maria. We have already said, that Maria always regarded Harry, as far as love was concerned, with indifference. But the moment she saw him now, something like a feeling of aversion, almost unconsciously to herself, sprung up in her mind. If she had ever suspected before that Harry loved her, she never gave the thought any serious entertainment. But now it suggested itself to her mind, and produced nothing but a feeling very closely allied to disgust. For the first time in her life, she regarded his company as a disagreeable intrusion.

" It is a fine evening, Maria," said Harry, as he entered the cottage; " are you inclined for a walk?"

" No! Harry," said she; " I am tired."

" Oh, then you have been out to-day!"

" No! I have not."

" How, then, can you be tired?"

" Why! can't a person be tired without walking out? I tell you I am tired, that's enough."

" There's Sally Hodgson and her brother, and Tom Morgan and his two sisters, gone a nutting this evening in Squire Colson's wood ; I thought you might like to go too."

" No! I don't like it; I don't like nutting."

" Oh! Maria, how can you say that? you know you are very fond of it."

" I tell you I am not fond of it, and I won't go."

" Well, Maria, there's no more to be said about Of course you have a right to please yourself. Shall I read to you?"

" No ! I have got a head-ache; I can't listen to ou."

"Maria," said her father, interposing, "this is all nonsense :—I say, Harry, finish that story you began last night; I like to hear you."

Harry began reading, and Maria got up and left the room. Her mother followed, and pressed her to return ; but she pretended illness, and went to bed. The youth soon took his leave, in a state of the greatest dejection.

As he went home he was puzzling himself to think what could be the reason of Maria's very altered manner. " It is not illness," said he; " for she was looking as well as usual." His mind was filled with a thousand vague fears, jealousies, and suspicions. His way lay through a lonely and woody valley, beyond which was his father's farm. On entering this he began again to soliloquize thus. " She never loved me," said he; " that I always knew. But never until this night did she treat me with dislike. It must be so. She has seen some one she likes better Yes !" continued he, raising his voice ; " she loves another, and she will never be mine : I shall never be happy,—never, never !"

The last word "never !" was immediately repeated in a deep and hollow tone. Harry started with momentary astonishment, and for an instant, —so absorbed had been all his faculties,—forgot that the place in which he stood was distinguished by a very remarkable echo. But in the mood in which he then was, this trifling incident heightened his melancholy. " Ah !" said he again, " it is too true; the Echo is a true prophet: she will never be mine—never!" and again the word "never" reverberated, in the same mournful tone in which it was spoken, through the lonely vale.

Very different reflections occupied the mind of Maria that night, and very different feelings agitated her bosom. Whatever scruples she might at first have felt about what she intended to do, were soon silenced by her vanity and the liveliness of her fancy, which dressed up the future in such brilliant colours. She remained awake the whole night, planning how she should go to the fair, and what preparations she should make for it. She was determined, if possible, to go alone; for if Harry or her father should accompany her, she was afraid it might be an obstacle to the expected interview. As to Harry, she knew the sensibility of his character; and she resolved, before the fair day, to give him some decided cause of offence—to hurt his feelings in such a manner, as to put his accompanying her totally out of the question. As to her father, it was possible that something might prevent him from going; and her mother, she knew, had no desire to go to such places. After much reflection she formed her plan. There was a relative of her father's, a widow, who resided in Polstead: this woman had an only daughter, some years older than Maria. To them she determined to go the evening previous to the fair, and pass the night with them: even if her father should go

to Polstead next day, there might be many means
of easily eluding his vigilance. The art of deceiving is soon learned by the female mind, the
instant it recedes a single step from the path
of virtue.

Having thus settled in her own mind what
to do, she at last fell asleep. But her sleep
was short and unrefreshing, and disturbed by
dreams of all that had passed on the preceding
day, and all the gaudy images of the future,
floating in fantastic colours before her heated
imagination.

Notwithstanding the reception of the night
before, Harry ventured to make his appearance
at the cottage the following day. He had also
passed a sleepless night; and in the course of his
reflections on his intercourse with Maria, found
reason to blame himself for over diffidence in not
having fully declared to her his real sentiments.
Notwithstanding his first depression of mind, at
her strange conduct the last evening, he began to
think that his fears and suspicions might be
without foundation.

True love, indeed, consists almost in a continual
transition from fear to hope, and from hope to
fear. Its very essence seems to be this perpetual
mutability. When hope is swallowed up in enjoyment and confidence, love soon subsides into a
tender voluptuous friendship. When hope is
utterly cut off, and the worst fears are realized,
love turns to hate, to indifference, or to profound

melancholy, according to the disposition of the individual. Harry, however, had not ceased to "lay the flattering unction to his soul," that he might yet win the heart of Maria. After many struggles with his own diffidence, he came on that day, determined to take an opportunity of declaring to her his affection, and hearing his fate from her own lips. Yet, as he approached the cottage, he trembled in every limb with apprehension. "I am going," thought he, "perhaps, to lose her for ever;" and the ominous echo of the valley again resounded in his "fancy's listening ear." But he felt that he could no longer endure the torment of suspense; and he "screwed his courage to the sticking place," and determined to know the worst.

When he entered, Maria was alone; she was sitting at a table. with her head reclined on her hand, and apparently in very deep thought. She started on the entrance of Harry, and regarded him with a look of displeasure which cut him to the very heart. She replied coldly to his salutation. He attempted to begin a conversation; but she gave him nothing but short, indifferent answers, and then relapsed into silence. Harry at last said, "My dear Maria, what is the matter? are you unwell?"

"No!" she replied; "I am very well."

"Have I done anything to offend you, Maria?"

"No! nothing."

"Then do tell me what is the matter!"

"Harry, you are very dull and teazing; I wish you would leave me."

"Maria! I have come here to-day——" Harry paused, and found he could not go on. She took up his last words.

"Well! I know you have; and I'd as lief you had stayed away."

Harry looked steadfastly at her. "Then my company is disagreeable to you, Maria?"

"All company is disagreeable to me at present: I wish you would leave me to myself."

"Maria," resumed Harry, with a firmer tone, "I can bear this no longer—I will not bear it."

"Maria looked at him with all the air of the heroine of a novel, and said—"And pray, Mr. Everton, who wants you to bear it? It is your own fault if you will stay to hear what is unpleasant. You may go, if you please."

"I will not go, Maria," said Harry, "until——"

"Oh, very well, as you please; but if you do not go, I will;"—so saying she arose, went into her chamber, and locked the door, leaving Harry in a state more easily conceived than described. He left the house utterly bereft of hope; and when he gained the neighbouring wood, being quite unable to controul his feelings, he burst into a flood of tears. Pride, however, soon came to his assistance: he saw too plainly that Maria not only did not love him, but disliked him; and he felt almost convinced that the true cause was her prepossession for another. He therefore

4

determined (until he ascertained whether this was the fact or not) to absent himself from her father's house.

Having thus disposed of Harry, Maria repaired to her relation's house at Polstead. She soon settled with her cousin that she should come there the evening before the fair, and spend the following day. On her return, she easily prevailed on her parents to consent to this arrangement, and learned, with no small pleasure, that her father would be unavoidably engaged at the farmer's who employed him, on the fair day. The farmer himself was to be there, and would trust nobody but old Martin to superintend his workmen in his absence.

The eve of that important day at last arrived. Maria chose out one of her prettiest dresses, which she carried in a bundle, and with a heart beating high with hope and anxiety, tripped off to her cousin's; yet, when she took leave of her parents, she felt a return of her misgivings, and when her mother kissed her, and said, " God bless you, my child, and keep you from all harm!" the tears started into her eyes.

CHAP. III.

Light graces dress'd in flow'ry wreathes,
  And tiptoe joys their hands combine;
And love his sweet contagion breathes,
  And, laughing, dances round thy shrine.

It may be well imagined by the reader, that the night previous to the fair was one of no small anxiety and agitation to Maria. She retired early to bed, but not to rest. The first half of the night was passed in all those varying sensations and ideas which had occupied her ever since her interview with the fortune-teller. Her mind was cast, as it were, upon a sea of doubt, uncertainty, and confusion. Now elevated by hope, now depressed by fear; passing with the rapidity of lightning, from one image to another of an opposite character;—sometimes dwelling on bright prospects of elegance, luxury, and splendour— sometimes filled with undefined apprehensions of disappointment and even misery; again thinking of the affliction of her parents should she make a false step, and reverting, not without some compunctious visitings, to her treatment of Harry, and his probable melancholy, dejection, and despair.

But she had undergone so much mental exhaustion, that tired nature at last claimed its prerogative, and slumber sealed her eyelids. The same images, however, which had occupied her while waking, continued, in sleep, to dance before her perturbed imagination. Her dreams, made up chiefly of her waking ideas, had, with all the fantastic inconsistency and sudden and improbable transitions peculiar to dreaming, something like a method and a meaning which rendered them remarkable.

She at first imagined herself sitting alone under a venerable oak, which protected her from the strong sun above : there was a green space around her, in which a snow white lamb was sporting, and the birds were singing sweetly on all the neighbouring branches : the sky above was of the deepest blue, and the sun in its meridian splendour. On a sudden appeared the fortune-teller, who instantly seized the lamb, and strangled it. The sky became immediately overcast, there was a violent thunder-storm, and the rain fell in torrents,—from which she was protected by the close and massy branches of the oak. The fortune-teller then, without saying a word, beckoned her to follow her. She obeyed : she trembled,— but they traversed several green fields together, and at last arrived, through an avenue of trees, at a splendid mansion. They entered an apartment elegantly furnished, where there was a table spread with the choicest viands and the richest wines: a very handsome man was seated at the head of it, who, as she entered, arose from his seat—approached her—and, having informed her that he had been long expecting her presence, he took her by the hand and placed her beside him. He had scarcely done so, when a cry of fire was heard, and the entire mansion was enveloped in flames.

Again—she dreamed that she was sitting with the very same person in a green arbour, and that he was making love to her—that Harry suddenly appeared, pale and agitated, and said in a hollow voice, " Maria, if you remain here another instant, you are lost!" She paid no attention to him : her companion and the arbour appeared at once to vanish, and she found herself stretched on a pallet of straw, in a wretched hovel, and a strange man standing over her with a naked sword.—Her last dream transported her, in fancy, to a long and barren strand. There she saw standing in line, at equal distances, the fortune-teller, her companion in the mansion and arbour, and the ruffian of the hovel with the naked sword, while Harry stood at some little distance to the left. She thought the two first beckoned her to approach them, while Harry called out loudly on her to desist. But the man with the sword exclaimed—" Let her do what she will, she must be mine at last." Even in the very instant of speaking, she thought he was changed into a skeleton, and exactly presented the imaginary figure of death. With the horror of this impression she awoke, as the first faint rays of morning began to gleam.

Maria was far from recovering immediately from the effect produced by those fearful dreams. She was not altogether untinctured with what some would call a feeling of superstition respecting dreams. But, indeed, she might have stood excused in this, if excuse were necessary, by the example of many of the wisest and best men in all ages. There is no absurdity in supposing that some dreams may be prognostic, though all are not. There is no absurdity in supposing that a dream, like other second causes, may become an instrument in the hands of a superintending Providence. "Dreams," says a celebrated writer, "are liars which yet sometimes tell the truth."

Be this, however, as it may, Maria's dreams were certainly not of the most favourable complexion. They all ended unhappily, and seemed obscurely to forbode misfortune: they brought back a return of her misgivings and apprehensions. She began to suspect that she was on the brink of a precipice, and half hesitated to proceed; but the predictions of the fortune-teller recurred to her mind, and, aided by her own youthful hopes and natural sanguineness of character, soon banished her doubts and vacillations. She arose determined to obey what she considered as the voice of destiny, and what was certainly most consonant with her inclinations.

It may well be supposed that Maria took no small pains in setting off her person to the best advantage on this occasion. She dressed herself, however, with great taste and simplicity. She was in white. Her beautiful waist was bound with a green sash, and her new Leghorn hat was decked with ribbons of the same colour. Her lovely brown hair hung in clustering curls on each side of her face, and her naturally fine complexion was heightened, by the vivacity of her feelings, to a bloom that art in vain would imitate.

She did not go out in the earlier bustle of the fair, but sat for some hours in the window, watching with intense anxiety all the passers by. But she looked for a long time in vain;—many a rustic and clumsy figure passed, appropriately mounted, but in none of them could she discern the slightest approximation to the hero of her fancy. At last a figure appears, the sight of which instantly struck her with the most trembling agitation from head to foot. She beheld at some distance a grey horse and a white hat! the person thus mounted was riding very leisurely up, talking to a man who was walking by the side of his horse. As he approached nearer she had a more distinct view of him. He was a very handsome man, about thirty years of age, well made,

and of middle size.   He was, properly speaking,
neither dark nor fair, though more inclining to
the former than the latter. He was very elegantly
dressed, in the best style of costume usual with
country gentlemen.   He sat his horse, which
was a fine spirited looking creature, very grace-
fully, in a style something between the jockey and
military seat, but with an ease and firmness that
announced a man well accustomed to the field.
As he came up towards the window where Maria
was sitting, he stopped to say something to his
attendant, who then walked forward rather
quickly, and as he wheeled round for the purpose
of returning, he looked at the window, and had a
full view of Maria.   He instantly halted point
blank, seemed for a moment lost in admiration,
and then, giving her a graceful and respectful
salute, passed on—not, however, without looking
back several times.

It would be quite superfluous to describe
Maria's feelings now. If ever any doubts had
remained upon her simple mind respecting the
truth of the fortune-teller, the appearance of
this gentleman completely dissipated them. She
had, however, but little time for the present to
indulge in reflection, as she was summoned to
dinner by her cousin.

To dinner she went, with what appetite I leave
the reader to imagine. Soon after, she and
Ellen Mayberry (that was the name of her

cousin), walked out to see the fair, not without some little additional attention to the duties of the toilet.

They were roaming about, amused (one of them at least) by the different objects which presented themselves, without anything more remarkably occurring than the passing salutations of some of the young sparks at the fair, with all that freedom of manner which belongs to the country. Maria was thinking of nothing but the gentleman with the white hat, whom she expected every instant to meet; but she was very careful not to make her cousin a participator of her thoughts.

She could not discern her hero anywhere for some time, and began to fear that, perhaps, he had left the fair; and that she, therefore, should not see him. However, she was soon re-assured by his appearance: he was on foot, and accompanied by the same person whom she had seen with him before. This was a young man about two or three and twenty years of age, of short person, respectably dressed; and though evidently not a gentleman, yet in his appearance above the lowest order. On seeing the girls, they approached, and Maria's little heart began to flutter rapidly. The gentlemen accosted them, and after some complimentary nothings in the usual common-place way, to which Maria was too agitated to make any coherent reply, proposed to them to quit the fair, and walk into a more

5

retired place.   This offer, after some little bashful
hesitation, which, on the cousin's part, was merely
affected, was assented to; and they walked forward through the fields.   The gentleman paid the
most particular attention to Maria, whispering
soft nonsense in her ear, while his companion
who seemed a young man of no common shrewd-
ness, was entertaining her cousin very much to
her satisfaction.   While Maria's lover (for so we
must call him now) placed her arm gently within
his, and engaged her very deeply in conversation,
the young man, his companion, drew off her
cousin in rather a different direction.   When they
were quite out of hearing, Maria was thus addressed by her companion :—

"You say you cannot believe that I love you—
how can you think so?"

"Because our acquaintance is too short; you
have never seen me before this day."

"Oh! charming Maria, you mistake;—to see
you for a moment, is to love you.   Years, months,
or even days, are not necessary to the growth of
true love: but, if they were, Maria, this is not
the first time I have seen you, though it is the
nrst time that you have seen me.   I have loved
you for many months past, but have had no
opportunity of declaring it until now."

"Ah," said Maria, "but our stations in life are
so different;—a gentleman like you——"

"Oh!" interrupted he, "do not speak of that.
love knows no such distinctions.   In short, Maria

I love you—dearly love you : I am ready to devote myself, my life, my fortune, to you—only say that you will be mine."

Maria, who, with all her simplicity, had a sufficient share of the coquetry of her sex, did not choose to give too easy an assent even to proposals which she deemed honourable, replied—

"I don't know what to say,—I have known you so little,—I have only just seen you: a little time——"

"Oh! Maria," said he, "what have lovers to do with time, except to improve it? I could not love you better, if I had known you for years."

"Perhaps not," said Maria; "but you may love me worse, when you have known me for a time. Gentlemen, I am told, are very changeable."

"Some may be so, Maria, but that is not my character; I never loved before I saw you, and now I feel I can never cease to love."

"Ah!" said Maria, "but I have only your own word for that; and I have often read, that gentlemen don't mind breaking their words in love matters."

"Maria, only try me; I am ready this very moment to prove to you the strength of my affection. Fly with me at once, my dearest girl! I will take you to my home, and to my bosom. My fortune is at your feet; my life shall be devoted to make you happy. You shall want for nothing; our days and nights shall pass on the wings of love: we shall be all to each other. Do," continued he, pressing her hand, "do consent—come this moment!"

"Oh!" replied Maria, "that would be very improper; besides, what would my poor father and mother do, were I to go off thus with a stranger? they would die of grief."

"My dear girl, your parents shall be my special care: say but that you will be mine, and come to my home at once."

"No!" exclaimed Maria, firmly, "that is impossible; I can go home with none but a husband."

The tone in which she pronounced these words, convinced him that she was not to be won by a *coup de main*. He altered his manner, and thus addressed her :—

"Maria, I now see how it is: I was too vain and presumptuous in supposing that you could love me;—there is some one else more favoured—you have a lover, and I must despair."

"No," said Maria, "I have no lover."

"Nor never possessed one?" added he quickly

"No!" replied she, with some little hesitation, "I never have."

"Then," said he, with a most insinuating tone, "you do not hate me?"

"Hate you? no! I hate nobody "

"My dearest girl, do not trifle with me; only tell me that I am not quite indifferent to you—that I may hope for your love."

"Well," said she, blushing, "if that will satisfy you—I—do say so."

"My dearest Maria," said he, enclosing her waist with one arm, "you make me so happy—and you really have never had another lover?

"Never!" replied Maria, "never!"

The word "never" had scarcely passed her lips, when a figure suddenly crossed the path—it was Harry Everton! The fatal word which he heard reverberated by the ominous echo of the vale, again struck upon his ear;—it was uttered by lips on which his destiny depended. He saw the form of her he so fondly adored, almost enclosed in the arms of another. He saw the face, upon which he had so often gazed with unutterable love, beaming with the smile of complacency upon a stranger—he halted suddenly, and looked at her with an air of astonishment and sorrow: he attempted to speak, but could not; all his faculties were confounded. She was at first confused and startled by his appearance; but soon recovering, she darted at him a look of displeasure and disdain. He clasped his hands, and passed on in silence.

This little scene was not lost upon her watchful and discriminating companion. His suspicions were instantly excited.

"Who," demanded he abruptly, "Who is that young man?"

"Only a neighbour of ours, a friend of my father's."

"Then you know him, Maria?"

"Know him? oh yes! I have known him since I was a child."

"But why did he not speak to, or salute you, instead of stopping and staring so impertinently? And how came you to give him such an angry look?" demanded the stranger.

"Why," said she, "he did something lately that displeased me—I have broken with him."

"Broken with him! then it was your lover, Maria, though you told me you never had one."

"I told you true; he never was my lover,—at least he never said so."

"Maria, I have an eye that cannot be deceived —I know what love is too well, not to see it in another. I marked the young man's countenance; —love and jealousy were written on it plainly enough; but let him take care how he crosses my path again."

"Oh!" said Maria, "he won't interfere with you."

"I hope not," replied he, with a smile of contemptuous pride; "but," he added, "the young man must have been your lover, Maria—your quarrel and his manner prove it."

"Surely," said she, (not displeased at the

idea of exciting a little jealousy) "you do not fear him as a rival?"

"I," said he, drawing himself up, while his dark gray eye flashed with fire, and his lip was curled with a haughty smile, "I fear him as a rival? No! but I may chance to chastise him as an intruder.

Maria, alarmed at his manner, begged of him to make his mind easy on the subject; and then explained to him the intimacy of Harry with her father, and the whole nature of his intercourse with herself.

"Then," said he, "Maria, you do not love him?"

"Love him! I never loved him;—I never thought of him but as a friend."

"Well! my love, it is enough, I am satisfied; but it is quite clear that he loves you:—that I can judge from what I have seen, and from all that I have heard from you. I cannot help fearing something: he can see you when he pleases: he is, too, a friend of your father's,—he may do much with him."

"No," said Maria; "I am sure my father would not oblige me to marry any one I did not like. I shall take care, too, that he shall see but little of me: if I ever liked him as a friend, I feel that I hate him now. Besides," added she, "you know you can see my father."

Our hero seemed a little startled at the suddenness of this proposition; but quickly recovering the self possession of which he was eminently a master, replied,—

"Yes, certainly; I can, and will see your father; but it is impossible for me to do so immediately. Reasons, my dear Maria, that I cannot get over, prevent me from seeing him for the present. It is necessary for my own safety, and also for your interest, that our love should, for a while, remain as secret as possible. —But," said he, looking up towards the sky, the evening is coming on fast, and I see your cousin returning to us. Meet me, my dear Maria, to morrow evening, and I will explain every thing to you—my name, my situation in all respects;—and, oh! believe that my heart is wholly yours; and that we will, we must be united."

Maria, after a little show of maidenly reluctance, consented to meet him; and, after cautioning her to secrecy, he took his leave, and retired with his companion, who had just come up along with her cousin.

The girls then directed their course back to Poltstead. Maria made very light of this recontre to her companion, and treated the gentleman's attentions only as a bit of harmless flirtation. Her cousin was a girl with a plain face, but good figure. She was very gay, light-hearted, and volatile; exceedingly fond of all kinds of flirtation and coquetry with the men, but more for amusement than with any other more serious view. When Maria asked her how she was entertained

"Oh! very well," said she, laughing; "very well indeed;—a pleasant, nice young man—quite gay—very good company."

"What was he saying to you all this time?"

"I don't know, I'm sure; a great deal of nonsense,—but he made me laugh.—However, you," she continued, "you have made a conquest indeed!"

"No such thing," said Maria.

"Do you know," said the cousin, "who that gentleman is?"

"No!" said Maria, "do *you* know? Have you learned?"

"I don't know his name, for my spark would not tell me; but he is a very great Squire, and has a fine house."

"Well," said Maria, sighing "that is nothing to me; I dare say I shall never see him again."

"But I dare say you will, for the young man told me that he was quite in love with you."

"Oh! nonsense,—how you do run on!"

"Ay," said Ellen, "I shall dance at your wedding; I am sure it will all soon be settled."

After some further conversation, the girls agreed that they would say nothing about this meeting to any one; and Maria took leave of her cousin, and proceeded home.

When they parted, the sun had set for nearly an hour; light was rapidly fading from the landscape, and the evening shades grew deeper and deeper at every step Maria made.

6

Nothing was heard but the indistinct hum of winged insects, usual at the final close of a long summer's day, varied only by the flitting of the bat, or the distant hooting of the solitary owl awakening to his evening prey. The moon had not yet risen, and the sky, that " majestical roof fretted with golden fire," was of that intensely dark blue which is never seen in our climate but in the hottest and finest midsummer. It looked like an immense overhanging concave, of the finest deep and polished marble.

Maria crossed the road, and entered a long, retired green lane which communicated with another cross road, that would lead her directly home. She had not proceeded far in this direction, when she fancied she saw a figure rapidly gliding on in her front. She lost sight of it immediately, and indeed her glimpse of it was so very faint, that she dismissed her first imagination and believed it to be nothing but the dark shadow of some tree in the distance, which she had mistaken for a human figure. She was tripping lightly along, her mind greatly elevated and excited by the recollections of the past day, and by a variety of confused yet pleasing anticipations of the future, when she arrived at a small close thicket, which grew at each side of the path through which she had to pass, in a woody valley. At this hour, the shade of the trees produced in this spot almost complete darkness

BARNARD.

and the stillness of the tomb was around. The time and place were not ill calculated to produce some degree of superstitious awe in a young and timid mind; but at present this impression was greatly weakened by the peculiar feverish buoyancy of her spirits. She entered the thicket, and had got about half through it, when she heard, uttered as it were behind her, in a deep and distinct tone, the following couplet :—

"Speed home—speed home,—with your heart so light,
For we're making your wedding ring to-night!"

She turned, but saw nobody near her; terror seized her—she stood for a moment as if fixed to the ground— a violent tremor shook her limbs, and she staggered a little to one side of the path, and leaned against a tree, quite exhausted. The voice was not repeated, and no other sound occurred to break the surrounding stillness and repose. At length she recovered her strength, and left the thicket with rapid steps. As she proceeded her fears abated, and recollecting the character of the words she had heard, and which she had no doubt were uttered by some supernatural agent, the favourable augury which she drew from them helped to restore her spirits. She reached the end of the lane just as the moon was beginning to peep above the verge of the horizon.

She was now on the road, on the left side

of which, a little way on, was a projecting bank, whereon arose an oak whose outstretching branches threw a deep shade across the path. She heard very distinctly the tramp of a horse's hoofs, and soon saw, emerging beyond the shadow of the tree into the moonlight, a man mounted on a grey horse, and wearing a white hat! Her astonishment at this sight was great indeed.—"Good God!" thought she, "there he is again;—what could have brought him here at this time?" She felt half afraid to go on, and her heart began again to beat. The horseman, however, approached leisurely, and drew up his horse before her. The moon threw a light fully upon his face and figure; she saw that he was not her lover of the fair, but an acquaintance of herself and her father. His name was William Barnard. He was a very young man, the son of a rich farmer in the neighbourhood. He knew her directly, having frequently met her before at and about Polstead, at little rustic parties.

"What! Maria Martin," exclaimed he, "is this you?"

"Oh, Mr. Barnard," said she, "I was quite frightened; I thought it was a stranger.

"And where have you been, Maria," resumed William.

"At my cousin's," said she, "and at the fair. I am now going home."

"Well, Maria," said he, "I will see you safe

the rest of your way." So saying he alighted gallantly from his horse, and leading the animal by the bridle, walked alongside of her.

" You have been at the fair, too, Mr. William, I suppose," said Maria.

" Yes," he replied, "I was there in the early part of the day, and bought two horses of Squire Colson's for my father. We sent them home by our John; and the Squire, who seemed pleased with the bargain he made with us, asked farmer Adamson and myself to dinner. There was one or two more there, and the Squire's wine was excellent. We cracked a few bottles, and here I am quite comfortable."

Young Barnard was by no means drunk, but very highly exhilarated by the wine he had drank.

" Squire Colson," said he, " is a real gentleman : he has no paltry pride about him ;—he is not ashamed to shake an honest farmer by the hand, and give him a good dinner. A fair day never passes but he has half a dozen or so of them to dine with him. If he should put up for parliament, he shall have plenty of votes in this country."

Barnard was then seized with a fit of gallantry, and began to pass a variety of compliments to Maria's beauty, which, as she was as much elevated as himself, though from a different cause, she replied to with much liveliness.

"I declare, Maria," said he, " you look uncommonly pretty to-night; that white dress becomes you well."

"Mr. Barnard," she answered, " I am sorry I can't return the compliment. You don't look even commonly pretty."

"Oh!" said he, " I can't help that; I don't pretend to beauty. But you know the old proverb —'Handsome is that handsome does;' and I am ready to do handsomely by you. Upon my word, Maria, I am quite in love with you."

"Nonsense," said she; "don't be so foolish." —(as he was drawing closer to her, and taking her hand).

"Foolish!" said he, "I think I am very wise."

"That's more than anybody else thinks, I am sure."

"I care very little what anybody thinks except you. And all I can say is, Maria, that I love you dearly; that I want a wife, and that if you'll have me, I'll make you as comfortable as you can wish."

"*You* want a wife, Mr. William?" said Maria; "why you are hardly older than myself; what would you do with a wife?"

"Oh! leave that to me; I'll tell you when you marry me."

"Then I fear I am not very likely ever to know."

"Well, Maria," continued he, "now let us leave

jokes apart, and speak of business. If you'll marry me, I'll make you as happy as a queen. You know my family is well off, and we shall want for nothing. Only say the word, and Parson Boodle shall soon do the business."

" You must be joking," said she.

" Upon my soul," continued William, " I never was more serious. I am ready to marry you to-morrow. I never was more serious in my life."

" Well, William! marriage is a very serious business, and requires a little thinking about. We are both too young to talk of such matters. You have a father, and so have I."

" True," said Barnard, "but my father will let me do as I please, and I am sure *your* father could not object."

" I don't know how that is. But let us drop the subject for the present. I am just at home, and that is your way."

" Well, Maria," said he, " but you'll think of it."

" Why, I suppose I shall;—good night."

" Good night!" echoed he, as he pressed her hand to his heart and assumed a seriousness of manner that surprised Maria, "Good night;—J love you, my sweet girl!—I have loved you long—adored you, Maria. God bless you !—But who is ..e you met at the fair to-day ?"

He paused.—She remained silent,—he pressed his lips to her burning cheeks and she felt that his was wet with tears. His emotion increased

—he broke from her arms, and having mounted his horse rode rapidly away.

This recontre produced a very strong impression on the mind of Maria. Although she never had an idea of Barnard's preference for her, his declaration of love produced a favourable effect on her heart. The fact of meeting this young man on a grey horse, and with a white hat, threw her into a sort of bewilderment: she began to think that perhaps *he* was the person meant by the fortune-teller. His father was known to be rich, and there was no doubt but that it would be a very good match for her to marry his son; but then she did not meet him at the fair, and he did not at all come up to the idea given by the fortune-teller. He was not a gentleman; besides, she had felt no particular partiality for him: he was well enough, but nothing to compare with her new acquaintance,—who was, indeed, a handsome man, and spoke and made love so differently. Oh, no! it could not be William,—it must be the other.

She had just settled this point, when she came to her father's gate. The moon was now fully risen in unclouded majesty, and shed a yellower verdure over all the surrounding landscape. Her father's white-fronted cottage glistened in its beams, as if washed with silver,—contrasting beautifully with the vine-leaves that thinly tapestried its walls, and the dark painted frames of the little windows.

All was quiet around her home: the birds had

long retired to rest—the insect tribe was hushed
—every wood and every field was silent. Not
a breath disturbed the calm serenity of the night,
—not a sound broke upon its profound stillness,
except the distant baying of some watchful dog,
the alert and faithful sentinel of the peaceful
cottage.

Just as she was about to enter, a female figure
appeared by the hedge, and beckoned to her:
she approached, and recognized the fortune-
teller. There was no difference in the woman's
dress from the first time Maria had seen her,
except that instead of the old black silk mantle,
she wore a handsome French shawl, evidently
the produce of a contraband trade; her head
was covered with a silk kerchief, green and red
mixed, and her handsome waist bound with a
girdle of some dark-coloured morocco leather,
fastened with a plain steel buckle under her left
breast. But, whatever might have been the
reason, she certainly appeared to have taken more
pains than usual in putting on her dress to the
best advantage. Her black hair, too, was arranged
with rather more attention than when Maria had
seen her last; and the latter observed something
like a gem, whether true or false, sparkling on
one of her fingers.

This woman's naturally fine figure, Maria
thought, looked particularly striking on this occasion she stood erect, and seemed taller than

7

before. Her dark eyes beamed with something like an expression of triumph, and a flush was observable breaking through her swarthy cheek, in spite even of the pale reflection of the moon-light.

"Well! my fair damsel," said she, "how have you sped?"

"Oh, you have told me all truth—I have seen him," said Maria.

So she detailed the entire of her interview and conversation with the gentleman. When she mentioned his asking her to meet him, the other interrupted her, saying,

"Meet him! meet him by all means; do not on any account fail. Let nothing prevent you;—your fortune will depend on this: fortune may do much for us, but we must do something for ourselves. Our fate is partly in our own hands,—fortune gives us opportunities, 'tis ours to neglect or improve them."

"But," returned Maria, "I met another man to-night as I was coming home; he, too, wore a white hat and rode a grey horse."

And she then gave her a full account of her meeting and conversation with William Barnard.

The fortune-teller felt a little surprised, but was silent, and seemed buried in thought.

"Perhaps," said Maria, "*he* may be the man, after all, that is to be my husband;—is it so?"

"My dear," replied the sybil, after a pause, "our knowledge is limited: we are permitted to look

MARIA MARTEN,

Having her picture told

a certain degree into futurity by our art. We see the truth, but not the whole truth: I knew, by looking at your hand, that, sometime on the fair day, you would meet with a man mounted on a grey horse and wearing a white hat, who was to be your husband; but I did not discover that you were to meet two such persons—that was not allowed me; and if you ask me now which of these two persons is to be finally your husband, I candidly own I cannot tell at present; —I must go home and consult my books. But which of them," continued she, "do you like best?"

"There can be no comparison between them," returned Maria: "the gentleman I met at the fair is everything that I could desire;—so handsome,—so well spoken. William is a young man I don't dislike, but I should not care for him as a husband."

"Yes, my dear," said the fortune-teller, "but girls are sometimes married to husbands they don't care about: and, as I said, there is no knowing exactly at present;— many a slip between the cup and the lip However, my opinion is, that the other is your man: I shall soon be able to know exactly; in the mean time, don't you fail to meet him.—But did nothing else occur to you to-night?"

"Oh yes," said Maria, "I was very much frightened indeed;"—and she told her of the strange voice she had heard and the lines which were repeated.

" Ah!" said the fortune-teller, with a smile of joyful surprise; " and what was the voice like ?"

" Like nothing human I ever heard," replied Maria.

" I dare say not," observed her companion; " it was not human."

" What was it, then?" said Maria.

" That," said she, looking mysteriously, " I am not permitted to reveal : there are secrets of the other world, which must not be lightly spoken by those who are favoured with some insight into them: it is enough for you to know that the voice was a good omen. Your marriage is certain, and your fortune is written in the book of fate in letters of gold. Marry which you may, you will be rich and happy; but don't fail—don't fail on any account, in your meeting to-morrow evening. Farewell ! you shall see me soon again."

Maria put a piece of silver in her hand, and they parted.

When the maid entered the cottage, her father was in bed, and she found her mother waiting up for her.

" Well, Maria," said the latter, " you are late to-night,—I thought you would have been here before : your father came home an hour ago, but he was so tired, he went to bed."

" I stopt at my cousin's sometime after the fair," said Maria.

" You did not come home alone," observed her mother, " at this time of night ?"

" No," said she, " I met William Barnard, who saw me to the end of the road."

" Did you see Harry Everton at the fair ?"

" Yes," replied Maria, hesitatingly, " I saw him—I just saw him."

" He has been here this afternoon," said her mother.

" Here !" exclaimed Maria, and felt alarmed lest he had mentioned their meeting; " did he say he had seen me ?"

" No," replied her mother, " he said very little on any subject. Poor lad, there seems something the matter with him ;—he looked quite ill and low-spirited. He and your father came in together."

" He and my father ?" repeated Maria, and her alarm returned.

" Yes; he met your father on his way home, and they walked in together."

" Indeed !"

" Yes, indeed!—you seem quite surprised ;— what is there so very odd in their coming in together ?"

" Oh, nothing," replied Maria.

" I never saw the poor lad look so ill," observed her mother, " he was as pale as a sheet."

(Here Maria felt something like a twitch of conscience.)

Her mother continued ;—" I am sure there is something preying on his mind,—he looks like one that is crossed in love."

Maria laughed.

"Ah, you may laugh; but I think, Maria, you are the cause of it all."

"Oh! mother," said Maria, "how can you say that? how can I be the cause of it?"

"That is plain enough,—you treated him so ill this night week;—I remember he went away quite melancholy."

"My dear mother," returned Maria," I did not treat him ill: if he thought proper to teaze me when I was unwell and tired, let him take the consequences. I have nothing to do with his sullen fits, and I am sure I care very little about them."

"Well," observed her mother, "I am sure poor Harry loves you very much, and you should not treat him so."

"Oh, mother, that is all foolishness."

"No, Maria, it is not foolishness. Harry, I am sure, loves you: he is a good young man, and both your father and myself would like to see you married."

"Well, mother," said Maria, (who wished to get rid of the subject, but was afraid to put a decided negative to her mother's wish), "let us talk no more about it now. I declare I am so tired and sleepy, I cannot keep my eyes open—I must go to bed;—good night, my dear mother."

So saying, she retired to her chamber, undressed, and went to bed; although, notwithstanding her declaration of being tired and sleepy, she never felt less inclination to repose : all that had passed that day, between herself, the gentleman, William Barnard, and the fortune teller, she turned over and over again in her mind. The mysterious voice again sounded in the ears of her fancy ; then she thought of the meeting that was to take place to-morrow night, with hope, with fear, and with anxiety.

The reader may have already remarked, from all that we have described, that Maria's feelings did not, as yet, partake precisely of the character of love : she certainly liked the gentleman she had met at the fair better than any other man she had ever seen. His person and his manners were both equally agreeable to her ; but there was as large a portion of girlish ambition and vanity mixed up with her ideas of him, as of any softer feeling. Be it also remarked, that she was not totally indifferent to Barnard : there was a similarity of years, and, at this time, something of a conformity of temper between them ; and, in case of missing the gentleman, she would not, in all probability, have made any very serious objection to accepting the matrimonial offers of the other.

Maria was employed in such reflections as these, and sleep was banished from her pillow, when she heard very distinctly, and evidently near her window, the following verses sweetly sung by two male voices :—

I.

There is a pearl within this cot,
Of greater price than wealth untold ;—
T۰ win it—oh ! be mine the lot,
And I will sigh no more for gold.

II.

There is a flower within this grove,
More bright than any flower that blows—
More fragrant than the breath of love,
And purer than the virgin rose.

III.

How blest, who wins to wear this pearl !
This flower where every sweetness lies ;
How blest is he, enchanting girl !
For whom thy guileless bosom sighs !

To this song she listened with a pleasing astonishment. She arose when it was concluded, and looked out of the window, but could not discern the slightest traces of any human being. The deepest stillness prevailed around, and the moonlight calmly slept on the hill, the valley, the meadow grass, and the tall trees around her. The effect was like enchantment on the mind of the maiden, and, having listlessly gazed on the blue arch above her for at least an hour, she retired to her pillow as from a fairy scene.

CHAPTER IV

But how shall I relate in other cantos
    Of what befel our hero in the land,
Which 'tis the common cry and lie to vaunt us
    A moral country? But I hold my hand—
For I disdain to write an Atalantis;
    But 'tis as well at once to understand,
You are *not* a moral people, and you know it,
Without the aid of too sincere a poet.

                                        BYRON.

IT will be now necessary to lead the reader a little forward in our history, and, quitting for the present Maria and her love affairs, to transfer the scene of our narrative to London.

Let him, then, accompany us in imagination from Suffolk to the metropolis—alight with us from the top of the coach at the Blue Boar in Whitechapel. We shall not stop to take any refreshment in that respectable inn, bating one glass of brandy and water, for which we shall pay eighteen-pence, and as our business is pressing, we shall walk arm in arm into the main street. When we have gone a few dozen yards along that ancient and polite vicinity, we shall turn up a long and narrow lane on the north side of the way, the name of which we choose, for the best of reasons, to conceal.

8

When we have arrived near the end of this lane, which opens upon the fields, we enter a public-house of no very respectable exterior. Whether such an establishment exists at present or not we cannot take upon ourselves to say, but certain it is, that it did exist at the period of which we are writing.

We pass the bar, and the common room where the chance customers drop in, and, crossing the yard, we come to an apartment, on the door of which we see PRIVATE ROOM in very imposing capitals. Availing ourselves of the privileges of authors in all ages, we make bold to open this door and enter, without at all disturbing the company, or indeed exciting any consciousness of our presence.

In this room, which is of a good size, is a round table, which very nearly fills it. At this table are sitting five persons of no very pre-possessing appearance. Their costume is neither altogether that of the town or that of the country.

It is a bizarre mixture of both, or, more properly speaking, an agreeable compound of the farmer, butcher, and horse jockey. In reference to personal cleanliness, and a peculiar species of dandyism, their exterior will be best depicted by the expressive vulgarism of " dirty swells."

The looks of these gentry were in perfect keeping with their dress. Coarse featured vulgarity, callous insensibility, sly cunning, or desperate ferocity, constituted their leading characteristics;

nor was the expression of the countenance, in this case, at all a fallacious index of the mind.

They were partaking of the generous beverages brewed by Meux. and distilled by Hodges, and each was provided with a long pipe, from which he was puffing volumes of smoke in ominous silence and solemnity. This silence remained for a little time unbroken, but was at last interrupted by a *gentleman* sitting at the head of the table, whom we shall take leave to call, for distinction's sake, the president.

This worthy might be about forty-five or fifty years of age. He was tall and very robust. His dark locks were rather grizzled, and his complexion was of that hue which appeared to be the joint produce of brandy, wind, and weather. He had a remarkably flat nose, wide and projecting mouth, and his small black eyes glistened like two little fiery points from beneath his monstrous bushy eyebrows.

"We muster thin to night," said he; "I wonder what's become of the rest of our lads."

"Flat catching to be sure," said a stout man at the other end of the table, in a grey frock coat and red triped waistcoat, and whose beauty was far from being improved by the loss of his right eye. "It is early yet; we shall have some of them here soon, and I hope with some game."

"I say, Captain Creed," said a young man on the left of the president, to his opposite neighbour, " have you done a good stroke of business to-day?"

The person thus styled Captain, was a man about five or six and thirty years of age, with very plain and vulgar features, and an appearance altogether indicating anything but the military or naval profession. Still, there was an expression in his face of the most irresistibly droll and solemn humour. He was styled Captain, in virtue of his being at the head of a young band of " *appropriators*."

" No," said he, " not a great deal,—only half a dozen silk wipers, brought in by Solomons and Ikey Jones;—a bad day's work, and therefore I gave the young rascals nothing. I read them a moral lecture on their conduct;—says I, you young vagabonds, how do you hope to earn your bread, if this be the way you attend to business? there is nothing to be done in this world without industry;—you were on the very best stand in London to-day, (they were in Pall-mall and St. James's street, and it was a levee at Carlton House, you know). You might, says I, have brought a dozen wipers a piece, at least. What do you expect to come to? You will be forced to turn beggars, or disgrace yourselves by going to service."

" By Gad, Creed," said the man with one eye, " it is a pity that you are not a parson, or a schoolmaster.

" God forbid !" replied the Captain ; " I hope to live and die an honest man."

" You certainly, however," rejoined the other, ' have a happy knack of instructing youth ;—the rising generation will be greatly indebted to you."

"Aye," replied the Captain, " I act upon the good old maxim, Train up a youth in the way he should go, and when he is old he will not depart from it."

" I suppose, my noble Captain," said the young man who first addressed Creed, " that you were yourself so trained up."

" No," said the Captain, " I was not brought up to the business of macing—I took it up from natural genius. I **was** bred in an attorney's office, but I was too honest to succeed in that line. Their method is too roundabout for me,—I like to do things straight forward ;—besides, I confess my weakness ; I am naturally soft-hearted, and I could not bear to see so many widows and orphans ruined by law."

"Yes, Creed," said the man with one eye, " we all know you have a soft heart and a tender conscience ; but methinks you were not brought up as an attorney for nothing: you have learned to keep on the **windy side of the** law. You make others your stalking horses, while you bag the game."

" Your comparison is bad," rejoined the Captain : " I use them as a sportsman does his dogs ; they run down the game and fetch it in without daring to bite "

" They have a nibble sometimes."

" Not often; they know the consequences."

" Well, you play a tolerably sure card—you keep your neck out of the noose."

" What the devil," said the Captain, " is the use of a man's head, if it can't take care of his neck. Our worthy president there, I know, is of a different opinion,—he does not care how often he runs the chance of swinging, or being shot. He wants a little of my wit."

" You want a little of my courage, Creed," said the president. " If you had it you would not be slinking about this smoky town, but live the wholesome life of a brave man. Curse London! I hate to come into it,—only one must dispose of his merchandize I'm never right, but when I'm on the salt seas, with a good smacking breeze, astarn. And if we have a bit of a tiff with the revenue sharks at times, all the better,—I like to make the bull-dogs speak."

" Aye, aye," said the Captain, " that's all mighty fine sport to you, but it might be death to me. You were born to be a hero,—I am a man of peace, although I am a Captain. You're all for dry blows ;—they may suit your sconce very well, but they'd give me a headache. You can live in salt water like a fish—the sea does not agree with me."

" But," said the smuggler (for such he was), " our trade is honourable, yours is low—we rob the king only, you rob the people."

" I never knew before," said Creed, " that you

were so very particular as to whom you robbed; and as for honour, 'What's honour? will honour set a leg?' as Falstaff has it. My leg is no great beauty," says he, raising his substantial pin upon a chair; "but it does very well for me; I'd rather have it than a wooden one. No, no! honour can't set a leg, nor put your head to rights after your neck is stretched;—damn honour,—I hate it almost as much as I do law."

"I say, Creed," said the smuggler, "did you ever come to the scratch in your life?"

"No," says the Captain, "I can't say I ever did; I am not bloody-minded,—I have no taste for wounds, bruises, and wooden limbs. And yet I drew an old rusty sword once."

"To toast cheese, I suppose," said the smuggler.

"No," replied Creed; "the story is worth your hearing. I was in Paris at the time—*parley-vood* but badly, and was without a tanner. I met a fellow that had run away from England, after robbing the Stamp Office of some thousands;—I knew him well,—he had plenty of blunt,—I asked him for some, and the rascal refused. I soon formed a plan to settle him. He was a stupid fool, and knew nothing of French, and very little of anything else. Next morning I put on a loose blue coat over my other clothes, and an old cocked hat, which I borrowed from one of my French cronies. and under this coat I had an old sword in a black cross belt. I was with my gentleman before he was out of bed, for I would not be

denied. 'Oh!' says he, ' is that you?' 'Yes,' says
I, (taking off my cocked hat, and opening my
loose coat, that he might see the sword and belt),
'and I am very sorry to disturb you so early, but
my business don't admit of ceremony.' ' In the
name of God!' says he, ' what's the matter?' ' Oh,
nothing,' says 1, ' only you're found out, that's
all.' ' Found out!' says he. ' Aye, by my
soul,' says I, 'found out, sure enough;—you have
been traced here, and application has been made to
the French Government, and directions given
that you should be arrested immediately. ' My
dear friend,' says he, ' I'm so much obliged to
you,—and you have come here to warn me!' ' By
my word, I have,' says I, 'and to do a little more
too. Don't you see my cocked hat and sword?
you left me so suddenly yesterday, that I had
not time to tell you that I am in the employ of
the police here : being hard up, I was glad of
the situation. And now they have sent me to
arrest you ; here's the order,'—and I pulled out of
my pocket a duplicate of a watch that I had
pledged a few days before at the Mont-de-Pieté,
for so they call the spouting establishment in
Paris, and as it is under the government, and its
papers are marked with the royal arms, the
duplicate looked exactly like an official paper,
and the fool knew no better. He was horribly
frightened. ' Come,' says I, ' its very disagreeable
to my feelings, but duty, you know, must be done.
Get up and dress yourself as quick as you can,

—I repeated, drawing the sword,— for my com rades below are in a hurry: we have to arrest five persons more before twelve o'clock,—two of them are Englishmen,—for like offences. The government here is determined that no offenders against the English laws shall escape.'

"On this he got out of bed, and put on his breeches, quite in a quandary. 'Come here,' says I, opening the window, ' and you'll see my comrades below. He looked out, and saw two very neat lads of my own—friends of mine, that I had brought on purpose: one was an Italian barber, that I had known here—a regular out-and-outer. He came to Paris to mace the French, but they were too much for him, and he lost all his money. This boy had as much hair on his face as would have set him up in his own trade of wig making. The other was a man of colour, a servant out of place, who had left his master in consequence of some little difference in money-matters. When my gentleman saw these, he was still more frightened ;—' and look,' says I again—pointing to two gens-d'armes that happened to be standing at a little distance—' if my comrades and myself should not be enough to secure you, there are two honest fellows ready to help us.'

"This completely finished him,—he fell on his knees, and begged of me to let him escape,— 'Oh, no,' says I, ' that's impossible ;—they are too strict with us. You think you are in London;

9

but the police here do business quite differently. If it was known that we let you escape, we should all swing.'

"'My dear friend,' says he, 'do let me escape. Here's twenty Napoleons for you, and let me go;—I have my passport made out for Brussels, and I shall be off before you can say Jack Robinson.' 'Why,' says I, 'what you say is pretty fair, and if it depended on myself I might let you off, but there's my two comrades; they would peach to a certainty.' 'Oh,' says he, 'surely you can persuade them.' 'Why,' says I, 'there's but one mode of dealing with these people; you say twenty Napoleons for myself—say twenty more for them, and I'll see what I can do with them.' 'Twenty, my dear friend?' says he. 'Oh, not a penny less,' says I; 'I could not offer them less, and I don't know if they'll do it for that, but I'll go and see;—in the mean time I must lock you in.' So saying, I took out the key of the door which I locked outside, and went down stairs.'

"I returned in about five minutes. 'Well,' says I, 'I have spoken to my comrades, and they are contented to let you go, on the terms, —but we must have five Napoleons more to give the soldiers.' 'My dear friend,' says he, (for he was damned fond of money), 'can't this be got over?' 'Oh, yes! says I, 'by coming with us to the police.' 'Well, well,' says he, fetching a deep sigh, 'if it must be, it must.' So he counted me down forty-five Naps, which he parted with like so many drops of blood. 'Now,' says I, 'my good friend, be off as quick as you can · we'll return and say you have escaped : but, if you stay in Paris another hour, the devil himself can't save you.' He took my advice, and posted off to Brussels ; took shipping at Ostend for America, and, contrary to the opinion of every one who knew him, was drowned on his passage.'"

"Certainly, Captain," said the one-eyed man, "that is a right good story; but if the fellow had had one spark of sense or courage, he must have found you out."

"Oh," said the Captain, "I knew my man : a greater ninny never breathed, or a more miserly scoundrel ; and he was a greater coward than myself."

The Captain had scarcely finished his last observation, when a person entered the room who was hailed at once with surprise and delight by the whole company.

"What, Stafford Jackson!—is it you?" was echoed by altogether.

This was a man about thirty, with handsome features, of the middle stature, or perhaps rather above it, dressed in a light drab top-coat with one cape, a black cravat, and a pair of mud overalls : he wore spurs, had a riding switch in his hand, and was well spattered.

"Yes, my boys," said he, "here I am, and a hard ride I have had for it."

" Well, what news?" said the president.

" The best of news, Warren, my boy," replied the other; "we got our cargo over safe; landed last night, and stowed it, you know where. A glorious lot of silk and lace. We dispatched off our lads directly;—three for London, two for the North, and two for the West. I took coach at four this morning as far as Rumford; there a horse was waiting for me: I mounted, but did not come the straight road,—I took a little circumbendibus—you understand me—did a small bit of business after dark,—and here I am."

" Well done," said the president, "by Gad! you know how to do the trick."

" Oh, leave me alone for that;—but I say, Warren, have you done all your business here?"

"Yes," replied the other;—"Tim there, and myself, got rid of the last lot to-day: I'm sure I'm glad of it,—I want to get out of this cursed hole."

" And that you shall, my boy," replied Stafford Jackson; " the Spanker is waiting for you, with five good hands aboard, and a boy; take her, and be off to the other side as fast as the wind will carry you: you are the only fellow I can trust her with, except myself. And there," continued he, tossing over to him a small leathern bag, " there's something to help the freightage, for the boys on the other side."

" But where's Jack Smith?" said Warren; " won't he come with me? Jack's the lad for a tussle;—there's no man, next to yourself, that I would sooner have alongside of me."

"I expect him here every moment," replied Stafford Jackson; "he left some hours after me: but I cannot part with him at present—there's business for us to do here."

"Aye," said Warren, "some of your old capers, I suppose. You and Jack have the same fault,—you lose too much time after the girls. I say, what's become of that little bit of goods you were along with at Polstead fair? Jack, too, had a finger in the pie: he was looking after another small cargo."

"Oh! mum for that," replied Stafford Jackson; but you're mistaken—it's for no such business Smith is wanting at present; he has caught a regular flat, down in Suffolk; he has had him in training for some months; quite a young one, as green as a leek: Jack has given him some good lessons. The old father of this chap is rich, and Jack has taught the son the road to the strong-box: he has plenty of blunt, and Jack is bringing him up to town for the first time, where, please the pigs, we shall soon release him of his burthen."

"Well then, Commodore," said the president, "I suppose I may be off immediately?"

"Not for the world," said Stafford Jackson; "to-morrow morning will be time enough; I can't have too many hands to-night. We must fleece the greenhorn,—he'll be here directly

Captain Creed, you're the man for him; and Warren, you're as neat a hand at all-fours as I know, the Captain always excepted."

" Thank you, Mr. Jackson," said the Captain; I think your own skill that way is not to be despised."

" Oh !" replied Stafford Jackson, " I never touch a card now, in company,—you understand me ?"

" Yes," said Creed, " you bet on the wrong side, and lose your money."

" Exactly so," said he; " I lost twenty pounds that way in Chelmsford, three weeks ago, betting with Jack Smith on an officer of the garrison, at billiards."

" Aye," said Creed, " but how much did you win ?"

" A trifle," said Jackson ; " we only divided five and twenty."

" That is a great deal though," said Creed, "for an officer to lose,—a quarter's pay."

" Oh, not for him," returned Jackson ; " he is a first rate dasher,—a captain of dragoons, with plenty of money."

" I wonder he played with Smith," said the Captain.

"Oh ! for that," replied the other, " he'd play with a chimney sweeper, or old Harry himself, he's so fond of the game."

A young man, apparently about five or six and twenty years of age, now entered. He was about five feet six inches in height, of a very smart and athletic make; his hair, eyes, and whiskers, were dark, and his complexion of a ruddy brown: his features were coarse, and he had, in an eminent degree, what is termed a knowing look.

"Hah! Smith," said Stafford Jackson, "here you come at last,—just arrived, I suppose?"

"You have hit it," said Smith; "*we* have just disembarked from the coach."

"*We!*" reiterated Jackson; "then you have got the trout on the bank?"

"Yes," said Smith, "hooked him nicely; I have just deposited him at the 'Three Nuns' Inn. I came here to give you warning to prepare your faces to play your parts; I shall now return and fetch him directly. But I say, my lads, none of you must know me, except Jackson."

"A word to the wise," said Captain Creed."

Smith retired, and Jackson thus addressed the party :—

"My lads, we must not let out before this youngster. As he's but newly fledged, we might frighten him, and he might take the wing. If it's not our own faults, we shall have many a jolly pluck at him. We must not go too far to-night: were we to strip him altogether to-night, it would not do. I should not object to it, if he had no more money than what he has brought up to town; but he can get many future supplies, and we must not excite his suspicions at the onset. Moreover, my lads, we must sink the shop as much as possible. he is not an ignorant man, nor a fool, though young and inexperienced. You, Creed, are a man of education and the world, and can entertain him properly: as for the rest of you, the less you talk the better. You, Warren, must take a hand at cards."

"The tiller suits my hand better," said Warren.

"Oh! never mind that for to-night," said Jackson; "you play well;—and, do you hear, keep, if you can, your contraband dialect to yourself. But, by George, I forgot! I must uncase before he comes, that I may look a little decent, as I must play the flat to-night."

So saying, he divested himself of his top-coat and mud over-alls, and appeared in a well-made dark green frock, which showed his fine figure to advantage, and a pair of dark grey pantaloons, and hessian boots. He took a key out of his pocket and opened a small closet, in which he deposited the top-coat and over-alls.

"Now," said he, "I think I shall do." And certainly, his handsome and even commanding features, and gentlemanly person, formed a considerable contrast to the appearance of those around him.

"By Gad! Jackson," said Creed, looking at him, "I don't wonder at the girls running after you,—you are not a bad looking fellow."

"Creed," said Jackson, "if you can't tell me anything newer than that, you may as well hold your tongue."

"Gad!" said Creed, "I did not mean it as new; but you know, as the Scripture says, 'Out of the abundance of the heart the mouth speaketh.' —But what's that sticking out of your pocket?"

"One of my tools," said Jackson; "but as we are to sink the shop, I shall put it up with the other toggery."

So saying, he pulled out a small double-barrelled pistol, and put it into the closet.

"I have seen that little pistol do some good work," said Warren, "before now."

"Oh," said Jackson, carelessly, "I believe it has done it's duty, but not better than other pistols;—your own, for instance, Warren."

"Ah!" said Warren, "but for that pistol, I should not be here now."

"Well, well, Warren," said Jackson, "no more of that; I hear footsteps crossing the yard. It is Jack Smith and the gull: mind,—don't be at all familiar with me."

His conjecture was right: it was Jack who entered, and with a very young man, apparently not twenty years of age.

Smith bowed slightly to the company in general, and, coming up to Jackson, took him by the hand, and said,

"Mr. Jackson, this is my particular friend, Mr Barnard."

So saying, Smith and his *protegé* seated themselves beside Jackson.

The latter preserved exactly that sort of manner

10

to the rest of the company that might lead the stranger to suppose that they were merely tavern acquaintances, and not to suspect any greater intimacy between them. As for Jack Smith, he was even more distant; for he had told his companion that he only came there because his friend, Mr. Jackson, occasionally used the house when in town, as being convenient for his business,—that his father was a great grazier in Devonshire, and had extensive dealings with all the principal killing butchers in Whitechapel: to which he added, that Stafford Jackson was a very dashing young man, fond of the amusements of London, had plenty of money, was as liberal as a prince, &c. &c

When they had sat down, Jackson called for a bottle of wine, of which he insisted on his two companions partaking. The rest of the company were drinking grog.

"Captain Creed," said Jackson, "this is a very good house: I don't know a better of the kind in London."

"Nor I," said Creed; "every thing is good and cheap. It is not always your houses with the most dashing outsides that are the best. How do you find the wine, Mr. Jackson?"

"Excellent," replied the latter; I have paid seven shillings a bottle for worse port at the West End.—Try a glass, Captain."

"Thank you, Mr. Jackson, I don't care if I do."

This bottle was soon finished, and Jackson called for another.

The conversation now began to grow more brisk; and Creed, in particular, told several amusing stories of his travels,—not, however, precisely of the character of the Paris affair; and Smith's companion began to be gradually excited, and grew rather lively. Jackson, observing this, and acting as if the wine had got into his head, though it was scarcely possible to affect him in that way, stood up and said,

"I am tired of this wine: one bottle of it is enough for a man, this cold weather. Allow me, gentlemen," addressing the whole company, "to treat you to a bowl of punch."

"I have no objection, Mr. Jackson, provided you let others take their turn," observed Creed.

"Certainly," said Jack Smith, "that's but fair."

"Oh, no doubt," said his companion.

"Well, gentlemen," observed Jackson, "you shall do as you like afterwards, but I'll order in the bowl."

He did so, and a very large bowl of hot and strong punch soon made its appearance.

This soon wrought its effect: the conversation grew highly spirited—Stafford Jackson made many lively sallies, and Creed was unusually comical.

"Mr. Jackson," said Smith, "push the bowl this way; my friend and I are aground."

"I am called Mr. Stafford Jackson, if you please, Mr. Smith; my father is Mr. Jackson: that's the way we are distinguished from each other."

"Well, then, Mr. Stafford Jackson, let us have the punch, if you please."

"No," said the latter; "damn me, we must sink the Mr.; I'll be plain Stafford Jackson."

"Very well," said the other, "and I'll be plain Jack Smith with you: so, plain Stafford Jackson, let us have the punch."

"Oh!" resumed Smith, "we are now aground, —its my turn now."

"No, Mr. Smith," said the Captain, "'tis mine; —you and your friend are strangers—your turn comes last."

"Gad!" said Smith, looking round the table, "one, two, three, four, five,—I'm afraid my turn won't come to night, if I am to wait for all of you."

"Don't be alarmed," observed Creed, "our worthy president there could drink the five bowls himself, if that was all."

"Aye," said Warren, "and five more to the back of them."

"I believe you," says Creed, "if you had only time enough. Allow me to ask you what was the longest drinking bout you ever had?"

"I'll tell you," said the other;—it was on the hgih seas."

Stafford Jackson gave him a look, as much as to say, "nothing contraband."

He replied by a sly wink, and continued.

"I was then in the Norway trade, and used to the regular voyages there. We were becalmed near the Orkney Islands, and for three days and three nights there was such a fog that you could hardly see your hand. We cast anchor, broached a cask of rum, and the mate and myself stuck to our grog for the whole time."

"The ship must have fared well," said Jack Smith, "while you were boosing."

"Oh, there was no fear of her," said Warren; "she had hands aboard that we could depend upon: besides, we ourselves were as sober as judges."

"Come, Captain Creed," exclaimed Jackson, "give us a song."

"With all my heart," said Creed; and sung with a very fine voice and good taste, "*Locks bolts, and bars.*"

"That's a professional song," said Warren.

"Yes," returned Creed; "I learned to sing it when I was in the waggon-train."

"He means the waggon," whispered Jackson in a low voice to Smith, whose companion was then talking to his neighbour on the other side.

"Now, Mr. Jackson," said Creed, "I call on you."

"I can't sing a solo," replied Jackson; "but I'll try a second with my friend Smith."

The latter, who had a good voice and ear, and was well accustomed to all the pot-house singing in London, assented; and they sung in very good style together, the duet of "*All's well.*" Stafford

Jackson, however, was evidently the more scien
tific singer of the two, and his second was
admirable.

After this, Creed proposed a glee; and he,
Stafford Jackson, and Jack Smith, sung "*Old
Van Tunck.*"

By this time it may well be imagined that
young Barnard was getting tolerably drunk. He
began to be very communicative with the company
in general; to relate stories and adventures connected with himself and his family, and to boast
of his own feats of horsemanship and skill in rural
sports.

"The country," said Creed, "is very well in
summer, and in winter too during the day, but it
must be dull in the evenings."

"Oh no," replied young Barnard, "we manage
to pass our time very well, over a flowing bowl
and a game at cards."

"Cards!" said Creed: "you play, then?"

"I believe I do," said he, with a look which, no
doubt, he thought extremely knowing.

"Do you play whist?" said Creed.

"No," replied the other, "not much of that; I
don't like the game: but, for all fours, I'll back
myself against any man in the country."

"Or London either, I suppose?" said the
Captain."

"Aye, or London either," replied the young
fellow.

"Well," said Creed, "I think I can find your match in London: I should not mind trying you myself."

"There's nothing I should like better," said young Barnard; "and if we had the cards now, I'd be your man."

"The cards can be easily procured," said Creed, "and I have no objection to play; but I must tell you before hand that I never play high;—no more than to give a zest to the game.'

"Oh!" said Barnard, " for my own part, I don't dislike a good bet on the game."

"Well," observed Creed, "I dare say you will find some gentlemen here to indulge you. If you like, your friend Mr. Smith and I will play with you and Mr. Jackson."

"I'd rather be excused," said Jackson; "I am no player, and like better to look on."

"Very well," said Creed; "then our worthy president will make one of the party."

"With all my heart," said Warren; "but, as I don't know how these gentlemen play, we may as well cut for partners."

"Why," observed Creed, "I'm willing to take Mr. Smith, of whose play I know nothing; and can't you do the same by Mr. Barnard? but I'm willing to content you. We can't cut until the cards come, but here's all the same; I'll toss with you for choice of partners."

"Done," said the other.

They tossed, and Creed won

"Well," said he to Warren, "to show you that I'm not particular, I'll take young Mr. Barnard : but let us send for the cards."

The landlord was sent for, and soon made his appearance. He was a very appropriate figure for the president of such an establishment. He was a tall and powerful man, about forty-eight or fifty years of age ; had been a heavy dragoon, and was marked with a deep scar, extending obliquely from the top of his forehead to below his cheek-bone on the left side.

"Landlord," said Creed, "have you got a pack of cards ?"

"Yes, Captain," said the landlord, "I have."

"Is it a new pack ?" demanded Jack Smith.

"No, Sir," rejoined the landlord.

"Oh, then," said Smith, "I won't play with it— I never play with old cards. I say, Mr. Barnard," continued he, addressing young Barnard ; "you and I will go out and fetch in a new pack. The shops are not yet shut : I know a stationer's in Whitechapel where I can get them."

So saying, he got up and led off Barnard along with him.

"Smith's a neat hand," said Creed ; "he knows what he's about. I say, landlord, is your pack bound up to look like new ?"

"Yes," said the landlord, "it *is* new ; we got it to-day : only took the cards out to mark them, and made it up again as nicely as ever."

"And where is it now ?" demanded Jackson.

"Where !" said the landlord, "why, in Mr. Smith's pocket, to be sure,—where else should it be ?"

Upon this they all set up a shout of laughter.

"But now," said Creed, "while they are away, let's hold a council. Shall we introduce him to the bones below stairs to night, Jackson ?"

"No," replied Stafford Jackson, "not to-night— too soon ;—we must fleece him gradually. In five or six days he'll be without any money. But he can get more ;—and more after that. We must not be too fast with him, lest he might declare off, —more haste, worse speed."

"Well," said Creed, "I leave it to your better judgment. But I say, Jackson,—share and share alike. Fair play's a jewel."

"Yes," returned Stafford Jackson, "you have reason to use that proverb.—But, Captain, wher did you see me act otherwise than fair? Is there any man who knows Stafford Jackson, who ever knew him to put a paltry pound into his pocket at the expense of his friends ? No, no! the world is wide ;—thank God, there are fools enough for us all, without preying on each other."

"I beg your pardon, my dear Jackson," said the Captain, "I did not mean what I said for you ;—but Jack Smith has this young fellow so much under his thumb."

"Oh!" said Stafford Jackson, "I can answer for Smith, as for myself. And even if I thought

11

he could be unfair, I'd soon settle him, notwithstanding our friendship. I'm a very easy going fellow, but I am not to be trifled with."

"I know that," said Warren; "and it is a pity, my gallant commodore. that you are forced to conjure the mocusses out of fellows' pockets in this numbug sort of way, instead of taking them boldly, as the right of a brave man, on the high seas, or,—elsewhere."

"Necessity, Warren," said Jackson, "necessity;—times are altered. This cursed peace has ruined us all. Ah! Warren, if there were another war, you'd soon see Stafford Jackson in his right element,—on the quarter deck of a privateer, cleared out for action,—all sails set, bearing down with a fine breeze on some rich prize,—like a falcon swooping on a dove."

"Aye," said Warren, "and if we were in the South Seas, we should not be very particular as to the flag."

"By the bye," said Jackson, "there is something to be done there, even now. And if all comes to all, and we can muster enough for a good fit out, it would be no bad spec. But as matters stand at present, I must, as an old general, whose name you never heard of, used to say, eke out the lion's skin with that of the fox."

"Aye," said Creed, "and you'll find the latter no bad addition. For my part, it's large enough for me without the other."

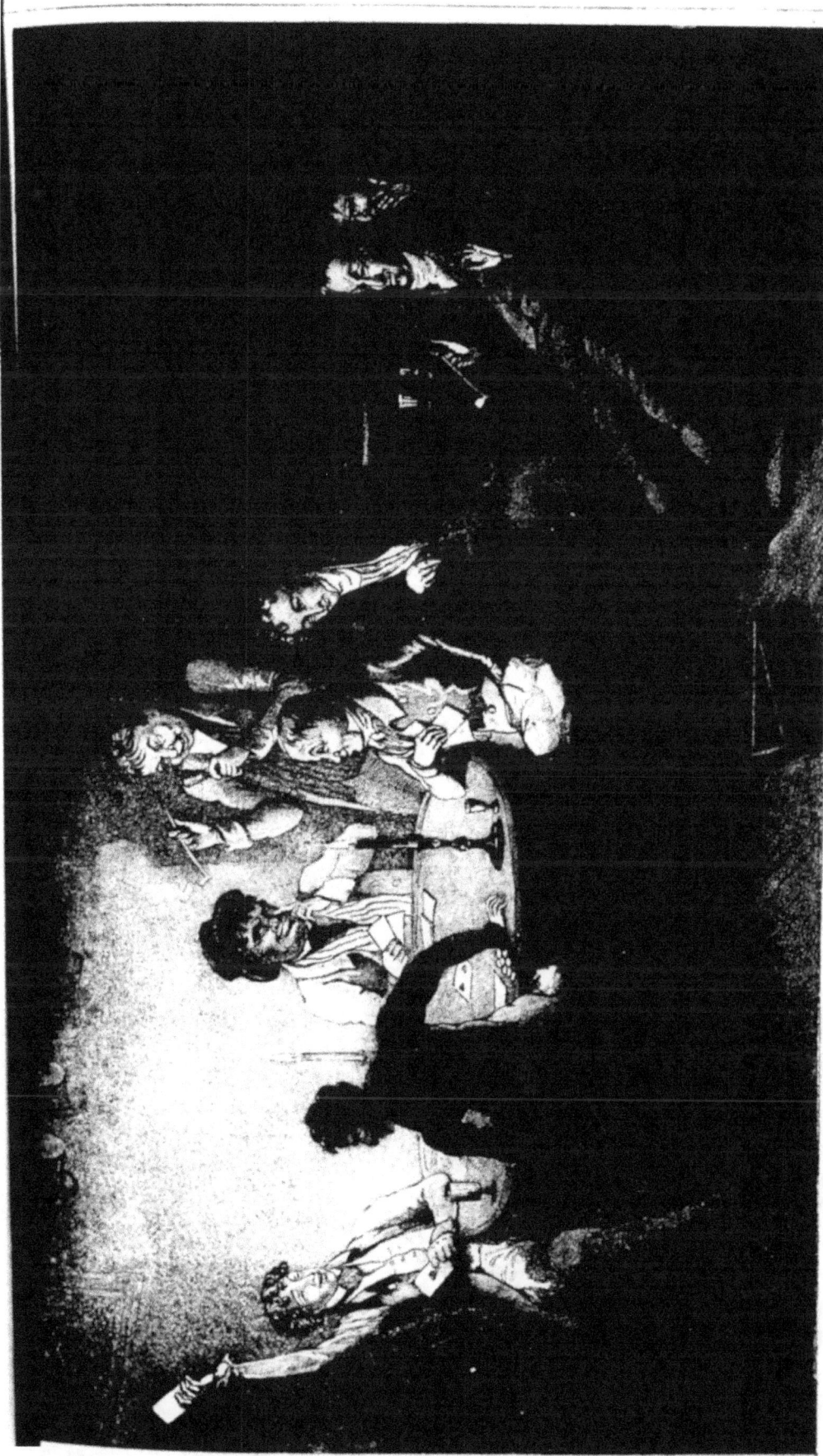

Designed & Etced by R.Seymour.

BARNARD disturbed at Cards in the Private Room.

Page 97

Jack Smith and young Barnard now entered, and, with Creed and Warren, sat down to their *partie quarrée.*

"What do we play for?" demanded Smith.

"I won't stand more than half a crown on the rub," answered Creed; "you may make your bye-bets as you please."

"I'll have a crown with you, Mr. Warren, on every game," said Jackson.

"Done," said Warren.

"Who'll bet with me?" said young Barnard.

"I'll have five shillings with you on the rub," said Smith, "besides our half-crown."

They played, and Creed and his young partner won the first rubber, winning the two first games running.

In the second rubber, Creed and his partner won the first game, and lost the second. All bets were doubled on the conqueror, which Smith and Warren won.

It would be tedious to the reader to follow up their subsequent play by any minute description. Suffice it to say, that after several well managed *fluctuations* of fortune, young Barnard arose from the table *minus* thirty-five pounds, which was all the money he had about him. Stafford Jackson pretended to be mightily affected by all the crowns which he appeared to lose to Warren. But Creed consoled him, saying, that it was all the fortune of war. Jack Smith conducted his juvenile charge home to the "Blue Boar," who, from the state of his brain, and his ignorance of London localities, might otherwise have failed in finding it. When they arrived, they finished the night, or rather morning, with a cold fowl and two glasses of brandy and water; leaving Barnard in a state of unenviable intoxication.

CHAP. V.

———" I saw him break Skogan's head at the court gate, when he was a crack, not thus high: and the very same day did I fight with one Sampson Stockfish, a fruiterer, behind Gray's-Inn. O, the mad days that I have spent!"

SHAKSPEARE.

BEFORE we proceed further with our history, it will be necessary to let our readers know who Stafford Jackson and Jack Smith really are, as they will both be found to have been very principal and efficient actors in most of the subsequent events that we shall have occasion to describe.

Stafford Jackson was the son of a gentleman of small fortune, residing near Ipswich. He lost his mother when he was very young, and his father was a man of a gay and social turn, fond of his glass, and passionately attached to hunting, shooting, and all kinds of rural sports. Stafford, who was a fine active boy, soon learned to excel in all kinds of country exercises. At ten years of age he could ride like a young Arab, and at fourteen could bring down a snipe or wood-cock with almost as much certainty as his father

Stafford Jackson was sent to school very early, as his father was determined that his education should not be neglected. There he made a very considerable proficiency in all the usual and some of the ornamental branches of education.

He was, without question, one of the idlest and most mischievous boys in the entire school. He past his school-hours in playing tricks of all kinds, making those who were disposed to idleness still worse, and preventing those who were inclined to study from so doing. Out of school he was the ringleader in every kind of school-boy wickedness,—foremost in robbing orchards, organizing plans of rebellion, and the like. There was no boy in the school that could excel him, when he was about thirteen or fourteen, in boxing, leaping, wrestling, running, or swimming. He was, therefore, regarded by his schoolfellows with great respect, and some degree of fear; but he had so much good humour and generosity of disposition withal, that he was loved full as much as he was respected and feared.

He constantly received severe castigation for his various pranks, but never for his lessons : in these he was always perfect, though he was never seen to look into a book. His plan was this :— though he was a boarder at the school in question, his father lived so near, that Stafford used always to go home on Saturday afternoon and return to school the following Monday. The great majority of this interval he devoted to hard study, and as his capacity was singularly good, he mastered, without much difficulty, all the tasks of the succeeding week.

During the vacations, he passed his time in all kinds of country sports He always accompanied his father to the field, and was his companion at table :—even when there was company, Stafford made one of the party, and at fourteen took his wine regularly like the rest. His manliness of appearance and manners, much beyond his years, and his sharpness, intelligence, and high spirit, made him a universal favourite with all his father's friends.

He left school when turned of fifteen. and it may be well imagined that he did not pursue very closely the line of study he had commenced there. He acquired, however, a taste for amusing reading, from the society of an old gentleman in the neighbourhood, who was very fond of him, and who had a large library entirely composed of plays and poetry, novels and romances. As many of the latter were in French, Stafford kept up his knowledge of that language by reading them, and acquired further facility by conversing with an emigrant French gentleman, who was a friend of his father's.

About this time a singular character came to reside in his father's neighbourhood ; one Captain Carribles, an old gentleman who, during three-fourths of his life, had been an officer in the navy. Not being provided with good interest, in spite of

his long services, and the loss of a right arm,
he never arose beyond the rank of a lieutenant;
and was put on half-pay, to which was added,
after long and patiently memorializing the Admi-
ralty, a small pension.   He retired into Suffolk,
which was his native country, and took a pretty
picturesque cottage near the sea-side.

Captain Carribles, notwithstanding his disappointments, had preserved an enthusiastic attachment to his profession.   He always wore his
naval undress at home, and invariably, when
he dined abroad, was in full uniform.   He could
not enter much into the field amusements of
the gentlemen of the neighbourhood, but he
was perfectly at home with them over the bottle,
and full of naval anecdotes, which he told very
circumstantially, and with much characteristic
spirit and humour.   His cottage was furnished
quite professionally.   As you entered the hall,
there was on a table a complete model of a
man of war.   The room where he sat, which
he called his cabin, was hung with marine
paintings, pictures of naval engagements, and
portraits of celebrated admirals.   Over the mantel-
piece were suspended swords, pistols, cutlasses,
tomahawks, and boarding pikes.   A mariner's
compass and a telescope completed the naval
apparatus.   Instead of chairs, there were camp
stools: and the table was fastened to the ground
with screws, to keep it steady in case of a hard
gale

The Captain had a servant, the only one he kept, who was as great an original as himself. His name was Tom Squires, a thorough-bred old tar, with a blind eye and wooden leg. Tom cooked for his master, brushed his coat and shoes, and swabbed the decks. Beds there were none to make, for Captain Carribles and his man Tom slept in hammocks.

When the Captain had no other company of an evening, he relaxed a little of naval subordination, and would allow Tom to sit in the cabin with him. There master and man used to take their grog together, talk of old times, and roar out sea songs in concert, until both were more than half seas over.

But Captain Carribles' great amusement in fine weather, consisted in making short cruises about the coast in a small sailing boat of his own, nicely trimmed. Tom always accompanied him on these occasions, although, in consequence of his wooden pin, he was of little use except to steer.

To young Jackson, Captain Carribles took an uncommon fancy; and Stafford, on his part, equally liking the Captain, they soon became uncommonly intimate. The youth would pass his evenings with old Carribles, and soon became an admirable proficient in grog. He accompanied him on his sailing excursions, and, by the instructions of the Captain and Tom Squires, very speedily attained some insight into the theory and

12   N

practice of naval tactics : he delighted to hear the naval anecdotes of the old sailor, and became quite enamoured with the profession. He pestered his father continually on the subject, until the latter, through the interest of a friend, got him rated as a midshipman on board of the Camilla frigate, notwithstanding that his age was rather beyond the proper time for entering the navy.

Stafford Jackson did not continue in the navy more than four years. During this time he made two voyages to the West Indies, and was engaged in two actions, in which he behaved with the greatest bravery. On his return to England, the vessel lay for some time at Portsmouth, and afterwards at Plymouth and Deal. In these places Stafford got in with a very wild and dissipated set of young fellows, and passed all his time on shore in debauchery, drinking, and gaming. He drew largely on his father for supplies very inconsistent with the finances of the latter, and was over head and ears in debt besides. His breaches of duty became more and more frequent; and at last he was sent to the right-about, for flinging a dish of fish in the face of the commanding officer, in a tavern at Portsmouth.

When the news of Stafford's behaviour reached his father's ears, he was excessively enraged, and would not suffer him to come home. The other, indeed, had no great inclination to do so, having acquired a most decided taste for an uncontroled life. Being, however, without money (for he could get none from his father), he was obliged to cast about for some means of existence. We have already mentioned his talents, when a boy, for dramatic recitation: these talents he had exercised and improved occasionally in the Navy; for the officers of the Camilla sometimes amused themselves in getting up private theatricals. He now availed himself of them as a means of subsistence, or rather as a preservation from positive want, and enlisted in a strolling company.

This mode of life he pursued for a time, and found it wretched enough. After many vicissitudes, he was sufficiently fortunate to make a tolerable engagement with a country manager. He now played the first line of light comedy, and, with a versatility not very usual, also distinguished himself as a tragic actor.

His stage career, however, proved but short: the manager, among his other theatrical apparatus, happened to have a very beautiful wife, who was likewise a sprightly, clever actress. Stafford Jackson, being a very handsome and insinuating fellow, soon got completely into this lady's good graces: he wrought so far upon her mind, as to persuade her to elope with him for London. They accordingly set off together one fine morning, --having first taken the judicious measure of securing the contents of the manager's treasury to defray the expenses of their journey. The latter took the loss of his wife with philosophica. indifference; but the abstraction of his exchequer occasioned the breaking up of the company, as he could not pay the actors' arrears.

Stafford Jackson now entered, for the first time, on a London life. He soon formed a numerous set of acquaintances, more remarkable for wit than honesty. He passed his whole time at cards, billiards, hazard, and "rouge et noir." Previously to his arrival in London, he had been no mean proficient in gaming; but he now became completely initiated into all the mysteries of that noble science. Stafford was not one of those fools who trust their hopes of success to the blind chances of fortune: he took care to ascertain the means of fixing the wavering and capricious goddess; and he employed them without any scruples of conscience.

The manager's capital, in such judicious hands, could not fail to be considerably improved. His fair rib continued for some time to be the companion of Jackson; and they lived in most excellent style on the proceeds of his new profession.

But, alas! human happiness is but a fleeting shadow: Stafford Jackson soon furnished a striking illustration of this trite remark. On returning one night to his lodgings, he found, to his great horror, that the fair Angelina had sheered off in a fog under a crowd of sail, with all the moveables she could conveniently carry, and his entire stock of ready cash.

This was a devil of a blow to Stafford, who

passed exactly two hours thirty-five minutes and seven seconds, in cursing and damning the entire sex. He soon, however, regained his philosophical composure: he knew that all searches after the fair one would, in all probability, be fruitless; and besides, he had very potent reasons against instituting any inquiries that might bring him and his affairs before the public eye Fortunately, he had about twenty pounds in his pocket, which he had won that night, and a good suit of clothes on his back: reflecting, then, "that what can't be cured must be endured," he took fresh lodgings, and determined to prosecute his profession with increased ardour and assiduity.

Fortune consoled Stafford for the disappointment of love, and he speedily realized a few hundred pounds: with these he made a trip to Paris, to try his luck there, and to amuse himself in the French capital. He had other reasons, too, which rendered a short absence from London, just at this time, rather convenient than otherwise: his face was beginning to be rather too well known, and some of the flats were growing rather shy of a contest with such a determined favourite of fortune.

Stafford did not meet with all the success in Paris that he anticipated: he found many there who were just as clever as himself, and who met him on equal terms. He was forced very frequently to play "*upon the square;*" and the consequence was, that fortune treated him in the same way that she does other people: he lost as often as he won, and began to find .that his finances were rapidly declining.

He now changed his plan of operations. Quitting altogether the public gaming-tables of the Palais Royal, Frescati, &c., he devoted his entire attention to cultivating the acquaintance of the English in Paris. By his gentlemanly exterior and insinuating manners, he succeeded in conciliating their intimacy; and soon made up, by private play, what he had lost by public.

It was at this time that Stafford became acquainted with the incomparable Captain Creed: he had seen him at the gaming tables, and was not long in observing that he might be made a very useful assistant for his own purposes. Creed's appearance and situation, precluded the possibility of Jackson treating him on a footing of equality in public; it would excite suspicion, and prove equally injurious to both. He, therefore, proposed that Creed should act as his servant: the latter readily agreed to this. Jackson clothed him in a handsome livery, and master and man lived famously for a while on the united produce of their ingenuity and industry.

But an accident soon occurred which rendered the climate of Paris rather too warm for the constitution of Stafford Jackson. A young officer in the English army, the son of a nobleman, lost a very considerable sum to him one night, playing at the game of ecarté. A gentleman present, who was a very attentive spectator of the play, took the young man aside, and told him that he would be very wrong to pay the money, for he had no doubt that all was not fair: the young officer returned to the table, accused Jackson of foul play, and refused to pay the cash. It was in vain that the other stormed, and swore, and bullied: it ended by the officer putting into his pocket the pack of cards which had been provided by our friend Captain Creed, and, walking off, declared that he would expose the affair all over Paris.

Jackson, and his worthy valet de chambre, knew too well that the cards would not stand the test of examination, and were far too prudent to await the result: they got their passports made out immediately for London. Before they set off, however, **Stafford paid a visit to a** gentleman of property, residing at St. Cloud, and told him **that** he was going to England, and would be happy to execute any commands. The gentleman, who, of course, had heard nothing of the true cause of Jackson's departure, said that it occurred very fortunately; that he wanted to send a carriage to England, and would be much obliged to his friend Mr. Jackson, if he would take charge of it The latter, it may be well believed, did not hesitate: he, and his right hand man, the captain, travelled in the carriage to Calais; brought it over; and when they arrived in London, sold it immediately, and divided the proceeds.

Stafford Jackson was obliged to keep himself remarkably close while he remained in London: therefore he took lodgings in an obscure part of town, and dropping the name of Jackson, called himself Mr. Stafford.   He had a good sum of money about him, but had not yet made up his mind what line of conduct to pursue: he felt the necessity of absenting himself for some time from London, where he could not possibly carry on operations at present with any safety; but he could not determine to what quarter he should steer his course.

While he was in this state of indecision, he went one evening to regale himself in an obscure pot-house in the neighbourhood: there he met with a seafaring man, an American, and entered into conversation with him.   The American spoke much of his own country, vaunted loudly of her riches and independence, and particularly dwelt on the wealth and splendor of New York and Philadelphia.   Stafford Jackson listened to him with great attention, and determined in his own mind on a voyage to America.

He soon got every thing in readiness, and within ten days was on his passage from Liverpool to New York.

Stafford Jackson found the *New Yorkites*, however unpleasant in many points, to be fully as much attatched to gaming as he could possibly desire: but, like the Parisians, they were tolerably old hands; and our hero did not reap among them a very plentiful harvest.   He was, however, no loser; and as he could not think of returning to England so soon, he was about to make the tour of the United States, when a circumstance occurred which altered his determination.

It is not easy for the most peaceably disposed subject to mix much in New York society without having a duel upon his hands. It may, therefore, be well supposed that Stafford Jackson, among whose vices fear was not to be numbered, did not escape the usual ordeal. He was called out by an American Colonel and fishmonger, in consequence of a dispute arising out of a game of cards. He went to the field accompanied by an Englishman, who called himself Captain Brown: when he arrived there, he found the piscatory Colonel waiting for him, armed with a blunderbuss loaded with slugs. Captain Brown attempted to remonstrate with him about the unfairness of this, but to no purpose. "Oh! damn the scoundrel," said Stafford Jackson; "let him keep his blunderbuss.'

They fired;—the fishmonger lodged two slugs in Jackson's left shoulder, and the latter shot his adversary through the heart, who instantly dropped dead upon the spot.

This affair led to a very close intimacy between Brown and Jackson. The former was a man about forty years of age, of short stature but herculean make, with an enormous pair of black mustachios. This man had received a captain's commission from the Mexican government, and had fitted out a small armed vessel to cruise in

13

the Atlantic and Pacific Oceans, where he trusted
very soon to be enabled to repay his expenses
He had come to New York for the purpose of
engaging some additional hands.

As soon as Captain Brown had learned that
Jackson had been in the navy, he asked him to
join him, and offered to make him his second in
command. " We give no pay," said he, "but
there will be a fair division of prizes, and plenty
of them." The proposal was too much to Jackson's taste not to accept of it. His wounds were
soon cured, and he and the Captain embarked
and put out to sea immediately.

The crew of this vessel was equally worthy of
the commander and his lieutenant, and of the
peculiar character of the service on which it was
employed. It was a pleasing melange of outcasts
and vagabonds of different nations—Mexicans,
North Americans, English, Mulattos, and Blacks.
"These rascals," said Brown, " fight well, but
I have the devil's work to keep them in order."
Well accustomed as Jackson had been, in London
and elsewhere, to the sight of ruffians, he was a
little startled at the first appearance of these
gentry : they realized all that imagination had ever
painted of bandits and pirates.

Jackson soon found that his friend, Captain
Brown, by no means confined his attention
exclusively to the enemies of the Mexican empire.
He was, in fact, no very scrupulous respecter of
neutrality, and paid much more regard to the

size and strength of the vessels he met with, than to their national colours. The flag of the United States, indeed, formed an exception to this rule—for the best of reasons. Brown knew too well that the American government would soon find the means of punishing his infraction of neutrality, and that he would also lose the principal, if not the only, market for the disposal of his prizes.

With Captain Brown, Stafford Jackson remained for nearly two years, during which period they had several sharp affairs with Spanish vessels, and committed a vast number of piratical as well as privateering acts. They had even the audacity to make two or three descents on different parts of the Spanish coast, plundering and murdering for the space of some miles, and then returning to their vessel.

During their courses they made many good prizes, and accumulated a good deal of money. Their conquests, too, were generally made without any very great expense of blood, as they generally engaged with vessels of much inferior strength: sometimes, however, they met with an unexpected resistance. They attacked a merchant vessel from Alicant, which, instead of striking immediately, as they expected, saluted them with a volley, and maintained for a little time a tolerable fight. It was, however, obliged at last to give in, and the master and crew, consisting in all of only eight hands, paid the forfeit of their imprudent bravery with their lives.

But this affair proved fatal to Captain Brown. He was wounded in his right groin, and died in two days after, in great agony. Jackson conducted the vessel to America, and disposed of the cargo at Boston.

Stafford Jackson now found himself worth three or four thousand pounds in ready cash. He resolved to quit the trade of piracy, and return to England, there to make some inquiries about his father. He left his vessel and crew at Boston, who, had they known of his intentions, would not have parted with him so easily, and travelled by land to New York, where he embarked for England.

As soon as he landed he set off for his father's residence in Suffolk. Not being quite certain of meeting with a favourable reception, he did not go to his father's house directly, but waited upon his old friend, Captain Carribles, whom he intended to employ as a mediator in his favour. He found the old boy exactly as he left him, in no wise altered by the lapse of years. He still retained his foreman, Tom Squires, who seemed to stand the best of time as well as his master. Carribles at first did not recognize Stafford, he was so much altered; but when he told him who he was, he shook him warmly by the hand, at the same time alluding, with regret, to his early conduct. Stafford told him a long and plausible tale of his adventures, and concluded with saying that he had now realized some property by commercial transactions, and was returned for the purpose of being reconciled with his father, and sharing his fortune with him. Old Carribles readily undertook the office of mediator, and easily prevailed on Jackson's father to receive his son again.

Stafford's father did not long enjoy the fruits of reconciliation. He died soon after, leaving his property (not very considerable) to his son, who, however improved it by marrying a young lady in the neighbourhood, with a fortune of two thousand pounds.

One would have imagined, that Stafford would have now settled himself down to something like a regular and respectable course of life. For a while, indeed, he appeared inclined to do so. His wife was an amiable woman, and he seemed, at least, to be attached to her. But his natural disposition, and the inveterate influence of habit, proved stronger than her attractions and his own original resolutions. He began to find himself like a fish out of water, and to long for a renewal of his former irregularities. His was one of those constitutions to which the stimulus of difficulty and danger seemed absolutely indispensable. He seemed as incapable of existing without it, as the habitual drunkard without his usual excitement.

He began by making frequent trips to London, under some pretext or other. There he recommenced his career of vice and dissipation, and soon got rid of the principal part of the money he had gained abroad, as well as his wife's fortune. He at last scarcely ever past any time at home, with the exception of coming down for the purpose of receiving his quarter's rents, which having done, he would return to town immediately. His wife's health, naturally delicate, at last totally gave way under a series of neglects and insults, and his repeated and notorious infidelities. She died of a consumption in little more than twelve months after their unfortunate union.

Jackson was now pretty nearly at the end of all his ready cash. His property, however, near Ipswich, yet remained, and with moderate habits would have sufficed for his subsistence; but for his wants it was totally inadequate. He therefore disposed of it for a sum of money to a merchant desirous of retiring from business, and recommenced his precarious and unprincipled mode of life.

About this time Stafford became acquainted with our friend Jack Smith, whom we have already introduced to the reader's notice.

Jack was one of those thorough-paced knaves that nature seldom produces in complete perfection. He was unredeemed by the slightest semblance of any thing like a virtue, unless we can honour the courage of a ruffian with such a title. He was the son of a Suffolk cotter, and having evinced very early an extraordinary precocity in wickedness, at the age of twelve begar to despise his parent's honest mode of life robbed him, and ran away to London. Here he formed suitable and congenial connexions, and soon became a thief and pickpocket of the most expert kind. As he ran risks of every description, all his cleverness could not extricate him out of serious scrapes. His feet became familiar with the stocks, and his neck with the pillory. He had sojourned in Bridewell and the Hulks, and taken no less than two short trips to the Antipodes.

At the time of which we are now writing, Jack Smith was connected with a desperate gang of smugglers down in Suffolk; but he did not, on that account, relinquish his system of land robbing. Between the town and country, he contrived to drive a very flourishing trade. He was married, and under his house near Polstead he had a cavern, which was a grand depôt for his spoliations of all kinds.

This accomplished gentleman was known universally among his companions by the *soubriquet* of *Beauty* Smith,—given him, not in reference to any physical peculiarities, but to the purity and moral excellence of his life and character.

At his suggestion, Jackson united himself to the smugglers, among whom was president Warren, aforementioned, and by his courage, naval experience, and superiority of intellect, soon acquired over them a complete ascendancy. He was, indeed, eminently calculated to command desperadoes of any kind: he knew how both to conciliate their attachment and insure their respect.

As the period to which we allude was previous to the establishment of the preventive service, Jackson and his friends drove a famous trade. He passed his time between making smuggling trips, and carrying on in London the business of swindling in general. When down in Suffolk, he had accidently seen Maria Marten, or whom he became enamoured ; and, perhaps, it is almost superfluous to inform our readers, that the gentleman with the white hat, whom she met at the fair, and his companion, were no other than our good friends, Mr. Stafford Jackson, and Mr John, alias Beauty, Smith.

Such was the foundation on which the innocent victim of superstition built all her hopes of future fortune!

CHAP. VI.

Boxers, parsons, wits, and bores;
Gamblers, swindlers, thieves, and w••••s
Duns and debtors—scores on scores,
        All in Life in London

                      Song Book.

WHEN we discontinued our regular story to introduce our readers to a more intimate acquaintance with Stafford Jackson and Beauty Smith, we left William Barnard in the "holy keeping" of the latter.

Barnard was, at this time, a very young man, with no great expansion of mind, and less know-'edge of the world. He was, as we have before mentioned, the son of a wealthy farmer; and his education was of that description which such persons usually receive from parents who retain, unimpaired by modern refinement, that wholesome system of bringing up their children, which, for centuries, was a main power in producing England's boast—a wealthy and happy farmer-hood. And although in Barnard cannot be found a proof of the superiority of such a system, yet it

14

may be questioned whether the *"improvements,"* which of late years have been added to the education of the young English farmers, exercise so beneficial an influence on such persons as is commonly imagined. Without imparting a much greater quantum of really useful knowledge, the sort of education to which we allude, is calculated to produce tastes, and foster propensities, which are not in the strictest unison with the peculiar destinies of such people. It is often adapted to create a dissatisfaction with their rank in life, and a love of expensive enjoyment above their sphere, and too often fatal to their true interests and happiness. It is too often adapted to detach them from the path of steady industry, by which alone their success in life can be insured. Pleasures incompatible with their resources become necessary to their existence, and they have recourse to means of procuring them alike inconsistent with integrity and safety.

William Barnard, with the narrow intellect and superficial education we have mentioned, was a man of strong passions and strong mental impulses. These, however, did not display themselves in short and violent ebullitions, but rather operated with permanence and regularity. He seemed, indeed, incapable of any sudden strong impression; however, an impression once made was not easily effaced, but proved a lasting motive to action Such a character, when its impulses receive a right direction, is capable of much good; and unfortunately, when the reverse is the case, is equally capable of much evil.

His personal appearance was by no means above his situation in life: nor was it, perhaps, equal to it, if we take robust health, athletic proportions, and frankness of demeanour as the standard. He was below the middle size, lightly made, and possessed a gloominess and repulsiveness of countenance, rarely to be seen in men of fair and ruddy complexion such as he was.

Barnard rose on the morning following the night we have described, with his head as little benefited by the drinking of the previous evening, as his pocket was by the gaming. He was not much pleased with the result of the latter, which left him minus all his ready cash; but he never for a moment suspected any foul play on the part of his worthy friends, and consoled himself with the recollection, that he was to receive £250 that morning for the sale of a quantity of corn belonging to his father. He dressed himself, and coming down stairs, found his good friends, the all-accomplished Stafford Jackson and the amiable Mr. Beauty Smith, waiting breakfast for him.

"Good morrow, Mr. Barnard," said Jackson; "how have you rested last night?"

"But badly," replied Barnard; "my head and stomach are not all right this morning."

"Allow me to be your doctor, Mr. Barnard," said Stafford; "I prescribe to you a bottle of soda water, with a glass of brandy in it: nothing so famous after a night's debauch : it's my regular morning's dose, without which I can do no business."

"Well," said Beauty Smith, "every one to their taste; for my part, I find the brandy do as well without soda water."

Barnard, however, thought proper to follow the prescription of Jackson, who, contrary to the approved practice of physicians, took a dose of his own medicine; while Jack Smith, with his unsophisticated taste, swallowed two glasses of brandy in its native strength and purity.

Now my gentlemen sat down to breakfast, and here their different tastes and characters appeared.

Stafford Jackson would have nothing but strong coffee, a devilled mackarel, finishing with a small glass of brandy; Barnard breakfasted on tea, toast, and eggs; while Jack Smith demolished half a side of a huge buttock of beef, which he washed down with one quart of the best triple X.

Being each of them now fortified in his peculiar way, Jackson said to Barnard,—

"Well, Mr. Barnard, I will not ask how you like London, you have seen too little of it yet; and certainly that little is not calculated to make you much in love with it. I fear, like myself, you were something of a loser last night."

"Oh! don't mention it," says Barnard; "a trifle —a mere trifle."

"How much?" said Jackson.

"Only thirty pounds," said Barnard.

"I am sorry for your loss," replied the other, "though I myself lost more in betting on you. That cursed fellow, old Warren, is always in high luck. By the bye, I shall have to hand him over five-and-thirty."

"That's nothing for a man of your property, Jackson," dryly observed Beauty.

"Not a great deal, to be sure," said Jackson; "but more than I ought to lose :—you know I am depending on the old fellow."

"Old Harry, I suppose," said Smith, *sotto voce;* then aloud, "Oh, he'll open his purse strings. What the devil are these rich old fathers for, but to supply us young chaps with the needful?—eh! Barnard, my boy, what say you?"

"I am entirely of your opinion," replied Barnard.

"Right, my dear boy," said Beauty, "and now, I say, my old cock, we'll show you a little of London life to-day.—Eh! Jackson, what say you—shall we take our friend Barnard the rounds to-day?"

"I shall feel most happy," replied Jackson, "in contributing to Mr. Barnard's amusement while he remains in town—if," he added, bowing, "if he has no objection, and is not better engaged."

"Oh," said Barnard, "I am your man; there's nothing I wish more than to see the varieties of London life. I have nothing to do except to call on my father's old salesman for £250, and then I am quite at your service."

"Then let us consult," said Jackson, "how

we shall pass the day;—the forenoon is rather dull; how can we get on until dinner?"

"Why," said Smith, "there will be good fun to-day, at the Fives Court. It is for Scroggins' benefit,—some prime bang-up sparring I can assure you."

"Very good," replied Jackson; "the very thing: it will amuse our friend greatly; who, as a countryman, must be fond of all manly athletic exercises."

"There's nothing I delight in more," said Barnard.

"Then, Mr. Barnard," said Jackson, "I promise you a great treat. You shall see some noble specimens of the science of self-defence. Who are to be there, Jack, to-day?"

"Why," replied Jack, "there's Neate and Scroggins, Cropley and Young Sam, Harry Holt and Jack Randal, Spring, Langan, and Whiteheaded Bob,—in short, all the prime lads of the fancy."

"Bravo!" exclaimed Jackson; "we shall have some good sport."

"Then let us toddle," said Beauty.

Off they set; and Barnard could not help observing how very differently Jackson appeared from what he did on the preceding night: he was what is technically termed *knowingly togged*—quite in the sporting style. He wore a very well made whitish drab surtout, with one small cape, a velvet collar, and lined through with silk. This, though appearing to be a top-coat, was in fact, a regular body coat made to fit tightly, and show the figure. He wore white cord breeches and handsome top-boots—a coloured handkerchief round his neck, with the ends falling down a little in front. A *white* hat completed his costume, and he carried in his hand a small ash switch.

Beauty Smith was habited as he was the night before.

They first went to where the old salesman lived, where Barnard entered alone, Jackson and his friend remaining in the street, as they thought upon the whole that it was more consistent with prudence not to make their appearance. They knew nothing of the man, it is true, but then it was just barely possible that he might know something of them, and might give Barnard some friendly hints touching the *taking* qualifications of his new associates. Indeed, to an old and knowing hand, their very appearance, especially that of Beauty, might inspire a very salutary distrust of the fitness of such companions for a young country farmer. All these considerations naturally suggested themselves to the minds of experienced and reflecting men like Stafford and his worthy compeer. Good generals in every point of view, they were not less cautious in avoiding an ambuscade and securing a retreat, than they were bold in pushing for a probable victory, and prompt in following up a successful blow.

When they arrived at the Fives Court, the

company had already begun to assemble. It was of the usual description, consisting of flats and sharps, pigeons and rooks, gentlemen amateurs and professional pugilists, young men of fortune who are anxious to get rid of their money, and men of no fortune equally anxious to get hold of it. The former influenced by the ambition of distinguishing themselves as men of *taste* and *fancy;* the latter once ruined by the same ambition, but now living by the fruits of their experience.

"*On commence par etre dupe, on finit par etre fripon,*" is a proverb applicable to all men who engage in the ruinous career of gaming, of whatever kind, whether on the turf, in the prize-ring, or at any games of chance or skill, where money is depending. The only exception to this rule, is when they have resolution enough to withdraw themselves from such pursuits in time to preserve a sufficiency to live on, or to engage in more honourable pursuits : but it too generally happens, that when a young man has lost all his money, the fascination of his former habits still continues, and perhaps operates even more strongly than ever. He cannot quit the scenes of his losses and his disgrace, but continues to haunt them as the ghosts of misers are fabled to hover round the places where their treasures have been buried. He is led to inquire into the causes of his ruin, and having ascertained them, to put them in operation upon others. He is led to associate

with sharpers and with swindlers, to study their
arts, and to practise their deceptions; and when
he has lost all, he cannot, like the gallant
monarch of France, have the consolation to except
his honour.

There are, indeed, a few lofty spirits, whose
career will not exactly admit of the application
of the proverb. Those gifted geniuses commence,
continue, and conclude, *"par être fripons,"*—
having from infancy some peculiar lumps or
bumps, the nomenclature of which we leave to
Messrs. Gall and Spurzheim,—they exhibit
always a decided propensity for cheating, and an
adequate capacity in its theory and practice: if
they ever fail to cheat, the goodness of their
intentions cannot be called in question;—either
circumstances render an occasional observance of
honesty expedient, or short-sightedness prevents
them from using the opportunity of deceiving. Such
men were the honourable Captain Creed and the
amiable Mr. Beauty Smith. These men would
cheat under all circumstances, and their friends
and companions were just as liable to be plundered
by them as anybody else.

Such, however, was not altogether Stafford
Jackson,—he was of a higher order: he had, it is
true, commenced the business of imposition so
very early, that it became to him a second nature.
But he had many redeeming qualities with all
his bad ones: he would not exercise his profession at the expense of an associate of his own

15

kind, or even of any man whom he liked, or to whom he was under any obligation. There was also a dash of chivalry and romance about his character, which rendered mere common swindling and sharping not altogether to his taste, notwithstanding his practice of them. He had a natural disdain for every thing on a petty and sordid scale. As indicative of intellect, he hated little frauds, but admired great ones. Under similarly favourable circumstances, he could have hoaxed an entire nation like as Law did the French. In the corrupt times of the Roman republic, he could have figured like Catiline, whom he resembled in his inordinate taste for vicious pleasures and expense, his total want of principle, his daring courage, and his extraordinary flexibility. In more lawless times, and more lawless countries, he would have been the formidable leader of a band of robbers : in the court of a Charles, he would have been like Rochester or Buckingham. In England, in the year 18—, he was a smuggler, a sharper, and a *roué*.

Disdaining, however, petty transactions, and not being devoid of generous sentiments, Stafford Jackson would not have willingly lent himself to the ruin of a young country lad like Barnard, merely for the sake of the gain which might accrue to himself from the transaction. But he felt the necessity of binding to himself such associates as Creed and Smith : he could not do without them ;—there were many things which he either could not, or would not, perform himself, in which such men were useful instruments. He, in fact, considered the generality of men either as his tools or victims; and no man possessed better the talent of conciliating each peculiar character. He had a Proteus-like facility of changing the phases of his manners and conversation. With gentlemen he could be a perfect gentleman, with blackguards a complete blackguard; to the learned he could talk of literature, to the fair of love; with the politician he could converse on politics, with the merchant on business. He was an adept in the mysteries of the prize-ring, and a cultivator of poetry and music. In short, he suited himself to the peculiar disposition, information, and profession, of every man. It was thus that by his courage, rough bearing, and naval dialect, he won the attachment of Warren; by his cleverness, quickness, and wit in roguery, he gained the esteem of Creed; and by his pretended total want of every right and natural feeling, that he obtained the regard of the amiable and interesting Beauty Smith.

At the Fives Court this day, there was some capital sparring, which highly enchanted Barnard, but of which it is not necessary to trouble our readers with a minute description. The merits of the various great men who have done such immortal honour to our country in the prize-ring and Fives Court, and the mysteries of the noble science, have been recorded by abler pens than ours, in the inperishable annals of pugilism. Lo! are not the same written in the chronicles of Pierce and Vincent? It would be presumptuous in us to infringe on the province of these great historians, and vain to emulate their excellence. We neither possess their profound knowledge of the subject, nor the incomparable eloquence with which they can adorn it. The task is far above us—far, indeed, above all but themselves. The harmonious name of Scroggins should never sound in any verse but the mellifluous metres of the one, nor roll through any prose but the sonorous periods of the other. None but Homer or Pindar should chant the achievements of heroes and of gods.

Still, though we refrain with pious awe from touching the mysteries of the science, we may be permitted to offer such remarks on the general effects of its practice as suggest themselves very obviously to the uninitiated observer. It cannot be denied that the art of sparring is in itself both elegant and healthful. It is admirably calculated to develope the muscles, and to expand the chest,—to give rectitude to the carriage and vigour to the frame. The whole business of training is also improving to the constitution and general health of the individual. Nor, as an useful art, is the art of self-defence with the weapons with which nature has provided us to be despised. Unfortunately, it may sometimes be expedient to know it, and necessary to exert it, in a metropolis like London. We may add that its general prevalence may be useful in equalizing the contests which must occur among the lower orders.

But when we have said all this, we have said all that can with truth and consistency be alleged in favour of pugilism. That it has any tendency to improve the national courage, is merely visionary. Englishmen were just as brave before the introduction of pugilism, as they are at present. No one will deny that the heroes of Agincourt and Cressy were as brave as those of Salamanca, Vittoria, and Waterloo. But what sets this question at rest at once, is the fact that the latter were as little indebted to the pugilistic art as the former,—for the best of all reasons, that the vast majority of them knew just as little about it. Moreover, we have been told by experienced officers, that the few pugilists who had enlisted in their regiments proved in general the worst soldiers.

Indeed, on the question of courage we might naturally expect that pugilism would exercise an effect totally different from what has been stated. True courage can be exerted only on occasions where the danger is great, and the mutual powers of resistance are at least fully equal. This may sometimes be the case in the prize-ring; but rarely, if ever, so in common life. It requires but little courage to engage in a contest, under the influence of a confidence inspired by our own strength, activity, and skill, and in the consciousness that the result cannot be fatal. Very different is the feeling, only worthy of the name of courage, which, produced by intellectual discipline, bears its possessor calmly through scenes of peril and of death, conscious of his risk, and conscious of his weakness.

But though pugilism cannot inspire true courage, it may foster a feeling very different and very pernicious. It may feed a quarrelsome spirit, and give occasion to the exercise of brutal ferocity. The man who has great confidence in his own strength and skill, will not always be very slow to provoke a conflict, where he is almost certain of victory, nor can the by-standers always interpose effectually to prevent the unfair contention. They may stop its progress sometimes, without being able to prevent its commencement from being seriously detrimental to the unequal adversary.

But the great and crying evil which has arisen out of pugilism, is its having been made the vehicle of gaming. This it is which has so degraded the character of its professors, and communicated so strong a tinge of depravity to all connected with it. A prize-fighter may think as highly of himself as he pleases, but a race-horse is incomparably the superior animal of the two. The latter is influenced only by a generous emulation of superiority. If he be made the instrument of the sordid purposes of man, it is without his concurrence, and he participates not in the debasing gain. The image of the Creator, and the divine gift of reason, are not obliterated and perverted in him. But the pugilist hires out his strength and skill for sale voluntarily; which would not be degrading, were they exerted for one useful purpose, but which produce no other result than degradation to himself, and the most fatal mischief to society.

Look at the countenances, hear the language, and observe the line of life, of the professors and amateurs of pugilism, and who will have the audacity to declare that their profession and pursuits are innocent and useful? If any illustration were needed of the evil tendencies of the pugilistic profession, surely we have it in the manners and conduct of those who cultivate it! The first are characterized by grossness and vulgarity, the second by profligacy and want of principle. Let any man, if he be fearless of contamination, stroll through the various recesses of midnight and morning debauchery, with which this mighty Babylon is infested, in spite of the integrity and vigilance of the police, and the sapient sagacity of our pinguified magistrates; who is he most certain to find there?—Pugilists, or the amateurs of pugilism, with their inseparable companions, --prostitutes, sharpers, and thieves. How many of the professors and amateurs have fallen premature victims to the vices and excesses in which their pursuit would appear inevitably to involve them!

It is become matter of perfect notoriety, that the battles of the prize-ring are now generally pre-arranged as to who shall win and who shal lose, so that the flats must be " gammoned," and the sharps come off triumphant. This we do not regret, as it may prove the means of putting a period to the evil. But what other result could be expected from men of the lowest birth, of no education, of profligate habits, and desperate fortunes, but that they should unhesitatingly sell themselves to the highest bidder?

It has been said that pugilism keeps up the spirit of the people, and the corollary drawn from this is, that prize-fighting is necessary to keep up the spirit of pugilism. We have already answered the first position: but, granting that it were desirable to keep up this pugnacious temper, we deny that the periodical exhibitions of the prize-ring are necessary for that purpose. Man, unfortunately, is too well inclined for the said pugnacity, to need any such incentive. Ay, but, say our opponents, if you remove pugilism, you introduce the knife and dagger, as in Portugal and Italy; or you have a dozen men trampling upon one, as in France and elsewhere; or the exquisite gouging of the eyes, as in Connecticut. No, no!—Englishmen have never been a nation of assassins and cowards.

In all that we have said of pugilism and its professors, be it remembered that we allow there are some honourable exceptions; but there are very few in number: still, their conduct is worthy of the greater credit, when we consider what is, and must be, the almost inevitable tendency of their profession.

To return from this, not perhaps unnecessary digression:—on the different " turn-ups " that took place this day at the Fives Court, there was betting to a considerable amount. Our worthy acquaintance, Captain Creed, was there, and as he knew well how to bet, was, we dare say, no loser. Barnard, as might be expected, was no gainer: he was eased of twenty pounds by his friends,—one, as usual, appearing to lose while the others won.

Jackson, Beauty, and Barnard, now left the Fives Court. It was yet early, and Creed proposed to adjourn somewhere for refreshment. They accordingly went to a tavern not a hundred miles from the east end of Holborn, kept by a noted pugilist. When they sat down, they observed two men in the farther corner of the room, busily employed in drinking ale and tossing shillings. When our friends came in, they stopped, and one of them, who recognized Creed as an acquaintance, saluted him. He was a stout and portly looking man, about thirty or upwards, with a florid complexion, and rather good-humoured handsome countenance. Some conversation ensued, and this man asked Creed to join in the game. Creed said he had no objection to toss for a bottle of ale, but declined playing for money.

16

The ale was tossed for, won by Creed, and drank, when the original proposer resumed his propositions to play for half-crowns.

"No, Mr. Pinks," replied Creed, "I never toss for money."

"Will *you*, gentlemen?" said the other, addressing Jackson, Smith, and Barnard.

The former two declined.

"I have no objection," said Barnard, in whom the ale had begun to inspire some confidence.

The other three, who did not choose that a stranger should have any of their pickings, strongly dissuaded him.

Barnard seemed still inclined, and was rising to move to the other table, when Jackson sprung up, and seizing him by the arm—

"Mr. Barnard," he exclaimed, "you are wrong, very wrong;—you don't know London. I must request—nay, I must insist, that you will forbear. I will not suffer you to toss with a stranger."

Barnard, over-awed by his manner, sat down.

"Stranger," replied the man who was thus designated; "I am no stranger to *some* of you. I suppose you have caught a flat among you, and want to keep him all to yourselves."

"Scoundrel!" exclaimed Jackson, "how dare you cast such an imputation?"

"Oh!" returned the other, "don't scoundrel me, —the name becomes yourself better; and if you continue this impudence, I'll soon kick you out of the room."

"Boasting liar! I'll soon show you the difference," exclaimed Jackson; and jumping over the table, with the quickness of lightning struck him under the right eye. The other was not slow in retorting, and a regular set-to was about to take place, when the landlord entered.

"Gentlemen," said he, "this room is no place for fighting—among all these chairs and benches. I don't know what your quarrel may be, but my maxim is, when gentlemen can't make up matters amicably, to let them have it out;—they are always better friends afterwards. I have got a long room up stairs, in which you may amuse yourselves if you have a mind;—these gentlemen and myself will see fair play."

"Come along then," roared out both the combatants.

Up stairs they went, and a regular scientific battle took place. Jackson's antagonist was rather the superior in size and weight, and exhibited no small degree of pugilistic skill; but the other was both more active and muscular, equally scientific in defence, had better wind, and was a quicker hitter. There was a great deal of fine play on both sides, and for a time the contest seemed nearly equal. At last Jackson planted several hits in succession with the rapidity of lightning, the last of which staggered his adversary, who fell into the arms of his friend and seconder. He seemed to be rather exhausted, and to want wind.

" I will wait for you, Mr. Pinks," said Jackson.

"Now gentlemen," said the landlord, " let me interfere. You have both done as prettily as possible—you could not do better had you been my own pupils. I think you ought, therefore, to be satisfied and shake hands. I like to see a neat set-to, but not too much of it."

Said Jackson, " If the gentleman be satisfied, I am. If he choose to have more, I'm ready."

"No, Mr. Jackson," replied the other, advancing, " you are a brave man. Give me your hand—I am sorry for what I said."

" I can return the compliment as to bravery," said Jackson, shaking hands with him; " and I wish nothing better than to be friends with you. So come, and let us drown our disputes over a bottle, at my expense."

"With all my heart," returned Pinks; so down stairs they went.

In the passage the following conversation took place between the antagonists, who let the others precede them.

" But I say, my good friend," said Stafford, " you should not poach on a neighbour's manor."

" Pooh! pooh!" said the other; " say no more of that. I did not mean to poach, but I thought we might just toss a little for amusement."

" Oh! damn your innocence," exclaimed Jackson; " I know what your tossing for amusement is. Is there a man in London *can* toss with you? Haven't you made it as certain as sun-rise?

The other laughed, and then asked him, where he had hooked his fish?

"He's none of my hooking," replied Jackson; "Beauty was the bait he bit at. But I'll tell you more to-night, if you come to Grubb's, or the Finish: in the mean time, mum's the word."

These two worthies (who, as it appears, knew each other perfectly well,) now entered a little room behind the bar, and the whole party sat down to ale and sandwiches, and lunched heartily. Jackson then called for a bottle of wine, and drinking Pinks' health, said " Well, Mr. Pinks, here's may we never meet again in anger; for damn me if I don't think I got very well out of your hands."

"I may say the same to you," replied the other.

"Well, well," said Stafford, "I should not like to repeat the experiment."

Thus it was that Jackson conciliated every man. He always threw his own merits into the back ground, and brought forward those of others. Thus, in this contest, though he had the most decided advantage, (and had it continued, his adversary's short wind must have determined in his favour,) yet he chose to give the whole glory to his opponent. If he thought highly of himself, he kept it to himself; for though he had much pride, he had little vanity.

Our party having finished lunch, Jackson proposed to pass away the time at billiards, until dinner.

" But where shall we dine?" demanded Smith.

" At the 'Sablonniere,' in Leicester Square," replied Jackson; "you like a foreign dinner, Captain Creed."

" That I do," said Creed, with a gastronomic chuckle.

" Well," said Jackson, "as we are showing our friend here 'life in London,' we will also show him a spice of French living in London. Mr. Pinks, will you and your friend be of our party?"

" I will," said Pinks, " with pleasure ; but my friend is engaged."

" Well, Smith," said Jackson, " go you to the Sablonniere, and order a crack dinner for five, at half past six o'clock. A private room, do you mind. And I say, my dear fellow, will you call at the Gloucester, Piccadilly, and tell them to send a portmanteau, which was left there for me, down to Leicester Square, and you can return to us at the billiard-rooms?"

" No," replied Smith, " I can't return, for I have to look after some matters of my own; but I shall meet you at dinner."

Beauty accordingly went his way. Mr. Pinks' friend took his leave, and the other four proceeded to the billiard-rooms together.

The rooms were crowded, as usual, with well dressed scamps of all kinds, and fools of every variety of calibre. There was my Lord Roger Komberkin, and honest Tom Ewer, who differed in nothing except that one had a title to an estate, and the other a title to the gallows. In exterior, in actual property, in virtuous inclinations, and in understanding, they were quite upon a par. But my Lord Roger had not shaved the wind quite so close as honest Tom, whose neck was once deemed in reasonable danger from the slight mistake of signing another man's name for him. But Tom assured all his friends, upon his honour, that it was done only to save the gentleman trouble. Tom was believed by one third of the world, disbelieved by another, and doubted by another. Fools thought it was truth, knaves knew it was a lie, and wise men doubted the fact. Tom, however, jogged on merrily, and stood cheek by jowl with my Lord Roger Komberkin, as accomplished a gentleman as himself. There was also the Honourable Stanley Atherton, who yielded to no man as a horse-jockey or a player of billiards and ecarté. There was little Tom Higgins, with his green breeches—an unrivalled flyer of kites ; Captain O'Brien, whose brogue and boots were equally *nate ;* Sir Harry Beaver, who was bottle-holder to Lord D——— when he fought with the Duke of A———, fifteen rounds for a thousand guineas, by way of lark, in C——— House. There were the twin brothers, one literary and the other divine : the literary hero, a "fellow in foolscap turned up with ink," a cogger of other men's thoughts—the divine a blue-bottle parson, who preached other men's sermons, and

one of the blessed "unpaid." There was P. G. H.
a decided *green*horn, and **T. H.** a decided black-
leg.   There was the celebrated family of the
Eusthathioi, true western Greeks.   There was
old Lord Cogham, famous for throwing sixes at
backgammon *by chance ;* and Captain Carnee,
one of the real *sowls* for either macing or malleting.
In short, they were all partly knaves and partly
fools,—not one of them capable of entertaining
a man of sense five minutes with anything like
rational conversation.   How inferior to Stafford
Jackson were such men as these ! even Beauty
Smith had more *νους* in his little finger, than most
of them .

Then there were foreign Counts, who had the
best of all right to their titles, for they were of
their own creation ; Russian noblemen, whose
nobility consisted in their green trowsers and red
whiskers ; Chevaliers of that very ancient order,
d'Industrie ; Hussar Colonels, whose commissions
were in their brass spurs and mustachios ; and
Clergymen, whose livings were on the spot which
they then occupied.

Be it known to you, gentle reader, if you are
not already initiated into the arcana of town, that
the billiard-rooms which we are describing, were
not simply billiard-rooms.   They did not merely
sport tables, cues, and balls : but were appropriated to far nobler and more important purposes,
as many similar establishments in London are.
There were besides billiards, chess and draughts

backgammon, the dice of which, in an adjoining
and well secured room, were found extremely convenient for the purposes of hazard. Cards too,
it is said, were not excluded from this repository
of agreeable and profitable amusement. The proprietor's motto was—

"Omne tulit punctum qui miscuit utile dulci;"

and accordingly, negus, punch, lemonade, &c.
were procured from a neighbouring house, as well
mixed as the nicest connoisseur could possibly
desire.

When our party entered, there was a grand
match playing in that particular room, for 100
guineas the short rub, between Mynheer Van
Hogendorp, a Belgian Baron, and Lieutenant
Colonel O'Kelly, of the Austrian Imperial Guards.
The profoundest silence prevailed; by-bets being
made continually, to a large amount, in low whispers. The players were unrivalled in skill, and
Barnard, who knew a little of billiards, was perfectly astonished at the inimitable science of their
performance. What amazed him most was the
lightning-like rapidity with which each game
was won and lost. Indeed, the fate of every
rubber depended entirely upon which player first
got the balls into his hands. When this fell to
the fortune of one performer, the other was considered to have little or no chance, and the odds
laid in favour of the striker were enormous; yet
it did sometimes happen that the balls assumed
a position which allowed the adversary to use his

17

cue ; in which case he was sure to win the game, though ever so far advanced.

Not seeing any chance of amusing themselves in this room, for the tables were engaged three deep, our party adjourned to another where the tables were free. Here a match took place between Jackson and his friend and late opponent, Mr. Pinks ; and, whether designedly or by accident, Barnard was permitted, in betting, to win back a few of the pounds which he had lost at the Fives Court.

The dinner-hour now approached, and they proceeded to Leicester Square. Arrived there, they found Beauty Smith waiting for them, and quite transformed as to the covering of his outer man. He had taken off his *slang* dress, and put on that of a gentleman,—though he could not muster much of the appearance of one, with all his pains. Jackson retired to a room, where the portmanteau he had given charge to Smith concerning had been left, and soon returned equally metamorphosed in a fashionable evening dress.

" What is the meaning of this change of costume, gentlemen ?" demanded Creed.

" Why," replied Jackson, " we have a notion of visiting one of the theatres this evening, or perhaps the Opera. Our object is to show Mr. Barnard as much as we can."

" But," said Barnard, casting an eye downwards on his boots and inexpressibles, " I am not exactly in trim."

" Never mind, Barnard," observed Beauty, " you

are well enough;—besides, I can lend you what you want,—we are nearly of a size."

They now sat down to dinner in high style. Every delicacy that could be procured was on the table; and their wines were claret, champagne, and burgundy. All this was quite in Jackson's taste, for he had the most decided turn for all elegant and expensive luxuries. His fondness for these, for all kinds of social pleasure, and, above all, his inordinate passion for the fair sex, led him into the greatest expenses; and, notwithstanding his success in gaming, and his admirable skill in " raising the wind," kept him always more or less in want of money. In fact, a princely fortune would have been insufficient to minister to his prodigality;—in this instance, however, he knew that Barnard should pay the piper.

They dined, and got very merry over their wine—singing songs, cracking jokes, &c. They did not, however, drink to excess, for doing so was not to Jackson's taste; nor was it consistent with the *profession* of the other gentlemen, Barnard excepted. When they called for the bill, it may be supposed that it was of a tolerable amount. They were about to settle it, when Pinks said, with a smile,

" Gentlemen, if Mr. Jackson can get over his scruples, suppose we toss to see who shall pay this bill ?"

"Oh!" said Jackson, laughing, "I have no objection in the world; it's only tossing for money that I dislike—and," added he, "with *strangers*. As for you and me, we have been too familiar this morning, to come any longer under that denomination."

"Well, then," said Pinks, "I will begin with you, Mr. Jackson,—two out of three," taking a sovereign out of his pocket.

We must inform our readers, that, by long practice, this man had acquired such extraordinary dexterity in the art of tossing, that he had reduced it to a perfect certainty. Heads or tails were alike to him: he could make either appear, just as he thought proper. In the present instance, in tossing with Jackson, it suited his purpose to lose

"Well, Mr. Jackson," said he, "you are clear of the scrape;—now, Captain Creed."

Pinks lost again, and also in tossing with Smith.

"Now, Mr. Barnard," said Pinks, "it is between us both; but as you are comparatively a *stranger*, I will give you every advantage. These gentlemen have allowed me to toss altogether, and a pretty hand I have made of it; but with you I will first toss once, to see who shall have the first play."

So saying, he threw up a sovereign, and covering it with his hand on the table, said, " Heads or tails, Mr. Barnard?"

"Heads," cried Barnard— and tails they were!

" The first toss is mine," said Pinks. He threw up the sovereign again, and Barnard then crying " tails," lost.

Barnard then tossed, and won.

" Now for the conqueror," cried Pinks; and the result of the third toss settled the dinner bill :—as the reader may well suppose, it was paid by Barnard.

They now broke up. Jackson, Smith, and Barnard, proceeded to Drury Lane Theatre; Creed and Pinks took leave, appointing to meet their *friends* again, after the play, at *Mother H.'s.*

It was near ten when our gentlemen entered the theatre; but as, like a vast majority, they went for any purpose but that of seeing the play, the hour was of small consequence. They were, however, in sufficient time to see a portion of the last act. It so happened that the play was " The Gamester." Barnard had before seen the play performed by a strolling company at Colchester, and was familiar with the plot. The terrible delineation, therefore, given by Kean in the concluding scenes, made a strong impression on his mind; and one which, if equally lasting, would not, perhaps, have contributed to further the pious purposes of his companions.

This did not escape the penetration of Jackson, who, immediately after the play was ended, hurried him off into the saloon, where Barnard soon forgot the impression of the drama in the blaze of elegance and meretricious beauty that surrounded him.

We, who have long been habituated nightly to witness the extraordinary scenes exhibited in the saloons of theatres, look on them with stoical indifference, and even almost forget the first impression which they made upon us; but on a youth fresh from the country, the effect is very much the reverse: to him, the saloon is fairy ground: the frail beauties that adorn it, dressed in the first style of elegant and expensive fashion, are like the houries of Paradise to the imagination of the enthusiastic Arabian. Their forms and faces, which, perfect as many of them are, lose their effect on us, from the ideas of mercenary depravity which we associate with them, have their full influence on him. Tell him what the women are, and he will hardly believe you, until he has witnessed a little of their conduct, manners, and conversation. These are as little in accordance with their features as with their dress; and to hear blasphemies and obscenities, which would disgrace the very lowest of our sex, fall from the lips of a Hebe, is a contrast truly hideous.

There is no absurdity, wickedness, or folly, in the world that has not found its defenders. Accordingly, those nightly exhibitions in the saloons of our theatres,—so disgraceful to our country, so subversive of public morals, and so insulting to the modest portion of the sex,—have had their advocates. The late Mr. Scott, in his " Visit to Paris," compares the cases of England and France in this respect, and gives the preference to the former. He says that this strong line of distinction between vice and virtue is necessary, for the sake of the virtuous part of the community. What nonsense all this speculative sort of reasoning is! What is the fact?—are not thousands of young men ruined by the system which he would uphold? are not numbers of young girls in middle life seduced by the apparent gaiety and happiness of these unfortunate women, and especially by their gaudy and expensive style of dress? and above all, by this strong line of distinction which he advocates, are not these unhappy victims prevented from returning to the paths of virtue—is not the door of repentance closed against them for ever?

Barnard, when the play was over, was conducted by his companions to that sink of iniquity, Mother H.'s. There he beheld the same women that he had seen figuring in the saloon, and many others. There, too, he beheld that assemblage of fools, sharpers, and roués, who, as to exterior all alike, are some of them the dupes, and some the associates, of prostitutes; many of them living on the wages of the prostitution of these wretched women, or allied with them in enter prizes of robbery and plunder.

There are few places more injurious to the youth of this metropolis, and to those who visit it than the place of which we are now speaking. Many a young man has been sent from this seminary of vice, to transportation or the gallows. There are billiard-rooms up stairs, where cheating and plundering proceed to an immense extent; while below, scenes of riotous debauchery last till morning. But this, I suppose, is one of the establishments necessary to be kept up, for the purpose of marking the strong line of distinction between vice and virtue! At all events, it appears, that such is the inefficiency of our laws, that they are unable to suppress it.

Here our friends were rejoined by Captain Creed and Mr. Pinks All the party, with the exception of Barnard. seemed pretty well known to most of the ladies who visited Mother H.'s. However Barnard may have felt inclined, his *friends* had such extraordinary care of his morals, that they prevented him from attaching himself to any of these fair ones. That would not have at all squared with their purposes. He had, they knew, upwards of £120 about him, and they were determined that none but themselves should share the spoil. They encouraged him, however, in his devotions to the rosy god; and with the aid of the execrable "old port" of Mother H., Barnard's brains began to be in a state most admirably suited for their operations.

"Shall we go to *hell,* Captain Creed?" whispered Mr. Pinks.

"No," said Creed, "we will first take a turn in

purgatory;—I have no notion of putting money into the hands of those cursed dealers."

"You are right," said Pinks; "but let us change the scene."

They withdrew, and just looked into the Shakspeare Tavern, then kept by a puritan, ycleped Grubb—one whose name, nature, and occupation, were in the most delightful harmony. The Shakspeare was then appropriated to similar purposes as Mother H.'s, but the order of Cyprians there were rather of a lower cast.

As it was waxing late, or rather early, these were gradually dropping off; scarcely any remained except those whose years and faded beauty had detained them until that advanced hour, in the faint hope of deceiving the indiscriminating vision of inebriety. Such places then present a most melancholy picture, to a mind at all capable of reflection. The first rays of morning beaming through the windows struggle with the expiring artificial light within, and both combined, cast a horrible reflection upon the pale and jaded-looking countenances of the midnight revellers. The fictitious colour worn from the faces of the women, leaves their years and wrinkles exposed to investigation, and exaggerated by fatigue and excess. The ravages, too, of disease can then be clearly seen, and, in short, every defect and deformity becomes more glaring. Then, too, the unmeaning eye of intoxication rolls on vacancy, and the livid skin and furrowed cheek announce, even in

18   T

the prime of life, what a wretched slave is the man of pleasure!

The scene here was not, however, quite so dull as it usually was at the hour of which we are speaking : it was enlivened by a contest between two madmen—the celebrated Bobbins, a constant frequenter of the place, and another, who was a stranger, but who could put in the most unequivocal claims to admission on the score of insanity. Bobbins, who, I suppose, like the Turk, could bear no brother near the throne, was for turning the intruder out, but the latter stoutly resisted the writ of ejection both by blows and vociferations. He sat himself down in a chair and swore that he would *never* walk out. In this particular he kept his word, for he was literally dragged out along the ground by the heels, and pitched into the street.

Our heroes, notwithstanding all they had drunk, contrived to demolish a bowl of bishop at the Shakspeare, after which, as Barnard complained a little of the state of his "upper works," Creed very judiciously proposed to adjourn to Robottom's, and *finish* the evening over a cup of coffee. This was to be the last scene of the drama they had been acting since the morning before. Here they were to make their "*grand coup*," which was to leave Barnard as bare of cash as a coot's head is of feathers, and, if possible, to involve him in engagements beyond the present extent of his finances.

To Robottom's they went. This house is generally considered as the climax of all that is villain-
ous on the Covent Garden side of town ; and, to
say the truth, its pretensions are tolerably well
founded. Nice connoisseurs, indeed, have their
doubts whether or not it be the very worst house
in London. There are others, perhaps, more exclusively devoted to the entertainment of genuine
ruffians of the lowest order ; but they are not so
dangerous, because a respectable person can
scarcely, under any circumstances, be enticed
within their walls. But here is to be found an
assemblage of all kinds :—low dressed and high
dressed ruffians—silken and draggle-tailed
prostitutes—burglars, boxers, gamblers, and
vagabonds. Here the pickpocket who rises early
to go through the business of the day, sits down
in delightful sympathy with the pickpocket who
has sat up all night that he may be up early.
Here the fine lady about to retire to rest, meets
with the market wench lately risen, and redolent
of gin. Flat-fish, too, come in shoals to this
ocean of iniquity ; for they are essentially requi
site to the support of its indigenous sharks.
Without the former, the latter must perish, and
the supply of the one will always be found nicely
balanced by the numbers of the other. Such
are the admirable contrivance, order, and harmony observable in the works of nature !

It must be confessed, that however revolting
such places as we are describing may be to minds

of taste and delicacy, and however totally unfit
for the young and innocent, they are the proper
places for the philosopher.   Here he has an opportunity of studying human nature, stripped of
the disguises which it too often assumes in the
ordinary walks of life, and of seeing fully developed
the genuine baseness of man. In the usual occupa
tions of life he is more or less disguised——he
wears the mask of friendship, of principle, of professional etiquette, of conventional decency, of
morality, and religion, for the purpose of imposing
on his neighbour, and benefiting himself——he
throws into the back ground his brutish appetites
and domestic passions : but in places like these,
his true nature breaks out : we see him as he is,——
brutal, selfish, sordid, unprincipled, and unfeeling;
intent on nothing but the gratification of his
cupidity or his lust ; not satisfied with a total
disregard of the feelings of others, but actively
engaged in the indulgence of his malicious propensities to annoyance.   In the *truth* of intoxication, we see him regardless of every tie of friendship, relationship, and acquaintance,——devoid of
common decency, and of common sense ! Such
we find to be one form of the interesting being
who has the impudence to term himself the
image of the Divinity !

In the upper room at Robottom's. they en
countered the gentleman with the one eye who,
our readers will recollect, constituted one of the
party at Whitechapel, the night of Barnard's

arrival. Whether he was there by accident or design, "deponent sayeth not."

They got into a private room at Robottom's, quite snugly, and ordered coffee; after which they sent out for some brandy, and the honourable Captain Creed proposed, when he saw Barnard, whom the coffee had recovered a little, thoroughly primed, the favourite game of all-fours. This was immediately agreed to, and by none more readily than Barnard. As our good friend, Robottom, was never without a *choice* pack of cards, he soon supplied them with their tools; and 'o work they went, heart and hand.

Creed and the one-eyed gentleman played against Beauty and Barnard, while Jackson and Mr. Pinks amused themselves by mock betting. Game succeeded game, and Barnard was a rapid loser:—at length, being drained of all his money, he stood up and said he would play no more.

"Oh! Mr. Barnard," said Creed, "let us go on; you may win back your money, and it is too soon to retire yet."

"I have no more cash about me," replied Barnard.

"That," returned Creed, "is not of the slightest consequence ;—your security, Sir, is good."

"Come, then, Mr. Barnard," said Smith, taking a gulp of brandy; "let us go to work, and here's luck."

Barnard took a deep draught, and they set to. playing for twenty pourds the rubber.

As might be expected, Barnard lost every

rubber; and continuing to drink, became more and more intoxicated.

"Now, I think," said Creed, "we had better leave off."

"Yes," replied the one-eyed rascal; "but per haps Mr. Barnard will give us his bill for the money he has lost, only for form's sake. It is just two hundred."

"Certainly, certainly," interrupted Smith; "my friend, Mr. Barnard, will do that.—What say you, Barnard, my boy?"

"Do as you like," replied Barnard, who was so overcome by the effects of liquor that he knew not what he was about.

"Rowy," said Creed, calling the worthy host, "have you got a stamp?" (Robottom was never without a few of those useful articles.)

"Yes, Sir," replied he; "for how much?"

"Two hundred," said Creed.

The stamp was produced, and handed to Barnard by Creed, who said,

"Now, Mr. Barnard, if you will give your promissory note at two months, it will do."

"Draw up the note," returned Barnard, "and I'll sign it."

The note was drawn up, and Barnard, with some difficulty, signed his name, laid his head on the table, fell fast asleep, and all attempts to wake him were to no purpose.

"Come," cried Beauty, "let us leave him here, —he's *did*—no use in disturbing him."

" I'll be damned if *I* leave him so, Mr. Smith,"
said Jackson; "we have done the poor lad's
business pretty well for one night—let us have
the humanity to take care of his person, however
his purse may have fared."

" Oh, certainly,' exclaimed Mr. Pinks, "that's
but fair."

" To move him is out of the question," said
Jackson, "now, in broad day-light. I say,
Robottom, have you got a bed for this young
man ?"

" Yes !" replied mine host, " if he can pay for
it."

" I'll pay for it, Mr. Robottom," said Jackson,
" that's enough for you."

" Certainly, Mr. Jackson, your word——"

"Oh ! damn my word, Sir," returned Jackson,
" you shan't trust to that,—here's the money for
the bed ; and here," added he, handing him over
two pounds, " give him this when he wakes, that
he may have something in his pocket, and explain
everything to him that has happened ;—and, d'ye
mind, don't forget to give him the two pounds, or
you know the consequences."

" He'll be sure to have it, Sir," said Robottom

Barnard was then carried up to bed, and the
others departed, Jackson muttering between his
teeth, as he went down stairs, " Damn this Life
in London !"

CHAP. VII.

O let me safely to the fair return,
Say with a kiss she must not, shall not, mourn!
O let me teach my heart to lose its fears,
Recalled by wisdom's voice and Zara's tears,
He said; and called on Heav'n to bless the day
When back to Shiraz' walls he bent his way.

COLLINS.

BARNARD awoke late in the day from that unrefreshing and horrid sleep produced by intoxication,—chequered by confused and disagreeable
images of the scenes through which he had passed
the preceding day and night. His head seemed
ready to split open with pain. and the nausea he
felt was almost insupportable. Of all the miserable
situations with which this *happy* life of ours
abounds, there is none which, for the time it lasts,
is more horrible than this! The awaking from
intoxication, the sense of physical oppression,
the moral feelings of compunction, the wretched
disinclination to exertion, and the inability we
bring, in such cases, to grapple with business to
struggle against difficulty, or to face danger,
render man a pitiable spectacle indeed. Such is

the effect of occasional drunkenness: habitual ebriety causes less corporeal inconvenience, but greater moral evil. It is a vice which must assuredly blast the fairest prospects: it deprives prosperity of all its advantages, and renders adversity sordid and disgusting. In his good fortune, the drunkard is without respect; and without compassion in his calamity. There may be vices of greater moral turpitude, but there is none which so completely degrades the individual. In pain, in sickness, in poverty, there is still a possibility of securing respect, and maintaining tranquillity; but the drunkard is invariably despised, and he dearly pays for a few hours of brutal stupefaction, in the gloom, remorse, and horror, of returning sobriety.

Barnard knew not where he was, and had, as yet, but a confused recollection of what had passed. He got up to ring the bell, but there was no machine of that kind in the room; so he opened the door and called loudly on the staircase; in consequence of which, Mr. Robottom immediately made his appearance.

Barnard inquired what house he was now in, and Robottom gave him a full explanation of all that had passed,—how he had lost his money, given his note for £200, and got so drunk that he could not be moved; concluding with telling him how Jackson had paid for his bed, and handing him the two pounds with which he had been entrusted by the latter.

19   v

Barnard made little or no observations: in such a state, a man of his character is not much disposed to talk. A thousand ideas chased each other successively through his brain, each of a gloomier colour than its predecessor. He got up, dressed himself, and made the best of his way to the "Blue Boar."

When he arrived, he inquired if Mr. Smith or Mr. Jackson had been there, and was answered that Mr. Smith had been at an early hour, and had taken away his things: as for Mr. Jackson they knew nothing about him.

"Did Mr. Smith leave no message for me?" said Barnard.

"None," was the reply.

He then retired to his bed-room, and flung himself into a chair.

"Well!" thought he; "so this is life in London! How much better are my own green fields, exercise, health, sweet sleep, innocent amusement, harmless mirth!—Ah, Maria!—would I had never seen London!"

He then bethought himself of the difficulties in which he was placed:—how to account to his father for the money he had lost?—how raise the sum for which he stood engaged? He was perplexed, bewildered, tormented. Sometimes he thought of never returning—of enlisting as a soldier or a sailor—of remaining to see what he could do in London:—but no; the thought of London was horrible.

At last his better genius interposed.—"I will return home," said he, "and ask forgiveness of my father;—I will tell him the truth—I will never touch a card again—I will come no more to this cursed town—I will attend regularly to my business; perhaps I shall be happy;" and he again thought of Maria.

Ill-fated young man! Happy indeed would it have been for him, had this frame of mind always lasted—had these resolutions been preserved unbroken!

With every mind which enters the career of vice and folly, and which is not originally utterly depraved, there are times when either conscience, —that warning voice within,—or our better angel, interposes to save us from destruction. Happy, if we attend to the suggestions of the divine monitor, who, if neglected, soon leaves us to the influence and counsel of our worst of enemies,— ourselves!

Barnard determined then to bid an eternal farewell to " Life in London"—to that life in the midst of which is death!—to that life extolled by artists, authors, poets, and dramatists of a certain order, and, we lament to say, too successfully; for, however their style and their subject may be revolting to minds of sound principles and good taste, both have had their fascinations for a very large class of society,—for a class, in whose morals and conduct society is very deeply interested,—for the major portion of the youth of the middle orders.

It is but a short time since a contemptible
and vulgar drama, the characters, the plot, and
the language of which were immeasurably below
all criticism, actually drove insane more than three-
fourths of the youth of this metropolis; where it
was patronized by rank and fashion, and its disgusting vulgarities listened to, and simpered at, by
female delicacy! It was on the middle classes, however, that it exerted its most pernicious influence:
the others were above or below its corruptions.
Who forgets the Tom-and-Jerry mania? To a common observer, its senseless and troublesome absurdity was its most distinguished feature.   But, if
we would look for its more fatal consequences, we
must consult the records of Bow Street, the trials
at the Old Bailey, and the "Newgate Calendar." If
such mischief could be produced by a compounder
of vapid farces, we have no reason to think public
morality secure, because her enemies seem to be
feeble.   Alas! it requires but little talent to
pander successfully to the vicious propensities of
our nature.

Barnard having adopted his resolution, was not
slow in carrying it into execution.   He called for
his bill, which amounted to five-and-twenty
shillings.   With the remainder of the two pounds
left by Jackson, in his pocket, he mounted the
coach, and the next morning saw him at his
father's house in Polstead.

It is now time for us to return to Maria.   We
left her, as the reader may recollect, on the eve
of an appointment with the *gentleman* with the

white hat, who was no other than our friend Stafford Jackson. She went to the appointed place, and remained some time; but no gentleman made his appearance. Stafford was then far distant, having been suddenly summoned away by business of more importance to him than the seduction of a young, innocent, and foolish girl. He had neither time nor opportunity to advertise her of his compelled absence.

She returned home, disappointed, dejected, and somewhat indignant.—Was he, after all, only sporting with her feelings?—A different train of reflection then arose in her mind: she thought and pondered over the fortune-teller's prediction. The idea of Barnard and his white hat occurred to her. After all, he might be the man—she had no aversion to him.—She did not know what to think;—she was perfectly bewildered.

On the other hand, Barnard himself was employed in a train of thought, the tendency of which was to lead him to the hopes of an union with Maria. As, on her part, she had no aversion to him; so, on his, he felt a very strong growing affection for her. After some little difficulty, and much paternal reproof, he succeeded in gaining his father's pardon for his London freaks, and his assistance in settling the embarrassments in which they had involved him. He began to recover his tranquillity of mind, and to turn his thoughts with serious resolve upon a settled, steady, virtuous course of life. With such a plan of a country life,

the idea of marriage would of necessity be associated, even if no prepossession for any individual
female had pre-existed. But where, as in the case
of Barnard, so decided a penchant had been
formed, it was naturally the very first idea that
would suggest itself.

There was little doubt but that the mind of
Barnard had undergone a salutary change for the
better, after his London excursion. He had been
disgusted with vice and profligacy by their detrimental results to himself. Happy would it have
been for him, if the strength of his virtuous
resolutions had lasted, or had circumstances
proved as favourable to their permanence, as
unfortunately they were otherwise!

Barnard dwelt so long on the idea of Maria,
that he at last resolved to seek an interview.
But as, from his connexion with Smith, and other
unfavourable reports of his late conduct, his
character did not stand very high in the estimation of the neighbourhood in general, he had his
doubts and misgivings relative to his eventual
success. "Perhaps," thought he, "she won't see
me: her mind may be set against me, in consequence of my late proceedings." But then he
reflected that, in the last interview he had had with
her, she certainly did not show herself unfavour
able to his pretensions. He never dreamed of
any feelings on her part in favour of another; or
if he did, his thoughts reverted only to Harry
Everton, for whom, notwithstanding general

report, Barnard had his own reasons for believing that Maria cherished no feeling of love. Also he was, or thought himself to be, so firmly fixed in his virtuous resolutions, that he imagined that he should find little difficulty in persuading Maria of his sincerity, and inducing her to overlook his late follies, and to listen to his addresses.

Having thus made up his mind, he determined to seek an interview with her at once, and therefore walked over one fine morning to her cottage; and, singularly enough, he happened to wear precisely the same dress which he had worn on the night of their last interview.

The sight of her cottage produced on his mind a very powerful effect. It was, indeed, all that fancy could picture as the appropriate residence of peaceful innocence, and happy, virtuous, wedded love. " Alas !" said he, " how delightfully my days might glide along in a retreat like this, blest with content and Maria's love : but I fear I am not worthy of such happiness."

She was seated at the door; and at the sudden view of Barnard, and more especially of his *white hat*, she was not a little startled. Her agitation, however, though the effect of sudden surprize, was not unmixed with pleasure. She quickly recovered, gave him her hand, and greeted his arrival in most friendly terms.

After the usual salutations on both sides had passed, Maria said—-

" William ; I have heard but an indifferent

character of you lately.   I am told that you have
been in London, and spending your father's
money."

"How did you hear all this, Maria?" said
Barnard.

"I am sure I don't know who told me," said
she; "but it is the common report."

"Common report, Maria, I am sorry to say,
is for once right.   I have been unfortunate enough
to lose my father's money, and, for a time, my
own peace of mind.   But the latter I have
recovered; I am forgiven by my father, and am
fully resolved to go astray no more."

"Such resolutions," said Maria, "are sometimes broken; at least, I have heard so.   You,
perhaps, may soon forget them."

"Never, Maria," replied Barnard, with energy;
"I have received a lesson I cannot forget: I was
never so miserable in my existence : I cannot—I
know I cannot, ever renew such scenes again.
A virtuous life I am determined to lead; and it
only depends on you, Maria, whether it shall also
be a happy one or not."

"How can it depend on me, William?" said
Maria, with a laugh and a blush.

"Maria," replied Barnard, "do not trifle with
me now; my happiness does depend on you.   I
am not a man of many words; but I have come
to-day, to renew the proposal which I made
to you before I went to London.   I was then
elevated with wine, and in good spirits; I am

now neither one nor the other, but my feelings are still the same. I know not much how to make love, as it is called; but this I know, I can be a faithful and affectionate husband."

Maria seemed affected by the serious sincerity of his manner. The fact was, that the disappointment she had experienced with regard to Jackson sunk rather deeply in her mind, and produced offended feelings. Had she been fully convinced that Jackson had wilfully disappointed her, she would probably have given her hand to Barnard from a motive something like revenge. But she was not fully convinced of that; he might, perhaps, return, and explain his conduct satisfactorily She did not like, as yet, to give up all hopes of him.

On the other hand, she did not dislike Barnard personally; and other considerations rendered him, as a husband, not to be despised. The fortune-teller might have erred, or she herself might be mistaken;—at all events, she no more liked the idea of giving up Barnard altogether, than she did that of giving up Jackson. Not being able to secure the one, she would assuredly have accepted the other; but circumstances kept her mind in a state of vacillation, and she gave a temporizing, though not exactly an unfavourable, answer.

"William," said she, "it is impossible for me to make up my mind at once, to a matter so serious as this. Do not press it any more at

20

present; we are both too young; let me have a little time;—perhaps I may ————"

Here she stopped suddenly, and cast down her eyes.

" Well, Maria," said Barnard, "only let me have some hope; let me think that you may yet decide in my favour: I cannot be happy if you will not say that, at least."

" Then," said Maria, "if that be necessary to prevent your being unhappy, I do say so; but more 1 cannot say."

" It is enough," said Barnard, " and I must be satisfied; but do not forget that my happiness, and perhaps my existence, are depending upon you."

They were both silent for a few minutes, when Barnard, as if the thought had just come into his head, suddenly resumed,

" Maria, I have one favour to ask of you."

" What is that ?"

" There will be a dance to-morrow in our Red Barn, the day before we bring home the harvest; will you come and be my partner? Your cousin, Ellen Mayberry, will be there, and all the young people about."

" Oh," said Maria, " I will grant you that favour with pleasure."

" Well, then, I shall come and fetch you."

" No," said Maria, " I had rather you would not come here, for my father has, in my hearing strongly spoken against your conduct. I expect him now shortly, and therefore you had better go,—I should not like him to meet you now. A little time may do away with his prejudice against you. Ellen and myself will leave this together, and you can meet us."

"Very well," said Barnard; "I take my leave.'

As Barnard was going out through the gate, the first person he met was Harry Everton. There was a strong cloud of melancholy on his fine countenance. They passed each other with a slight salute, for though personally known to one another, their acquaintance had never been intimate. As for Barnard, he considered Everton as his inferior, because his father was less rich than his own ; and Everton's habits and disposition were incapable of any assimilation with those of Barnard. There was, therefore, so far from anything like congenial feelings between them, a sentiment something not very unlike a decided antipathy. This, it is true, never broke out into anything like overt hostility ; but it went far enough, even before this, to betray itself by symptoms of unequivocal dislike.

Thought Barnard, as Everton passed towards the cottage, " I wonder what that fellow is about now ;—I would bet ten to one that he is going to slander me." The idea of betting did not produce the pleasantest recollections in Barnard's mind. " Ah!" said he, thinking aloud, " After all he has some reason to speak against me: but I do not fear him with Maria ;—I am quite sure she does not love him. Besides, there's no comparison between our situations. Yet I have no doubt but that he has succeeded in poisoning her father's mind against me."

Harry had not seen Maria since the evening of the fair. He had studiously avoided going near the cottage; but he had been led by some circumstances to suspect that Barnard was paying his addresses to her. He had also heard some vague reports relating to Jackson, by no means favourable. Although he was forced to give up the idea of Maria's loving himself, yet his affection was as strong as ever. He came, therefore, for the last time, to give her the warning of a friend, and to snatch her, if possible, from impending ruin.

When he entered, Maria was still more startled by seeing him, than she had been at the sight of Barnard. But her feelings were very different: her agitation in the last instance had no intermixture of any pleasureable sensation ; it was composed of fear, surprize, and anger. She addressed him with a cold and haughty air.

"Mr. Everton," said she, "this is quite an unexpected visit ;"—and her looks announced that she considered it not less disagreeable than unexpected.

"Maria," said Harry, in a melancholy, yet firm tone, "I have not called for the purpose of troubling you about myself. I have had but too much reason to know that my feelings—that my happiness or misery, must be a matter of perfect indifference to you; but *your* happiness can never be so to me. I have come, therefore, to discharge the duty of a friend, and to warn you from the precipice over which I see you ready to rush headlong."

" Indeed, Mr. Everton," replied Maria, " you are very sharp-sighted. For a stranger, you seem to understand my affairs tolerably well."

" I have, indeed, been a stranger of late," said Harry; " but I have been so because you evidently desired it; and, as I said, if my own private feelings alone were concerned, I should have continued to be so: but your happiness is at stake,—I know it, and I come to warn you of it."

" Well, Mr. Everton, go on,—I suppose I must hear you out."

" I tell you then, Maria, that you are on the verge of a precipice; and whichever side you fall over, it must be your ruin."

" I wish, Mr. Everton, you would speak plainly, —I cannot understand your fine speeches."

" Well, I will speak plainly :—the gentleman, with whom I saw you at the fair, with the white hat, I have every reason to believe to be a dangerous and improper character. The man who was in his company I know to be so."

" All this," replied Maria, " is nothing to me; I have seen neither of those gentlemen since: and

we cannot help if gentlemen will speak to us .
—there is no use in being rude and uncivil."

"It is not, however, from those," continued
Harry, "that I conceive you to be in the greatest
danger;—they, I believe, have left the country.
Nor would I, perhaps, have come about them
alone, unless I had seen them again : but there
is another against whom you should be warned.
I mean the young man who has just left you ;—
he is the associate of profligates and gamblers,
and is himself a gambler. Beware of him :—
should you marry him, you will not fail to be
miserable,—if, indeed, he have any idea of
marriage."

"Mr. Everton, this is really too much : as if I
could listen, sir, to any one who did not mean
marriage! I consider your language as quite
insulting; and you have no right whatever to
speak to me on such subjects."

"No right, certainly, Maria, except the right
of a friend and well-wisher. As both, I could
not avoid speaking to you on the subject ; more
especially as I am about to leave this country ;
and," continued he, in a voice a little broken,
"we now meet, in all probability, for the last time
May you never have cause to recollect my last
words with sorrow !"

So saying, he arose and departed.

Maria was not quite so destitute of feeling as
not to be impressed with what Harry had said,

but she was too proud to let him perceive that such was the case. Yet, when he was gone, she felt sorry for her harshness, and would have willingly recalled him. She felt for the youth— she pitied him, for her heart was susceptible to the most genuine tenderness; and she had seen the terrible picture of his feelings in his face as he retired from her—the marked lines of love-care, the trembling lip, and the bursting eye labouring to retain its manhood. Her companion from infancy was Harry—she regarded him with tenderness, and but for the whirlwind into which her girlish vanity had thrown her, would have been happy in maturing tenderness to love. She now felt her heart for a moment in its right place, and she burst into tears without knowing why; but those tears—that heart could have told her, had she consulted it,—were shed for Harry Everton.

Maria soon recovered her former state of mind, and began to think whether there might be any foundation for Harry's warning. The absence and apparent light conduct of Jackson, seemed to import that there was some foundation for Everton's suspicions concerning his character. Yet, after all, they were evidently only suspicions, for Harry had specified nothing. As to Barnard, Harry had only echoed the reports which had come to her ears before; and to which, from Barnard's evident repentance, sincerity, and affection for herself, she was inclined to attach no great weight. Moreover, as she could not be ignorant now of Harry's attachment to herself, she imputed his conduct to a feeling of jealousy and disappointment, and also to the personal dislike which he bore to Barnard, and to which she was no stranger.

" No," said she, " there is nothing in it: he hates William, and is jealous of him ; that is the reason of his talking so. I have as much reason to believe William as him." She thought again of Barnard's unsophisticated earnestness, and was satisfied.

The case, however, was somewhat different regarding Jackson ;—concerning him, she would not make up her mind. What Harry hinted of him might be altogether true; yet, when she thought of his elegant person and insinuating manners, she was loth to give him totally up. Still, the result of a variety of complicated impressions upon her mind was favourable rather than otherwise to Barnard ; and this effect was by no means diminished by the visit of Harry.

Twenty-four hours passed rapidly away, and the time was arrived to repair to the rustic ball. Maria was not unstudious of ornament on this occasion,—and what girl of eighteen ever is, even where her motives are less powerful than were those of our heroine, for setting off her person to the best advantage? Maria, indeed, had as large a portion of the little vanities and coquetries of her sex, as is to be found among belles of higher rank. The idea of looking well in the eyes of Barnard did by no means pass uninfluentially through her mind; nor was she quite indifferent to the approbation of the other young men whom she was likely to meet. For the fact is, that women are never indifferent to the admiration of our sex;—no! not even the most virtuous, and those whose affections are engaged. In this respect, the sex is universally alike;—rank, age, virtue, ugliness, or beauty, makes no difference. The admiration of man is a natural homage to the charms of women, which is never received with disapprobation. It is not less grateful than was the steam of sacrifice, or the libation of wine, to an ancient priest of Jupiter or Bacchus.

But let me do justice to the fair sex, in confessing that a similar feeling is entertained by our own respecting them. We desire to please them, as much as they can possibly desire to please us. There is no man who entertains for the sex the sentiments which he ought to do, who is not gratified by receiving any portion of their attention; nor does an attachment to one woman, however great it may be, lessen the pleasurable sensations with which he contemplates female beauty in general.

And this is as right and natural on both sides, as it is assuredly mutual. Those who aver that the reverse is the case, either know little of the true character of either sex, or are desirous to impose. They judge from a narrow standard, and wish to

21

substitute conventional dogmas, derived from artificial life, for the genuine impulses of nature. They
labour to diminish the sum of innocent enjoyment,
and to deprive disappointed love of the remotest
possibility of consolation.

Though Maria, as I have said, was attentive to
the tasteful adornment of her person, yet her
toilet did not last quite so long as that of the
more fashionable belles of our metropolis. Its
mysteries, too, would, in all probability, have
better stood the test of elucidation. She needed
not the assistance of art, to repair or improve a
complexion impregnated by health with the
roseate dye of morning, to render more fair a
bosom that already rivalled the virgin snow in
purity and whiteness, or to rectify a shape on
which nature had set the seal of faultless symmetry. She was not, however,

"When unadorned, adorned the most;"—

a sentiment, by the way, which contains more
antithesis than truth; for the finest person is
susceptible of improvement from the judicious aid
of ornament. But her's was of that character,
which, from the union of simplicity and grace, was
best calculated to set off the advantages of nature.

Her cousin Ellen now entered. As it is sometime since we paid our respects to this young lady,
it is as well to mention that her disappointment,
from the absence of her admirer, was not less
than that which Maria suffered respecting Stafford.

Jackson. At this our readers cannot be surprised, as they have not now to learn that her admirer was no other than our honourable and accomplished friend, Mr. Beauty Smith! A gentleman of such refined and insinuating manners, united with a physiognomy so prepossessing, could not fail to make a very serious impression on the heart of a young lady!—But, to be serious, the rascal was not entirely without his good points. His person we have already described, which was not one of the worst; and he could, amongst women, divest himself of that very coarse vulgarity which sometimes distinguished him. He could lie and flatter, if not in such elegant language as Lotharios of a higher order, yet just with as much effect on the kind of women to whom he addressed himself. He could be entertaining when he pleased; and it is not wonderful that he should have succeeded with a lively but uneducated girl like Ellen Mayberry, and that she should regret his absence. This she was more likely to do, as her plainness, in all probability, secured to her no great number or choice of admirers.

But the truth is, that any man, however plain in person or deficient in mind, may, if he please, secure the affections of some one woman. Tastes are various; and when we consider that such amiable and accomplished gentlemen as West-country Dick, White-headed Bob, and Frosty-faced Fogo, have been successful lovers in their way, we cannot be surprized that Beauty Smith

should be the favourite   swain of some congenial
shepherdess.

The evening had already long commenced,
when the girls left the cottage : it was one of
those mild ones, so common in the decline of the
year, and which succeed an autumnal day of the
description so admirably drawn by the poet of
the Seasons :—

" When the bright Virgin gives the beauteous days,
And Libra weighs in equal scales the year ;
From heaven's high cope, the fierce effulgence shook,
Of parting summer ; a serener blue,
With golden light enliven'd, wide invests
The happy world.   Attemper'd suns arise,
Sweet-beam'd, and shedding oft through lucid clouds
A pleasing calm, while broad and brown below
Extensive harvests hang the heavy head.
Rich, silent, deep, they stand ; for not a gale
Rolls its light billows o'er the bending plain :
A calm of plenty ! till the ruffled air
Falls from its poise, and gives the breeze to blow ;
Rent is the fleecy mantle of the sky ;
The clouds fly diverse ; and the sudden sun,
By fits effulgent gilds th' illumined field,
And black by fits the shadows sweep along.
A gaily chequered heart-expanding view,
Far as the circling eye can shoot around,
Unbounded tossing in a flood of corn."

Such was the day to which the still evening
succeeded, dropping from her dewy wings delicious fragrance. The sun, just set, had left a
glowing streak of red, to mark his departure in
the western sky ; while, from the opposite quarter
of the heavens, the moon, like a fair and timid
nymph, arose in silent gracefulness from her

bed of silvery clouds. She pursued her course, sometimes uninterrupted through the deep azure, sometimes half enveloped in a mass of clouds, whose broken edges, reflecting her light, might easily be assimilated in imagination to the rugged summits of lofty mountains covered with eternal snow. She gradually assumed a deeper and more vivid brilliance, which gleamed through the dark foliage, illumined the recesses of the woods, or danced in glittering sparkles over the crystal wave. The air was calm and serene; the freshness of night fell upon the earth, and cooled its burning heat. All nature presented a scene of still magnificence, repose, and beauty. Such a scene would tempt one to exclaim, in the enthusiastic language of an eminent French poet, to whose beautiful lines our feeble translation car render but inadequate justice—

Yet for awhile withdraw, O! sacred sleep,
Thy poppies,—leave to my admiring gaze
This lovely orb of night, tranquil as thou!
This pure and melancholy vault of heaven,
This demi-day just risen over nature!
These spheres which, rolling through the void immense,
Seem at this hour to slack their silent course,
As if their heavenly music changed its time,
To mark a march of slower majesty:
This silvery light which in a thousand rays
Sports in the broken mirror of the stream;
Or casts within these woods, through many a branch,
Uncertain day—a mild and soften'd hue
Falls o'er the face of things; the quiet scene
Awakes the soul to meditations high.
Queen of the night! beneath thy sacred beam
The lover sighs, the saint and sage adore!"

Barnard and Maria met in a retired spot, Ellen having known her duty too well to intrude herself; and they became so interested in conversation, as to continue rambling until sometime after the moon had risen. In fact, they had almost forgotten, for some hours, that they were to attend the dance in the Red Barn; and when it recurred to their minds, they were half a mile from the rural ball-room, in a secluded and lonely part of the country. This, however, did not much affect their minds or their speed, and they bent their way to the Red Barn in the lovers' loitering gait.

This building stood on a hill, and was completely insulated, there being no habitation near it, except one small hut or cabin at a short distance. It was built of wood, and the denomination of *Red Barn* was given to it from the colour with which it had been originally painted.

There was something in the appearance of this ·isolated spot, as the lovers (if we may yet call them so) approached it by moonlight, of a wild and melancholy character. At least, it seemed, from the savageness of its seclusion, to be a place that might be devoted to purposes very different from a repository of the products of useful labour, or a scene of rustic festivity. Strong imagination could easily convert it into the haunt of the midnight robber—the rendezvous of the daring smuggler—the secret theatre of nameless deeds of darkness and of death!

This night, however, on entering it, such

Maria Marten's first Visit to the
RED BARN.

associations would vanish. It was enlivened by the cheerful strains of music, and rung with the sounds of rustic revelry. Its interior was spacious, and well adapted for the lively dance. There were two little rooms, of equal size, on the right and left of the entrance; one for the purpose of receiving the corn as it was brought from the field, and the other to hold it when thrashed and winnowed. The remainder was one open space, which was now cleared out for the accommodation of the present party.

That party consisted of the majority of the lads and lasses of the village of Polstead, and the neighbouring cottages. Some of the old people were seated on benches provided for the occasion, looking on at the dance, and partaking of the wholesome beverage of malt and hops, unsophisticated by the more active ingredients introduced into it by " the march of intellect."

If this party was not quite so refined and elegant, it was, at least, as cheerful and agreeable, as many of higher pretensions. If there was not as much grace as at Almack's, there was at least as much spirit; and some who contemplated the blooming countenances and pretty figures of the girls, with their white dresses and green and red ribbons, their clustering locks adorned with some simple natural flowers, thought, perhaps, that there was nearly as much beauty. Let not the reader, however, imagine for an instant that we are so unorthodox as to join in opinion with such schis-

matics.—No, no! fashion forbid!—Our tenets
are too pure to admit that there is anything
graceful, lovely, or interesting, beyond that very
comprehensive circle which embraces the " *haut
ton*," properly so called.

As for the youths of this assembly, all that
could be said in their favour was, that they were,
for the most part, tall, well-built, ruddy, good-
looking, young fellows, from the age of eighteen
to three-and-twenty, sons of respectable farmers.
They were full of life, health, spirit, and activity;
and the commanding officer of a dragoon regiment
would have seen much to approve of in their light,
athletic forms.   But they were lamentably and
utterly deficient in the air—the "*je ne scais quoi*,"
of West-end fashionables.   They had nothing of
it about them, as our readers may well suppose;
nor do we think that, under any circumstances,
they would be capable of acquiring it.   Like the
talent for poetry, it must be born with the
individual, and is never found except among the
aristocratical part of the creation.   We have even
our doubts whether our rustic beaux could have
competed with the underbred of Finsbury or
Russell Squares; but we forbear to make up our
mind on this unimportant question, until we shall
have consulted that discriminating oracle of
second-hand fashion, Mr. Romeo Coats.

Barnard and Maria now joined the dance.
Though the former had not much to recommend
him in point of figure, he was no bad dancer.

As to Maria, she performed as well in that way as any young lady that has not been in France could do, or who has not had the felicity of paying her devoirs at the shrine of Terpsichore, under the auspices of the scientific Mr. Wilson.

In point of beauty, Maria certainly outshone the other rural belles there assembled. She looked and felt happy, and her sentiments grew more and more favourable to Barnard: he on his part felt, as he then thought, more and more in love. Fortunate would it have been for them both had such sentiments remained unaltered—had no circumstances interfered to change them, or had he had sufficient steadiness to resist the fascination of the tempter!

The first dance had now concluded, and the young parties were taking some refreshment, when a figure which arrested instantaneous and universal attention, entered the barn It was a female of dark complexion and commanding stature. She was dressed somewhat wildly, but with infinite grace. She wore a sort of turban of yellow muslin, with a handsome brooch, or rather gold buckle, in front. From this her raven locks escaped on each side, in thick and clustering curls, which also hung down a little way on her neck behind. She wore a dress the upper part of which was of crimson stuff, prettily worked, and admirably fitting her elegant form. It was so low that, notwithstanding the addition of a tucker, it did not half conceal her beautifully rounded,

22

swelling bosom. The inferior part of her dress was of white muslin, with a variety of fanciful flounces. On each arm, which was quite bare from the shoulder, she wore a black bracelet.   A neat shoe and white stocking completed her costume ; the lower part of which, moreover, was so slight as to display, when she moved, the fine contour of her full and lovely limbs.   She was, in all respects, such a figure as would not have disgraced the chisel of Phidias, or the pencil of Titian.—It was Hannah Woods, the fortune-teller !

Maria, of course, instantly recognized her, and was seized with an involuntary trembling.   To some of the company she was known, but only by sight.

She apologized for her intrusion in easy, un-embarrassed terms. She had heard, she said, of the dance, and was come to join in the festivity, if she might be allowed ; in return for which, she would tell the young people their fortunes.

They, as may well be imagined, desired nothing better.   The old ones had retired, and there was now no restraint upon their gaiety.

The handsome fortune-teller addressed each, telling them something in a manner that seemed half jest, half earnest. To Ellen Mayberry, for instance, she said, " You will either be married in five years, or not at all ;"—a prediction of a very safe descrip-tion, considering the person of the girl for whom it was intended.

Thus she went round the circle ; but, when she

came to Maria, she stopped short, and whispered in her ear, " Those are happy who choose best !"

Barnard was the last of the young men to whom she addressed herself. She fixed her full black eyes upon him with a languishing air, and gave him one of her irresistible smiles. " You," said she, in a lower whisper, " are destined for something better than a farmer's life : be not too quick to decide; losses may be repaired, and the arms of love stretched out to receive you— though not where you imagine."

As Barnard looked at her, he thought he had never beheld so fine a woman; and it is by no means unlikely that he was right. But her face and person, fine as they were, derived much additional attraction from the sweetness of her voice and the seductiveness of her look and manner. A man, at the sober age of forty, could not easily resist such a woman, were he to try : it may, therefore, be well conceived with what facility she could kindle the inflammable temperament of youth.

The dance was now recommenced. Hannah directed a look of invitation at Barnard, which he was not slow to comprehend. If he had mis-understood it, he must have been dull indeed— so peculiar was the expression of her speaking eye, so intelligible the smile that played upon her ruby lip. But Barnard was not one of those dull young men who require to be spoken to in good round terms—who must be plainly asked before they can understand the wishes of a woman; neither was he of that cold temperament as to be indifferent to the charms of female beauty. On the contrary, he was too much alive to all such feelings, and too easily led away by any appearance of partiality on the part of the other sex. He arose, therefore, instantly, and having asked her to dance, both joined the merry throng.

Hannah's style of dancing was very different from that of the village lasses. There was a graceful softness, a rich luxuriance about her movements, strongly contrasted with the lively tripping style of her companions. Hannah had studied the art of dancing in a very different school, and in very different scenes, from those in which they had learned and practised it. A connoisseur in those matters would pronounce that there was a little dash of something theatrical in her manner—something approximating to the wanton twinings of a columbine, and not at all characterized by simplicity or modesty. She did not merely dance with her feet, as young country ladies are wont to do: every look and gesture was highly expressive, and expressive of what certainly does by no means accord with the most straight-laced notions of propriety. Although the character of the dance itself was not such as to admit of much of this kind of embellishment, yet she did contrive to throw as much of it into it as she possibly could.

On Barnard she lavished all her looks and all her blandishments; she turned on him ever a seducing smile, and an eye whose liquid lustre spoke tenderness and passion. As they passed along the dance, his hand would every now and then receive from hers a gentle but very sensible pressure, always accompanied by a corresponding glance and smile. Occasionally she would approach a little closer to him than the rules of the dance absolutely prescribed, and almost touch him with that heaving bosom which seemed, as it were, " panting to be pressed."

All this produced on Barnard the full effect which it was intended that it should do. His senses became intoxicated—he could see nothing but the fascinating object before him—he could hear nothing but her silvery tones—he could feel nothing but her tender pressure. He was under the irresistible spell of the enchantress, which, to him, was scarcely less powerful than the witcheries of Armida to the hero of Tasso. For the moment, he actually forgot that Maria was present.

She was dancing with a handsome young man, whose rural gallantry was by no means disagreeable to her. It gratified the momentary impulses of vanity; and she paid little or no attention to the spreading of the meshes in which poor Barnard was getting fast entangled.

The dance was now over, and the hour of parting arrived. Hannah was standing by the

side of Barnard : she gave his hand a warm pressure, unnoticed by any of the company, and disappeared with the quickness of lightning without
uttering a word ; he looked round, and she was
gone. To the rest of the bystanders she seemed
actually to have vanished, rather than to have
made her exit in the manner of ordinary mortals.

Barnard stood for a while in a deep reverie,
from which he was aroused by Ellen's asking
him to return with herself and Maria. He accompanied them accordingly to the gate of her
father's cottage. On his way he spoke but little ;
his thoughts were in the Red Barn, and with
Hannah. Her luxuriant form swimming through
the dance was present so vividly to his mind's
eye, that he might almost be said physically to
behold it still. His whole soul had undergone
a complete revulsion ; and while Maria was
leaning on his arm, her image was fast fading from
his heart.

But she perceived nothing of all this : she
was in high spirits. What the fortune-teller
had whispered to her that evening, admitted of a
double interpretation ; and circumstances disposed her to put the construction on it most
favourable to Barnard. She and her cousin
talked and laughed together ; and Barnard felt
almost unconsciously to himself that the presence
of the latter was a relief to him. Previously to
the dance he would have thought very differently ;
he would have preferred being alone with Maria :

now he would have dreaded it as a source of embarrassment.

Barnard having left the girls at the gate, walked slowly back. Now alone, he gave full scope to his feelings and reflections. The beauty and fascination of Hannah recurred to him with treble force. He thought, on the other hand, of **Maria**: he felt that this sudden and violent penchant was not quite right;—that it ought not to be indulged—that it was unjust to her, and criminal in itself;—that the woman who had excited those temporary feelings was, must be, unworthy of his regard, and that Maria was alone deserving of his affection.

With his mind in this state of vacillation, though more inclined to his original virtuous resolutions after all, he retired to bed, but not to sleep.

CHAP. VIII.

And must I still be guilty, still untrue,
And when old crimes are purged, still charg'd with new?

OVID.

WHEN Barnard arose next morning, the intoxication which his senses had undergone the preceding night, was, in a great measure, dissipated. His reflections again turned on the impropriety of his feelings towards Hannah, the absurdity of supposing a lawful connexion with such a woman, and the culpability of any other. The effect produced on him by her beauty and her wiles was growing fainter and fainter, and becoming rapidly superseded by his returning feelings for Maria. His mind was about to resume the original rectitude of its position, like a bow when the string is slackened ; or it rather resembled the waters of a torrent suddenly checked in their course by some opposing dam, but which rush forward with increased impetuosity the moment the impediment is removed

We have said that he was a young man not very liable to the influence of sudden strong impressions. We did not mean, however, to say that his senses were not liable to be led captive by those transitory influences which operate on other men; but such impressions were not sufficient of themselves to impel him to a permanent course of action. For this purpose it was necessary that they should be reiterated, and that they should be strengthened by corresponding circumstances. It was necessary that his senses should be steeped, as it were, in enjoyment— that he should drink deeply of the poisoned cup of pleasure, before his reason became thoroughly enthralled, and the triumph over his virtue was complete. It is more than probable, nay, it is certain, that had the temptation of the preceding evening been never repeated, its effects would have been entirely obliterated; nor would he voluntarily have sought its renewal.

Some little struggle did certainly take place within him, before he could resolve to give up all thoughts of Hannah. That struggle, however, was successful; and he now determined to act at once from his present feelings, to prevent the possibility of again backsliding, and to make to Maria direct proposals of immediate marriage.

Accordingly he proceeds at once to the cottage. He finds her alone; for, at this hour of the day her father was always from home, and her mother

23   A A

generally busily engaged. She was in a temper ot mind the best calculated to receive his addresses favourably. Of the re-appearance of Stafford she quite despaired, began to be fully persuaded that William Barnard must be her destined husband. and to feel the friendly regard she possessed for him fast ripening into something like love. The moment was propitious for his wooing, and his better stars seemed to smile and promise him success and happiness.

We have before adverted to the person of Barnard ; and the reader has seen that, in this respect, Nature had not been over bountiful to him. But if he imagine that personal qualifications on the man's part are of the first importance in a female's eye, he must be very young, and very inexperienced in the ways of women. Where love exists, it can discover beauty in deformity itself: and where it cannot be said precisely to exist in full force, where there is calculation and wavering, and more especially where there is, as in the case of Maria, a superstitious sense of destiny, personal attractions, weigh but little in the scale. Barnard, it is true, did not atone for their absence by the possession of those insinuating ways which prevail so far with the softer sex ; but then, the strong manifestations which he gave of sincerity and affection, united with similarity of years and congeniality of character, were not ill-adapted to supply the place of all he wanted, and under the peculiar circumstances which we have detailed, to generate an attachment in a simple girl like Maria.

Impelled by the full tide of his returning feelings, Barnard was more tender and eloquent than usual in the prosecution of his suit. He pressed her for an immediate favourable answer: even proposed that she would permit him to speak to her father, to have the business completely settled, and a day appointed for their marriage.

" Your father, William," said she, " is in such different circumstances from mine, that perhaps he may not consent."

" My dear Maria," replied Barnard, " my father will do anything to make me happy: he is the best of fathers. Besides, what is the difference between our conditions? My father may be a little richer than yours, but he cannot think it any degradation that I should marry the daughter of an honest man, who, though poor, is by his industry independent,—and such a daughter! Do not, my dear Maria, refuse any longer;—consent—we shall have the business immediately settled, and we can be married directly.

He could not, however, prevail upon her to concede quite so far; but he succeeded in gaining from her a promise to marry him shortly, if both parents should consent; but requested him not to hurry matters.

With this promise he was obliged to rest satisfied; and he was the more delighted with it, as

Maria's manners evidently testified the favourable state of her inclinations towards him He remained with her for more than an hour; and they might now, in fact, be pronounced declared lovers But as the conversation of such lovers, when they feel quite happy, is peculiarly interesting to nobody but themselves, we shall spare our readers the infliction of its detail even, though we might gain, like Anne of Swansy, a few pages by a contrary proceeding.

Barnard left Maria full of joy and exultation. He was pleased with himself, and pleased with everything; yet he did not feel completely satisfied. He had certain indefinable longings after more perfect bliss, which were half inexplicable to himself; though one would imagine that the scene which had just passed was well calculated to fortify him in his virtuous resolutions; and though it certainly would have had that effect with a firmer or a colder character, yet with such a man the excitation it produced had some tendency to lay him open to the attacks of temptation.

The day was remarkably fine—the sun, in its meridian splendour, pouring intense heat, was such as Thomson thus describes:—

> " 'Tis raging noon, and vertical the sun,
> Darts on the head direct his forceful rays.
> O'er heav'n and earth, far as the ranging eye
> Can sweep, a dazzling deluge reigns; and all,
> From pole to pole, is undistinguished blaze.
> In vain the sight dejected, to the ground
> Stoops for relief.
>   *   *   *   *   *

And scarce a chirping grasshopper is heard
Through the dumb mead.　Distressful nature pants,
The very streams look languid from afar,
Or through the unshelter'd glade, impatient seem
To hurl into the covert of the grove.

     *   *   *   *   *

Thrice happy he ! who, on the sunless side
Of some romantic mountain, forest crown'd,
Beneath the whole collected shade reclines ;
Or in the gelid caverns, woodbine wrought,
And fresh bedew'd with ever-spouting streams,
Sits coolly calm ; while all the world without,
Unsatisfied and sick, tosses in noon.''

It was, indeed, an hour in which he who was exposed to the burning ray, would be tempted to exclaim, in the language of that poet of whose unrivalled descriptive muse we have already availed ourselves—

" Welcome, ye shades, ye bowery thickets hail!
Ye lofty pines ! ye venerable oaks!
Ye ashes wild, resounding o'er the steep,
Delicious is your shelter to the soul,
As to the hunted hart the sallying spring,
Or stream full flowing that his swelling side,
Laves, as he floats along the herbaged brink.''

Barnard walked slowly along, thinking of Maria, and indulging in all the delicious reveries of the lover, when, after a short time, he found himself near the Red Barn ; and as it offered a most convenient shelter from the oppressive heat, and a seclusion where he might indulge his reflections undisturbed, he entered it, and flung himself down on a heap of newly-reaped corn.

A delightfully refreshing coolness pervaded

this place, the windows, while they admitted
air, only allowed a softened shadowy light to prevail, relieving the sight which had been fatigued
by the broad glare of noon.   The isolated character of the barn seemed to secure it from intrusion,
and all the country immediately around was still
and silent.

The noon of a burning day like this which we
have described, is not less tranquil than midnight.
The songsters that usually enliven the fields are
hushed, and universal nature, faint with heat,
appears to sink for the hour into deep repose.
There is no time better adapted than this to produce and cherish voluptuous sentiments in the
mind of the young and idle.   It is a dangerous
moment, even for the severest virtue, if Cupia
and his beautiful mother should set temptation
to work.   A train of vague and pleasurable sensations were passing through the mind of Barnard.
He thought first of Maria, and on the virtuous
pleasures of love ; then on a sudden the image of
Hannah—of her luxuriant form—of her melting
glance—of her soft and gentle touch—of all her
witcheries, flashed across him.   He made an effort
to repel the intrusion of such ideas, but did not
succeed : they still floated before his mind's
vision ; his imagination ran riot ; the place in
which he was seemed to exercise a spell over
him—to renew the impressions of the preceding
evening—to stimulate his senses, and to fire his
brain—until at last he almost fancied that she

stood before him in all her dazzling beauty ;—when, to his unspeakable astonishment, the door opened, and he beheld with his corporeal eyes the enchanting reality!

Language cannot depict the sudden feelings which seized upon Barnard at the sight of Hannah. She was more plainly dressed than when he saw her the evening before, but looked, if possible, more lovely and enticing. A country-made straw bonnet, the straw of which was left of its natural colour, with a wide front, was tied under her chin with red riband, and hung almost on the back part of her head ;—under this was a row of narrow lace, which, added to her clustering curls, gave a peculiar look of youth and softness to her face. A gown of very pretty striped cotton, and made remarkably low in front, exhibited her swelling bosom, which seemed ready to burst from its confinement as she carelessly threw aside a dark green shawl which covered it She cast a sort of sidelong glance at Barnard with her darkly rolling eyes, which penetrated to his very soul.

"You did not expect to see me here," said she disclosing a row of the purest ivory, which contrasted beautifully with the dark glow that flushed her cheek and the deep coral of her lip.

"I own I did not," replied he.

"And are you displeased at it?" she resumed, sitting down beside him, and taking his hand.

"Displeased!" exclaimed he, with all the

energy of growing passion, and returning the warm pressure of her hand; "enchanting woman! who could be displeased at seeing you?"

"William," rejoined the sorceress, "it is three weeks since you and I first met;—long, long weeks."

"Long!" returned Barnard; "you cannot call it very long."

"Long, for this heart," continued Hannah; "long, for the bosom that has been burning with passion for you."

Barnard started, and blushed deeply.

"Yes, for *you* William—burning with love for you. There are women I know, who would not own as much; but the love of Hannah is as far above disguise, as her character is above that of other women."

She looked him full in the face, and dropped her head upon his shoulder. Barnard pressed his lips to hers in ecstasy—a short silence followed.

Having thus wrought upon his feelings, the syren saw that she had the vantage ground, and suddenly raising her head, she continued, with well acted seriousness of manner,—

"Yes, William! I love you—dearly love you; but I cannot share your heart with another. Hannah must have no rival. Before I consent to give you full proof of my affection, you must renounce every other woman. I don't want to bind you in the vulgar chain of marriage *My* love is pure and disinterested. I am not like *some* who would accept your hand, for the sake of your wealth, while their hearts were another's,—who wait only for the security which a marriage with you would give them, to throw themselves into the arms of their *real lover*. No! no! I love you for yourself alone. But much as that love may be, I will never see you more, unless you swear to give up every other woman."

Barnard looked confused, and was silent.

"You will not, then?" resumed Hannah; "Barnard, I know you love another;—weak young man! that other's heart is none of thine : though she would take your hand, that she might more cruelly deceive you—she would wear you as a cloak to hide her baseness."

Barnard, starting up, exclaimed, "You mean Maria Marten !"

"Sit down," said Hannah,—"I do.—Did you not see a gentleman with a white hat at the fair of Polstead ?"

This circumstance had until this moment totally escaped the memory of Barnard. He had had a glimpse of Stafford Jackson walking with Maria as we have already seen from his conversation with her on her road home; but the adventures he had since gone through had totally driven the matter out of his head, and, in fact, he had not given it any serious consideration at the time. When he met Stafford in London, he could not recognize him, for the glimpse which he had of

24   B B

him was transient, it occurred in the dusk of the
evening, and besides, Barnard was uncommonly
near-sighted.   But now, this incident, thus artfully insinuated by Hannah, rushed upon his mind
with full force, and completed the effect which the
sorceress was labouring to produce. The wounded
feelings of jealousy and pride concurred with
the almost irresistible charms by which he was
assailed, and he succumbed at once under the
temptation.   Explanation and detail were needless. He saw, as he thought, the entire affair at
a glance.   Maria was carrying on a secret intrigue
with the stranger; and she was willing to conceal
her disgrace, and continue her criminality, under
the cover of his protection as a husband. This
accounted, in his opinion, for the hesitation with
which she had at first listened to his addresses,
and her subsequent compliance. All appeared
nothing but an artful train of conduct, for the
purpose of entrapping him.

All these thoughts passed through his mind in
a second; and indignant and ashamed at the idea
of being made a dupe, he hung down his head,
and continued silent.

"Weak young man!" resumed Hannah, with
a smile of pity; " I knew it all—I was anxious to
save you. *He* was,—*he* is, the favoured lover;"
—and then changing her voice to the softest,
tenderest tone, taking his hand, and gazing on
him with eyes in which the tear appeared **ready**

to start—" and so, William, this is the girl that you refuse to renounce for Hannah,—for one whose whole soul, whose every thought, is yours?"

"I will never see her more," said Barnard.

"Swear it," replied Hannah.

"I do," cried he; "I swear it solemnly, by al' that is sacred."

"Then I am thine for ever!" exclaimed the syren, and sunk into his arms.

Hannah Woods was a woman deeply versed in all the arts of her own sex, and well acquainted with the character of ours. She was particularly formed to exercise the most imperious influence over a young man like Barnard, of weak intellect and strong passions : she knew how to administer to the gratification of the latter, without producing satiety. She knew how, too, to adapt the style of her fascinations to the different ages of her admirers. With a man of more mature years and experience than Barnard, she would not have been so prompt and forward. Such men are to be caught by affected modesty, by apparent reluctance, by amorous delay; but with an inexperienced youth the case is otherwise. He is never so completely enthralled as after his passions have been partly gratified: an experienced woman then has him completely in the toils: the spell she can exercise over him is little short of what is fabled of witchcraft. Such was now the case with Barnard; his intoxication, his infatuation, was complete. He forgot everything but Hannah: he gazed upon her full eye, instinct with liquid fire—he kissed her glowing cheek and burning lip—he pressed her in his arms, and felt her swelling bosom beat warmly against his own. For the first time the Circean cup of terrestrial love was presented to his lips, and he drank deep draughts of the delicious poison, but only to thirst for more. The spell was ended—the charm was perfect—his destiny was fixed for ever; his better angel fled affrighted, and the triumphant demon claimed him as his own.

They had met at noon, and they parted not until the sun's broad disk stood upon the western edge of the horizon, pouring a ruddier light over the extended landscape, and dying with the richest crimson the fleecy robes which began to invest the eastern sky.—Time flies swift indeed on the wings of rapturous enjoyment!

CHAP. IX.

They little knew the human breast
Could pant for sordid ore ;
Or, of a faithful heart possest,
Could ever wish for more.

HELEN WILLIAMS

IT is now necessary to explain to our readers now a woman like Hannah Woods could have acquired that evident superiority of education which she possessed, so much above her station and which enabled her to exercise so great an influence as she did over Barnard, in conjunction with her personal attractions. We are therefore obliged to give a sketch of her history, which we shall make as brief as possible, that the main action of our story may not be long interrupted.

Hannah was the daughter of a captain of a merchant vessel, who was in the habit of trading to the West-Indies. Her mother was a woman of African descent, being two removes from the Black, or one shade lighter than the Mulatto. She was an uncommonly fine woman, and Captain Woods, meeting her in Jamaica, fell in love

with and married her.   Hannah was the only
offspring of the marriage.

Her father being in good circumstances, placed
her, when very young, in a genteel boarding
school in the neighbourhood of London, where
she received the usual rudiments of female education.   He took lodgings, also, near at hand for
his wife, where she might remain during his
occasional absences, and visit and inspect the
education of Hannah.   This lady, the warmth
of whose constitution was not inferior to that of
most tropical females, formed, while her husband
was away on one of his voyages, a connexion
with a handsome young officer of artillery, whose
friends happened to be her opposite neighbours.
This went on for some time, and one of the very
usual consequences in such cases ensued, namely,
a total neglect of her child.   She abandoned her
entirely to the care of the mistress of the boarding school, without condescending to interfere in
any way, or give herself the slightest trouble
concerning her welfare.

Another consequence, equally natural, resulted
from this intrigue—Mrs. Woods became pregnant.
Concealment was impossible, and dreading the
immediate return of her husband, she threw herself into the arms of her lover, who took her
altogether to live with him.

When the Captain returned, he instituted a
prosecution against the young hero, who had property independent of his commission, and he

·eceived five hundred pounds damages. Mrs. Woods continued to live with the artillery officer, but died shortly after, in bringing into the world the fruits of her illicit love.

Hannah was still kept at school by her father, who, from the nature of his pursuits, could exercise but little surveillance over her education. She was now turned of fourteen, very finely formed, and almost prematurely womanly in her appearance. She could speak a little French, play a little on the piano, and danced uncommonly well; but in a moral point of view, her education was utterly neglected, and no principles of religion had ever been instilled into her mind.

She was beginning to grow excessively tired of the irksomeness and restraint of school, when she was relieved from it by a young gentleman of fortune, who persuaded her to elope with him and put herself under his protection. This could scarcely be called, with any propriety, a case of seduction, as she threw herself most willingly into his arms—not so much from any strong affection for him, as from an impatience of scholastic restraint.

With him she lived for some time. He was a young man of fashion and the town, and being exceedingly fond of theatrical amusements, he was constantly in the habit of taking Hannah with him to the theatres, where she also imbibed a strong taste for the stage.

Among the friends of her protector, was a

young man of slender fortune, gay habits, and remarkably handsome person. This youth was likewise passionately attached to theatricals, and himself no mean amateur performer. Hannah fell violently in love with him, and he succeeded in prevailing on her to quit her friend.

This gentleman, finding that his means of living were rapidly declining, determined to try his fortune on the stage. He failed in London, but succeeded in obtaining an engagement in the country, whither Hannah accompanied him.

She also adopted the theatrical profession, and evinced no small degree of talent. The manager found her extremely serviceable as a general actress; but she excelled more particularly as a stage dancer. At the Opera, or either of the Theatres Royal, she would have probably made no great figure; but in a provincial theatre she was a star of the first magnitude.

She had been for some months thus situated, when her lover was taken very seriously ill. He was beginning, however, to recover, when unfortunately he swallowed a dose of oxalic acid instead of Epsom salts, through the mistake of an ignorant or careless apothecary, and died in a few hours, in intense agony.

Hannah was at first quite inconsolable for his loss; for, in fact, he was the only man for whom, at any time, she had felt a real attachment. She soon, however, suffered herself to be comforted by a dashing colonel of dragoon-guards, then quartered in the town where she was performing. His protection she the more willingly accepted, as her small salary was totally inadequate to her support, after the death of her former lover.

The colonel was a good-natured man, and treated her with much kindness and attention. To these she made but an ungrateful return : she intrigued with all the officers of the regiment ; and at last her infidelities became so open and notorious, that the report of them reached the colonel's ears. Without suffering his temper to be ruffled, he coolly informed her of the facts which had come to his knowledge, presented her with twenty pounds, and advised her to make the best of her way out of the town as speedily as possible.

Hannah took his advice, and came up to London.

Here she attempted to renew her theatrical pursuit, but without much success. She was employed, however, as a dancer at one of the minor theatres ; and by this engagement, and a sly system of intriguing with the other sex, she managed to live in very good style. Her financial measures, however, began to be known ; and the manager, whose *morality* was shocked by such proceedings, dismissed her from his company.

She now began regularly to pursue the mode of life adopted by such numbers of unfortunate women in this great metropolis. She met with vicissitudes which are incidental to such a course of living,—sometimes in splendour and luxury, and at others in the lowest wretchedness. Her utter improvidence and taste for expense, rendered her occasionally liable to the severest privations; and she soon began to be heartily sick of female " Life in London."

About this time she became acquainted with Stafford Jackson. That eminent discriminator of human character, who so well understood the art of employing others according to their capacities, soon discovered that Hannah might be made a useful instrument. He proposed to her, at first, to become an agent in his smuggling trans- actions. Her cleverness, education, and manners, made him think that he could succeed admirably in the disposal of contraband articles, especially among the ladies: she accepted his offer, and succeeded to admiration. It was by his advice that she assumed the character of a fortune-teller, as a good disguise in travelling through the country; and which her features and dark com- plexion, assisted by the peculiarity of dress, well adapted her to personate. In this character she agreed, for mercenary considerations, to become, as we have seen, an agent in the seduction of Maria; and this she undertook the more readily, as she had not the slightest spark of affection for Jackson himself, and was actuated by no considerations but those of self interest. She was constantly up and down between London and Suffolk; and when in the latter county, she resided in the small hut on the road side, within a mile of Polstead, with an old couple to whom Smith had recommended her.

Of Barnard she had known something previously to the night of the dance. She was aware of the state of his feelings regarding Maria, and she determined to detach him from her in the way that we have seen, and thus at once to further her own designs and those of Jackson. She hoped to be able eventually to persuade Barnard to marry her; or, at all events, to draw most liberally on his property, as long as it lasted.

We must now return to Maria. Her feelings, after Barnard had left her, were still rather of a complicated and conflicting character. She had promised, it is true, to marry him; and when she gave that promise, it was dictated by her feelings. But, as is often the case when we pledge ourselves to a line of conduct respecting which we have been vacillating, after he was gone she began half to repent that she had given so decided a promise. She again ruminated on the possibility of Jackson's return; and she felt, that if such were the case, her inclinations would very easily return in his favour, if he could give any reasonable explanation of his conduct. But again she dismissed this notion from her mind, and reflecting on Barnard's sincerity and affection, and not without adverting to his comfortable circumstances, she thought there was every probability of their being happy together.

Such was the tone and temper of her mind

when she sat down to supper with her parents, just after night-fall. They had scarcely commenced their humble meal, when a loud knocking was heard at the cottage-door. It was opened, and a young man entered, who stated that a gentleman's postchaise had just broken down hard by, and entreated old Marten's assistance to repair the accident. "A hammer," said he, "and some nails will do the business; and we can patch it up some how for the present."

This man Maria instantly recognized, and felt no small degree of agitation at his appearance. It was no other than the companion of her admirer at the fair, the lover of Ellen, the aid-de-camp of Jackson—the inimitable Beauty Smith! He smiled and winked expressively to Maria, as much as to say, "He is here—he is come at last." And she understood him as perfectly as if he had spoken it in so many words.

Mr. John Smith now proceeded to the postchaise, where his friends, Stafford Jackson, Esq. and the Hon. Captain Creed, were waiting for him. With the assistance of old Marten and the postilion, the accident, which was slight indeed, was speedily rectified; and the gallant trio proceeded into Polstead, and established their head quarters at that most excellent house of entertainment "for man and horse," the "Cock."

The sight of Beauty had wrought a most astonishing revolution in the feelings of Maria · she felt certain that Jackson was now returned—

the man who, of all others, had best pleased her youthful fancy, whose person and manners were everything she could desire, and whose fortune she imagined must correspond with his appearance. Without doubt, he was fully able to assign a sufficient reason for his sudden disappearance, and his neglect of the appointment which he had himself made. A thousand things might have occurred: he might have been taken suddenly ill—some untoward accident might have prevented him from coming or communicating with her. After all, she felt that he must be the man whom the art of the fortune-teller had pronounced to be her destined husband.

But she had made a promise to Barnard;— what would she not have given now to recall that promise!—how could she possibly have been so foolish as ever to suppose for a moment that he could be the person? She recalled to memory the exact words of the fortune-teller,—"Your future husband is young, handsome, and rich." Barnard was certainly young, and might be said to be rich—but handsome! certainly little of that except according to his own mode of interpretation, "handsome is, that handsome does,"— a proverb, after all, not strictly applicable to the general line of conduct pursued by Mr. William Barnard. She was to see her destined husband at the fair—but she did not see Barnard at the fair;—there was to be nobody there like him. That might certainly apply to Barnard; but not in the sense of his superiority of appearance, in which sense her present sentiments led her to understand it. "You were born for great things," (as most women are, or wish to have been,) but what "great things" could be expected from Barnard? he was comfortably off, and that was all. No, no! it must be the other!

Yet the promise! the fatal promise!—how could she ever think of making it? But then again, how could it be binding?—if it was not her fate to be married to Barnard, what signified her promise? Promises ought not to be binding, that are contrary to our destiny, or to our——inclinations.

Such were her thoughts as she retired to her chamber, but not to rest. She sat ruminating for nearly an hour, sitting at her window gazing on the tranquil landscape, silvered over by the pale moonlight. But it was not with the beauty of the scene that her ideas were busy: it only served to recall the first time that she had met Jackson, and the sweet strain of vocal music with which she had been that night saluted.

On a sudden the deep stillness of the night was broken—and broken by the very same duet which she had heard on a former night under her window, repeated. The same words—the same voices—the same style of singing.

She opened the casement, and listened with

the most intense feelings. A pleasing tremor seized upon her frame—her heart palpitated with joy and fear.

The song was ended, and a figure approached the window from the garden of apple trees which it overlooked. This figure was not to be mistaken: it was the graceful step, the light athletic form, the erect carriage of Stafford,—" There was none indeed like him at the fair !"—the white hat completed the effect, but he wore a black crape around it.

He was alone: his companion had retired,— his presence was not necessary now. He waved his hand to Maria, and coming directly under the window, requested her, in a soft whisper, to descend.

She complied ;—she stole down stairs with trepidation, and softly unbarred the door. Her father and mother were locked in the embraces of that sound repose, which is the constant attendant of peaceful labour and contented simplicity.

"Dearest Maria," said Jackson, "I am here at last."

She could not reply : he took her arm gently under his own, and they walked forth a little together. At last Maria said,

" I thought I should never have seen you again."

" My dear girl," resumed Stafford, " I have suffered, since I saw you, the most bitter torments. I was summoned hence at a moment's

warning to attend the dying bed of a father. I
had no means of seeing you or sending to you,
previously to my departure, and I did not dare to
write,—lest my letters should fall into other
hands than yours. You can have no idea of
what I have endured. The melancholy occasion
on which I was recalled was of itself sufficient to
awaken the keenest pangs of sorrow; but added
to the thought of losing you, it wrought me up
almost to madness. I slept neither night nor
day, partook of little food, and when I had laid
my beloved parent in the earth, (for he died in
three days after my arrival,) I was myself seized
with a fever, and for a short time pronounced to
be in great danger. The strength of my constitution, however, surmounted the disorder, and
the moment I was able to leave my bed, I was
about to return here : but the physicians would
not permit me then to move, and it was with some
difficulty that I have at last escaped them, to fly
to you upon the wings of love."

Maria seemed moved by this well told tale,
and expressed her sorrow.

"But, my love!" said Jackson, "I hope that my
absence has not changed your feelings. When I
last saw you, you gave me some hopes that you
would listen to my suit. Has no happier lover
availed himself of the interval to prepossess your
mind against me, and plead his own cause successfully ?"

Maria blushed, and was at first silent and con-

fused. She had too much nature and simplicity
to reply in the negative. She could not make
up her mind to tell an absolute falsehood, though
she was well disposed to conceal the truth.

Jackson saw her hesitation, and said, " Maria,
I fear much that such has been the case, if so,
speak, and pronounce my doom for ever."

The most sincere of the sex will never tell a
man the entire truth in a case like this; nor,
indeed, is it to be expected that they should do
so. The heart of a woman is never thoroughly
known to any man; no! not even to him whom
she loves the best: and, in many instances, it is
very fortunate for the lover that it is not.

———" Where ignorance is bliss,
'Tis folly to be wise."

Maria confessed that a young man had made
to her proposals of marriage; but she forgot to
add, that she had received them with some degree
of complacency.

" Who is he ?" enquired Jackson.

" You don't know him, I believe," replied
Maria: " he is a rich farmer's son; his name is
Barnard."

" I have heard of him," said Jackson : " a
young man of profligate habits, and a most unfit
husband for you. But believe me, he was not
serious; or else his designs were of an evil nature."

" I can hardly think so," said Maria, " he
seemed so sincere."

26   D D

" It is easy to *seem*," returned Jackson; " but I see how it is—you love him, Maria."

" No, no !" hastily interrupted she, her feelings getting the better of all attempts at female coquetry; " I do not love him—I can never love him."

Jackson, who valued Barnard very little as a rival, and had his own private reasons for being perfectly easy about him, nevertheless affected great alarm ; and, by his artful, insinuating style, soon drew from her a full confession of what had passed between her and him ; though she forbore to tell him what had been the precise state of her feelings towards the latter.

" So, then, **Maria, you** actually promised to marry him."

" What could I do ?" simply returned Maria; " I never saw you but once, and I thought I should never see you again ; and, besides, I felt a little angry with you."

This last expression highly pleased Jackson, who knew very well that anger, in certain cases, is no unfavourable symptom of a woman's affection. He continued—

" Probably, Maria ; you did not wish ever to see me again,"—tenderly pressing her hand, and adding, " if my presence is now disagreeable to you, I will banish myself for ever ; but it will be to that country whence no traveller returns."

Maria was much affected by his manner, and replied, " Do not speak so;—I am sure I did wish to see you again."

"Lovely Maria!" he exclaimed, throwing his arm around her waist; " you make me the happiest of men. I own you had some cause to think me unworthy;—but are you satisfied with my explanation?"

" I am," returned Maria.

" And will you consent to be mine?"

"Yes," she replied in a low and tremulous tone; " I consent to —— marry you!"

" Enough, enough," cried he, in affected rapture; and kissed with ardour her burning cheek.

Jackson did not think proper to press the affair any further at present, for two reasons :— first, he saw very plainly, from Maria's manner, that her virtue would not yield except to proposals which she deemed honourable;—her conduct, during his absence, relating to Barnard, was a further confirmation of this :—and, secondly, it did not suit his purposes to quit Polstead so soon as the proposal of immediate elopement would render necessary.

He now, therefore, turned the conversation; and telling Maria that it was time she should know who he was, gave her a long and glowing account of himself, which it would be as unnecessary to detail to our readers, as it is to inform them that it did not contain one word of truth. Suffice it to say, that the sum and substance of it was—that he was a man of independent fortune; and that all he wanted, to render him completely happy, was the possession of her sweet self.

After more than an hour spent in this way, and in mutual endearments, the lovers parted, having agreed to meet the following night. Maria returned to her chamber, and Jackson rejoined his friends at the Cock.

It is proper here to mention that the breaking-down of the postchaise was not accidental, but part of a premeditated plan. Jackson had come down to Polstead for two reasons ;—first, for the seduction of Maria; secondly, for the further plunder of Barnard. Smith contrived on the road, at a place where the postillion was watering the horses, very ingeniously to derange a spring, so that the chaise came gently down just in proper time and place, and thus gained an opportunity of securely advertising Maria of the presence of Jackson; and afforded a pretext to Barnard for the appearance and stay of that gentleman, Smith, and Creed, at Poltstead.

CHAP. IX

———————like an open friend
I treated, trusted you, and thought you mine:
When, in requital of my best endeavours,
You treacherously practised to undo me.

OTWAY.

BARNARD had not yet risen, at mid-day; for he had passed most part of the night awake, thinking over the scenes of the preceding day; and when he did sleep, it was but to dream of the voluptuous enchantress who had steeped his senses in forgetfulness of all but herself. Again, he was encircled in imagination in her clasping arms, pressed to her palpitating bosom, and intoxicated by the nectar of her dewy lip. Never was there a man more utterly, more completely enthralled by the syren-spells of a fair and fallen angel than he was.

From these dreams of enjoyment he was roused by Mary, the servant, who entered his bed-room, exclaiming,

"Oh, Mr. William, there are two such nice gentlemen below wanting you."

"Who are they?" demanded Barnard

" I don't know their names, Mr. William , but one of them is the handsomest man as ever I seed ; and so finely dressed."

" You are an excellent judge," replied Barnard ; " tell the gentlemen I shall be with them directly."

Mary proceeded to obey, ejaculating repeatedly, as she went down stairs, " What nice gentlemen !"

These *"nice gentlemen,"* it is almost superfluous to inform our readers, were our friend Jackson and his companion, our still more amiable friend, Beauty Smith. They were both admirably well dressed, and the appearance of Jackson was particularly imposing. He was in a sort of half mourning (to keep up the hoax of his father's death); wearing an elegantly made black coat and black silk waistcoat, with white summer trowsers. Beauty was dressed in a more foppish manner; but contrived, nevertheless, to retain much more of the Newmarket style about him than that of the gentleman. His exterior, however, announced the possession of wealth; and his glorious impudence made up for all the deficiencies.

When Barnard came down stairs, he found his two *friends* in high conversation with his father. Jackson's manners had already advanced him considerably in the good graces of the old gentleman. He entered into a dissertation on farming— the different qualities of soils—the value of land, &c. on which subjects he descanted with as much fluency as if he had passed his whole life in rural topic of country sports, and quite astonished the old blade by his profound observations on fowling pieces, shot pouches, hares, partridges, and pointer dogs.

When young Barnard entered, the two heroes shook him very cordially by the hand, and were warmly greeted by him.

"We were on our way to my shooting-box, when my carriage broke down just as we entered Polstead," said Jackson: "but I understand that there is capital shooting in your neighbourhood; therefore I am not sorry for the accident."

"Excellent," replied Barnard; "and I shall be happy to accompany you on excursions of that kind."

"Well," said Jackson, "we shall stop at the "Cock," and make a party to-morrow: to-day we have not quite prepared for this sport."

"But, Barnard, my boy," said Beauty, "we shall dine with you to-day,—if you will give us something to eat."

Old Barnard, with all the hospitality of the genuine English farmer, replied that nothing would give him more pleasure than to entertain Messrs. Smith and Jackson; "and," added he, "I'll give you a plain country dinner; but you shall have a bottle of the best old port in the country."

"My dear sir," said Jackson, "don't put yourself at all out of the way for us; we are easily pleased in the eating way."

"Yes," interrupted Beauty; "for my part, I can manage anything, from a pork chop to a haunch of venison."

The visitors prolonged this visit more than an hour; walked over the grounds with old Barnard, who was quite delighted in showing all his farming mprovements. They were not less pleased at all the substantial evidences they received of the old man's wealth. He showed them his cattle, pigs, and poultry. He took them to his stable, where there were four capital hunters; and, finally, they visited the Red Barn, where they inspected his stock of corn, which was worth several hundred pounds. They never, of course, in their conversation, made the least allusion to young Barnard's London affairs.

They now took leave, promising to return to dinner; and Beauty, freed from restraint, gave full vent to his sentiments.

"Well, Stafford," said he, looking back on the old man's farm, "here is a pretty prospect for us —I told you the old boy was snug. These dirty acres are no bad things:—we'll turn factors for the old gentleman: that corn is wanting in the London market."

"Yes," said Jackson; "and we shall make out life here, too, pretty well, while we remain. Creed, too, must come in for a share: I know that he has no objection to a fowl and bacon at times.'

"Not he, by my soul!" said Smith. "If he remains here long, the old chap's pigs and poultry will soon travel the way of all flesh."

"But," resumed Jackson, "all will depend on our proper management of the young fellow : we must be cautious and dexterous in that."

"No doubt," said Smith, "but I am sure that I can wind him over ;—I know every point about him well. He may think himself capable of keeping good resolutions; but he has a taste for pleasure that will be sure to ruin him : besides, I rather suspect that his business is pretty nearly done already."

"You mean by Hannah ?" said Jackson.

"I do : it is through her that we shall succeed best ; and I have no doubt that she has already commenced operations."

"Well," said Jackson ; "our part is to get him into all kinds of fun and gaiety, for the present. But we must have no gaming down here ;—that would spoil all : we must make him 'drink deep ere we depart.'"

"Yes," said Smith; "and have him up to London we must and will : Hannah is the proper person to do that."

After this worthy dialogue, the two gentlemen rejoined their admirable compeer, Captain Creed, at the Cock; and all three resolved to storm Barnard's dinner-table on that day.

It is now proper to notice to the reader, the impression made on Barnard's mind by the re-appearance of Smith and Jackson. He was startled by it so completely, that his self-possession was utterly overturned. The whole time they were rattling away with his father, he was on thorns,—fearful they would mention the London affair: besides, he could not exactly make out the true cause of their coming; and their presence did not revive the most pleasing recollections in his mind. Not that he personally disliked either of them; for Jackson he entertained great respect, and was flattered by an acquaintance with a man of such gentlemanly manners and exterior: as for Beauty, he had something for him of a still more congenial feeling. There was a certain conformity of nature between them, which, though not yet fully developed in Barnard, led him to like the society of Smith. But he feared much to have the subject of his misconduct renewed: and though, in consequence of his passion for Hannah, his thoughts were quite averted from Maria; yet he had not given up, or at least he flattered himself he had not given up, his virtuous resolutions in a general point of view.

Such was the state of his mind when they parted from him and his father; and he even regretted that they were to return that day to dinner. However, there was no help for it now; and so come they must: but he determined to take an opportunity of cautioning them not to allude, in his father's presence, to the late gaming transactions.

When the guests were gone, old Barnard in quired of his son who they were: he replied, that both were men of considerable property, and of high respectability, particularly Jackson;— that he had met them in London, where they had treated him with great hospitality, and that it was only right that he should now make them some return. To these he added a few more lies of the same description, which were well calculated to impose on an easy, ignorant, and weak man like his father, whose vanity was also flattered by acquaintances so much, apparently, above his son in manners and station.

Old Barnard now bustled about, and gave his orders for an excellent substantial dinner. He was a joyous old boy, fond of good living and a hearty glass; but very simple in his character, and quite unacquainted with everything but a rustic life. It was, therefore, easy for such men as Smith and Jackson to impose on his credulity by the dashing plausibility of their appearance. He was, besides, entirely under the control of his wife, whose absence at this time (for she was on a visit at Ipswich) gave him full scope to act.

Smith, Jackson, and the noble Captain, now quitted the "Cock," for the purpose of carrying old Barnard's confidence and good things by a *coup de main*. If impudence could secure success, in any instance, their stock was amply sufficient for the purpose. Impudence, however, like most other qualities, takes a tinge from the peculiar character of the individual. The impudence of these three heroes differed much in each of them respectively. The impudence of Jackson was elegant and gentlemanlike; that of Smith, callous and blackguard; while the effrontery of Creed had all the dry, grave humour about it, which was natural to him.

The unexpected presence of a third guest, and such a guest as the Captain, equally startled young and old Barnard. It must be owned that Creed's appearance, if destitute of the "swell" foppery of Smith, and the elegant style of Jackson, was at least equally characteristic with that of either, and far more remarkable.

We have before observed that the gallant Captain's person was somewhat of the stoutes., and much more distinguished for substance than symmetry. He thought proper, on the present occasion, to envelope it in a body-coat of light grey cloth; to which the addition of jet buttons presented a pleasing contrast. His waistcoat was of the brightest canary buff; which colour was tastefully relieved by a red silk handkerchief round his neck. His nether man was covered with white cord breeches, very loose, and light drab gaiters equally roomy in accommodation; a massy gold chain, with two ponderous seals, hung down nearly to his knees, and a large straw hat completed this eccentric figure. He was followed by two very large and filthy dogs, whose muddy paws can never be forgotten by Mary, the servant, whose duty obliged her to wipe out their manifold marks from her highly polished tables and chairs.

These gentlemen came with the charitable intention of giving old Barnard "a thorough benefit," as they called it. While their object was to dupe the son, they also thought that they might amuse themselves a little at the expense of the simplicity of the sire. It was for this purpose that Smith and Jackson brought Creed along with them, in such a free and easy style.

When they entered, they found old and young Barnard waiting for them, also miss Julietta, the latter's sister :—Stafford, with easy impudence, taking Creed by the hand, thus addressed the old gentleman :

"Mr. Barnard, allow me to present to you my respected and gallant friend, Captain Creed, late of the Waggon Train, now of the Scarafooca Rargers;—a worthier officer never smelt powder."

Beauty, at this sally, was seized with a violent fit of coughing, the result of a desperate attempt to suppress his laughter. Indeed, the appearance of Creed was so utterly at variance with all received notions concerning the exterior of a soldier, that it required muscles of no ordinary rigidity to stand the application of a military character to him : with the Barnard family. however, it went down as all gospel.

Creed, who seldom changed a muscle upon any

occasion, approached with much gravity, seized old Barnard's hand, and shook it with extraordinary energy, saying at the same time—

"Mr. Barnard, I am proud to know you: men like you, Sir, who support the honourable character of an English farmer, are at once an ornament and a service to our country."

Creed then shook young Barnard by the hand, and taking off his "*chapeau de paille*" next saluted Miss Barnard with much mock politeness; who returned his salutation, and the more easy ones of Jackson and Smith, with a gentle and affected simper.

The party now sat down to an excellent and substantial dinner. The gallant Captain seated himself beside Miss Barnard, and amused himself by paying her the most fulsome compliments during the whole of dinner time. Beauty placed himself at the foot of the table, and commenced the dissection of a roast goose with a dexterity that would have done honour to a most practised anatomist. Jackson sat on the right of the old man, and opposite to Miss Julietta, who was employed in alternately ogling his elegant person, and simpering at the pleasantries of the witty and polite Captain.

After dinner old Barnard produced some excellent port wine, to which his guests did ample justice. The glass circulated freely; and the old boy began to get extremely merry, and highly

Creed proved excessively entertaining; and he and Jackson vied with each other in telling the most enormous lies concerning their adventures in foreign parts. Creed, for instance, told of his making one of a party at the capture of a whale which measured five hundred feet in length;-- Jackson swore that he believed it, for that him self had known a case of a whale having swallowed the long-boat of a man-of-war, with all her crew. Thus they went on with a variety of extravagancies; and after Miss Barnard had retired, they became worse and worse,—telling stories of all shades, and singing songs of all colours, in the midst of a loud chorus. As if determined completely to astonish the old farmer, Jackson jumped out of the window after a handsome ruddy wench who was passing by: she, being one of the servants, took refuge in the kitchen, whither he followed her, and began to romp violently with all the maids. Beauty, hearing the noise, ran out and joined heartily in the sport. He was followed by Creed, who meeting Miss Barnard in the passage, fell on his knees before her, and began to make love in high heroics, quoting furiously from Romeo and Juliet. This quite delighted her, although she thought that the Captain was drunk, which he pretended to be. He acted that peculiar style of inebriation, which is agreeable to a woman from the confidence and elevation which it produces, and presents a good excuse for any little freedom or extravagance of manner which it may give rise to.

While this scene was going on, young and old Barnard sat staring at each other, not very unlike two simpletons. As for the old man, he thought his guests were positively mad; and the young man did not well know what to think about their freaks. While they were in this quandary, a desperate crash was heard in the passage; and running out to see what was the matter, they found that Jackson, in pursuing a servant maid who endeavoured to make her escape through the passage, had overturned the Captain, who was kneeling before Miss Barnard. Jackson, the maid, Creed, and the young lady, were lying at heads and points in the hall; and Beauty, who had left the kitchen in search of further mischief, was riding about the yard on the back of a very large pig, which seemed just then very well disposed to carry his rider directly to the scene of action. Several dogs, (among others those of the Captain,) attracted by the uproar, now approached, and marvellously increased the confusion. Two of them attacked the animal on which Beauty was mounted, which ran directly into the passage, and right against old Barnard, who, giving way to the shock, fell flat on his face; while Beauty, losing his equilibrium, tumbled off on the other side. Meanwhile, the hog and dogs rapidly pursued their course into the back yard, capering without compunction over the bodies of the fallen.

William Barnard was the only person who had kept his legs in this scene of confusion; and seizing a stout cudgel, he proceeded forthwith to still the quadrupedal tumult in the yard. Jackson then arose; and giving a signal to Beauty, they both vanished in the twinkling of an eye, leaving Captain Creed to settle accounts with the worthy host.

The latter made an attempt to rise, but succeeded only so far as to support his body on his right elbow, while Creed reclined opposite to him exactly in a similar position at the feet of Miss Barnard. She had contrived to rise up, and had thrown herself on a bench close by in a state of great real or affected agitation. It was a scene worthy of the pencil of George Cruikshank.

As soon as the old man was able to speak, he said—

"Well! but this is the strangest thing I ever saw: in the name of God, Captain Creed, are your friends mad? or is this the way that your young London chaps usually go on?"

"My dear Sir," said Creed, with a solemn drollery of expression, quite irresistible, "I am marvellously grieved at this affair. The fact is, that your excellent wine got into the heads of those young fellows; and there is no accounting for what the wisest of us will do in such a state I came out here to endeavour to stop their pranks,

28   F F

if possible, but could not succeed. After all, my dear Sir, they meant no harm, and will be very sorry for what they have done when they get sober. Nay, you may see that they are already ashamed of it; for they have run off, not daring to face you at present."

So saying, he got up and assisted old Barnard to rise. He then turned round, and apologized in most inflated language to Miss Barnard for the conduct of his companions,—whispering softly in her ear, that it had interrupted the most delicious moments of his existence. She simpered a reply, and said that she entirely acquitted him of all share in the disturbance.

Creed succeeded so completely in pacifying both father and daughter, and insinuated himself so far into the good graces of them both, that he was invited to stop to supper; and he left them between ten and eleven o'clock, in a state of high satisfaction with himself, and a favourable dis-position to pardon the follies of his comrades.

The next morning Jackson himself made a par-ticular apology, and all was soon forgotten.

Young Barnard now passed almost his entire time with the visitors. The day was employed in shooting, and making excursions about the country; the evening in drinking and carousing at the "Cock." They frequently dined also with old Barnard, but without precisely renewing such scenes as the one we have been just describing: but they were extremely gay and pleasant, and

Vincent in Farmer Barnards Hall at Polstead.

became, all of them, most decided favourites with the family.

All this while they were gradually endeavouring to draw the mind of William Barnard back to the dissipation of London. They did not yet venture to make a formal proposal of the kind to him: but their whole conversation at the Cock, and elsewhere, turned entirely on the vast superiority of life in the metropolis—the successive scenes of endless pleasure that awaited those in London who had plenty of money—and the advantages of living like independent gentlemen without the degradation and drudgery attendant on labour and business.

Jackson would often say—" My dear Mr. Barnard, you have seen nothing of London ; and I own, the little mishaps you experienced there are not much calculated to make you pleased with it : but it is not fair to judge of such a place as the capital by one or two days' residence in it; nor is it just to suffer an unlucky accident, which one night would easily repair, to prejudice us against any place. You have, I repeat, seen nothing of London,—nothing of Vauxhall, the Opera, Concerts, Balls, and a thousand other enchanting places, where woman shines in her highest charms,—where music, and mirth, and wit, and gaiety take their eternal round. You are young, Mr. Barnard, and should take advantage of your youth, to see and enjoy life. For my own part, sooner than bury myself in a place like this, I would be contented to become a senseless clod of the valley. Besides, if you make up your mind to live here, what can you do? nothing but live on the jog-trot life of your father, without enlarging your ideas, bettering your condition, or improving your property. But, in London, a thousand glorious and easy modes are open to a young man like you, by which you may exalt your rank and increase your riches. With the means and the talents which you possess, you cannot fail to make your fortune, and, what is still better, to enjoy it like a man."

Such harangues of Jackson's had great weight with Barnard, who looked up to him quite as a superior being. The very elevation of the other's language above the level of his own mind, wrought a greater effect upon him. Stafford was older, better educated, more accomplished in everything, than himself. He was thoroughly acquainted with life, and must know best what was the most advantageous mode of conduct.

Beauty, also, was a most powerful auxiliary in furthering the schemes of the party. He attached himself more and more to Barnard; professed the greatest possible friendship for him, the most intense regard to his interests. There was something, too, as we have said, congenial between them. Their intellects and education were more nearly on a level, and there was a similarity of disposition between them. In fact, it was possible, that a similar course of circum stances might have rendered Barnard exactly such a man as Smith. His late good resolutions were, perhaps, more the result of his rustic bringing-up, his losses acting on a timid mind, and his fleeting passion for Maria, than of an inherent disposition or taste for virtue.

Smith was, then, continually urging him to give up his rustic life and return to London; and using all the arguments in his power to persuade him to that course.

Yet it is difficult to say whether the trio would nave eventually succeeded, had it not been for the aid of another, and a far more powerful, coadjutor in the person of Hannah. She and Barnard had met frequently since the rencontre in the Barn which we have described; and this artful woman had contrived to keep his passions in a high state of inflammation—never cloying by too much of her society,—always alleging some pretext or other for shortening their meetings. She was, also, continually throwing out hints and insinuations that she might be forced, at no great distance of time, to quit the country ;—perhaps they might meet again, perhaps not,—'twas hard to say ;—no knowing what might happen. Thus she was perpetually sporting with his feelings, alarming his fears, exciting his passions, and keeping him in a constant state of mental agitation.

When a young man has conceived so violent a passion for a woman, as Barnard had for Hannah; —when this passion has been ministered to in such

a way as it was by her; and when obstacles
or apparent obstacles arise, while yet it is in
its meridian;—there is scarcely anything that
he may not be prevailed upon to do, to gain his
object. Then it is, that a clever and charming
woman has him completely in her power, and
can persuade him to do what she pleases. He
remembers the ecstatic but transitory enjoyment, from the repetition of which he is now
debarred, and may be debarred for ever!—The
thought is madness! He dwells upon the delights
which he has but tasted, until his brain becomes
on fire, and his whole frame is fever! Then let
him meet the woman he adores, and she may turn
him any way she thinks proper!

Such was precisely the state in which Barnard
found himself, returning one evening rather late
from the " Cock." The influence of the wine
he had been drinking was not at all adapted to
lessen the violence of his feelings; for drinking
always gives a heightened colour and an exaggerated dimension to the ideas which have pre-
possessed our minds, from whatever cause arising.
Those who fly to wine, to enable them to forget
their cares and sorrows, generally find it but a
treacherous auxiliary. Those grievances which
oppress us only during the actual period of
their operation, it may make us forget for the
time; but they must be such as do not make the
deepest impression on the mind. The debtor, for
instance, whose notions of payment are rather

vague, may forget his debts, under the influence of the bottle, when he knows he is safe from arrest and imprisonment. The drudge of mechanical and ill-paid labour may thus, when he has a few hours of respite, enjoy himself in the lap of oblivion, but, to the lover, wine will only recal the idea of his mistress, associated with pleasant or disagreeable feelings according to the peculiar predicament of the case. The statesman or the soldier, unjustly branded with disgrace or infamy, cannot wash the stain from his recollection in the sparkling bowl. The patriot cannot so forget the wrongs of his country, or the secret murderer drown " the worm that never dies." The om-nipotence of wine cannot

> " —— minister to a mind diseased,
> Raze from the memory a rooted sorrow,
> Blot out the written troubles of the brain,
> And, with some sweet oblivious antidote,
> Cleanse the full bosom of that perilous stuff
> That weighs upon the heart."

Barnard, as he walked home, was thinking of Hannah, dreading the idea of losing her, and worked up almost to distraction by the recollection of past and the doubt of future enjoyment, when he saw, not far from the Red Barn, by which his route lay, a figure which he immediately recognized to be herself, notwithstanding a large dark cloak in which she was enveloped.

He approached her, and thought that there was a cast of melancholy over her features, greater than he had observed before. She took his hand without speaking, and they entered the Red Barn together.

They sat down, and Hannah took off her cloak; she had a white dress beneath it, and looked uncommonly lovely.

"William," said she, with a deep sigh, "what I dreaded has at last arrived: I must quit the country;—we must part, I fear, for ever!"

"Good God! Hannah," said Barnard; "how can you torment me thus?—we must not cannot part."

"We must," she resumed, in the same unaltereu melancholy tone; "our destinies are not united. I must go; you, I know, dare not—will not follow."

"How dare not?" said he. "What do you mean?—explain yourself."

"William," she replied, "I am the victim of persecution, and I must fly. I ar. no fortune-teller; it was love which made me assume that character,—love for you, William: it was folly, of which I am now the victim. I have been marked out by the magistrates, and I must go hence to London."

"Can you not remain concealed here?" said Barnard: "cannot I find for you a place of concealment?"

"Impossible!" she rejoined: "their vigilance is not to be so deceived; I should be discovered and brought to punishment: I could not survive the disgrace of it."

"But," exclaimed he, "is there no other way of settling this business? cannot some intercession be made with the magistrates, and you remain here with me, in some asylum of peace and safety?"

"No," she answered; "they would listen to nothing of the kind. We must fly, my dearest William! alas!—what did I say, *we?*—no, *I* must fly, and leave all that is dear to me behind. We must never meet again, William—never kiss—never embrace again."

She put her hands across her eyes, and began to weep, (for tears are ever at the ready command of woman).

Barnard was most powerfully affected, and, without speaking, threw his arm round her waist. She raised her glistening eyes, and looking up into his face, said, with an expression of the tenderest love,

"No, my dearest William! we must have no more mutual endearments. It is all over now. I was vain enough to promise myself years of happiness with you,—but it was not to be; and Hannah must now proceed alone through the world—a poor, helpless, solitary wanderer!"

She sunk upon his bosom. The tone and look with which she pronounced the last words were touching beyond the power of description to pourtray. The tearful eye of a lovely woman is never bent on any man in vain, (at least I hope not.) Thrice the firmness of Barnard might have

29

yielded to the irresistible fascination—thrice his penetration might have been deceived;—nay, such a woman could have persuaded where she could not convince, and the wisest would have walked into the snare with his eyes open.

"No! Hannah," exclaimed Barnard, "it must and shall be. We shall not part;—I will follow you—I will fly with you, anywhere,—everywhere."

Raising her head, and half encircling his neck with one lovely arm, she said,

"No, William! it shall not be said that I *seduced* you from your parents and your home: though no parents can love you as I do, or no home receive you half so warmly as this bosom."

"I tell you, Hannah, you are all the world to me. I will fly with you instantly to London. Exist without you, I cannot."

"Well, William," she replied, after a pause, "if it must be, I ——, but we cannot go to-gether,—that might excite suspicion. I will proceed to London directly, leaving you an address where to find me. You may follow as soon as convenient to yourself."

"Well, be it so." said he;—"but, Hannah, though I am not to go with you, you must receive from me the means of travelling." As he said these words he drew from his pocket a sealed letter, which he broke open, and took from it a £20 note, and presented it to Hannah.

"Never, William!" she replied; "you do

RED BARN, POLSTEAD.

injustice to my love. 'Tis true, I am poor, but I can find the means of getting up to London without putting you to expense. Even were I to walk, I would not do so; and I would go through much more than that fatigue for you."

" Take it :—why should you refuse ? are we not one ?—is not all I possess yours ?—you will only be receiving your own."

After some further pressing on his part, and well acted disinterested refusal on hers, she was at last prevailed on to accept the note; which she did, saying,

" William, I must consider this as but a loan : in London I can support myself by my own work. I have been well educated, and can do many things to gain a living. Our connexion must be disinterested."

She then gave him the direction where to find her. It was agreed that he should follow within four days, at farthest; and after a long, long embrace, they parted.

Scarcely had Barnard disappeared, and Hannah, resuming her cloak, quitted the Barn, when a figure, above the middle size of manhood, was seen running from the shade of the trees into the broad moonlight, and crossing the field towards her, also enveloped in a cloak, with a foraging cap upon his head. He approached and addressed her—

" Well, have you succeeded, good lady ?—is he safe within the toils ?—is he ours—is he yours ?"

" He is *mine*," said Hannah, " as securely as the triple chain of love can bind him;—that he shall be yours, Stafford, will depend upon yourself."

" I care not for him," said Jackson, " nor would I share in the paltry plunder: this head, and this good right hand, will always minister amply to my own personal necessities. I would not dirty my fingers with the gold of the clown, were it not for the sake of my comrades;—they must be secured."

" So must *I*, Stafford; I cannot labour for nothing: if your comrades are to have the wings, I must have the body."

" And the *soul* too, I presume," said he, " sateless woman! will nothing satisfy you but his utter ruin?"

" How marvellously compassionate you are grown, Mr. Jackson," retorted Hannah; "but why not extend your pity to an innocent girl, whose ruin seems necessary to satisfy you?"

" Fudge!" said Jackson, " there's no ruin in the case: but you have touched a subject that concerns me more nearly than the fate of Barnard. I meet with more difficulties in that quarter than I expected: your further assistance will, I fear, be necessary."

" Well, Stafford, you know the terms—I do nothing for nothing."

" I know it too well," replied he; " your avarice is as insatiable as your other passions."

" Beware what you say, Jackson," said Hannah,

her dark eyes flashing fire; "if I desert you, you will not only fail in your present scheme, but you shall hear from me further."

"Your threats," said Jackson, coolly folding his arms, "are like the idle wind. Did I not raise you from misery—from the precarious life of prostitution, and place you where your lap shall be filled with treasure; yet you hesitate to render me a trifling service, without being paid down for it. If *I* desert you, you will be poor indeed."

"Stafford," replied Hannah, "I know you to be proud as Lucifer, reckless of danger, fearing neither God nor man. But there is one point where you are vulnerable, and there I can touch you;—a word from me, and Maria is lost to you for ever."

"Hannah," returned Jackson, "we are necessary to each other: altercation between us is useless and absurd.—What sum do you desire?"

"Fifty pounds cannot be too much," replied Hannah.

"Well—well," said he, "you shall have the money."

"It must be soon done," said Hannah; I must have this before Barnard can arrive in London."

"To-morrow night," said Stafford, "we shall meet and arrange the whole,—an hour after midnight."

They separated as they had met,—cold and passionless: there was no love or sympathy between *them*. Stafford was like an angel fallen from his sphere, sullied with terrestrial propensities, though haughty and high crested still. She was an incarnate fiend, deaf to every inspiration but that of Mammon.

Hannah glided like a spirit into the valley, and Stafford passed into the road, as the village clock, tolling the hour of two, echoed through the silent fields; while the moon's pale orb slowly sunk, and left the horizon in temporary darkness.

CHAP. XI.

"Not one for thee, a friend or mate,
    Sweet daughter of the lowly dale!
O leave them to their lordly state,
    And think thee of thy parent vale."

M. BAILLIE.

——————————

JACKSON, instead of returning to the "Cock" proceeded to the cottage of Maria, resolving to try the full powers of his eloquence in persuading her to elope with him directly, and thus avoid the further intervention of Hannah in that quarter. It may be necessary to inform our readers that these lovers had had nightly meetings regularly since the last which we described, in which Stafford Jackson had tried all his persuasive powers to no purpose, she making marriage a *sine quâ non* of her consent to be his. Still her attachment to him grew stronger and stronger, more especially since the unaccountable absence of William Barnard, of whom she had heard or seen nothing since the day on which she gave him an indefinite promise of marriage. This, though it surprised, was far from displeasing her, as she considered it a tacit dissolution of her promise. But Jackson had not given her any sufficient explanation of the reason of his not coming openly forward to demand her from her father. He had only stated in vague and general terms, that motives of the greatest weight rendered a temporary secresy necessary. Therefore, though she admitted those clandestine meetings, yet her reason and her virtue were both still sufficiently strong to prevent her from proceeding further.

Jackson had a particular signal by which he used to advertise Maria of his approach. This signal was giving three gentle taps under her window, which she always left half open, in the expectation of his coming. At this, time however, he thought proper, from some whim or other, or perhaps thinking it would produce a greater effect, to preface his usual signal by the following song of his own composition, sung in a gentle but very impressive style. Stafford, as we have already seen, was both a poet and a musician; and the taste and feeling with which he sung this ballad proved him no ordinary singer.

> Sweet are the breezes of night,
> When the forehead is fevered with care,
> And sweet is hope's roseate light
> When it dawns on the night of despair.
> But thy lip is sweeter far
> Than the balmy breath of night,

And thine eye is a milder star
Than young hope's first dawning light.

Sweet are the opening flow'rs
That awake to the breath of spring;
Sweet are the silent show'rs
That drop from the South's soft wing:
But sweeter far is thy sigh
Than spring's awakening flow'rs;
Brighter thy glistening eye
Than April's tenderest show'rs.

After this, Jackson tapped thrice at the window, and Maria immediately descended.

He now commenced, as usual, to depict the ardour and sincerity of his passion, in the most glowing colours—to complain of her cruelty and delay—and to press her to an instantaneous elopement, under the promise of future marriage.

She replied gently, but firmly, that she never could become his under any other condition than that of an open marriage, and with the cognizance of her parents.

"Then," said he, "Maria, I perceive all my hopes are vain. Cruel girl! you drive me to madness and despair!—you care nothing for me;—you love another."

"It is not so," answered Maria; "I do not love another; but I must not act wrongly—I must not wound the hearts of my parents."

"Maria, you have no confidence in me—in my honour—in my affection."

"Yes, I have—too much. Is not my meeting

H H

you in this secret manner a sufficient proof of it? But you would persuade me to do what is wrong —you would take advantage of my foolish love."

"Oh, Maria!" rejoined he, "I would only persuade you to consult your own happiness and mine—to listen to the suggestions of the fondest and truest heart that ever loved."

"You have told me," said Maria, "that you have reasons for not speaking to my father now; but you have not told me what those reasons are. I have some cause to complain of *your* want of confidence."

"Hear me, then, Maria,—my existence is at a stake;—the safety of my life depends upon concealment. My love to you, even at this moment, exposes me to imminent danger in coming into this part of the country. I stand accused of murder, and the emissaries of justice are abroad to seize my person, and bring me to punishment."

"Great God!" said Maria, shrinking from him with horror, "a murderer!"

"Yes, Maria, I am called a murderer, but I am not one. I have killed a man, 'tis true, but it was in self defence; he might as well have killed me."

"How did it happen?" said Maria.

"I received from a gentleman the grossest insult which another can receive,—the lie and the blow: manhood could not bear it;—I challenged him to the field. We met in a secret place, each attended by a friend, and a surgeon accompanied us: we fired, and my opponent fell instantly dead upon the spot."

"But, I imagine—I have read, at least," said Maria, "that such cases were pardonable by law."

"True," rejoined Jackson, "when it can be clearly proved that all has been fairly conducted; but, unfortunately, in our case, this cannot be done. The only witnesses we had have unaccountably disappeared; therefore, until they can be found, I stand in the light of a murderer, and must infallibly be condemned and executed, if brought to trial now."

"Good God! how shocking," exclaimed Maria; "but still you might trust my father—he would never reveal the secret."

"Maria, I can trust no one but you: my friend, whom you have seen with me, is in as much danger as myself. He was my second: I dare not compromise his life, however careless I may be of my own. God knows that your cruelty renders it but of little value;—I care little now how soon it may be ended."

Maria was deeply moved,—her feelings were strongly excited; and had Jackson contented himself with pressing the elopement only, he might, perhaps, have succeeded; but he thought the opportunity favourable for a complete conquest. He embraced her—he kissed her; and, impelled by wild passion, urged his suit in terms that alarmed Maria: she struggled, and springing from his arms with a sudden strength lent her by innate virtue, was inside the house, and had closed the door in the twinkling of an eye.

Jackson stood confounded, ashamed, and indignant. He cursed, at one time, his own precipitance, by which he feared that he had entirely lost her; and, at another, his own fatuity and folly in thus wasting his money, his talents, and his time, in pursuit of a simple country girl. Sometimes he thought of giving her up altogether; but, again, he thought of her charms; and the difficulties he experienced, increased his estimation of the object he desired, and his ardour in its pursuit. His vanity, too, was piqued, and he deemed his honour to be interested in the success of his enterprize.

Stafford was a man who had been highly successful with the other sex;—he had found beauty, rank, and fortune, easily accessible: most of the women with whom he had intrigued had met him half way. He had never before been engaged in a case of seduction, properly so called; and the thought of being baffled by an untaught rustic country girl, at once perplexed, puzzled, and enraged him, and rendered him more eager and determined on her possession.

Such was the train of thought in which Jackson returned to his inn. He slept a few hours, and, on rising in the morning, soon settled within his own mind the plan of operations he should pursue. It was first of all necessary to repair the blunder into which his precipitant passions had hurried him; he, therefore, sat down, and penned the following billet-doux, which he entrusted to his worthy compeer, Mr. Beauty Smith, to take an opportunity of delivering into Maria's own hand, unperceived by any one else. It ran thus:—

"DEAREST MARIA,

"Can you forgive the error—the madness of love? I own my crime, but you are my apology. Who, alas! can look on heavenly charms like yours, and preserve his reason? Forgive me—oh! forgive me, my dearest Maria, and see me once again. I shall be at your window at the same hour as when I saw you last; and do give me five minutes' hearing: I cannot—will not, survive your refusal; and my death must rest on you.."

Beauty took this note to Maria's cottage when her father and mother were out, and delivered it to her, saying from whom it came; and, hinting that he himself ran some risque in being abroad at that hour, speedily withdrew.

The girl's state of mind may well be conceived, —though better, perhaps, by my fair readers than any others.

The conduct of Jackson, the night before, had, at first, both alarmed and offended her; but she loved the man—and love, like charity, covereth a multitude of sins. If he was afraid that his conduct had lost her to him, she, on her side, was not without her apprehensions that he might be lost to her. "Perhaps," thought she, "he will come no more;" and the idea of losing him was one pregnant with pain. In this state of mind she received his note, and her feelings in his favour were renewed. She forgave his audacity, pitied his dangerous situation, which was confirmed by Smith; but still determined not to elope with him on the mere *promise* of marriage.

The reader may be surprised at this firmness on the part of Maria in this point—a girl, otherwise so susceptible, so open to the temptations of vanity, and so simple, and even giddy in character. It was partly the result of being brought up in a strict veneration for all religious institutions, and partly of a little female policy, that led her to endeavour to secure thoroughly the splendid establishment to which she deemed herself destined, but now, her affections were engaged,—and when that is the case, both principle and policy will in time give way; still time is necessary.

The day, the evening, and the night, had passed, but passed on leaden wings to all the parties concerned in this affair. Hannah was anxious to secure her reward, and be off to London; Jackson was anxious to bring matters to a conclusion; and Maria was anxious to be thoroughly convinced that he was a man of honour, and to extend to him her forgiveness.

The midnight hour had stolen by, and the bell was now tolling one, when Jackson and Hannah met again, according to appointment made on the preceding night. Characters like them seldom exchange salutations, or waste time in ceremony. Jackson abruptly broke silence.

"Go," said he, "now is the time; give three taps under her window—she will think it is I, and will come down: the rest I leave to your own judgment and address,—only observe to impress upon her mind the safety of her trusting me."

"But, Jackson, remember our contract."

"Away!" replied he, "my word is passed—it is enough."

He threw the folds of his ample cloak over one shoulder, and disappeared. Hannah proceeded to the cottage.

It may be supposed that Maria was not asleep: she was up, and in anxious yet fearful expectation of her lover, though the appointed hour was not yet arrived. The signal, so well known to her, is heard,—she descends in silent rapidity—opens the door—a figure appears in the shade—she pauses —the figure advances, and Maria beholds the fortune-teller.—Her astonishment was unbounded.

"Great God!" said she, "is this you? What can bring you here at an hour like this?"

"Your welfare;—I watch over you, Maria, as the guardian angel over his charge—all hours are alike to me."

"But that signal!—how could you learn that? I thought there was but one——"

" Is my art nothing, child?" returned the Sybil; " is my intercourse with beings of brighter spheres nothing?—But let us not waste words, for I have far to travel ere the morning dawn; nor can I be always with the children of the earth :—speak, have you seen him?"

" I have," said Maria, " more than once."

" I knew it before you spoke—I saw it all in the glass of vision. Spare yourself a further recital,—you have seen him, heard his proposals, and refused your consent. Maria! you may, if you please, dash the cup of fortune from your lips, but it may not be presented to you again."

Maria was silent and confused. The sorceress resumed—

" Have you forgotten all that has passed?— have not all my predictions been fulfilled? Have you forgotten the supernatural voice that saluted you from the thicket?"

Maria trembled, yet replied, " But you know I was in doubt between two persons."

" Let that doubt, then," said Hannah, " be dissipated for ever : Barnard can never be yours, —he loves another;—he is irrevocably pledged to her;—their destinies are sealed above."

Had she said *below*, it would have been nearer the truth.

Maria felt not a little surprised; but Hannah's words perfectly explained the hitherto unac- countable absence of Barnard.

" As for him," said she, " I never loved him."

" You encouraged his addresses, though," said Hannah ; " nay, you promised to marry him."

Here Maria testified the utmost surprise, and owned it was true—and that, from the other's absence, she thought Barnard might be the man.

" You see," resumed the Sybil, " I know everything; will you trust me now ?—he was not—is not, the person : the other is, and yet you refuse him ;—why do you act thus ?"

" Because," said Maria, " I fear to go without the consent of my parents ; and, perhaps, he may not marry me."

" Weak victim of incredulity !" exclaimed Hannah, " why should you doubt him ?—he is young, handsome, rich, and full of honour. Has he not told you his reasons for concealment ? Mark my words ;—it is in your power to make or mar your fortune; so take your choice."

" Then you counsel me to accept his offer," said Maria.

" I do," she replied ; " I exhort—I conjure you, for your own sake, to do so ; you will find in the end that I counsel wisely. Remember, wavering girl, who it is who speaks to you ;—one whose predictions, regarding you, have all been fulfilled —one who has told you everything—one who holds communion with the world of spirits—to whom the veil of futurity is rent away, and who can read your inmost thoughts. Go with him and be happy—stay and be wretched !"

Maria was, as we have mentioned in an earlier part of this history, extremely superstitious. This appeal, therefore, of Hannah, after all the manifestations she had given of her superior intelligence, added to Maria's own feelings for Stafford, proved, for the time, irresistible : she promised to agree to the elopement with him.

Hannah, having thus gained the object of her mission, now left her, and acquainted Jackson with her success.

Maria had but little time to reflect on the scene which we have just described, when she heard the three taps repeated under her window; and going down, found Stafford himself below.

She received him with the most trembling agitation. He commenced by entreating her forgiveness for his conduct at the preceding meeting, imputing it to the desperation of his love, &c. He then reiterated his prayers that she would agree to an elopement; and, in her then state of mind, drew from her a promise to that effect. Maria told him nothing of the fortune-teller, for these are subjects that girls of all classes invariably keep secret from their lovers.

Before they parted, it was agreed that Jackson should come the following night at eleven o'clock to an appointed place near the cottage,—that Maria should meet him there,—proceed with him, and,—quit her peaceful home for ever.

Jackson returned to his inn, flushed and triumphant with his success; and Maria retired to her bed with very different feelings. When she arose in the morning, she began to reflect more collectedly on the occurrences of the previous night. She trembled when she recollected the promise she had given, and trembled still more at the idea of keeping it. That promise had, in a manner, been extorted from her under the influence of the strong excitement of love and superstition combined. The principles of religion, and of general rectitude, which had been early instilled into her mind—her warm attachment to her parents, and that vague sort of terror which every young person feels at the idea of quitting home for the first time, and of quitting it clandestinely,—all concurred to make her regret the pledge which she had given, and to wish most earnestly to recall it. When she was no longer overawed by the presence of Hannah, or persuaded by that of Jackson, these motives re-assumed their original force over her mind. The fortune-teller had certainly given her such apparent proofs of her skill and knowledge, as had very considerable weight with her; but then she flattered herself that this step of elopement was not necessary to the fulfilment of her predictions in the main; and the more she dwelt upon it, the more she felt her mind abhorrent from the measure.

As for Jackson,—his safety, &c., she thought that he could not be compromised by a private marriage, with the consent of her parents. This last, indeed, was the point which weighed most

with her; for though she did not hesitate to conceal from her father and mother the commencement and progress of this amour, she could
not resolve to take the final step without their
knowledge and concurrence.

In short, the more she reflected on the subject,
the more she was determined against the elopement: her virtue and her firmness were restored,
and she resolved to meet Jackson that night, and
put a decided negative on the matter. She felt,
indeed, that her own peace of mind required that
she should do so.

Meanwhile, Jackson took consultation with his
comrades, and their whole plan was concerted: he
was to carry off Maria with himself alone, while
Smith and Creed were to remain behind to bring
up Barnard to London to rejoin Hannah. The
public-house, in Whitechapel, was to be the place
of rendezvous for them all to determine concerning
future operations.

However, on the night of the day on which
this matter was arranged, a circumstance occurred
which occasioned some slight change in their intended measures. They had sat in the parlour of
the "Cock" to despatch a second bowl of punch, and
were waiting for the time appointed: it was now
about ten o'clock, when they heard a stentorian
voice, which seemed to come from the kitchen
of the public house, bellowing out—

> " My name, d'ye see, 's Tom Tough,
> I've seen a little service."

" WORTHY COMMODORE,

" This comes to let you know that the Spanker is safe in the old cove. We first pushed for Flushing, and sent some lads up to Antwerp, where a little business was done: we have cruised since along the north coast of France. Our cargo is pretty fat; but we can do nothing here without you: so come with the first fair wind. Old Blinker, that I left with you in London, told me where you have dropped anchor;—let go as quick as possible.

" Yours,

" WARREN."

"Confound it!" said Jackson, " this is awkward; but go I must, or everything will be topsy-turvy among these dunder heads. But for her:——I have it,—she must go too. You, Captain, and Smith, will wait to *convoy* Barnard, as Warren would say."

Jackson took a pen and ink, and wrote something on the back of the paper, then going down, he returned it to the sailor, saying,

" Well, my lad, this is very good, *mind you take care of it;*—here's something to help your journey."

" Long life to your honour!" said Ricketts, giving Jackson a sly wink, to let him know that he understood his directions.

The hour of appointment with Maria now rapidly approached, and Jackson repaired to the place of meeting. He had previously prepared everything for his journey to the coast, and had a postchaise in readiness : he was in a travelling dress, and well armed.

He came to the appointed place a little before the time. Maria was not there. "If," said he to himself, "she should trick me after all! Doubtless she is vacillating still—but surely she will keep the appointment.—After all, what am I about? Is not this most egregious folly? Is it not something worse than folly? Ah, Stafford! Stafford! I shrewdly suspect that you are something not very unlike a villain.—Nonsense ! I love her, and I will never desert her. But how do you know whether it will be in your power to keep this resolution? are not your means of living dangerous and precarious, and does not your own existence hang by a thread?—Well, I cannot help it—I must have her."

Scarcely had he finished this soliloquy, when Maria appeared in view. The instant he beheld her, he saw how the case stood : she was dressed exactly as usual, without the least appearance of any preparation for a journey. But she looked unusually lovely. Her chesnut hair escaped in thick and clustering ringlets from under her bonnet on each side. Her dress was white, and her slender waist was cinctured with an emerald-coloured zone. The night was calm, and the leafy boughs under which they stood scarcely moved, and the moon was brightly shining.

"My dearest Maria," said Jackson, "are you

ready to go! but," continued he, looking at her, "that surely is no dress to travel in?"

Maria looked down, and did not answer.

"I see how it is," said he, "you mean to go back from your promise. Maria, this is unkind, unjust, and cruel."

"Hear me, Stafford," said she, collecting unusual firmness; "I feel that that promise was wrong—was contrary to the laws of God, and my duty to my parents,—that I ought not to have made it, and, therefore, that I ought not to keep it."

"'Tis well," replied he, "love has but little influence over you. Were your love like mine, it would surmount every other consideration. But I see how it is—you are putting me off by foolish excuses, that you may bestow yourself upon another."

"As Heaven is above me!" exclaimed Maria, "it is not so. There is none on earth that I prefer to yourself; but I cannot—will not do what is wrong."

"Maria," resumed Jackson, in the tenderest accents, "dearest Maria, will you see me die at your feet?"

"Jackson," said she, "I cannot hear you,— I must not hear you."

"Maria!" he exclaimed, dropping on his knees and seizing both her hands, "you must,—you *shall* hear me."

"I will not," said Maria, endeavouring to disengage herself—"I must away."

"Well then, Maria," said he rising, "I will compel you to your own happiness;" so saying, he enclosed her waist firmly with his left arm, while he took, with the other hand, a small silver whistle from his breast, suspended by a black ribbon, and blew a loud and shrill call. In an instant three men made their appearance. Two of them were muffled up in cloaks, with which they half concealed their countenances ; the third was an herculean figure, in the dress of a sailor.

These men instantly seized Maria, who was half dead with surprise and terror, and carrying her off, put her into a postchaise which was waiting in the adjoining road. Jackson followed, and entered after her. The sailor mounted the seat with the driver, and the two others, waving their hats, one crying out in French, "*Adieu, au revoir,*" rapidly disappeared.

It is now necessary to explain to our readers how this affair took place. Jackson, who all along feared the vacillation of Maria, was too good a general not to provide against the contingency of her refusal. He had, therefore, stationed in ambuscade, at a convenient distance, Captain Creed and Beauty Smith, who were the two gentlemen in cloaks, and our new and worthy acquaintance Tom Ricketts, who, divested of his factitious leg and black eye-patch, and with his left arm at full liberty, was there in *propriâ persond,* sound of wind and limbs, the broad, bold, and brazen, ruffian.

While this matter was thus proceeding, Barnard had prepared everything for his departure for London: and for the purpose of gaining his father's consent to this measure—which, after all, was little more than a matter of form—a regular and pressing invitation had been made to him by Jackson, and the old man readily assented. He supplied his son with money for the occasion.

The invitation given to young Barnard seemed, in the eyes of his father, a thing just in season; for the visitors had concluded a bargain with the old man, by which he agreed to part with corn and hay to the amount of £178, to be paid for in bills drawn by "Stafford Jackson, Esquire, of Jackson Hall, near Truro, county of Cornwall, and Captain Creed, of the Scarafooka Rangers!"—This corn was to be forwarded to London without loss of time, and consigned there to the care of Don Josiah Xiutototle, a Mexican merchant, and a special agent of Jackson's, while young Barnard was to superintend the arrival and delivery of the cargo.

A note was left for young Barnard by Stafford Jackson, explaining that business of some consequence had obliged him to go to Ipswich in a great hurry, but that he would soon rejoin him in London. And the following morning, at five o'clock, the former set out for the capital, under the sacred superintendence of Mr. John Beauty Smith, and that distinguished officer of *Light Infantry*, Captain Cornelius Creed.

CHAP XII.

By art the pilot, through the boiling deep
And howling tempest, steers the fearless ship;
And 'tis the artist wins the glorious course,
Not those who trust in chariots and in horse.
                                    POPE'S HOMER.

WHEN Maria recovered a little from her sudden fright, it was in vain that she attempted to remonstrate with Jackson on his violent and treacherous conduct, and implored him to return and set her free. Her prayers, entreaties, and tears, were all to no purpose. Jackson answered them only by protestations of eternal love, and eternal fidelity. He declared,—he swore, that his intentions were nothing less than honourable that he was about to marry her; but that, from her wavering and distrustful conduct, he found himself obliged to compel her into a measure necessary to their mutual happiness.

How far this rhetoric might in the end have prevailed upon Maria, it is hard to say. Certain it is that she loved the man, and love will do much—but at present she felt both frightened and irritated by his conduct. The thought of quitting home in such a manner, the state in which her parents must be on missing her, and her vague apprehensions of the future, all rushed with full force upon her mind, and almost reduced her to a state of distraction. At the present moment, and under the influence of such feelings, she would have done anything to escape. If an opportunity offered, she would not have hesitated to jump out of the carriage to accomplish this purpose.

They had now moved rapidly on without interruption for about sixteen or seventeen miles. The moon had long sunk below the horizon, and darkness had overspread the face of heaven. It was that cold and melancholy hour which precedes the break of day, in the after season of the year. The gathering clouds increased the gloom of the scene, preventing the star light, and the twilight struggling in its birth, from diminishing the palpable obscurity. As far as it was possible to discern, the landscape around was a wide and barren waste. One of those lonely moors which, in the eastern parts of this kingdom, occasionally fling a wide interval between the opposite limits of cultivation, like the ocean rolling between verdant islands, or the patches of desert which intervene in Africa between rich and fertile lands.

"A dreary plain, forlorn and wild,
The seat of desolation, void of light."

Just in this spot, and at this hour, the travellers were suddenly arrested and astonished by a violent shock, accompanied with a loud crash. Something had evidently come in instantaneous contact with a wheel of the chaise; but before Jackson had time to inquire the cause, he heard the following dialogue take place outside, not in the softest tones imaginable.

"Helm's a-lee; shiver my timbers, Tom, but we have run foul of a frigate."

"Ay, ay, Sir; this comes of navigating in these narrow guts by night;—there is no sea-room here."

"D—n your eyes!" roars a voice from the seat of the chaise; "there's plenty of sea-room if you knew how to steer, you lubber."

"D—n *your* eyes again!" rejoined the former speaker; "I knew how to steer before you could splice a hand-line, you great ill-looking porpus."

"Sheer off, I say," roared Ricketts from the top, "or by the holy Pope we'll pour a broadside into you;—that's flat. D—n me, I'd sink your cockle-shell with a two-ouncer."

"Come, come, shipmates," said the first speaker, in a fine mellow naval tone, "let us not fight about straws,—we all carry the same flag here: this is an accident that will happen sometimes in these narrow straits,—let us try to get clear as well as we can."

There is (if I may be allowed to use a figure of speech bordering on a blunder), a sort of physiognomy in the human voice, by which character is indicated. Something there was in the honest, open, clear, and manly tones of the last speaker, that would impress any hearer with an idea of his good nature, sincerity, and courage. Such, at least, was the impression which they made on the mind of Maria, who was struck with a sudden thought that the opportunity of escape was now presented. Obeying without hesitation the almost instinctive impulse of the moment, she cried out,

"Whatever you are, take pity on a helpless young girl, who has been dragged away from her parents and her home against her will;—if you are men, you will have pity on and help me."

"Halloa, Tom!" exclaimed the last male speaker, "here's a pirate we've run foul of;—an Algerine, by Jove! with a prize in tow."

"Aye, ay, master, I sees as how it is."

"Well, Tom, we must try and re-capture:—hang the sailor that would not fight for a pretty girl, if he was as old as the Royal George."

"So says I, master," rejoined the person addressed, descending from the gig and coming round to the carriage-horses' heads.

"Drive on, I say, postillion," cried out Jackson; "I command you, Sir, drive on."

"I'll be d—d if he does though," said the person in front, who held back the horses.

"If you don't let go the horses' heads I'll shoot you!" roared out Jackson.

"No blustering, young man; save your fire for a better opportunity," returned a voice.

"You are highwaymen."

"You lie!"

"Will you let go?"

"No!"

"Then take the consequences, scoundrel," said Jackson, discharging a pistol through the front window.

He failed, however, in hitting the person intended. The other descending from the gig, was just about to fire into the chaise, when he recollected there was a female within, and checked himself. Ricketts now jumped from the chaise, and knocked the pistol out of his hand. They then grappled.

Jackson now jumped out, leaving Maria nearly senseless with fright, and rushing to his horses' heads, aimed a blow at the person there with the butt-end of his pistol. The latter received the blow on his left arm, and wielding a sturdy cudgel in his right hand, directed a stroke which, had it fallen as it was intended, on the head of Jackson, would have left him in a very ill condition for further fighting. But he avoided it with the rapidity of lightning, and, by a simultaneous movement, tripped up the heels of the other with his foot, and levelled a blow at the side of his head, which instantly laid him prostrate. Jackson now striding over him could perceive, by the imperfect light from the chaise lamp, that he had a wooden leg; and on looking closer, recognized him to be no other than Tom Squires, the ancient foreman of his respected friend, Captain Carribles!

But for this discovery it might have gone hard with poor Squires; for though a powerful man, his wooden leg and the difference of age rendered him no match for Stafford Jackson. The latter, however, contented himself with keeping him in his prostrate position.

Meanwhile, Ricketts and Captain Carribles (for it was no other) were engaged in a very unequal contest. The loss of his right arm, though he could use his left extremely well and was otherwise a very powerful man, was a tremendous disadvantage to the Captain: still he fought extremely like a tough old tar. Ricketts, however, soon got the better of him, and was in the act of planting a blow of a bludgeon that would have settled his antagonist for ever, when the giant and now ferocious slayer was himself suddenly felled to the earth by an unknown arm. He was struck in the neck, just under the ear, and down he fell at the feet of his antagonist perfectly senseless.

Carribles looked round for his deliverer, and saw, by the light of the lamp, a tall athletic young man in the dress of a soldier, with a knapsack on his back.

Jackson, still standing over Squires, beheld this scene. On seeing Ricketts fall, he ran to him directly, attempted to raise him up, but found him completely senseless. He looked around, and saw Carribles engaged in shaking hands with the soldier, and praising him for his bravery, instead of following up their advantage.

Jackson was a man whose presence of mind never forsook him: he saw at a glance that the field was lost. His companion was senseless, and could render him no assistance, and he would have been no match alone against three adversaries. On the post-boy he could not calculate; besides, a discovery, in the present instance, and the being prevented from going to the coast, would decidedly be fatal to him.

All this, which has taken us up so many words to explain, passed through Jackson's ear in the twinkling of an eye. He acted upon it with the most instantaneous promptitude: having struck out the lamp, all was involved in obscurity; he then, by a powerful effort, raised Ricketts in his arms, and carrying him to a low wall on the opposite side of the road to where Carribles and the soldier stood, threw him over it into a field, and immediately leaped after him.

Old Carribles, after having nearly shaken off the hand of the young soldier, bethought himself that there was some more work to do.

" But where are these pirates?" cried he, groping

about; " they were here just now,—one of them at least. Holloa, Tom! where are you ?"

" Ay, ay, Sir," echoed Tom, trying to rise, but to no purpose "here I am at the forecastle."

" Come astern, then," roared Carribles.

" I cannot rise without help: bear a hand here, your honour, and give us a heave."

Tom was not disabled by the present action,— it was his wooden leg which obliged him to require a hand.

The young soldier ran round and helped Tom to rise. They then commenced a search for the fugitives, but, of course, to no purpose: and they were most confoundedly puzzled to think what had become of them.

" Split my mizen," said Tom, " but I think it was the old boy himself, and his right-hand man, Beelzebub—I never felt such a grip in all my born days."

" Stuff!" said Carribles; " the scoundrel that I tustled with was flesh and blood,—bone and muscle, I should rather say, for he was as tuff as an old oak ;—still my gallant young friend here, the marine, felled him nobly :—d—n me, I shall think better of a red coat as long as I live. But the rascals have sheered off somehow, so let us look after the prize."

So saying, he opened the chaise door and spoke to Maria. She had recovered by this time, and to the questions put to her by Carribles, replied, that she had been forced away from her home, as she suspected, for no good purpose; and that she did not know what to do, or where to stop, until to-morrow.

"Oh! my precious dear," cried the old Captain, "don't be uneasy about that; I have a snug little cabin for you to-night, close by, to the right of the road; there you shall have all the accommodations that an old sailor can give you : stay where you are for a moment, until we ease off this gig wheel of mine from the chaise. Here, Squires, clear away the craft, and let the marine hold the horses' heads."

Tom Squires obeyed, and the Commodore, advancing towards the soldier, who had posted himself at the gig horse's head, addressed him thus :—

"And you, my brave red-coated friend, shall be my guest to-night :—d—n me, if ever I call a soldier a lobster again. Where are you bound for, friend ?"

"A long voyage," replied the young soldier, with a deep sigh; "I am going to the East Indies. My regiment is at Ipswich, and I am on my way to join them."

"Well, my boy," said Carribles, 'you can stop with me till morning,—you shall have a glass of grog, and a hearty welcome. D—n it! what signifies the difference between a red and a blue coat?—we both serve the same king and country, and we both like a pretty girl equally well, and don't hesitate to expose our lives to save her from ill usage."

The young soldier made no answer, but fetched a sigh still deeper than before. Carribles observing this, said,

"Come, my lad, don't be down-hearted; you have left your sweetheart behind, I suppose: you will see her again, and if she's a true girl, she will think of you; if not, she won't be worth thinking of."

"I have left none behind, Sir, who will think of me, except my parents."

"Well, then," said Carribles, "you will have a hundred sweethearts in India, only they are black ones; so make yourself easy:—besides, there's a few white ones there too."

"Never!" said the soldier, with peculiar emphasis.

"I see how it is," said Carribles; "you have been crossed in love; but never mind, the lasses are like eels,—they will slip through our fingers at times. Never mind, I say, there's as good fish in the sea as ever was caught."

The wheels being now unlocked, Carribles helped Maria out of the chaise; and having assisted her to get into his gig, took his seat beside her, cheering her in the unsophisticated language of his heart. Tom and the soldier got up behind, and away they drove, leaving the chaise in the middle of the road alone with the horses, for the post-boy, in his fright, in the early part of the scuffle, had run aside somewhere to hide himself.

We must now explain to our readers, how this rencontre · took place. Captain Carribles had been dining with a friend, at some little distance, and had sat rather late. Tom Squires (as was his custom on such occasions) had brought the gig to fetch his master home. Carribles stayed to supper, and Tom was also provisioned by the gentleman's butler, who was very fond of Tom's company. Both master and man, on leaving, had their grog aboard; and Tom, who was rather out of his element on land, and did not understand how to manage the reins quite so well as the rudder, had, by steering rather too much to leeward, fallen foul of the post-chaise, and thus given rise to the adventure, which, for the present, occasioned the rescue of Maria.

While all the latter part of this scene was taking place, Stafford Jackson remained very snugly behind the wall, listening to what was going forward. Though forced, for the present, to give up Maria, he was rejoiced to find that he had a certain clue to her; for the site of Carribles' cottage was perfectly familiar to him. He did not, therefore, despair about her; but his present business to the coast brooked no delay, even if he had sufficient force to attempt to reclaim her now. He, therefore, when the others had departed, again raised up Ricketts (who still remained senseless), threw him over the wall, followed, and, after some difficulty, got him into the post-chaise. He then roared out for the post-boy, who came crawling out of a neighbouring ditch; and entering the chaise himself, he proceeded on his journey, if not with so fair a companion as his last, with one, at least for the present, equally helpless.

The other party now arrived at the cottage of Carribles. This original abode, with its peculiar paraphernalia, we have already described. The Captain had made no alteration in his establishment from the time we allude to, except the having hired an old woman as cook and housekeeper. To her care, the old Captain, immediately on his entrance, with a delicacy that would have done honour to a more polished character, confided Maria, who retired with her; while he himself, with his two companions, entered the "state cabin."

Tom Squires now put some salt junk on the table, and brewed some famous grog, not "too strong of the water." Maria had begged to be excused from joining them, and remained with the housekeeper. During supper, the old hero dilated on the event which brought the party together, with as much pride as he was wont to do when detailing the action of Trafalgar, at which he lost his arm. Tom Squires also put in his opinion when he could, with true nautical warmth; to all which their guest listened with politeness, but, from depression of spirits, could not join them with his heart. Carribles perceived this, and wished him to drink, as he said it, " like a sailor."

" Come, my hearty," said Carribles, giving his hand to the young soldier, " make yourself at home. Be happy like me. I'll give you a toast, my boy,—' May our sailors and soldiers never meet but in friendship, or part but in peace!'"

They had just concluded the honours of the toast, when Maria entered for the purpose of thanking her noble deliverer, ere she retired to rest. The young soldier had stood up with his face to the mantel-piece, admiring the arms which were suspended over it. His figure was tall, slight, and elegant, and appeared to much advantage in a very handsome light-infantry uniform. He had not yet undergone the military crop, and his brown hair curled luxuriantly behind his ears.

" Sir," said Maria, addressing Carribles, " I have come to thank you most sincerely for——"

The young soldier started, and turned round at the sound of the voice. She could proceed no farther, but sunk upon the floor.—It was Harry Everton who stood before her!

He flew to her assistance, raised, and placed her on a chair.

Recovering a little, she exclaimed, " Good Heaven! is it you, Harry,—and in this dress?"

" Yes, Maria!" replied Everton, " this dress is

most suitable to me now. The man who has no hope at home, cannot do better than go abroad, and sacrifice his life for his country."

She was overwhelmed with confusion: a sudden torrent of the bitterest feelings rushed upon her soul. The early ties of infantine association, and youthful friendship, recurred forcibly to her mind. Her feelings had been much changed from those of her early days: she had learned to love; and now, at least, she knew how to pity a hopeless passion, though she could not return it. The amiable character, too, of Harry; his long and silent love; the desperate step he had taken, of which she could not but accuse herself; and the idea, also, that she might have been much happier with him than any other;—all served now to torment and afflict her. After a long and painful pause, she exclaimed, " Oh, Harry! I am the cause of all this," and burst into a flood of tears.

" Don't weep, Maria," said Harry, while the tears started into his own eyes; " your tears unman me. To-morrow I bid farewell for ever to my native land: my destiny is fixed, but my feelings must remain unchanged, in whatever climate of the earth fortune may cast my lot. I loved you, Maria, but you could not love me: I resolved to banish myself from your presence, though your image must remain for ever impressed upon my heart."

" Do not talk so, Harry," said Maria; " for God's sake do not—you torture me to death."

"I shall say no more on that subject," said Harry, resuming his firmness; "such thoughts ought not to be expressed now. But I rejoice, Maria, that you have escaped this night, and that I have been a partial instrument in protecting you. I hope, at least, that you will now remember the warnings of my friendship, which you so utterly disdained when I saw you last."

"Oh!" said she, "I will—I will;—do not—do not, talk to me now."

Carribles and Tom Squires looked on this scene in silent amazement: the former saw how things were, and was greatly affected: at last he broke silence, saying,

"Come, come, my children, dry up your tears; you may come together yet, and be happy."

"That is impossible, Sir," said Everton; "she never loved me—never can love me: I know it too well, and her happiness is far dearer to me than my own. Besides, am I not bound to a distant land?—Does not the voice of honour call me away? Even were her feelings different, there is now an impassable bar between us;—I am the property of my king and country—they must do with me what they please."

"But," said Carribles, "you may get out of the army."

"What, Sir!" replied Everton, erecting himself proudly; "have I not sworn to serve my King and country—and shall I break my oath?— and for what?—I know too well that she cannot

THE RED BARN. 267

love me : ask her, Sir, and be satisfied. Speak, Maria—speak with sincerity."

"Harry," said Maria, after a deep pause, "I always esteemed you as a friend,—as a brother, —but——"

"Enough, enough," interrupted Everton; "you see how it is.—Honoured Sir," continued he, "I thank you for your hospitality, and must take my leave."

"No, no!" said Carribles, "you must stop until morning."

"Dear Sir," replied Harry, "I cannot—I shall be late with my corps. Besides, I could not remain here in my present frame of mind. I must plunge on into business to forget my feelings. Farewell, Sir ;—farewell, my honest friend *(to Squires ;)*—adieu, Maria," said he, taking her hand in a hurried manner, and pressing her wildly to his breast, while his voice became broken with emotion, "remember me as a friend!"

So saying, he raised up his knapsack, and rushed out ; while Maria sobbed aloud,

"Harry! don't, don't go,—we may be happy yet."

The words came too late;—Harry heard them not—he was gone for ever.

Carribles ran out into the road after Everton, exclaiming,

"Stop, young man ; you have saved my life this night. Think you that old Joe Carribles ever forgot a service done him?—take this," handing him his purse, " to help your voyage."

" Sir," said Everton, putting back the purse, " I am paid by my King, and I have done nothing but my duty. I should have assisted any one else who was fighting against odds, in a just cause: I desire no reward but the satisfaction of having acted rightly."

" Well, well," said Carribles, " my brave lad, I did not intend to offend you; but you must not go without some token of my friendship and gratitude :—this watch you must take, and a better never kept time in every latitude."

It was in vain that Harry refused to take the silver watch: he saw that the old man would have been offended, if he persisted in his denial; therefore, he accepted it. Old Carribles shook him again and again by the hand, and was about to urge a hope of Maria, when the youth rushed away, and disappeared in the gloom of the night.

When Carribles returned in, Maria had retired. Her agitation had quite overcome her strength, and she was led to bed nearly in a state of insensibility by the old housekeeper.

" Well, Tom," said Carribles to his old valet, " how do you feel now?"

" Sir," answered Tom, " I'm surtain there's *ingins* about somewhere, my eyes water so. I never recollect the like afore, except when I parted with poor Moll Davis at the Nore. Moll, you know, Captain, was——"

"Nonsense," interrupted Carribles ; "I have heard that story fifty times, and more : it's a sign you have got your grog aboard when you begin on that tack. But now let us turn in ; for hang me if I haven't got the melancholies :—go to your hammock."

"Ay, ay, Sir," rejoined Tom, and both retired.

CHAP. XIII

All feed on one vain patron, and enjoy.

POPE.

WHILE the transactions which we have just described were taking place, Barnard and his two worthy friends were on their way to London. They arrived there without any accident deserving of record, and stopped for the first night at the old quarters, "The Blue Boar." Here on his arrival the following note was immediately put into the hands of Barnard by the waiter, who first inquired his name.

"MY DEAREST WILLIAM;

" You will find me at No. 9, Kepple Street, Edgware Road. Come, my love, as quickly as you can after the receipt of this note, for I am dying to see you.

" Ever yours,

" H W."

Barnard, on the following day, took coach at an early hour, and went to the place indicated in the note. He found it a small but very elegantly furnished house, and this Hannah occupied altogether, with one maid servant. The latter conducted him to the drawing-room, where her mistress was prepared to receive him reclining on a sofa. Her present appearance struck Barnard, if possible, more forcibly than ever. She had entirely doffed the exterior of humble life, and assumed that of a perfect lady, which her fine face and figure most admirably qualified her to personate. She was elegantly attired in a robe of pale yellow muslin. Her luxuriant black hair was most tastefully arranged under a rich lace cap, and her brown complexion judiciously relieved by a slight addition of artificial colour. Hannah was a perfect mistress of the science of the toilet; and on the present occasion she had put all her skill in requisition with such effect, that she looked not only most exquisitely beautiful, but appeared to be many years younger than she really was.

On Barnard's entrance, she arose and embraced him, and placing him beside her on the sofa, with his hand within hers, said—

"My dearest William, I am so delighted to see you. Now I trust we shall never part. This house must be your home from this time;—all that is in it is yours—myself included," added she, smiling, and throwing herself into his arms.

"Hannah, my love, I am content; but only on condition that I shall bear the expense."

"Do not talk, William, about paltry money matters," she replied.

"On no other terms can I possibly consent," emphatically returned Barnard.

"It is no consequence which of us bears the expense," resumed she;—"as long as we love each other: what I possess is yours:—however, if you will have it so, the expense shall be mutual, and so let us say no more on that subject."

Barnard remained with her for nearly three hours, during which time she gave him a long and fictitious but plausible history of herself. She told him that she was the widow of an officer who had died in the West Indies. She also found it necessary to account for the appearance she made at present, by informing him that since she returned to London she had been so fortunate as to recover some prize-money to which her husband had become entitled at the taking of some of the French Islands during the war.

To the reader, an explanation of this fact is almost unnecessary. Her connexion with Jackson, the money she had made by smuggling transactions, and other modes of finance, which his penetration may enable him easily to guess at, will suffice to account for the capacity of her exchequer.

It was agreed, before they parted, that Barnard should return to dinner, bring his luggage from the "Blue Boar," and establish himself in his new quarters from that day forth. He begged leave to introduce his two friends, who had come up with him from Polstead, to dinner; to which Hannah, who, as the reader knows (though Barnard was ignorant of it), was well acquainted with them, most readily assented.

Barnard accordingly returned to his inn, and for the first time communicated to Creed and Beauty the secret of his amour. They rallied him a little on his good fortune, and complimented him on the mysterious secresy with which he had hitherto concealed it. Of course they accepted his invitation, and Barnard, having packed up his trunks, returned to dinner with his two companions.

It was not without some difficulty that the two heroes preserved their countenances unmoved, on being formally presented, by Barnard, to their old acquaintance, Hannah Woods. She, however, acted the part of a stranger admirably well, and received them with a most lady-like demeanour. Still, a very scrutinizing observer might have discovered something like a smile on her lips, when she bowed at the introduction of " Captain Creed, of the *Scarafooka Rangers !*"

The Captain, however, did not appear in the costume which his humour had led him to assume at Polstead ; but actually affected something of a military dress, and wore a blue frock coat braided with black, hooked up to the throat.

Still his appearance was grotesque enough; for, by way of being ultra-military, he adopted the addition of white kerseymere breeches and silk stockings, wore a white cravat like a field-marshal, and carried a "*chapeau de bras.*" The irresistible *unmilitariness* of his natural air rendered this assumption most intolerably ludicrous; and fortunate it was that as they came along, a coach concealed his person from the prying eyes of the ignoble vulgar.

It is not less true than strange, that many men, otherwise not devoid of common sense, display a taste in dress equally absurd and incongruous. This is particularly the case with men who have risen from obscurity, and are desirous of rendering themselves remarkable, and of playing a character for which neither nature nor habit has fitted them. It is not less singular, that many men of similar pursuits to those of our noble Captain, should adopt an eccentric style of dress, which, one would imagine, must render them dangerously conspicuous: but folly and knavery are very closely allied.

The reason of Creed dressing in this peculiar style now, was that he meant to go that night to the Opera to superintend *business;* or, in military phrase, to take command of his *light bobs.*

The party sat down to a good dinner, and en-joyed themselves afterwards over some excellent wine until about nine o'clock, when Creed and Beauty departed, leaving Barnard to the full enjoyment of the society of Hannah,—not without each of them wishing that, for that evening at least, he was himself in the same desirable predicament.

The young farmer became every day more and more intoxicated with the charms of Hannah, and more and more pleased with a London life. He began to acquire a most decided relish for good living, and drinking good wine; and as Creed and Beauty constantly visited him, they did all in their power to maintain and strengthen this improving taste. He likewise became a coxcomb in his dress: the flattery of Hannah, added to the insinuations of the others, having actually had the effect of persuading him that his person was agreeable. The idle life, too, that he was leading, was greatly to his fancy; and, as hour after hour, and day after day, glided over his buoyant heart, he felt a greater and greater aversion to the idea of returning to one of business and industry.

Affairs were exactly in this position, when Beauty received the following letter from Jackson, which he immediately took an opportunity of communicating to Hannah :—

"*From the Coast, Sept. 29th, 18—.*

"DEAR JACK;

"After an adventure of no pleasant kind, which I shall mention by and by, I arrived at the old spot, and found, as I expected, everything topsy-turvy. The vessel, after the cargo was landed, had pushed off to the Dutch coast with a few hands (the only prudent measure that was adopted). They had, however, been so clumsy in conveying the goods ashore, and stowing them away in the place near the Cove, that the Revenue sharks got scent of the matter, and eight of them made their appearance immediately after my arrival. Concealment was out of the question, so exact had been the information of the rascals respecting the spot where the goods had been deposited. There was, therefore, only one mode left—namely, to fight it out. We were eight in number also; but I was obliged to dispatch three to translate the goods. While they were thus employed, Warren, Ricketts, myself, and two more, set upon the Revenue chaps in the following manner:—we awaited their approach in a narrow pass on the road, at a particular point where there are two old walls, one on each side. The road sinks very deep in this place, and from it the walls may be about twelve or fifteen feet high; but, on the other side, in the field, the earth was raised so much, that a moderate-sized man may look over the wall. I had eight or ten old hats fixed on these walls, and placed three fellows inside with pistols, and plenty of ammunition. The moon was up, but the sky was very much overcast with clouds. The Revenue fellows were marching in a body, well armed. When they entered the pass in question, Warren, Ricketts, and myself attacked them suddenly, rushing out from a place where we had been hiding. At first they made a stout resistance, but on my calling on those behind the wall to come on 'in a body,' as I said, the three lads there commenced a sharp fire; when the astonished sharks looked up, and seeing the hats and the pistols flash, they threw themselves into complete confusion—for they thought we had a numerous party—and took to their heels immediately. Our friends, in the interval, thus gained time to transport the goods to a place of safety.

"Now for the rascally adventure which took place before this. For the present, my dear Jack, I have lost Maria! we were going on at a spanking pace, when a gig with two fools in it ran right against one of our chaise wheels. Who, think you, did the two mischievous asses turn out to be?— Why, nobody else than old Carribles and his man Squires, whom you have heard me mention so often. There was some cross firing about the accident, between Ricketts and the latter, when the girl suddenly took it into her head to roar lustily to Carribles for help. The old boy and his man Tom took up the cudgels for her, and the four of us had a regular set-to. We should have soon settled their hash, as you may suppose, if the devil had not determined it otherwise. I had just upset Squires, when in popped a rascally soldier, and fetched Ricketts such an infernal blow in the lug, as laid him senseless.

I saw, then, it was all up, so I took Ricketts and got him behind a wall, where we both lay concealed, until Carribles was off, and Maria with him. I then took up the huge hulk, who was still senseless, shoved him into the chaise, and drove off. There he lay like a sack, and never recovered until we had got eight or ten miles farther on, I cursing my unlucky fate the whole way. This accident, however, I shall soon repair. I am determined she shall not escape me. No! I'll have her in spite of the devil and all his angels.

"The goods are safely lodged, Jack, in your cave, and Ricketts has the care of them. I shall remain for a while in this neighbourhood, and, if necessary, write for you and Creed to come down. I hope you have the young clod-hopper in proper tune. You must introduce him to Xiutototle at the counting-house, and let the matter be managed so that he shall have a strong opinion of the concern. Hannah, no doubt, has him well meshed by this time. D—n these women, they are the ruin of us all!—Believe me, dear Jack,

"Very truly yours,
"STAFFORD JACKSON.

" P. S.—Compliments to the *Commander of the Scarafookas.*"

Hannah and Smith laughed heartily at Jackson's losing Maria; with which adventure they

were not less amused, than they were pleased
with his successful management of the smuggling
business.

Smith and Creed, especially the latter, gained
more and more on the mind of Barnard every day.
The former was peculiarly successful in sapping
and destroying all remains of good principles in this
young man. He wormed himself completely into
his confidence, and was continually hinting the
superiority of his own rascally mode of existence,
to the jog-trot style of Barnard's former life. He
often dwelt upon the shameful inequality that
existed in the distribution of property ;—the injustice that one man should revel in every enjoyment, while another was compelled to labour and
privation. Every man, he would say, had an
equal right to partake of the pleasures of this
life; and if he had no hereditary property, it was
proper that he should seek, by any method he
could employ, the means of enjoying himself.
Fortune had bestowed wealth on some men, and
nature had given wit to others ; and it was perfectly according to the order of things that the
latter should prey upon the former. As for laws,
they were made by the rich for their own protection and the disadvantage of others. It was the
business of the strong to break, and of the witty
to evade, them. Religion was a mere humbug,
invented by knaves to frighten fools, and worthy
only of the contempt of the wise!

Such was the general substance of the lectures

daily delivered by Mr. Beauty Smith, professor
of ethics. The reader must not, however, imagine,
that he let out the whole of his villainy at once.
He took his measures with more caution, and
proceeded step by step. He commenced by
fostering Barnard's idleness, his love of pleasure,
and his taste for gaming. He then demolished
all the outworks of morality and religion, and
brought him gradually to look with indifference
on the violation of every principle of justice and
honour, and with fearlessness on the legal consequences contingent on such violation. In doing
this he had no very difficult task: he found a
ready pupil in Barnard, whose naturally coarse
and vicious mind only wanted the rays of such a
sun as Smith to bring forth an abundance of rank
weeds. No spontaneous twitchings of conscience
dictated an opposition to the doctrines thus
instilled into him, nor did a doubt of their danger
ever enter his head.

The impression produced on his mind by Smith's
liberal discourses, was mainly strengthened by his
peculiar situation. The funds which he had
brought with him to London were fast melting
away. He lost several small sums from time to
time at play with Beauty and Creed; but the
principal instrument in the dilapidation of his
finances was Hannah. The expensive establishment which she kept up, and which it is almost
needless to hint to the reader, was supported entirely on the strength of Barnard's purse, soon

rendered him ready to listen to any advice that he thought might tend to relieve his embarrassments.

The reader has been apprized that one of the pretences on which Barnard came up to town, was to consign the corn, purchased with bills by Jackson, to that meritorious but cacophonously named individual Don Josiah Xiutototle. Barnard, accompanied by Creed and Smith, waited on the worthy merchant, whom they found in his counting-house in Three King Court, Lombard Street. This firm consisted of two partners—Xiutototle and Killganders—the latter an Englishman. In the outer office were two clerks, whom Barnard thought were about the most ill-looking and dirty rascals he ever saw. Creed, however, whispered to him not to mind their appearance, inasmuch as foreigners of all nations were very careless as to dress,—and asked one of them, in French, whether the Don was within. He was answered in the affirmative, on which they were shown into an inner room.

Here, seated at a desk of the most awful height, ramparted round with rails on all sides, sat, as on a throne of state, the ineffable Xiutototle. He was a tall stout man, about fifty years of age, with a complexion like mahogany; wore a bushy black wig, green spectacles, and mustachios about three inches long. He was dressed in a complete suit of snuff-coloured brown, and had on a green hat, with a leaf six inches wide, and a very low crown. There were piled upon his desk

o o

several heaps of what appeared to be gold coins, and several leather bags were suspended around, seemingly containing money.

Barnard was about to mention the nature of his business, but had not time to utter a syllable, when the Don roared out in a voice of thunder—

" Vat you vant, young gentaman ? "

Barnard declared his business, but to no sort of purpose ; for the Don either could not or would not understand one word he said. In reply, Xiutototle thundered—

" Be plast! be plast! Io not know los Inglas. Man join me—he come a while ago—be plast!"

This language was just as unintelligible to Barnard as his had been to the worthy Don. Creed, however, appeared to understand it extremely well, and said to Barnard—" He means to tell you to sit down: he does not understand English, but his partner will be here directly."

Down they sat, and the partner, Mr. Killganders, made his appearance. He was as great an original as the head of the firm, but in a different way. He could not have been more than five feet in height at the most,—but extremely corpulent. His face was round and red, his hair quite grey, and his cheeks shaded with a profuse growth of sable whiskers. With such a person, and such a face, he was dressed in the very extremity of fashionable foppery.

"Well, gentlemen, what's your business?" *(He spoke with the most astonishing rapidity of intonation)*

—" what's your business ?—hot day,—very hot day" (wiping the perspiration off his forehead with a cambric handkerchief).

Barnard explained.

" Aye—aye, very good,—very good. I know Mr. Jackson,—Jackson Hall,—good customer, sir, —good customer,—rich, rich, sir,—rich as a Jew: very good, sir,—very good, sir,—your business, sir, is done—done, sir, to a T. I'll give you the acknowledgment, sir, in the twinkling of an eye."

He then rushed up to the desk at which Xiutototle was sitting, and scribbled away like lightning over a piece of paper.

"There, sir," said he—" there ; all's right, sir, now. Mr. Jackson, sir, is a good man,—excellent man,—wallowing in riches,—fine mark, sir—fine mark, sir—your're a lucky man, sir;—his bills are as good as the Bank, sir. Lucky man, sir, to fall into such hands,—plenty of dibbs, blunt, and stumpy, sir;—good morning, sir, good morning,— we must mind business,—excuse ceremony, sir, —good morning."

So saying, he literally thrust the astonished Barnard out of the office by the shoulder, while Creed and Smith followed, nearly suffocated by the attempt to suppress their laughter.

"These are strange people," said Barnard, when he got into the street.

"Yes," said Creed, " odd fishes ; but it's the way with mercantile people,—not much cere- mony: but they are as rich as Crœsus. Did you see all the money bags, and the gold piled on the desk?"

"Yes," said Barnard ; "they must be worth a deal of money."

"Half a million, at the least," replied Creed.

As our readers are not very likely to divine who these wealthy merchants were, we may as well inform them : in a few words, the firm of Xiutototle and Killganders was no less than a regular swindling establishment, supported by Jackson himself—a place of reference, and a pass to assist his smuggling transactions. Don Josiah was personated by an old acquaintance of ours,—no less a personage than the one-eyed gentleman who had assisted in robbing Barnard at Robottom's, and was now disguised with wig, spectacles, and mustachios, and had his complexion darkened to a true Mexican hue. The other partner was a Jew, who had returned from a transportation of fourteen years; and trusted to the alteration, wrought by time, in his hair, his huge whiskers, and general appearance, to escape recognition. The "gold," piled on the desk, was nothing but counters excellently gilt; and the "money" in the bags was lead and tin.

Matters went on with Barnard, Hannah, and Company, swimmingly for three weeks, when the former's finances were approaching to a very low ebb. Hannah had informed him that the first division of prize-money which she had received was nearly gone, but that she expected to receive a further supply in a few weeks. His own purse was reduced to a very few pounds. He could not, however, resolve to give up his present way of life, nor could he by any means endure the thoughts of separating from Hannah,—that, under any circumstances, was totally out of the question.

He was sitting one morning alone, ruminating on his condition, and revolving various projects in his mind, when Smith appeared. He came, as Barnard thought, extremely *à-propos*, that he might ask his advice.

"Well, Bill," said Beauty, "how do you do this morning? Why, man, you're looking cursedly down in the mouth."

"Jack," replied Barnard, "I'm very low spirited."

"Low spirited, man?—pooh!—what's the matter?—a pound of sorrow never paid an ounce of debt."

"You have hit it," said Barnard; "I am in debt, and cannot pay."

"And do you really think of paying?" resumed Smith; "I did not believe that you were quite such a greenhorn. What's the nature of your debt?—is it a gaming business?"

"No," said Barnard; "I owe money to some tradesmen."

"What!" exclaimed Beauty, "you're uneasy on that score, are you? You think of paying a rascally tradesman?—well, after that, I give you up."

Barnard, half ashamed, answered, "But what can I do? I shall be arrested."

" Nonsense," said Smith; " you can remove from where you are, and they cannot find you."

" But," rejoined Barnard, "I have no money either to remove or supply my occasions."

" O ho !" answered Beauty, " that's a horse of another colour : but if you have no money, your father has ;—apply to him."

" I dare not," said Barnard; "I have over-drawn on him already. If I thought he would stand further, I would have no objection to try the old boy again."

" But he has plenty of cash, William. Now hear me ;—I will give you my advice, but only on one condition."

" What is that?" said Barnard.

" That you never prate about paying debts again. D—n me! I was beginning to be a little proud of you as a pupil—I thought you were a man of liberal notions ; but that idea of paying debts was a desperate slap in the chops for your humble servant."

" Well," replied Barnard, " say no more about it. Your advice—how shall I raise the wind ?"

" Thus," resumed Smith; " write to your father ; —tell him of the wealth of Jackson, and that copper-faced Don with the jaw-breaking name. Tell him that they have offered you the best price for cattle to export :—he'll send you up a drove of oxen, and the devil's in it if we cannot manage to raise the wind then. But you must write very plausibly,—just like a good steady son, as you are."

" Humph !" said Barnard, pausing ; " but what shall I do when he asks for the money?"

" Leave that to time ; you'll win ten times the sum that the cattle will fetch, and thus make all square. All you want to enable you to win, is a good sum to start with."

" I'm afraid it won't do, Jack," sighed Barnard; " have you no other advice to offer ?"

" Yes,—go home—quit the joys of London— leave Hannah, and go bog-trot, and drink ale for the rest of your days in the country."

" Not I, Jack," said Barnard, ringing the bell; " bring me pen, ink, and paper *(to the servant)* ; I will write instantly."

He sat down and wrote to his father, after Smith's dictation,—that he was getting on remarkably well ; vaunted in high terms the immense wealth of Jackson and Xiutototle; boasted of the admirable connexion to be made through them ; and finished by stating the high prices they were disposed to give in ready cash for cattle for immediate exportation, and requesting his father to send up several head immediately. He concluded his epistle by a moral comment on the vice and folly which he was of necessity obliged to witness in London; grieving that he could not, conveniently with his father's interest, return to Polstead instantly; and hoping that when he did return, he should never be again called upon to quit, for a single night, his happy home, and a father whom he so respected and loved !

In the course of four or five days the cattle arrived in London,—the representations made by Barnard of the wealth of the high contracting powers, having wrought upon the weak and credulous mind of the old man. Beauty and Barnard very speedily disposed of them in Smithfield market, and they brought exactly £320 to the latter.

The sight of this money aroused the cupidity of Smith, who determined on having a share of it. He was annoyed by the idea that Hannah should have the entire plucking of the pigeon, and was resolved, at all events, to pick up some of the feathers. The mode which struck him at the present time, as most promising of success, was to seduce Barnard that evening to a gaming table, where he might himself have a good opportunity of borrowing a considerable portion of the money.

For this purpose he invited Barnard to dine at a tavern on the day of sale. He made the hour of dinner very late, filling up the interval from the time in which the cattle was sold, by taking him about from place to place, but always at a considerable distance from his home. They took sundry pints of ale, &c. with the purchasers of the cattle, which though they had not the effect of intoxicating, yet served a little to confuse the head of Barnard, and render him indisposed to return home to dinner.

They proceeded to the neighbourhood of Covent Garden, where they dined and drank pretty freely of wine. In the course of the second bottle, Smith said to Barnard—

"William, how do you mean, now, to manage with this money you have received to-day?"

"Why," said Barnard, who was getting a little primed with the wine, "spend it like a man, to be sure, and enjoy myself with my friends."

"That is all very well," replied Smith, "and quite right; but a man should look beyond the present enjoyment. What will you do when the money is out?"

"Trust to Providence," said Barnard.

"Believe me," rejoined Smith, "the less you trust to Providence the better: Providence is a slippery customer, and may chance to leave you in the lurch. You must yourself provide for the enjoyment of the future out of your present means. Trust the word of a man who knows the world better than you do—the time for making money is when you have money: cash begets cash, if the right way be taken."

"Then what do you advise me to do?" said Barnard.

"Try your fortune to-night at *rouge et noir*,— I'm sure you'll win."

"But if I should lose?" said Barnard.

"I have got a system," said Smith, "by which you cannot lose; besides, don't risk all your money—hazard only £150. Give me £50 out of this to play for you, and try £100 yourself,—we cannot both lose. You, I have no doubt, will win sufficient to enable you to get over all your embarrassments, reimburse your father, and enjoy yourself for some time to come. You must do something to keep yourself constantly afloat, if you do not mean to return to a dull country life, and give up every pleasure."

"Well, then," replied Barnard, "I will try my luck to-night :—here's fifty, Jack, for you."

"That's right, my boy; and here's success to us!"

They finished their wine, and repaired to a house well known in the West End. This was the first time that Barnard had ever been in a regular gaming house; for hitherto it had been the policy of his associates to keep him out of such places, that they might reserve all the plunder to themselves. Under the passport of Smith, he easily entered; and on going up stairs, he was perfectly astounded with the splendour of the establishment. The lights, the furniture, the sideboard spread with cold viands and expensive wines, surprised him not a little. He observed around the table many of the faces he had formerly seen in the billiard-rooms which we have described; and in addition to these, many others whose countenances were expressive of anything but benevolence and contentment.

The company frequenting all places of this kind consists of three distinct classes;—those who fleece, those who are in a course of being fleeced, and those who are completely fleeced.

The first are the old, knowing, cautious players, who have long made a regular trade of the game, and who have no other means of subsistence: such men may be known at a glance. There are not many of them young, yet their features are furrowed more by sordid care than the natural operation of time. In vain you look into their countenances for any traces of human feeling: you find nothing there but the cunning of the fox, or the ferocity of the tiger. They have long been accustomed to contemplate with apathy the ruin of the young, the noble, the ingenuous, and the brave. Sordid avarice has long eradicated from their hearts every principle of honour, and every sentiment of humanity.

The second class is constituted of those young men who are better provided with money than wit. Many of these have been originally led by accident into gaming, and encouraged to proceed by the fatal fascination of early success; others have entered into it voluntarily, from the absurd notion of its practice being necessary to the character of a man of fashion; but the great majority consists of such as are flattered into the preposterous hope of realizing a fortune by the pursuit.

The third class is filled up from the second.

When these unfortunate young men have lost all their money, and are completely ruined, such is the effect of habit that they cannot quit the scene of their destruction. There you may see them, night after night, overlooking the players, and when they can borrow a counter, trying their fortune, and invariably losing. Their appearance indicates their situation; their clothes are seedy— their looks announce a dejected and broken spirit. Many of them have nothing to eat or drink, but what, by the *liberality* of the keeper of the establishment, is gratuitously supplied to his customers.

From this class some migrate into the first: others are made *useful* about the establishment itself, as decoy ducks, &c. Many are reduced to the lowest infamy and degradation, destined eventually to swell the population of our prisons, to figure on the scaffold, or to wander on the shores of Australasia.

But it is superfluous for us to dwell any longer on a subject which has been so often and so ably handled. Still it must be granted, that every effort, however humble, to assist in the extinction of these nurseries of ruin, and hot-beds of vice, is not only meritorious but necessary.

Barnard and Smith now commenced to play. The latter was unsuccessful, soon losing the fifty pounds given him by Barnard, and borrowing fifty more with which he had no better success. Very different was the fortune of Barnard. He had never played at *rouge et noir* before, and had not the least idea of the game. He was merely told by Smith to place his money upon whichever colour he fancied. He did so, and with the extraordinary luck which will sometimes attend young players, while Smith was losing the hundred pounds, he won no less than £1800.

Smith was astonished and nettled at the success of Barnard: he was vexed to think that the latter should have won, while he himself had lost. Though an old and knowing player, Beauty could not adopt, in the present instance, any of the means by which he usually contrived to secure the good graces of fortune. He resolved, however, that he should be no loser by the success of Barnard.

By his advice, the latter left off play when he had won the sum above-mentioned. They went out together, and Smith dissuaded Barnard, by all means, from his intention of going home. It was very dangerous, he told him, to go such a distance, at that hour, with such a sum of money about him,—he had better stop at his (Smith's) lodgings in the Strand until morning, where there was a spare bed for him.

Barnard consented, and the following morning, at breakfast, his Mentor thus addressed him:—

"Well, my dear fellow, you have been uncommonly lucky last night;—I told you that you would win. I think I am entitled to your thanks for bringing you to that place."

"You are entitled to much more than these, Jack," rejoined Barnard; "and if two or three hundred are of any use to you, they are at your service."

"I thank you," said Smith, "but I will not touch a penny: I do not want money at present: but allow me to ask you how you mean to manage with the sum you have won?"

"Why," replied Barnard, "I shall clear off all my embarrassments, reimburse my father, and enjoy the rest."

"If you will take the advice of one older than yourself, and who knows life much better, you will do no such thing."

"Why not?"

"Because you have now a glorious opportunity of making a splendid fortune—an opportunity that may never occur again. Your debtors and your father can wait awhile,—there is no hurry about them: but if you want to make a good hit, you must keep your money, for the present, in a lump."

"And how shall I turn it to account?" said Barnard.

"There are many ways of laying out money to advantage in London; but it requires some consideration to choose: meanwhile, you should have your money secured."

"Secured!" cried Barnard, "how do you mean?"

"I mean," said Smith, "that you should have it deposited in safe hands;—you cannot be so weak as to think of carrying such a sum about with you. Why, man, there are a thousand ways in which you may lose it; or even, if you don't lose it, you may waste and fritter it down to nothing."

"Then what do you advise me to do, Smith?" responded he.

"I advise you to lodge the money in proper hands."

"In the Bank?" said Barnard.

"Fudge and nonsense!" cried Beauty; "do you want to lose your money? I tell you no bank is safe, not even the Bank of England—to say nothing of the trouble you will have in drawing your money when you want it."

"What can I do, then?" said Barnard.

"Take my advice,—keep one hundred pounds for your occasions; lodge the rest in the hands of some wealthy merchant, who will pay you a fair interest for the time he holds it. Thus it will be safe from accidents of all kinds, as well as from your own nibbling fingers; and you will have it in a lump, when an opportunity offers of turning it to profit."

"Who do you recommend should have the care of it?" said Barnard.

"For my own part," said Smith, "I have no very great acquaintance in the City; but, from all I know, I think you could not entrust it to better hands than those of Xiutototle and Killganders."

Barnard still appeared to hesitate; and, after a pause, replied—"I think I had better get rid of my embarrassments first;—yes, I will do so."

" Well, do as you like," observed Smith ; " it is no business of mine "

We may as well inform the reader, that getting rid of his embarrassments was the very thing of which Barnard had not the remotest intention. He was anything in the world but a man of natural rectitude, though timidity might induce him, in some cases, to keep in the path of justice. Nor was he averse from lodging the money through distrust; but he was swayed by a weak and boyish feeling of exhibiting his winnings to Hannah, and pouring the treasure into her lap. This was what Smith feared;—he had too much discrimination not to perceive that principle had no hold on Barnard : but he was dreadfully afraid of the influence of Hannah. He resumed the conversation.

" All I want you to do, William, is to secure your money ; you can draw it out any time at a moment's warning, for whatever purpose you may want it : meantime it will be producing to you a good interest."

At this moment a knock came at the street door, and Captain Creed was shown in.

" Good morning, Captain," said Smith, " you are come in good time ;—your advice is greatly wanting. Mr. Barnard has been so lucky as to win £1800 last night, at *rouge et noir*."

" Indeed !" exclaimed Creed, " that was a famous hit."

" Yes," resumed Smith, " and I have been

advising him to lodge the money for security in the hands of Xiutotótle and Co. ; he can draw it when he likes : they will pay good interest, and he will have the money in a lump to lay out to advantage when a favourable opportunity offers. I appeal to you, Captain Creed, as a man of sense, and a man of the world, whether my advice is not right ?"

" To be sure it is," replied Creed ; " the very best that could be given."

" You see there," said Smith to Barnard. " But, Captain, he wants to get rid of two or three hundred, in paying off what he calls embarrassments."

" That would be very wrong," rejoined the Captain, " very wrong indeed, Mr. Barnard Take my word for it, there is a maxim concerning money, which admits of no exception,—it is this—*never break bulk*,—that is, don't fritter away a good sum when you have it, which may be applied to some great and advantageous purpose: besides, as to what you say about embarrassments—excuse me, but that is all nonsense; there is no embarrassment but want of money Debt is nothing;—if you have money, you can live as well in ' the Rules' as anywhere else. None but a fool ever troubles himself about his debts."

" But," said Barnard, " if I pay off what I owe now, I shall get credit again."

" Pray," rejoined Creed, very solemnly, " have you been asked for the money ?"

"Yes," said Barnard, " more than once."

" Then, believe me," said the Captain, " you'll get no more credit under any circumstances. I know the London tradesmen better than you, Mr. Barnard,—if once they ask you for money, your credit is dished. Payment can't recover it, and therefore the best plan is never to pay at all."

" I'll take my oath of that," said Beauty.

" But," resumed the Captain, " what you have to consider is your own interest : you have got a sum of money, which may, with proper management, prove the means of realizing a splendid fortune. Your first step is to place it in a state of security, and then you can look about you. I am decidedly of Mr. Smith's opinion."

" I am sure," said Smith, " my dear Barnard, I would not advise you to anything but for you own good. It is needless for me to say that I have no interest in the matter;—I advise you as I would a brother."

" I believe it well," said the Captain, slightly contracting his forefinger, but unperceived by Barnard.

" And do you not think," resumed Beauty, " Captain Creed, that Xiutototle and Killganders are the proper men to lodge the money with ?"

" To be sure I do," replied Creed; " the best

men in London : their word is good for three hundred thousand pounds, at any time; and they are excellent fellows, with all their oddities. Killganders, is the most honourable man I ever knew, and the most liberal : he has lost immense sums by his liberality—but he did not mind it— trifles to him."

" He is a very charitable man, too," said Smith; " is he not, Captain?"

" Oh yes! very charatible indeed ;—he is a large contributor to the Foundling Hospital."

" Indeed!" said Smith; " what a worthy man ! The fact is, Barnard, you cannot do better than entrust your money in such wealthy and honourable hands."

" So say I, Mr. Barnard," said Creed; "safe bind, safe find, as the old proverb has it. You will be always sure of a good account of your cash, from Xiutototle and Killganders."

In short, without dwelling on details, it is sufficient to inform the reader, that these two gentlemen finally succeeded in talking Barnard into the measure proposed by Smith. When he gave his assent, Beauty exclaimed—

" Now, then, let us go right smack to business : when a man has made a good resolution, the next best thing he can do, is to act immediately upon it. Will you come with us, Captain, to the City ?"

" With all my heart," said Creed ;—and away they hauled Barnard to Lombard Street.

When they arrived at "Three Kings Court,"
they found the two ill-conditioned clerks in the
outer office, writing away like wildfire. Inquiring
for the partners, they were told that Mr. Killganders was alone in the inner office. They
entered, and found the man of commerce seated
at the lofty desk deeply engaged in thought, with
his head imbedded in his hands, and poring over
a huge ledger. The scene that followed must be
reduced to a dramatic form, to render it perfectly
intelligible to our readers.

Barnard.—" I have come, sir, for the purpose——"

Killganders—(his head still down).—" Six and
two are eight—eight and six are fourteen—
fourteen and six are twenty."

Barnard.—" I have come, sir——"

Killganders.—" Twenty thousand—five thousand three hundred and thirty-two ;—twenty-five
thousand three hundred and thirty-two."

Barnard.—" I have come, sir, I say——"

Killganders.—" Thirty-two—damn it ! there's
some mistake here—we have overpaid five hundred
and some pounds."

Barnard—(losing patience).—" I have come,
sir, I say, to give you seventeen hundred pounds."

Killganders—(starting up).—" Lord, sir, I beg
your pardon,—gentlemen, I beg your pardon.
'Fore God ! I did not know there was any one in the
office ;—I really am very abstracted—shockingly
so. Business—business, gentlemen, 'fore God

I'm quite stupid with business. Sir, what may you please to want?"

"This gentleman, Mr. Killganders," said Captain Creed, "is desirous of lodging in your hands the sum of £1700, being convinced of the stability and liberality of your house."

"Sir," said Killganders, "he does us honour; and he will, I trust, find his confidence not misplaced—but we must wait for my partner. Eugene!" (roaring out to one of the clerks outside, who entered), "when did the Don go out?"

"Von heure, saar, exact."

"Did he take the phaëton?"

"No, saar; he did but walk to de store, to see de ten tousan cask of rum put in."

"Sit down gentlemen, sit down—he'll be here directly."

Scarcely had he spoken, when the unutterable Xiutototle entered.

"Don Josiah," said Killganders, "I am glad you are come; this gentleman comes to lodge with us——."

"To lodge wid us! hah! hah!—we have not de lodging!"

"He comes to give us money, Don Josiah!"

"Money! hah! hah! ver good—we take best care of money;—keep his money fast."

"No doubt," said Killganders; "we will take all possible care of the gentleman's money. I wished you to be present when the tender was made."

"Tender! oh, si! we sall be very tender."

"Have you the money about you, Mr. Barnard?" said Killganders.

"Yes, sir," replied Smith; "Mr. Barnard has the money quite ready."

"Then I will write an acknowledgment," said the merchant.

While he was thus employed, a lad about fourteen or fifteen years of age, very badly dressed, and looking very pale, entered the office. As soon as Xiutototle beheld him he intonated forth—

"Vat you vant, juvenal vello?

"Charity, your honour," said the boy.

"Sharitee! sharitee bee dam. Eugene! push out dis here ladron—vat for you let im in?"

Killganders on this raised his head; and with more pompous enunciation than usual, said—

"Retire boy, I never give to beggars— I subscribe to de medicity.—No charity to give to beggars; begone, I say, boy."

He now handed a paper to Barnard, who then reckoned down the sum of £1700, which the worthy merchant immediately deposited in his desk.

"Depend upon it, sir, we shall take care of this money for you," resumed he; "we dare not give you more than the legal interest: but sir, when you come to draw your money, there's such a thing as a bonus, sir—I say nothing, sir—time will tell—you shan't find us illiberal, sir. When you come to draw your money, depend upon it, sir, you'll be very much surprised—won't he, Don Josiah?"

" Aye, aye; dat he vil—ver mush soorpreeze indeed."

Killgander now bowed the gentlemen out of the office with much bustle and vociferation, repeating his assurance to Barnard of the great care with which his money would be treated, and the surprise that awaited him when he should come to draw it.

"What an excellent man, this Killganders!" said Smith.

" A most humane character !" ejaculated Creed.

" He has travelled ?" resumed Smith.

"Yes!" said Creed, " from motives of the purest philanthropy—for the good of his country and mankind."

Barnard now returned home to Hannah. She had been very uneasy in consequence of his absence, and very much annoyed—not in consequence of any feeling for his safety, but fearful (as was really the fact) that he had been led into the disposal of the money arising from the sale of the cattle, in a manner prejudicial to her interests. When he returned, she questioned him eagerly as to where he had been, and what he had been about. He detailed to her all that had occurred, even to the minutest circumstance, since they had last parted.

Her indignation at this recital was extreme, and it was with difficulty she avoided the manifes tation of it. She even had some thoughts of disclosing the true character of Smith and Jackson to Barnard, and developing the prime humbug of Xiutototle; but she reflected that, by so doing, she would be betraying herself, and injuring her own interests: she therefore kept silence on that subject, contenting herself with remarking that Barnard had been somewhat quick in his measures, and hoping that all was safe. He excused his precipitation by the urgent instances of Smith, and expressed his full conviction of the security of the deposit.

Barnard was rather fatigued after his walking, and more especially as he had had but little sleep during the last four-and-twenty hours: he therefore laid himself down for a couple of hours; and while he was enjoying his repose, his fair partner took a coach and drove off directly to Smith's lodgings.

Being informed that he was within, she hurried up stairs without further ceremony, and found Beauty and our noble Captain enjoying themselves over some sandwiches and a bottle of sherry.

" Well," said she, " Mr. Smith, this is very pretty conduct of you!"

" What conduct, Madam?" said Smith, with an affectation of surprise.

" Why, to urge Barnard to part with his money in the manner he has done, without consulting me."

" Surely, better advice could not be given to

the young man," replied Beauty, "than to put his money in a place of safety?"

"And so the money," said Hannah, "is in the hands of that one-eyed rascal?"

"I don't know whom you mean by the one-eyed rascal," said Smith; "it is in the hands of that most respectable merchant, Don Josiah Xiutototle."

"I am determined, Mr. Smith, that I will not bear this."

"What!" cried Smith, "you think the money is not safe:—I assure you it's as safe as a church."

"Why," said Creed, "my dear lady, what better security could you desire, than the ancient firm of Xiutototle and Killganders?"

"Besides," added Smith, "you know Barnard has got an acknowledgment for the money."

"Upon which," said the Captain, "he can sue them in any court of law."

"He may proceed by common action for debt; or by indictment, in case of extremity," cried Smith.

"Yes," said Creed; "and call us as witnesses."

"But there will be no occasion for that," rejoined Beauty.

"Not the least," said Creed; "the men are too honourable."

"They'll pay with interest," cried Jack.

"Aye, and give a bonus," said the man of war

Here Hannah lost all temper, and flew into a torrent of the most violent abuse against both

Smith and Creed,—using epithets with which we do not think proper to disfigure our pages. Beauty allowed her to proceed without interruption ; and when she had finished, replied, with the utmost *sang froid*,—"Where's the use of putting yourself into this violent passion ? I assure you, upon my honour, that the money is quite safe."

" If you do not believe us," said the Captain, " you can ask Killganders himself, or the Don with the hard name."

" This is all mighty fine, gentlemen," cried Hannah ; " but I will contrive to mar your mirth. I'll have my revenge, depend upon it ;—I'll blow you all up."

" And yourself along with us," said Beauty, quietly.

" No matter !—I'll have my revenge."

" Why, hear me, Mrs. Woods," said the Captain ; " what amazing folly this is ! Revenge! for what ?—for securing money which will be equally divided, and of which you will have your share ? All we want is even justice ; and for this you would madly destroy both yourself and us. Does not your fortune depend upon us and Jackson ?—Are you not supported at present, without expending a farthing that you make ?—And who brought you into all this ? Don't let your passion get the better of your reason,—it is unworthy of a woman of your superior understanding. You'd sacrifice, for a few hundreds now, thousands to come : but what do I say ?—

you'd sacrifice them for nothing,—you would not gain a farthing; it is only through us that you can touch a penny of this money. It remains, therefore, with you to consider whether you will put three or four hundred pounds in your pocket; continue in the way of making a splendid income; or, by ruining us, lose everything, and be ruined yourself for ever. *I* am satisfied that, upon reflection, your own good sense will point out to you the folly—the madness, of such a proceeding."

"Well, but," said Hannah, in a much calmer tone, "you should not have been so precipitate—you should have consulted me, and made me a party to the affair :—I felt hurt that you did not."

"There was no time to be lost," answered Smith; "if I had not acted as I have done, Barnard would have paid his debts, and returned to the country. He expressed his full fixed determination to do so; and I appeal to Creed, whether we had not the utmost difficulty to dissuade him from this, and to induce him to remain."

"There is no doubt of it," said Creed; "he even talked of leaving to-morrow."

"What!" said Hannah; "and would he have left me?"

"That he would," replied Beauty; "and I advise you to keep a tight rein upon him ·—I know his temper."

"He shall not escape so easily," said Hannah,

"I will weave a triple net around him, which his strength shall not be able to break, nor his art to disentangle."

"Right!" said Smith; "and our aid shall not be wanting."

Thus this affair was settled; and the worthy trio, restored to mutual amity, finished the bottle of sherry together and parted.

CHAP. XIV.

"She's gone—the lovely village maid!
Now droop the flowers her care hath fed."

SHEPHERD.

ON the morning which succeeded the night of
Maria's abduction, her parents rose as usual with
the break of day to their respective labours,—the
father to the field, the mother to her household
duties. Maria, being an only and much indulged
child, was not habituated to leave her bed for an
hour or two later. The father, on going out, had
observed that the door was not bolted inside; but
as, of course, he had not the slighest suspicion of
the truth, he took no particular notice of this
fact, but attributed it to casual neglect.

Maria's ordinary time of rising was now past,
and, to her mother's surprise, she did not make
her appearance. The latter, however, thought
she might either have slept badly in the early
part of the night, or that head-ach, or some

other such cause, might now detain her in bed.
But when eight o'clock arrived, the old woman
began to get alarmed: she went to Maria's
chamber; and her alarm was not diminished by
finding the door half open, as the girl was
generally in the habit of locking it inside. She
entered, drew back the curtains of the bed, and
found that it was not only empty now, but had
evidently not been tenanted at all the night before!

To describe the sensations of a mother, on such
an occasion, would be no easy task. Maria was
gone! but how?—but when?—but where? Of
these questions, the second was the only one to
which any answer could be given by her parent
Her daughter had retired apparently to rest at her
usual time, and, therefore, must have gone out in
the middle of the night. That was no time for
visiting her cousin, or any of her female acquaintance in the village:—she must have eloped
with some man.

Was it with Harry Everton?—Impossible!
Harry, the mother knew, had long quitted the
neighbourhood, though she knew not what had
become of him: besides, she knew him to be
incapable of seducing away her daughter;—he
had no occasion to do so. He might have had
her, with the full consent of her parents, if she
were herself so inclined: but she also knew that
Maria was not so inclined; that she had a dislike
rather than an attachment to him:—it could not,
therefore, be Harry Everton.

Her thoughts then reverted to William Barnard. She was not ignorant that her daughter had given some encouragement to this young man. She herself, as well as old Marten, had no very high opinion of his character: she thought him very capable of a bad action : but, for some time, she had heard or seen nothing of him ;—she did not know whether he was in the country or not. Besides, why should they run away ? If marriage were the object, it might have been brought about easily without that, if Barnard (as Maria had once told her) was quite reformed. The match was a good one, and old Marten might have readily been induced to give his consent ;—but, perhaps, marriage was not Barnard's object :—she knew not what to think ; still her suspicions inclined to rest on him.

The father now returned to breakfast.

"Oh, Jack !" said old Mrs. Marten, " our Maria is gone."

" Gone !" cried the father ; " gone where ?"

" I don't know, I am sure, my dear," replied she ; " her bed is empty, and she has not lain in it last night."—And then she told him all.

The father's astonishment, confusion, perplexity, and grief, were equal to the mother's. He, however, indulged a hope that Maria might return in the course of the day, and all might be explained : meanwhile, he desired the mother to go and make inquiries in the village.

When Marten returned to dinner, he questioned

his wife on her success.   She told him, that of
Maria she could learn nothing. She had not
been amongst any of her friends.   But she did
find out that three strange gentlemen had been
stopping at the " Cock,"—that one had departed
the night before in a post-chaise, and that the
two others had gone off this morning, and young
Barnard with them.   But Maria had not been
seen with either of the parties.

The father did not know what to think ;—Maria
might have been with them, though she had not
been seen :—all was doubt and darkness.

The evening of that day passed, and night
came on ; but no Maria appeared. The old couple
sat desolately down to supper.   She who used
to busy herself in getting all ready, sit by her
father, read and sing to him, embrace her parents
before retiring to rest, and beg their blessing,
was not there.   The old couple looked at each
other,—words were not necessary to express
their feelings, nor could they give them language.
The mother cried aloud—the father buried his
face in his hands, and groaned deeply.

Even in their broken slumbers the painful
thought of their loss pursued them, and the
mother's dreams were frightfully vivid. She
thought she saw her daughter sitting, as usual in
fine weather, at the door, busy with her needle ;—
suddenly four men appeared, who, in spite of her
resistance, carried her off by violence.   After
this, she saw her dragged forcibly into a cottage,

and the door violently closed. But, strange to relate, the prominent figure in the dream was young Barnard. This, indeed, might be accounted for by her previous suspicions of him.

In fact, there was nothing in this dream particularly remarkable, or which might not easily be accounted for under the circumstances. But it, nevertheless, made a deep impression on the mind of the old woman. She told it to her husband in the morning, and expressed her full conviction that Maria had been taken away by force, and that Barnard was the chief agent in the business.

That day too elapsed, and the next, and the next, but no tidings of Maria came;—the mother abandoned herself to the bitterest grief, and the father was plunged in the deepest melancholy Everything about them served to remind them of their lost child. In one corner lay her work, in another her books. Her singing-birds (for she had two or three in cages) were now neglected. The kitten received not its milk from her hand as usual, nor the house-dog his accustomed encouragement from her tongue. The little shrubs, that she used daily to water, were beginning to wither for want of her care. All, in short, served to heighten the pangs which her parents suffered, and to increase their despair.

There was a difference, however, between the grief of the father and the mother. That of the latter was open and querulous : but Marten felt like a man;—his eyes, it is true, refused to weep, but his heart was deeply lacerated. He doated on his daughter—to her he looked as the only comfort and consolation of his declining years. To see her happily married, was the first wish of his heart; and for her welfare he had cheerfully supported a life of constant labour, and abstained from all those little indulgences that men of his age and class in life are usually in the habit of taking. He seldom drank, even in the most moderate degree, and never joined the society of his equals at any of their places of meeting. All his happiness was centered in his humble home, and his only, lovely child. The feelings of such a man may be better conceived than expressed.

A week had passed in this way, and the old and miserable couple were sitting one night, in gloomy silence, over the embers of a declining fire. The mother first broke this silence by saying—

"She is gone, Jack—gone for ever. My poor Maria!—she must certainly be dead: she would never leave us this way, without letting us hear from her, if she were alive."

"Mary," said old Marten, "do not talk about it. I thought to have died quietly and happily in her arms and yours. I now feel I must go soon, and very differently—my heart is broken."

Scarcely had he uttered the last sentence, when the rattling of wheels was heard upon the road without, at a little distance. The old couple started, and listened attentively. They both thought within themselves, without expressing it— " if this should be Maria!"

The vehicle, whatever it might be, was now approaching the house, for the sound grew clearer. At length it made a sudden stop, and was pulled up evidently at the gate of the cottage.

Voices were then heard, but the words were not distinguishable. Immediately came a loud knocking at the door; it was opened by Mrs. Marten, and—her daughter flew into her arms!

" Poor thing—take care of her!" cried old Carribles, who was close behind. " Here she is back for you, safe and sound. We've got her now into harbour, clear of pirates, rocks, and quicksands."

The old father now rushed out, and in a transport of joy embraced his daughter. " Oh, Maria !" said he, " I have you once again.

The old man could utter no more. The sudden revulsion of feeling was too much for his aged frame, and he sunk exhausted into a chair!

Carribles at once drew from his pocket his travelling flask of brandy, and having applied some of its contents to the lips of old Marten, he soon recovered.

" Oh, Maria !" said her good mother, " you have made your father and me so miserable. How could you go off in such a manner?"

" Dear mother," said Maria, " I was taken

away by force, and, but for this good gentleman, I should not be here now: you have to thank him for my safety."

" No thanks!" cried Carribles; "I have only done the duty of an honest tar,—rescued the weak and innocent out of the grasp of the strong and the wicked."

" Tell us, my dear child, how this happened," said Mrs. Marten.

Maria, with some hesitation, began her story, and told the whole substance of what had passed between her and Jackson, from the beginning of their acquaintance—with the suppression, however, of some circumstances. She mentioned how she had met her lover at the fair, of their subsequent communication, of her opposition to his proposals of elopement, and, finally, of her forcible abduction, and rescue by Carribles. She thought proper, however, to say nothing of the fortune-teller; nor did she allude to the share which Harry Everton had taken in her delivery, as she knew that that would be painful to her parents.

She concluded with telling them that she should have returned the next morning after her departure, but that she had been taken extremely ill; and expressed, in the strongest language, her gratitude for the kind attentions of Captain Carribles and his housekeeper.

" Maria," said her mother, " you should not have kept this acquaintance so secret from your father and me: you see the consequences."

"I know it, my dear mother," replied Maria; "I know I was very wrong;—I will never act so again: I was very—very wrong."

"We forgive you, my child," simultaneously ejaculated both parents, and strained her alternately in their arms.

The veteran tar was much affected by this scene: he was thanked in the warmest terms by the father. Carribles seized his hand, and said—

"No thanks, my dear friend:—this is a great pleasure to me, I assure you: to see honest folks happy is my delight. But it is not to me alone ——"

Here a look of entreaty from Maria made him pause:—she knew he was about to mention Harry, and she had before requested him not to do so before her parents.

Carribles took the hint, and resumed—

"But, young lady, I think you mentioned the name of the Corsair who was carrying you off: what do you call him?"

"Jackson, sir, is the gentleman's name."

"Jackson—Jackson," cried Carribles; "I should know that name. What was his other name, do you know?"

"Stafford, sir," said Maria; "Stafford Jackson."

"Stafford Jackson!" exclaimed Carribles, at the top of his voice; "why, shiver my timbers, but I know the man well: how is he built?"

"Built, sir?" said Maria.

"Aye, girl; I mean what sort of a man is he?"

"A tall, handsome young man, with dark brown hair," replied Maria, blushing.

"I know him," said Carribles, "well;—the son of a late respected friend of mine; a brave and gallant youth, but as wild as the devil: still, I did not think he would force away a young girl from her parents. A sailor, too, the rascal has been."

"I believe he meant honourably," said Maria; "but he wished to be concealed, in consequence of having fought a duel."

"Just like him," said Carribles; "he was the most desperate boy I ever knew, and has all his life been in one scrape or other, I believe:—but do you take care. If he mean honourably, he will ask you from your worthy father here; and I do not think he would make a bad husband, for he is a good-hearted fellow, in the main; but don't you listen to him on any other terms."

Mrs. Marten was proceeding to lay on the table all the refreshment the cottage could afford, when Carribles interposed, and prevented her hospitable exertions.

"No," said he; "no refreshments for me—I must steer home. We should have been here sooner, but for my grey mare: she could not mend her pace, if Old Nick was astern of her."

"But, sir," said old Marten, "we will make up a bed for you here to-night, and take care of your horse;—there is an out-house where he can be put, and I will get some hay: it is late for you, sir, disabled as you are, to go home now."

"No, no, my friend," cried Carribles; "home I must steer; and as for danger, d—n me, I have a pair of bull-dogs that will guard me from the land-pirates: besides, I am alone—what signifies my old hulk now? It has been well battered for five-and-forty years, and will be soon no longer sea-worthy: d—n them, what can they get of a cat but its skin?"

Further pressing was of no use: the old boy would be off, in spite of wind and weather, and every other obstacle. He shook the parents by the hand, kissed Maria, told her to take care of herself and have nothing to do with Jackson, unless he would splice fairly, got under way, and proceeded homewards at old Grizzle's usual rate of two knots and a half an hour.

Maria was now, as she thought, fully resolved to give up all further ideas of Jackson, unless he should come openly forward and demand her of her parents. In forming such a resolution, however, she reckoned without her host. Like a great many others, she knew little of her own character, and of the real nature of her own feelings: it is much easier to make resolutions contrary to our propensities and inclinations, than to keep them. What seems facile enough in theory, is difficult in practice; and Maria was like the man of whom Voltaire writes, who rose in the morning with a full determination to be a perfect philosopher, considered nothing more easy than the subjugation of all his passions, and ceded, in less than an hour, to the first temptation which presented itself.

Jackson did not make his appearance; yet, in spite of her resolutions, he was the only subject of her thoughts. Indignant as she had been at his violence, (or rather at the violent measure which he sanctioned, for he had committed no personal violence himself), the sophistry of her love now began to make excuses for it—it was the strength of his passion—the violence of his attachment for herself, that induced him to act as he did—she herself was the cause of it—and this idea at once flattered her vanity and excited her regret. She was now very sorry for her own obstinacy (for in such a light did her former firmness appear to her mind at present), and she was much afraid that she had now lost him for ever. The observations thrown out about him by Carribles, had no tendency to counteract these feelings; for, on the whole, they were favourable rather than otherwise. The worst the Captain could say of him was, that he was wild; and there is no woman who does not think herself capable of taming any man, when she is once married to him. This opinion, too, I believe to be correct in most cases,—your marriage is a sore, decayer of your young men's wildness.

The general solitude in which Maria lived at present, tended much to nourish and support this particular train of reflection; and the only society of which she occasionally partook, served to corroborate it still more :—the society which I mean, was that of her cousin, Miss Ellen Mayberry.

We have been so extremely busy with the principal personages of this history, that we have not had time to look after this young lady and her concerns: for this enforced neglect, we ask pardon, and hasten to make atonement. The reader must not suppose that while Jackson was laying siege so vigorously to Maria, Beauty had been altogether idle with regard to Ellen :—no such thing !—the intervals of leisure, allowed him from the serious occupation of tutoring Barnard, he devoted to the relaxation of courtship : thus passing his time in the manner most suitable to his amiable and philanthropic character—between the duties of friendship and the enjoyments of love. He and Ellen had frequent clandestine meetings : what passed at those meetings, it is not necessary for our purposes fully to detail. Suffice it to say, that the insinuating and tender elegance of Beauty's conversation completed that conquest over the fair one's heart, which his prepossessing physiognomy had commenced. She was, indeed, a girl of a very different character from Maria ;—one by no means disposed to carry resistance in love matters to any outrageous extremity, but who would much sooner capitulate on reasonable terms, than reduce the assailant to the *dernier resort* of storming the citadel.

Ellen was very sorry for the departure of Smith, who, however, consoled her with the strongest assurances of his speedy return. When she heard of Maria's disappearance, she could give a tolerably shrewd guess at the cause of it; but, with the true secrecy of a woman, when her own interests are likely to be compromised (the only time when a woman observes secrecy), she remained as silent as the grave.

After she had heard of Maria's disappearance, she was in daily expectation of hearing from her, that she was happily settled, &c. &c. Her surprise was great, after the lapse of a week, to see Maria herself; and her surprise was still greater, when the latter detailed to her every particular of the transaction: this surprise, however, was equalled by her disapprobation of Maria's conduct; and her comments were not calculated either to render her cousin satisfied with the present, or guarded for the future.

"Well, Maria," she would say, "I am sure you are a very odd sort of girl; you love this gentleman, you confess, and yet you won't have him: you actually forced him, by your foolish, stupid obstinacy, to run away with you—and then your nonsense in calling out on the road to two strangers;—I am sure I should not call out, if I was in the carriage with such a dashing fellow. I wish, with all my heart, that *somebody* would run away with me."

"That I believe," said Maria; "I could guess, too, who that somebody is."

"Oh!" said Ellen, laughing, "I'm not ashamed

to own it,—I like the young man very well indeed;
and when he wants me to go with him, he'll have
no occasion to use force. I won't die an old maid,
through any foolish scruples, like you."

" But what could I do, Ellen ?" said Maria.

" Do ! why, go with the man quietly that you
love, and that loves you, and be happy."

" But my father and mother," said Maria.

" Oh, nonsense ! don't you think you would
have made them much happier by coming back to
them well married, or by letting them know that
you were so, than by returning as you have done ?
Besides, did you want the man to expose his
life for your whim, and for no use ? It's my
opinion that you'll die an old maid after all ;—
William Barnard is off, and Harry Everton is off,
and now I am afraid Mr. Jackson is off too."

" You don't think so ?" said Maria.

" I don't know, I'm sure," said she, " how he
will act; but I think, if I was half so badly
treated, I'd never come back."

" Then, perhaps, I shall never see him again,"
said Maria, with a sigh.

" Why," said Ellen, " that may very well be ;
for how do you know what's become of him : you
know, from the old Captain's account, that he
was missed quite suddenly the night of the scuffle ;
—he may have been seriously hurt, for aught you
know, and may be dead by this time."

" My dear Ellen," said Maria, " don't say that,

—I cannot bear it; if that were the case, I should never be happy again."

" Well, my love," replied Ellen, " don't take it so much to heart,—Mr. Smith has promised to see me soon, and Mr. Jackson may return to you also.: but, if he does`come, I advise you to treat him better than you did before."

Such conversations, while they militated strongly against the resolutions of Maria, were but too much in accordance with her inclinations: they served to foster her love, to increase her regret for her firm and virtuous conduct, to make her wish for the return of her lover, and to prepare her to cede with greater facility to a renewal of his propositions: they also had a tendency to undermine the strictness of her principles, and to blunt the keenness of the moral sense within her. Nothing is more dangerous to the youth of either sex, than a companion, the levity of whose temper, or the strength of whose passions, disposes them to cast away the restraint of rectitude. Sympathetic feeling is soon engendered; and such is the infirmity of nature, that the contagion of loose principles is propagated with far more facility than the love of virtue. The virtuous are more easily corrupted by the society of the vicious, than the latter are benefited by the example of the former.

About five or six days after her return, Maria was walking in the dusk of the evening, in a retired place, at no great distance from the cottage. Her thoughts were in the train we have been describing : she was regretting the harshness with which she had treated Jackson ; fearing, at one time, that she had lost him for ever; indulging, at another, an undefined hope of his return ; and again, with the inconsistency so natural to woman, trembling at the bare imagination of seeing him. She commenced to think aloud,

" I am afraid he is gone for ever—my conduct must have offended him much. Oh! if I could see him again !"

" Behold him here !" said a voice behind her ; " the ill-treated, but still constant Stafford."

She turned round, beheld her lover, and fell into his arms.

Jackson had come prepared to make an eloquent defence of his own conduct ; but what he had overheard suddenly determined him to change his mode of operation. Instead of defending himself, he turned the tables on Maria, and commenced to reproach her with hardheartedness and cruelty.

" Maria," said he, " dearest Maria, you have made me truly miserable. Would that I had not recovered on the fatal night we were last together !—would that the villain who struck me senseless to the earth, had given a more effectual blow !—I should not have awaked to the torments of disappointed love, and the horrors of despair."

"What do you mean?" said Maria; "*you* were not hurt that night."

"All I remember," replied Jackson, "is having been struck to the earth by some unknown hand, while I was engaged with the villain at the horses' heads. When I recovered, I found myself lying by the side of the road, and the honest sailor, who rode outside the carriage, was stretched still senseless by my side: the chaise, the gig, you, and our assailants, had all vanished. I was left alone on a dreary road—a black and gloomy morning, in a state of exceeding weakness from loss of blood, with a helpless, senseless man for my companion :—for this situation, Maria, I had to thank your kindness. What a return for love like mine !"

"Oh, Heavens !" ejaculated Maria; "what have I done ?"

"If you regret it, Maria," resumed Jackson, "I shall rejoice in what I have suffered; and were it ten times greater, I should think it but a cheap purchase of your affection. I rose," proceeded he, "with some difficulty, and endeavoured to recover my companion : I could not succeed— he had been very seriously injured indeed. I marked the place, and proceeded slowly forward, I knew not whither, in search of aid : fortunately, I was soon overtaken by a man in a waggon-cart,—I told him the case, and requested his assistance. We returned to where my companion lay, hoisted him into the cart, I entered myself, and we drove to the next village. There we were fortunate enough to procure some medical assistance, such as it was : but the consequence of what I had gone through was a high fever, which confined me to my bed until within the last few days. I resolved, however, to seek you as soon as my strength would at all permit, to throw myself at your feet, to ask forgiveness for the apparent violence into which the strength of my love had led me, and to hear my final doom from your own lovely lips."

So saying, our hero suited the action to the word, fell upon his knees, and again exclaimed—

"Dearest Maria, how could you treat me with such cruelty ?"

She replied, "I know not—I did not know what I was doing : I did not know what you meant to do."

"Oh, Maria! how could you doubt my truth, my honour, my affection ?—what could I mean but well ? I feel that I could not live without you ; and I thought that the only means of securing the possession of all that can render life valuable to me, were those which I adopted. God knows I have suffered enough for it, both in mind and body. But I swear by the sacred power of love, that I will not rise with life from this position until you say that you forgive me."

"Rise, then," cried Maria ; "I do forgive you, —rise."

"Not yet," said Jackson; "you must promise to be mine, or see me die at your feet."

"I do," said Maria, "I will never be another's."

"One promise more," added Jackson, "before I rise: this our meeting must be a secret; to reveal it will be my sure destruction."

Maria, after a pause, promised not to reveal it, and Jackson rose.

They walked forward and continued their conversation. Jackson inquired into all the particulars that occurred to her after their parting; and she told him all. When she mentioned the name of Carribles, and his mentioning his acquaintance with Jackson, the latter exclaimed,

"Good God! my honoured friend, Captain Carribles!—what an accident! I hope he received no hurt:—what a mistake!—that man, then, at the horses' heads was Squires, though I knew him not from the darkness. But there was a third; who was he?"

"I know not," said Maria, while her conscience reproached her for the untruth, and the colour flew to her cheeks; but it was not perceived by Jackson.

The latter then informed her that he himself was living concealed in the neighbourhood, that he would take immediate measures for their marriage, which must be private; and again extorting a promise of secrecy from her, they parted, having first made an appointment to meet again the following day.

The spot where Jackson, for the present, lay *perdue*, was no other than the cottage belonging to Smith; under which was a subterraneous apartment of very considerable extent, into which, the smuggled goods lately brought from the coast had been conveyed, and placed under the surveillance of Ricketts. This cottage was situated in the midst of a very romantic and hidden dell, so much concealed that not many persons in the neighbourhood were aware even of its existence. It was remote from the road, surrounded on all sides with shrubs and thick underwood, growing in such profusion as to render all access to it extremely difficult to any person not well acquainted with the locality. There was, however, one narrow path leading to it, which was not readily discoverable to a stranger. It was even very possible for a person to pass by the cottage itself without notice. It lay in a hollow, backed immediately by a small hill entirely overgrown with furze and brushwood. It was built so very low, that the thatched roof, inclining from the hill, seemed in front within a foot or two of the turf. The small window was actually on a level with the ground; and the door, which was at one side, was invisible at first, being sunk below the surface, and having a descent to it of a few rude and very abrupt steps. Notwithstanding this, there was considerable room inside, as the floor had been sunk several feet below the level of the soil, and, independently of the secret cavern, excavations had been carried back to some extent in the body of the hill.

No one in Polstead had the slightest idea of the purposes to which this cabin was appropriated, or that it was the property of Smith. He, indeed, had left the neighbourhood so very young, that on his return, which we have described, he was not recognized by a human being. Few, in fact, had ever known much of his family, which was very obscure, and had left the place soon after his original departure. The cabin was tenanted by a miserable looking old woman, who pretended to live by knitting stockings, &c. Her appearance did not much invite communication, and the common people around, who had ever seen her, were not without their suspicions of her holding an illicit intercourse with the prince of darkness. Had they seen the *gentleman* who was her present lodger, such suspicions might have received additional confirmation; for Tom Ricketts might have well passed, if not for the " Most Low" himself, at least for an accredited agent of the court of Pandemonium.

With these amiable companions was Jackson for the present domiciled. He did not, however, bestow upon them any extra allowance of his conversation. He had a very comfortable room, snugly furnished, there was an abundance of provisions, and, when he was not abroad, he contrived tolerably well to dissipate *ennui*, with the assistance of burgundy, claret, and champagne, most assuredly "neat as imported," and perfectly unsullied by the intervention of the revenue code. Not that Jackson was a disloyal subject, or bore any personal antipathy to his most gracious Majesty; but, like Nanty Ewart, he could not afford to pay duty.

Jackson and Maria met next day according to appointment. He commenced a long and round-about tale of the measures he had taken for their speedy marriage;—how, when everything was done, he would then present himself to her parents;—immediately after, they must leave the country for his house in London. He told her that he was in daily expectation of the duelling affair being quite settled, as he had now got a clue to the witnesses; but in the mean time the most profound secrecy was indispensably necessary to his security.

He then expatiated with vast eloquence on the unbounded happiness that awaited them. He painted, in the most glowing colours, the warmth and purity of his passion, boasted of his own high sense of honour, and swore that he would die ten thousand deaths, sooner than take the slightest step that could compromise her welfare. Nay, so transcendently sublimated was his affection, that he had rather renounce her possession for ever (though that would be worse than death), than expose her to the remotest chance of one moment of uneasiness.

By these and such like discourses, he prevailed

over all her former resolutions. He got her to agree to the private marriage, and to entire secrecy. She who, a day or two before, was fully determined to hold no communication with him, unless he acted openly, and consulted her parents, now completely gave in to all the clandestine measures he proposed. Her virtuous firmness, her moral principles, her filial piety—all gave way to the ardent and persuasive eloquence of her seducer—vanished, like the dew of night, before the rising beam of morning.

Such is woman! The creature of present impulses, varying like the camelion, and uncertain as the idle wind!—of too soft materials to carry the stern impress of principle, or preserve for a moment undefaced the broad, distinctive characters of rectitude. You might as well write upon the strand, which is washed by the restless ocean, or on the watery plain itself, as attempt to fix her wavering will, or determine her unstable conduct. She is caught, like the mackarel, with some gaudy bait, and led by the ignis fatuus of vanity into the swamps of destruction and despair. Unhappy they, whose interest, whose honour, whose happiness, are in her keeping ; and yet still more unhappy those, who have never basked in the sunshine of her smiles, tasted the nectar of her lip, or sighed within the Elysium of her circling arms !

There was a 'poet whose name I know not, but who is quoted in the illustrations of Martinus

Scriblerus, in the Essay on the " Art of Sinking," and who puts this very modest request to the supernal powers—

> " Ye Gods, annihilate both space and time,
> And make two lovers happy !"

Now this prayer, absurd as it is, in the application intended by the author, who speaks of two absent lovers desirous of meeting, is often realized to the minds of lovers who are together. This was the case in the scene we have been describing between Jackson and Maria. By the latter at least, time flew unheeded, while she listened to the silvery tones and soft persuasive eloquence of her lover. Nor were her ideas of space one atom more distinct than her ideas of time. She wandered on without adverting either to the extent or the direction of the ground she was traversing. Jackson, however, was far more geographically disposed. He contrived, while pouring soft nonsense into her ear, very artfully to lead her steps to the entrance of the dell in which stood the cottage of the inimitable Beauty. They entered together the narrow path which led to it; and when arrived at its site, Jackson made a full stop, and pointed it out to Maria's notice.

" Dear me !" said she, " what a low roof !"

" Beneath that low roof," said Jackson, " is my present retreat for retirement and safety. Come in, my love, and see it."

Maria at first hesitated to enter; but her

scruples were soon overcome by Jackson, and she consented to go in.

They descended the steps, and knocked at the door. It was opened by the old woman, whose appearance did not much prepossess Maria in her favour, though she had been dressed for the occasion with peculiar care and neatness. There. was a sinister expression in this woman's coun- tenance which no art could relieve, or no hypocrisy disguise. It was in vain that she attempted to dress her face in smiles : the mouth might be distorted into something like a smile, but the cold pale eye never changed its character of hardheartedness and cunning. We cannot avoid remarking here a most excellent provision of nature. In the great majority of instances, an evil disposition, and evil habits, give a stamp to the countenance that cannot be mistaken : it is hung out as a beacon for the warning of the unwary; and the wicked carry, like the vagabond Cain, a mark upon their forehead, that all who see them may shun them. When this is not the case with persons whose pursuits are culpable, we may be assured that nature has given them some redeeming qualities, and designed them for better things.

Jackson now led Maria into a small sitting- room, very neatly furnished : she observed, lying on one of the chairs, a guitar and a music book. A small mahogany case, filled with volumes, very neatly bound, stood on a table next the wall :

on another table, in the centre of the room, a cloth was laid as if for dinner.

Jackson looked at his watch, and said,

"My dear Maria, it is now five o'clock,—your dinner hour is past, and you must stop and take some refreshment here."

He did not give her time to reply, but ordered the old woman to bring in dinner, which she did immediately. The repast was excellent; and when it was concluded, a bottle of capital wine was placed upon the table.

Nothing could be more tender and respectful than the whole of Jackson's behaviour to Maria during dinner, and after. He did not presume to take the slightest liberties : not a gesture, word, or look, escaped him that could alarm the most apprehensive modesty; but all his conversation was of love, of connubial happiness, of unspotted truth, and unchangeable fidelity. He expatiated on these themes with so much eloquence, and accompanied his language with looks of so much affection and apparent sincerity, that his words fell upon the ".charmed ear" of Maria like the sweetest music, sunk deep into her soul, and melted her heart to a reciprocation of tenderness. If she loved him before, she was now most thoroughly enamoured : his soft and respectful demeanour had banished all her fears, and she gave herself up to the full enjoyment of the society of the man she loved, forgetful of the past, and careless of the future.

Jackson was not slow in perceiving the deep

impression which he had made.   He thought the present was the proper moment to press his suit, and gain her immediate consent to be his: but he had seen enough of her character to make him forbear, even in the present most favourable instance, to persuade her to yield, without the preliminary of marriage; and he was too manly to try to accomplish his wishes by violence. Deceit, however, with women, in such cases, he thought perfectly admissible; and such is the creed of many honourable libertines, who, in their ordinary transactions with our sex, are far more scrupulous than was Jackson.

He drew his chair nearer to that of Maria, and taking her hand, whispered in the softest voice—

" My dearest love, I told you that I would take measures for our immediate union: I have done so;—everything is prepared, and we may be united this very moment, if you will only consent to be mine immediately. Do not refuse, my dearest, only love."

" How is it possible?" exclaimed Maria; " now! —why it cannot be."

" It can and will, Maria, if you but consent: there is a clergyman, a friend of mine, near this, and he will join our hands at once."

" Oh! but," said Maria, " it is so abrupt. My father and mother ——"

" Dearest Maria," cried he, " have I not your promise that you will consent to a private marriage?—your parents shall know it in proper time. Abrupt!—surely, now that all is ready, the sooner it is done the better : I cannot, Maria, —I will not, live without you any longer."

He used a great deal more persuasion in the prosecution of his suit, and Maria's denials and excuses grew fainter and fainter. At last she yielded, tremulously saying,

"Well, Stafford, I consent,—I throw myself entirely on your honour and protection."

"Dearest Maria!" exclaimed Jackson, "now, indeed, you make me happy!" and folded her in his embrace.

He arose immediately, took pen, ink, and paper, and wrote the following :—

"DEAR AND REVEREND SIR,

"I have received the consent of my beloved Maria, and only wait your arrival to make me completely happy. My domestic will conduct you to me.

"Yours,

"Dear and Reverend Sir,

"STAFFORD JACKSON."

He rung a small hand-bell, and the old woman entered.

"Is Ricketts in the way?" demanded Jackson.

"Yes, sir," replied the woman.

"Tell him to take this note where it is directed."
The old woman vanished.

While waiting for the parson, Jackson did not suffer Maria to indulge in any reflection : he continued his former strain of amorous conversation, accompanied with the most insinuating endearments. He made her also take another glass of wine ; for wine is a great auxiliary to the lover,— it confuses the reason, enlivens the imagination, and excites the passions.

The Reverend gentleman, for whom they tarried, now made his appearance, and was presented to Maria by Jackson.

He was dressed in the clerical style : his hair brushed back from his forehead, both at the top and sides, and most profusely saturated with powder, which extended itself over the collar of his black coat, and half way down the back : the coat was very long, remarkably full in the skirts, and altogether too big for him. His waistcoat, of black silk, was also very long, with pocket-flaps reaching to his thighs. His black velvet breeches, all in wrinkles, were fastened at the knee with black buckles. Black silk stockings, shoes with very large buckles, a small white cravat without a collar, and a bishop's hat, constituted the rest of the outward man. He carried in his hand a large silk bag.

It is here necessary to observe, that a few days before the time of which we are now writing, Captain Creed received, in London, the following pithy communication by post.

"MY DEAR CAPTAIN,

"I must trespass on your friendship to do me a small favour. All I wrote to you about, in my last letter, is settled: come down to Polstead immediately on receipt of this, and bring with you the necessary things. We must afterwards go to Ipswich, on the business I mentioned.

"Yours, very truly,

"JACKSON."

"P. S. On no account delay, as you love me and good wine. Not a word to Smith or Hannah."

The gallant Captain, on reading this epistle, instantly made all ready, took coach for Suffolk, and arrived in time to attend Jackson's wedding. —In short, the *Reverend* gentleman, who now stood before the expecting couple, was nobody else but himself—Captain Cornelius Creed, of the Scarafooka Rangers!

"Reverend sir," said Jackson, formally addressing Creed, "I have sent for you on the happiest occasion of my life;—you must unite this amiable young lady and myself in the bands of holy matrimony. Come, sir, a glass of wine."

"Not yet, thank you, Mr. Jackson," replied his *Reverence*; "business of this kind must be performed by one of our holy calling with dry lips. I suppose, Mr. Jackson, you have taken all the preliminary steps?"

"Yes, sir," replied Jackson, "I believe I have."

"Have you the licence?" rejoined the *parson*.

"Oh yes!" said Jackson, opening a scrutoire,

and presenting him with a piece of parchment folded up; "here it is."

Creed very gravely received the parchment, took a pair of gold spectacles out of their case with great deliberation, and clapping them upon his nose, mumbled over the parchment for some seconds.

"Stafford Jackson,—um—um; Maria Marten, spinster,—um—um. You are sure, Mr. Jackson, the names are right?"

"Certain," cried Jackson.

"That is well—that is well, Mr. Jackson; for otherwise the marriage might be void. Have you the ring, Mr. Jackson?"

"Yes, please your Reverence."

"That is also well—very well, Mr. Jackson. And now, young people," continued he, with vast solemnity, "I suppose you have reflected well on the grave nature of the contract on which you are both about to enter?"

"We have, your Reverence," said Jackson.

"That is also well—very well, Mr. Jackson; and who is to give the bride away, and witness the ceremony?"

"On my word I have not thought of that, your Reverence."

"Oh! but you should have thought of that, it is a form we cannot dispense with: any one may do it."

"Then," said Jackson, "there is my honest

follower, Tom Ricketts—a blunt sailor, but a good-hearted man."

"He will do very well," rejoined the pseudo-ecclesiastic.

Jackson now called in Ricketts and the house-keeper. The former was newly "rigged" in naval style,—white trowsers, blue jacket, and black silk handkerchief with sailor-knot.

"Tom," said Jackson, "I am going to be married."

"God bless your honour!" said Tom; "I shall be glad to see you happily spliced—if I sha'nt, damme."

"Don't swear, mine honest friend," said the *reverend* Captain.

"Beg your Reverence's pardon," said Ricketts; "no offence, I hope."

"Tom," said Jackson, "you must give away this young lady."

"That I will," cried Tom, "with pleasure;—but to no one but your honour."

The gallant *parson* now opened his silk bag, took out a surplice, and band; and having arrayed himself leisurely "*in pontificalibus,*" produced his prayer-book, and read with much solemnity the marriage service.

Jackson then embraced Maria, who was extremely agitated during the whole business; Ricketts and the house-keeper retired; and the parson, divesting himself of his canonicals, sat down to enjoy a glass of wine with the *new-married* couple.

" Now," said he, " business being done, enjoyment may follow.   When we have discharged the calls of duty, we may attend to the calls of nature : frail flesh needeth refreshment.   Mr. and Mrs. Jackson, I wish you both many years of happiness and prosperity."

" I thank your Reverence," replied Jackson ; " and in drinking your health, allow me to offer you a small tribute of gratitude for the happiness you have been instrumental in introducing me to." —And he handed over to the parson a bank note folded up.

" Mr. Jackson," said the Light Infantry ecclesiastic, " you insult my friendship.   I have known and esteemed you for too many years, to require payment for my services : take back your money, Mr. Jackson."

" Nay, but, my dear sir," cried Jackson, " I do not offer you this as payment ;— I only request you to accept of it as a token of friendship."

" Oh !" said the *parson*, " that is quite another affair :—as a token of friendship, Mr. Jackson, I accept your money.   Take a pinch of snuff, sir," (presenting a massy silver box).

Jackson took the box, and taking a pinch out of it, returned it ; but Creed pushed it back to him again, saying,

" When I presented you the box, Mr. Jackson,

I did not mean to receive it again. You have given me a token of friendship, accept from me another in exchange : put the box into your pocket, or I shall be offended."

This was a serious whim of Creed's. Though a man quite destitute of principle, he was not incapable of the feelings of friendship; and Jackson was the only man for whom he had such feelings. Now, though his notions of justice were in general so loose, he would not only not plunder his friends, but he made a scruple of receiving money from them, without a *" quid pro quo."* Jackson recollected this, and, with a bow, put the snuff-box into his pocket.

Creed, having helped himself to as many goblets of claret as he could, without infringing on Jackson's precious time, now rose and said, " My children, I must leave you : to-morrow will be Sunday—I have to officiate for a brother clergyman, at Ipswich, and must depart early. Good night !—I wish you all happiness."

The mock-parson departed ; and—over all that followed we must draw a veil.

So fell Maria,—the victim, not of her own vicious inclinations or passions, but of a course of systematic deception by which the most virtuous might have been ensnared. Few girls of such inexperience—and few, indeed, at all—, would have resisted so long as she did : multitudes would have succumbed in the first instance, if assailed by so accomplished and insinuating a

seducer as Jackson.   And, after all, she was not,
properly speaking, seduced;—her principles were
not perverted, nor was she led to act wilfully
against the dictates of virtue : she complied with
nothing but what, to her apprehensions, was
perfectly lawful;—her only error was in ac-
ceding to a clandestine intercourse in the first
instance, and then swerving from her resolution
not to renew it. But, surely, in a girl of such
simplicity, inexperience, and susceptibility of
heart, such an error will not be deemed worthy
of the severest reprobation. Many women, who
have preserved their chastity, or at least their
reputation, have been far removed from the possession of such purity of soul as belonged to
Maria ; and if the most prudish of the sex should
be inclined to condemn her, let them examine
their own hearts, and let her " who is without
sin among them, cast the first stone."

CHAP. XV.

Here, Virtue spurns me with disdain;
  There, Pleasure spreads her snare;
Strong habit drives me back to vice,
  Religion lends no care:
I strive, while passion gnaws my heart,
  To fly from shame in vain:
World, 'tis thy cruel will!—I yield,
  And plunge in guilt again.

LEWIS.

WHILE the incidents, whose description has occupied our latter chapters, were taking place, Barnard had scarcely ever bestowed even a passing thought upon Maria. If he did think of her at all, it was only with feelings of indignation and contempt. He thought of her only as a girl of depraved mind, who would have made use of him, as a cover for her shame, and a security for the continuation of her illicit intercourse with another. Tenderness and regret were not mingled with his sentiments respecting her.—He congratulated himself on his escape, and rejoiced in his immunity.

But the fact was, that such thoughts rarely crossed his mind. He was far too much occupied, and agitated by present feelings and incidents,

Y Y

to indulge in much reflection on the past. He
was kept in a continual whirlwind of dissipation,
between the pleasures of society, and the bottle,
and the caresses of his syren mistress. Her
influence over him became more and more
unbounded, his appetite grew by what it fed on,
and he soon began to think that the true end of
existence was perpetual amusement and perpetual gratification.

In the midst, however, of all this mental
intoxication, an unpleasant suggestion of conscience would occasionally intrude itself,—that
" still small voice" which will make itself heard,
even by the most vicious breast, until a long course
of practical depravity, aided by theoretical perversion, shall have silenced its warnings. Barnard had been brought up with a respect for the
principles of religion. He had never for a
moment been led to doubt of the truth of Christianity; and little as his conduct accorded with
its precepts, he was not without a certain reverence for its authority. It was no better feeling,
it is true, than the force of custom and the prejudice of education ; but it was sufficient to make
him feel that he was not acting right—to render
him now and then uneasy under a sense of his
misconduct, and fearful of punishment in another
life.

Under the abuse of certain forms and doctrines
of religion, we have heard of many vicious men,
who proceeded comfortably enough in their course

of criminality, without either renouncing their faith, or suffering any twinges of remorse. Thus, with some, the compliance with certain exterior ceremonies is sufficient to atone for the greatest vice, and ward off the vengeance of offended heaven; with others, the doctrine, that where the faith is correct, and election insured, conduct is a matter of total indifference, answers the purpose of quieting their consciences equally well. But where religion is taught to be insepa- rable from moral conduct; where the only offering stated to be acceptable to the Deity is a pure heart; and where true faith is only admitted to exist from its natural fruits of temperance, jus- tice, and charity—there the religious belief must be demolished, before the mind of the sinner can be at ease under the weight of his iniquities. Such was as yet the case with Barnard; like the devils, he "believed and trembled."

This last check, however, on his career of vice and folly, was destined speedily to be removed. His friends Smith and Creed were thorough-paced infidels. The latter had travelled, was a man of some education, and a systematic disbeliever,— having imbibed in France, both from reading and conversation, the pernicious dogmas of infidelity. As for Smith, he had never received any religious instruction in youth, and had never given the subject a thought of any kind until lately, when he suddenly became a proselyte of Mr. Carlile. The doctrines, of which that gentleman became

so active and notorious a disseminator, were too
suitable to the inclinations and practice of Beauty,
not to be embraced by him with the warmest
avidity: he soon became a preacher and propa-
gator of the new opinions he had adopted; and
when the subject of Christianity was mentioned,
he indulged in the most violent philippics against
our holy religion, and the most blasphemous
ridicule of its sacred mysteries.

The motive and object of persons like Carlile,
who are so ardent in the extermination of religious
opinions, cannot for one moment be mistaken.
They are not actuated, as they themselves give
out, by a philosophic love of truth, and a philanthropic regard to the human species: were this
the case, we might pity their error, while we condemn it and strenuously oppose its propagation.
But their direct object is the furtherance of their
own sordid interest; and their great aim is to
sap the foundations of morality as well as religion,
and disturb the basis of political order. They do
not hate religion so much for itself alone, and in
the abstract, as because it is the great cement of
moral and social happiness: they would willingly
support any system of superstition, that allowed
them to indulge their gross passions to the full,
and to plunder their neighbours with impunity;
but they hate a religion which enjoins temperance,
soberness, and chastity, justice to our fellow-men,
and obedience to the laws. This we cannot
doubt, when we invariably find the character of

the infidel apostle united with that of the political incendiary ; and that Mr. Carlile's morality is no better than his religion, will be evident to any one who takes the trouble of perusing many of his publications, professedly unconnected with the subject of religion.

The persons who suffer most from the spread of opinions hostile to Christianity, are the lower orders, and the half-educated among the middle ; the rest, though open enough to the contagion of infidel principles, have yet, from circumstances, so many guards over their conduct, that, however we may deplore their errors, they are not productive of such extended mischief. It is unfortunate, indeed, for any individual to be destitute of religion ; he is thereby deprived of the greatest source of happiness, and the strongest motive to uniform purity of life : but still, men of certain stations and certain professions, must of necessity keep up the appearance of decency The taste which education imparts, may prevent them from being grossly immoral ; and their interest must induce them to support the system of social order : but when persons of vulgar habits and no education are freed from the restraints of religion, the most fatal consequences to themselves and to society may be expected to ensue. Without taste for the beauty of virtue, judgment for the policy of honesty, or philosophy for the regulation of appetite, they will soon abandon themselves to the most dangerous crimes and the most disgusting and brutal vices.

Barnard, as I have hinted, was not without an unpleasant twinge now and then, when the idea of hell suggested itself: but it was nothing but the base and servile feeling of fear that operated upon him; he had no horror at the deformity of vice, no regrets for having quitted the paths of innocence. All the feelings which acted upon him when he returned from his first trip to London were gone by, never to return: the seeds of virtue were blasted and dried up within him; but the fear of hell remained—the only check to the last extremity of wickedness.

He was sitting one evening with Creed and Smith, at the lodgings of the latter, and the conversation happened to turn on the fate of a man who was hanged that morning for murder. The case was of a very aggravated character, as the murder had been perpetrated in cold blood, upon a woman, and with many other circumstances of cruelty. Creed expressed his reprobation of the deed in very strong terms, in which he was joined by Smith, who, bad as he was, was incapable of sympathizing with a cruel, cold-blooded murderer.

"If there be anything," said Creed, "which deserves hanging, it is an act like this."

"I agree with you," said Smith: "not that I have quite so much respect for human life as you have; I would not hesitate to kill those who stood n my way, fairly and openly;—but a weak, defenceless woman!—faugh! it is a stain on manhood that nothing can wash out but blood. I almost wish, for the fellow's sake, that there was a hell."

"I have frequently heard you," said Barnard, "talk as if there were none; but I am very much afraid there is, after all."

"Fudge!" said Smith; "all old women's tales and priestcraft!—that doctrine might have gone down very well a hundred years ago; but we are not to be humbugged that way now, thanks to 'the march of intellect,' as my friend Carlile says."

"But how can any one tell," rejoined Barnard, "that there is not such a place?"

"I'll tell you, Mr. Barnard," said Captain Creed; "because, upon my principle, it is the height of nonsense and injustice. Half an hour's roasting would be, I should think, punishment enough for the greatest criminal that ever yet existed—even for the scoundrel who was hanged this morning : but roasting eternally is rather too much of a good joke."

"Yes," said Smith, singing; "by the powers! it is rather too bad."

"Besides," resumed Creed, "before you can prove a hell, you must prove that there is an existence of any kind after death."

"And don't you believe that there is?" said Barnard; "don't you believe that the soul lives after the body?"

"Indeed I do not, Mr. Barnard," replied Creed; "and allow me to ask you in return, What is the soul? did you ever see your soul? It would be a fine thing, as Voltaire says, if we could see our soul."

"No," said Barnard; "I have not seen it, but we are told that there is such a thing."

"So we may be told," said Creed, "that the moon is made of green cheese. The soul! a mere phantom! What is the soul? if it be anything, it is the thinking power within us. And permit me to ask, Mr. Barnard, in what state that power, or soul, is with you, when you are drunk? when you are dead asleep? when you are very ill?— Does it not depend altogether upon the state of your body?—Can you write a letter as well after a hearty dinner and a bottle of wine, as when you are cool, collected, and fasting?—Don't tell me about a soul that can do nothing without the body, or in spite of the body. If its actions are impeded by the slightest ailment of that body, is it reasonable to believe that it can act at all when that body is destroyed?"

"But I recollect," replied Barnard, "to have heard our parson say, that all you have now mentioned only proves that the soul and body are united here; that in the present state the soul cannot do without the body; but that hereafter it will be able to do without it."

"My dear sir," said Creed, "what proof is there of this? Not one. Before we can believe that the soul can act without the body, we should have some proofs of its capacity to do so. But we never see any such thing; therefore we have no reason to believe it. Until I see one instance of the mind (which is the soul) acting without the body, I will never believe that it can do so. But the fact is, that the soul, or mind, is nothing but the brain; on the state of which, and the general state of the body, the thinking power depends."

Barnard remained silent, and seemed puzzled and confounded. He was incapable of replying to the sophistries of Creed, and was, besides, but too well disposed to receive them. The Captain resumed—

"You should read on these subjects, Mr. Barnard, and enlighten your mind."

"Yes," cried Smith; "read Paine's ' Age of Reason,'—that's the book for you."

"Paine is very good," said Creed, " for exposing the humbug of the Bible,—he demolishes that in prime style—therefore you should read him;—but Paine had his weaknesses. He was inclined to believe in the immortality of the soul. In this respect, indeed, he was more absurd than the parsons. He would only allow himself, and a few other clever fellows, to have immortal souls, while the rest were to be annihilated. But if you want to come at true philosophy, Mr. Barnard, read Mirabaud's 'System of Nature,' and Palmer's 'Principles of Nature;' those will soon set your mind at rest on the subjects of Hell and God Almighty."

"Ay," said Beauty, "and read Carlile's little book, called, 'WHAT IS GOD?' If you bother yourself about such nonsense ever after, I'll forfeit my head for a halfpenny."

Barnard followed the advice of his two friends, and soon became deeply versed in all the mysteries of infidelity. He sucked in the poison with the utmost avidity, and it produced its intended effect, for his mind was a proper recipient for it. His new doctrines accorded completely with his mode of life: he congratulated himself on his escape from hell fire, and wondered at his former besotted credulity. His mind became, now, fully prepared for the commission of every excess—for the violation of every principle—for the perpetration of every atrocity. The fear of hell being removed, but one check remained— the fear of the gallows,—a fear which has too often been found insufficient to keep men virtuous.

Barnard, not finding that any advantageous mode of employing his capital occurred, allowed it to slumber, as he thought securely, in the hands of Xiutototle and Co. The £100, in addition to some moderate winnings at gaming, kept him in funds for some little time longer. But his and Hannah's expensive style of living soon reduced his exchequer to the last farthing. This, however, gave him no uneasiness, as he calculated so securely on the deposit in the City.

It may not be amiss to remark here, that the style in which Barnard lived was far more expensive, comparatively speaking, than that of persons who make a much superior figure in life. Men who *muddle* away (to use a vulgar but expressive phrase) money in taverns and public places in pursuit of pleasure, do often spend a greater numerical sum in the year, than gentlemen who keep regular establishments, and even an equipage. The money goes, they cannot tell how; —they have nothing to show for it, and are perfectly astonished themselves, when they find it all expended. The fact is, that they pay for everything twice, or three times, as much as anybody else : they utterly disregard the old proverb —"Take care of the pence, and the pounds will take care of themselves ;" and when they have lavished their all, they find that they have purchased nothing but fatigue, dissatisfaction, and disappointment.

Barnard, now completely short of cash, resolves to draw on his friend, Xiutototle, for a few hundreds. He communicates his intention to Hannah, who regrets the necessity of "*breaking bulk*," but, of course, is forced to accede to it. Away he posts to the City, in the full confidence of receiving the cash : he goes to "Three King Court,"—hope elevating, and joy brightening, his crest. The first thing that excites a shadow of misgiving, is his not observing the names of Xiutototle and Killganders on the landing-place, where they formerly cut so conspicuous a figure. This, however, makes no very deep impression on him: he proceeds up stairs to their office on the first floor. From there, wonderful to relate, the names had also disappeared: the doors, too, were fastened up, and not a trace of a human being, or a vestige of any notice of the worthy merchants, to be found!

Barnard, to use the expression of old Moses Thick, of the "Salisbury Arms," was "struck all of a heap." He thought at first he must have been mistaken in the office, and galloped up and down stairs three times in a vain search for the names of Xiutototle and Killganders. He went into some neighbouring sets of chambers with no better effect; nor could he see any one of whom to make inquiries.

On coming down into the court, he observed a fellow sitting at a sort of stall, with the implements of shoe-blacking before him.—Barnard addressed him.

"Friend," said he, "can you tell me what is become of Xiutototle and Killganders?"

"Who, your worship?" cried the fellow, opening a mouth from ear to ear, and shutting one eye.

"Xiutototle and Killganders," replied Barnard; "the great merchants who lived here."

"Ah! your worship," resumed the shoeblack,

displaying a glorious set of rotten teeth in a
most inimitable grin; "it won't do—I'm not to
 done, your worship."

"Done! you rascal; what do you mean? I ask
you if you know anything about Don Josiah
Xiutototle, the great Mexican merchant, whose
counting-house was here?"

"Hah! hah! hah! your worship's merry," said
the Huntite, applying the thumb-nail of his open
hand to his nose; "but it won't do: it a'n't the
first of April;—I'm not to be had."

"Impudent scoundrel!" cried Barnard, "are
you laughing at me?—I'll teach you to laugh the
wrong side of your mouth."

He had just raised his stick, which was about
to descend on the bald pate of the unfortunate
shoeblack, when his attention was arrested by a
figure at the end of the court, which he thought
he knew. On approaching, he recognized to be
that of one of the ragged clerks of the evaporated
firm, whom he had heard addressed by the appel-
lative of Eugene. He came up and spoke to him.

"Your name, I think, is Eugene;—do you
recollect me?"

"Oh ees, saar, recollect vel,—Monsieur Barnard, I tink?"

"Yes;—what is become of Don Josiah, and
Mr. Killganders?"

"Dom Josiah!—hah! hah!—you do not know
den?"

"No; but I want to know."

" Den I vil tel you ;—by gar, me do not know vat dey become. Mais ècoutez—dey are gone off!"

" Gone off!" exclaimed Barnard ; " but where?"

" Dis is dạt vich I can no say ; dey hire us—autre garçon, you see, and moi. We come one morning, find all shet—big fellow outside vid paint-pot, painting de name all over: we ask him vat for he do dat, and where be our master ?—he bid us go to de deble, and swear, if we do not, he vil throw his paint-pot over us ;—we go, and never hear more of Dom Josiah, or Monsieur Kill-de-gander."

" And have you no idea where they are gone?" said Barnard.

" Oh si," rejoined honest Eugene ; " I suppose de Dom Josiah be gone back to Mexico, and Mr. Kill-de-gander to de deble."

" This is a pretty business!" said Barnard ; " my seventeen hundred pounds are gone too."

" Ees, saar," said Eugene, " dey take off all de money. Mr. Kill-de-gander did say, you be mush soorpreeze ven you come to draw your money :—ha! ha! by gar, saar, he vas right—you much soorpreeze, sans doute."

" Confound the swindlers !" said Barnard, walking off in no very pleasant temper.

His reflectioṇs were of the most distressing character, as he walked along,—he had not the least idea what he could do. He cursed the *foolish* advice of Smith and Creed ; and he cursed his own folly in pursuing it. How should he manage with his father?—how should he manage with himself and Hannah?—he was thoroughly vexed and bewildered.

In this mood, he turned into a tavern to try the effect of a glass of brandy. The first person he saw sitting there, in a box by himself, when he entered, was Don Josiah Xiutototle!—not, however, as the Mexican merchant, in masquerade; but in his natural character, plainly dressed in black, as the one-eyed gentleman, or rascal, for in his case the terms were synonymous.

He professed the greatest degree of pleasure and surprise at the sight of his good friend, Mr. Barnard, whom he had not had the pleasure of meeting for so long a time; inquired affectionately after the health of Mr. Smith and Captain Creed, and insisted on having the honour of treating Mr. Barnard to a glass of brandy and water.

"People may talk as they like, Mr. Barnard," said he, "about drinking before dinner; but drink, sir, with moderation, is good at all times— the hour makes no difference; and men, fatigued by application or perplexed with care, require refreshment at all times."

"The last is my case," replied Barnard; "I never was so perplexed and annoyed in the course of my life, as I am just now."

"Pray what is the cause of your annoyance, Mr. Barnard, if I may be bold enough to ask?"

"I have lost seventeen hundred pounds," said Barnard.

"My God, sir! at the old work, eh!—the cards. Do, sir, let me caution you against card-playing; I have not touched a card since I last played with you, and then I was, in fact, inadvertently *seduced* to play."

"No!" replied Barnard; "I did not lose the money at cards,—that would have been some consolation to me; I should have considered that only as the fortune of war: but I was robbed, sir, —robbed infamously of my money."

"Dear me! then you were out late in the neighbourhood of Hounslow Heath—or Bethnal Green, peradventure; or perhaps you were drunk, Mr. Barnard, and went from the Finish to Mrs. Mendoza's,—dangerous place for young men with money."

"No such thing!" roared Barnard; "I was robbed, sir,—robbed by worthy merchants in the City."

"Nay, now, Mr. Barnard, you're facetious— you are trying how far I can be hoaxed. Well, well! I can take a joke as well as another. Robbed by worthy merchants!—hah! hah! hah! —that's a good one."

"I tell you, sir," said Barnard, "I was never less inclined to joke in my life: I entrusted seventeen hundred pounds with merchants in the City; and this morning, on going to draw a few hundreds, I found their counting-house shut up, and themselves gone, God knows where."

" Oh ! my dear sir, I beg your pardon," cried the one-eyed hypocrite. " I am truly, sincerely sorry.—Alas ! sir, there are many ticklish characters in the mercantile world. No knowing whom to trust, sir, now-a-days. No man knows that better than myself.—But, sir, who were these merchants ?"

" The firm of Xiutototle and Killganders," replied Barnard, and then gave a minute detail of the whole business. When he had concluded, the other with the utmost gravity observed,

" Ah ! sir, how unfortunate it was that you did not meet me before you lodged your money with these swindlers. I am acquainted with everything in the mercantile world, and could have directed you where you might have lodged your money safely. I am myself chief conducting clerk to the house of ' Buckles, Bagster, and Buchanan,' and I have the first commercial information of every kind. There would have been some chance for you, if you had fallen into any other hands : but, sir, you have fallen into most infamous hands. I know this Xiutototle well— a greater rascal does not exist, *between you and me*. He owed our firm £500, which is gone for ever."

" Then you think," said Barnard, " I have no chance of recovering the money ?"

" Not the slightest," replied Polyphemus : " I wish with all my heart I could give you some hopes ; for I sympathize most sincerely with your misfortune. But I know the fellow too well, and his blessed partner, Mr. Killganders. Take my word for it, sir, you'll never get a rap."

"Then their acknowledgment is of no use," said Barnard.

"Not worth a button!—They have left the kingdom; and, besides, they had not a fraction of property."

"But how did they contrive to deceive people ?" said Barnard.

"I'll tell you," replied he of the single optic. "In commercial life there are great opportunities for cheating. I know the history of this firm well. They entered into business, pretending to be Mexican merchants of great wealth. They opened an account at a respectable banking house, by way of reference. They then drove a famous trade in bills, so contriving it that all the bills should become due at once. They began, for instance, by accepting bills at twelve months, then nine, and so on, shortening the time until within a month of the expiration of the year. Now the bills being all due, the worthy merchants have decamped."

"Then, indeed," said Barnard, "there is no chance."

"I am sorry, Mr. Barnard," said he, rising and shaking him most cordially by the hand; "very sorry for you indeed. But I cannot give you any hopes. Your money, sir, is gone! lost to you as certainly as if you had thrown it into the river. I am very sorry for you, but you may rest assured you will never see one farthing of the money. Good morning, Mr. Barnard, good morning!--I am truly sorry for you."

The one-eyed gentleman made his exit, leaving, by some unaccountable lapse of memory, his friend Barnard to pay the piper.

Barnard now proceeded home with a heavy heart and light purse, where, on his arrival, further consolation and sympathy awaited him. He told the case to Hannah, who of course affected to be overwhelmed with grief and astonishment. He consulted her on what he could possibly do,— and she told him that he had better advise again with Smith, who perhaps could assist him, or, at all events, point out some plan to retrieve his finances. "See him, my love," said Hannah; "hear what he has to say, and let me know. Among us all, it is hard if we cannot contrive something."

Barnard approved of this counsel, and, in pursuance of it, called on Beauty, whom he found alone."

"Well, Smith, this is a very pretty affair," began Barnard; "and I have to thank your advice for it."

"What's the matter?" said Smith.

"Nothing," said Barnard, "but that Xiutototle is gone off, and my money is gone along with him."

"Is it possible?" exclaimed Beauty, with a look of deep sympathy.

"It is too true," replied the other, and told him all we have described.

"What a shame!" cried Smith; "who'd have thought it?—men so well recommended, and apparently so wealthy! You, however, are not the only sufferer,—Jackson has lost at least £2000 by them."

"How could you have given me such advice, Jack?" resumed Barnard.

"My dear fellow," said Beauty, "am I a prophet, that I could foresee what has come to pass?—am I a conjuror, to dive into men's thoughts? They have deceived multitudes as well as you: Jackson has lost his property. I was weak enough to take a bill of theirs myself, ten days ago, for £100: it has thirty days to run yet, and I must pay it or be arrested, for I have passed it away."

"Well, Jack, I don't know what to do; I have no money—my father has been writing about the payment for the cattle;—in short, I am perplexed and harassed excessively."

"Take courage, man," cried Jack; "faint heart never won fair lady: difficulties are the element of the ingenious. For my part, I love dearly to be in hot water:—we'll soon strike out something."

"Can you assist me, Jack, with a little cash?"

"My dear Barnard," said Smith, "my purse

is at your service; but, unfortunately, it is very light just now. Its amount is ten pounds, which I will most willingly share with you; but that won't help you far: you want a good round sum."

"How shall I get it?" said Barnard.

"Before I tell you," replied Smith, "allow me to put a question or two to you."

"Certainly," replied Barnard.

"You know," resumed Smith, with vast gravity of manner, "the pains *we* have taken to enlighten your mind on all subjects of importance. We (I mean Creed and myself) have introduced you into real life; we have given you proper rules for your conduct; we have tried to beat out of your head all those nonsensical ideas about honesty, &c., which you brought with you from the country; and, above all, we have endeavoured to root out of your mind that useless of all things, religion. Have we succeeded, William Barnard?"

"To be sure you have," replied Barnard.

"You are certain that you have lost all respect for that common honesty, which, as a great author (published by Carlile) well observes, is one of the surest non-conductors of the best feelings of the human heart?"

"No doubt about it," replied the catechumen.

"Moreover, you are quite rid of your superstitious notions, and have no fear of Heaven or Hell?"

"I regard them as mere phantoms," said Barnard; "in my last conversation with Carlile, he settled their hash."

"'Tis well," said Smith; "now hear me:— you want money,—you can't get on without a good sum. There are but two ways of raising it at present;—by chousing your father, or committing a robbery. Now, I never recommend the latter, except in a case of absolute necessity."

"I suppose not," said Barnard, laughing; "but, seriously, how do you recommend me to go to work?"

"You can raise no money from your father, until you have settled for the cattle: you must pay for them first, before you can draw any more blood from the old boy."

"Nay, Jack," cried Barnard, "this is ill-timed jesting. You know I have not a farthing, and you talk of my paying for the cattle."

"I am quite serious," replied Smith; "you shall pay for the cattle, and yet it shall not be a farthing out of your pocket."

"Explain yourself," said Barnard.

"Don Josiah Xiutototle has swindled you out of your money, I think?"

"Too true: but what of that?"

"He has literally robbed you of seventeen hundred pounds?"

"He has, he has," cried Barnard, impatiently.

"The worst of it was, too," continued the imperturbable Smith, "that it was all in hard cash."

"It was, it was; but what of that, in God's name?"

"Had it been goods," proceeded the inveterate tormentor, "there might have been some consolation; for the goods, you know, might have been damaged, and not worth the entire money."

"That's true," said Barnard; "but I don't see ——"

"Or if you had only given your bill for the money, there would have been a good chance, as you might have shirked payment."

"What are you driving at, Smith?" cried Barnard, most impatiently.

"Be easy," said Beauty, "and hear me. I don't mention Xiutototle for the purpose of reminding you of your misfortunes, but that you may be able to extract some good out of the evil that has befallen you. The wisest of us may be taken in, but it is only the fool that cannot profit by experience. You have got an acknowledgment for your money from this Xiutototle?"

"I have," answered the other; "but I have been told it is not worth a button."

"You were told rightly: in a commercial point of view it is worth nothing; but it will go hard if we cannot make it worth something to us. Have you got it about you?"

"Yes," said Barnard, "here it is."

"The very thing," said Smith; "now you shall see what it is to be a man of genius: we will make Mr. Xiutototle reimburse part of your

money.   Write immediately to your father.
Apologize for not having written before, on the
score of having been extremely busy, and also
having wished to give him an agreeable surprise.
State that you sold the cattle for £350, which was
the fact—that you were about to remit him the
money, when you met a person from America,
who proved to you that by investing it in the
purchase of both corn and cattle, to sell again for
exportation, you might make a good profit—that
you did so, and realized a few hundreds—that
this encouraged you to proceed—and, in short,
that you entered regularly into the corn and cattle
trade, made the sum of eighteen hundred pounds,
seventeen hundred of which you lodged for
security with Xiutototle and Killganders (who
are better than the Bank), and that you now send
their acknowledgment to him, thinking it will be
more safe in his hands than yours; and also that
he may have the satisfaction of being assured that
you have not misspent his money."

"This is very well," said Barnard; "but I don't
see how this is to induce my father to send me
any money: on the contrary, he won't think
that I want money; or, if I did, I might take it
from the deposit."

"You are dull, William,—'duller than the fat
weed that rots itself with ease on Lethe's wharf.'
We don't want your father to send money,—we
want him to send money's worth. Add a post-
script to your letter, that an opportunity has just

offered of disposing of horses to great advantage:
he has no use for his four hunters—he never
hunts;—let him send them up to you. Tell him
another cock and bull story about grain and hay;
—let him send you as much as he can. We'll
raise the wind again, and trust to Providence and
Don Josiah to discharge our debts,—the only
thing I would trust to them for."

"I will do it immediately," exclaimed Barnard.

"Do so," said Smith; "and now you will
have no occasion to make excuses to your father
for your stay in London. Business, you know,
must be attended to."

Barnard wrote a long letter to his father, the
substance of which we have already given; and
the style underwent revision from the critical
hand of Beauty. It was dispatched, and a few
days after it brought back the most favourable
answer from the old man, who was quite over-
joyed with his son's success, and highly pleased at
his address in business, thriftiness, and prudence.

The hunters, hay, and corn, "followed hard
upon." They quickly travelled the road that
the cattle had pursued before, and fetched altogether the sum of £520.

This money Barnard was fully determined not
to entrust to the keeping of any worthy merchant,
nor did Smith use any of his persuasive powers to
that effect at present;—on the contrary, he
advised him this time to give the money into the

keeping of Hannah ; with which advice Barnard, without delay, complied.

Hannah, we should have mentioned before, had given her full approbation to the mode suggested by Beauty for raising the cash.

It is, perhaps, almost superfluous to inform the reader, that the seventeen hundred pounds, lodged with the worthy Mexican, had been equally divided among the depredators; and that the present sum of £520 shared the same fate.

Barnard was now very rapidly approaching to the gulph of irretrievable perdition. His passions had received the full rein, his principles had been utterly destroyed, and nothing was wanting but further embarrassments, and the impossibility of drawing any more from his father in any way, to lead him to the consummation of any crime. He was approximating to the devil with a velocity, the ratio of which increased in proportion to the diminution of the distance; and something soon occurred which lent an additional impulse to his hellward career.

A week had passed on right jollily, in feasting, drinking, frolic, and debauchery, when, one morning, two men knocked at the door where Barnard lived, inquired for Mrs. Woods, walked up stairs, and arrested her without ceremony for the sum of £800. They took her off directly to a spunging-house.

Barnard was not within at the time this occurred, but returned home very soon. He found the servant-maid in the greatest grief and confusion imaginable. She told him the piteous tale, with all that embellishment of style and pathos with which the fair sex so well understand how to give effect to their stories of disaster.

Barnard was thoroughly confounded: he asked the maid if she knew where her mistress had been taken to. She answered, that she had heard one of the men say that they would take her to No. 19, Chancery Lane, until the business was settled.

Barnard posted off immediately to this address. Inquiring for Mrs. Woods, he was shown into a room, where he found her sitting at a table, her head leaning on her hand, and deep dejection painted on her countenance. She rose suddenly on his entrance, rushed into his embrace, and burst into a flood of tears.

"Oh, William!" said she, "I am truly unfortunate."

"My dear Hannah," cried Barnard, "explain this business. How comes it that you have been arrested?"

"I will tell you," said she, "in a few words. My late husband was a very extravagant and improvident man: he got considerably into debt with his agent here. After his death, I got a small yearly pension, and continuing to employ the same agent, I was foolish enough to become responsible for my husband's debt, and signed a bond accordingly. The agent agreed to take so

much every year, by instalments, until the debt
was paid. Unfortunately, he has become a
bankrupt, and the persons who now manage the
estate have resolved to arrest every one who
was in debt to it. The portion of my late
husband's debt remaining unpaid, and some little
money that necessity obliged me to overdraw,
have raised their claim on me to £800, for which
I have been arrested this morning, and I have no
means whatever of paying."

"But," said Barnard, "perhaps the parties can
be brought to some terms."

"I fear not," said Hannah; "there is one particular person who directs all these proceedings,
and with him I know there is no chance: he is
the most inflexible and unfeeling of rogues."

"Who is he?" asked Barnard.

"His name is Whitehead," replied Hannah;
"he is what is termed a public accountant,—that
is, a fellow whose business it is to make up the
accounts of bankrupts in such a manner, that the
quantity of money owing to them shall be
increased, and the quantity that they owe decreased,—thus enabling them to come better out
of the hands of the Commissioners. Now this
fellow, moreover, has a strong dislike to me; for
you must know that, after my husband's death,
he thought proper to make love to me. I treated
him with contempt, and now he takes this mode
of being revenged upon me."

"What a scoundrel!" said Barnard; "but

perhaps he'll take half the money, and *our* security for the rest."

"I'll try him," said Hannah; "but I have no great hopes of success;—I'll send for him to come here."

"Do so, my love," rejoined Barnard, "and meanwhile I'll go and look for Smith and consult with him. He's a clever fellow, and may be able to set us all to rights again."

Barnard then set off for Beauty's lodgings, but on his arrival there was told that Mr. Smith had just gone out. Greatly disappointed, he posted off to the residence of Creed, where he was equally unsuccessful—the noble Captain had also sallied forth for a promenade. He then employed more than two hours in a fruitless search for them in all their usual daily haunts. He returned, fatigued and rather vexed, to Hannah. Her countenance seemed inflamed with anger, and her eyes looked red, as if from weeping.

"Have you seen him, Hannah?" said Barnard.

"Yes," she replied; "the wretch has been here."

"And will he come to no terms?" rejoined the young man.

"None," said Hannah, "but such as I would die ten times over sooner than submit to."

"What are they?" asked Barnard.

"Oh! my dear William, I cannot tell you."

"Nay, but," said Barnard, "let me hear; perhaps something may be done."

"You shall judge then," replied she. "I offered him half the debt, and security for the remainder. And what do you think was the answer of the villain?"

"I cannot guess," said Barnard.

"He said he had no objection to accede to the terms, provided I would yield myself into the bargain."

"I'll cut his throat!" exclaimed Barnard, in a paroxysm of rage.

"My love," replied Hannah, "how can you be so violent?"

"Violent!" cried Barnard; "methinks I am very mild;—curse the rascal, I could stab him in the dark. I could trample him into paste," repeated he, stamping desperately on the floor.

Barnard's naturally unprepossessing countenance assumed, on this occasion, an expression that alarmed even Hannah. His face became pallid and convulsed—his cold blue eye was fixed in stern regard, and there was something fiendish in his whole aspect.

"My love!" said she, approaching him, "don't be thus agitated. This is an unfortunate affair—I must only go to prison."

"Never!" cried Barnard: "I will sacrifice everything—I will do anything first."

"You have already sacrificed too much for me, William, you shall sacrifice no more."

"But I will though: I'll sacrifice my father, my whole family, and myself. You shall never go to prison—still less —— oh! curse the villain!"

"Nay, my dear William, no more of that," said Hannah.

"Well, Hannah, the scoundrel must be paid, and shall be, even if I were to die for it. I have not been able to see Smith,—I must go look for him again. Farewell, my love; you shall not see me until I bring your deliverance."

So saying, he departed. He had not gone many yards, when he met the very man whom he wanted most particularly to see, viz. Mr. Beauty Smith.

"Smith," said Barnard, "I have been looking for you the whole day."

"I heard," answered Beauty, "that you were at my lodgings; but what's the matter, man? you're looking like a ghost."

Barnard took him by the arm, and explained the whole business. He concluded by pressing him earnestly for his advice and assistance.

"William," said Beauty, "this is an awkward affair; but we cannot discuss it in the street. Come into Jack Randall's, and we'll excogitate the matter over a glass of ale. In knotty points I find ale useful."

"Come along, then," said Barnard.

They entered the mansion of honest Jack, (now, alas! no more—the unsuspecting victim of genuine Deady), and got into a little room by themselves. The ale being brought, Beauty took a deep draught, and then opened his mouth, which to Barnard was like the oracle of Delphos.

"William," said he, "this woman is a source to you of great expense; it has often struck me that you'd be better off if you got rid of her altogether. A good opportunity now offers. You can't pay this debt of £800, and therefore you may as well cut the connexion."

"What!" said Barnard, "and let her go to prison? You can't be serious."

"Let me tell you," resumed Smith, "that people live better in prison than you think, especially the ladies;—King's Bench no bad place for them. But as for prison, I don't think she need fear it. I am of opinion that that gallant gentleman, Whitehead, would not allow her to go to prison. If you were to quit Hannah, they'd soon make up matters, you may depend upon it; therefore, my advice to you is, to bother yourself no more about the affair."

"Mr. Smith," said Barnard, "if you have no better advice than this to offer, you might as well have held your tongue. I'd have you to know, that I will never desert Hannah: I love her better than the whole world; and if I cannot keep her out of prison, I will go there and live with her myself. And as for the scoundrel whom you just mentioned, I'd tear him piecemeal with pleasure."

"Oh! ho!" cried Beauty, "I did not think you were so far gone. As Colonel Oldboy says,

'When love gets into the youthful brain,
Instruction is needless, and caution vain.'

But really, my dear fellow, I beg your pardon. I was not serious—I only meant to try you: Hannah is a most admirable woman, and well merits all your affection. But, upon my soul, this *is* a ticklish case."

" Can you suggest nothing ?" said Barnard.

" Why, you see," replied Smith, "there is no use in writing to the old fellow now, and I don't think we can get any more out of Xiutototle."

"But," cried Barnard, "you must know of other ways of raising the wind."

" I do, William ; but I am afraid they require more strength of mind than you possess."

" Why should you doubt me ?" said Barnard.

" You are quite sure, then, that you have got rid of all your moral and religious scruples ?—are you quite sure that there is no more of the yellow clay sticking to you ?"

" Where's the use of all this catechizing ?" replied Barnard. " You talked, sometime ago, of a robbery in case of necessity—if it be necessary now ——"

" Stop !" cried Smith, " I am satisfied : you seem to be up to trap. Now hear me ;—a robbery is not necessary at present—I mean a direct robbery—nothing in the way of burglary or arson : but there is some money to be made in the bill line,—you understand me."

" I can't say I do exactly," answered the other.

" Then I must speak plainly :—if I had a good bill I could get it cashed; —your father's, for instance."

" But my father would not accept," said Barnard.

" But can't you accept for him ?" said Smith; "where's the mighty trouble of writing your father's name across a stamp ?"

" But that's forgery !" exclaimed Barnard.

" Forgery—nonsense !" cried Smith; " just now you would not stickle at a robbery, and yet you prate of forgery. Forgery, indeed ! do you think your father would hang you ? I tell you, Barnard—I tell you, you must do this, or abandon Hannah to your friend Whitehead."

" Enough," said Barnard; " it is done."

" But," resumed Smith, " we want a thousand pounds, at least : this is too large a sum to draw on your father alone for ;—we could not so easily negociate the bill. Has your father no friend whose name you think you might use with safety?"

Barnard paused a while, and replied, " Yes; there is Mr. Roper, the banker of Chelmsford,—he is a friend of my father."

" He'll do," said Smith; " and now come home to my lodging, and we'll draw the bills."

They went accordingly, and drew two bills, one on old Barnard for £460, the other on the banker for £540 ; and, by an ingenious turn of humour, suggested by Smith, they made the banker the drawer on old Barnard, and old Barnard the drawer on the banker.

"Now," said Smith, "how are we to get these bills cashed?"

"Why," replied Barnard, "I thought you could do that."

"Why, so I can," said Smith; "but the person who would do them for me is out of town, and you must wait three days for his return: that's a long time, you know, for poor Hannah to be immured in that horrible spunging house. Don't you know any one who would do them immediately?"

"Yes," said Barnard, "I know two salesmen who, I think, would cash the bills, as they know me and know the parties."

"Let us be off to them directly," said Smith.

Not to tire the reader by minuter details, Barnard succeeded in getting the bills cashed. He returned in high spirits to Hannah, got from her the address of Mr. Whitehead, and went there with Smith to pay the debt.

They found that gentleman, after some difficulty, in a small obscure court in [the neighbourhood of Fetter Lane. Having clambered up a narrow staircase in a shabby looking house, they knocked at a door on the second floor, to which they had been directed, and a gruff voice cried out, "Come in."

The room was small and dark; and, seated

at a table covered with papers, they saw apparently a very old man, with a profusion of white hair as coarse as a goat's beard, goggles on his eyes, and a large loose dressing gown of grey cloth upon his body. When Barnard saw him, he recollected his own jealousy, and could scarcely refrain from laughing aloud.

" A pretty rival!" whispered Smith to him. " We have come," continued he, aloud, " Mr. Whitehead, to pay the debt for which you have arrested Mrs. Woods."

" 'Tis well," grumbled Whitehead, in a voice of extraordinary harshness; " I'll take the money, and write a receipt."

Smith then handed over the money, which Whitehead reckoned with great care and deliberation, and then wrote a receipt.

" Now," said he, " gentlemen, here is my bill of costs, for I am an attorney as well as an accountant, and conduct my own actions;—the amount is £15 7s. 6d., which, if you will please to pay, I will write an order for the discharge of the prisoner."

There was no help for this, and Barnard, who knew no better, paid this shameful bill, and received the order

" Now," said Smith, " Mr. Pendinger, let me give you a parting word of advice :—confine your attentions for the future to your parchments, and do not meddle with the ladies. Believe me, you are much better adapted to make an impression on green wax, than on the soft heart of woman."

" Let me recommend you, young man," rejoined Whitehead, " to mind your own business."

" Sir !" said Barnard, getting enraged ; " your conduct ——"

" Stop," said Smith, putting his hand on his companion's mouth ; " recollect that you are in the house of an attorney : he'll have an action of assault and battery against you before you can say trap-sticks.—Come along."

And who, gentle reader, do you imagine was Mr. Whitehead, public accountant and *soi-disant* attorney ?—Why, no one else but that accomplished actor who so successfully had personated Don Josiah Xiutototle, viz.—the one-eyed gentleman.

Barnard and Smith now repaired to the spunging-house, and conducted Hannah home in triumph ; not, however, without first discharging one of those very moderate bills usually consequent on a short residence in any of those hotels of cheap and temporary accommodation.

It was late in the evening when they arrived, and Barnard ordered in a splendid supper from the nearest tavern, and plenty of champagne. Captain Creed was of course sent for to partake in the general rejoicing. He and Smith were loud in their encomiums of Barnard's generous and noble conduct ; and as for Hannah, her gratitude and pathos were inexpressible. She gave Barnard many a fatal, languishing, side-long look of love, while the champagne went briskly round, and Smith and Creed, with no mean taste and execution, were singing the duet of " Drink to me only." Barnard drank deeply both of champagne and love, and was as happy as Alexander when the lovely Thais sat beside him ; and though it would be profane to compare Captain Creed with Timotheus, yet, as he sung " Is there a heart that never loved ?" his influence over the enamoured youth was not less complete than that of the mighty master of the lyre over the unconquered hero of Macedon.

And, after all, if we could forget the means by which such moments of pleasure are procured, we would pronounce them worth all the rest of existence : compared with such a *present*, the past and the future are but tedious, lifeless blanks. We do not mean to justify the conduct of Barnard, but, perhaps, there are few of us that would not have sunk, for a time at least, in the delicious illusions in which he was immersed. Life is such a choice of evils, such a perpetual alternation between *ennui* and vexation, that to seize with avidity on the fleeting bliss which so rarely presents itself, is natural and excusable in man : but it is the stern decree of fate and nature, that such enjoyments must be purchased at the price of honour, and followed by the penalty of remorse. Man finds out, too late, that the pursuit of pleasure ends but in pain ; and that terrestrial happiness has not been the object of his existence. This reflection may escape him in the hey-day of youth, and the full tide of prosperity; but time, a monitor that must be heard, will not fail to inform him of the fatal truth. He whose prime of life is consumed in pleasure, must expect neither comfort nor respect in his latter years, and will descend to the grave without a name remaining amongst men.

CHAP. XVI.

"Still pleasure holds him in his headlong course
To danger blind, unshaken by remorse."

SHEPHERD.

IT is almost superfluous to state, that, in spite of the supplies so nefariously raised by William Barnard at the expense of his too credulous father, embarrassment succeeded embarrassment; and he was daily, hourly, plunged into fresh difficulties. To meet these, he could not again venture, for the present at least, on the means which had hitherto been attended with success. He was fearful of rousing at once the suspicions of the old man, of wearing him out by reiterated experiments, and of entirely cutting off all chance of any future resources from the same quarter.

The reader, on adverting to our description of this youth's career, as far as it has gone, will perceive that he commenced by being a perfect dupe. He was not, however, the dupe of the unsuspecting simplicity of a mind naturally ingenuous, but of his own ignorance and inexperience, united with headstrong passions, and a native propensity to vicious pleasures, but feebly counteracted by any moral sense, and uncorrected by education. He then became partly a dupe, and partly a rogue;—he deceived others, only to be himself deceived by his associates. To the latter he had now almost ceased to become a desirable object of prey; but his taste for vice, and aptitude for villany, began to render him an eligible co-partner. In short, he had now arrived at the conclusion indicated by the French proverb which we have once quoted, and finished by being a thorough "*fripon*."

Under the auspices of Beauty and the Captain, he now began to get a good insight into the arts of sharping and swindling. By these he contrived to keep, as the vulgar saying is, his head a little above water; but the sums he gained in this manner were altogether insufficient for his purposes. His cheating was of necessity upon too small a scale to minister to his own numerous and factitious wants, and still less to support the expensive profligacy of Hannah. Avarice, and an unbounded passion for luxury, were the predominant propensities of this dangerous woman. No Eastern sultana could be more insatiable in her thirst for splendour and voluptuous enjoyment: nothing would satisfy her but the most expensive dresses, the most exquisite viands, and the richest wines. Every day she appeared in some new costume—each more magnificent than the last. Her toilet might have rivalled, in expense and research, that of Agrippina or Cleopatra: it was spread with a profusion of cosmetic preparations, many of them the costly products of other climates. Expensive vases of cut glass, of porcelain, of silver, and even of gold, were there: cabinets of cedar and mahogany, tastefully inlaid, stood around. All the furniture was of the most elegant description, and the atmosphere of the chamber itself was redolent of perfumes.

But though Hannah delighted in all these luxuries, yet such was her avarice, that she would expend upon them as little as possible out of her own private purse: she preferred, as long as she could do it, making her paramour provide for wants of this kind. Nor must the reader, for a moment, imagine that her fidelity to Barnard was such as to prevent her raising contributions from occasional admirers. Quite the reverse,— she was almost every night at theatres and other public places, where she made many a private and profitable assignation. The rich and the old of our sex were the chief objects of her attention; and while she had the art to manage her intrigues, without exciting the suspicion of Barnard, he proved a most convenient cloak for her character in the deceptions she was practising on other men.

Hannah was utterly incapable of the sentiment of love. For Barnard she cared nothing, or for

any other man with whom mercenary motives led
her to cultivate an acquaintance : but she inherited the tropical constitution of her mother,
and that large portion of the animal which invariably accompanies the slightest infusion of
Ethiopian blood.   In sensual passion she was
scarcely inferior to Messalina herself : she, therefore, was not without her secret favourites, whose
herculean proportions constituted a more powerful
recommendation, than the elegance of their persons,
minds, or manners.

Meanwhile, Barnard dreamed of nothing of the
kind, but thought she was as exclusively his, as he
was hers.   The influence which she possessed
over him increased daily, and his appetite seemed
to grow by what it fed on.   He was under the
fascination of a basilisk's eye,

> "Beneath whose beauteous beams, belying heav'n,
> Lurk searchless cunning, cruelty and death ·
> And still false warbling in his cheated ear,
> Her siren-voice, enchanting, draws him on
> To guileful shores and meads of fatal joy."

Barnard, as an additional mode of recruiting
his finances, began to study military tactics,
under the auspices of that experienced officer,
Captain Creed, and made such rapid progress, that
his instructor appointed him to the command of
the Western division of the Scarafooka Rangers.
We may as well, at once, fully explain to our
readers the organization and constitution of this
celebrated corps, at whose existence we have

hitherto but obscurely hinted. The idea of its
institution was not altogether original with the
Captain, inasmuch as gangs and knots of thieves
and pickpockets have flourished from time im-
memorial : but it must be confessed that it received great improvement and developement from
his fertile genius. He began by organizing a
small band of depredators, all of them boys under
the age of fourteen : of these he constituted himself the captain and patron. To him the young
heroes brought all their boot which he, through
certain channels, soon disposed of,—paying his
troops a stipulated sum, and reserving to himself
a reasonable overplus. He kept these youths in
their allegiance, by holding the law over them
in terrorem : and they were prevented from ap-
propriating any thing of consequence out of their
plunder, by the difficulty of disposing of it ; for,
in consequence of an understanding with, the
Captain, none of the *regular dealers* would receive
anything from his troop, except through his own
hands, and the attempt to get rid of it elsewhere
would be attended with danger. In consequence
of this, though some trifling article might occasionally be secreted, everything of material
value was duly delivered into the Captain's
keeping.

The Scarafooka Rangers, at first few in
number, gradually increased under the energetic
and skilful exertions of their accomplished leader.
They, at last, became sufficiently numerous to be

formed into divisions, which were nominated from the quarter of the metropolis especially devoted to the peculiar operations of each. Each of these divisions was superintended by a lieutenant appointed by the Captain himself, and who was obliged to make regular weekly reports at head quarters. Barnard had now the honour of commanding the largest and best disciplined division of the Scarafookas, whose range of action extended from Temple Bar westward, as far as the House of Commons in one direction, and the end of Piccadilly in the other, including Covent Garden and the Haymarket.

Our new-made lieutenant was actively employed in his first campaign, the fatigues of which were agreeably alternated with the recreations of love and wine, when a visitor arrived in town, whose presence he least expected and least desired. This visitor was no more or less a personage than his own father. The fact was, that the old man had begun to suspect his son's rectitude: he was roused out of his long slumber of credulity very suddenly, and rather unpleasantly, by that most unceremonious of proceedings—an arrest. The reader may remember that previously to Barnard's coming to London, in his last conversation with Hannah in the country, he had presented her with a £20 note, which he took out of a sealed letter. This letter and its contents had been confided to him by his father, to deliver to a person to whom the money was due. This person, not receiving his debt at the expected time, and being a very great rogue, and in league with a still greater rogue, an attorney, into whose hands he was constantly playing, instead of applying for his money, had old Barnard arrested, that he might put costs into his friend's pocket. This, however, led to an *eclaircissement* which opened the father's eyes a little to the conduct and character of the son, and induced him to come up to London, that he might have a personal opportunity of inspecting into his proceedings.

When a person, naturally credulous, is once undeceived, the progress of his suspicions is generally very rapid. Old Barnard began now to think that it was not at all improbable that William had been carrying on a regular system of hoaxing since he left the country. Impressed with this idea, he determined, before he saw his son, to make inquiries relative to the firm of Xiutototle and Killganders. The success with which such inquiries were attended, the reader may well surmise : old Barnard could find no traces whatever of this respectable firm, at the address which was attached to his acknowledgment for £1700. On mentioning the business, however, to an acquaintance of his, a salesman, who had a very intimate knowledge of all City affairs, the latter put him in possession of the true state of the case—giving him the history of the rise, progress, decline, and evaporation, of Xiutototle and Killganders. He also stated the precise period of their disappearance, which, on comparing dates, was found to be exactly a fortnight prior to his son's transmission of their acknowledgment. Mr. Barnard's friend also put him in the way of finding out his son's address, by taking him to the porter of the " Blue Boar," at which house he knew the young spendthrift had set up. Half a crown, and the expense of a coach, soon opened the way to the address of the youth; whither arrived, he prepared to overwhelm him with reproaches, and give him what is called in the bowers of Academus a thorough *Jobation.*

When he arrived at the house, he knocked at the door, which was opened by a very spruce young lady, dressed in the very first style of London *waiting-maidishness:* he inquired for juvenile Barnard, and was shown up stairs. On his entrance, a scene presented itself well calculated to astonish the weak mind of the venerable clodhopper.

It was eight in the evening, and young Barnard was seated with Creed, Smith, Hannah, and the one-eyed gentleman, at a table which was covered with wine, fruit, and confectionary. The quintetto were engaged in deep carousing, and Barnard was in a pretty far advanced stage of intoxication. He was sitting next Hannah, with one arm round her neck, and the other holding a full bumper, and was singing, or rather roaring, with windpipe most dissonant, " Life let us cherish ;"

a volunteer solo : Smith, Creed, and their one-eyed friend, were amusing themselves by vying with each other to see who would make the most *expressive* grimaces, in which, though the exertions of the two former were highly praiseworthy, they were left at an immeasurable distance by him of the deficient optic. The distortions of this fellow's countenance were so ludicrously horrible, that they would almost have bid defiance to the art of caricature to represent. While the guests were thus employed, there was in the back ground, at a sideboard, a servant boy taking advantage of their abstraction, and guzzling down a bottle of wine with the most rapid desperation.

When old Barnard entered, he stood astounded at the scene before him. He was not, however, suffered to stand quietly very long; for, instantly on his entrance, two large and ferocious dogs, belonging to Creed, flew at him, and seizing him by the skirts of the coat, one on each side, held him fast, until summoned away by the voice of their surprised master. The party were not less astounded at old Barnard's appearance, than he was at the predicament in which he found them. Young Barnard came to a full stop in his obstreperous song; the three grimacers resumed their natural *perversion* of countenance; and the frighted boy, who had been guzzling down the wine, let the bottle fall in his amazement, which was dashed to pieces on the floor. For some time, none of them could find their tongues,—even

Hannah was confused and silent. At last young Barnard contrived to stammer out,

" My father !"

" Yes, William," said the old man, " it is your father—come in time to find you, as he expected, destroying his property in drunkenness, (looking at the wine), in lewdness, (casting a glance on Hannah), and in gaming, (fixing his eye on a little table in a corner, on which were three or four packs of cards and a dice box or two)."

" Why, father," replied Barnard, who was still a little sheepish, " where's the harm of a little amusement ?—I attend to business in the morning."

" You do," cried the sire; " you attend to the business of cheating and imposing on your poor old father."

" How ?" said Barnard.

" Thus, sirrah," replied the old man, "by putting into his hands securities like these, to induce him to part with his property—the acknowledgments of fraudulent and run-away bankrupts."

" I was myself deceived there," said the son.

" You were not, sir ;—you knew, at the time you sent me the acknowledgment, that the scoundrels were gone. Nay, sir, no further paltering—I have learned every tittle of the business since I came to town :—besides, sir, where is the twenty pounds I gave you in a letter to deliver to Biggs ?"

" He has it, I suppose," answered Barnard.

" He has," said the old man, " but not the

twenty pounds I trusted to you. Look here, sir, here is his receipt for the money,—here is the bill and receipt of the rascally attornev he employed to arrest me.'

Young Barnard was dumb-foundeᴅ, anᴅ could not reply. The father resumed,—

"You are right to be silent—you cannot defend yourself: the money you got by the cattle, the corn, and the horses, you need not speak about, —I see the road it has travelled, and I would not believe a word you could say. William! William! you have cruelly deceived me, and I shall never trust you again : but still, bad as you are, you are my son ; and if you return with me to the country, leave off your wickedness, and promise to live quietly for the time to come, I will receive you and support you : but I will entrust you with no more money while I live ; and when I die, I will leave you sufficient for your maintenance in he country, but no more."

William Barnard had, by this time, recovered from his confusion, and his natural frontless audacity returneᴅ, assisted by the wine that he had been drinking. He saw, after what had passed, that he had no chance of duping his father any more. The kind of life that the latter had proposed to him was by no means to his taste: he was too deadly immersed in vice and crime, too much the abject slave of passion and ʰad habits, to dream of returning to anything like a virtuous path. In short, he was become a thorough reprobate, and now, flinging off all disguise, as he found there would be no further use for it, he answered in his true character.

"Old gentleman," said he, looking at his father with matchless impudence of face, and then filling a bumper of wine, "I have the pleasure of drinking your very good health. I am very much obliged to you for your kind offer; but, I thank you, I have no taste for a country life;—I'll stay here, if you please."

"Stay here!" exclaimed his father; "and how will you support yourself?"

"Oh! don't trouble yourself about that, my good sir," said the dutiful youth; "I shall get on very well."

"Ungrateful boy! is this the return you make for all my kindness? Alas! I have been far too indulgent a father to you. You are bent, I see, on a life of wickedness, which will end in misery, and you will repent when it is too late."

"Well," said Barnard, "you may talk as you please, I shall live as I please. I am too old to be lectured, and I shall do just as I like; so I advise you to return to the country, and not to bother yourself any more about me;—every one is the best judge of his own business."

"Very good advice," cried Beauty, who, with the rest, had been hitherto silent; "and I recommend you to follow it, old gentleman."

"Hah, sir!" replied old Barnard, "is that you?

I have heard of you also; your character is not quite unknown to me : you have been the means of corrupting and seducing my son."

" I advise you, my old buck," said Smith, "to keep a civil tongue in your head;—you will get no good by brawling here, I can tell you."

" I have nothing further to say to you, sir," rejoined the old man; "but between you and me, Captain Creed, there is an account to settle. Yours and Mr. Jackson's bills are now due, and I trust they will be settled."

" Have you the bills in your own possession, Mr. Barnard ?" asked the Captain.

"I have," replied old Barnard; "I did not pass them."

" If you have them about you," said the Captain, " I'll pay you now."—And he pulled out a handful of bank-notes.

The old man, attracted by the sight of the money, pulled out his pocket-book, and said, " Here they are."

" Let me see them," said Creed, putting on his spectacles.

The old man's suspicions were too strong now, regarding all his son's companions, to let the bills out of his own hand.

" Sir," said Creed, " I see you are afraid to entrust me with the bills; but you wrong me much,—I am ready to pay both my own and Mr. Jackson's."

So saying, he reckoned out notes to the amount

of £178. He put into old Barnard's hands five twenties, seven tens, a five, and three sovereigns.

"Now," said he, "Mr. Barnard, here's the money, and I'll trouble you for the bills."

The old man took the money, reckoned it rapidly, and delivered the bills.

"Captain Creed," said he, "I thank you;—you, I see, are a man of honour, and I wish you would use your influence to persuade this wretched boy to return home."

"I never meddle in family affairs, Mr. Barnard," was the short and cool reply of the Captain.

"Father," said Barnard, "all that you, or Captain Creed, or anybody can say, is perfectly useless: I have determined to remain in London, and to attempt to alter my determination is preaching to the wind. And now that you have got your money from the Captain, I think you have nothing more to detain you here."

"Undutiful boy!" replied his father; "how am I to get the money you have robbed me of, and the value of the property out of which you have cheated me?"

"That's your business, not mine," answered the youth, with the most imperturbable composure; "get it how you can; perhaps I may pay when it is quite convenient; perhaps not: but for the present, I think you're only wasting your time here."

"Unnatural son," cried the old man, deeply affected by this callous levity, "I ought to curse you, but I will not yet. For this time I leave you. Hardened as you are, you may yet repent, when poverty and wretchedness shall overtake you. You will then be abandoned by your profligate associates, and you may think, perhaps, of your unfortunate father." So saying, the old man withdrew.

We may here remark, that a very material alteration had been gradually taking place for some months in the character of young Barnard. Perhaps, however, we ought rather to say, that it was his natural character which was now coming out, but the developement of which had hitherto been retarded by nothing but his rustic inexperience and that awkwardness and "*mauvaise honte,*" which a newness to society must produce, more or less, in all. But nature had endowed him with flinty nerves, and the most determined obstinacy of disposition. We have seen, it is true, some traces of feeling about him, on his return from his former visit to London, and in his intercourse with Maria; but the sources of such feelings were purely selfish, arising from regret for his losses, and the desire of physical gratification. But his latter campaign in London had nearly obliterated all the little sensibility he once possessed;—it had lent him a firmer determination in the courses of villany, and a reckless composure respecting the consequences of his crimes. Against these he would, to be sure, make such provision as he could; but in case of failure, he had disciplined his mind to meet the result with a cool intrepidity worthy of a better man. This was the cause of that impudent and unfeeling levity which he displayed in the meeting which we have just recorded with his father.

Even Smith himself, with all his cool rascality, could not entirely sympathize with the conduct which Barnard had displayed on this occasion. Still less could Creed do so. Regardless as he was of the rights of property, and the principles of integrity, he was not without touches of humanity and natural affection. He had children himself, whom he fondly loved, and for whose sake, perhaps, partly, he continued to persevere in his swindling and thievish pursuits; of friendship, too, we have already seen that his heart was far from unsusceptible. He was, in fact, one of those mixed characters of which nature composes the majority of men; and we rarely find that persons possessing the talent and the relish for humour that belonged to Creed, are wholly devoid of sensibility. He could not look on this parade of unfilial conduct with an approving eye. He therefore remained silent, as did also Smith.

But there was another silent spectator of this scene, on whom it operated very differently: that spectator was Hannah. She was far from being in the least shocked by Barnard's behaviour as a son, but she was employed in calculating whether now, as all hopes of future finance from his father seemed to be cut off, it would not be prudent in her to desert him.   The result of this calculation was, that she determined to persevere in the connexion, as long as it promised hopes of gain from any quarter.

"Well," said Barnard, "I think, my lads, I have dispatched the old fellow nicely:—what say you?"

Creed and Smith were silent, but the one-eyed gentleman resumed,—

"Yes, Mr. Barnard, it must be owned that you enact the dutiful son in good style."

"I'll be hang'd if I care whether I do or not," rejoined Barnard.

"Did you ever read the story of Tommy and Harry?" said the one-eyed gent.

"Don't tell us about such nursery nonsense," said Barnard: "but I say, my lads, what are we to do to-night?"

"The first thing I advise you to do," said Creed, "is instantly to change your lodgings."

"Why so?" asked Barnard.

"Because," said Creed, "you have everything to fear from the irritation of your father. He may have you taken up to Bow-street, I can tell you, if he pleases ; and you may be certain that he will look in here again, more especially when he finds out the manner in which his *bills have been paid*."

"Aye," observed Beauty, "how did you manage that business?"

"Time will tell," replied Creed   "A word to

the wise; but be that as it may, I strongly advise Barnard to decamp,—and that without beat of drum."

" I am entirely of your opinion," said Smith.

" Then," replied Barnard, " I am off directly; but I must have your help to move off everything; —and where shall I go ?"

" I have a house at your service," said Creed, " at the other side of the water, so situated that I would defy Old Nick himself to find you out, if it were not that he is so constant an attendant on your lordship."

" Thank you for that," said Barnard; " but let us go to work."

" We must manage matters cautiously," said Creed, " not to excite suspicion in the neighbourhood. The best way will be for each of us to go out separately, at different times;—one can take a coach, another walk; and, with the help of the boy and girl (whom you know we can trust), we'll soon leave an empty house; which, as all the world knows, is better than a bad tenant."

" The furniture !" cried Hannah; " how can we move that ?—and what can we do without it ?"

" Make yourself easy about that," said Creed : " allow me to direct the line of operations—I am privileged to do so, from my experience in military tactics. There is plenty of furniture for you in my house; therefore we'll sell yours. Go you, Smith, to *our friend* in Long Acre,—he'll down with the dust directly; and he can leave some one here until morning, and then remove the furniture. Hannah shall pack up all her's and Barnard's moveables, and take a coach to the Golden Cross, where she can manage to change coaches, and proceed to our destination. The rest of us can easily carry off all that will not fit in the coach."

To business these worthies went immediately: the affair of the furniture was soon managed. Hannah then took coach, and was off with the best part of the other goods. The rest then departed, including their trusty servants,—one of whom had held a distinguished rank in the Scarafookas, and the other had been an inmate of another description of establishment, rented by the noble Captain in a different quarter of the town. The broker's man was left in the house, who, at a very early hour, removed the furniture, and flung the key over the garden-wall.

When old Barnard arose next morning, after a night of no small mental agitation, he called for his bill at the inn where he was stopping. On the bill being brought, he presented the waiter with a five pound note to change. The latter was absent for some time, and the old man, getting impatient, rung the bell. Instead of the waiter, the landlord made his appearance with a face of the most profound gravity.

"Where's my change, landlord?" said old Barnard

"If I were not convinced sir," replied the

landlord (who was a very discreet and civil man), of your respectability, I should be inclined to think that you meant to cheat me; but, sir, you must either intend a joke, or there is some very serious mistake here."

"Why, what's the matter, landlord?" replied the old farmer: "joke! I can assure you I never had less cause to be merry in my life."

"This is the note you gave my waiter,—look at it, and read it, sir, if you please."

Old Barnard took the note: and to his utter astonishment, read as follows.

£5.   BANK OFF ENGLAND.

I promise to pay the Bearer on demand, the Sum of Five Pounds of Chaff, sterling value received.

                              HEN. HASE.

𝔉𝔦𝔳𝔢 𝔓𝔬𝔲𝔫𝔡𝔰

The style, &c. of a bank-note was exactly imitated, and several names were scrawled on the front and back of the note.

The old man turned to his pocket-book, in the utmost trepidation, and soon found that all the notes he had received from Creed were precisely of the same description. This led him to examine the sovereigns, which he soon perceived were nothing but gilt counters, and which, by the way, came from the flash exchequer of Xinto totle and Co.

Old Barnard communicated the whole affair to

the landlord, who advised him by all means to apply at Bow Street for relief. But the old man who considered that he could not do so withou involving his son, and whom his weak good nature still induced him to spare, rejected this sensible advice. He contented himself with going to the place where he had been swindled, in the illusive hope of seeing some of the parties. When he arrived there, he found, of course, that all the birds had flown,—and there was a bill in large .etters on the window—THIS HOUSE TO LET, INQUIRE OF MR. SPRUCE, AUCTIONEER, HACK-NEY. This bill had been written and stuck up by Beauty previously to his departure.

The old man returned; and being prevented by the salutary counsel of the landlord from wasting his time in a wild-goose chase after Mr. Spruce, who, it is needless to say, was what the school-men would term a nonentity, set out for Polstead that evening.

The son continued his course of abject depravity, recklessness, and dissipation; still contriving, however, to raise the wind pretty well, and to minister to the profligacy of Hannah, by his copartnership with Smith and Creed. The two latter were now quite above board with Barnard,—neither attempting to impose upon him any longer, nor to conceal a tittle of their nefarious courses. He, an apt scholar, soon equalled his instructors in the art of duping, and far exceeded them in cool audacity and total want of feeling.

They even ventured so far as to inform him how

ne had been himself originally imposed on—and how Jackson lived by smuggling, and raising the wind in many other modes similar to their own. Even the affair of Xiutototle came out in the following manner :—

One evening, Creed, the one-eyed personage, and Smith, were sitting together at the lodgings of the latter over a bottle of wine. Barnard suddenly came in, and said,

"Well, my lads, who do you think I have just seen ?"

"Whom ?" asked Smith.

"Why, that cheat Killganders," said Barnard: "he was coming down the next street; and I am sure the villain saw me, for he turned back and was off like lightning."

At this the three others set up a shout of laughter.

"What are you laughing at ?" cried Barnard.

"Would you like to see his partner ?" said Smith.

"Aye, that I should !" cried Barnard.

"Behold him then !" said the one-eyed gen-tleman.

"Where ?" inquired Barnard

"Here," replied the other; "I am his partner, —was, I should say, rather,—the late Don Josiah Xiutototle."

"You !" exclaimed Barnard; "how can that be ?"

The entire hoax was then explained, much to

Barnard's astonishment, and not at all to his gratification. He laughed at it, to be sure, and pretended to treat the matter lightly; but it made a very deep impression on his dark and remorseless mind.

"We tell you this now," said Smith, "as a pledge of our future sincerity: you must think nothing of it,—it is the mode in which we treat all young hands at first. When we find them good for anything, we undeceive them as we have undeceived you; but this is a sort of apprenticeship which all must undergo: I have undergone it myself,—so don't think the worse of us or yourself on this account."

"Oh! by no means," said Barnard; "not at all, I assure you—I think nothing about it."

"Yes," observed Creed; "this is a noviciate which all must serve: but when we find the novice turn out a clever fellow, like yourself, we teach him our trade, as we have taught you. Lastly, we inform him of the trick which has been played upon him; and when we find him take it with the temper that you do, we conclude him to be fit for anything."

Barnard was now a dupe to Hannah only. He had no suspicion of her collusion in the cheats which had been practised on him; for it may be well supposed that the one-eyed gentleman did not inform him that he had played the part of Whitehead with as much success as that of Xiutototle. To her, therefore, he was still entirely devoted: how long he was destined to remain so, will appear by the sequel.

About this time, Jackson arrived in town. Having passed the *honeymoon* with poor Maria in the country, he brought her up to London, and took lodgings at the West End. He had cajoled her with a variety of plausible reasons why he should not yet communicate with her parents; and he had succeeded in rivetting the girl's attachment so firmly, that she easily credited anything he said, and was easily persuaded to any measure which he counselled.

The place of rendezvous, between Jackson, Smith, Creed, &c., was, as the reader will remember, the house in the neighbourhood of Whitechapel, where we first had the honour of introducing him to some of the leading characters of this history. The private room there was the secret divan, where the chiefs of the gang connected with Jackson, both in smuggling and swindling, were wont to assemble. It was pretty generally visited nightly by Smith or Creed, and the one-eyed gentleman; and latterly by William Barnard, who, having taking all his degrees, was now an acknowledged fellow of the society.

The quartetto in question were sitting in this room in deep confab, at a very late hour in the evening, and Smith had been just expressing his surprise at having heard nothing from Jackson lately, when the very man who was the subject of discourse suddenly entered, accompanied by

Warren. All appeared equally surprised and pleased to see him. After a few questions and replies, relative to the state of affairs, Smith arose, and presented Barnard to Jackson with much ceremony.

" Jackson," said he, " I had the honour of first introducing Mr. Barnard to you : but I now think it necessary to introduce him again, inasmuch as he is not at all the same man that he was when you first met him in this room ;—he was then a novice—a greenhorn : now he is as accomplished a cove as any of us, and a worthy member of our society:—allow me now to present to you Lieutenant Barnard, of the Scarafooka Rangers, and a privy counsellor of our special cabinet."

Jackson fixed his eye for a moment on Barnard, and replied,

" Had you not told me of this change, Smith, I could have discovered it myself : his appearance is enough,—determination and talent are written on his countenance."

" In the first, at least," replied Barnard, " I shall never be found wanting."

" I believe it," said Jackson.

" It must be owned," said Creed, in a low whisper to Warren, " that he looks like a determined villain. But," continued he, aloud, " where have you left Ricketts, Jackson ?"

" He is still in charge of the goods in the cave."

" Don't you think," said Smith, " that it was time that these goods were disposed off ?"

"Yes," said Jackson, "I have come to town to arrange that affair with you all. From your speaking so freely, I perceive that you have let Mr. Barnard into the secret."

"Yes, yes!" answered Smith, "he is now one of us,—we have no secrets from him now."

"'Tis well," said Jackson; "and now, my friends, I have something to mention to you. We shall have the goods up immediately, but it is necessary that we should agree on the division of the profits."

"How!" said Smith, "surely that requires "no consideration; the profits must be equally divided, as they always have been—equal justice is our motto."

"I am as great a friend," answered Jackson, "to equal justice as you are; it is therefore that I speak. An equal division, in the present instance, would, I conceive, be anything but equal justice."

"What do you mean?" cried Smith; "how can that be?"

"I'll tell you," replied Jackson: "the goods in question have been placed in a predicament: all has not gone on, in this instance, fairly and smoothly, as heretofore. But for the exertions of the brave fellows who were with me, we should have had no goods to talk about; nor, perhaps, have been here ourselves to talk about anything else."

"And what of that?" said Smith.

"Thus much," replied Jackson; "that it

3 G

would be unjust indeed if those brave fellows should have nothing extra for their important services."

"Oh!" exclaimed Smith, "I see how it is,—you want to come in for an extra allowance yourself, Jackson."

"And supposing that I did," said Jackson, coolly folding his arms, "who, let me ask you, has a better right to it? Have I not been the whole soul and life of your proceedings?—Could you have done without me?"

"Could you have done without us, Mr. Jackson?—answer me that," retorted Smith.

"Yes," replied Jackson, "I could; the world is wide, and there are many men in it as brave and as clever as yourself, to whom my services would be acceptable. But you mistake me—I want nothing additional for myself; however, I am determined that my brave companions shall not go unrewarded."

"And I am determined," said Smith, "that we, and the rest of us, shall not be humbugged;—I will not suffer it."

"Indeed!" said Jackson: "you are started into mighty power all of a sudden; but, fortunately, the thing does not depend on you,—it will be decided by general consent. And I say again, that I am determined my brave comrades shall not go unrewarded."

"Reward them, then," said Smith, "out of your private purse; which, no doubt, is well stocked, Mr. Jackson: but remember, you reward them out of the profit of the goods at your peril. I can tell you that ——"

What!" cried Jackson, looking fiercely at him; "do you think to intimidate me? I have been heard and obeyed by men, amongst whom you would not have dared to lift your voice; and I can tell you that you shall not bully me out of my just intentions."

"There is a way of doing things," said Smith: "all is not carried in this world by force."

"There are ways of doing things," responded Jackson, "which cowards and traitors may employ, but which brave men detest and despise."

"Coward!" exclaimed Smith, rising from his chair; "do you call *me* a coward?"

"Not now," replied Jackson, coolly; "but I shall call you a coward and a traitor, if you deserve it, as you seem disposed to do."

"You dare not for your life call me a coward," said Smith; "you have not a tongue to do so."

"Away, vain boaster!" cried the other; "I have not only a tongue to call you a coward if you deserve it, but an arm to chastise you as a ruffian."

Smith was now attempting to make his way over to Jackson, when Creed and Warren seized him by the arms, and forced him to sit down. The former then said,

"Gentlemen, gentlemen! this is very foolish work—very foolish work indeed: if we quarrel this way among ourselves, we shall be ruined

Union is our only strength, and our only chance of success; and to see two of the foremost men amongst us thus quarrelling, is grievous. For my own part, I am inclined to coincide with the opinion of our friend Jackson, and think that something extra should be allowed to those who have saved the goods: but let me recommend that the subject be dropped for the present; and when the goods are sold, let the money be divided according to general consent. In the meantime, don't let there be any quarrel between two such old friends."

"You speak well, Creed," said Jackson; "I am contented with the measures you propose. I never meant to quarrel with Smith, but I am not to be bullied by any man."

"I know that," said Creed; "nor did he mean to bully you. It was only a difference of opinion; and let me entreat you both to be friends, and not ruin us by your divisions."

"With all my heart," said Jackson; "I repeat that I have no quarrel with him, but the threat he held out ——"

"I meant nothing by it," said Smith; "it was only in a moment of anger."

"There's my hand, then," replied Jackson.

Smith shook hands with him, and apparently acquiesced in the reconciliation; but the heart went not with the hand, and rancour took a deep seat within his bosom.

The party soon broke up, and, in going out,

Barnard and Smith took one direction, and Creed and Jackson another. As the two last walked along, Jackson observed,—

"I confess I did not think that Smith could have behaved in the manner he did to-night."

"Jackson," said the Captain, "you and I are old friends : I should be sorry to see you wronged or injured; and I can't help thinking that you run some chance of being so."

"Why do you think so ?" demanded Jackson.

"I have some insight," replied Creed, "into human character, and some experience of its indications ; and I am very much mistaken if Smith means any good to you."

"He must be most ungrateful, then," cried Stafford, "and a fool to boot ;—I have put more money into his pocket than he could have ever gained without me. To say nothing of other matters, he could never have succeeded with Barnard as he has ; and, God knows, he has gained more by that concern than I have."

As for his gratitude," said Creed, "I would not calculate much on that: he is a man who makes no distinction between friends and enemies, when his interest is concerned."

"But it is not his interest to quarrel with me."

"If he thinks it is, that is all the same;—the prospect of an immediate gain is enough for Smith—he is incapable of looking farther; neither has he the feeling to observe fidelity, nor the sense to perceive its necessity. Young Barnard, too, whom we all thought such a greenhorn, is as bad, or rather worse, than Smith : they are very closely linked together at present, and neither of them is to be trusted."

"As for Barnard," said Jackson, "I wonder how you came to trust him : I should not be surprised if he were actuated by feelings of revenge against us all."

"Nor I," answered Creed; "but it was Smith's doing, not mine. I would not willingly have trusted him, but I was forced to concur. Men of *our profession*, Stafford, are obliged to do many things against our judgment as well as our feelings, when we have any."

"Alas, Creed! you speak too truly," said Jackson. "Would that I had never adopted such courses, or that I could dare to relinquish them even now; but the die is cast, and I fear it is too late to repent."

"Repentence," said Creed, "is folly,—it cannot alter what has been done, and seldom can it better the future; for one false step in life inevitably leads to a thousand others. I, too, could have wished myself a better pursuit, but it is vain to think of that now; still, though to the world we are otherwise, we may be men of honour amongst ourselves: we are not all, I hope, equally bad."

"I know it," replied Jackson; "on your friendship and fidelity, Creed, I know I can depend."

"You can," said the Captain, "but not so on Smith : trust me, he is a dangerous man."

"He may be so, but I fear him not."

" Still," said Creed, " beware of him."

Beauty and Barnard, instead of separating to go each to his home, entered a convenient house of accommodation, which was open to such as they at all hours; and sitting down in a private room together, called for some of their favourite beverage, brandy and water Smith commenced the conversation, and began to open his mind a little freely to Barnard.

" Well, William," said he, " what do you think of Mr. Jackson's conduct this evening?"

" Why," said Barnard, " I think his proposals very unfair."

" Shamefully unfair!" ejaculated Smith.

" I see no reason," rejoined the other, " why these fellows should have more than you."

" Or than *you*, William," added Beauty.

" As for me," said Barnard, " I don't know that I can claim anything."

" Oh, but *I* do," cried Smith; " you have as much right as any of us, now."

" I think," said the other, " that Jackson assumes a great deal."

" He does," responded Smith; " more than he has any right to do: he would fain be lord and master; but that he shall never be, in money matters, while I live. He talked of being heard and obeyed by better men than we. He meant when he was captain of a band of pirates,— fellows like Warren, without any brains. But he'll find himself mistaken, if he thinks to roister over us.   He'll find he has to do with men as sharp as himself."

"I own, I don't like his manners," said Barnard; "he is too proud and imperious."

"I tell you, William," cried Smith, "you have no cause to like himself or his manners;—now hear me.   It was through him that you have been cheated of your money.   He it was that planned it all—he it was who reaped the principal benefit.   I own that I engaged in the thing, but I was forced to do so : I was in fear of my life—for he is a desperate fellow; but I determined to take the first opportunity to compensate you : that opportunity now offers ;—we can enrich ourselves, revenge ourselves, and ruin him."

"How?" said Barnard.

"The thing is easy," said Smith, "if you will only be firm, and faithful."

"Depend on me," answered the other.

"Do you know," said Smith, "that Jackson, not contented with robbing you, has made you the subject of ridicule ?"

"The deuce he has ?"

"He called you, in a letter to me, 'the young clodhopper.'"   A sardonic smile passed over the features of Barnard.

"Do you wish to be revenged ?" added Smith.

"I desire nothing more."

"Do you wish to pull up your losses tenfold ?"

"How can you ask me such a question ? Only

say how it is to be done.—Shall we waylay him, and —— ?"

"No," interrupted Smith; "that would be poor revenge, and we might pay the price of it with our lives. I have a better plan, if you will only join one in it."

"Name it at once," said Barnard.

"The goods," said Smith, "that we were talking of, are now deposited in a cavern under a little cottage of mine in the country. No one unacquainted with the place could possibly find them out. They are now under the care of one man, a fellow named Ricketts, who with an old woman is the only tenant of the place at present."

"Then your plan is, that we should go down together, murder Ricketts and the old woman, and seize upon the goods."

"No," replied Smith; "how fond you are of murder! Ricketts is a perfect Sampson in point of strength, and a devil in the way of desperation. We could not both escape him;—and even if we succeeded, there are certain consequences not so easily avoided."

"Consequences are nothing, if the deed be concealed," remarked Barnard.

"If—" rejoined Smith: "but, at all events, we could not so well manage the removal and disposal of the goods. We should be thwarted and impeded there. My plan is safer and more certain. You and I shall go down, give informa- tion to the officers, and receive half the value of

3 H

the goods as a reward for our services. Thus I shall be put in funds, you will be compensated for your losses, and we shall both be revenged of Jackson. A warrant will be had against him, and he will either be taken or obliged to fly."

"Your hand upon it," said Barnard : "I am your man."

"There is no time to be lost," said Smith.

"No," said Barnard ; "we must be off with the earliest coach."

"Earliest fudge!" rejoined Smith; "we must be off now, my boy—this moment. We are young and strong.—We can walk until daylight and take advantage of the first quick conveyance we meet. I know Jackson's vigilance too well; —I am sure he suspects me ; and we must, therefore, anticipate his measures."

The two heroes accordingly took immediately to the road; and having walked until about six next morning, found themselves at Colchester: they then took a post-chaise, and arrived early in the evening at Stoke, a town situated but a short distance from Polstead, where they commenced operations with the revenue officers.

Smith, however, had done no more than justice to the promptitude of Jackson;—quick as he was himself, the other was still quicker. When Creed and he parted, he returned immediately to the public-house where Warren slept. He found the latter in the act of undressing, and about o "turn in."

"Warren, my friend," said he, "you must dress yourself again, and set off with me for Polstead directly."

"For Polstead!" cried Warren, in astonishment; "and at this hour?"

"Yes!" replied Jackson, "we have not an instant to lose. I am satisfied that Smith is a traitor, and means to *nose* the goods. We must be beforehand with him, and save them if we can. It will be a business quite in your way, for I am sure we shall not part without fighting."

"That is meat and drink to me," said Warren: "d—n the fellow! I thought as much by his dark looks. I don't like that pale-eyed younker neither."

"I am disposed to think that they understand each other," said Jackson.

"Well, we'll give them as good as they bring," cried Warren, huddling on his clothes; "but how are we to be conveyed, my noble commander?"

"I have two of the fleetest roadsters that ever sniffed the wind, in the stable in the lane," replied Jackson. "We'll ride as long as we can, and then take post."

"Good!" exclaimed Warren; "though a sailor, I can ride as well as your landsmen.—Let's be off."

They went to the stable, of which Jackson had the key, saddled the horses, and were on the road before Barnard and Beauty, and, consequently, arrived sooner in Polstead.

When they came to the cottage, they deliberated as to what measures should be taken for the security of the goods. Jackson was quite decided that they should be moved. But where? and when?—there was but another secret depôt in the country, which was near Ipswich; but which was now rendered quite unsafe, by the information which the officers had received, and which led to the rencontre described in Jackson's letter. As to the *when*, no removal could be attempted until night.

Thus circumstanced, they formed the following resolution,—viz. that Jackson and Warren should carry off as much of the goods as possible that night, to London : leaving Ricketts with the rest until their return. In the interim they barricaded the cottage, and remained under arms, to protect their booty, in case of attack, as well as they could.

That attack was nearer than they imagined,— for Jackson, notwithstanding all his foresight and promptitude, had no idea that Smith was yet in the country. His measures were merely precautionary, and pursued under the influence of a maxim by which he generally regulated his conduct, which was to leave as little to chance as possible. In further pursuance of this maxim, he made his companions secure on their persons all the articles which were light enough to be carried in that way, and did the like himself

The night came on, and proved extremely dark

and stormy. The trio were sitting in the cottage, each of them armed with a blunderbuss, a cutlass, and a case of pistols. They had left no appearance of light, having nothing but a dark lantern: they had even taken the precaution of extinguishing the fire, though the weather was cold.

While they were thus prepared, a knock of a very peculiar kind was made at the door. It was the signal knock, known only to Jackson, Smith, and Ricketts:—there could be no doubt of the person who had given it.

No answer was given from within,—all was hushed and dark, and silent as the grave. The signal knock was repeated three times with no better effect.

A low voice from the outside then called, " Betty, Betty, open the door!"

The voice of Smith was recognized by all the parties.

" Shall we give him one volley?" whispered Warren to Jackson.

" No," replied he; "rascal as he is, I don't want to kill him."

Th s was an impolitic clemency on the part of Jacks n; for, had they fired, they might, by means of the darkness of the night, have deceived the enemy as to their own numbers, and caused them to retire. This, however, was but a chance, as the revenue party outside were strong.

" My lads," said Smith, outside, " I see we

must break open the door. Hand me an iron crow."

Of the iron crow, however, Smith had no occasion to make use; for he had scarcely uttered the last words, when the door flew open, wonderful to relate, apparently of its own accord.

The fact was, that Jackson, with all his judgment and foresight, had made one capital error. This was, in neglecting to dismiss or secure, in some way, the old housekeeper. This woman was alarmed for her own safety, and in the dark had cautiously and silently withdrawn the bolts; and she suddenly threw open the door, when Smith called for the crow, and taking to her heels, escaped.

"We are betrayed, Warren," exclaimed Jackson; "that infernal hag has opened the door. Do you two escape out of the window, if you can, and leave me here to my fate."

"Never," said Warren; "we'll stand by you to the last."

"Hah, hah!" cried Smith; "come on, my lads! —the ringleader himself is here. Now, Barnard, is your time for revenge."

Two men immediately rushed down the steps, and entered the cottage. Jackson, who stood foremost in the passage, with the quickness of lightning, laid them both prostrate at his feet.

"Follow me, my friends," cried he, running up the steps; "all we have for it, is to cut our way through them as well as we can. First (whispered he) discharge your blunderbusses."

They did so, and wounded two of the other party. The confusion created by this, and the darkness, their own knowledge of the paths, and the ignorance of the others respecting localities, were all in their favour. They succeeded in escaping, but the cottage and the booty became the prize of their adversaries.

Having got to a considerable distance, and the others being too busy and confused to pursue them, and not knowing, indeed, what direction to take through such an entangled country, our three heroes halted and held a council of war. Short and speedy were their resolutions. It was agreed that Jackson should proceed immediately to London, and get over to Ostend as quickly as possible; while Warren and Ricketts should make their nearest way to the coast, and find some means of joining their associates on the other side. All were provided with money and valuables sufficient for their immediate purposes.

Jackson was now in a very serious predicament: if discovered, taken, and identified as one who had resisted the King's officers in the execution of their duty, his fate would be by no means doubtful. He threw away his cutlass, and retaining only his pistols, struck into a by-road, by which he avoided Polstead, where it would not have been very prudent for him to have ventured. He walked all night; and at the first market town he came to, secured a chaise and proceeded to London.

The goods were now seized *secundum artem*; and Barnard and Smith, having settled matters to their satisfaction with the officers, resolved to proceed to Polstead, as there was no accommodation in the cottage. The former had his arm tied up, for he was one of the men struck down by Jackson; and, although not wounded, his arm was considerably hurt.

It was a bleak tempestuous night, suitable for deeds of darkness, and harmonizing well with the heart which is abandoned to gloom, remorse, and desolation. It was not a night for the innocent, the gay, the happy, to be abroad : their place was in the social circle or the brilliant assembly, where wealth and luxury create a climate of their own, and bid defiance to the warring elements without; or on the downy couch, lulled in serene slumber, and dreaming of cloudless skies and verdant bowers, and ever-green islands of the blest, crowned with eternal summer. But this was a night for the children of sorrow, of crime, and of despair. Not a glimpse of moonshine—not a star appeared : volumes of black clouds, surcharged with rain, filled the lower atmosphere, and seemed occasionally to touch the earth, as they were swept along before the south-east wind. The storm howled in wild ravings; and a strong and superstitious fancy might well deem that the angel of desolation was abroad, wielding the elements, and directing the blast, to visit with vengeance the offending children of men.

Smith and Barnard had proceeded some distance, when a lustrous flash of lightning, bursting from the bosom of a livid cloud, overspread the horizon with instantaneous light. It was followed by a tremendous peal of thunder, reverberating through the skies: the descending rain then suddenly fell in an overwhelming torrent.

"This is a dreadful night, Smith," said Barnard; "is there no place near where we can shelter?"

"Yes," replied Smith; "a little to the right there are the remains of an old ruined building."

Thither they instantly hied. What this building might have been, is not very easy to decide: it was of some antiquity, but of little note. At a distance it appeared nothing but a heap of stones overgrown with moss. When you came nearer, however, the remnants of three walls were very perceptible, and it was easy to observe that they had been solidly built. The two side walls were very low; and the back one, which was higher, stood against a hill, which afforded a shelter from the east. There was no vestige of a regular roof, but a sort of shed, rudely formed with stakes, covered with sods, thrown across the back part, extended a very little way down the sides: it was sufficient, however, to afford a temporary refuge from the storm. The floor of this place was of a hardened clay; and, in fine weather, some of the country lads were in the habit of repairing hither to amuse themselves with a game of fives.

Barnard and Smith took shelter directly under the back wall: the rain continued to come down with tremendous violence. Neither of them were much inclined to speak; for there is something in such a night as I have described, that makes an awful impression, however temporary, on the most hardened minds.

They had been here but a few seconds, when something very like a deep sigh, uttered by a human being, was heard.

"Good God! what's that?" exclaimed Barnard; "did you hear nothing?"

"Yes!" said Smith, "very plainly; there is some one here besides ourselves: speak, or I'll fire."

"For heaven's sake don't murder me," cried a female voice, in the most piteous tone.

"Murder you?—no!" said Smith; "we don't murder women. Speak,—who are you?"

"A wretched, unfortunate female, the victim of falsehood and perjury: and O!" continued the voice, and seeming to come nearer; "whoever you are, take compassion on me."

Scarcely had she ceased to speak, when another electric flash suddenly illumined all around, and revealed to the eyes of the astonished Barnard, Maria Marten!

"Maria!" exclaimed he.

"Hah!" said she, "I should know that voice!
—who are you?"

"William Barnard," replied he; "surely you
know me."

"Oh!" cried Maria, "this is too much, that
you should be a witness of my shame and misery!"

"What, in the name of heaven, brings you
here?" cried Barnard. "Whence come you?—
whither are you going?"

"To my grave," replied she; "the only refuge
now left for the wretched Maria."

Barnard, corrupted and callous as he had become, was not unmoved by her distress: he entreated her to explain the reason of her being in
such a situation. After much pressing she did so.

"I have been deceived and cruelly deserted,"
she answered. I have been married since I saw
you, William,—at least, I thought so: I was
happy, for a time,—oh! how short a time." Here
her utterance was choked by a convulsion of grief.

"Married!" exclaimed Barnard; "to whom?"

"No matter," said she, recovering; "to one
whom I—yes! I fondly, foolishly, loved him:
—oh! that he should treat me thus. Stafford!
Stafford! I did not expect it from you." A flood
of tears came to her relief.

"Stafford!" ejaculated Barnard, "Stafford!—
do you mean Stafford Jackson?"

"What!" said Maria; "you know him, then!
Yes, in truth, it was he: I was married to him

here—in the little cottage under the hill. There we remained for some time, when, about a week ago, he took me up with him to London."

"And how came you to part?" said Barnard.

"I know not,—it was his doing. I was sitting alone one evening last week, in the lodgings we occupied, expecting his return:—He always came home very late: I heard a knock at the door, and thought it was his. The landlady came up, and put a letter into my hand, which ran thus:—

'DEAR MARIA,

'We must part,—ask not why, or wherefore. You can return home, if you please,—I enclose you the means of doing so. It is right I should tell you we are not married;—he who married us was no clergyman. Farewell! I shall never see you again.'

There was a note enclosed in the letter for fifty pounds."

"And what did you then?" said Barnard.

"I know nothing of what happened afterwards, until the following morning: I fainted away, and was, I suppose, carried to bed. Next morning, the landlady came into my room before I was up, and told me I must leave her house immediately —that she had been mistaken in my character, and go I must. I told her that I knew not where to go. She said it was no matter—I must leave her house. I got up, dressed myself, and looked for the note which had been enclosed by Jackson: it was nowhere to be found. When I asked about it, I received nothing but insult;—'Do you take me,' said she, 'for a thief?' It was very kind of her to let me go without paying for my week's lodging. In short, I was obliged to leave the house immediately."

"And what could you have possibly done then?" asked Barnard.

"I inquired my way towards the road which led from London to Suffolk; and, after much trouble, found out from whence the van departed for Colchester: I got a seat in it as far as that town, and the rest of the way I walked. I was taking a cross road to reach Polstead, to go to my cousin's, when the storm came on, and forced me to take refuge here."

This tale made a deep impression on Barnard; and if he had feelings of revenge against Jackson before, they were now doubly heightened. He turned, and addressed himself to Smith.

"Why," said he, "you never told me anything of this—did you know of it?"

"Yes," said Smith, "I knew it all. I was with Jackson when he first met this young lady, and I have seen her more than once since; but I did not think of mentioning it to you, because I was not aware that you knew her."

"Oh, Mr. Smith!" said Maria, "are you there too?—but I have nothing to blame you for."

"I hope not," answered Smith. "I am sure I

thought Jackson meant honourably ; but you now see, Barnard, what a rascal he is in everything."

" Who married them—or, rather, pretended to marry them?" demanded Barnard.

" When the affair was finished, I learnt that it was Creed who acted the part of clergyman on the occasion," replied Smith.

Barnard's astonishment at this information was as great as Maria's, and both uttered ejaculations expressive of their feelings.

" But Jackson is the real injurer," observed Smith.

" He is, indeed, a scoundrel," said Barnard; "and, I trust, I shall be completely revenged on him yet. But, Maria, you must go home ; this gentleman and myself will conduct you : the rain is now abating."

" Alas !" said Maria, " I dread going home, after what has passed. How can I face my poor father and mother ?"

" Don't think of that, Maria," said Barnard; "what is done cannot be undone. After all, you are little to blame : any girl might have been deceived as you have been. Your parents will be happy to receive you again : you must forget this worthless villain."

" Would that I could !" said Maria : " but I will go home. I'll go with you—I dare not go alone."

Smith and Barnard then lent her their arms, which were indispensably necessary to support her sinking frame. After a while, they reached the cottage, in which a light was still perceptible. They knocked, and the door was opened by old Marten.

"We bring you," said Barnard, "your poor daughter Maria. '

The old man started back with astonishment; which, however, very suddenly gave place to indignation, and he exclaimed, on recognizing Barnard,—

"Is it you, villain? and have you the assurance to bring me my daughter, after having ruined her?"

"You mistake, my good sir," replied Barnard; "I am no villain,—I have not seen your daughter for several months, until to-night, when we met by accident. But," continued he, looking at Maria, who was deadly pale, and utterly unable to speak; "you see the state she is in. Let her be conducted to bed, and I will explain everything to you."

The mother now made her appearance, and uttered an incoherent exclamation of surprise and reproach, at the appearance of her daughter, who stood weeping and trembling before her.

"For God's sake," said Barnard, "don't speak to her so: you see she cannot answer you—she is fainting."

The mother then led Maria away, and Barnard and Smith went into the parlour with old Marten. The former told him all that he had heard from

Maria. The father, lifting up his hands and eyes, exclaimed, when the tale was concluded,—

"Oh, merciful God! my poor girl, then, is ruined!"

"Never think so, sir," said Barnard: "she has been unfortunate and deceived; but, in heart, she is as virtuous as ever."

"But," said the old man, "her prospects are blasted. What respectable man will ever marry her now?"

"It need not be known," answered Barnard: "besides, no respectable man could think the worse of her, if he did know it. She believed that she was lawfully married; therefore the fault rests not on her."

"Well, Mr. Barnard," said Marten, "you give me comfort, and I thank you. I am very sorry for what I said to you;—you'll forgive a foolish old man."

"Don't mention it, my dear sir," said Barnard; "but, in truth, you wronged me. I certainly once had some thought of your daughter, but it was in an honourable way;—circumstances put an end to that. But this gentleman can bear me witness, that this is the first day I have been out of London for some months."

"That I certainly can," said Smith; "and, moreover, I can bear testimony as to the real seducer."

They now took their leave—Barnard recommending the old man, by all means, to be gentle with his daughter, and promising him to come and see him again. Smith and he then went to Polstead, and took up their quarters for the night at the " Cock."

A few words of explanation, in addition to the story of Maria, will serve to throw a complete light on the very culpable conduct of Jackson, in this affair.

When he first formed his connexion with Maria, he certainly did not intend to desert her. He was not altogether so abandoned as to have conceived a premeditation of this kind ;—nay, he even fancied that the strength of his attachment was such as would render him always faithful to her : but he most widely miscalculated his own powers of remaining constant. The fact is, that Jackson was, like the vast majority of hackneyed libertines, utterly incapable of a steady attachment to any one woman. It is not likely that the most accomplished female could have succeeded in rivetting his affection ; it was still less to be expected that a country girl, like Maria, could have done so. She was not like Cleopatra, whose " infinite variety " custom could not " stale." Jackson had only regarded her with the eye of appetite ; and when that was gratified, there was nothing mental to relieve the monotony of domestication, or to keep up the delusion of the senses. Besides, Jackson was one of those general lovers who is caught with every new face, and whose attachment to the sex, at large, utterly precludes the possibility of constancy to an individual.

There was also another very peculiar trait in the character of Jackson, which tended most materially to influence his conduct in the instance on which we are commenting. This was an outrageous hatred of the slighest shadow of anything like personal restraint. He inherited from nature a sort of savage love of unbounded freedom; and this disposition had been trebly strengthened by the vagrant habits of his life. In this respect, he was a perfect Bedouïn Arab; and would have spurned from him with disdain, if he could, the most ordinary loads of social life. He did so as far as he was able : he was never so happy as when he had no fixed place of abode; when, in London, he was living in taverns, coffee-houses, and gaming-houses; when he was flying about the country on his swindling speculations; or scudding with full sails before the blast as tumultuous as himself, and over the waves, as restless and as inconstant.

There is another point also necessary to notice, which has much bearing on this question. Jackson's finances were beginning to get low,—that is, low in his own estimation, and in proportion to his insatiable thirst of expensive pleasure : he, therefore, began to find, or to fancy (which was all the same), that Maria was both an actual incumbrance to him, and a serious impediment to his activity. The chain which he had himself forged, and with which he had fettered his freedom, began to gall him; and he was now as eager to get it off as he had been originally to put it on. In short, he very soon became tired of Maria, but he had too much feeling to tell her so bluntly. Several times was he on the point of breaking to her the necessity of a separation, but he lacked the power to do so: his resolutions, firmly fixed during her absence, were perfectly disarmed by a simple smile, or some artless display of her affection, when she was present. His mind was kept in a perpetual state of contention, between the imperious passion for restored freedom, and the sentiments of pity which he cherished for her. He had resolved, at first, to leave her behind him in the country. This, certainly, would have been the wisest and fairest way he could have acted, independently of cherishing and protecting her: but she pressed with such affectionate earnestness to accompany him to town, that he could not refuse her. But the same feelings, resulting from satiated appetite, vagrant fancy, and the untameable impulse to freedom and activity, pursued him to the metropolis, and at last determined his resolution: still he could not muster sufficient cruelty to inflict the wound personally. He chose rather to communicate his determination by letter; and the enclosure of the fifty pounds was, in his ideas, quite a sufficient atonement for having destroyed her reputation and peace of mind, and quite a sufficient salvo to his own conscience.

Much has been written on the fatal effects and
high criminality of seduction; but enough can
never be said against it. Putting out of the
question men of such loose habits and principles
as Jackson, there are many others who would be
shocked by a comparison with him, who yet think
very lightly of this most heinous sin. They consider the deception of an innocent female, at
most, as nothing more than a very venial trans-
gression. But if the criminality of actions be at
all to be estimated by their consequences (and we
are not aware that there is any other more rational
mode of estimating it), seduction will be found
to rank very highly indeed on the list of human
offences. In the most favourable view of the case,
namely, when the seducer does not desert his
victim, still the consequences of seduction are far
from being innoxious. The woman is degraded
from the station which she previously held; and
the loss of charater, and the weakening of moral
principles, must, unquesionably, exercise a
baneful influence on her general conduct. She
has learned, at all events, to consider chastity as
of little value; and a slight temptation is often
sufficient to render her faithless, even to her
generous seducer.

But this is, indeed, a very favourable view of
the case; for, in ninety-nine instances out of a
hundred, desertion infallibly follows seduction:
this desertion is frequently unavoidable on the
part of the man, but that does not excuse the act
which led to it. If the seducer could but see,

distinctly and vividly pourtrayed before him, the long train of misery and vice which he is about to originate, he might, in many instances, be led to pause in the pursuit of his guilty gratifications. If he could see the blooming and innocent tenant of the cottage, transformed into the pale, haggard, and profligate inmate of the brothel,—if he could hear the tongue which now utters only harmless vivacity and folly, become the organ of blasphemous obscenity,— if he could see the eye, now beaming on him with love, fixed with demoniac rage, or rolling in the vacancy of intoxication,—if he could pursue his unfortunate victim, through all her successive scenes of misery and degradation, to a workhouse death-bed, and a parish burial, he might, perhaps, stop before he accumulated on his own head such a tremendous weight of accountability. And there is almost always time enough to reflect; for seduction is usually, as its name implies, a premeditated act. For the victims, indeed, of sudden and overwhelming passions, there may be some excuse; but for the deliberate seducer there can be none in the eye, either of man or God : and the death-bed of such a man, if he have any feeling left, is as little to be envied as the death-bed of his victim.

CHAP. XVII.

But now there came a flash of hope once more.—BYRON.

PooR Maria remained, as may be well believed,
for many weeks, in a very low-spirited and depressed situation. Her health became seriously
affected by the agitation of mind which she had
undergone, and her exposure to wet and cold on
the night of her meeting with Barnard. The
foundation of a pulmonary complaint was then laid,
which, though it was not in the decrees of destiny
that it should prove the agent of her dissolution,
did materially injure her health.

In the course of time, however, she gradually
grew reconciled to her home, where she was
treated by her parents with all possible kindness.
Her health became tolerably reinstated, and her
mind began to revert with more tranquillity to the
subject of her lover, and of his shameful desertion

of her. Her conscience had not any very many severe reproaches to make her, for she had considered herself as a lawful wife, and had acted accordingly: all she could be blamed for, was the too credulous facility with which she had listened to the persuasions of an insinuating and accomplished seducer.

But what more particularly came to the relief of Maria's mind, was religion. This sovereign " balm of hurt minds," which can administer not only consolation, but joy, amid the bitterest ills of life—this only prop on which the faint, the weary, and the broken in spirit, can rest with security, was not wanting to the unfortunate, though comparatively guiltless, Maria. She had been brought up in the highest reverence for the dictates, and correctly instructed in the genuine principles, of Christianity. With, however, the levity natural to youth, she had not yet reflected very deeply on the subject; but adversity, that " tamer of the human breast," led her to think seriously on what she had been taught, and to fly for comfort to the one great source of it. She recollected the invitation of the Deity himself, when he took upon him a mortal body for the redemption of mankind,—" Come unto me all ye who labour and are heavy laden, and I will give you rest." To him she fled for refuge, and in him she found it.

But there was nothing of the fanatical, or enthusiastical, in the religious feelings which now actuated the breast of Maria. She did not imagine that faith released her from the necessity of repentance for the past, and circumspection for the future; or that the mere adoption of an orthodox system of belief, was to act as a garment, like charity, covering a multitude of sins. No! she was well aware of the necessity of sincere sorrow for her transgressions, and stedfast resolutions of amendment. She knew that the faith, which did not exhibit itself in purity of life and manners, was barren and worthless, and would stand the professor of it in little stead before the awful tribunal of his Creator.

One of the principle causes of Maria's entertaining such just sentiments on the subject of religion, was the visits of a clergyman residing in the neighbourhood of her father's cottage. This gentleman was a pattern of genuine and rational piety, and of everything, in fact, which the clerical character ought to exhibit. He was a man in years, and of exceeding suavity of manners: his whole attention was devoted to his flock, his entire time absorbed by the duties of his profession. He did not conceive, as some clergymen do, that these duties were sufficiently discharged by preaching a sermon once a week, or receiving the fees for performing the burial or marriage service. Every hour of his time was devoted to the instruction and edification of those committed to his care; and in such pious attentions, he made no distinction between the cottage of the peasant and the mansion of the squire. In this respect, he followed the example of the great founder of our religion, who considered himself as especially sent to the meek and lowly.

This gentleman used often to look into old Marten's cottage. His pious discourses proved a very great source of consolation to poor Maria: her case was revealed to him by her parents. He did not make her any severe reproaches on the subject; but, while he blamed her too careless and confiding credulity, he acquitted her of wilful vice.

Maria, in the way we have been describing, so far recovered her peace of mind, that she might almost be said to be more happy than when in the enjoyment of her delusive hopes. She experienced a calm serenity of mind to which she was before a stranger: her present and her previous states were like the mild tranquillity of a summer's eve, compared with the feverish heat and fatiguing brilliance of noon. Her health also returned, and with it the natural charms of her person, now more interesting from the pensive cast which circumstances had thrown over it.

Barnard remained but a short time in the country, after Maria's return: his *business*, and his inclinations, soon recalled him to London. While he did remain, however, he called several times at the cottage; and his behaviour to Maria was that of respectful tenderness.

But a surprise awaited Barnard, on his return to London, for which he was but little prepared,

and which wrought a very material revolution in
his destiny. On his arrival, he, of course,
hastened to have an interview with Hannah. It
was night when he arrived in the neighbourhood
of their habitation, which was situated at the end
of a small green lane. As he proceeded up this
lane, he heard voices before him; and, on a nearer
approach, he very distinctly recognized the well-
known tones of Hannah herself: it was so dark
that he could not be distinguished. Hannah and
her companion now stopped at the door of the
former's present residence, as if the latter were
about to take leave of her. Curiosity induced
Barnard to listen for awhile before he discovered
himself, when the following precious fragments of
a dialogue reached his astonished ear.

"*He!*" said a voice that he could not possibly
mistake for any other than that of his mistress;
"he! you cannot be serious in supposing that I
ever cared anything about him: it was only the
fellow's money that I wanted."

"I can very well believe it," replied another
voice, which Barnard immediately recognized to
be that of the one-eyed gentleman; "for I think
he is as ill-looking a fellow as I ever saw. I should
as soon think you could fall in love with me for
my beauty."

"Yet you were the cause of jealousy in the
fool, nevertheless," said Hannah.

"Oh!" replied he, laughing; "you mean
when I played Whitehead:—yes! that was a

good one. Did you ever know a fellow so humbugged as he has been all along?"

"What else was he fit for?" said Hannah: "but
the clodhopper was fully persuaded that I was
dotingly fond of him."

"He has been a good harvest to you."

"Yes; but I have now drained him pretty nearly
of all his cash, and I shall presently have done
with him."

"You had better have a final pluck at him,
when he comes from the country. He and Smith
have got, I am told, their share of the goods for
betraying them into the power of the Revenue
officers."

"Yes," replied Hannah; "Barnard has written
me word of it: when he comes we'll cheat him
out of his remaining cash, and then turn him
adrift. I can't keep up the farce of pretending to
love him any longer: he is not worth losing any
more time with."

The impression made by this conversation on
Barnard may be well supposed. He forbore,
however, to discover himself,—being determined to
hear all that he possibly could. After a pause,
Hannah resumed—

"But you have said nothing yet respecting
your last meeting with the old fellow."

"It's all right," answered he; "he is caught,
and you may work his purse now famously. I
have told him that you would see him to-morrow
evening, at nine precisely."

"Where?" said Hannah.

"Here," replied the other, "at your house. But, Hannah, as I have put this job in your way, which cannot fail to be a profitable one, you must behave fairly. Even shares, you'll recollect, is our agreement."

"Certainly," rejoined Hannah; "you'll never find me acting otherwise. We have divided the plunder of Barnard equally, and we'll do the same with respect to this old fellow."

"Very well," said the fellow; "you'll see him to-morrow night, and you can easily get a check or bill out of him."

These two worthies now parted,—the one-eyed gentleman turning the corner of the lane, and Hannah entering the house.

The first impulse of Barnard was to rush after her, and suddenly overwhelm her with his reproaches; but, on second thoughts, he checked this feeling, and determined to defer seeing her until the following evening, when he meant to come at the very hour which he had heard appointed for her interview with the stranger. He then took his way back into the City, revolving in his head a variety of plans of vengeance. He was furious at the idea of his having been made so complete a dupe; and still more galled by the biting personal remarks which had been made on him by Hannah, and her open avowal of utter disregard, than even by the loss of all his money.

He thought, at first, of consulting his friend

Beauty, and taking him with him on his intended visit to Hannah : but then, again, he hesitated at exposing his own degradation to another; and the recollection of the very prominent part which Smith had played in the system of dupery which had been carried on upon himself, rendered him very little disposed to seek for his aid and confidence again. He felt quite assured that the latter had been all along in the secret of Hannah's baseness, and that he had been as well acquainted with the Whitehead hoax, as with that of Xiutototle.

After much wavering and cogitation, he determined on proceeding alone to Hannah, loading her with reproaches in the presence of her new lover, and unmasking to him her true character. As a necessary precaution, he provided himself with a brace of small pocket-pistols for the occasion.

Accordingly, he set out for the place in question the following evening, after dark, and arrived there precisely at the hour appointed. Instead of knocking at the street-door, he climbed over the garden wall, which was low, and got into the house very quietly through one of the back windows; for Barnard, by this time, had profited so well from Beauty Smith's lessons, as to be able to enter almost any house in any way but by the front entrance. He directed his steps immediately to the drawing-room, suddenly pushed open the door, and entered.

Hannah was seated on a sofa, in an elegant sort of half Grecian costume, having one side of her bosom completely uncovered. By her side, and with his hand round her waist, sat a gentleman-like looking man about sixty years of age : on a table before them stood wine, fruit, and biscuits.

All Hannah's assurance and self-possession were at first completely overturned by the surprise of Barnard's sudden appearance : she could not speak, and her paramour was not less astonished and disconcerted than herself. Barnard stood near the door with his arms folded; his countenance was deadly pale; there was a cat-like ferocity in his light grey eye; but he was evidently struggling to prevent his rage from getting the better of his self-possession.

After a pause of some seconds, he uttered, in a voice of great assumed calmness,

" So, madam, this is the style in which you are going on during my absence !—this is a fine specimen of your fidelity and gratitude !"

Hannah, who had, by an instantaneous effort, got the better of her confusion, now answered him, in her usual cajoling accent,

" My dear William, I grant that appearances are against me; but when I have explained, you'll find that this gentleman is ———"

" Another dupe of your perfidious art," interrupted the young man; " but I am to be one no longer. I have bought my experience pretty dearly ; but my eyes at last are opened."

"Will you only hear me in explanation, William?" replied she.

"Not a syllable," said he; "I heard quite enough last night. I overheard your conversation last night with the blind scoundrel, who has been so principal a coadjutor in your knaveries, —the fellow who assisted to cheat and rob me, and is now playing the same part for this worthy gentleman here."

This completely stopped Hannah's mouth, and she could not utter one word in immediate reply.

"Sir," resumed Barnard, addressing himself to the gentleman, who had hitherto remained in silent astonishment, "had not accident completely discovered to me the true character of this infamous woman, I might have addressed you more roughly. As it is, I only regard you as the subject of deception, like what I have been myself. She has cheated me out of several large sums of money, by false representations, and by pretending an affection which she is incapable of feeling for any one. She is now trying to do the same by you. I heard her and her villanous assistant agree last night on the division of your spoils. I therefore give you fair warning, if you should be duped by her, it will be your own fault now. As for myself, I discard her altogether; and when I tell you, sir, that this is my house, I hope I need add nothing more to show you the propriety of withdrawing."

The gentleman, who began to think that he had got into an unpleasant predicament, and whose love had been thoroughly cooled by his apprehensions, arose for the purpose of taking Barnard's advice, when Hannah suddenly started up in a violent paroxysm of rage. Her dark eyes flashed fire, and her whole countenance assumed an expression truly fiendish.

"It is false !" she cried, "as false as hell. The house is mine.—All he has said is false, and he is himself a common thief and sharper."

The gentleman's suspicions of danger were not at all removed by this last assertion. On the contrary, he thought himself in very unsafe company, and in a very unsafe situation, at night, in such a lonely, isolated part of the suburbs. Therefore, quietly observing that he would leave them to settle their disputes by themselves, he walked down stairs and quitted the premises with all convenient speed.

"Ruffian and scoundrel!" cried Hannah, when she saw that the gentleman was gone; "you have done me all the mischief in your power, but you shall pay for it: you shall not live to boast of this."

So saying, she seized a knife that lay upon the table, and made an attempt to stab him. But Barnard was instantaneously upon his guard, and pulling out his pistols, presented them at her, crying, "Stand back, or your own life shall be the forfeit."

She threw herself back on the sofa, quite overcome with rage. Barnard resumed.

"Now," said he. "I leave you for ever, I

have, thank God, spoiled one customer for you—
that is some satisfaction for me: and I rather
doubt if you'll find so good a one in a hurry as
him you call the *clodhopper*."

"I did call him so; and I call him now, to
his face, fool, dolt, and clodhopper. Did you
imagine that a woman like me could regard you
with eyes of love? Learn to know yourself better.
It is not for such a caricature on human shape
and features as yourself, to inspire the sentiment
of love. I have made you my dupe, and I glory
in having done so: and I tell you, that you may
also prove the victim of my vengeance."

"I fear you not," said Barnard, with great
coolness; "you have done me all the injury you
shall ever do me."

"Don't be so certain of that," replied Hannah.
"I can tell you that you are a marked man,
and that I can bring the gripe of the law upon
you."

"At your own peril be it," said Barnard;
"you are yourself as much involved as I am."

"A lie!" retorted Hannah: "the law can hang
you; and I can, when I choose, put you in the
power of the law;—remember your forged bills."

This deadened the force of Barnard's rage: he
assumed a less violent tone, not forgetting to hold
out certain threats against Hannah, which, in
their turn, had their effect; and after some further
violent railing on the part of Hannah, and some

3 M

cool thrusts and parries on that of Barnard, this virtuous pair separated.

Barnard left her in possession of the house, which, in fact, belonged to Creed, and contented himself with removing his own property, which was of no great bulk. He proceeded into the City, where he now took up his head-quarters.

Thus ended a connexion commenced in passion and folly on the one side, and mercenary perfidiousness on the other, and continued, as long as it lasted, in profligacy and vice. The consequences, however, of it did not end with the connexion itself. The effects which it produced on the character of Barnard did not cease with their originating cause, which left an indelible stamp behind it, not to be obliterated by time itself. It was during this connexion that the taste of this wretched young man for profligate expense and sensual gratification became matured into an habitual, ruling, irresistible passion, that all his principles of religion and morality were utterly undermined, and that he became nearly as careless of the laws of his country as of the commandments of his God.

The breaking of the connexion did not, therefore, alter his habitual course of life in London. In one respect, indeed, it produced an effect more injurious, perhaps, than its continuance would have done. While Barnard was living with Hannah, his attentions were confined to her

alone ; but after their separation he held indis-
criminate intercourse with various women of the
town, many of whom were of the very lowest grades
in depravity and vice.   Even the semblance of
marriage, in the illegitimate union with one
woman only, with whom fidelity is observed, is
some preservative of virtue, or, at least, a preservation against the grossest and most disgusting
modes of vice ;—it compels, to a certain extent,
some slight observance of decorum and regularity :
but when a man once abandons himself to an in-
discriminate intercourse with vicious women, he
loses every shadow of the sentiments which he
ought to entertain for the sex,—is degraded in his
gratifications below the instinct of many brutes,
—forfeits his own self respect, and all his claims
even to toleration, as a member of civilized
society.

With many of these wretched women Barnard
formed alliances of profit as well as amusement.
The plunder of their dupes was shared with him,
and the profits of his knavery with them : they
played into each other's hands, and supplied one
another in turn with customers.   Nor were his
male associates a whit more respectable : independently of Creed and Beauty,—with whom
interest still induced him to preserve his intimacy,
though he cherished no very good feelings for
either, in consequence of the share they had
taken in his plunder,—he was linked with many

far below both in the depths of crime and profligacy.

Things went on in this way for some time longer, when both Smith and Barnard got into a very ticklish scrape, which induced them to leave London with the utmost precipitation. This was nothing more than a case of robbery, the detection of which would have secured for them, if not the gallows, at least transportation for life. They contrived, however, to escape undetected, and they took refuge in the neighbourhood of Polstead, which, from its retired situation, afforded them a convenient shelter.

Barnard arrived just in time to witness the expiring moments of his father. The poor old man was brought to the grave, perhaps sooner than he would have been by the usual course of nature, in consequence of the profligate line of conduct pursued by his son. The pecuniary embarrassments to which that conduct had reduced him, and his distressful feelings at the undutiful behaviour of Barnard, unquestionably expedited his fate. The last and heaviest stroke he experienced was the detection of the son's forgeries on himself and his friend the banker: this came on him like a clap of thunder.

The parties, however, who held the bills, entertained a high respect for the old man, and accepted a compromise which rendered the loss somewhat less oppressive to him. Still, it fell heavily on the old man's spirit, accompanied, as it was, with such bitter reflections; and by the time that Barnard arrived in the country, the old man's strength was quite exhausted, and he was on the point of death.

The son, who knew nothing of all this, proceeded immediately to his father's house; for he had come down with the determination of playing the part of a penitent, and adopting an hypocritical style of external reformation. When he arrived, the first person he met with was his mother, who told him that his father was at that moment actually dying. Hardened as he was, this news affected him deeply. He requested to be allowed to throw himself at the feet of his aged parent, to declare his sincere repentance, and ask a dying pardon.

When he entered the chamber where his father lay, the scene he then witnessed might have made an awful impression even upon a more abandoned person than himself, and on one whose personal feelings were wholly unconnected with it. The old man was stretched upon his bed, his head raised with pillows, and his daughter also supporting it on one side with her arm; on the other side, kneeling on a cushion, was the venerable clergyman whom we have already mentioned, engaged in fervent prayer. He paused on the entrance of the mother and son; the former of whom then said,

"My dear husband, I bring you our son

William, a sincere penitent, who begs for your forgiveness."

William then knelt beside his sister, and uttered, in a low voice, "Dear father, do not curse me!"

The old man's face was so pallid, and his features so attenuated and drawn in, that he could scarcely be recognized : he was evidently in the paroxysm of death. Still, at the mention of his son's name, his glassy eye assumed something like an expression of consciousness : he attempted to speak but could not; he put forth his skeleton hand, and while the son was in the act of kissing it, the father's spirit fled for ever.

The reverend clergyman who attended, chose the present opportunity of impressing deeply on Barnard's mind the necessity of repentance and reformation. "To his wild and evil courses," he said, "it was too probable that his father's death was partly to be attributed. It was true that, in the course of nature, he could not have lived very long; but his days might have been extended, and his latter end, come when it would, not have been embittered by the undutifulness of a son. Still," added the clergyman, "you may console yourself by reflecting that your father has died in peace with you, as well as with all the rest of mankind. He has not bequeathed to you that most tremendous of all legacies, a parent's curse : he has forgiven you, as our heavenly Father will also forgive you, providing that you sincerely repent and thoroughly reform; for, without the last, the first is fruitless. The only atonement you can make for a past life of impiety and folly, is a future one of religion and uprightness: you are yet young, and there is time enough; and were you a greater sinner than you are, there would be yet room to receive you in the bosom of infinite mercy. Your part is plain to act: you have still another parent left,—make up, by your tenderness and attention to her, your want of duty to the other. That parent, and a sister, now depend on you for support,—exert yourself to make them happy, and yourself respectable. You may not be rich, for the pecuniary embarrassments you have entailed on your father have diminished his income; but you will have competence by your own honourable labour, and a self-satisfaction resulting from integrity and virtue, which countless millions can never produce, when they are the wages of iniquity. God bless you, my son, and reform your heart and conduct, and make you wise, virtuous, and happy!"

The old clergyman spoke with an earnestness and fervency, that made, or seemed to make, an impression on the young man: probably, the impression was real, for the present; for such a scene and occasion could scarcely fail to make the hardest feel, at least for the time. Barnard expressed his thanks to the minister of God, for his advice and exhortation, declared the fulness and sincerity of his repentance, and the firmness of his resolutions of amendment. The old gentleman then rose and took his leave.

William Barnard now became the head of his family. The first thing he did was to superintend the final ceremonies due to his deceased parent, at whose funeral he was, of course, chief mourner. He next examined into the state of his affairs, and found, notwithstanding the dilapidations which he had himself caused, that enough remained to support, in decent competence, the remainder of his family and himself. By proper attention, exertion, and economy, he still might improve his income, and recover the losses he had occasioned.

He now put on all the external appearances of a man completely reformed. He was attentive to the comforts of his mother and sister, kind in his manners to them, and to all with whom he was connected; temperate in his habits, and most assiduous in his general application to business. He managed the affairs of the farm with industry and cleverness; and, to the eye of the world, appeared, in a temporal point of view, to be doing extremely well. He would work occasionally himself among the labourers, as well as superintend their operations. He became, too, peculiarly remarkable for the suavity and extreme mildness of his manners: he was never known to be out of temper; and he gained the reputation, throughout the whole neighbourhood, of being a most kind-hearted, good-natured young man.

But we regret to say that all this was false and hollow: the impression made upon him by the deathbed of his father, if any indeed were made, passed rapidly away. His virtuous bearing was all external, his piety wholly assumed, his decorum a garb for the concealment of depravity; his mildness, suavity, and kindness of manner, all acting : he proved a most accomplished hypocrite. His powers of self-command, and of countenance, we have more than once had occasion to notice ; and he exercised them, in the present instance, to their fullest extent. He thoroughly imposed on every one, and passed for a model of goodness ; but, in spite of his sanctimonious demeanour and gentleness of exterior, he remained, at bottom, what circumstances fully proved him to be,—an unprincipled profligate, and a cold-blooded ruffian.

Even now, while he was daily employed in acting the part of the good son, the kind brother, the industrious farmer, and the amiable acquaintance, he was still closely linked in the bond of iniquity with his old friend Smith, and a partner in many of his nightly depredations. That gentleman passed his time between London and Polstead ; and, when in the latter neighbourhood, he always sojourned, in secret, in the cottage which was the scene of Maria's seduction, and made the cave which was under it the depôt of his spoliations. He lived there in such profound concealment, that no one in the country was aware of his residence, except Barnard. Nor was he without a companion in his retreat : Ellen, the unfortunate cousin of Maria, was now his *chère amie.* This girl, whose disposition and principles had never been what they ought to be, soon became thoroughly depraved under Beauty's corrupting auspices : she called herself his wife, and was the confidante and partner of his villanies. During his absence, she kept house and watched over the spoils.

It may surprise our readers, why Barnard, who was now externally a man of competence and respectability, should persevere secretly in those nefarious courses. It may be thought, perhaps, that he could not want money, and that, situated as he was,—obliged to live moderately in appearances,—he could have had no outlet for profuse expenditure ; and that a country place, like Polstead, was not likely to furnish the means of indulgence in profligacy and excess : but those who are disposed to guilty gratifications, will find them even in the bosom of retirement. Barnard and Beauty, in the retreat of the latter, enjoyed many a secret revel and midnight debauch : there they partook of the most expensive wines, and the most costly viands. Barnard, also, had formed connexions with many women of bad character, far and near, throughout the country, which drained him of considerable sums : besides, be it observed, that a day's journey would, at any time, bring him to Whitechapel ; to which he paid occasional weekly visits, under pretence of business. He never ventured to proceed into London; but in the purlieus of that ancient vicinity, with which he was so well acquainted, he found ample means and opportunities of dissipating his money in the society of drunkards and gamblers, of thieves and prostitutes. Here he would now and then pass a week; and when he had got rid of all his money, return to the country, to be a puritan by day, and a robber by night.

While in the country, he used to pay continual visits to the cottage of Maria, who was now living with all the retirement and strictness of a modest widow; and might well be regarded by any candid person as being virtually such. She had now, to a wonderful degree, recovered her tranquillity of mind; and passed her time between reading, working, and attending to household duties. The old couple had also grown happy again; and the cottage had resumed all the air of comfort, simplicity, and innocence, which it wore before the departure of its loveliest inmate.

The visits of Barnard, as I have said, were frequent, but they were secret. From his own relations he kept this intimacy profoundly concealed: they entertained a most inveterate dislike to the entire of the Marten family, and more especially to Maria. They looked down on them with all that pride of superiority, which, be it observed, almost always exists in the highest degree in the lower walks of life. Those, whom station has very little removed above the humblest rank, are generally at the greatest pains to support their fancied dignity, and the most profuse of their contempt towards those whom they are pleased to style their inferiors.

Such persons, indeed, present a caricature of aristocratic pride, which ought to convey a salutary lesson to their betters. Pride of all kinds is, indeed, equally ridiculous and unbecoming to the worms called men. Nor is it less useless than absurd—for the proudest can never hope to have his claims to distinction allowed to the extent of his own estimation of them. In fact, the most deserving never have their claims fully admitted, and an assuming manner is precisely that of all others the least likely to vindicate them successfully.

It was to Maria, in particular, that the female part of the Barnard family bore the most decided antipathy. Her beauty was a source of envy to them; and her pretensions to dress as well as they did, an unpardonable insult. This, indeed, was poor Maria's weak side; and this is what one female never forgives to another. Besides, their suspicions had been excited by William's former attention to Maria, and rumours that he had intended to make her his wife. This idea was perfectly intolerable. It was not to be endured, that a low girl like her should have the presumption to aspire to an alliance with the high family of the Barnards.

But Barnard himself had never been troubled with any scruples of this kind. At the time he had thought of making her his wife, he never dreamed of any obstacles arising from the pride of birth. And even now, though, of course, he had entirely dropped that idea, he still had a great liking for her person. His libertine habits had totally cured him of everything like sentiment, which he held in the utmost derision: but Maria was a desirable object in the eyes of a general lover of the sex; and, perhaps, more so now than ever. Her person had acquired all the tempting fulness of womanhood, her cheek had recovered its bloom, and her eye its liquid lustre. Her countenance, though no longer illumined by the gay vivacity of youth, yet beamed with a pensive sweetness that was still more interesting and attractive.

Maria, therefore, was now the cause of Barnard's visits to the cottage. Since he had cast away the chains of Hannah, he had met no woman like her. Maria was her equal in beauty; and to Barnard, now matured in experience, if not in years, her youth and beauty lent her additional charms. But his passion was entirely sensual; her person was the object of his desire, and her person he resolved to obtain.

But he went systematically to work. He was far from declaring his passion at once. He never spoke of it,—but he persevered in a plan of constant, delicate, and tender attention, by which he trusted eventually to succeed.

The hypocrisy, art, and insinuation of Barnard, succeeded as well with the Martens as they had done elsewhere. He became a prime favourite at the cottage, where, when at Polstead, he usually passed some portion of every evening. The father and mother became attached, and he began insensibly to gain ground in the affections of Maria. At this the reader will be the less surprised, when he reflects what the state of her feelings respecting him had formerly been. Had it not been for the return and interference of Jackson on the one side, and the interposition of Hannah on the other, she would doubtless have been married to William, with her own free and full consent. Nothing is more natural, more common, or more excusable, than for a young and affectionate female, deserted as Maria had been, after the first transport of sorrowful feelings has gone by, to be accessible to a second return of the tender passion. It sounds mighty fine, in Novels and Romances, to talk of the impossibility of a woman's feeling love a second time; of eternal constancy to a shadow, to a name! But this is neither human nature, nor probability, nor fact: if such be ever the case, —which I marvellously doubt,—I suspect that the woman who is an illustration of it never felt love at all. The female who has once truly loved, must love again, if severed eternally, by any circumstances, from the object of her first attachment. She must always have something to love. There is, in almost every female breast, an imperious necessity of loving, which must be obeyed. It is the dominant feeling of her mind, and the whole business of her life. Men, as a highly gifted poet well observes, have many other matters to occupy their attention, to distract their minds, to console them for their disappointments: but woman has nothing but love; and in that one word is written the entire history of her life.

It would, therefore, have been extremely natural for any young man, of insinuating manners, to have gradually won on the affections of Maria, under the circumstances in which she was placed. But it was doubly natural that a man like Barnard, for whom she had certainly cherished some affection before, should do so. Moreover, be it remembered, that Maria justly considered herself most shamefully deceived and deserted by one whom she had looked on as her husband. His conduct had been so cruel, that time alone would have sufficed to wean her thoughts entirely from him,—and finding that she was not really married, she naturally considered herself free to accept any man she might like for a husband.

Barnard's visits she soon felt to be habitually necessary to her. The state of retirement in which she lived; that monotony of existence which she felt more than formerly, since the feelings of her heart had been so much excited, made his presence a relief, an amusement, a pleasure: they would converse and read together for hours. Barnard was now by no means an ignorant man: he surpassed Maria in the knowledge of books, almost as much as he did in the knowledge of the world. He acted, in some measure towards her, the part of an instructor: he lent her books, read with her various portions of history, and works on literature in general. He, in some degree, formed her taste, and even corrected her style of composition.

The mind of Maria was flexible, and, like the twig, was easily inclined. We have mentioned that, from education and habit, she had a strong reverence for the precepts, and in the hour of disappointment had derived comfort from the lessons of religion: but she had not an understanding competent to the discussion of its truths, and she had received them, as the majority do, without examination: she was not prepared, according to the advice of St. Paul, to give a reason of the hope that was in her. Dr. Goldsmith used to say, that he took his religion from the priest as he did his coat from the tailor,—leaving the fashion of the one to the first, and that of the other to the second. This saying, which would have better become a worse man, is very applicable to the greater portion of those who call themselves

Christians : that the faith of such should be easily shaken, by plausible and persuasive sophistry, is not to be wondered at.

Barnard's notions concerning religion we have already described : he had graduated in the school of Carlile, and was one of his warmest disciples. It is not, therefore, to be supposed that many of the books which he recommended to Maria, or the ideas which he inculcated, were favourable to Christianity. With his own family and friends, his hypocrisy on the subject of religion was the same as in everything else; but with Maria he was more open, because it suited his own purposes to be so. He gradually insinuated into her mind doubts concerning the infallibility of religion. If he did not succeed in imbuing her thoroughly with his own atheistical principles, he, at least, succeeded in giving a material shock, both to the religious and moral feelings in which she had been brought up.

Although Barnard was not so accomplished, so handsome, so gentlemanlike, as Jackson, yet he was a seducer far more insinuating, artful, and sophistical. He did not often allude, in his conversations with Maria, to her affair with her former lover— but when he did, he always assumed an apologetic tone for her conduct. He reprobated the other for his deception and desertion of her, but always insisted that she was totally free from every shadow of culpability. He went further, and took upon himself to defend the propriety of an illegitimate intercourse between the sexes: he said, that even if she had not been deceived as to the validity of the marriage, that still she would not be to blame for having yielded to her inclinations;—that marriage was useful, and, in some cases, necessary; but still that it was nothing but a human institution, not founded on the laws of nature or of God.

The winter had more than passed away, in the manner we have been describing, and Barnard found that he had made a very great progress in the affections of Maria: for himself, his passion for her possession, united with a certain sort of vanity in the conquest of a young and pretty girl, grew stronger and stronger: still he forebore, as yet, to come to an open declaration of love. But he soon saw that little else was wanting, and accordingly he seized a favourable opportunity of making such declaration.

Maria answered, as he expected, by a confession of reciprocal attachment on her part. He then declared that it was his full and firm determination to marry her, but that marriage must be delayed for a little time, in consequence of the inveterate dislike of his relatives to the connexion. Time, he said, was necessary, either to overcome that dislike, or to place him in such a situation as to be independent of their feelings.

After this eclaircissement, Barnard's attentions grew more and more constant, and the strength of Maria's attachment increased. He began to press her to give him the last proof of that attachment; and though she refused to do so for a considerable time, her denials at last grew fainter and fainter. He told her, that though the ceremony was delayed, she was not the less his wife—that he considered her as such in the eyes of heaven—and that though he looked on the mere form as nothing, yet the earliest opportunity that should offer, he swore most solemnly, that for her sake —for the sake of securing to her his property, it should be performed

Still he could not yet completely prevail; but, at last, he bethought himself of a method by which he should overcome all her scruples. He prevailed on her to consent to meet him by moonlight at the Red Barn, where they should go through a sort of religious form—taking vows of eternal fidelity to each other, and calling God to witness their mutual sincerity. She listened— she consented,—and they met under the pale moonlight near the Red Barn, at the spot where Barnard had, all innocent, at a former period, wandered with her—ere his heart had been estranged from virtue and its sweet consequences; —here, on this spot where he had made the first step towards the loss of that virtue, and yeilded to the false glare of Hannah's beauty—here did he now meet his victim with a heart—O, how changed from its early self!—how false—how dark! Had poor Maria known, she would have shrunk from him as from the withering touch of a pestilence. Here they pledged their mutual faith in the most solemn terms,—each called upon the Deity to witness their vows; and Barnard, not content with this, called down the most tremendous imprecations on his own head, if he should fail in the performance of his oath. He then pressed her to his heart, saying—"Now, Maria, you are mine for ever!"

"Oh, William!" she sighed, "if you should prove false?"

"False!" he exclaimed; "I am as likely to do so, as to stab this bosom which is now throbbing against mine."

"If you deceive me," said she, "you will pierce it indeed."

Thus fell Maria, a second time, to rise no more. In the first instance, she proved the victim of an accomplished libertine, who, though unprincipled and vicious, possessed many traits to redeem him from utter reprobation :—though inconstant, he was generous,—though sensual, yet refined,—and though regardless of the rights of society, not without some sense of honour. In the second case, she was the dupe of one who had little to recommend him, either personal or mental, except a portion of intelligence and artfulness turned to the worst purposes ; and a gentleness and suavity of manners, assumed as a cover for inward depravity and secret fierceness. In neither case, however, could she have been said to have made a wilful sacrifice of her virtue : if she erred at all, she erred through weakness ; and the worst blame that the most rigid could have attached to her, was a want of such firmness and intelligence as it would be ridiculous to look for in a girl of her age, circumstances, and rank in life. In the one instance, she was deceived by a solemn burlesque of the sacred ceremony of marriage, accompanied by every circumstance that could impose upon an ignorant and inexperienced female ; in the other, by vows made and attested in the presence of the Deity himself. If she had been culpable, what were her seducers ?

CHAP. XVIII.

As a beam o'er the face of the waters may glow,
When the tide runs in darkness and coldness below;
So the cheek may be tinged with a warm sunny smile,
While the cold heart to ruin runs darkly the while.

THE secret intercourse between Barnard and Maria was now regular and constant. Their place of private meeting was always the Red Barn. After some months, however, the fruits of that intercourse became so apparent that longer secrecy was impossible. She revealed her situation to her lover, and after many consultations, it was agreed between them, that that should be done which, indeed, could not be avoided.

A full confession was made to the parents of Maria. They were not so much surprised as vexed at the circumstance. From the long and close attentions of Barnard, they had previously suspected the state of the young people's affections. He, however, made the same protestations

to them that he had made to Maria. He swore
that it was his firm intention to make her his
wife the very moment he should be so situated
as to be enabled to do it—that at the present
moment he considered her as nothing else, and
that while he had breath he would cherish her as
such. It was, therefore, agreed between them all,
that Maria's situation should be concealed,—which
was easily done, as she lived in such privacy at
home; and that when the time of her accouch-
ment drew near, she should go to Sudbury, a
village not far distant, to be delivered.

Barnard affected a vast deal of tenderness and
satisfaction at the present state of *his* Maria, and
to be highly delighted at the idea of becoming a
father; but his real feelings on this subject were
vastly different. The fact of Maria's pregnancy
filled him, in secret, with the most fiendish rage.
The idea of a burthen being thus imposed upon
him, when he had contemplated nothing but the
gratification of his passions, rendered him furious.
When alone, he abandoned himself to the full
force of these demoniacal feelings. At the cottage
he was all smiles, soothing, and gentleness : the
instant he quitted it, and thought himself secure
from observation, he was transformed into a fiend.
He would then stamp and swear, indulge in the
gesticulations of a maniac and the blasphemies
of a devil. He could be compared, on such
occasions, to nothing but the arch enemy of mankind, as described by Milton, when, after appear-

ing as an angel of light, he abandoned himself,
unnoticed, as he thought, to all the paroxysms
of his fiendish nature, on the mount of Paradise.

This union of a generally mild and calm, and
even cold demeanour, with the internal com-
motion of the worst passions, was a striking
feature in the character of Barnard. He had it
from his infancy. He very rarely suffered the
ebullitions of stormy feelings to break out—exer-
cising, in this, a degree of self-command which
increased with his increasing years : he could
assume the calmest and the gentlest outside,
while the most malevolent passions were raging
within. One or two instances have occurred, in
which this usual circumspection in company
forsook him ; but they were only momentary.
In this peculiarity, however, Barnard was not
singular,—it belongs to many others, and perhaps
is always characteristic of those whose feelings,
of whatever kind, are the strongest and the
deepest. The outside is no criterion. The earthquake may slumber in the deep caverns beneath
the surface of the most placid waters;—the
smiling verdure on the slope of the volcano, and
the snow upon its summits, afford no indication
of the fires that boil within its bosom.

When the time approached, the unfortunate
Maria went to Sudbury, where she might more
easily escape the censoriousness of the villagers
of Polstead, and more readily receive the medical
assistance which her situation required. She was

delivered of a fine infant; and when her strength was sufficiently recovered, she returned with her child to her father's cottage, where she continued to live with greater privacy than ever.

Barnard continued his tenderness of manner, and poor Maria, now almost entirely occupied in the pleasing duties of a mother, began really to taste again of happiness. She forgot the sorrows and disappointments of the past, and began to indulge a golden dream of lasting contentment, felicity, and love: but she was too soon, too suddenly, to be awakened! Oh, happiness, thou fleeting shadow!—thou illusive phantom, ever dancing before thy pursuer, and eternally eluding his grasp!—Misery! thou only thing below that is certain and substantial—the never failing inheritance of the children of the earth, though divided among us with no very impartial hand. Mysterious providence! the largest portion of evil too often falls to the lot of the virtuous and unoffending, while temporal good is the possession of the wicked: but their hour of retribution must arrive—if not here, hereafter. Their crimes are written with a pen of adamant on tablets of brass; and the talents they have wasted will be reclaimed by an inexorable judge, whose scrutiny no subtlety can escape, and whose rigour no prayers can soften.

The malignant feelings of Barnard were not altered by the sight of his innocent offspring. On the contrary, they were rather increased: he was perpetually brooding in his gloomy mind over the burthen which his own unbridled passions had entailed upon him; and which all the ties of nature, feeling, and duty, called upon him to support. This, however, he was determined to do no longer than he could help it : he knew that as long as he remained in the country he must do so, either voluntarily or by compulsion. To leave the country, at present, or for some time to come, did not suit him : he turned his mind to other schemes of emancipation.

Nor were his feelings, now, towards the mother, much more favourable than towards the child. Of all passions, there is none so soon satiated as lust; and mere lust was all the feeling that Barnard had entertained towards Maria. It is also the most debasing of all passions, when unmixed with any finer sentiment : its votary is always sure to turn with disgust from his victim, when the brutal appetite is once satisfied; and if circumstances will not allow him to quit her, his former liking is apt to turn into a deadly hatred. When this once takes place in a mind of such depravity as Barnard's, it is scarcely possible to conceive the enormities it may produce. Demoniacal cruelty, infanticide, and murder, are the offspring of this hell-born passion.

Barnard became soon fully resolved to get rid of a burthen from which he could not escape, and the idea of which grew more and more irksome to him every day. But the most depraved seldom

THE RED BARN. 475

determine on crime for its own sake; and even when the motive to the crime is nothing but a sordid and fallacious view of self-advantage, they will endeavour sophistically to persuade themselves that the action which they contemplate is justifiable on some other ground. Perverted reason is ever ready to lend its aid to unbridled passion, or heartless depravity: we all of us easily find cogent arguments for doing what we like.

Thus Barnard attempted to convince himself that the removal of the child would be a benefit both to Maria, himself, and the infant. Being determined not to provide for it, he soon found that he could never muster the means without denying himself the necessaries of life; *i. e.* the means of all kinds of riotous gratifications, which habit had now rendered so necessary to him, that he could not exist without them. Again, he considered that to relieve Maria from the burthen would be right and proper. How could she support the child?—and, as for the child itself, he considered that he should be doing a kind action in removing it from inevitable want and misery. He even called his memory and his reading to his assistance, and defended himself by the practice of individuals, and even nations, with whom infanticide was common, when there was no means of supporting the offspring. But, above all, he fortified himself by the reasonings of his infamous friend, Mr. Carlile, who has recommended the prevention of child-bearing, in such cases; and whose theory Barnard would have willingly reduced to practice with Maria, but that he had not the audacity to propose it to a girl of her principles, or so completely to unmask his own vile character.

As to the idea of committing murder, that did not at all shock him, especially in the case of the *benevolent* murder which he was contemplating. " What signifies," thought he, " the life of a mere infant? a thousand things may occur to destroy it before it reaches the age of five years. And what an immensity of pain and misery I shall save it from, by the mere pain of a moment!— nay, probably, without inflicting any pain at all : children, so young, must have little pain in dying. And, after all, what is human life itself, at any age, and under any circumstances? What is its value?—nothing! it is subject to ten thousand accidents : the most trifling thing may destroy it; and go it assuredly must, at one time or other. An early death may often be accounted happy : perhaps it would have been happy for me had I died at the age of this infant."

He was not aware, at the time he made this reflection, of its entire truth. Unfortunate and abandoned youth! it would, indeed, have been happy for yourself, and all connected with you, had you not entered the portal of life, or had you died upon its threshold!

By continually revolving reflections of this

kind in his mind, Barnard, at length, came to a determined resolution of putting an end to the existence of his own child!

The next question was, how should it be done?— the coalition of Maria, in such an infernal business, was not to be expected. That mighty feeling, by which the system of animated nature is not less preserved, than by the procreative instinct,— the feeling of maternal affection, which no brutes are destitute of, except a few in human shape, existed in its fullest force in her kind and gentle bosom. She was completely wrapped up in the life of her infant: its care absorbed every instant of her time, and every thought of her mind. She doted on it with the most affectionate fondness: she did not love it less than she did its wretched and unworthy father.

It happened, rather favourably for Barnard's detestable purpose, that the child was about this time taken ill. It continued so for some time, and, being a weakly infant, would, in all probability, have soon died in the ordinary course of nature: but the amiable father determined to seize this opportunity of hastening the mortal crisis, and expediting the passage of his child into eternity.

Accordingly he went to Sudbury, under the pretence of purchasing medicine for the child, as the village apothecary was absent from Polstead at the time; and even were he present, Barnard observed that he would not trust to him. When he returned, he came to the cottage, from which both the old people were absent; and the little girl, who attended Maria and the child, told him that the former was asleep. He asked for the child, and was informed that it was in a cradle adjoining the room where the mother had just lain down: he entered, mixed a powder in a tea-cup, and, taking up the child, administered it to it. While he was thus employed, Maria, waking from the child's cries, looked immediately through a small crevice in the wall, and saw very clearly what he was about. Having no other idea than that he was kindly administering medicine to the sick infant, she was delighted at his paternal kindness; and resolving to give him an agreeable surprise, suddenly entered the room.

" My dear William," said she, " this *is* kind of you."

Her entrance was unexpected, for he thought she was asleep: his presence of mind was over-turned, and his agitation would have been palpable to any one but Maria. He stammered out, " Yes! I have given it some medicine from the doctor."

His hand trembled excessively, and he uncon-sciously dropped the paper containing the powder.

Maria, turning her attention to the child, did not then notice the confusion of Barnard. He made some excuse to quit the room—not being able to endure her presence.

Scarcely had he withdrawn, when the child was seized with the most fearful convulsions: Maria was in the most dreadful alarm, not knowing what to do. There was no one in the house with her but the little girl. She knew that the village apothecary was absent, and she could have no assistance : she sent the little girl to look after William, to try what he could do. In her absence, she happened to cast her eyes on the ground, where the paper lay which Barnard had dropped : she took it up, and, to her unspeakable horror, she found it labelled "POISON !"

Her next look was upon her infant. The poor innocent was in the agonies of death : its features were frightfully distorted, its skin had assumed a deep livid tinge, and every limb was shaken with convulsion. In a second or two it expired.

Maria shrieked aloud, threw herself on the floor, rose again, and hung over the child in the most intense agony of feeling. She called upon its name, used the little terms of endearment which she had been accustomed to apply to it in life, raised it in her arms, kissed its livid cheek, and pressed its lifeless form to her bosom. She fell into an agony of tears.

The girl returned,—her search for Barnard had been fruitless ; but he made his appearance directly after her entrance. He had withdrawn for the purpose of re-collecting his self-possession; but, as he had anticipated the immediate death of the child, he knew the necessity of his immediate return. He now came prepared to act his part,— the cool, hypocritical, whining villain.

Scarcely had Maria seen him, when she exclaimed, "Traitor! you have poisoned our child! the dear, dear infant is murdered!"

"Poisoned?" cried he, raising his hands and eyes.

"Yes, poisoned! and by you: look here, villain!" and she showed him the paper.

He started, but he was prepared for this: his acting was consummate. He let his head fall upon his bosom, (a motion which, by the way, was rather usual with him,) he struck his hands violently against it, and cried out,

"I am the most miserable of men, Great God! what have I done? but I will not survive it."

So saying, he rushed over to the mantelpiece, and seized a brace of pocket pistols belonging to himself, which hung there. He was in the act of applying one of them to his head, when Maria seized his arm.

"Madman!" said she, "what do you mean?"

"To follow my child," answered he. "Oh, Maria! I have, I have poisoned the dear infant; but it was by mistake. I bought a powder at Sudbury, a medicine for our infant; I unluckily purchased some poison for rats also, and—oh! my God! it was the poison I gave to the child, by mistake—and I am—I am its murderer."

He threw himself on the floor, and groaned aloud.

Maria was completely deceived by his acting, and became not less alarmed for her husband, as she always called him, than agitated by the death of her child. She stooped, and put her arms around him, saying,

"For heaven's sake, William, do not be so violent—do not alarm me in this manner. We have lost our child—do not rob me of my husband too."

"Oh! Maria," said he, "I cannot, will not live,—I am too unhappy!—besides, if I do not kill myself, I must perish by the law. If this be known, I cannot escape; I had better, therefore, die by my own hand;"—and he again seized one of the pistols, both of which had dropped when he threw himself down. Maria wrenched the pistol from his hand, which indeed, he did not hold with the firmest grasp, and threw it to the other end of the room.

"For the love of God, William, forbear," said she, "or kill me too. It shall not,—must not be known."

"I am unfortunate," he exclaimed, after a pause, "but not guilty; yet it is all the same— I must equally suffer, if this be known. I have no witnesses in my favour."

"Am not I a witness?" said Maria.

"No," replied he, "your evidence would not be taken. It would be said that we were in collusion to murder the child."

"Oh heavens!" cried she, and sunk on a chair.

Much more of this sort passed between them; and his repeated solemn asseverations, and

3 Q

parade of mock feeling, succeeded, for the present at least, in completely persuading Maria of
his innocence.

They finally agreed, that as the manner of the
child's death was known only to themselves,
they would keep it a profound secret. The old
people were to be told that the child died of
convulsion, so suddenly that timely assistance
could not be obtained.

But the death of the child produced a very
serious effect on the mind of Maria. Previously
to that event she had begun to recover the happy,
cheerful disposition which was natural to her,
tempered, it is true, by such a remembrance of her
past trials, as prevented it from re-assuming the
light and thoughtless character of her early
vivacity. But now a shade of the profoundest
melancholy began to overcast her. She scarcely
ever left the body of her infant while it remained
unburied, and passed her entire time in sighs and
tears. The jaded passion of Barnard was not
stimulated into renewed activity by this change in
her temper.

He was particularly anxious that the child
should be buried with all convenient speed. He
felt himself neither safe nor comfortable as long
as it remained above ground. He was terribly
alarmed lest the manner of its death should be
betrayed in some palpable marks on the body.
He therefore urged Maria to its immediate
burial. He told her, moreover, that the burial

must not take place at Polstead—first of all, for the very obvious and natural reason that it might be the means of promulgating their connexion in the neighbourhood, which, for the present, must be avoided ; secondly, that any examination of the body, which by some accident or other might take place, would, notwithstanding his innocence, put his life, and perhaps hers, in the most imminent danger. They determined, then, that the hapless babe should be secretly buried in the neighbourhood where its ill-fated mother had given birth to it—namely, near Sudbury.

CHAP XIX.

"————Thou sure and firm set earth,
Hear not my steps which way they walk, for faw
The very stones prate of my where-about,
And take the present horror from the time
Which now suits with it.

SHAKSPEARE.

MARIA and Barnard now prepared to proceed to Sudbury with the body of the infant. They procured a small coffin, in which its poor mortal remains were enclosed, and set out together, after night-fall, on their melancholy mission on foot.

It was moonlight, but the moon was continually obscured by detached and fleeting clouds, ever and anon traversing its silvery disk. They seemed like the scattered fugitives of a retreating army, as they were hurrying along to join the cloudy rack which was flying before the north-west wind : but the air was dry and sharp, with no symptoms of approaching rain.

Our travellers plodded on their dreary way in profound silence, through a narrow, lonely, melancholy road. How different were the feelings of the two bearers of their first, their last, their only child! Maria was wretched—and yet without being able to assign to herself a sufficient cause for her wretchedness. It was not altogether the loss of her child, aggravated, as it was, by the mode of its dissolution: this loss might have been borne. There was a chance of its being repaired, and a prospect of happier days; but her mind, in spite of herself, was filled with the most gloomy presentiments of the future. She shuddered with vague apprehensions of—she knew not what—a death-like dampness hung over her spirits, utterly subduing all their energy and elasticity. In vain she tried to rally them—in vain she summoned hope and resolution to her aid. By every mental effort, she sunk lower than before; and the tears, which she would have repressed if possible, flowed silently down her pale cheeks, as she slowly paced along.

The feelings of Barnard were different—but was he happier? Oh no! could the murderer of his child be happy?—could the extinguisher of his own blood taste of joy or peace? He was not quite so callous as totally to escape the scourge of conscience, or those pangs of feeling which outraged nature must inflict: but his chief source of uneasiness was sordid fear. He considered that his life was no longer secure: another was the depository of a secret on which his fate depended. Even though that other was Maria, he could not be satisfied: incapable himself of anything like a pure affection, he did not credit its existence in others. His decreased, I might almost say now extinguished, passion for Maria, was another cause of his distrust: those whom we cease to regard, we begin to suspect. Besides, the consciousness of his own guilt, and the fear that Maria was not deceived by his protestations, or that though she might be so at present, she might yet cease to be so, tormented him. He felt that he must escape—that he must take some step, by flight or otherwise, to secure his own safety. He was exactly in that frame of mind in which a man like him —so disposed, so circumstanced—would not long hesitate to commit one crime to shelter himself from the consequences of another. His fears were growing thick upon him ; and, as he proceeded along, the idea of his being about to bury his murdered child, made him start at every noise, lest, by any chance, his crime might have been discovered, and the agents of justice be in pursuit of him.

They had now arrived at a very picturesque part of the country. To the right of the road which they were traversing, was a very considerable extent of open ground, chiefly pasture-land and meadow. It consisted of an undulation of hill and vale, or rather of small rising slopes and gently sinking hollows: the rising grounds were all covered with clumps of thick and low trees, the close masses of whose foliage in the moonlight, contrasted in dark patches with the surrounding landscape. It all appeared to be the work of unassisted nature, for the divisions of the fields were not marked so as to be visible; and the absence of all arable land increased this illusion.

On the right of the road was a thick and verdant hedge which rose considerably above it, or—to speak more properly, the road sunk below it, for the ground on the other side was so high that a moderately tall person standing there, might be visible for more than half his height: on that side the moon shone. Along the length of this hedge, on the field side, were planted, at unequal distances, several large sycamore trees.

They had just reached a projecting corner of this road, where it winded round a little more to the right, and were proceeding on, when a voice called out, in a full, clear, deep, and thrilling tone,—

" Barnard ! stop !"

Terror seized on both the travellers; but Barnard, in particular, felt the greatest perturbation : he trembled from head to foot. The cold perspiration fell in large drops from his forehead; his teeth rattled within his lips; and his face, which was naturally florid, assumed a hue of deadly paleness, rendered still more ghastly by the reflection of the moon.

" In the name of God, William, what is that ?" exclaimed Maria.

"I know not," cried he, hurriedly; "come along."

The voice had appeared to come from behind them as they walked along; but now, on the other side of the green hedge, close by a sycamore, and directly between Barnard and the moon, stood a tall figure enveloped in dark drapery : it waved its hand, and beckoned to him. He, however, attempted to disregard it, and was hurrying quickly forward, when, in a deeper and more commanding voice than before, it called,

"William Barnard! stop!—I command you."

It would be vain to attempt to pourtray the agitation of Barnard. The surprise was so unexpected, and took place under circumstances so calculated to inspire alarm and awe, that he could not maintain his self-possession : the strength of his nerves forsook him, and he trembled like an aspen leaf. His impression was, that it was an officer of justice who had addressed him, and that the avenger of blood had overtaken him.

As for Maria, her confusion and terror were great, but, of course, she could comprehend or conjecture nothing respecting their cause.

Barnard was in that state in which a man is, whose courage is so paralyzed that he has not even the power to run away; still, even in all his agitation, the selfish, sordidness of his character broke out.

" Here," said he to Maria, in a faltering voice,

" take this, (pushing the coffin towards her); — take it—take it—I must see who calls me.'

Maria, with trembling hand, took the coffin, and walked slowly on; Barnard returned trembling to the place where the figure addressed him. It descended from an open part of the hedge, and came into the road. He came up : the figure was enveloped in a large dark cloak. It removed the hood on his approach, and, to his utter astonishment, confusion, and rage, it proved to be— Hannah Woods!

Barnard's audacity now returned, and his first feeling was to strike her to the earth ; but, recollecting that Maria was within sight and hearing, he paused, checked his feelings, and listened patiently.

" Barnard," said she, " it is in vain that you attempt to shun me :—I must be heard."

" What brings you here ?" replied he : " wherefore do you persecute me ?"

" Necessity !" answered Hannah.

" I cannot minister to your necessity," said Barnard ; " and it may not be for your interest thus to pursue me."

" I care not—I am reckless,—consequences are nothing to me now. I see who is with you."

" What of that ?" said Barnard.

" Much," replied Hannah ; " much more than you are aware of. But I must see you again, and talk with you : it is for your own interest, welfare, and security. Your life is in my hands, William

3 R

Barnard; and if you regard it, you will meet me
to-morrow evening, after dark."

" Why should I meet you?" said Barnard: "I
will not meet you."

" Then you will take the consequences. I care
not;—if you do not meet me, you shall deeply
repent it."

" Where would you have me to meet you?"
said Barnard.

" At Smith's cottage,—there you will find me,
after dark."

" Well—I—will meet you; and now let us
part."

" Don't fail, Barnard, at your peril;—for your
own sake you will not. Recollect, I hold the
scales of your destiny in my hands, and a touch
of mine can incline the balance. Meet me, if you
regard your existence."

So saying, she re-ascended, and quickly disappeared over the hedge.

Barnard and Maria now pursued their journey,
until they arrived where the narrow road they
had been traversing struck into the highway.
They crossed the latter, and turned into some
fields, through which there was a path: this
finally conducted them to a lonely, isolated,
uncultivated valley, surrounded on all sides with
thick low brushwood. A limpid stream flowed
through the midst of this little spot, over a sandy
bottom: it seemed to be a place completely shut
out from the rest of nature,—such as the genius

of solitude might be supposed to choose for his most favorite haunt.

Here Barnard suddenly halted, and said to Maria, " This is the place where we shall bury the child ;—remain here for a few minutes, until I return."

So saying, he ascended the nearest eminence, and disappeared through the brushwood.

Maria laid down the coffin, and seated herself on a broad stone at the foot of the hill. The wild and barren scenery—the uncertain light of the moon, as the clouds which successively obscured it flung their dark shadows across the valley—the silence of midnight, unbroken, save by the hooting of the owl heard from the distant wood—and the light gurgling of the stream, as it surmounted some opposing pebbles in its descent from the hill,—harmonized well with the sadness of her desolate heart. She looked on the coffin containing the relics of her beloved infant, raised her eyes and hands to heaven, and wept bitterly.

Barnard remained absent for nearly half an hour, and Maria began to feel alarmed at her lonely situation. He returned, however, at last, carrying a spade upon his shoulder; how he had procured it is not known.

He spoke not a word, but proceeded, in gloomy silence, to dig the grave. The spot he chose for this purpose, was a little hillock not far from the source of the gushing stream.

Maria was attentively and silently watching the

vrogress of his labour.   He continued to work for
more than half an hour: she, at length, observed that he was making the grave of a much
greater magnitude than was necessary for a small
infant.   She noticed this :—

"Aye," said he, the grave should be large ;"
and he looked at her with a mysterious and undefinable expression of countenance. She trembled,
but knew not wherefore.

Barnard finished.   He flung down the spade,
folded his arms, and looked intently for some
minutes in the new-made grave.   He then raised
his eyes, looked at Maria, and then looked down
into the grave again.   He now walked round it,
paced up and down a few turns, with his arms
still folded, and with an air of the greatest abstraction.   He seemed like one who was de-
liberating about something of intense interest, and
could not make up his mind.

He returned to the grave, looked into it again,
and, after a long pause, observed,

"It is large enough."

"Too large," replied a hollow voice, which
actually, to his frighted ears, seemed to issue
from the bosom of the hill.

Maria sunk on the earth with terror,—Barnard
started with the most fearful agitation. When a
little recovered, he exclaimed,

"Who are you ?—answer, I charge you."

There was no reply.

Maria and he now listened in trembling silence,

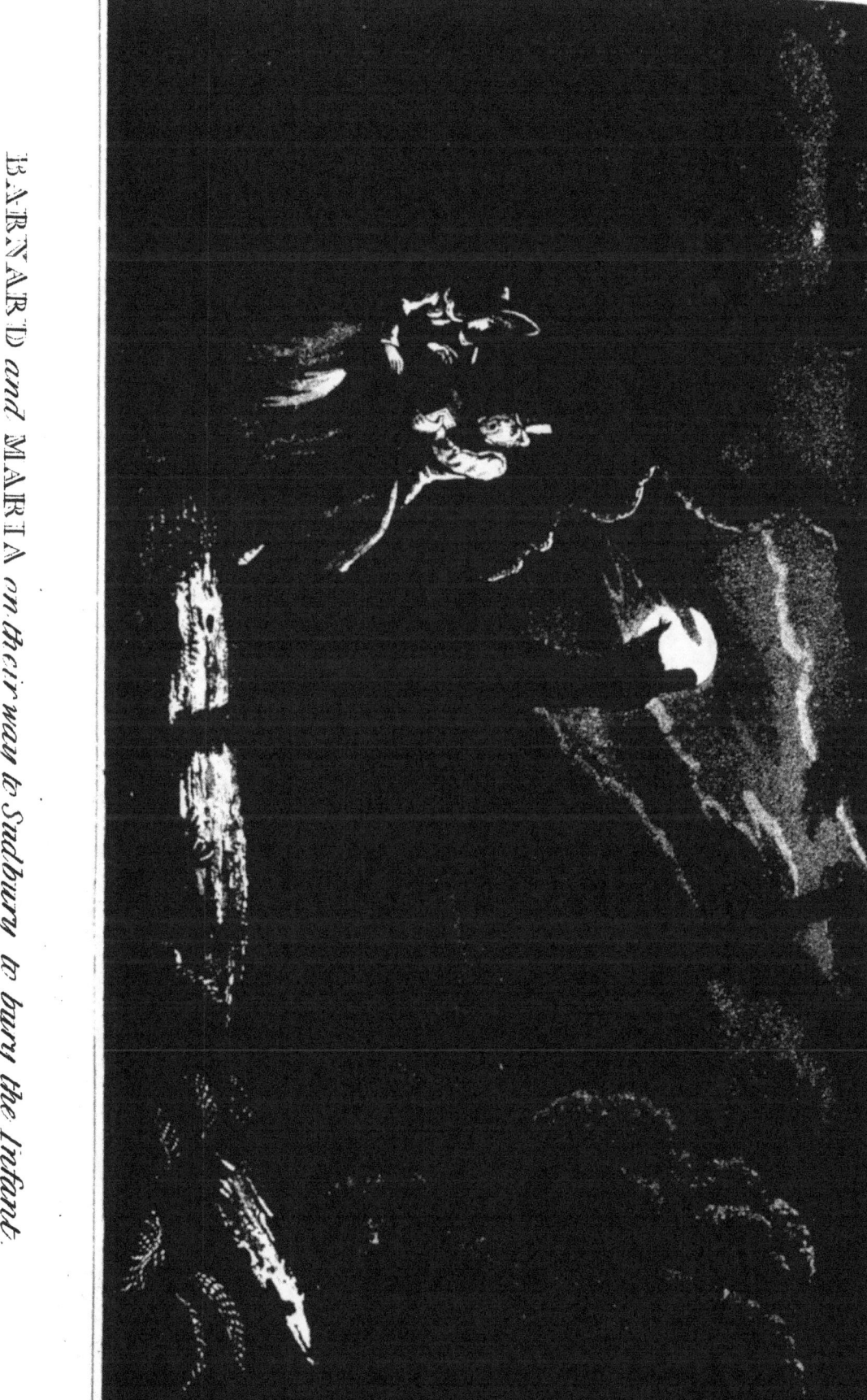

BARNARD *and* MARIA *on their way to Sudbury to bury the Infant.*

See Page 287.

for a few seconds; but they heard no sound save the plaintive murmur of the rivulet.

"Give me the coffin," said Barnard; "we must dispatch, and leave this place."

They deposited the coffin in the ground. Barnard covered it with nervous precipitation, and replaced, as well as he could, the green sods which he had dug up.

"Farewell, my dearest, dearest child!" sobbed Maria, as the last turf was replaced on the new-made grave of the murdered innocent; "never, never, shall I see you more."

"Come on, come on," muttered Barnard; "we are not safe here."

They quitted the valley, and having entered on the field-path, walked on for some time without speaking. Maria, at last, said,

"What could that voice have been, William?"

"I know not," replied he; "probably nothing but the echo of the place."

"That could not be," said Maria; "I think it was the voice of a spirit."

"Nonsense," answered Barnard; "there is no such thing—let us talk no more about it."

"But who," said Maria, "was that who spoke to you on the road?—that voice I certainly have heard somewhere before."

"Don't ask me now," said Barnard; "I'll tell you hereafter—I cannot talk at present."

They now proceeded homewards, and gained the cottage, after an hour's walking, without further interruption : there they parted—Barnard giving Maria an hypocritical embrace. She retired to a sleepless bed, to bathe her pillow with tears,—he wended homewards his solitary way, distracted by a variety of the most fearful reflections, and revolving in his remorseless mind deep and dark designs of villany.

He was haunted, as by a demon, with the perpetual thought that his life was in danger : he did not, however, repent him of the enormous crime which he had committed, but regretted its imperfect concealment. He believed that Maria more than half suspected the truth; and the idea that she, or any other human being, should be the depository of this dreadful secret, was terrible to him. He was already three parts inclined to send the mother to keep company with the child. His extraordinary abstracted manner at the grave was the result of a sudden impulse of this nature; and had it not been for the voice by which he was startled there, it is far from improbable that Maria might never have returned from the valley where her infant was buried.

Again, on the other hand, he was greatly troubled and alarmed at the re-appearance of Hannah : here was danger from another quarter. He knew that he was in her power also : she could lodge informations of a very serious kind against him, in consequence of his London pranks : besides, had she no knowledge of his last crime? He could not account to himself for the possibility of her possessing such knowledge; and yet he could not divest his imagination of the idea that she did possess it. The voice by which he was startled in the valley, he was convinced, was hers. She saw him, then, bury the infant in a clandestine manner, in unconsecrated gound;—that would be a sufficient foundation for her to injure him, and he knew, too well, that she had the inclination.

He resolved, however, to keep his appointment with her the following evening, that he might ascertain the full extent of the risk to which he was exposed, and take the best measures that circumstances might suggest.

Barnard accordingly repaired to his appointment. He went to the cabin which, for some time back, had been tenanted by Smith, Ellen, and the old hag who had been originally placed there as the ostensible occupant. At present, however, he found nobody there but the last mentioned and Hannah: Smith, he knew, had gone up to town some days before.

When he entered, he found Hannah sitting in the parlour, at a small table, by the embers of a half-extinguished fire, and with a pale and solitary light before her, which might almost be said to render darkness visible. She was poorly attired, and had lost all traces of her former beauty: the pleasing expression of countenance, which she had known how well to assume, had all vanished. It had given place to a calm, cool, determined look of recklessness, with a sort of

chastised ferocity in the eye, which was rendered
not the less alarming from the evident attempt to
restrain and temper it.   Her naturally strong
features and swarthy complexion were totally
unrelieved by any artificial aid from the art of the
toilet; and she looked full ten years older than
when Barnard had last seen her.   How changed
from what she was!—how changed from the
voluptuous syren—the luxurious Egyptian—who,
aided by all that art, and dress, and manner,
could bestow, had given an added zest to the
Epicurean banquet, the Bacchanalian revel; who
seemed to possess the power of pepetual excitement; whose soft and thrilling accents of love
would strike an alarum to the heart of an an-
chorite; and within whose arms was all that is
fabled of the eternal virgins of Paradise!   The
fire of love, or of simulated passion, no longer
illuminated her eye; it was cold, and dark, and
gloomy: yet her form still possessed much of its
original and native dignity.   She was ruined, but
it was the ruin of the archangel.

> "————————Care
> Sat on *her* faded cheek, but under brows
> Of dauntless courage, and considerate pride
> Waiting revenge."

She looked like a being who was not to be trifled
with,—who had fortified herself as with triple
steel to execute all that she had resolved—to
whom life and death were equally indifferent—
who, to better her existence, would not hesitate

at the chance of losing it; and rather than not gain the point she had in view, would perish in the attempt.

She raised her eyes on the entrance of Barnard, and said,

"It is well,—you are faithful to your appointment."

Hannah was sitting between two tables,—or rather, there was a small table a little towards her right hand, while her left was leaning on the larger table at which she sat. The latter table filled the room so as to render it rather difficult for Barnard to come round to her side. She rose up, threw back an old black cloak which she wore, took from her girdle a pair of pocket pistols, and laid them very deliberately on the smaller table—at the same time suffering to appear very visibly the handle of a poniard which protruded from her bosom. How unlike the Hannah of the rustic ball, of the first private meeting at the Red Barn—the Hannah that he regreeted in London, on his second arrival there—or even the artful and voluptuous wanton, in Grecian state, whom he had detected with the old gentleman: she looked utterly unhumanized, unsexed. She seemed an object that it would be impossible to think of with any sentiments of desire or love the woman had vanished, and nothing but the fiend remained. But she was calm, cool, and collected—wholly unruffled by any symptom of

3 ı

63

passion whatever. She repeated, in a deep and tranquil tone,

"You are come, William Barnard:—I am glad of it, for your own sake."

Barnard did not contemplate her appearance and behaviour without a certain degree of alarm: he saw very clearly that a bullying conduct on his part would be of no use. He replied, after a pause,

"Yes; I am come :—what would you with me?"

"That will explain," said Hannah, handing him a letter.

The contents of this letter were as follow :-

"DEAR WILLIAM;

"I am pinned at last,—decidedly nibbled. Information was laid about our last concern, and I am bagged : the least I can expect, is a trip over the herring pond. Ellen is here, and sometimes sees me : she is now a free trader, on her own bottom: I can't help that. Good bye, my dear Barnard; keep your sails up, though your keel be striking the ground. I send you a lock of my hair: good bye. Remember that if I am topped, I'll die game :—I hope you will do the same if it should be your luck to go that way.

"Yours, very truly,

"J. SMITH.

"London, Newgate, 10th Feb. 18---."

"A pretty epistle," said Barnard, as he finished it; "but what is all this to me?"

"Everything," replied Hannah; "you were engaged with him in this robbery, and your liberty, if not your life, is in danger. You are in my power—not only for this, but for other matters. You are in his also."

"Well," said Barnard, "I can't help it;—you must do your worst."

"Barnard," replied Hannah, "you mistake me: I do not come here to injure you—I come as a friend, notwithstanding all that has passed. I own that I have once deceived you, but I do not pretend to do so any longer: I speak to you now, as a man of sense and of the world. I do not pretend to keep up the farce of love."

"Proceed," said Barnard; "I am all attention."

"Smith is ruined," replied Hannah; "they are all ruined. You can hope for nothing more in that mode of life; nor can you live long as you do at present."

"This is all very true," said Barnard; "I know I cannot: but what do you counsel me to do?"

"To raise your fortune by marriage," said Hannah.

"By marriage!" replied Barnard, and paused awhile. "Yes; I believe there is something in that: but how go about it?—it requires introduction."

"I have a plan," said Hannah, "by which you cannot fail to succeed; but my assistance will be necessary, and I cannot afford to give it for nothing."

" Name your plan," said Barnard.

" This it is," said Hannah: " you go to London, advertise in the papers for a wife; I will resume my character of fortune-teller, and find out some girls of property, from the addresses to the answers, whom I will persuade that they are to be married to a man exactly like you, and through the medium of an advertisement."

" Well," said Barnard, " and, in case of success, what do you expect?"

" While I remain here, a protection from want; and, in case of success in the matrimonal specu-lation, one hundred pounds; otherwise, William Barnard, you shall have no assistance from me, and I shall be forced to make unpleasant dis-closures concerning you."

" Well," said Barnard, " you talk fairly: it is our interest to be friends—I accede to your terms. My present means are but scant, but I will do all I can."

" You have a connexion in this country which you must break, William Barnard," said Hannah.

" How do you know anything about it?" ob-served Barnard.

" No matter how," said Hannah, " I know it; and I know more than that,—your life is not very safe here, William Barnard."

He started. " What," cried he, " what do you know?"

" Did not I see you," said Hannah, " burying your child by moonlight, in unconsecrated ground. What could that be for?"

" Secresy," replied Barnard.

" I believe you," said Hannah, expressively ; " but," added she, " re-assure yourself—I will not betray you. While you act fair, I shall be faithful ; but, mark my words—no longer."

Barnard now departed, having first supplied Hannah with a little money. Here was a new coalition formed between them, very different from their original one. That had been an union of sensual passion and sottish confidence on the one side, and duplicity and avarice on the other ; this was a consolidation of interest and exertion on both sides, for the avowed purpose of undisguised villany. There was no love on either side, but the love of self—no confidence, except that which, like the courage of a coward, is the inspiration of fear.

Matters continued in this state for some time longer. Barnard could not yet arrange things so as to be enabled to depart for London, or make up his mind as to the disposal of Maria. He felt himself now in a state of double slavery. His means were seriously contracted, by reason of the supplies he was forced to advance, and his mind was perpetually tormented by the though* that he was in the power of two women, either of whom, by a single word, might seal his destruction.

Thus situated, he came to the resolution, that of either of them he must decidedly get rid, by some means or other. He could not fly—he could not escape. His property was in such a state that he could not convert it into cash, without some time, difficulty, and trouble. If he were to withdraw himself from the country, he would withdraw himself from the present means of subsistence, and resign the indispensable foundation of his future hopes. Besides, he would leave himself open to the vengeance of two enraged females, and his very flight would be a tacit confession of guilt.

He began then to argue with himself, which of these two females he had better trust to—which of them he should determine to remove. For that either of them must be removed, and removed by death, he had fully decided. Was Hannah to be his victim? Here he came to a dead pause. His interest was now obviously connected with hers. She might always be induced either to act or to conceal anything, for money. She was absolutely necessary to his future measures. He could not do without her. She must be the stepping stone, not merely to his fortune, but to his security. Moreover, were he even resolved to kill her, had he decided that such would be the most expedient measure, could he do it? Here he paused again: Hannah was a very dangerous woman to meddle with—her genius overawed him. The promptitude and determination of her character, which lent her an apparent ubiquity, gave her, in his eyes, something of a supernatural cast. In plain language, he was afraid of her: the interview which he had with her at the cottage, as we have described, proved to him that she was on her guard. Every subsequent interview confirmed this fact to demonstration: she never went un-armed, and she always took care to let him see that she was not so. His own life might be the immediate forfeit of any attack on hers: violence she was prepared to resist, and he could never hope to overreach her by art, or lull her suspicions and win her confidence by smooth-tongued hypo-crisy.

Hannah was, then, out of the question; but Maria remained. Maria, an obstacle to his hopes not to be surmounted, but which must be re-moved. He could do nothing until she was dis-posed of;—she was a clog on his every movement. She was also a thorn in his side: his life was especially in her power. He felt convinced that she was the depository of his most dreadful secret. There was no safety for him while she lived,— no peace of mind, no tranquillity, no pleasure, by day,—no rest, no oblivion, by night. His agita-tion of mind was terrible: his health was affected —his appetite was gone—sleep was banished from his pillow. The hated cause of all this must be removed.

Had he wavered at all in this, his final deter-mination, a conversation which took place be-

tween Barnard and Maria, about this time, was
sufficient to fix his decision. Latterly, they had
many altercations. Barnard, from day to day,
had postponed, under a variety of pretexts, the
performance of his promise of marriage : Maria,
wearied of guilt, incessantly urged him to the
execution of it. To her intreaties, those of her
parents were strenuously united. The connexion
was beginning to be more than whispered
through the village; in fact, it was almost
publicly known. Maria's character, of course,
suffered severely : she lived very privately ; but
still she heard and saw sufficient to convince her
of this fact. If she ever did venture out, the girls
of her acquaintance passed her with a contemptuous sneer, and often with a very audible expression of their notions of her character. This
preyed deeply on her mind, and she was continually urging Barnard to do her justice, and
restore her to the enjoyment of her pristine
reputation.

It is needless to say that all this was ex
ceedingly disagreeable to him, and often excited
his anger in no small degree. One day, when
they were both speaking on this subject, the conversation turned on the death of the infant. Maria
stated to Barnard that, on the day before, when
she had been at Sudbury, she had gone to the
apothecary from whom the powder which had
been administered to the child was said to have
been bought. She had gone to him merely to

procure some simple for her mother,—and that he told her he did not sell Barnard *two* powders, but only *one,* on the occasion stated by him ; and she asked Barnard how he could have been mistaken. This alarmed him :—he replied in his usual hypocritical strain, and succeeded, at least, in silencing Maria on this dangerous topic. But from that moment he felt that he stood on a terrible precipice. He did not fear Maria herself —but she might speak of the circumstance to her mother : the thought shook him with fear, and he felt that while Maria lived he could not be safe.

CHAP. XX.

"And the complexion of the element
Is tev'rous, like the work we have in hand."

SHAKSPEARE.

IT is not to be supposed that Barnard determined quickly, or at once, upon the murder of Maria.　A sudden impulse to commit it certainly did seize his mind at the burial of the infant: time, place, and opportunity, then seemed to concur so favourably for the atrocity.　But in the case of all premeditated crimes, it almost always happens, that even the greatest ruffians must familiarize their minds for a time with the idea of the act they are about to perpetrate.　The habit of contemplating a forbidden action will gradually render us less averse to its performance, when good, or fancied good, to ourselves is to be the result.　On every repeated contemplation it loses, in our estimation, a portion of its natural deformity.　It is not in human nature to choose crime for its own sake. There must be first a powerful temptation, and the understanding must be blinded by the passions, before the worst of men can make up his mind coolly and deliberately to the perpetration of a great enormity. It is quite a mistake to suppose that criminals see their own guilt in the light that others see it. They either pursuade themselves that the act they have in contemplation is not so bad as it is represented, or they are supplied, by the sophistry of self-love, with the most invincible reason in favour of its commission.

Such was the case with Barnard. The idea of his connexion with Maria became every hour more and more irksome to him. It hung with a dead weight upon his mind—a clog without the removal of which there was no hope of freedom, no prospect of prosperity. He might fly, it is true, with some little difficulty; but if he should so, what would be the consequence ?—the certain risk of his life. Such a measure would, he was certain, cause the disclosure that he had so much reason to dread. There were, he conceived, but three possible choices for him, and all of them evil. He might fly, and have his life in perpetual danger, and his mind in constant uneasiness—he might remain, in which case he must have married Maria, and, without getting rid of his fear, have lived unhappily with a woman he could no longer love, and must have given up all his hopes of fortune—or, he might remove the object which stood between him and present peace and future prosperity, and trust to management and good fortune for the concealment of the deed. In an evil hour he determined on the last. The fiend which had been long planning his eternal destruction, now succeeded in achieving the final blow. The net of guilt, in which he had been long entangled, had its last meshes now completed. The concluding link was now forged of that fatal chain which was to bind him to the throne of the Prince of Darkness—perhaps for ever!

Having made up his mind to the commission of the atrocious deed, the next thing to be considered was, how was it to be done?—This question involved no small degree of consideration. It behoved him to proceed with the utmost caution, and to make all possible provision against discovery. Time, place, and manner, were all to be provided for.

While his mind was in this state of deliberation, another circumstance occurred, which was not calculated to make him slacken in the execution of his infamous design. As this circumstance also will throw some light on another character in this story, we shall relate it. Sometime before what we have been now relating had taken place, Jackson, who had not altogether forgotten Maria, and who wished still to make all the further atonement in his power for deserting her, sent her by post a letter containing £50. He had met with some success, and his first thought was to impart some assistance to his unfortunate victim. He sent the letter from Brussels, where he then was, and requested that she would write an acknowledgment of its reception to an address in London, which he inserted.

It so happened that when the letter arrived at old Marten's, there was no one in the cottage but William Barnard: he took the letter in, and evidently felt that there was an enclosure in it. Without ceremony, he broke the letter open, and read it; then put the money very quietly into his pocket, considering it as an excellent windfall, and threw the letter into the fire.

Jackson, having waited for some time, and received no reply from Maria, wrote again. Barnard was not so successful in intercepting this last epistle as the former: Maria received it; and read it with the utmost astonishment.

The first thing she did, was to communicate this discovery to William Barnard. He exhibited some confusion on the occasion; but, pretending to treat the business lightly, said that he supposed it was some miscarriage of the post, and bade her think no more of it. He told her, moreover, that he was glad of it, as he did not desire that she should receive assistance from any one but himself, and least of all from Jackson.

It so fell out, however, that in a few days after this conversation with Barnard, Maria Marten chanced to meet the village postman. She stated the facts which we have now related, and, to her great surprise, he assured her that he had brought the letter in question to the cottage, and that it had been taken in and paid for by Mr. William Barnard!

This conduct, on the part of Barnard, both astonished and displeased Maria : she thought it both unkind and unprincipled; and when she next met him, she reproached him with it. He, seeing that a denial was of no further use, now openly confessed the fact.

He said that, in the first place, he did not like the idea of any communication between her and Jackson; and, in the next, that he was, at the time he opened the letter, in a state of great embarrassment, in consequence of a bill of his having just come due, and for which there was no immediate provision; he, therefore, he said, had ventured to borrow the money with the full intention of repaying it at the earliest opportunity. He had no other means, he said, at that time, of saving himself from the jaws of a prison; and he solemnly swore, that the very instant certain monies should be paid which were then owing to him, he would put £50 into her hands, which she might either return to Jackson, or dispose of in whatever other way she thought proper.

Maria said that it was not the consideration so much of the money that displeased her, as the want of confidence on his part. However, after some further gentle reproaches on her side, she heartily and freely forgave him.

But this circumstance, which, in a different state of things, might have been unproductive of any effect, whetted his resolution still more to the immediate execution of his atrocious design : he felt that every moment's delay was pregnant with danger. By this discovery, he concluded that he must have lost every tittle of her confidence—that she was not in any degree to be trusted—and that there was no security for him but in her destruction.

But how was that destruction to be accomplished ? Barnard at first thought of poison ; but he soon relinquished that idea. He was afraid of detection, and he did not like to have recourse again to a mode in which he had already partly failed—failed, if not in execution, at least in concealment : such a failure, in the second instance, must be fatal. Poison was not difficult of detection ;—the purchasing of it was dangerous—the administering of it both difficult and dangerous. Its operation was not always to be depended upon : Maria might live long enough under its influence to ruin him. Its marks might become so apparent as to be obvious to detection : a thousand accidents might lead to discovery ; and should any accident lead to suspicion, that suspicion would hardly fall on any one but himself.

Poison, then, was not to be thought of : he must take some mode more certain in its execution, and more easily concealed.

He also revolved in his own mind where the dreadful deed which he was contemplating should be performed. It must not be done in the cottage, or in any place where the body could not be properly concealed. Sometimes he thought of inveigling Maria away with him to some considerable distance. Then again he reflected that a long absence would expose him to great suspicion, and that in any quarter the localities of which he was not well acquainted with, he should find a great difficulty of concealment.

The idea of Smith's cottage then occurred to him. "Down," thought he, "in the cave, the deed might be perpetrated with safety, and the body concealed." But then it could not be done without the knowledge of Hannah,—and he was determined to have no confidante to his guilt, and least of all such a one as she. He was far too deeply in her power already—he did not choose to involve himself any farther there. That might necessitate the commission of another crime; and, steeped as he was in guilt, he still trembled at the idea of a concatenation of murders

At last he bethought himself of the Red Barn! He kept the key of it himself—the place was at present particularly isolated—he would be liable to no interruption—and he could hide the body there, as he thought, so as to defy the possibility of detection. He imagined, too, that this place, though possessing many requisites for such a deed of horror, would yet be generally thought an unlikely place enough for the commission of a murder.

On the Red Barn he then fixed, as the theatre in which to perform his bloody tragedy: he also fixed upon the instruments which he should employ. He determined first to try the pistol, and if that failed, to have recourse to the sword.

Respecting the use of the latter weapon, he adopted a measure which discloses a most marked trait in his diabolical character: he took a curved sword, which had been for some time in the possession of his family, to a cutler in the neighbourhood. He gave him directions to make this sword as sharp as he possibly could; and though not called on to give any reason for this, he added, with careless impudence and levity, that within a few days he was to be present at a wedding; and that he intended, merely as a whim, to make use of this weapon as a carving knife!

Having now made up his mind, digested his plan, and prepared everything for its execution, all that remained was to inveigle Maria to the intended scene of action. For this purpose he visited the cottage, and introduced himself, quite contrary to his usual custom, the subject of their marriage. Before this, he scarcely ever mentioned it, except when it was forced on his attention by the urgency of Maria or her parents. Now he commenced it himself—telling them that it had been too ong deferred, though unavoidably;

3 u

and that he was now determined that the ceremony should be performed without delay : still, he observed, that the greatest privacy was indispensably necessary, to keep it from the knowledge of his relations—that Maria and himself must leave Polstead secretly, and get married at Ipswich, by licence, to avoid the publicity and delay incident to being called in church.

The old people and Maria were quite delighted at his proposal ; and the latter bestowed many caresses on the hypocritical, subtle, murderous villain, which, had he possessed any feeling, must have been like so many daggers in his heart. Feel them he did, in spite of all his callousness ; but his personal fears, and strong determination on crime, were not to be overpowered. He appointed to come the next day to take Maria to Ipswich, and then withdrew as soon as he conveniently could, lest the contending feelings by which he was agitated should betray him.

As he was returning home, he was met by Hannah Woods.

" Barnard," said she, " you are losing time—you should be in London."

" I know it," replied he ; " but I cannot go yet awhile.'

" You cannot resolve to give up this girl, I suppose?" said Hannah.

" I shall soon get rid of her," said Barnard ; " she is about to leave the country."

" For ever ?" said Hannah.

There was something in the tone and look, with which she pronounced these words, that disturbed him. She, probably, meant nothing by them; but the natural peculiarity of her manner, added to his own consciousness of premediated guilt, produced a shuddering feeling through his frame.

"Yes!" he replied, with a voice a little faltering; " I hope for ever."

" I hope so too," said Hannah; " when she is gone you may be free—but not till then."

No more passed between them; but this was sufficient to strengthen him still more in his diabolical determinations.

The following morning Barnard came to the cottage about ten o'clock. He then stated that their departure must yet be deferred for a day or two;—that his mother was unwell, and he could not, with propriety, be absent until she got better. He said that they should go on the following Thursday, if possible.

The fact was, he had been that morning at the cutler's, and found that his sword had not been sharpened; nor could it be finished for a day or two, as the cutler was unavoidably absent. This was the true reason why the villain thought fit to defer their departure.

In the interim which elapsed between that and the day appointed for the marriage, Maria suffered very much from mental depression: she could not tell why, or wherefore; but she had an undefined feeling of some dreadful calamity im

pending over her. She thought perpetually on
the fate of her poor child, and was constantly
bursting into tears. Her nights were for the
most part sleepless; or, if she did at any time
close her eyes, her rest was agitated by vague and
terrific dreams. She would suddenly start from
sleep—awakened by some horrid image, too
dreadful to be borne; and utter an involuntary
scream of terror. Her mother, alarmed, would come
to see what was the matter, and find her trembling
every nerve, and her face bedewed with a cold,
damp, and death-like perspiration

She thought, too, sometimes of Barnard with
an unaccountable feeling of distrust: his conduct,
relative to the money, occurred to her. She then
thought of the child :—could he have intended to
poison the child ?—But no !—that was impossible;
—she could never believe it. Who could be that
mysterious person that met them on the road ?—
Barnard had never given a satisfactory explanation
of that. A thousand little indescribable peculiarities in his manner had lately struck her: he
was reserved, abstracted, silent, seemed often lost
in thought, and gave most incoherent answers,
and impertinent to the subject. He would sit
with her sometimes for an hour together without
opening his lips, and then get up, take his hat,
and walk away without bidding farewell. She
also could not avoid observing how careless he
was grown in his dress. This was the more remarkable as he had hitherto been always notorious

for the reverse: he had evinced a strong tendency to be a coxcomb—now he was culpably negligent even of cleanliness.

She sometimes would ask him the causes of all this, and what was the matter with him. He generally replied, that he was unwell—that he felt his health severely affected; and, indeed, his thin and haggard looks bore testimony to the truth of this statement. His florid complexion had given way to a deadly paleness; and, instead of having the elastic step and erect gait of youth, he stooped considerably.

But Maria's distrustful feelings concerning Barnard were merely temporary, and, as it were, instinctive: her understanding did not concur with them, and she could not bring herself to think really ill of him. The fact was, that, with all his unworthiness and apparently repelling qualities, the unfortunate girl sincerely loved him; and against those we love, it is impossible to retain any permanent suspicion. We cannot help thinking that they feel as we do; nor can we easily be brought to suppose that they would act towards us differently from what we would towards them.

On the Thursday, Barnard came and made some pretext for deferring their departure a little longer: his mother, he said, was not completely recovered, nor was his sister perfectly well. He did not then appoint any definite day for them to go, but said that it should be in a day or two at farthest.

On the following day, however, William Barnard called at the cottage about noon : Maria was then up stairs with her mother, and he sent for her to come down and speak with him. When he saw her, he said,

" Well, Maria, I have come for you at last We must go—so get ready immediately."

" Why, William," she replied, " that cannot be —I cannot get everything ready.   You said yesterday that it should not be for a day or two ; and this being nearly the end of the week, I am not prepared."

" Never mind preparation," answered he ; " it is not as if you were going a long journey, or to marry a stranger."

" But surely," said she, "a day or two can make no great difference."

" No, no !" he replied ; " there must be no more delay : you have been disappointed too often,, and you must come now."

After some further conversation, he opened a parcel which he carried, and took out a male dress—telling Maria that, for the purpose of avoiding observation, she should put on that dress; and that, instead of going out together, they should meet at the Red Barn, where she was to resume her female dress, which he would carry thither.   After some more talk on this point, the measure was agreed to, and Maria went up stairs to change her dress, while Barnard seated himself for a few moments by the parlour fire.

Maria went up to her bed-room, where her mother still was. She laid the dress, which Barnard had given her, on the bed; and throwing herself into a chair, burst into an involuntary flood of tears.

" What is the matter, Maria ?" said her mother; " and what is that dress for ?"

" I am going, my dear mother," answered Maria; " going at last."

" Going, Maria ! where ?"

" To be married," said she; and again wept bitterly.

" Why, I thought William said yesterday, that you could not go for a day or two;—how he changes his mind ! And what is that dress for ?"

" I must wear it to escape observation : I shall put on my own again at the Red Barn."

" At the Red Barn !" said the mother.

" Yes! William and I will meet there;—we must not go out together."

" Maria !" said her mother, " all this seems very strange to me. I don't know how it is, but I don't half like your going now;—I had a dream last night."

" Oh, mother !" said Maria, rising, and wiping her eyes; " there is no use in our talking about it—go I must : I feel that—my character——"

" True," said the mother; " yet I wish it had been on any other day;—Friday is an unlucky day "

"Well, well," said Maria, preparing to dress herself, "it must be."

While Barnard was sitting below, old Marten entered, and found him with a pair of pocket pistols in his hand, which he was snapping and examining as if to see that the flints were in proper order. He started at the father's appearance; but quickly recovering himself, asked him how he did, and told him that Maria and himself were now going to be married.

The old man, who had nothing of the feelings of his wife on the occasion, expressed his entire satisfaction at the news, but added very abruptly,

"What are you going to do with those pistols, William?"

"Oh!" said Barnard carelessly, "I never travel without pistols. Nothing like being prepared for whatever may happen: but it is getting late," continued he. "God bless you, my dear sir! I must go out before Maria."

"God bless you, my son!" said old Marten; "and I hope and trust you will take care of Maria."

"Don't be afraid of that," said Barnard; "I'll take the best possible care of her."

As he was going out, he called to Maria to make haste, or they should be too late. He received a bundle from her, and directing her to take a private path-way to the Red Barn, while he should take the public road, hurried off with the most unceremonious precipitation.

Maria now finished dressing, and came down stairs with her mother. The parting with her parents was deeply affecting: she was bathed in tears.

" Don't cry, Maria," said her father; " you are going, I hope, to be happy."

" Yes," said Maria, " I know I am; but I can't help crying."

" Husband!" said the mother, " I don't like Maria's going: I am terribly afraid some accident will happen to her;—I had a dream last night."

" Pooh, pooh!" said Marten, " don't tell us about your dreams,—the girl will be happy enough. Villiam's a good lad, and will protect her,—he has his pistols with him."

" Pistols!" rejoined the mother: " well, God protect her !"

The parents then folded their unfortunate child in their embraces, and pronounced a long, a last farewell! and Maria crossed that threshold, over which she was never, never to return.

It was now high noon: the sun shone brightly in a cloudless sky, and not a breath disturbed the calm serenity of the atmosphere. Nothing could be heard but that low buzzing sound which almost seems to render silence itself more palpable. How little in accordance was the horrid tragedy, about to be performed, with such a day!—and yet, how tenfold more horrible from the contrast! There was something, too, in the death-like still-

3 x

ness that prevailed around, to excite and cherish apprehension and foreboding, in a mind already depressed, from whatever cause. It was like the terrific calm which is said to precede the first shocks of an earthquake.

Maria felt a most unconquerable depression of spirits : she knew the necessity of haste, but her limbs seemed to fail her as she walked, and to refuse to obey the dictates of volition—as we often fancy they do in some frightful dream, in which we appear to be making abortive efforts tc escape from instant and tremendous danger

She stopped, and leaned against a tree : the cottage where she had been born was still in sight. There it stood—its white walls gleaming in the sun-light, and partly shaded by the climbing rose trees, whose more than half-blown honours were shedding their fragrance far around. Within a little time they will fade, wither, and die, thought Maria ;—but they were not destined, like herself, a fairer flower, to be cropped in their bloom of beauty by a ruffian hand !

The sight of the cottage, and its surrounding scenery, produced a strange effect upon her mind : every object about assumed a vivid and painful distinctness to her eye; and the recollections associated with it rose in review before her fancy. In an instant of time, her whole life passed like a panorama before her mind's eve her playful infancy, her careless happy youth, all the events that had occurred within so short a space to excite and afflict her feelings, passed before her.

She felt a sudden impulse to go back to the cottage: again, the necessity of her marriage pressed upon her mind. Something seemed inwardly to tell her that, in spite of all reluctance, she must proceed,—that there was no going back now. Her heart was sinking within her; but on she felt she *must* go: a mysterious voice, more powerful than her fears, commanded her forward.

> " Some say, the Genius so
> Cries *Come !* to him that instantly must die."

It was the voice of irrevocable destiny, and she obeyed it: her days were numbered,—her last hour was at hand. Innocent victim of delusion !— culpable in nothing but a foolish fond credulity, an overweening confidence in the base and villanous !—Sacred Heaven ! why was there no protecting hand to succour and to save her?—why did not thy lightnings consume the wretch in his yet vague and formless conceptions of murder ?— why did not the thunderbolt—— but stop !—let not the weak presumptuous voice of mortal dare to arraign the decrees of eternal wisdom.

But where was Barnard now ?—where was the layer in wait for blood ?—the incarnate fiend who could coolly premeditate the destruction of her who so sincerely, so fondly loved him ? At the RED BARN,—on the very stage where he was to act a part, almost without parallel in the annals of human atrocity. All was prepared;—the weapons of death were ready, and the instruments of concealment.

What were his feelings? Were they calm, cool, collected?—was he so hardened in guilt as to have no touches of compunction?—so nerved in villany as to have lost all conscience? Not so;—he was still agitated by a tempest of contending feelings: the demon and the coward were struggling in his bosom; but the former gained the ascendancy, and the latter was silenced, if not subdued: he had screwed up his determination, if not his courage, to the sticking place. He could not rid himself of the physical sensations of fear and horror, but he palsied their moral influence. While his bosom faltered, his heart palpitated, and his hand trembled, his mind was firmly, steadily bent on the execution of his direful purpose.

Maria now came in sight of the Red Barn—before the entrance of which Barnard was slowly pacing, with downcast looks and folded arms. He was like the prowling wolf, awaiting his unwary victim.

" You have been a long time coming, Maria," said he, as she approached; " we shall be late: come in, my dear, and change your clothes in the *bay* of the Barn. Did anybody see you as you came?"

" No," replied Maria.

" Did you see any body?"

"Not a soul," answered she; "the workmen are gone home to dinner.—Heavens! how lonesome we are here, William!"

"So much the better. Come—come in."

They both now entered: Barnard thought himself quite prepared. He stood apart while she was undressing, but so as to see her perfectly through the wide crannies of a partition which stood between them. She wore a part of her own dress under the male attire which he had provided for her. As she was removing the latter, he cocked one of his pistols.—He looked at her: her lovely hair, having escaped from the combs which confined it, hung dishevelled over her snow-white bosom, while her bright eyes were raised towards heaven suffused with tears. It was a sight that might have moved the Prince of Hell himself to pity. The monster presented the pistol at her through an aperture in the partition,—hesitated—trembled —his arm fell. He was almost wrought on to relinquish his design.

But he thought of his murdered child—his danger—his interest: if he should fail now, he might never have such another opportunity;—he might be discovered. By a desperate effort, he rallied his determination, and suppressed his feelings. Thrice he raised the fatal weapon—thrice his trembling hand refused to obey the dictate of his hellish mind, and fell inefficient by his side. The fear of missing his aim, and horror of hitting, made his whole frame shudder: he walked to and fro in the greatest agitation.

" William," said the ill-fated girl, " come here and tie this ribbon on my hair."

He approached.

" Heavens !" she cried, " how you tremble, love !—what's the matter ?"

" Death !" exclaimed the villain ; and at the same moment levelled his pistol at her head : he fired, and she fell at his feet with a deep and heavy groan.

The report of the shot deprived him of all consciousness for a moment : he stood fixed to the spot in a paroxysm of terror ! Cold drops rolled from his forehead.

Aroused by a deep and piteous moan, he started up : he ventured to look at Maria. She was extended on the earth, but not dead !—it was a dreadful sight ! Her bosom heaved with convulsive throes—blood was flowing from her neck and part of her face—her eyes were open, but sightless. Barnard did not dare to look again, but rushed from the Barn in horror.

After some minutes in the open air, he recovered the consciousness of his situation : the imminent, tremendous danger in which he was placed, flashed across his mind. Maria was not dead !—she might recover,—he must then be discovered. One immediate impulse of self-preservation now effaced every other feeling, and hurried him back to the horrible scene.

He returned : Maria was still alive ; but the ball which had entered the neck and come out near the eye, had deprived her both of speech and

reason : she might have survived several hours in this state. She was now awfully convulsed ;—her fair bosom laboured for breath, and her white limbs quivered. Should she yet live to speak his atrocity !—the thought was fearful.

There is an intoxication, an infatuation, a madness, about crime, that in the very commission of it destroys reflection, and impels almost instinctively the criminal to proceed in his atrocity. Barnard seized the short sword which he had provided, in case of the failure of the pistol : he was about to strike, when the eye-ball of the dying woman turned horribly upon him ! There was no meaning in the vacant stare; but it was terrific beyond the power of language to pourtray. He flung down the sword, and rushed out again.

But his purpose must be fulfilled. He fancied that he saw some one cross the road below, at a distance : the necessity of securing himself reverted to his thoughts. He returned, locked the door, took up the sword again, and, without daring to look at the dying countenance, plunged the weapon into her heart—that hapless heart which once had throbbed with warm affection for him ! There was no groan,—the blood rushed profusely from the wound, and, with one convulsive stretch, the unfortunate girl expired !

Barnard gazed in stiffening horror at the dead body for a considerable time—he felt almost senseless, when he was aroused by voices without. He started—self-preservation restored his half sunken faculties : he listened—the voices died away. Two of his labourers were passing the Barn, returning from their dinner to their work— it was their voices he had heard.

No time was now to be lost : he at first had intended, after the murder was accomplished, to make the grave immediately, and had provided spade and pickaxe for the purpose, but his powers were unequal to the task. He dragged the body, with some difficulty, into the chaff-house; and having locked the Barn-door, left the place to recover himself a little, before he could attempt the burial of his victim.

He soon returned; and in that isolated place— beneath the midday's sun—alone with the dead body of his affectionate Maria—did he labour at the hard earth, with a harder heart, until he made her grave. There he buried her; and with stealthy pace left the Barn, to offend the innocent light of day with his odious and accursed look.

But we must now draw to a conclusion this melancholy portion of our narrative. We should not, indeed, have dwelt so much on its details, had we not considered that the interests of truth, morality, and religion, required us to do so. It was necessary to point out the gradations which led to folly and vice, to the highest degree of criminality, and to develope fully the extent of atrocious depravation, which will prevail in a mind that has once discarded the rules of virtue and religion.

Such was the fate of the unfortunate Maria: in the bloom of youth and beauty she became a sacrifice to the guilty fears and demoniac cupidity of a villain whom she loved—to whom she had borne an infant—and who had solemnly pledged himself in the presence of the Deity to protect and cherish her for ever. She left her home to meet a husband, and found—a murderer! Her destiny reads a most awful lesson to all those who dare to turn from the strictest path of rigid virtue; for though her deviation was but slight—though it was, in fact, a deviation rather in form than substance, yet it entailed the most dreadful consequences. She was summoned without preparation before that awful tribunal, at whose scrutiny the purest souls may tremble.

CHAP. XXI.

Sho came—she is gone—we have met—
And meet, perhaps, never again :
The sun of that moment is set,
And seems to have risen in vain.
Catherina has fled like a dream,
(So vanishes pleasure, alas!)
But has left a regret and esteem
That will not so suddenly pass.

Cowper.

On the day which followed the bloody tragedy which we have detailed, between one and two o'clock, a postchaise suddenly drove up to the gate of old Marten's cottage. A great bustle and loud talking took place between the driver and a man who sat along with him.

"Come, my hearty," cried the latter, "we drop anchor here."

"I doant knaw what you mane by drop anchor," said the postboy.

"Pooh, pooh! my lad, I mean stop—halt the gig."

"Gig! why this bees a chay, mun—gig, indeed!"

"Well well! stop, I say, in plain English."

"Well, then, in plean Henglesh, I wool."

On hearing this noise, Marten and his wife came out to the door, to see what was the matter. As they approached the chaise, an old gentleman put out his head, saying,

"Ah! Mr. and Mrs. Marten, how do you do? —how do you do? All hearty—eh?

They recognized immediately the protector of Maria, and our old and much esteemed friend, Captain Carribles!

The worthy Captain looked as well, as strong, and as hearty as ever : the lapse of time seemed to have little or no effect upon his iron frame, nor could the cold and darkling clouds of age diminish the warm and cheerful sunshine of his soul. No envious care, no rankling passion, had contracted his manly brow ; but his open and serene aspect at once announced a guileless life, and a heart over-flowing with the best feelings of philanthropy. Time, which had shorn the honours of his head, had left his strength unimpaired, and his temper unaltered : he was like the oak of the forest bereft of its leaves, but whose trunk might yet for ages bid defiance to the storm.

"Well, my worthy old folks," said he, as he descended from the chaise and entered the cottage; "you must come off directly with me, both of you, down to my cabin."

"Lord, Sir!" exclaimed the husband and wife; "what for?—why should we go with your honour?"

"I'll tell you that," said Carribles, "when we get home: I have not come here to take you away for nothing, I can tell you—I'll make you both as happy as your hearts can wish. But where's my little charge—and how is she?—vour pretty Maria."

They did not, of course, tell him exactly what had become of her; but answered that she had merely left home for a day or two.

" Shiver my timbers !" said Carribles, " but I'm sorry she's not here. A sweet creature—I'll make her happy, too : but come along, my good people, we've no time to lose—come along."

Mrs. Marten made some excuse about her not being sufficiently well drest, &c.; but the pressing and promising manner of the veteran was irresistible.

. ' Nonsense," said Carribles, " nonsense. You are quite well enough—just as you ought to be,—so come along. There's room enough in the chaise for us three ; and there's my honest old shipmate, Tom Squires, will ride outside, as convoy. Come along, my dear people—no time to lose."

So saying, he actually forced them into the chaise—scarcely allowing the old lady to put on her best bonnet, or the old gentleman his Sunday coat,—all wonderment and puzzle, and then drove off as rapidly as the horses could go.

When they arrived at old Carribles' cottage, they alighted and entered : his housekeeper had, by her master's directions, provided refreshment ; to which the old couple sat down, and partook of heartily. Old Carribles had directed the chaise driver to remain still in waiting; and all the while Marten and his wife were refreshing themselves, he was rubbing his hands with the highest glee imaginable.

" Yes, yes !" he would say, " I'll make you right happy ; but we have to go a little farther yet. I'll give you an agreeable surprise ;—you shall see some one that—— but no! I must not tell you yet—that would spoil all. D—n it, there's nothing like making our fellow creatures happy— when they deserve it."

The old people could not possibly tell what to make of all this ; they were perfectly amazed and confounded. But they forbore to ask any questions; and knowing the kindheartedness of their host, trusted themselves entirely to his conduct.

" Now, my good friends," said he, " we must just embark again for a short sail,—I will not keep you much longer in suspense. You will be surprised, I can tell you."

Again they mounted into the chaise, and were driven along a fine level road for about a mile or two. The chaise stopped at a gate which was evidently the entrance to some rich domain. This gate formed the centre of a semicircle of stone work, with the usual architectural ornaments of such entrances to country mansions ; and all was so thickly overshadowed with wood, that there was no prospect beyond. The driver, by the direction of Carribles, rang at the gate, which was opened by a porter from an adjoining lodge. The chaise drove in through the gate, and they proceeded on a winding gravel road through a thick shady grove quite impervious to the rays of the sun. When they had got out of the grove, they were saluted by the prospect of a fine, extensive, gently sloping lawn, through which the road continued in a strait line to a splendid mansion, situated on the highest part of this spacious lawn. The house was very lofty, and built altogether of free-stone, with a handsome portico, pillars in front, and a double flight of white steps leading up to the door. Its situation and appearance were equally imposing, and it commanded a fine prospect of the adjacent country. The end of the lawn, opposite the house, was bounded by low hills very thickly wooded; on the left side it was completely excluded from the road by a continuation, in another direction, of the shady grove through which they had passed; and on the right was an open, unbounded, magnificent prospect of the champaign country, with its waving fields of green corn, its pastures of rich clover, and its meadows of tall grass now courting the sickle of the mower. The country here was more rich than picturesque, as it wanted the variation of hill and dale, wood and water; but it was a glorious exhibition of cultivation, industry, wealth, comfort, and happiness. The sun shone brightly above in the cloudless azure, in harmony with the smiling scene below, while the deer were skipping lightly over the smooth and numerous herbs, and flocks were scattered over the rich pasture lands far and wide.

The chaise stopped at the foot of the steps: Carribles and his companions got out, ascended, and the Captain gave a loud knock at the door. It was opened by an elderly and very respectably looking male servant, who had not in his countenance the slighest traces of that insolence so proverbial, and, unhappily, too frequent, among the pampered domestics of the rich. He bowed respectfully to Captain Carribles, who enquired,

"John, is your master at home?"

"No, Sir; but he will return in a few minutes; and he has given directions that, if you called, I should request you to be good enough to wait."

The servant now showed Captain Carribles and his two humble friends into a spacious and magnificent apartment. It had four windows on a level with the floor, looking out upon the lawn: they were hung with curtains of the richest crimson. The mahogany chairs were ornamented with inlaid brass, and their cushions were covered with red morocco. A large and most beautiful round table occupied the centre of the room; and a splendid book-case was on the side opposite the windows, with green silk curtains inside the glass. The mantelpiece was of the whitest marble, covered with expensive ornaments, and above it was a large and most magnificent mirror: another of the same description was or the opposite side of the room, and the floor was covered with a rich Turkey carpet. In short, every article of furniture announced at once both the wealth and good taste of the proprietor.

The Martens were completely astonished: into an apartment of such splendour they had probably never before entered in the whole course of their lives. Of such places, indeed, they had heard descriptions, but the effect of seeing is very different from that of hearing: their senses were completely dazzled, and their understandings overwhelmed. They thought to themselves that this place must be the residence of some nobleman. or. at the least, of the lord of the manor.

"Well, my old friend," said Carribles to Marten; "what do think of this place?—snug little box for a single gentleman—eh!"

"Lord, Sir!" replied old Marten, "I was never in so fine a place in all my born days—it is fit for a king."

"It's not too good," said the Captain, "for the princely fellow that owns it."

Scarcely had he uttered these last words, when a gentleman, elegantly drest, entered the room: he appeared about seven or eight and twenty. He was above the middle height—of a light but admirably turned figure: his features were very handsome, and his complexion rather embrowned by the influence, perhaps, of a warmer climate.

The expression of his countenance was a little pensive, but it announced a feeling and reflective character.

When he entered, Carribles arose in the most abrupt and unceremonious manner, and took up his hat.

"Now, Mr. and Mrs. Marten," said he, "I leave you and this gentleman together. I shall not interrupt your conversation; and I trust you will soon be better acquainted."

On which the eccentric old Captain quitted the room.

The Martens were quite overwhelmed with confusion at being thus left in the presence of a stranger, and of so fine a gentleman: they could not utter a word, but stood in the most awkward manner imaginable. At last, old Marten, twiddling his thumbs, began to stammer out by way of excuse, that he was brought there by Captain Carribles—he knew not why—hoped no offence to his honour, &c.

The stranger, who had hitherto remained silent, eyeing them both with an agreeable and contemplative smile, now said,

"Is it possible, Mr. Marten, that you don't know me?"

"I think, Sir," replied Marten, "I have seen a face like yours, and I have heard a voice like yours somewhere, but I don't know your person."

"Have, then," said the stranger, "a few short

3 z

years so altered him, that Harry Everton is not
known to his earliest friends ?"

"Good Heaven !" exclaimed the old couple;
" can it be ?—is it possible, Sir, that you are
Harry Everton ?"

" Indeed, my friends," answered Everton, " it
is not only very possible, but quite true ; and if you
have any doubt about it, look here,"—pushing
back his dark hair from the side of his forehead,
and showing them a very remarkable mark which
he had borne there from his infancy, and which
was quite familiar to them both.

Old Marten, on seeing this, exclaimed,

" It is, it is Harry Everton, indeed ! but
you are so much changed that I did not know
you at first : you are so much darker, Henry, and
also stouter. Besides, how could I think of
meeting you in so fine a house as this is ?"

" True," said Harry ; " but, my good friends,
I will soon explain all that to you. In the mean
time, let me ask you how is Maria ?"

" Very well," replied the mother; " she is
gone from home for a few days."

" Well," said Everton, " my dear friends, I
have something very particular to talk to you
about ; but, first of all, I'll tell you how I came
into the situation in which you see me. But,"
continued he, ringing the bell for the servant,
" we'll call in our worthy friend, Captain Carribles."

The Captain soon came; Harry called for some

wine, and then commenced the relation cf his adventures, the substance of which we shall present to the reader in our own words, as briefly as
possible.

When Harry Everton took leave of Captain
Carribles on the night, or rather morning, of the
rescue of Maria from Jackson, he of course joined
his regiment without delay. The corps soon
embarked for India, where Harry was very
speedily engaged in active service. He soon distinguished himself by the steadiness of his
conduct, his attention to duty, and rapid improvement in military discipline, but, above all, by his
courage and intrepidity in the hour of danger.
Thus attracting the notice and approbation of
his officers, he was soon raised to the rank of
serjeant.

In this situation he acquitted himself with the
utmost credit; he was beloved by the men and
respected by the officers. His manners, and appearance, and education, were so far above the
level of his comrades, as to constitute an object of
attention even to his Colonel; and a service
which he rendered to the latter, proved the
cause of his further advancement.

Even private soldiers in India, as is well known,
have a large portion of leisure time on their
hands, except when engaged in actual warfare.
They have their native attendants, and the situation of a non-commissioned officer among them
has advantages beyond that of a subaltern in

Europe. The leisure that Harry thus obtained he devoted to the best purposes, namely, the study of his profession and the general improvement of his mind. He read much, and, among other pursuits, applied himself to obtain a knowledge of the language of the country, in which he soon made so great a proficiency as to be enabled to understand and speak it with no small facility.

Colonel Oswald had, of course, a number of native attendants in his service. The natives of India are, in general, men of great fidelity, much to be depended upon, and, when treated with kindness, susceptible of a very strong attachment; but, on the contrary, if offended or injured, are exceedingly inveterate and revengeful. This is particularly the case when their religious prejudices happen to be shocked, or their superstitious observances become the subject of derision. It is for such indignity they bear a deep and lasting hatred against their Mussulman conquerors.

Colonel Oswald had two servants whom he unfortunately, though unintentionally, offended in this way. He happened to do something or other which proved the means to these men of losing *caste*, as it is termed. This inspired in them a rooted malignity and a determined spirit of vengeance, and they resolved to seize the first opportunity of assassinating the Colonel.

Before they had an opportunity of executing this intention, one of them died suddenly. The other, however, did not relinquish the design, but determined to perform it alone. There is nothing to which an Hindoo is more indifferent than death. This man thought nothing of sacrificing his life for the gratification of his revenge; and indeed the loss of *caste* made him wish for destruction, as soon as his vengeance should be satisfied.

Accordingly, one morning as the Colonel was walking alone at a little distance from his quarters, this man came behind him for the purpose of stabbing him with a *crees,* or dagger. It was the first opportunity that he had of finding the Colonel unattended, and, as he thought, remote from any assistance; but scarcely had the assassin raised his arm to strike the fatal blow, when a sword was passed directly through his own body, and he fell prostrate on the earth. The Colonel turned round, and beheld the lifeless Hindoo, and Serjeant Everton withdrawing his faithful weapon from his body. Harry had observed the native following the Colonel with his drawn dagger, and knew the fact of his having lost *caste* He instantly conjectured what he was about, pursued him with the rapidity of lightning, and just got up in time to save the life of his commanding officer.

The Colonel's gratitude to Harry for this service was so great, that he immediately exerted all the interest of which he was master, and procured for the young man an ensigncy in his own corps.

The regiment was soon after this affair sent to
Calcutta. The Colonel continued his patronage
of Everton, and, in spite of the fastidious feelings
entertained too generally in British regiments
against deserving officers raised from the ranks,
Harry became an exception to the operation of
this prejudice. Against so decided a favourite of
the commanding officer this feeling was not likely
to exhibit itself strongly; but, independently of
that, so gentlemanlike were the manners, so
respectable the entertainments, and so high the
reputation for courage, of our young Ensign, that
on his own account alone he was highly esteemed
and respected by the entire corps.

Everton was a constant guest at the private
parties of the Colonel, which were always attended
by some of the first military and civil characters
in Calcutta. It so happened that, on one of these
occasions, a gentleman was introduced of his own
name. This gentleman had, for many years,
filled, with great credit to himself, a number of
offices in the civil department in India, and had
amassed a large fortune. Struck with the identity
of name, he entered into conversation with Harry,
and questioned him closely as to his family and
the place of his nativity: Harry told him ingenu-
ously every circumstance respecting them. The
conversation ended by the old man folding him in
his arms, and saluting him by the title of nephew!

The facts of the case were briefly these:—
Harry's father and this gentleman were the only

two sons of a respectable farmer living near Yarmouth. The youngest of these sons, Harry's uncle, was a wild lad, and, when very young, had run away to sea, and his relations never heard any more about him. Harry's father, on the death of his own parents, had removed to Polstead, where he settled and married : his brother, by a series of fortunate incidents, had arrived to the possession of the rank and property which he enjoyed. He wrote many times to his family in England, when he began to thrive in the world ; but, in consequence of the removal of his brother, the letters never came to hand : Harry's father had, therefore, long concluded that his brother was no more.

The first inquiry made by Harry's uncle, was whether his brother was still living. To this Harry replied in the negative. When he left England his father was alive ; and such was the fidelity of this most excellent son, that even while a non-commissioned officer he contrived, by economy, to save money, and had remitted several sums to his father, which were duly received through the hands of a banker in Suffolk. In answer, however, to his last letters, Harry, then an officer, was informed by this agent that his father had died some time before, that the small farm which he rented of course reverted to the proprietor, and the very small personal property he was worth did little more than suffice to pay the expenses of his funeral. Harry's mother had died several years before.

His uncle now grew more and more attached to him every day. Mr. Everton was a very worthy man, but not without his prejudices. One of these was a strong dislike to the profession of arms,—not that he had any aversion towards the members of the army as gentlemen, but he disapproved of the pursuit for a young man. He made his will in favour of Harry, but it was on this condition—that he should quit the army. This the latter consented to, though with some regret; nor was his Colonel less concerned at losing him as an officer, nor his brother-officers as a companion in arms: soon after, his uncle died and left him in possession of a very large fortune.

Harry, who had now nothing to detain him from his native country, determined to return to it. India, though the place for making fortunes, seems not to be the best one for their enjoyment. Independently of that consideration, however, there was another thought which, in Harry's present circumstances, would have induced him to return to England.

That thought was—Maria! Never, during his absence, had he forgotten or ceased to love her: her cherished image was ever present to his mind in all his wanderings and changes of fortune, and no other could supersede it. Her own ill-treatment of him, time, distance, nothing could banish it; and now the favourable change in his circumstances induced him to encourage the idea that, if she were still single, she might yet listen to his addresses. He piqued himself on the opportunity thus afforded him of showing the permanence and strength of his attachment, and the disinterested character of his passion.

Full of this idea, Harry, after making all necessary arrangements respecting his property, took his passage on board a vessel bound for England. When he arrived in London, he found that of necessity he must be detained there some time in the regulation of his affairs. He wrote to his agent in Suffolk to make, if possible, a purchase of an estate and residence for him in that county. The latter succeeded in doing so; and Harry, by one of those extraordinary coincidences that so often happen, arrived at his new and splendid mansion on the very day on which the unfortunate Maria was murdered in the Red Barn, by the monster, William Barnard.

Almost immediately after his arrival, Harry called on Captain Carribles. The latter was absolutely in ecstasies, when he learned the good fortune of his yound friend and preserver. Harry told him of his feelings and intentions respecting Maria, if she were still disengaged. The old Captain shook him by the hand, swore that he was an honest fellow, and made the proposal that he should himself go up to Polstead, for the pur-

4 A

pose of surprising the family in the manner we have described.—This is the brief history of Harry Everton's good fortune.

" Now, my good friends," said Harry, when he had concluded the narrative of his adventures, " here you see I am, in possession of all that wealth can bestow upon me; but one only thing is wanting to my happiness. If Maria be still unmarried, and can think of a man who has loved her so long and so sincerely as I have, I am ready to bestow upon her all my fortune, and to devote the remainder of my life to make her happy."

Old Marten and his wife remained silent, and looked at each other with sadness in their faces.

" What! my dear friends," said Harry; " you don't speak. My heart misgives me;—she is married, then ?"

" Oh! Mr. Everton," replied the mother, "she went to be married yesterday !"

"Then," said Everton, " all my hopes are blasted for ever! I had thought—something had told me that we might have yet been happy;—it was all delusion :—but the will of heaven be done !"

" Well!" said Carribles, " this is the most provoking thing I ever knew: I had made up my mind to see the young people happy—I hate to see any one otherwise ;—I saw them when they last parted, and——"

" Last parted, Sir ?" said old Marten.

" Yes, to be sure," said Carribles; "at my house.

She would not let me tell you; but this was the noble fellow who not only rescued her, but preserved my life. *I* saw them, I say; and though she could not make up her mind about it, I saw that they were made for each other; and now, when my brave young friend has come home with all the means to make her happy, to think that —— D—n it!—it's enough to make a saint swear."

"It is a melancholy thing," said Marten, looking at his wife. (Little the poor father knew *how* melancholy it was!)

"Indeed it is, Thomas," replied the latter.

"To whom," said Carribles; "to whom, in the Lord's name, is she gone to be married?—to that scamp, Jackson—eh?"

"Oh no! Sir," replied the mother; "to a young man named Barnard."

'Barnard!" said Everton; "I knew him. The last man on earth I could have wished to be her husband: indeed, I warned her against him before I left the country."

"Oh!" said the mother, "he is much changed for the better; and I hope he will make her a good husband."

"I hope so too," said Everton, with a deep sigh.

"I had much rather Mr. Everton had been her husband," said old Marten.

"So had I," said the mother.

"And so had I, ten million of times," said Carribles, "though I know nothing at all about the other."

" Well, well," said Harry, " let us say no more of this;—I wish her happiness, with all my heart and soul. May she never have cause to regre her choice! May he watch over, protect, and cherish her, as I would have done! May they live long and happy! and as for you, my dear friends, I will shortly visit you ; and all I say is, if ever you want a friend, you know where to find one. While Harry Everton lives, never apply to any other."

The old people now took their leave—Harry having first made each of them an appropriate present. Carribles saw them into the chaise, gave the driver directions to take them back to Polstead, and call at his house, on his return, for the fare. He then shook hands with them, saying

" Good bye, my old friends ; I hope that youth, whoever he be, will prove kind to poor Maria : if he should not, he will deserve to be hanged."

It may be well imagined that the reflections of the old fold folks, as they returned home, were not the most agreeable : they regretted much the loss that their daughter experienced of such a husband as Harry Everton. But their feelings were somewhat different : the mother considered the matter in a worldly point of view, and was grieved that matters had so far gone with Barnard ; and, had it been in her power, would have broken off the match : she thought, if that had been done, nothing would remain but to marry Maria to Harry Everton. But the father thought very differently: he did not so much esteem Harry's fortune, as he did Harry himself. He regretted that they had not been married in the first instance, and that his daughter had not secured so amiable a husband, although he would not, perhaps, have ever been so rich; but he felt that, after her connexion with Jackson and Barnard, it would be neither just, nor fair, nor honourable, for him to sanction a union between her and Harry—that Maria herself would never have agreed to it;—in short, that the thing was utterly impossible:—the time was past—destiny had ordered it otherwise.

Otherwise, indeed!—While the fond parents were thus speculating respecting their beloved child, she was lying a mangled corse in her new-made untimely grave!

CHAP. XXII

Ob! tyrant conscience, how dost thou afflict me !—SHAKSPEARE.

THE first impressions on the mind of the blood-stained Barnard, after the perpetration of his accursed deed, were horrible; nor did they soon give way to the natural callousness and depravity of his disposition: he was disturbed—distracted —agitated—absent. He went home in the evening. Had the slightest suspicion existed of what had been done, his behaviour must have betrayed him. To the questions put to him by his family, he replied incoherently. He went out again after nightfall, for he did not dare to go to bed,—the idea of that filled him with terror. As he walked along, he shook like an aspen at every breath of wind, and started at every bush as if it were an officer or a ghost.

He resolved to try that resource which is so often

flown to by the wretched, the remorseful, the
guilty, and which may create temporary oblivion,
though it can never remove the cause of their
sufferings. He walked some distance, and
entered a very low public-house on the road: he
was afraid to show himself at the "Cock" that
evening, lest he might be recognized by some of
the townspeople. By himself, miserable, in a
little room, he sat and drank, glass after glass, of
brandy-and-water with the utmost rapidity;
but no effect like intoxication ensued. His mind
was in no state for that,—there was too strong a
counteracting principle at work within him. In
some states of bodily distemper, inebriating
liquors may be drunk to a great extent without
producing their usual and natural effect. It is
the same way when the mind is diseased: grief,
remorse, despair, counteract intoxication, as certainly as typhus, spasm, or vascular inaction.

But the liquor, which did not intoxicate Barnard,
removed his nervous agitation: he began to reflect
that he had secured himself as far as possible
against the chance of discovery. There was no
living being aware of his guilt: the place, the
time, in which the crime was perpetrated, could
never be suspected. For the concealment of the
body he had done all that, at present, could be
done; the key of the Barn was in his pos
session, and none could enter there without his
permission. That key he resolved not to let out
of his hands for some time.

Thus he flattered himself;—no eye had seen him perform the bloody deed. Wretched man! an eye had seen him that never winks,—the all-seeing eye of everlasting justice. There was no tongue to tell of his misdeeds. Mistaken fool!—

> "———Murder, though it hath no tongue,
> Will speak with most miraculous organs."

He thought himself secure from punishment; but he was already marked out by the unerring hand of almighty vengeance. He should escape, he thought, the trial and condemnation that awaited him at the bar of his country. He was already tried and condemned at the bar of Heaven!

He, at first, had felt the impulse to fly—to quit Polstead as soon as possible; but he now altered that resolution. To go immediately might excite suspicion;—he would remain until harvest time, and see the Barn *well filled*—the grave well covered; then depart, and rest perfectly secure, as he thought, from all detection.

Having eased his mind very considerably by this train of reflection, he continued to drink on until his thoughts acquired a sort of demoniac elevation. He had now, as he fancied, securely removed the great obstacle to his future prosperity, and a splendid vista of fortune was opened to his infatuated vision. He possessed, in spite of his personal defects, a large portion of vanity; and he looked forward with hope, and confidence, to the prospect of a matrimonial connexion which should establish him capitally in life: through the cleverness of Hannah, he thought he could not fail of succeeding. As for her, he proposed to continue his connexion with her as long as his interest dictated its continuance; and when it should become inconvenient, to cut it short in his own neat way.

Barnard continued his deep potations until long past midnight; and now, being firmly nerved and much exhilarated, but still reluctant to go to bed, he resolved to visit Hannah in Smith's cottage. Accordingly he left the public house and proceeded thither. Late as it was, Hannah had not retired to rest. She was in the habit of taking but little sleep: her restless, ambitious, scheming, disappointed mind kept her perpetually sleepless. She was seated, reading, with a single pale light burning on the table. The old hag was stretched on a pallet, in a corner, fast asleep. The fire was nearly out, and shed a faint light on all around.

" Ha! Barnard!" exclaimed she, at his entrance " and at this late hour?"

" Yes!" replied he; " what are hours to us? I have gone through much business to-day, but I could not sleep."

" I am in want of money," said Hannah.

" Take my purse, then," said he, flinging it on the table.

" William," said she, " I must still reproach you

4 B

with delay. You are tardy: you procrastinate your fortune."

" I cannot help it at present, Hannah,—here I must stop for some time longer. I cannot yet raise sufficient money."

" That girl—that girl!" said Hannah.

" Name her no more!" cried Barnard, with a smile of infernal exultation; " she is disposed of —she will trouble us no more."

"What!" said Hannah, " is she dead?"

"Dead!" echoed Barnard, starting; " no! she is not dead—she was alive when I last saw her; but she has gone a long journey."

" Well, well, Barnard, I ask you no questions about her,—I have no impertinent female curiosity. She may be dead or living for aught I care; but it is your business to provide that she interfere with you no more."

" Make yourself easy about that," said the ruffian; " she is safe enough, I assure you. But let us talk no more about her: I will get out of this as soon as I can muster the means; but I must stop until the harvest is got in."

" Why?" said Hannah; "you can get money enough to go up to London before then, and try our plan of advertising. You can return, you know, at the harvest time."

" No, no!" said he, "impossible—I must stay here. My presence here is indispensable."

They then had some further conversation respecting the matrimonial scheme, which continued until the first rays of morning broke through the little windows of the cottage. He then returned home, threw himself on his bed, and through sheer fatigue slept soundly for two hours.

The following night, Barnard ventured to go to bed at his usual hour; but he passed a night of tremendous horror. Scarcely had he closed his eyes, when the image of the murdered Maria stood before him: he awaked, streaming with perspiration and paralyzed by fear, and fancied that he saw her still. She appeared to his imagination in a standing posture, but with the fixed and horrible aspect with which he saw her after her fall from the pistol-bullet. He arose, walked about, opened the window, and made a strong effort to dispel his imaginary terrors, and to calm his agitated mind. He succeeded in some degree, and lay down again, but not to sleep: the excitement had been too great. He tossed from side to side all night upon his feverish bed—his mind agitated by dreadful thoughts Sleep seldom came to his pillow, and when it did, it was but to torture him with horrid visions.

On the following day, however, which was Sunday, Barnard had wonderfully got the better of his agitation, and soon quite re-assumed his habitual coolness and self-command. At nine o'clock on that morning, he mustered sufficient effrontery to call upon the Martens. He found the mother only at home, who immediately

THE RED BARN.

questioned him, on his appearance, as to what he had done with Maria, and whether they were yet married? He replied in the negative to the latter part of the question; saying that, on their arrival at Ipswich, he had got a licence, but he found that it was necessay it should go to London to be signed, and that they could not possibly be married in less than a month or six weeks. As for Maria, he told her mother that he had consigned her to the care of a female relative of his own, who resided at Yarmouth, whither they were now gone. He had supplied her, he stated, with money; and she was, in all respects, as comfortable as could possibly be desired. To her mother's observation that Maria, during her absence, might possibly want the rest of her clothes which were at the cottage, he replied that his cousin would supply her with every requisite in the way of dress.

As long as Barnard remained at Polstead, he was in the habit of continually seeing the Martens, —even sometimes two or three times a-day. This was no small argument of the callous, cold-blooded cast of the villain's character. How he could continue in the same scenes where he had so often wandered with the unfortunate Maria, pouring false vows of love into her too credulous ears— how he could calmly look on the countenances of the parents whose child he had basely murdered,— may seem inexplicable to those whom nature has ifted with feelings of humanity, and in whom ducation has produced a becoming horror of crime. But experience and observation teach us, that when a certain point has been passed in the career of villany, every natural feeling becomes seared or perverted, and the whole man is metamorphosed into the demon. No feelings, in fact, remain, but such as are founded on the most sordid modification of brutal selfishness.

During this time, Barnard invariably used to tell the unsuspecting parents that Maria was well, and living most comfortably with his cousin. He would occasionally leave Polstead for a day or two, and say that he had been with Maria, who continued in excellent health. He meant, he said, to bring her home at Michaelmas to his mother's farm, and openly acknowledge her as his lawful wife.

The mother would frequently express her surprise, that Maria never wrote to her or to her father. For this, Barnard framed a variety of excuses. At one time she was too busy to write—at another, she was incapacited from doing so, by an accident, which temporarily deprived her of the use of her hand. He was always ready with some pretext or other, which sufficed to impose upon the slight discrimination and easy credulity of the rustic parents.

When the harvest was ripe for gathering in, Barnard busied himself most actively about it. The key of the Red Barn had never been for a moment out of his possession, from the period of the murder up to this time. He now opened the

Barn, and assisted himself in placing the corn there,—a thing be had never been known to do before. That bay of the Barn where the body had been buried, was the part first filled; and Barnard took especially on himself the principal part of that operation. He placed the ground-work of straw, with the utmost care and accuracy, and had that portion of the Barn filled as full as it could possibly hold; thus, thought he, I am secure. I shall now quit Polstead, and sleep in peace. Alas! how insecure is guilt! Little thought he that mountains cannot cover it from the eye of retribution.

That the worm of conscience was secretly preying on this wretch, in spite of his callous disposition and assumed calmness, was evident from many circumstances. That retributory power never sleeps; it will pursue the criminal, when human law and justice lag behind. Often did Barnard, writhing under its lash, contemplate suicide; and nothing but a still lingering thought of hereafter prevented his consummating it.

He now thought that he was completely secure: the Barn was filled—the corn would remain there many months—the body would soon become thoroughly decomposed, so as, even in case of it being accidentally taken up, to defy all chance of recognition: therefore, having raised all the money he possibly could, amounting to four or five hundred pounds, he made all preparations for his immediate journey to London.

He went to Hannah, and made his arrangements with her. It was agreed that she should
precede him to the metropolis; and an address
was fixed there, where they should meet on his
arrival.

Barnard kept up his systematic, hypocritical
effrontery to the last. When he was about to
depart, he came to the cottage to take his leave
of the old people. He told them, that he was
now going down to the water-side to marry
Maria; that everything was settled; he had
obtained, after much entreaty, the sanction of his
mother to the match; and that they should shortly
see their beloved daughter, as his lawful wife,
living with him at his own farm. In corroboration of this, he had the assurance to exhibit to
them a gold ring, which, he said, was to be the
wedding-ring on the occasion.

On his arrival in London, he had an interview
with Hannah, and they drew up an advertisement
between them, which was inserted in one of
the morning papers. Strange to relate, he was
soon favoured with a number of replies. This
readiness to pick up a husband anywhere, or
on any terms—to rush blindly into the matrimonial state with a person of whom they could
know nothing,—speaks more in favour of the
disposition of the ladies of the metropolis to
lawful wedlock, than of their prudence or
discrimination.

The replies were submitted to Hannah, who

selected from them a few addresses, and en-deavoured to get access to the fair writers,—this took up a little time and trouble; and while she was thus employed, Barnard was amusing himself in town.

He plunged into dissipation of every kind, with a view of escaping from reflection The chief source of his uneasiness was not so much repentance, or any touches of remorse for his grievous guilt, as vague apprehensions and fears of discovery, which would still haunt him at times in spite of the precautions he had taken; and also certain terrors of punishment in another world, which, notwithstanding the course of philosophy he had studied under Carlile, would sometimes prove very unpleasant intruders into his bosom. To drown these feelings he had recourse to the bowl; and in the midnight and riotous conviviality of ruffians like himself, or in the loveless arms of some hireling prostitute, he would seek a temporary oblivion from his torments.   But outraged Nature still asserted her right, and the scorpion whip of conscience was exerted ever and anon with unrelenting severity.   Sleep seldom rested on his " penthouse lids;" and when it did so, it was only to bring with it a train of ghastly images and fearful forebodings.   He flew from place to place, and from pleasure to pleasure, in vain. He could find no medicine to rid him of the worm within, or to allay its secret, deep-felt gnawings. —He could not escape from himself

"Where'er he went was Hell, himself was Hell"

In the turmoil of society and dissipation, he could mask his feelings with outrageous levity, and contrive for the moment to be callous to them. But when alone, all his misdeeds would rise in array before him,—his unprincipled profligacy—his dying father—his poisoned child—his murdered wife, betrothed to him in the face of heaven.

"His conscience had a thousand several tongues,
And every tongue brought in a several tale,
And every tale condemned him for a villain."

Among his other peregrinations, he called secretly on his friend Beauty Smith, now under sentence of transportation. Him he found changed indeed from what he had been. His well made and muscular form had lost its roundness and expression of strength and activity. Long imprisonment and uneasiness of mind had worn him to the bones. His dark eye had lost all its fierceness and its fire, and his bold front no longer exhibited the tameless audacity of his spirit. Care had engraven its deep characters on his contracted brow, and reckless desperation had given way to gnawing regret. Yet was his lot enviable in comparison to that of Barnard. There was hope for him yet. He was no murderer! His crimes were manifold, but his soul was not stained with the blood of the innocent. He was about to expiate his offences against his country

4 c

and mankind, by an eternal exile from his native land. Yet on that distant shore to which he was bound, he might atone, by a life of integrity and good conduct, for all the past. He might become .. new man, and a useful member of society. Imprisonment and solitude had taught him to reflect, and his understanding being naturally strong, he was almost persuaded to believe that virtue, after all, was the safest path, and honesty the best policy. Banished for life, for such a man there is yet hope of reformation and happiness

" And is there nought for him but grief and gloom,
A lone existence, and an early tomb ?
Is there no hope of comfort and of rest,
To the seared conscience and the troubled breast ?
Oh, say not so ! In some far distant clime,
Where lives no witness of his early crime,
Benignant Penitence may haply muse
On purer pleasures and on brighter views ;
And slumbering Virtue wake at last to claim
Another being, and a fairer fame."

When Barnard had saluted Smith, the latter took him by the hand and said:—

" My dear William, I am glad to see you You find me on the point of leaving my native country for ever. I have learned, since in prison, for the first time, seriously to reflect on our mode of life; and, from reason alone, I find every cause to condemn it. It is dangerous—it is precarious— and after all it produces no present pleasure; no solid happiness can attend it. I am now speaking to you, Barnard, for the last time in my life; for though I may live many years, I do not think we shall ever meet again. To-morrow I am to be removed for embarkation: hear me, therefore, as you would hear the voice of a dying man. Take warning;—leave off our old courses, pursue a steady path of industry, marry Maria, and you will be happy! Would I had done so by poor Ellen in proper time!"

Every word of Smith's sunk like a dagger into the heart of Barnard; and, at the name of Maria, he started, trembled, and turned deadly pale. They soon parted for ever, and the unfortunate but not totally hopeless Smith was shipped in a few days for the Antipodes.

Yet another interview awaited Barnard, to stimulate his conscience into tormenting action, and wound him deeply. In the course of his wanderings through scenes of vice and profligacy, he bent his course one night to that temple of infamy, the oyster-shop opposite Drury Lane Theatre. There, where the gaudy prostitute covers with the vain splendors of dress a broken heart, or a ruined constitution,—like a tomb covered with garlands of flowers, or the apple of the Dead Sea shore, fair without, but ashes and bitterness within,—he was about to enter; when one of these unfortunate creatures, who, from the meanness of their attire, will not be permitted to come within that "*sanctum sanctorum;*" but who, like the unburied ghosts on the banks of Styx, love to hover round its brink, took him by the arm and solicited his assistance. Barnard was about to shake her rudely off, in the brutal, unfeeling manner so characteristic of the *swell* gentlemen of London, when, by the lamp-light, he recognized her features.—It was Ellen, the *chère amie* of Smith—the unfortunate cousin of Maria!

" Oh! William Barnard," exclaimed she, hiding her face and bursting into tears; " do I live that you should see me thus ?"

She was pale, wan, and wretchedly dressed— the picture of disease, broken heartedness, and misery—-the mere wreck of a London prostitute. Her figure had lost all its attractions, which had been very considerable; and her features, naturally plain, had assumed the sharp outline which is produced by fatigue, and want, and mental suffering. Oh! how unlike the healthy, lively, thoughtless girl, that had accompanied Maria on the first visit of the former to the Red Barn!

Even the soul of Barnard was touched at the appearance of this miserable victim of " Life in London." But when she inquired after Maria, and expressed her hopes that she, at least, would never experience such a wretched fate as her own, the murderer started back with horror thrust some money into her hand, and hurried away from her, to hide his head in some low den of vice, and steep his senses in the oblivion of ebriety.

Hannah had now succeeded in gaining admission to two or three young ladies, who had answered the advertisement of Barnard; and she had worked considerably on them, in the character of a fortune-teller. She informed them that they were to be married to a man exactly of the personal appearance of Barnard, of which, without departing too much from truth, she yet gave a flattering description. On the excellence of his disposition, she dilated more considerably, and with much less regard to truth. She stated him to be an independent gentleman, moderately rich; and, above all, she particularly mentioned that they would meet through the medium of an advertisement in the papers.

This was quite sufficient. Each of them then separately confessed to Hannah that they had answered an advertisement of this description, which they had seen some days previously in the papers. Their answers, they said, had, however, been merely those of inquiry as to the person advertising, &c. Hannah urged them to make decided appointments to see the advertiser, and offered herself to undertake the management of them in such a manner that their delicacy should be in no wise compromised. They consented to this, and Hannah now came to report progress to her worthy employer.

These appointments were kept; but the two first were attended with no satisfactory result— if, indeed, we may be justified in calling the disappointment of a heartless ruffian, and the escape of two innocent though foolish women, an unsatisfactory result. The first of these was a widow, with only a moderate life annuity, which Barnard discovered was not at her own disposal: this he did not conceive would suit him, and so he broke off the negociation. The second was a young lady of good expectations, but who, the moment she beheld the countenance of the advertiser, had the good taste to declare off in spite of her predilection in favour of the occult sciences : it might, she thought, be her destiny to marry a man who had advertised in the papers, but it could not be her destiny to marry so evil looking a fellow as Barnard. In the third instance, however, he proved more successful. A young lady, possessed of a considerable sum of money, in her own control and living with her mother, met him according to appointment: they were mutually pleased with each other, and had several meetings. At last, everything was arranged between them; and in an evil hour, a respectable, virtuous, well-educated young lady gave her hand at the altar to a man whom, had she known, she would have found to have been guilty of theft, forgery, and murder,— one in whom all the feelings which redeem human nature from detestation and contempt were utterly annihilated, and in whose bosom nothing reigned predominant but sordid avarice and brutal sensuality.

Were not the fact so clearly demonstrated, no

rational man could ever bring himself to believe that marriages could be brought about in such a manner as this, or that matrimonial advertisements were ever anything more than waggish and mischievous "*jeux d'esprits?*" Who could suppose that any woman of the most ordinary degree of sense or reflection, after being introduced to a man through such a medium, and on three week's acquaintance, would entrust her fortune and the happiness of her life in his keeping? But the fact is, the evil does not arise from the want of sense on the part of the other sex, so much as from the inhospitable system of exclusion practised by the generality of families in London. There is a difficulty of access into private society here for any man, unless he belong to the immediate circle of family connexions. By this, the acquisition of many valuable acquaintances is lost; while, on the other hand, the personal freedom enjoyed by the younger members of families, of either sex, enables them to form improper connexions abroad. Greater general freedom of admission would be better policy: the bad would be thus detected, by the superior discernment and experience of heads of families, and soon got rid of, while the worthy would be cherished. Acquaintances that would not be allowed at home, are met with abroad, and cultivated simply because there are no acquaintances to be met with at home. We would say to the heads of houses in London :—either open your doors more hospitably to the worthy and respectable youth around you, or curtail the personal freedom of your sons and daughters. If you do not, the corruption of the former by swindlers and gamesters, and the marriage of the latter by elopement or advertisement, are among the least of the evil consequences which you will have to deplore from your own system of illiberal exclusion."

CHAP. XXIII.

"And thou say'st true ; these weeds do witness it—
These wave-worn weeds—these bare and bruised limbs.
What would'st thou more ? I shrink not from the question.
I am a wretch, and proud of wretchedness."

MATURIN.

BARNARD was now settled as a married man, and filled a station of respectability in the middle class of life. A station far, indeed, beyond his deserts : but his profound hypocrisy enabled him to succeed in establishing a character for steadiness, sound principles, and good feelings, among the connexions of his wife, as he had done before in the country among his own. His acting was as consummate here as it had been there: his wife became passionately attached to him, and he became a high favourite with all her relatives.

During all this time, we must observe that Barnard wrote different letters for the purpose of cajoling the old people at Polstead. In one he informed old Marten that he had married his daughter, and expressed his surprise at no answer

4 D

having been sent to a letter of hers, describing the same occurrence. At another time he wrote, that business had called him to London, and that he was about to take Maria to the Isle of Wight, and that he had made inquiries at the post-office about her last letter, &c. In this manner he continued to amuse the parents of the murdered girl for many months,—hoping, by this means, to lull suspicion and prevent inquiry, until such time as no search or discovery could be dangerous to him.

Meanwhile his friend Hannah still remained a burthen on his hands. Her he was obliged to support, in fulfilment of his contract ; and because he still held her in some degree of awe. However, he soon grew tired of advancing money to her, as she could no longer be of any use to him, and very impatient of the sort of check which he fancied she held over his free agency. He would not, however, attempt to rid himself of her in the way that he had of poor Maria ; he resolved, for the future, to keep his hands clear of all offences of that kind ; but, as he could not remove Hannah, he determined to remove himself : and as no particular business now detained him in London, he set off, with his wife, to the Isle of Wight, without making the least previous communication of his movements to his guardian mistress.

When Hannah, on inquiry, found that he had departed in this manner, she was excessively enraged. She could not attribute the step he had taken to any motive but that of getting free from her solicitations.

In a day or two, however, she received from him one of those Machiavelian letters, which he so well understood how to write. Therein he declared, that in consequence of his wife's fortune being so situated, that he could not touch the principal at once, he was reduced to sudden embarrassments. That he had been discovered by some of his old creditors, and was obliged to quit London with precipitation, to avoid being arrested. He, therefore, was quite unable for the present to supply her with money; but he promised that as soon as he could bring his affairs into any thing like a proper train, she should have at least £200.

Hannah was a woman of too much penetration to be imposed on by shallow devices of this kind. She also knew her man too well for that. She had herself contributed to the developement of his talents, and the progress of his education; and she could pretty well appreciate his capabilities of imposing, and the depth of his sincerity. She saw clearly that,—to use a vulgar term,—his object was to " cut her completely ;" and she was fully determined that he should not do so, without very serious consequences to himself.

There was another feeling which acted in conjunction with disappointed interest, to stimulate her desire of vengeance. Hannah, notwithstand-

ing the masculine cast of her understanding, and
her want of the usual tender susceptibilities of
her sex, was, after all, a woman. Now, though
she had never loved Barnard, and though all
intercourse of any tender kind had so long ceased
between them, yet she could not divest herself
of something like a sentiment of jealousy about
him. It was pride, that was wounded and offended
at the idea that any other woman should possess
the place which she once held. She had entertained this feeling respecting Maria; and from
this, as much as any other cause, had she been
urgent with Barnard to put an end to that
connexion. She was, also, the more galled by
this idea, from her present situation; for her
faded charms, and want of money to call in the
assistance of art to repair them, placed her in a
predicament where she could hope neither for
equivalent nor retaliation.

She was sitting one night in a miserable apartment which she occupied, in a court off Drury
Lane, brooding over schemes of vengeance with
regard to Barnard, when a loud knock was heard
at her door. She called out to the person to come in;
and a man entered the apartment, in appearance
thin, pale, haggard, and not very well dressed
With all this, however, there was an air of commanding superiority about him, that marked him,
even to the superficial observer, as no common
man. Intelligence and resolution were written
on his manly though pallid countenance. He

looked the wreck of something that had been high and noble.

Hannah looked at him, and beheld with astonishment the ruin of Stafford Jackson!

Nor was his surprise at her appearance, an atom less. They stared at each other a moment without speaking, when the following ejaculations burst simultaneously from their lips :—

" Hannah !"

" Jackson !"

" Yes," said he; " it is Jackson : doubtless I am altered much, if in your appearance I may see any reflection of my own."

" Times are changed with me Jackson," said Hannah, " and doubtless with you too."

" They are," said he; " but notwithstanding that, and the change in our persons, our minds remain the same; at least mine does."

" And mine," said Hannah : "but, Jackson, how did you find out this wretched place ?"

" I'll tell you," said he, sitting down.—" On my first arrival I went to look for Creed : but him I was unable to find. I learned, however, that he was obliged, some time since, to fly to America, with scarcely any property, that he might escape the hands of justice. Some say that he had committed forgery; but I cannot think that a man of his peculiar caution could so lay himself open. However, be that as it may, he felt it necessary to run for his safety."

"I am sorry for him," said Hannah; "he was a man of wit, intelligence, and judgment."

"He was," said Jackson; "and, what was better than that, he was a kind and generous friend. It is true, his notion of *meum* and *tuum* were not quite orthodox; but it is no part of ours to find fault with him for that. Not being able to find him, I next sought after you."

"How did you find me?" said Hannah.

"Through a girl that lived with you, when Barnard and you were together, and whom I met accidentally."

"But how comes it, Jackson, that you are so much reduced?"

"Disastrous fortune, and, let me add, time; I am not what I was. Hope no longer can inspire me to deeds of enterprise. My spirits are no longer buoyant and elastic. But I am reckless of the future, and desperation shall supply the place of hope."

"But," said Hannah, "speak the particulars."

"My fortunes are completely ruined; my companions all killed or taken. I alone have escaped, with just sufficient money for a few days."

"What led to all this?"

"In brief, I'll tell you. When I escaped to Ostend, after the rascals, Smith and Barnard, had betrayed me (of which you, of course, have heard), I had a tolerable sum of money. With this, I commenced business; and travelling through the entire of the Belgique, proved rather successful. I went to Brussels after, where there was a run of fortune against me. I, however, saved enough from the wreck, and went to Flushing, where I joined Warren and our crew. We then made several successful trips; but our last expedition was fatal."

" How was that ?"

" Thus :—We purchased a new vessel, our old one being no longer sea-worthy; expended all our money on the cargo, which was very valuable, —and, had all things gone right, we should have been independent for life, and might have relinquished our dangerous pursuits. We pushed over for the western coast of England, from Brittany. It was the commencing dusk of the evening when land appeared; the breeze was favourable, and we had every prospect of landing safely, near Penzance, in a secret creek, where we had frequently harboured before. I was on deck, cheerfully conversing with poor Warren, when the man at the forecastle cried out, ' A sail, a sail!' "

" What was this ?"

" You shall hear : I ran forward, took my glass, and very plainly descried a revenue cutter bearing down upon us. We clapped all sails to, and bore away before the wind. But she was the better sailer, and soon coming within range of shot, fired from a swivel into our stern."

" What followed ?"

" I saw there was no further use in attempting

to escape.—' My lads,' said I, ' we must fight it out ; only remember that your lives and fortunes depend upon your courage.' I was answered by a shout, and we discharged a volley of small-arms into the cutter ; this was returned, and the action now became very warm. Our fellows fought like lions, but the enemy were too much for us."

" I wonder that the night did not favour your escape."

" Impossible ;—they were too close to us. Four of our men fell at the second volley. Poor Warren——"

" What of him ?"

" A musket-ball took him down, close by my side. He exclaimed, ' Jackson, I am killed—it is all over with us—escape if you can.—Thank God, I die on my native element.'—I stooped down to raise the poor fellow, but he was gone for ever."

" And how did you escape ?"

" They now boarded us. There were only three of us remaining,—myself and two others. One of them was soon disabled ; the other said to me, ' For God's sake, Mr. Jackson, let us save ourselves ; follow my example ;'—so saying, the brave fellow plunged into the waves,—whether he sunk, to rise no more, or escaped, I know not."

' And you followed him ?"

" I was on the gunwale of the forecastle. The commandant of the cutter came up and struck at me with his cutlass. Somehow, he overstretched himself,—perhaps deceived by the darkness and shadows—around, and falling against me, we both tumbled into the sea. Fortunately, he did not seize me in the water. I was always a good swimmer; the coast was near, and I reached it in safety, and ran along for about a mile: the darkness favoured my escape."

"And how did you manage for money?"

"I had my purse secured about me, with some gold in it. I walked all night, my clothes dripping wet. I had on a sailor's dress. Towards morning, I met the coach for London—mounted, and got on without suspicion, by acting the part of a jack-tar—told a story that satisfied the coachman—and when I got to London exchanged my sailor s dress for the clothes which I now wear.—But what's become of that scoundrel Barnard, and also of Smith?"

"The fate of the latter is fixed," said Hannah; "he is now under sentence of transportation."

"He deserves worse," said Jackson, "for his ingratitude and perfidy."

She then informed him briefly of Barnard's breaking with her—the renewed coalitions that took place between them—his late conduct—with a variety of comments upon his infamous character.

"Maria—have you heard aught of her?" said Jackson.

"She formed a connexion with Barnard, soon after your departure—she bore him a son."

4 E

73

" Humph !" said Jackson. "With *him*, after *me* ! well, well—I blame her not—such is the nature of woman. Where is she and her child ?"

"The child is dead and buried. I overtook both her and Barnard, and saw him bury the infant clandestinely, in a field near Sudbury. From all that I saw, I have strong suspicions that there has been foul play there. As for Maria, I know not where she is ; Barnard says, she is gone to some relation of her's. But his manner is very suspicious ; and I often think that he may have made away with her somehow. I believe him capable of the darkest atrocities."

"The infamous scoundrel !" cried Jackson ; "would I had trampled out his accursed life, the night of our encounter in the cottage of Smith !"

" You may yet be revenged," said Hannah.

" How ?" cried he.

"Hear me, Jackson. This man and Smith have been the primal causes of your ruin. I have a long score, too, against him. Our causes are the same ; let us join, and we can destroy him."

" The manner ?" said Jackson.

"That he murdered his child, I have little doubt—that he has destroyed Maria, I more than suspect. But, at all events, he was positively a party to the robbery for which Smith is condemned ; and I know other matters which might go near his life. Let us lay information against him."

"No," said Jackson; "I cannot agree to that —at least, I will not join in it."

"Why not?" said Hannah; "is the fellow deserving of any forbearance?"

"I consider not his deserts, but my own character, Hannah. I have done much that the world will blame; but nothing to degrade me utterly in my own estimation. I have transgressed the conventional rules of society—I have invaded the rights of property; but I have never taken a sneaking, cowardly advantage of any man. My revenge is open. Bring me face to face with my enemy, and my right arm shall avenge my wrongs;—but I will never descend to be an informer."

"Well, well, Jackson, I know your high character and feelings, and I will not press this further. An opportunity, no doubt, will yet offer for our just revenge. But what do you mean to do now?"

"I must seek some temporary asylum, where I may be secure from the pursuit of government, in consequence of the fight—live as well as I can —and when the thing is blown over, we shall see if anything is to be done."

"Where do you propose to seek this asylum?' said Hannah.

"I know not yet; but somewhere, I think, in London."

"You are wrong, Jackson—quite wrong; London is no place for you : you are too well known here. I could advise you better."

"Speak on," said Jackson. "Where can I be safer ?"

"In Smith's cottage : it is left in possession of the old woman. A little will satisfy her; and you can be there in safety. I will accompany you, and between us we shall yet be able to devise some plan to redeem our fortunes and revenge our wrongs."

"I like the idea well," said Jackson ; "and I will go immediately."

Hannah's principal object, in proposing to go down to the country, was, that she thought she could better carry on there her machinations against the life of Barnard ; for notwithstanding what she said relatively to her being able to give information as to the robbery, she feared that she could not give such evidence, on those points, as would prove fully satisfactory for his inculpation. But she strongly suspected his more deadly guilt down in the country, and she thought it more than possible that she might, by her intervention, be able fully to develope the entire extent of his criminality. Independently of her desire of revenge, she was in this design also actuated by the hope of gain, for she thought it probable that some reward might be attached to the instrument of discovering this horrible atrocity.

For Jackson she was not altogether devoid of some feeling, almost like friendship. She therefore advised him to go down into Suffolk, partly with the consideration of his present safety, partly with the view of her own temporary support there through his means, and partly from the desire of keeping up a coalition between them, which might yet, through the cleverness of both, turn out mutually advantageous; for Hannah knew the world too well not to know that little success is ever to be expected from exertion without coadjutors. It is also to be observed, that she had no person in the world now to look to for any co-operation but him.

As for Jackson himself, his motives were perhaps less defined. He was in such reckless state of mind, that he probably cared little to what quarter he directed his steps. The ruin of his hopes, the loss of his companions, sunk deeply in his mind. He was growing careless with regard to futurity, and rapidly acquiring a thorough distaste for existence. He now felt strongly what he had occasionally felt before, namely, that he had made a most erroneous choice in his mode of life ;—that, hurried on by passion and the love of pleasure, he had madly flung away the prospect of honourable distinction—perhaps of high rank, of solid happiness, and of peace of mind. He felt, when it was too late, that nothing but steady perseverance in a right path, can secure all these blessings, and that he who deviates widely from the prescribed road of rectitude and prudence, must expect to be entangled in the wilderness of misery, and plunged into the morasses of despair.

He was now quite alone in the world. The companions of his dangers—his frauds—his desperate enterprizes—his convivial hours, were gone;—many of them to render a serious account to the Author of their existence for their manifold abuses of his gracious gifts. In this state of isolation, the society even of Hannah was something to him. Though no feeling like love had ever existed between them, nor was very likely to be engendered under their present circumstances, yet an analogy in misfortune and downfall excited something like a sympathy of sentiment. Guilt and misery produce strange and degrading alliances, of which truth the coalition of Hannah and Jackson is no imperfect illustration.

They proceeded to Suffolk, and were domesticated in the cottage This was Jackson's third visit to this wretched place. The recollections which he associated with it, were of no very agreeable kind: it had been the scene of his deception of the unfortunate Maria, for the gratification of a fleeting passion, which had entailed upon its unfortunate victim such direful consequences;—it had been the scene of luxurious enjoyments, purchased at a bitter price indeed From this place he had been driven by the perfidy of a man whom he had considered as his bosom friend, deprived of the fruits of his illegal gains, and thrown into new vicissitudes, disappointments, and misfortunes, terminating in overwhelming ruin. To this place he was now returned, broken in constitution, broken in spirits, bereft of hope, and sickened of existence. With a body debilitated by premature age, and a mind to which even prosperity could now hardly administer a balm. Just, retributive Providence! the thoughtless, or the careless originator of evils must suffer for his misdeeds, as well as the perpetrator of darker atrocities.

Jackson confined himself, during the day, entirely to the cottage, and was in the habit of taking long walks at night, indulging gloomy reflections of the past, and unfavourable presentiments of the future, He would often say to himself, " Oh! what I might have been!" This, though an useless reflection, as far as the past is concerned, is yet the readiest to suggest itself to our imagination, when we think of wasted time, of lavished fortune, of golden opportunities lost for ever; of feelings which might have proved our own happiness and that of others, perverted into engines of self-torment ; and of talents abused, frittered away, destroyed, which might have raised us to eminent utility and honourable fame. Happy those who make this reflection when it is not quite too late— who have not yet wandered so far into the desert of vice and folly, but that they may still retrace

their footsteps—for whom there is a future stil
open, where they may in some measure redeem
the past—who are yet young enough to atone,
in their riper years, for the dissolute disorder of
their greener days.   Such was not the case with
Jackson. His manhood had been as desperate
as his youth was dissolute; and the consequences
had deprived him of the promise of an age of
redemption.   What he might have been was,
therefore, a reflection that brought with it nothing
but anguish. He might have been the delight
of his friends, and the ornament of his country
What was he?—The mind turns with pain from
the contemplation of the picture.

Some time had now elapsed since Barnard
last wrote to old Marten, and the latter and his
wife had begun to feel very uneasy, anxious,
and suspicious, about the fate of their child.
They were continually talking on the subject.
Her not writing was so strange!—she that had
so loved her parents! Never sending for
things which must have been indispensably
necessary to her comfort. They turned over every
particular connected with her disappearance, and
the more they reflected on the subject, the more
were they persuaded that all was not right.

The ever-designing Hannah, without mentioning
her intention to Jackson, contrived to introduce
herself to the cottage of the Martens : this she
found little difficulty in accomplishing. She frequently sat down by the cottage gate, where sne

had first accosted the ill-fated Maria, and conversed with Mrs. Marten.

They would talk on the subject of the daughter's mysterious absence; and, by a series of artful questions, Hannah soon drew from her every circumstance connected with it. One day, in particular, the following conversation took place between them.

' You say, Mrs. Marten," said Hannah, " that on the day Barnard came here to appoint the meeting at the Red Barn, he had his pistols with him ?"

" Yes; he was snapping them by the fire."

" That was suspicious. You also say that, on the evening of that day, he was seen descending from the Red Barn with a pickaxe on his shoulder."

" Yes; but I questioned him on that point, and he denied it,—said it was another man."

" But did not the person who saw him, know him ?"

" Yes; for I have spoken to that person since Barnard's departure, and he declares that it was no one else, and that he could not in any way be mistaken."

' Well, you know, if that be the case, he could not possibly have gone to Ipswich with Maria on that day."

" That is true," said the mother; " besides, I have since spoken to the man whom Barnard stated to have been mistaken for himself, and he says he was not in that neighbourhood the whole of that day."

7-t   4 r

" This," returned Hannah, "is a clear proof that Barnard is a liar, and meant to deceive you ; and if he did not go to Ipswich—as it is quite evident he did not—it is very unlikely that Maria went there by herself. Has anything else transpired, since his departure, to confirm your suspicions ?"

" Yes; I have heard that he told different stories about Maria to different persons. To one he told that she was gone to France, and to another that she was living very near us."

" Have you heard from Barnard since he left Polstead ?"

" Yes :"—(and here Mrs. Marten told Hannah about his letters, and the pretended miscarriage of Maria's letter).

" Well, Mrs. Marten," said Hannah, " the suspicion that Barnard has made away with your daughter appears to me very strong indeed : your not hearing a word from her—his palpable lies,—every thing, in short, seems to prove it. Do you know that I should not be at all surprised if he had murdered her in the Red Barn, with those very pistols which you saw him snapping."

" Good God ! you cannot think so ?" said the mother.

" Indeed but I do though ; and I think, that if you would have the Red Barn examined, you would find it out; for, if he killed her, he could not have hidden the body with safety anywhere else."

This made a deep impresion on the mind of Mrs Marten, and she had a long conversation with her husband on the subject. He, however, could not at all be brought to enter into her suspicions of Barnard's being a murderer: he thought his conduct somewhat mysterious, but could not believe that he was capable of such villany.

Full of what Hannah had said to her concerning the supposed murder of Maria in the Red Barn, Mrs. Marten retired to rest, and remained for some hours awake, deeply reflecting on the horrible suspicions excited in her breast. Towards the middle of the night she fell asleep, and dreamed a singular dream;—not singular from its subject, for her waking thoughts had led to it, but from its remarkable accuracy and prophetic character.

She dreamed that she was looking in through the door of the Red Barn, and that she saw the body of her daughter lying on the floor in the right hand bay, covered with blood : Barnard was close by, without his coat, working alternately with spade and pickaxe, making a grave. She saw him complete his work, and, when he had finished, deposit the body in the earth, cover it over, and then spread the ground with straw. She then fancied that she entered the Barn—stood upon the grave—removed the straw and the earth with her hands from the body—and plainly saw the features of her daughter ; at which a scream burst from her, and she awoke trembling with horror. She told her husband this remarkable dream ; and added her full conviction that Maria had been murdered by Barnard, and buried in the Red Barn.

The old man still remained incredulous. "My dear," said he, "dreams are nothing. It was natural you should dream all this after what you had been saying to me last night. But I cannot believe that William Barnard could do such a thing."

"You may talk as you like, husband," said she, "but I feel sure it is so."

The poor old woman passed the whole of that day in a state of the greatest melancholy and depression of mind. The following night she dreamed precisely the same dream as the night before, without the variation of a single particular.

Again she spoke to her husband on the subject and told the second dream; at which he was startled, and without hesitation determined to search the Barn.

Accordingly he proceeded to the cottage of a neighbour and friend of his, told him what he was about, and asked him for his assistance. The other, very much surprised, consented to accompany him. So, having procured the key of the Red Barn, and having entered the place, they went to work immediately in the left bay, where Mrs. Marten had dreamed that her unfortunate daughter lay buried.

The corn had been thrashed out, but the litter

still remained in the Barn. On lifting up the straw, several great stones appeared in the centre of the bay, and the earth there had evidently been disturbed and rooted up. On this spot they began to dig.

The earth was removed without much difficulty, it being quite loose and unfirm. They had worked down about a foot and a half, when they felt something stop them. They then cleared away the adjacent earth a little, and, to their astonishment and horror, most clearly discovered the remains of a human body. It was dressed in female attire, and a green handkerchief was observed round the neck—announcing to the unhappy father the terrible fate of his daughter.

Who can picture to themselves at this moment the feelings of the unfortunate man? He was utterly unable to speak; the spade fell from his nerveless arm, and he would have sunk upon the earth, had he not been supported by his two companions, and borne into the open air.

It was agreed that the body should not be touched or removed, until information should be given in the proper quarter.

The wretched father, heartsick, returned home, and informed his wife of the result of his labours. He still had some slight hope that the corpse might not be that of his daughter. The first question he asked her was, what kind of handkerchief Maria wore round her neck on the day of her departure.

"*A green one,*" was the reply.

"Then," said Marten, "it is too true: our daughter has been murdered, and buried in the Red Barn; and, I fear, by Barnard."

The unfortunate mother hurried off to the fatal spot, where she beheld the corpse of her beloved daughter, and identified every article of dress which remained.—We shall not attempt to describe her feelings: they can be better imagined than described.

As she was returning home, she met Hannah Woods, and told her all. The latter, affected by nothing but her feelings of revenge against Barnard, exclaimed, with a look of triumphant malice,

"'Tis well! I shall have the satisfaction of seeing the villain hanged."

So saying, she posted away to communicate the news to Jackson.

CHAP. XXIV.

"'Twas strange, they said, a wonderous discovery!
And ever and anon they vow'd revenge."

HOME.

HARRY EVERTON, according to his promise, now prepared to visit Polstead, and see the Marten family. Carribles and Tom Squires accompanied him in a chaise to the village, and they arrived at the cottage of old Marten on the day subsequent to the discovery of the body of Maria!

Having descended, and entered the yard, they were met at the door of the house by old Marten, whom Carribles was beginning to address with " Well, my dear old friend, here we are come!" ——when, on looking at the other, whose expression of countenance denoted something dreadful, in a manner too plain for the most superficial observer to mistake, he exclaimed,

" How now, man? what, in God's name, is the matter?—You look the very picture of terror and distress "

" Oh, sir !" sobbed out the unfortunate old man, " my daughter, my daughter !—My poor dear Maria !"

" What of her ?" cried Carribles.

" What of her ?" cried Everton.

" Oh, gentlemen !—dead—destroyed—basely murdered !"

" Murdered !" cried Everton; " murdered ! how ? when ? where ? by whom ? Great God ! it is not possible."

" Oh, Harry, Harry !" cried the mother, running out, with her eyes swoln with weeping, " poor Maria is dead !—destroyed by a ruffian !"

" But, for God's sake, my good friends," said Carribles, " tell us about it. How happened this horrible business ?"

" Come in, gentlemen," said old Marten, " come in ; and we will endeavour to tell you all."

In they went ; and the old people related minutely every circumstance which is already known to the reader concerning the discovery of the body, and their persuasion that William Barnard was the murderer.

When the melancholy and horrid tale was concluded, Everton rested his head on both his hands and uttered not a word. He appeared so astounded as to lose for a while the use of all his faculties. Carribles started up ; and with an oath, the profanity of which might perhaps be excused by the most pious, from the burst of generous indignation which inspired it, exclaimed.

"Infernal ruffian!—desperate, abominable monster!—but every search must be made;—the fellow cannot—shall not escape. Maria's death must be avenged."

"Avenged, Sir!" cried Everton, starting from his stupor, as if roused into recollection by the sound of the last words of Carribles; "avenged!—yes—not all the powers of hell shall screen him from vengeance. I will sacrifice both life and property, if necessary, to bring the villain to justice;—I would hunt him even to the centre of the earth, if he could take refuge there. No spot of the habitable globe shall be secure for him—I will pursue him to the remotest corners of the world."

"Well said, my friend," cried Carribles; "and I will help you, tooth and nail. Curse me, but I would hang him myself at the yard-arm, if he lacked an executioner, rather than that he should escape justice."

"And so would I, master," said Tom Squires.

"But, alas! my dear friend," said Everton, "she is gone,—the young, the beautiful, the harmless. Never shall these eyes again behold her;—she whom to be near was happiness—with whom I have sat so often in that window—whom, when we were both children, I have helped to make that little garden, whose flowers we have nursed together! My dear friend, bear with my weakness—you will, if you have ever loved."

"Harry," said Carribles, taking him by the hand, "I do. I have known what it is to be

4 G

young, and to love; but remember that you are a man, and have a duty to perform. You cannot better prove your affection to the memory of the deceased, than by revenging her foul and heartless murder."

"Enough!" said Everton; "that idea nerves me again; I will not rest until the ruffian be brought to justice. Come, my friend, let us about it straight: let us take the first steps—there is no time to be lost. My dear old friends," said he, addressing himself to the Martens, "let us dry up our tears, if possible: the destroyer of your child shall be brought to punishment,—his life will be but a poor atonement for his atrocious guilt. Farewell, for a while;—I go to use all the influence I am master of in this county: meanwhile, bear this in mind—though you have lost a daughter, that while I live you shall never want a son."

"Heaven bless you!" cried the old couple, weeping bitterly.

"Carribles, Everton, and Squires, now departed. Everton expressed a wish to visit the Barn, to see the body; but his friend Carribles, with a good sense, prudence, discretion, and good feeling, highly praiseworthy, would not permit him. His mind, he said, had already been quite sufficiently agitated and distressed; and to view the mouldering remains of all that he had adored when living, could serve no other purpose than to render him still more unhappy.

The news of the discovery of Maria's body spread like wildfire through the village and its neighbourhood. Numbers flocked to the Red Barn, and all united in execrations against the perpetrator of so accursed a deed. That the murderer was no other than Willam Barnard, every one, who heard the particulars of the dreadful tale, most firmly believed.

But who can describe the feelings of Jackson, when Hannah told him the tremendous news. The others who had been connected with Maria, who had hitherto heard the fact, were affected simply by horror, or by heart-felt grief—with the exception of Hannah, who, incapable of pity, thought of nothing but her vengeance upon Barnard. But with Jackson, the feelings of horror and of anguish were mingled with a deadlier draught—the bitterness of remorse. He felt that he himself was the primal cause of all. He it was who had laid the train which ended in this dreadful explosion. He it was, who by a cool, systematic plan of seduction, by unworthy artifice, and base deception, by a burlesque on the sacred ceremony of marriage, and by a heartless desertion of the victim of his wiles, when appetite was sated,—he it was, who had laid the foundation of this dreadful catastrophe. He could hardly consider himself as less guilty than the actual perpetrator of the deed; so deep, so terrible was the impression made on him by the story of Hannah.

"Well," said she, " I was right; I guessed he was the murderer."

Jackson looked steadily at her for several minutes, without speaking. The expression of his countenance was awful. He started up, and struck his hand against his forehead.

" *I*," exclaimed he—" *I* am her murderer."

" *You!*" said Hannah.

" Ay, I! and you too—you assisted ;—we have murdered her, by first deceiving her."

" As for me," said Hannah, " I am guiltless of her death ; and as for deceiving her, you employed, instigated, solicited, bribed me to that. On your head be that portion of the responsibility."

"Yes," said he ; " yes, it is too true. It was this cursed head that planned it all. Why should I attempt to cast the burthen of my guilt on its worthless instruments? As well might the ruffian who performed the infernal deed, lay the blame upon the weapon which he used. But no! the weapon was unconscious, you were not ; it was no free agent, you were ; you might have refused. Besides, you are guilty of this murder in another way. You corrupted Barnard—you led him into the labyrinth of vice and infamy. You trained his mind ; you led him from one degree of guiltiness to another, until he was capable of this direful consummation of crime."

" Did no one help me, Jackson?" said the female fiend, with a sarcastic sneer ;—" who originated his ruin ?"

"Not I—you know it was not I!"

"You sanctioned others; you lent your powerful influence—an influence that was, probably, indispensable to success."

"Well—be it so. On my head let my portion of it rest—it is weighty enough. But you have your share; and a heavy one it is. If there be, as the wisest of men have believed, a dispenser of eternal justice, and an hereafter of retribution, you are deeply, awfully responsible."

"Vain imaginations!" said Hannah; "they touch me not. I fear not the hell hereafter—the one that is here is enough."

"That you will yet feel. Mark me—I am going, I know not whither; but we are not likely to meet again. I am careless of my fate: my offences are great, and I must suffer the just punishment of them. Be it so—repentance is too late. I go to my doom—but mark my latest words. You have passed your life in heartless infamy; and, for the sordid consideration of gain, you have ever been the ready tool of villany and of crime. The hell you speak of here you will feel. Deserted and despised of all, forlorn, and poor, and wretched, you will drag out the remnant of your days in misery and contempt. Your arts will no longer deceive: the charms by which you held fools in thraldom are vanished; the mental powers which you have abused will become your torment. Madness will not come to your relief; and you will preserve a vivid memory of past guilty enjoyments, with a consciousness of the miseries of the present. You will finally be reduced to the lowest degradation that age, disease, and penury, can cause ; and you will die without consolation, and without hope !"

The manner in which Jackson pronounced this dreadful prophecy was awfully impressive. His sonorous voice was re-echoed by the hollow cavern over which he stood; the deadly paleness of his countenance contrasted with his dark bushy hair, which hung around his face in neglected profusion. His eye glared wildly on the object he was addressing, who was perfectly overawed and struck dumb by the fearful energy of his delivery. When he had concluded, he seized his hat and pistols, and hurried forth from the cottage, never to return.

He directed his steps to the Red Barn. "I will take," said he, " a last view of the sad consequences of my guilty folly."

Evening was approaching. It was the month of April. The sun, upon the extreme verge of the west, darted his crimson beams over the landscape ; but a mass of livid clouds, with their dark edges tipped with red, denoted, in the eastern sky, a coming storm. All the scenery was familiar to Jackson, and associated with the bitterest recollections of the lost Maria. He took a path which gave him a distant but distinct view of her cottage. He stopped, and looked at it. He was just facing the corner window from which she had so often looked out on him, in all her virgin beauty, at their various nightly assignations. He thought upon what she was then, and what she was now! He thought upon himself, too—how lost—how ruined! His manly heart sunk under the recollection, nor could he restrain a flood of tears.

He recovered himself, and proceeded forwards. He had a horror of visiting the fatal spot; and yet he felt irresistibly impelled towards it.

He entered the Barn. There were a few peasants there. The body was not yet removed; but remained for the inspection of the Coroner. It was in the place where it had been buried. The earth had been now completely removed from about it. Jackson approached, and looked stedfastly at the sad remains of what he had once loved, and what had fondly, dearly loved him. Instead of life, and youth, and loveliness, what did he behold?—all the revolting ravages of mortality!

He rushed with horror from the scene: a second look he could not endure. His feelings were wound up almost to frenzy, and he proceeded in a hurried pace along a path which led him far from the Red Barn—but whither, he neither knew nor cared.

When he found himself in a wild and silent spot, apparently far from the haunts of mankind, he seated himself under a tree, close behind a hedge which bordered the road. Night had now come on; but neither moon nor stars were visible;

for the dark clouds which had been gathering in the east had now involved the whole horizon.

Here Jackson gave utterance to the feelings which lacerated his bosom :—" So, this is my handiwork !" said he ; " I have been the artificer of death and ruin.   Oh ! if I had acted otherwise ! If I had remained faithful to her, even after having first deceived her, she would have been still living, and I should have been happy !—She loved me ; —her heart was all purity, and innocence, and affection.   Wretch that I was, to have seduced her !—doubly so, to have deserted her !"

He then pictured to himself how happy he could have been with Maria.   How he might have retired with her to some remote and sequestered spot, where, having renounced his irregular pursuits, he might have lived, forgetful of the world and its allurements, happy only in her simple and confiding love. There he might have atoned for his errors by a virtuous course ; have lived in tranquillity, and died in peace.

" But, no !" thought he again, "that could not be. I was too deeply immersed to have emerged—I was too far gone to return.   I could not subsist except as I did.   I had made my choice of folly and of vice long before, with my eyes open, and I was obliged to stick to it.—I shall quit," said he, " the country, which has been the scene of my vice and folly. I shall fly far away from this scene of horror, and hide my head in some distant region of the earth, where I shall not hear the sound of my native language, or encounter aught that will excite the remembrance of my country. I will go and wander with the Tartar of the plain, or the Arab of the desert;—or I will go, and transport myself to some remote island in the boundless main, where the untutored savage roams through his native woods, untainted by the vices of civilization. —But, fool that I am! what am I talking about? where can I go without means? I am a beggar— I have no money, and I know not where to get it. To get it honestly is impossible;—I will not get it meanly. There is but one alternative. I must get it bravely, though foully. Yes; I have no hope else. This must I do, and then away from England for ever."

Scarcely had he made this last reflection, when the wheels of a carriage came rattling along the road. The impulse to stop it instantly seized upon his mind. It was a moment of dreadful desperation with him. The risk of his life he did not value—it was nothing. This attempt might make him or mar him for ever.—He might procure the means of quitting the country at once. Reason and reflection were banished from his mind; he scarcely thought of what he was about, and was in a state little short of madness.

He started up, clearing the hedge with a single bound, rushed up the road, met and stopped the horses, and demanded the purses of the passengers. A young man instantly opened the door

75

of the carriage, and jumped out, armed with a brace of pistols. Jackson called on him to deliver his money—that he did not wish to take his life. The other refused, and both fired simultaneously. Jackson fell :—he was mortally wounded, but retained full possession of his senses.

At this instant another person descended from the chaise, and called out—

"What, ho! Harry, have you crippled the pirate?"

"I believe so," replied Everton ;—for it was he and Carribles, who were returning in the chariot of the former. They had, after quitting Polstead in the morning, dined with a neighbouring gentleman, with whom they had been consulting about the immediate measures to discover the murderer of Maria.

Everton took one of the lamps off the chaise, and came up to see if the robber were actually dead. Jackson lay on the road, half reclined on his elbow, —he was wounded in the side.

"Whoever you are," said he, in a voice which, notwithstanding his wound, was sufficiently firm, "you have given me my *quietus*, and I thank you for it with all my heart,—it was the best turn you could possibly have done me now."

"Surely," cried Carribles, approaching, "I should know that voice—I have heard it before."

He looked at Jackson's face by the lamp-light, but could not recognize it: Jackson however, instantly knew the Captain.

"My friend!" he exclaimed; "my father's

friend !—Captain Carribles ! Just heaven !—what an attempt I have made ! I thank thee for my death,—I have been saved from a worse crime than any I have been ever guilty of yet."

" Who are you," said Carribles, " that know my name so well ? Your voice I have heard before, but I do not know your person."

" I wonder not at that—misfortune makes great changes. She has so altered Stafford Jackson, that he is not known to him who was his own and his father's friend."

" Heavens !" cried the Captain ; " is it possible ? are you—*can* you be, Stafford Jackson—the son of my old friend ?"

" It is too true," said Stafford ; " and little cause have I to rejoice in the name."

" Unfortunate young man !" said Carribles ; " how is it that I meet you in such a character ? —a robber !—a highwayman !"

" Misfortune,—desperation,—madness !" replied Jackson : " my life has been a course of folly, of vice, of violence ; and it is right it should end thus. Accident to-day led me to where I beheld a ruin—a dreadful ruin, of which my own unprincipled passion was the primary cause. Struck to frenzy by contemplation of the horrid scene, I rushed away—determined to fly for ever from my native country ; but I had no money, and, under a momentary impulse of desperation, I stopped your carriage. Thank heaven ! I have been prevented from adding the murder of my friend, or of your friend, to the black catalogue of my crimes. But I faint—I am dying —O! give me a little water."

Carribles was never without a small pocket-case of brandy about him, and he now applied it to the lips of Jackson.

"Come," said he, "my unfortunate boy! my house is close by,—we'll remove you, and send for a surgeon."

It is useless," said Jackson; "my wound I feel is mortal;—I cannot live—I do not wish it."

"You shall not die here, at all events," said Carribles ; "it shall not be said that old Carribles let his friend, and the son of his friend, die like a dog on the high road—however guilty and unfortunate he might have been.—Come, Mr. Everton, help me."

Carribles, Everton, and the driver, now gently raised the wounded man, and placed him in the chaise. They stopped the flowing of the blood from his side, by binding it with handkerchiefs, and drove quickly to the Captain's cottage; where having brought him in and set him on a couch, they sent for a surgeon, in spite of Jackson's opposition.

"It is useless, my respected—my injured old friend!" said Stafford ; " my life is ebbing fast, and will not last his coming. But, before I die, I wish to confess to you the full extent of my errors ;—ı do not desire that you should think me better or worse than I am."

He now briefly touched on his irregular life, detailed his intercourse with Maria, and his feelings and resolves when he had discovered the dreadful catastrophe.

Everton listened with intense attention; and when he had done, exclaimed,

" Gracious heaven ! you, then, were the person I met with her at the fair of Polstead, dressed in the white hat."

" I am," said Jackson ; "but who are you ?"

"Do you not remember a young man who passed you in the evening ?—you marked me well then—it was not far from Maria's cottage."

"I do, I do !" said Jackson.

" I am he," replied Everton.

Here Carribles explained Harry's attachment to Maria, and honourable designs.

" Just heaven !" said Jackson ; " the retribution was doubly due ;—I have fallen by the man I have most injured. Give me your hand, my friend—for I must call you so :—I thank you again for my death. I have been very reckless through my life, both of divine and human laws ; but the injury to Maria, and and its consequences, are what press most deeply on my heart in this my dying hour. Those excepted—though I have greatly offended otherwise—I have never stooped to aught that was mean and petty. I have betrayed no friend—I have taken no cowardly advantage of a foe: early love of pleasure, early imprudence, has led me to this end. One false step produced a thousand others : I foolishly left an honourable profession, and was then thrown upon the world under the influence of strong passions and of evil councils. Habit made me irreclaimable, and necessity forced me to persevere in the course that folly had begun. But I am going—my course is run: I am about to render an account of my follies and my crimes;—heaven have mercy on me! —Farewell, my old—my early friend ! forgive me ! —Oh! forgive me !——"

These were the last words that Stafford Jackson ever spoke. In a few minutes he expired, as he had predicted, before the arrival of the surgeon.

" Unfortunate boy !" said Carribles, leaning over him; "you are the wreck of all that was gallant and high-spirited. Oh, Everton, I used to love this boy as if he had been my own son I taught him to sail, to row, to hand, reef, and steer. A lad of more daring mettle never trod a quarter deck—or of quicker wit; and, in spite of all his errors, his heart was generous and noble. But thoughtlessness, folly, headlong dissipation, bad company—look, look at their consequences, Harry. But of you there is no danger—your principles are too good ; you are too steady in the paths of virtue and of honour, to need such an example."

Carribles, after all proper investigation had taken place respecting this affair, saw, himself, the last duties paid to the son of his friend.

CHAP. XXV.

"——— Then is sin struck down like an ox."—Shakspeare.

Meanwhile, the infamous and wretched author of the atrocity had returned to London. At the time the body of Maria was discovered, Barnard was settled with his wife near the metropolis, where they lived in great respectability. He could not, however, totally rid himself of his fears, nor of the stings of an evil conscience. During his waking hours, he had so far disciplined his mind as considerably to overcome, or at least to suppress, such feelings ; but in the relaxation of sleep, when reason yielded her empire to fancy, his torments would return.

He had retired to rest one night oppressed with melancholy feelings—a dim light burned near his bed—the house clock had struck the hour or midnight, and his eyes closed in something like sleep, and he dreamed that he was standing in the fatal Red Barn, beside Maria's grave Suddenly the earth under his feet gave way, and he fell through it into a place of utter darkness. The darkness, however, did not long continue; for a tall figure, in long black drapery, entered, bearing a flaring torch. By the light of this, Barnard found himself in a charnel-house, where heaps of skulls and human bones were piled all around: the figure with the torch then vanished, and left Barnard again in darkness. After this, with the extravagance of dreaming, he imagined that the torch re-entered by itself, and, moving across the place, seemed to rest on a heap of human skulls. By the light, he now discerned, seated on an adjoining heap, Maria, with her child in her arms. Their appearance, at first, was such as it had been in their life-time; but a sudden and horrid change took place :—the mother appeared with the wound in her face, the dreadful staring eye-ball, and a deep gash in the side, from which was issuing a fountain of blood :—the face of the child was black with decomposition; its body was uncovered, and the limbs appeared half dropping into dust. Suddenly the ground opened at his feet, and he stood on the brink of an apparently interminable pit of darkness : all around the edge of this yawning gulf, he could discern the horrid countenances of demons and furies. The earth which sustained his feet now gave way—flames arose around him—and he fell headlong into an ocean of fire.—On this he awaked in an agony of terror, shrieking aloud so as to alarm the house : his wife and her mother rushed affrighted to his room, and found him pale and breathless. He contrived, however, to muster resolution enough not to betray himself, and merely complained of illness.

Notwithstanding the dreadful impression of this dream, he managed, when he was thoroughly awake, to recover the appearance of self-possession. He walked into his garden, and reasoned and reflected within himself for some time on the dangerous situation in which he must be placed, should the body be discovered. The dream foreboded something of this—he could not dispossess his mind of it—it haunted him through all his reflections, and he almost thought that it was his death warning. Yet, eleven months had now elapsed since the commission of the murder, and he must, he thought, be secure : the body must have become so completely decomposed, as to render its identification impossible. Even if it should be discovered—a thing in itself exceedingly improbable—still that discovery could not hurt him : he might, indeed, be suspected, but it could never be proved that he was the murderer. He knew that no circumstance but the identification of the body could inculpate him : his life, therefore, was safe. What had he to fear ?—why should he torment himself with imaginary terrors? What was conscience?—a name—a shadow—a phantom, to use the favourite expression of his friend Carlile :

4 I

nonsense !—he was perfectly secure—he was living in seclusion and in comfort—in the enjoyment of a good income, and of a respectable connexion in which he was esteemed—what was there to fear for him ? It was unwise, then, to trouble himself. He ought to enjoy, undisturbed by foolish visions, the happy lot which fortune and his own cleverness had procured him : to improve that lot should be his care. Like the rich man in the Gospel, he was disposed to say within himself, " Soul, thou hast much goods laid up for many years : take thine ease ; eat, drink, and be merry "—but he was soon destined to hear, in a voice of thunder, " Thou fool ! this night thy soul shall be required of thee."

Calmed, composed, and even exhilarated, by this train of thought, he sat himself down to breakfast in company with his wife and mother in-law, and two other ladies. His conversation was gay and mirthful ; and he was quietly minuting by his watch the boiling of some eggs, when a knock was heard at the street door. The servant came up stairs, and announced that a strange gentleman was desirous of speaking with Mr. William Barnard, on urgent business ; on which he desired that the gentleman should be shown into another room, and immediately waited upon him. —It was an officer of police who appeared before him, bearing a warrant to arrest him for the murder ! and Barnard's conscience told him so, even before the awful fact was announced to his ears. He trembled within—his face grew pale as death—his eyes almost lost their sight—his lips became dry—and his tongue faltered, as he replied to the officer of justice that he was not the murderer—that he never knew the name of the murdered Maria! But the lie availed him not—truth was written on his front, and the grasp of iron justice was upon him. The fatal weapons with which he committed the dreadful deed,—his pistols and dagger—were even in the very apartment where the officer charged him with the crime, and secured before him. So certain had he felt that he was out of all danger of being discovered as the criminal—so blunted in his feelings,—that he had hung these very instruments and memorials of his villany in the apartment to which he daily resorted!—He was arrested, bound—and from fancied security, in the comforts of affluence, dragged before a magistrate, and thence sent to Polstead, under the care of the officer who apprehended him; where an inquest took place on the body of Maria, and a verdict was brought in against him of WILFUL MURDER.

The remains of the unfortunate girl were then interred in the churchyard of Polstead. The weeping parents followed her coffin, and Harry Everton and Carribles appeared as mourners at the funeral. No stone marks the humble grave of the innocent victim of seduction and villany; but long shall the villager recognize the spot where she lies, pity her melancholy fate, and execrate the memory of her heartless destroyer.

As the carriage, which was to convey him to Bury Gaol, rolled away with the criminal through his native village, where every object was so familiar to him—where his innocent hours of boyhood had been spent—where his happy home lay, from which he was now parting for ever,—his head sunk —his frame convulsively shuddered—and he threw himself back on the seat, where he sat completely overwhelmed with mental agony. "Here," thought he, "I might have still been happy—I might still have enjoyed the blessings of this peace ful and delightful spot—here I might have still been respected and beloved by my neighbours and my kindred,—had not the false glare of worldly pleasure, and infidelity to my Creator, turned me aside into the wilderness of vice. And now, where am I going?—to quit home, friends, relations—all; to die on a scaffold—execrated by the world!"

In this train of reflection he remained, until the carriage stopped at the gate of the Gaol—out of which he never passed, but to his trial and his execution.

Thus perished William Barnard, in the prime of youth. Such was the just and awful vengeance visited by unerring heaven on the head of a murderer. Such were the consequences of lawless appetite, of vicious society, of unprincipled folly, and blasphemous infidelity. Such were the consequences of a young man being insnared within that fatal circle, " Life in London,"—the atmosphere of which is pollution, pestilence, and death ; where every good feeling grows extinct—where every bad passion, every hateful propensity, is cherished. From which, taste, refinement, sense, and honesty, are banished : where virtue is a scorn, and crime a jest. Where even our very language itself is perverted from its proper use : where a dialect is spoken not less expressive of the heartlessness than of the vulgarity of its adopters ; and which is, at once, the emblem, the preservative, and, in a great measure, the source of depravity; for words, after all, are too often things : nor can certain styles of expression be adopted with impunity to the character. *The gentlemen,* who imagine that they can habitually employ the language of ruffians, thieves, and prostitutes, without ceasing to be gentlemen, are indeed very grievously mistaken ; and the disposition to adopt such phraseology, from whatever cause generated, argues little for their taste, good sense, or morality. Such, in short, only added another victim to the many who have fallen within the scorching and pestilential breath of London pleasure.

Neither was Barnard the only victim to this vicious course, among the personages of this history. Smith is now wandering an outcast for ever from his country, on the shores of New

Holland; but he remained, after his embarkation, a sufficient time in harbour to hear of the dreadful fate of his pupil, his associate, and friend. The catastrophe of Stafford Jackson is already fully before the reader. Creed, whose guilt was not of the darkest die, is yet suffering the just penalty of his total want of principle, in a state of the lowest indigence in America. Warren, a man of violence, perished by violence. Ellen, a wretched, houseless prostitute, died in the streets from starvation; and the one-eyed scoundrel, who came to be a personal witness of the end of Barnard, was but then beholding what soon awaited himself.

As for the principal agent in producing the crimes and calamities which it has fallen to our lot to describe, the prediction of Jackson concerning her has been pretty accurately fulfilled. Utterly deprived of beauty by increasing years, and infirmities, equally the result of former vicious excesses and present privations, she sunk into the lowest and most degraded poverty. Haggard, filthy, and revolting in her appearance, she subsisted, for a time, precariously on casual charity, often bestowed by the young peasantry around as much from fear as from pity,—for her wild, withered, and witch-like appearance, was not ill-calculated to excite apprehension in a youthful and superstitious mind. She added to the list of her other vices, an habitual indulgence, as far as she was able, in drunkenness. After having remained some time in the neighbourhood of Polstead, she suddenly disappeared, and nothing certain concerning her fate ever transpired. About the time, indeed, of her disappearance, a female body was cast on the coast in the neighbourhood of Clacton, and some imagined that it might have been hers; but it was so disfigured by the waves, as to render it impossible to identify it.

Captain Carribles still survives, and is as healthy and as happy as ever, except when he reflects on the deaths of Maria and Jackson. He maintains the closest intimacy with his friend Harry Everton, who is most highly respected in the country. The latter still remains unmarried, and is still likely so to continue; for he cherishes, with a feeling not likely to be soon obliterated, the memory of his lost Maria.

If, in the earlier portion of this history, we have dwelt rather in detail on scenes of London life, it was for the purpose of showing how dangerous, how fatal, is their tendency. No character which we have described as figuring there, has failed to suffer the infallible punishment that awaits vice and folly. We trust that we have taken a moral for our end; and if our story prove the means of deterring any youth, who is on the brink of the gulf of vicious pleasure, from being plunged in and lost for ever, our labour will be recompensed to the extent of our hopes.

Colchester
George Inn
Wednesday
night 10 O'clock

Dear Brother

I scarcely dare
presume to address yo
having a full knowledge
of the shame disgrace
and I may truly add
sorrow a strain upon
my family friends and lost
formed connextions I have
but few minute to write
and being unfortunately
labouring under this
serious charge I have
solicit that you will
receive Mr Moore on
friday morning with it
probably may be my injur
lawfull and I must do h
itt justice to say worthy

I have always experienced
from every branch of
their family the Kindest
treatment hope and trust
the same will be returned
from you the short time
they continue in this part
of the Country which I am
sorry I have to state is
to hear the event of this
dreadful castrophe I
am happy to hear you
are tolerable well consi,
dering the present
circumstances I may
perhaps be allowed an
interview with you
in a day or two but that
I find is very uncertain
must beg to subscribe
myself your unfortunate
Son
W Corder

Mrs Corder

TRIAL

OF

WILLIAM CORDER,

FOR

The Murder

OF

MARIA MARTEN.

No event, of a domestic occurrence, since the murder of Mr. Weare by John Thurtell, has monopolized more of the public interest and sympathy throughout all parts of the country, than the savage assassination of Maria Marten, at Polstead, in Suffolk, and the recent trial and condemnation of her tiger-hearted assassin, William Corder, at Bury St. Edmund's—and few, indeed, if any, have been marked with a more cold-blooded atrocity, a more premeditated execution, or a more callous minded or pitiless disposition.

The vile murderer was William Corder, who is now condemned to pay the only earthly atonement he could offer for the magnitude of his offence, and the wretched victim of his barbarity was Maria Marten.   Both were natives of the county of Suffolk.   Corder, the only surviving son of a respectable farmer lately living in the vicinity of the village of Polstead, and the ill-fated Maria, the daughter of a poor but industrious man, who supported his family by mole-catching, and resided but a short distance from the cottage of Mrs. Corder.

A darker deed, or one more malignantly and barbarously accomplished, than that perpetrated by Corder, happily blackens not a page in the annals of human iniquity; but yet, while reviewing it, this satisfaction remains to us,—that outraged humanity, and the violated laws of God and man, will be partially, if not fully, avenged in the criminal's ignominious and merited death.

In detailing the incidents consequent upon this appalling offence, we assume the task with much hesitation, and more reluctance. It is an office from which the best feelings of humanity recoil; but yet, as it is one the performance of which may give a practical and useful proof of the baneful fruits of a life of immorality—serve as a beacon to those who, the slaves of ungoverned judgment, or heated by youthful passion, are about to make their first step in the career of crime, and warn them of its certain and ignominious termination,--we shrink not from its execution. And did we entertain any doubt of the propriety of its discharge, all

4 K

scepticism would vanish on the recollection of the ascertained and incon‑
trovertible fact, that even a solitary instance of punishment, treading,
though slowly, certainly on the heels of guilt, and it coming within our
own knowledge, and its existence verified by the most conclusive testi‑
mony, operates with greater force, and exercises a more powerful in‑
fluence over the rule and conduct of life, than a thousand theoretical and
supposititious cases.

Confining ourselves to truth, and repudiating, as much as possible, those
feelings of indignation and animosity, which will spontaneously and almost
irresistibly arise from the contemplation of so unprecedented a murder;
we shall simply lay before the reader those circumstances that have been
under our own observation, and such illustrative incidents as, after making
diligent inquiry, we are convinced are correct.

The barbarous deed, which has more the appearance of a melo-drama‑
tic romance, than an occurrence in a civilized country like England, pos‑
sesses, inherently, so fearful a reality, that it requires no fiction of the
imagination to add to its horrors—it needs not any embellishment—it de‑
mands not any ideal colouring—and, in truth, we are so lamentably as‑
sured, "that such things are," that to enlarge upon them, or enhance
their horror,—it cannot be enhanced,—would be as disagreeable as it would
be superfluous.

The murder itself was discovered as if by the interposition of Provi‑
dence. The work, which "shunned the light," was discovered by a
dream,—an incident not the least singular in this "crime of mystery," and
a circumstance which not only reminds us of the imaginative tales of our
childhood and the nursery, but one which, were it not so distinctly authen‑
ticated, would scarce obtain belief from even the most credulous.

The facts, each simple in themselves, but each furnishing, though a
small, yet a necessary, link in the chain of evidence confirmatory of the
guilt of the accused. His midnight perturbations—his disturbed mind—
his sleepless walks—his singular matrimonial advertisement—his almost
predestinated union with his broken-hearted helpmate—the purposed exe‑
cution of the deed of conveyance of the school at Ealing-lane, on the
very morning on which he was apprehended—his forgery on the Hadley
and Manningtree banks to complete the purchase,—are all circumstances
which, though viewed individually, may appear unimportant, are yet, when
taken collectively, of great magnitude; have been the instrument of dis‑
closing as unmotived and unprovoked a murder as has for ages been heard
of; and testifies, if testimony were necessary,

"That murder most foul will out;"

and that

"Justice, tho' halt, she's sure,
And will o'ertake the quick-paced criminal."

The first announcement of "the Polstead Murder," for such is the
name by which it is at present characterized, and the appellation by
which, in all probability, the diabolical tragedy will be transmitted to
posterity, appeared in the leading London Journal, "The Times," of the
22d of April, 1828. A simultaneous account was also given in a country
paper, the "Suffolk Herald;" but as it was, in the ordinary style of country
journals, overcharged where it was unrequired, and dealt in too much of
the romance of paragraph-making, its correctness cannot be depended on;

and it is altogether undeserving of notice, except so far as it furnishes one or two subsidiary circumstances (of the accuracy of which we have no knowledge) which "The Times" has omitted.

In "The Times," the murder was well described as a deed hitherto unheard of; unprecedented in cruelty; and distinguished by a concentrated malice that could have only been expected from the head of a demon ; and an outline of the apprehension of Corder, and the grounds on which it was thought proper to transmit him to Polstead, to await the verdict of the adjourned inquest holden on the corpse by the Coroner, Mr. Weyman, was published.

The announcement alluded to we subjoin; and the interest it created, though considerable, was raised to an irritable height of excitement, by the appearance, in almost the entire of the Metropolitan Newspapers, of a report from the Lambeth-street Office of Police, dated Wednesday, the 23d of April, in which the particulars were given with a great degree of minuteness, and, as the result has proved, with the utmost fidelity.

To preserve a regular order in the narrative, and to give the reader the opportunity of drawing his own conclusions, we shall here insert it, as also the extract from the "Suffolk Herald."

"The Times," April 22, 1828.

"On Tuesday evening, a constable from Suffolk, of the name of Ayres, made an application at Lambeth-street Police Office, stating that a strong suspicion was entertained that a most diabolical murder had been committed in Suffolk, by a person named William Corder. An inquest had been that day holden on the unhappy victim, which stands adjourned until Friday. In consequence of this communication, James Lea, an officer of this establishment, in company with Ayres, apprehended Corder; and a few minutes before the office closed on Tuesday evening, he was brought in custody before M. Wyatt, Esq. the sitting magistrate.

"From the statement, on oath, of the constable Ayres, it appeared that the murdered woman, whose name is Maria Marten, aged 26 years, was decoyed, in male attire, on the 18th of last May (1827), from the house of her parents at Polstead, in Suffolk, by the prisoner, who desired her to meet him at his *Red Barn*, promising her that they should go to Ipswich to be married by license.

"The unsuspecting girl accordingly attended at the time and place appointed, but from that day to this she had not been heard of. Since that period, however, many letters have been received by the parents of the unfortunate girl, from the prisoner, in which he uniformly stated that he and their child were living most happily together in the married state; and, in the last letter he wrote, he said that he should soon return and resume the occupation of the farm. He feigned many excuses for the absence of the deceased from time to time.

"The mother of the girl at length became alarmed, and the subject preyed so much on her mind, that she *dreamed* that her daughter was murdered, and her body buried under the floor of the barn of the prisoner, and where he appointed to meet her on the night of the 18th of May.

"The corn, which was in the barn, having been recently threshed out, the mother requested that the floor might be taken up, which was accordingly done, and then, to her horror, she discovered the remains of a sack, in which was contained the mangled corpse of Maria Marten! The body was of course in a state of decomposition, but it was identified by the teeth in the jaw-bone being wanting, which was her case. She was also dressed in the same male attire as she wore on the fatal night. The prisoner was apprehended at Ealing, and in his house were found a passport for France, dated the 17th day of December, and a brace of pistols, which were bought at Ipswich. He said nothing in his defence, and was remanded until the following day."

Such was the account in "The Times," and, as will be perceived, though it did not then go into detail, it embraces the principal facts of the occurrence in a clear and perspicuous manner, and serves as a preface to what at an after period was developed.

The version of the provincial Journalist is more diffuse, but not so clear; and wishing to give every information that can throw a light on the subject, we insert it also.—After a very hackneyed and Grub-street kind of introduction, the editor says, "A murder,"—we leave out his epithets and metaphors,—" has been brought to light within these few days, at Polstead, in this county. The circumstances which have reached *us* are these :—Maria Marten, a fine young woman, aged twenty-five, the daughter of a mole-catcher in the above village, formed an imprudent connexion, two or three years ago, with a young man, named William Corder, the son of an opulent farmer in the neighbourhood, by whom she had a child. He appeared much attached to her, and was a frequent visitor at her father's house; on the 17th of last May she left her father's, stating, in answer to some queries, 'That she was going to the *Red Barn* to meet William Corder, who was to be waiting there to convey her to Ipswich, where they were to be married. In order to deceive observers (Corder's relations being hostile to the connexion) she was to dress in man's attire, which she was to change at the *Red Barn* for her bridal garments.' She did not return at the time expected; but being in the habit of leaving home for some days, no great alarm was expressed by the parents. When, however, several weeks had elapsed, and no intelligence was received of their daughter, although Corder was still at home, the parents became anxious in their inquiries. Corder named a place at a distance, where he said she was, but that he could not bring her home for fear of displeasing his friends; her sister, he said, might use her clothes, as she would not want them. Soon after this Corder's health became impaired, and he, in real or pretended accordance with some advice he said he had received, resolved on going abroad. Accordingly, he left home in last September, expressing great anxiety, before he left, to have *the Barn* well filled. He took with him about £400. Several letters have been received by his mother (a widow) and sister, as well as by the Martens, in which he stated that he was living with Maria in the Isle of Wight. These, however, bore the London post-mark. He regularly desired that his letters should be burned, which request was not complied with. Strange surmises lately gained circulation throughout the neighbourhood; and one person stated, as a singular circumstance, that on the evening when Maria Marten disappeared, he had seen Corder enter the Red Barn with a pickaxe.

The parents became more and more disturbed and dissatisfied, and their fears were still more strongly agitated by the mother dreaming, on three successive nights last week, that her daughter had been murdered and buried in the Red Barn. She insisted that the floor should be upturned; and on Saturday morning the father, with his mole-spade, and a neighbour, with a rake, went to examine the Barn; and soon, near the spot where the woman described, her daughter lay buried, and only about one foot and a half under ground. The father turned up a piece of a shawl which he knew belonged to his daughter, and his assistant, with his rake, pulled out a part of a human body. Horror-struck, the unhappy father and his neighbour staggered back from the spot. The remains were afterwards disintered, the body being in a state of decomposition. The pelisse, shawl, Leghorn bonnet, and shoes, were, however, distinctly identified as those belonging to Maria Marten. The body has been closely inspected; but, owing to its decayed state, no marks of violence have been discovered, except some perforations in the bones of the face, as if by small shot. There can be little doubt but that this unfortunate young woman fell a victim to her unhallowed passion, and was inhumanly butchered by the monster on whom she relied for future protection as a husband. An inquest was held before J. Weyman, Esq., Coroner for the liberty, on Sunday last, and adjourned until Friday, in the hope that some intelligence may be gained of Corder, so as to lead to his apprehension. The murdered remains were buried on Sunday night, in the presence of an immense concourse of spectators.

" The mother of Corder appears to have been singularly unfortunate; and, it may be more easily imagined than described, what feelings must agitate a parent at the thought that her son has been guilty of so heinous a crime: but she has long been used to grief and misfortune. About three years since she buried her husband, and last Christmas twelve months one of her sons was drowned. Since that period, consumption has carried off two of her family."

Such is the statement of " The Suffolk Herald," and for the reasons hitherto mentioned we give it a place in our work. Though the outline in " The Times" is most accurate, yet it is but an outline, and we shall fill up the blanks by giving more of the details. On the evening of the 22d of April, Corder was brought before M. Wyatt, Esq., the magistrate sitting at the Lambeth-street Police Office, in London, in the charge of James Lea, an officer belonging to that establishment, and Ayres, a constable of Polstead, who was despatched expressly, by Sir Wm. Rowley, to London, to discover the supposed murderer. Knowing little of the Metropolis, and unauthorised to apprehend a person in Middlesex on a mere suspicion of criminality, he made an application, on the previous day, for a warrant of apprehension and the assistance of an officer, to Mr. Wyatt. Under these circumstances this was readily granted, and Lea, as an intelligent man, was selected for the pursuit. After fourteen hours most active search, without any direction, save his own sagacity, to guide him,—Ayres, the country officer, supplying him with no clue, nor, indeed, scarce knowing where he was, or what measures he should adopt, —he ascertained that the culprit had recently married the daughter of a Mrs. Moore, and that he was then, with his wife, conducting, in partnership with Mrs. Engleton and her daughters, the Grove-house Boarding-school, at the lower end of Ealing-lane, near Brentford. He immediately repaired thither, and on the culprit's being identified, secured him, and brought him, in the evening, before Mr. Wyatt, at the district office His primary examination was short, and merely consisted in his recog-

nition by Ayres, and his production of the under-jaw bone of the unfortu
nate Maria Marten, which, her frame being decayed and features quite
obliterated, it was thought necessary to exhibit, in order to the positive
ascertainment of her being the person with whose murder he was
accused.

The examination, as we have said, was brief, but yet not uninteresting.
The magistrate, Mr. Wyatt, was quite shocked with the barbarity of the
crime; and expressed an opinion that scarce any human being, diabolical
as might be his disposition, and murderous his propensities, would be guilty
of so incredible an atrocity. He asked Ayres, what the bone he exhibited had to do with the horrible transaction? And Ayres replied,
that it was the principal means they possessed of proving that the body,
discovered in the Red Barn, was that of Maria Marten, with whose assassination the prisoner was, on the strongest grounds, charged. It would
hereafter appear, that the murdered girl had lost two teeth, one of them
the eye tooth, in that part of the jaw where these were missing. "The
clothes," he added, "could be sworn to, that remained undecayed, and
which were found where the body was interred; and had it not been,
fortunately, for this discovery, it would, from the reduced condition of
the corpse, and it being literally a skeleton, have been impossible to
identify it as that of Maria Marten."

On this examination nothing more transpired; and, in obedience to
the orders of Mr. Wyatt, Corder was, for the night, detained in the
watch-house, and directed to be again placed at the bar on the following
day, prior to his transmission to Polstead.

While at the bar, on this occasion, he seemed perfectly at ease, and
displayed a self-possession which could hardly be expected from even
those who had the strong support of conscious innocence to sustain them
while subject to so serious and disgraceful an accusation. He was
dressed in a gentlemanly suit of black, over which was thrown a military
Spanish roquelaure; and he leant negligently, and in an indifferent and
lounging manner, on the front rail of the dock. For the Tuesday night
he remained at the parochial watch-house; and at an early hour (eleven
o'clock) on the next morning he was again brought before Mr. Wyatt,
when the following disclosures and proceedings, which in this stage of
the inquiry are momentously explanatory, took place. By them will be
perceived the recklessness of hardened guilt, and from them we may clearly
deduce that "foolish are the wise in their own imagination;" and that in
the boldness of guilt,—a boldness originating in a temporary impunity,—
the criminal will, with a heedless confidence, overlook even the most ordinary precautions, and preserve, with what may be designated a retributive fatuity, such unconsidered trifles as will ultimately lead to the discovery of his guilt, and render him subject to the laws, the injunctions of
which he has broken.

The account of the 29th of April, and that which we have spoken of as
having heightened the before aroused excitement of the public, is as
follows; we give it from the person who wrote it, and was a witness of
what he describes :—

On the night of Tuesday, the 22d of April, William Corder was brought
to the Whitechapel Police Office, under the charge of Lea, an officer of
the establishment, and a Suffolk constable named Ayres. He was then

briefly examined by M. Wyatt, Esq.; and the crime with which he was accused, was the perpetration of the foulest murder that has heretofore wounded the feelings of society.

The merciless offence was committed near a year since; and on the morning of the day referred to, far from the scene of his iniquitous offence, and while in satisfied but imaginary security, the culprit was seized, and made accountable to that justice, the sanctuary of which he had so cruelly and so wantonly invaded.

The monster's sacrifice was a fond and confiding female, in "the spring of life," who had borne him a child; whom he had pledged himself to marry; and who, previous to her deplorable fate, lived in peace and tranquillity at her father's cottage. It was at an inconsiderable distance from her murderer's house, and thus afforded him a facility of intercourse, which, did it but exist, the deluded girl might have been still living. She was young and beautiful, and in the very "bloom of existence." Frail she might have been; but that frailty arose not from any predisposition towards vice, but was the consequence of constant importunity, and the unremitting solicitations which a rustic beauty, and "the flower of the village," expects and demands. Her fall was natural, and its penalty most severe; it was enforced by the friend of her bosom, and she expired by the hand of a ruffian, whom

"She lov'd not wisely, but too well."

For the interests of society, immorality deserves its chastisement; but yet its executioner, though it may add to its bitterness, should not be the author of the crime he punishes; and, in the present melancholy instance, the expiation has been more than proportionate to the deviation from the straight and narrow paths of chastity.

The unfortunate victim of an overweening vanity was Maria Marten, and the only accountable motive for the annihilation of a life which its destroyer had declared he would "support and cherish," seems to be a fear of her disclosing a former very aggravated and felonious delinquency of which he had been guilty. It was his surreptitiously obtaining a letter sent to Maria by Mr. M. (the son of the Lady of the Manor), and abstracting from it a note of some amount, which he had transmitted for the maintenance of his illegitimate child. Of this theft she was aware; and, apprehensive that she would disclose it, he committed the inhuman crime, which he must expiate at the gallows.

On Wednesday he was brought up for a short interrogation, anterior to his being transmitted to Polstead, the theatre of his deep dyed guilt. Judging from his appearance, though there is a cat-like ferocity about the eyes, and a somewhat sinister expression of countenance, we should not infer that he had been so cold-blooded a murderer. His age does not exceed twenty-four years, and his complexion is lightly florid—but this, while under examination, varied momentarily, and changed from the most deadly pale to a high coloured crimson; his dress was fashionable, and appeared to be somewhat studied; and when taken into custody, he, in conjunction with his wife and a Mrs. Engleton and her daughters, kept a female boarding-school, of some estimation, at the Grove-house in Ealing-lane, Middlesex.

Here it may be proper to give some account of the manner in which he became acquainted with Miss Moore, now Mrs. Corder. On the

25th of November, after the murder of Maria Marten, he inserted the following Advertisement in " The Sunday Times."

" MATRIMONY.—A Private Gentleman, aged twenty-four, entirely independent, whose disposition is not to be exceeded, has lately lost chief of his family by the hand of Providence, which has occasioned discord amongst the remainder, under circumstances most disagreeable to relate. To any female of respectability, who would study for domestic comforts, and willing to confide her future happiness to one in every way qualified to render the marriage state desirable, as the Advertiser is in affluence. Many very happy marriages have taken place through means similar to this now resorted to; and it is hoped no one will answer this through impertinent curiosity; but should this meet the eye of any agreeable Lady who feels desirous of meeting with a sociable, tender, kind, and sympathising companion, they will find this Advertisement worthy of notice. Honour and secresy may be relied on. As some little security against idle applications, it is requisite that letters may be addressed (post paid) A. Z., care of Mr. Foster, stationer, 68, Leadenhall-street, with real name and address, which will meet with most respectful attention."

This Advertisement was not lost sight of by the ladies who sigh in single blessedness; more than fifty answers were received to it, and amongst them one from Miss Moore, with whom an interview took place at the pastry-cook and confectioner's shop nearest the Temple, in Fleet-street, which shortly afterwards resulted in a marriage with Corder.

Many rumours are afloat relative to his offence, but the only particulars that can be depended on as far as they have yet transpired, are as follows:—

For some years past, Corder, who was a person of some property, and who, at the time of the committal of the murder, was resident at Polstead, kept company with Maria Marten, the daughter of a person in humble circumstances in the village. An illicit intercourse ensued from their acquaintance, and a child was the fruit of their commerce. This, it is rumoured, was murdered by the prisoner; and the mother being aware of the horrible fact, as well as of his having obtained Mr. M.'s letter and plundering it of its contents, she made use of it as a threat, and received from Corder a distinct promise of marriage.

On the 18th of last May he called at her father's cottage, and there expressed his willingness, and indeed anxiety, to have the ceremony performed; but in order that it might be private, and as much concealed as possible, he said he was desirous of having it celebrated by licence, and not by banns; for that the latter would occasion an unnecessary notoriety.

The following day was that appointed for the discharge of his long-pledged vow. At Ipswich it was to have been fulfilled; but still, apparently, wishing for an almost impenetrable privacy, he urged the luckless young woman to dress herself in his apparel, and accompany him to a part of his premises called the *Red Barn*. There, he observed, she could exchange them for her own; and there, he assured her, he would have a gig in waiting, to convey her, on the ensuing morning, to the church at Ipswich. Yielding to his representations, and wishing to heal her character, which was then suffering by the malicious scandal of a country village, she complied with his request. Both, on his persuasion, then left the cottage—Maria by the back-door, and Corder by the front; it being, at the same time, arranged that some of the clothes of poor Maria should be sent back to her father's.

Instead, however, of Corder's taking her, as he had assured her, to Ipswich, he treacherously, and with the most malicious premeditation, murdered her; and inhumed her body in that part of the barn where it has since been discovered. No doubt of his iniquitous purpose can exist. as on the night when he stated he was with her at Ipswich, he was seen by her young brother crossing from the *Red Barn* to his mother's house, with a pickaxe on his shoulder.

The Red Barn is about half a mile from the Marten cottage. It stands on the brow of a hill; and in the hollow below, and not a stone's throw from it is a cottage, at which a shriek might almost be heard.

A Rough Sketch of the Ground Plan.

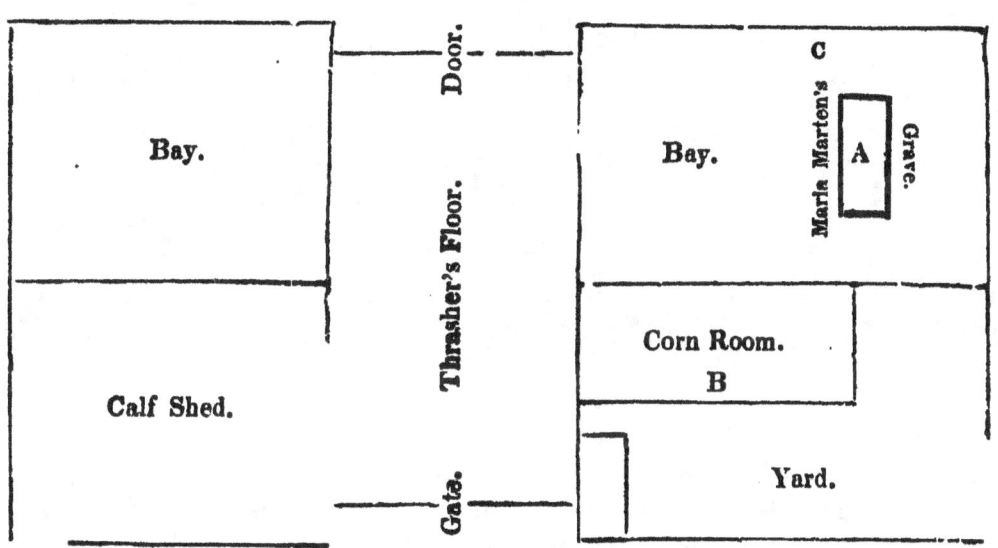

The spot marked A, is the grave where the body was found, about eighteen inches under the surface. At C, there are the marks of a charge of small shot on the side of the Barn, about five feet from the ground, which appears to have been fired from B, the corn-room; and it has been conjectured, that while she was changing her male dress for her female attire, she was shot at from the corn-room, but not wounded, as the whole charge is evidently lodged in the side of the Barn, and afterwards despatched by stabbing or strangulation. The corpse exhibited marks of violence on the cheek, as if a blow had been given by some round weapon; and though no ribs were fractured, there was the appearance of the chest having been beaten inwards, as if by treading or kneeling.

The grave is about five feet long, and eighteen inches deep. It is regularly formed, and was evidently the work of some time. It was, probably, dug in preparation for the intended victim; and the whole plan of the murder must have been the result of long previous deliberation We present our readers with a correct view of the grave, as it appeared a short time ago.

It is hardly possible to describe the great sensation which this occurrence has created. Crowds flock from all quarters to witness the scene of death, and the Barn is almost torn to pieces by the multitude. The grave is left open, and has a wild and singular aspect. There are two cottages within about fifty yards of the Barn; and it is singular that such a murder could be perpetrated, as it must have been, between twelve and four o'clock in the day, and was within ear shot of the houses we have mentioned; but they were so well known to be in the habit of meeting at this Barn, that it excited no sort of attention. What became of her male dress, except the great coat, is not known. The coat was thrown into the grave, probably from having some marks of blood upon it. The girl's father had always some suspicions of what had occurred, and has often walked about the Barn, determined to examine it, but always was deterred, lest he should find nothing, and be supposed to have raised an unfounded report.

On the Sunday after Corder committed the vile assassination, he called upon Maria's mother, and to her earnest inquiries after the situation and residence of her child, he replied that she was comfortably settled at home, where he had left her, as it would take more than three weeks to procure a license, and go through the required forms. This explanation satisfied her for a time; but some weeks elapsing without any intelligence being received, the agitated parent was more urgent in her questions, and to calm the importunity, which was now becoming most troublesome, another excuse was made—which was, that Maria was most happily settled at the house of an old school-fellow, and that, until her marriage could be accomplished, she was to remain with ois family at Yarmouth.

Several months passed over, and whenever the parental affection of Maria's mother induced her to make a further inquiry after the condition of her daughter, Corder's invariable reply was that she was well and happy; and on two occasions, it being observed that it was extraordinary she did not communicate with her friends, he met the remark by saying that her hand was injured by a severe whitlow, which prevented her holding a pen; that her business, as a milliner, was so pressing, that she had no time to devote to correspondence; and that all her leisure moments were so devoted to conjugal attentions, that any communication with her relatives was a matter of secondary consideration. These vague though plausible excuses were received as satisfactory, until last September, when he unexpectedly left the country, and went up to London. Before his departure, he endeavoured to guard against the consequences of his guilt; and to remove all lurking suspicions, he called upon the parents of the murdered girl, and then told them that he was hastening to his Maria, and that shortly that union would be effected which had been so long in contemplation. From that time until the day of his (Corder's) apprehension, the daughter had neither been heard of or seen, nor was it ascertained whether she was secretly made away with, or yet in existence. Occasionally there were letters from Corder (all bearing the London post-mark), in which he represented that he was married to the girl, was as happy as " human wish could make him," and desired to have his honey-moon congratulations presented to all his friends. The circumstances that have led to the discovery of a crime, characterized by an atrocity that, depraved as human nature is, has no precedent, are of a description at once extraordinary and almost incredible. A few weeks since, the afflicted mother had a prophetic dream, which demonstrated the fate of her daughter. The influence consequent on it considerably agitated her mind; and on two several nights she dreamed that her child was murdered, and that her corpse was buried underneath the right-hand bay (as she named it) of the further side of Corder's *Red Barn*. The impression created by a vision of this nature, the mind, perhaps, being excited by a previous anxiety on the subject, was proportionately deep; and so much did it occupy her imagination, that she felt convinced of the truth of its augury, and her dreams became a topic of conversation between her and her husband. Her uneasiness hourly increased; and, after some importunity, her husband was prevailed upon, more from a disposition to satisfy the suppositions of his aged wife, than from any reliance he placed in the verity of dreams, to gratify her wishes, and to search the Barn. He applied for permission to Mrs. Corder, the prisoner's mother, and also to Pryke, her bailiff, to examine the building,—not, however, mentioning what his object was. This was readily granted; and he merely said that he wanted to go there, to see if he could find some of his daughter's clothes, which he thought might have been forgotten when she was last in the barn.

The dream proved but too true, for, on his turning up a small portion of loose earth, at the very spot which his wife had desired him to examine, he found, not above eighteen inches beneath the surface, the corpse of his daughter. As may be supposed, but as cannot be described, the wretched parent was paralysed in feeling, and quite incapable of uttering a word, or shedding a tear that would give relief to his agonized sensations. He saw before him the remains of his child;—the dream of the mother was realised; and there lay before him the skeleton of a daughter that was once lovely, virtuous, and the pride of his cottage.

The fragile remains of mortality were enveloped in a piece of coarse sackcloth, a circumstance that, in itself, indicates a violent death, and also shows a desire to conceal the murderous crime. Maria's clothes were somewhat perfect, and by them she was identified. Her ear-rings, a silk handkerchief, a tortoise-shell comb, a Leghorn bonnet trimmed with black ribbon, were almost as fresh as when she left the cottage; and on her skeleton limbs were found the very shoes which she wore on the night that she was inveigled away by Corder and so barbarously murdered. Another strange event attendant on this horrifying catastrophe, in the identification of the body, sprung from the exclamation of Maria's sister, who, on its being removed from its covering, said, that it could be at once known whether it was that of her relative, by examining the lower jaw, in which two of the larger teeth were wanting. The examination was made, and the deficiency, quite corresponding with that which the sister had mentioned, discovered.

Information of the crime, and which, from its enormity, has thrown the village of Polstead into the highest state of excitation, was communicated with the utmost rapidity to J. Weyman, Esq., the Coroner for the liberty of Polstead. Though resident at some distance (Bury St. Edmund's), he lost not a moment in entering on an inquiry; and, from the circumstances that transpired on it, he was induced to dispatch a country constable in pursuit of William Corder. The constable arrived in town on Monday, and having applied at Lambeth-street for the assistance of an efficient officer, and advice as to how he was to proceed, Lea was appointed by the sitting magistrate, Matthew Wyatt, Esq., to accompany him, and to give the assistance which he required. Lea had a difficult duty to discharge;—he was to apprehend Corder, but had not the slightest trace to where he could be found; he, as he himself states, went from place to place, until at length, after a chase of many hours, he ascertained that he had been at one time living on Gray's Inn Terrace; from thence he tracked him through a number of intermediate places, and finally discovered that he was domesticated at the Grove-house, Ealing-lane, where his wife superintended a female boarding-school. Some stratagem was necessary to obtain an entrance; and the officer, fearful of alarming him, accomplished it by representing that he had a daughter whom he was anxious to place under the care of Mrs. Corder. On going into the house, he found the criminal sitting in the parlour, at breakfast, with four ladies, unapprehensive that the hour had arrived in which his guilt was to meet its punishment. He was dressed in a morning gown, and had a watch lying before him, by which he was minuting the boiling of some eggs. Lea called him apart, and they retired into the drawing-room: he then informed him that he was a London police officer, and had to apprehend him on a most serious charge. He seemed startled at the intelligence; and on being made acquainted with the character of the offence, he disclaimed all knowledge of its committal, and denied ever having heard of the wretched Maria.

Lea, after having secured him, proceeded to search both his person and drawers, and discovered a number of letters from his sister, and a person named Gardener; in the latter of which, warnings were given and cautions held out of a very singular description. He also found a case of detonating pocket-pistols—maker's name, *Harcourt, Ipswick*,—which are supposed to have been purchased on the day antecedent to the murder. There were also a powder-flask and some balls, and a passport for France, dated the 20th of December, 1827; from which it appears that he purposed leaving this country for the Continent, but, fortunately for the ends of justice, he did not carry his intention into effect, but still, like the moth, lingered about the flame that was to consume him.

The pistols were inclosed in a black velvet reticule, which has since been sworn to as the property of Maria Marten, and the same which she took with her on the night of her going to the *Red Barn*. There was in it, then, over six pounds, no account of which had been, as yet, obtained; but the presumption is, that Corder, to the crime of murder, has super-added that of robbery, and appropriated the contents to his own use. Previous to his removal to town, his brother-in-law, Mr. Moore, a re-spectable jeweller residing in the neighbourhood of Gray's-Inn-lane, having, by some means, ascertained the inhuman atrocity with which the culprit was charged, questioned his sister as to the length of time she had known him before she so irrevocably bound her fate to his? She an-swered, for three weeks only: that she first became acquainted with him at Seaford; that she next met him, casually, at a pastrycook's shop in Fleet-street; and that her marriage arose out of a matrimonial advertisement, in which a reference was given to Mr. F., a stationer in Cheapside. The marriage ceremony was performed in last November, at the church of St. Andrew, Holborn; and she was then, as now, quite ignorant of his ever having given any cause for censure.

Mr. Moore expressed an indignant surprise at the hasty and unreflect-ing manner in which she had engaged in so serious a transaction, and de-clared, that for his part, he would by no means shelter a person who could be capable of even imagining so barbarous a crime. At three o'clock on Wednesday, Corder was transmitted, by the Defiance coach, in the keeping of Lea, to Colchester, from thence to be removed to Polstead, to await the result of the Coroner's investigation, which was to be resumed on Friday.

During his detention at Lambeth-street, his wife, whose impression then was that the charge against him was that of bigamy, visited him in the strong room, and remained with him the greater portion of the forenoon. So intense was the interest that prevailed in Suffolk, that Sir William Rowley, M.P., and one of his brother magistrates, proceeded expressly to town to lend their assistance towards the discovery of the murderer.

Not alone did an anxiety prevail in Suffolk to develope this mysterious occurrence, but so much did it monopolize the attention of the metropolis, that the principal journals in London thought it necessary to send special reporters to furnish the fullest particulars, both of the incidents connected with the murder, and of the testimony given on the Coroner's Inquest; and from their accounts we collect, that the deed, committed under circum-stances partaking more of the character of fiction than truth, had created an excitement beyond the power of description, in Colchester, and through Suffolk and the neighbouring counties.

Corder arrived at the George Inn, in Colchester, at nine o'clock; but his being taken into custody being anticipated, it is scarcely necessary to observe, that immense crowds were congregated to gratify their curiosity, and see the man whose imputed guilt had shocked the better feelings of humanity. While on the road from London, he conducted himself with an unfeeling levity that indicated the baseness of his mind; and, as he ap-proached the town he recognized many persons, but they returned not his salute; and those who had previously known, anxiously shunned him, and appeared to feel a shuddering on beholding him. No one expressed the slightest commiseration for his condition; but hisses and execrations, both loud and bitter, pursued him till he had retreated into a private room at the George. Lea proceeded to Mr. Smith, the Governor of the Castle, a building made use of as a place of imprisonment, and requested him to receive Corder into his custody for the night; but this he refused, saying, "I can't take charge of him, for I have nobody to look after him; and being charged with so dreadful an offence, it may so happen that he will lay violent hands on himself, for which I should be held accountable." Lea then accompanied the Governor to the residence of Mr. Able, a magistrate, and having explained to him the character of the crime with which his prisoner was accused, requested that he might be lodged in a secure place for the night.

Mr. Able said, that the Castle was the most secure; but Mr. Smith replied, that he could not be taken there, as it was out of his (the magistrate's) jurisdiction; and that, as no warrant of commitment had been produced by the officer, he must decline receiving the prisoner.

It was next proposed that Corder should, for the short time he had to remain in Colchester, be confined in the Town Gaol, but it being discovered that that prison was insecure, the intention was abandoned; and it was ultimately determined that he and the officer, handcuffed together, should remain at the George. The prisoner ate a hearty supper, and seemed to be very little concerned at the awful situation in which he was placed. He retired to bed at an early hour, and, for his greater security, it was considered prudent to tie one of his hands to the bed-post, and lock the other to that of Lea, with whom he slept. On the ensuing day he arose about eight o'clock, and partook of a slight refreshment. He was visited in the forenoon by Sir William Rowley, M.P., and several of the country magistrates; but to every advance they made towards a conversation on the crime with which he was accused, he turned a deaf ear. The Rev. Mr. Seaman, a minister of the established church, also called upon him, and, prior to his doing so, several considerate individuals furnished him with a number of serious and religious publications. On his introduction to Corder, Mr. Seaman informed him that he had been formerly personally acquainted with his family, particularly his brothers, who were since dead, and that he was anxious to render him every assistance and consolation that was in his power; and, with that view, he presented him with a New Testament and a Hymn book, and earnestly and emphatically directed his attention to reflection and spiritual consideration. Mr. S. interrogated Corder concerning his participation in the murder;—the word participation is used, because it was confidently rumoured that more than one person was engaged in the crime;—and pressed him very closely to confess his guilt, and disburthen his mind of the weight under which it must labour; but, to every entreaty, he continued obdurate, and replied in the same words he had made use of during his journey from London—"I shall say nothing now." During the earlier part of Thursday, he occupied himself in writing, and filled two sides of a sheet of paper, which, scarcely had he done, when he started up in an uncontrollable agitation, and flung it into the fire. This, since his apprehension, was the only occasion on which he gave any evidence of his not being utterly insensible to feeling. He wrote, also, a letter to his mother on the Wednesday night, of which the following is a copy, and of which we lay before the reader a *fac-simile.*

" Dear Mother,

"I scarcely dare to presume to address you, having a full knowledge of the shame, disgrace, and, I may truly add, for ever. a stain upon my family, friends, and late-formed connexions. I have but a few minutes to write; and being unfortunately labouring under this unfortunate charge, I have to solicit that you will receive Mr. Moore on Friday morning, with whom, probably, may be my injured, lawful—and I must do her the justice to say—worthy and affectionate wife. I have always experienced from every branch of their family the kindest treatment;—hope and trust that the same will be returned from you the short time they continue in this part of the country, which, I am sorry I have to state, is to hear the event of this dreadful catastrophe. I am happy to hear you are tolerable, considering the present circumstances. I may, perhaps, be allowed an interview with you in a day or two; but that, I find, is very uncertain. I must beg to subscribe myself your unfortunate, *though unworthy* son,

W. CORDER."

[The words "though unworthy," were erased, but are yet distinguishable.]

Addressed—"Mrs. Corder, Polstead by Stoke,
Favoured by Mr. Catchpool."

This letter he afterwards thought proper not to send, and intreated of Lea, into whose possession it had got, so important did he feel were its contents, to commit it to the flames. This, as may be supposed, was not complied with, and it was expected to form a part of the evidence produced on his trial.

In the course of the evening Corder referred occasionally to the books which had been supplied him, and, at one time, in an incidental allusion to his wife, he exclaimed—"Oh! would that I were as innocent of sin as she is!" At about nine o'clock two gentlemen arrived at the George, and having an interview with Lea, told him that, in addition to his other crimes, they had to prefer a charge of forgery against Corder, committed under such peculiar circumstances as demonstrated that he was a culprit of no ordinary magnitude, and a person who had head and heart to execute the most cool, deliberate, and barefaced iniquity. One of the gentlemen, Mr. Taylor, who is the principal clerk in the banking-house of Messrs. Alexander and Co., the proprietors of several country banks, stated, that on the Monday week before, a man of respectable appearance passed a forged check for the sum of 93*l.* on the Manningtree Branch, whose person corresponded to an accuracy with the description of that given of Corder. He was about five feet six inches in height, wore a drab great coat, a plaid lilac handkerchief, a black dress coat, and blue pantaloons, and had rather a large nose, a small face, and a ring on the little finger of his right hand. The check which he produced, and on which he obtained the money, was forged, and was in the following form:—

" *Hadleigh Bank, Suffolk,*
" *Stratford, April* 12*th*, 1828.

" No 19.

" Dykes Alexander, Samuel Alexander, jun., Richard Dykes Alexander, and Henry Alexander, pay Mr. Cook Ninety Three Pounds.

" £93.

" R. ATKINS."

Lea having the letter written by Corder to his mother about him at the time, he privately compared its handwriting with that in the body of the check, and found that they must have been written by the same person

Mr. Taylor was accompanied by Mr. Dale, the landlord of the White Hart Inn at Manningtree; and, at his desire, they were at once introduced to him, but with the necessary precaution of having, at the time, several other persons present, in order to guard against any after-doubt being raised of Corder's identity. On entering the apartment in which he was confined, Mr. Taylor immediately pointed out the offender, and, extending his hand in a most marked manner, said to Lea, "That is the person who got from me, on last Monday week, 93*l*. on a forged check." Corder, on the recognition, was quite confounded; he lost all that cool ness and presence of mind which, up to this moment, he had exhibited; and on the unexpected announcement of the discovery of another of the deeds on his catalogue of crime, he suddenly appeared as if under the influence of the torpedo, and became powerless both in mind and body; his head dropped languidly on his bosom, and all his recollection and self-possession, which were taken as an evidence of his innocence, vanished ere the lapse of a second; and, in a word, there was, for the time, a pitiable prostration of the physical and mental powers. On his recovery from his lethargy, Mr. Taylor, addressing him for the first time, said—"Come, sir, pay me the 93*l*. you have so fraudulently robbed us of: look at me like a man; don't conceal your face, but view me directly." Corder still remained silent for nearly a minute, and seemed quite unconscious and abstracted. Memory then resumed her seat, and, throwing his hands over his eyes, as if with the intention of excluding from his sight an enemy positive and distinct, and whose declaration of his minor, but not less capital offence, now appalled him, he sank gradually into a chair which happened to have been behind him. Mr. Taylor, commiserating his situation,—a situation which merited not the slightest pity,—closed his interview, and retired from the apartment.

In the course of the night he communicated to Lea the circumstances, which were corroborated by Mr. Dale, under which the forged check had been discounted. On Monday, the 14th of April, Corder arrived, at an early hour in the morning, at the White Hart Inn, in Manningtree, and being in conversation with Mr. Dale, its landlord, he mentioned, as the reason of his coming to that part of the country, his having some business to transact at the banking-house of the Messrs. Alexanders. This was situated directly opposite to the White Hart, and Mr. Dale, anxious to accommodate his guest, though the Bank was not then opened, told him that if his business was very urgent, he would speak to the clerk, and have it despatched before the ordinary hour at which the doors were thrown open. To this kind offer, for which Corder expressed his thanks, he replied, that he was by no means in haste; but it turned out that he was; and while Mr. Dale was shortly afterwards standing at his door, Mr. Taylor happened to pass by, and he then informed that gentleman, that there was a visitor at his house, who, he understood, had some business to transact at the bank. In about an hour after the bank was opened, Corder presented the check to Mr. Taylor, and asked for cash for it. Mr. Taylor, in reply to his demand, said that he was unacquainted either with the drawer, Mr. Atkins, or with Mr. Cooke, in whose favour it was made payable; and that it was not customary with their house to discount any checks unless they knew the parties. This rebuff by no means daunted Corder, and he represented himself as Mr. Cooke; and said that he was a farmer at Wenlam-Hall, and that he had taken the check, on the preceding Saturday, from a Mr. Atkins, a butcher at Stratford, in payment for five head of cattle which he had sold to him. Mr. Taylor observed, that he had never seen the name of Atkins to a Hadleigh check before, and that therefore he had his doubts of its correctness. Corder assured him that every thing was right; that he was well known in the neighbourhood; that he kept an account with the Hadleigh Branch, and that Mr. Dale, the landlord of the White Hart, could tell him who he was. Acted on by these assertions, Mr. Taylor said, that if such were the fact, and if Mr. Dale came over and said he knew him, that would satisfy him. Mr. Dale shortly afterwards came with Corder to the bank, and having known him by sight, and before seen him frequently,—a circumstance that he mentioned,—the check was discounted. In payment, he received eighty-five pounds in five pound local notes, and the balance, eight pounds, in one pound notes. Corder immediately left the place, and proceeded with rapidity to the Branch Banking Establishment, at Ipswich, where he obtained gold for the notes. On the same night, Mr. Taylor had occasion to send to the Hadleigh Bank, and he there ascertained that the check was a forgery; and also learned that Mr. Atkins, who is a respectable butcher in the village of Stratford, had no knowledge of its being drawn. The check itself was filled up on a printed form of the Hadleigh Bank, and it is supposed that he had obtained it at his mother's, who was formerly in the habit of keeping an account with that establishment. The only observation Corder made, when convinced that there was a charge of forgery preferred against him, was, " I dare say they will try and make enough of it."

In a conversation which took place between Lea and Mr. Taylor, the former said, that he had it in his power to state a fact confirmatory of the second charge advanced against his prisoner. When he took him into custody at his house in Ealing-lane, he removed him to the Red Lion public-house in the neighbourhood,—which by the way was, as if by a more than usual fatality, formerly kept by the uncle of his wife,—and having there placed him in safe keeping, returned to the Grove House, and examined it carefully; when he came back to the Red Lion, Corder asked him, had he not found eighty sovereigns in a private drawer of his writing desk? He told him that he had not; and Corder then said, " My wife must certainly have taken them out;" send for her. Mrs. Corder shortly arrived, and she gave to her guilty husband twenty sovereigns, admitting at the same time that she had taken the sum looked after from the secret drawer of the desk.

At 12 o'clock on the Thursday night, Corder was removed from the George, under an escort, and conveyed with the greatest celerity to Polstead, where he was accommodated with a bed at a small inn, or rather public-house, called " the Cock." His departure at so late an hour was in accordance with the advice of Sir William Rowley, M.P., who, with as much prudence as humanity, suggested that it would prevent the explosion of any popular effervescence, and the congregation of an incensed and curious public; but independent of this, as the prisoner would be obliged, in his transmission, to pass under the window of his aged and respectable mother, it would be an outrage on human nature to render her, perhaps, a witness to the disgraceful circumstances in which he was placed, while conducting to his then destination, and passing the roof in which he had at one time lived unblemished and undishonoured.

On the morning of Friday, the day to which Mr. Weyman had ad-journed the inquisition, crowds of persons, among whom were some gentlemen dispatched by the London journals, to ascertain, from personal observation, the truth of any rumours that might be afloat, visited the Red Barn—the place where this unparalleled tragedy was committed: it is situated in a valley, at about a mile's distance across the fields from the cottage of Maria's parents; this stands on the brow of a hill, and is rather picturesquely situated; the Barn is of that description which in Suffolk is called double, and a view of which we lay before the reader. The discovery of the murdered girl's remains was made by her father, and a neighbour of the name of Pryke; the dreaming story possesses some portion of incredibility, and it would, were it not that the fact has been so well testified on oath, appear altogether undeserving of attention. One feature in it would be supposed to have been taken from the tales of old, and bears a strong resemblance to an incident detailed in the Romance of "The Old English Baron;" it is that of the parent directly going to the spot designated in his wife's vision as the place of his daughter's sepulture. Whether influenced by a supernatural interposition, or instigated by his wife's entreaties, he, on entering the Barn, certainly did so; and as, in another part of this work, has been mentioned, was assured that his partner's impression was correct, and that his complying with her wishes was only acting in obedience to the decrees of an all-seeing Power. Lying on the corpse of his wretched offspring were a number of loose stones, and on them was placed some earth, which, probably operated on by the decomposition undergoing beneath it, had not combined or cemented in so close a manner as, from the interval that had elapsed since the murder took place, might naturally have been expected. The first thing that presented itself to the astonished view of the old man, was a portion of a shawl, which he instantly recognized as Maria's; and such an effect had the discovery on him, that in a state almost delirious, he speeded to the clergyman of the parish, when, in a manner almost frantic, he informed him that they had at last discovered the corpse of his murdered daughter.

Mrs. Martin, the step-mother, and not the mother, as has been erroneously but unintentionally stated, did not accompany her husband on the occasion of his appalling discovery; and, from this circumstance, great doubt existed among the people in the vicinity, of the veracity of the announcement that this most wicked event was brought to light at so remote a period as Eleven Months after its perpetration: these doubts have, however, now vanished, and the dream or excitement of imagination created by the mind constantly dwelling on the subject, proves the mysterious, though unexplanatory, means by which Providence illustrates the punishment of the dark-minded assassin, and shows, by means inscrutable to man, the murdered

'Blood of a brother will cry out from the ground."

When old Marten returned, the exhumation was proceeded with; but the lower part of the frame was so decomposed, that it afforded not the possibility of being identified. Her bust was in a different condition, and so remained for some time, but not so long as to undergo the primary view of the Coroner's Jury: at the bottom of the pit was found a new coat, which she wore on the day on which she left her father's house, and on the night on which she is supposed to have been murdered ; it was quite bloody, and from this it is inferred that it was buried with the body. The gown, if there had been any, had decayed, but round the waist was a portion of a pair of stays. The bonnet, ear-rings, shawl, and a comb, were identified as having belonged to the deceased. On the recovery of her corpse, it was placed on a door, and while placing it in its position, one of the hands fell off. From the length of the grave, and its depth, and the hardness of the soil it was sunk in, several hours must have been occupied in its excavation. And this, when combined with other circumstances, shows a hardihood and a determination in the atrocious murderer, seldom attendant on the most vicious. The present impression is, that Maria was changing the male attire for her female, when she was assassinated; and on going to the place of appointment, it was ascertained that one party departed at the front door, while the other went out at the back. Corder, at the time, had a gun in his hand, which he accounted for by saying that he had been out shooting crows.

As a further confirmation of the accused's guilt, it appears that on the afternoon of the fatal day, he called at a cottage at about 50 yards' distance from the Barn, and borrowed a spade from one of the inmates.

The corpse was removed to the Cock public-house, where it was submitted to the inspection of a medical man; and after his having made a minute examination, he declared it as his opinion, that the *os frontis* had been penetrated. It was tied up in a sack before it was buried, a small portion of which only remains, which adhered to the neck, and is of the width of about two inches. On the legs was a silk handkerchief, in a rotten state, which was thrown over them into the grave. Corder is his mother's youngest son, and was considered as her favourite. About eighteen months ago, his two brothers died, when he fell into the possession of property of above 1000*l.* in amount, and he then returned to Polstead, professedly to manage the farm. He then renewed an intimacy which had previously subsisted between him and Maria, but it is but justice to say, that he was not the first seducer; she had been before on terms of an illicit intercourse with a Mr. Matthews, a gentleman of respectability, and a near relative to the Lady of the Manor, by whom she had two children. She subsequently bore a child to Corder, who having intercepted some letters containing sums of money sent to her by Mr. M. for the support of his children, and the fact having come to that gentleman's knowledge, he preferred a charge against him before a magistrate; but ultimately was compelled to abandon it, as Maria refused coming forward to furnish the required evidence. The child of which Corder was the father, died very suddenly; and on being questioned on the subject, old Marten admitted that Corder had removed its corpse, in a box, from his cottage at 12 o'clock at night, but where to he could not say; though his impression was, that it was buried in the barn. Search has been made for it, but to no purpose. A rumour was very prevalent that it also had fallen by the hands of Corder, but the grandfather does not credit it, and expresses a conviction that it came fairly to its end. Corder's motive for murdering his paramour, is said to be her having threatened to bring him to justice for the murder of his infant; but as there is not sufficient proof of this, it must be taken as an idle rumour.

In further explanation of this revolting murder, we give another extract; and we do so the more readily, as we are anxious to supply the most authentic details.

Corder reached his destination at the Cock, at 2 o'clock on the morning of Friday, and had a short but restless sleep. He conversed with the officer as the chaise was passing his mother's house, on some family affairs, and alluded to the number of deaths that had taken place within it for the last two years. About eighteen months ago, one of his brothers was drowned in a large pond; and before that period, he lost his father; and since then, his remaining brother. He mentioned his mother with great apparent affection, and said that he feared not death on his own account, but did on hers, as he was apprehensive that his disgrace would bring her to the grave.

The village of Polstead, the vicinity of which has been the scene of Corder's imputed offence, is a miserable place, and in a most secluded situation. It contains but one public-house, which was occupied by the Coroner and the witnesses, and about forty small houses, which are principally cottages. The Coroner and Jury, after the latter was impanelled, proceeded to visit the Red Barn, and on their examination, found, in one of the doors, some shot marks; and on the floor some stains of a bloody hue. Since the murder was perpetrated (and never before, which is an additional link in the chain of evidence) Corder always assisted in stacking the wheat, and he himself invariably placed the straw and first layers, over the spot from whence the corpse was disinterred. This was a task he had never before attempted, neither did he, prior to the May of 1827, express any wish to procure the key of the Barn; but from that time up to the period when he left home, he never let it escape from his possession.

Many individuals, who have examined the premises, are of opinion that the young girl was murdered in some of those dark paths which lead from her father's to the Barn, and that her remains were afterwards dragged there, and interred. This supposition, however, appears improbable; and particularly so, when we recollect that the *Red Barn* was the customary place of *their* interviews, and that there they had passed many hours together.

INQUEST ON THE BODY.

The Inquest, which was adjourned from the previous Sunday, again assembled at half-past 10 o'clock on Friday, the 25th of April, at the Cock public-house, Polstead; and the Coroner having taken his seat, the Jury were about to resume the inquiry, when that officer, perceiving a number of gentlemen in the inquest room, connected with the London press, interposed for a time, and addressing them, said :—"Gentlemen, as the present is merely a preliminary inquiry, but yet one affecting the life of an individual, who stands charged with the inhuman crime of murder, and as I presume that the purpose of your attendance is to give publicity to the evidence, I cannot, in the conscientious discharge of my duty, allow you to take notes of the proceedings. It has been decided, that the publication of evidence affecting the life of an accused person, before trial, is a misdemeanour; and if I granted a permission or sanction to your giving publicity to such evidence as may be brought before the Court, I should be aiding and abetting you in the commission of that which the law has pronounced an offence. In stating this much, I do not venture to offer my own private opinion as to the good or harm that may result from publishing the evidence in a case of this description; but even supposing that my private opinion inclined to publicity, I cannot, sitting here as Coroner, countenance that which the law has condemned."

A Reporter.—I admit, Sir, by a recent decision, a Coroner has the power to prevent notes being taken; but he has also the discretion, either to exercise that power or not, as he might judge proper. Lord Tenterden's decision did not extend to the exclusion of the public.

Another Reporter asked the Coroner whether it would not be better to permit notes to be taken, in order that a correct report of the depositions on oath might be published, rather than by enforcing an authority very few Coroners thought it expedient to exercise, that a garbled, and necessarily inaccurate and incomplete, account of the proceedings should go forth to the public?

The Coroner.—I feel no inclination to argue what might be best, nor shall I, as I have before said, give my opinion upon the expediency of the law; I have found it as it is, and I am bound to abide by it.

Another Reporter.—He would take the publication, with its consequences, on his own individual responsibility, if the Coroner would only permit him to take notes.

The Coroner.—The question of publishing evidence has already been decided on in the case of Rex v. Flint, the proprietor, I believe, of a Brighton paper, and the decision was against him for publishing the proceedings antecedent to the trial.

Some further conversation of an unimportant nature then took place between the Reporters and the Coroner; at the close of which the former put up their books, and the inquiry was proceeded with. If there are any inaccuracies in the report, they must be attributed to the obstacles the Reporters have experienced, and their being obliged to depend altogether on memory.

The first witness called, was

John Baalham, who, on being sworn, deposed that he was a constable of Polstead; he had not, at any time during the month of May last, nor at any subsequent period, informed William Corder, the person who was charged with the murder of Maria Marten, that he had a warrant for her apprehension for giving birth to illegitimate children that had become chargeable to the parish.

Coroner.—The reason I have put this question to you is, that Mrs. Marten, the mother of the deceased, in her depositions of last Sunday, stated, that the pretext the prisoner, William Corder, made use of to urge his marriage with her daughter, was, that he (Baalham) had told him that the Rev. Mr. Whitmore, the rector of the parish, and a justice of the peace, had issued his warrant to apprehend her on charges of bastardy, of which she was guilty prior to her connexion with him.

Mr. Humphries, a solicitor from London, here entered the Inquest-room and informed the Coroner that he attended as the representative of the prisoner, William Corder; and, in that character, he applied, that his client might be permitted to be present to hear the evidence adduced against him, and thus be enabled, with the assistance of his professional adviser, to put such questions to the several witnesses as might lead to his exculpation of the grave charge which was preferred against him.

The Coroner replied, that, in his opinion, the accused could claim no right of being present: within his experience, he never knew of an application of the kind being made or granted; and, in now refusing the solicitor's request, he conceived himself warranted by the circumstance, that a party charged with a capital offence was not legally entitled to a copy of the depositions on which he had been committed for trial.

Mr. Humphries said, that it could not be expected, and, in point of fact, it was impossible, that his client could meet so grave an accusation unless he went into Court prepared with something of the evidence which had previously been advanced against him; and the Coroner must know, by the statute of " Philip and Mary," that in a case of felony, the persons charged had a right to hear the evidence given against them on examination before the justices, previous to trial.

The Coroner asked Mr. Humphries if he could cite an analogous case from the books; or one showing that a person accused of murder was entitled to be present during the proceedings on the Inquest holden on view of the body of the murdered party?

Mr. Humphries replied that he could, and quoted the case of Richard Patch, whom he (Mr. H.) prosecuted to conviction for the murder of Mr. Bligh. Patch was not only present at the Inquest, but was allowed to give evidence. The jury, on that occasion, returned a verdict of " Wilful Murder" against some person or persons unknown.

The Coroner.—Patch was not, at the time he was examined, in custody, therefore I cannot consider this as a precedent.

Mr. Humphries.—Well, Sir, I can give you one directly in point, that occurred in the murder of Mr. Weare: Hunt and Probert were charged with the capital felony, but they were, nevertheless, permitted to attend before the jury at Elstree, and, in fact, their testimony was received by the Coroner. Some further conversation took place on the legality of Corder's witnessing the proceedings between the Coroner and Mr. H., which terminated in the latter gentleman saying that he would not then press the point, provided it was understood that his client would be permitted, at the close of the inquiry, to hear the several depositions read over before the witnesses were bound over to prosecute. This was agreed to, and the Coroner then read over some evidence supplied by *George Marke*, a lad of about fourteen years of age, and the half-brother of the deceased, in addition to that which he had given on the preliminary investigation; from it it was collected, that he, the deponent, saw the prisoner, he having a bundle at the time, and the deceased, go from his father's house together, at about twelve o'clock at noon, on the 19th of May, 1827; his sister had then men's clothes on. He also saw the prisoner leaving the Barn about two o'clock on the same evening, and he then had a pickaxe in his hand.—The testimony of *Phœbe Stowe* was next read; and the only fact of importance which she had sworn to was, that the prisoner had borrowed a spade from her on the afternoon of the day on which, there is every reason to believe, that the murder had been committed.

Francis Stowe, her husband, deposed, that he knew nothing of the spade being lent to the prisoner. During the foregoing year he had worked for his mother, Mrs. Corder. The first corn they had cut down, last harvest, was placed in the layer where the body was found; the prisoner superintended its being laid down. On one day, during the harvest, the prisoner came to him, and said he would give him a one pound note if he would cut his throat; but he told him he would do no such thing. The Red Barn was constantly kept locked; and before the wheat was put in, the hay was well littered down with straw. The prisoner was present when the first and second loads were stowed away. He never heard of any extraordinary smell being perceived in that part of the Barn where the body was discovered.

William Ionns examined.—I am a labourer, and work for the prisoner's mother. During the last harvest the prisoner directed the laying of the wheat ; .there was, before that, a good deal of litter strewed on the floor where the body was found, but he did not know that it was freshly laid on, since the harvest before. Last year's corn was all out before Stoke fair, which takes place on the 16th of May. He had no recollection of the prisoner's saying to Stowe that he would give him a one pound note for cutting his throat. Both the bays of the Barn were littered.

Ann Marten examined.—She is the sister to the deceased, and knew the body that was found to be that of her sister, by the absence of a tooth in one of the jaws, the clothes, ear-rings, comb, hair, and shoes, which were shown to her, she could identify as her relative's. On the night before-mentioned, the deceased and the prisoner, William Corder, left her father's together, and Corder said they were going to be married. The deceased was dressed in a suit of the prisoner's clothes, and on leaving, they went towards the Red Barn ; when they got there the deceased was to exchange her dress for her own clothes, which the prisoner took with him in a bundle. They departed nearly at the same time, one by the back door, and the other by the front : this they did to escape observation ; and arranged that they were again to meet each other. The deceased was not pregnant at the time.

Thomas Marten stated, that he was the father of the deceased Maria Marten. She had borne an illegitimate child to a gentleman named Matthews, and one to the prisoner, William Corder. He remembered the day when she went with him for the purpose of being married ; it was on the 19th of last May. The prisoner said that he had got a licence, but that it must be sent to London to be signed, and that it would be three weeks before their marriage could take place ; in the mean time, he said, that the deceased was going to reside with a lady, named Rowland, at Yarmouth, where she was to remain until the ceremony could be performed. In a few days afterwards the prisoner told him that the deceased was well and happy, and was then stopping at Yarmouth. After a long time had elapsed, and not hearing from her, he asked the prisoner why she did not write to her friends,—she being able to do so ? He replied, she was unable, from having a sore hand. On Friday last, he entered the Barn, in company with a man of the name of Pryke, and, on making a strict search, discovered the body of his daughter in a hole about two feet deep The child, which she had by Corder, died very suddenly, and at a late hour of the night ; its corpse was enclosed in a box and taken away by him to be buried.

Ann Marten stated, that she was the wife of the last witness ; and, as she believed, the reason of the deceased going out with the prisoner in a man's dress was to prevent the parish officers seeing her : the prisoner before that had told her that Baalham, the constable, informed him that a warrant was issued to apprehend her for having borne some bastard children ; and that he was anxious to marry her, in order to prevent her being taken into custody ; the warrant, he said, was issued by the Rev. Mr. Whitmore. The deceased consented to accompany Corder to Ipswich, where he promised they should be married. They had some conversation, in the course of which her daughter said, that if she could arrive at the Barn in men's clothes, she could then exchange them for her own, and leave the village with Corder unnoticed by any one. When he left the house he had a loaded gun in his hand, and a bundle containing the deceased's clothes ; among the articles she took with her, was a black velvet reticule, which, if she saw, she could recognize.

At this period of the inquiry the remains of the deceased were exhibited to the witness, and she distinctly identified the bloody neckerchief which was found around the throat, and the bonnet, shoes, and earrings, as those which Maria Marten had worn on the night she left home.

James Lea examined.—I am an officer of the Lambeth-street division of police in London ; I apprehended the prisoner, William Corder, at the Grove-house Boarding-school, in Ealing-lane, near Brentford, on Tuesday last. I took him into custody on a charge of having murdered a female, named Maria Marten. When I saw him, I told him that I was a London police officer, and had come to apprehend him on a most serious charge, and that then he was to consider himself as my prisoner. The remark he made to me was, " Very well, Sir." I told him, that the cause of his apprehension was respecting a young woman, named Maria Marten, with whom he formerly kept company at Polstead, in Suffolk, who had been missing for a length of time, and that there were strong suspicions attached to him concerning her fate.

He said that he never knew such a person, even by name. I desired him to take time, and took the prisoner to the Red Lion public-house, at Brentford. On the way thither, I told him that the body of Maria Marten had been found. He made no reply at first, but when we had got about twenty yards, he asked me when it was found.

William Towns, the foreman to the prisoner's mother, examined.—Last harvest, the prisoner ordered the bay in the Red Barn to be filled with wheat; I think the fodder or litter had remained there since the year before. The bay was cleared of corn last year, before Stoke fair, which begins on the 16th of May. William Corder managed the farm after his brother's death.

Mr. *Robert Offord* examined.—I am a cutler, and live at Hadleigh. About this time last year, or a little before, William Corder came to my shop with a small sword, with a cimeter blade, about twelve inches long; it had an ivory handle, and was mounted with brass. He wished it to be ground, and be made as sharp as a carving-knife. He said he had a cousin going to be married, and that he should sit at the head of the table to carve with it! I did as I was directed, and he called for it the same evening, and paid for it.

Mr. *John Lawton* examined.—I am a surgeon, and live at Boxford. I was present when the body was viewed by the gentlemen of the Jury, and made as minute an examination as I could. I first took off some pieces of sack which covered it; the body was lying upon the right side, with the head forced down upon the shoulder. There was an appearance of coagulated blood upon the cheek, and there appeared to be blood upon the clothes and handkerchiefs. The green handkerchief round the neck had been pulled tight, so that a man's hand might be put between the knot and the fold, and under it there was the appearance of a wound from a sharp instrument, but that part was so decomposed, I can only say that it had that appearance. The internal bone of the orbit of the right eye was fractured, as if a pointed instrument had been thrust into it, and the bone dividing the nose was displaced; the brain was in such a fluid state, that I am unable to say whether it had sustained any injury or not. Such a stab as I have described might have penetrated the brain. I found no injury in any other part; but there were two small portions of bone in the throat, which might have passed thither from the nose or orbit of the eye. I think the handkerchief was drawn tight enough to have caused death; the neck of the deceased appeared very much compressed indeed. The sack had evidently been tied after the deceased* had been put in head foremost. I had the mouth of the sack in my hand.

Mr. *Humphries* then proposed, that as the evidence had been gone through, his client should be permitted to come into the room to hear it read.

The *Coroner* ordered the officers to be sent for, and commanded them to produce Corder.

During the Inquest, Corder had been confined in an upper room, accompanied by a constable; and when Lea told him for what purpose his presence was required below, he scarcely made a reply, but prepared to accompany the officer.

Lea then ushered the prisoner into the room, properly handcuffed, and every eye was fixed upon him. He was enveloped in a large Spanish cloak, and appeared extremely exhausted and agitated; indeed, he scarcely seemed capable of supporting himself from fainting. This being observed, the Coroner ordered him a chair, and then commenced reading the evidence which had been adduced against him. While the Coroner was thus employed, the prisoner sometimes appeared very much agitated, and at others so absorbed in thought, as to be apparently inattentive to what was passing; his mind and body seemed to be completely over-

---

* In a supplementary deposition, since the exhumation of the body, this witness gives it as his decided opinion, that a pistol ball entered the neck about the jugular vein, and proceeded, in an oblique direction, to the eye on the opposite side of the head, which would have produced the fracture before alluded to on the orbit.

whelmed. When the depositions taken on the Sunday, when the Marten family were examined, had been read, Mr. Humphries, the solicitor, advised the prisoner to retire, and confide in him for the rest, in which request the prisoner seemed willing to acquiesce.

Before he left the room, the Coroner addressed him, and said, " William Corder, you are charged with the wilful murder of Maria Marten, and I shall be very happy to hear anything which you have to say, or listen to any evidence which you can adduce, in proof of your innocence. You have heard what some of the witnesses have said against you, therefore you are at liberty to invalidate their testimony if you can, or be silent, as you may think proper." After advising with his attorney, for by this time the prisoner had become more composed, he rose, and bowing to the Coroner, as if to thank him for his kind advice, retired with the officer without uttering a word, and he was re-conducted to his former apartment to await the verdict of the Jury.

Mr. *Weyman* then addressed the Jury, and observed, that, as the evidence was concluded, he would recapitulate the whole of it if they thought proper, and make such comments upon it as might appear necessary, as he deemed no exertion of his own too great in an affair of such momentous importance. That a murder had been committed, there could not be the least possible doubt; and the question for the Jury to consider at present was not by what instrument or weapon the deceased came by her death, but merely to say whether there had been sufficient evidence to convince them that the prisoner was the murderer.

Mr. *Green*, the Foreman, having conferred with his brother Jurors, informed the Coroner that they did not wish him to read the evidence, but they begged to be allowed to retire to consider their verdict.

The Jury were then conducted to a separate room, where they remained for about half an hour, and, on their return, the Coroner inquired whether they were agreed?

The *Foreman* said, " Yes, unanimously. We return a verdict of WILFUL MURDER AGAINST WILLIAM CORDER."

The Coroner immediately issued his warrant, directed to Mr. Orridge, the Governor of Bury gaol, to receive the prisoner into his custody, and him safely to keep, until he be brought to trial at the Assize and Gaol Delivery for the County of Suffolk, then next ensuing.

Soon after the conclusion of the Inquest, the prisoner was conveyed to Bury gaol in a postchaise. On his way thither, he frequently conversed with Lea, the officer, who accompanied him. Among other things, he said, he could not help thinking that there was some truth in dreams, and that he believed there was some reliance to be placed in the prognostics of fortune-tellers; for about twelve years since his fate had been foretold by an old woman, who declared that he had a great number of misfortunes and troubles to undergo, and that every undertaking in which he might engage would be unsuccessful. He added, "All her prophecies regarding me have come to pass, for everything has been unsuccessful."

He then made repeated allusions to the depositions which had been read to him by the Coroner, and remarked that they contained several untruths, and expressed regret that he had not continued in the room and heard them all read

During the period of his confinement in Bury gaol, even up to the time of his trial, his conduct was uniformly decorous. He manifested great self-possession, and was to all appearance unmoved, either by the allusions of scriptural discourse, or the near approach of the awful decision of his fate. Occasionally there was an appearance of agitation, but he quickly recovered his usual serenity, approaching almost to thorough indifference. His wife, who was far advanced in pregnancy, visited him daily. Her unmerited affliction excited universal sympathy. The prisoner was also visited by his mother and sister, we believe, more than once.

THE TRIAL.

IT is impossible to describe the state of confusion which prevailed from an early hour in the vicinity of the Court. Chief Baron ALEXANDER (who presided) had given peremptory orders that no person should be admitted until he had taken his seat on the Bench : the consequence of which was, that the crowd, composed of a mixed group of barristers, magistrates, jurors, constables, and yeomen, continued to accumulate, so as absolutely to obstruct the entrance of the Judge when he drove up, and created nearly one hour and a half of tumult and confusion, before the Court was in a condition to obtain that degree of order which befitted the proceedings.

At twenty minutes before ten o'clock the prisoner was put to the bar. He appeared to be about thirty years of age, of middle height, of a fair and healthy complexion, large mouth, turn-up nose, large eyes, which had a fixed and glazed aspect, and his features bore rather a smile than any other expression. He was dressed in a dark-coloured frock-coat with velvet collar, black waistcoat, and blue trowsers.

The Clerk of the Peace read the Indictment, which charged William Corder with having, on the 18th of May, 1827, murdered Maria Marten, by feloniously and wilfully shooting her with a pistol through the body, and likewise stabbing her with a dagger. The Indictment consisted of ten counts. The following is an abstract :—

First Count.—The jurors of our Lord the King, upon their oath, present that William Corder, late of the parish of Polstead, &c., Suffolk, yeoman, on the 18th of May, &c., with force and arms, &c., in and upon one Maria Marten, not having the fear of God, &c., then and there being, feloniously, wilfully, and of his malice aforethought, did make an assault, and that the said William Corder, a certain pistol of two shillings value, then and there charged with gunpowder and one leaden bullet (which pistol he the said William Corder, in his right hand, then and there had held), then and there feloniously, wilfully, and of his malice aforethought, did discharge and shoot off at, against, and upon the said Maria Marten ; and the said William Corder, with the leaden bullet aforesaid, out of the pistol aforesaid, by the said William Corder discharged and shot off, then and there feloniously, wilfully, &c., did strike, penetrate, and wound the said Maria Marten in and upon the left side of the face of her the said Maria Marten, &c., giving her the said Maria Marten one mortal wound, of the depth of four inches, and of the breadth of half an inch, of which said mortal wound she the said Maria Marten then and there instantly died ; and so the jurors aforesaid, upon their oaths, &c., do say, that the said William Corder, her the said Maria Marten did kill and murder.

Second Count.—That the said William Corder, on the 18th day of May, &c., upon the said Maria Marten, against the peace of God, &c., feloniously, and of his malice aforethought, did make an assault, and that the said William Corder, with a certain sharp instrument, to wit, a sword, of the value of one shilling (which he, the said William Corder, in his right hand, then and there held), her the said Maria Marten, in and upon the left side of the body of her the said Maria Marten, then and there feloniously, wilfully, &c., did strike, thrust, stab, and penetrate, giving unto the said Maria Marten then and there with the sharp instrument aforesaid, in and upon the left side of the body of her the said Maria Marten, between the fifth and sixth ribs, one mortal wound, of the depth of six inches, and of the breadth of one inch of which ......tal wound she, the said Maria Marten, then and there instantly died ; and .....o the jurors, &c., present, that the said William Corder, her the said Maria Marten did, by the means aforesaid, feloniously, and of his malice aforethought, did kill and murder, against the peace, &c.

Third Count.—Same as the last, except the wound is alleged to have been inflicted with a sword in the right side of the face of her, the said Maria Marten, and that he inflicted a wound of the depth of four inches, and of the width of one inch, of which said mortal wound she died, &c.

Fourth Count.—Same as the last, except alleging that the mortal wound was given by means of a sword, on the right side of the neck of the said Maria Marten.

Fifth Count.—That the said William Corder, on the 18th of May, &c., in and upon the said Maria Marten, and wilfully, maliciously, &c., did make an assault, and that the said William Corder, a certain handkerchief of the value of sixpence, about the neck of the said Maria Marten then and there wilfully, &c., did pull, fix, and fasten ; and that the said William Corder with the handkerchief aforesaid, so as aforesaid, wilfully, feloniously, &c., pulled, fixed, and fastened about the neck of her the said Maria Marten, her the said Maria Marten then and there feloniously, &c., did choke, suffocate, and strangle, of which said, &c., she the said Maria Marten then and there instantly died, &c.

Sixth Count.—Alleges the offence to have been committed with   gun, of the value of ten shillings, then and there charged with gunpowder and shots, which the said William Corder fired off, &c. ; and the said shots so fired off by the said William Corder, in and upon the left side of the face of her the said Maria Marten inflicted one mortal wound of the depth of four inches, and the breadth of half an inch, of which said mortal wound she died, &c.

Seventh Count.—That the said William Corder, on the 18th of May, &c., her the said Maria Marten into a certain hole, dug and made in and under the floor of a certain barn, situated in the parish aforesaid, &c., of his malice, &c., did cast, throw, put, or push ; and that the said William Corder over and upon the head, face, and body of the said Maria Marten, into the said hole so being cast, thrown, put or pushed, as aforesaid, and in the same hole then lying and being, then and there, &c., of his malice, &c., with both his hands did cast, throw, and heap divers large quantities of earth, to wit, five bushels of earth of no value, and divers quantities of clay, to wit, five bushels of clay of no value, and divers large quantities of gravel, to wit, five bushels of gravel of no value ; and that the said William Corder, with the said large quantities of earth, clay and gravel, over and upon the head, and face, and body of her the said Maria Marten, feloniously, wilfully, &c., did choke, suffocate, and smother ; of which choking, suffocating, and smothering, by the said William Corder, in manner and form as aforesaid done and perpetrated, she the said Maria Marten then and there instantly died ; and the jurors aforesaid, upon their oaths, do say that the said William Corder, by the means aforesaid, did her the said Maria Marten feloniously, &c., kill and murder.

Eighth Count.—Same as the last, except it describes the hole to be of the depth of two feet, of the width of two feet, and of the length of six feet.

Ninth Count.—Charges the crime to have been committed both by stabbing the said Maria Marten with a sharp instrument in the side, and by fixing a handkerchief round her neck and strangling her.

Tenth Count.—Charges the murder to have been inflicted with a pistol, loaded with shots, fired against the side of her face ; also, with a certain sharp instrument (not describing it as a sword), by stabbing her on the left side of the body, between the fifth and sixth ribs ; also, with a sword, value one shilling, by stabbing the said Maria Marten, on the right side of the face, and upon the right side of the neck ; also, with a certain handkerchief, fixed round her neck by the said William Corder, by which he choked and strangled the said Maria Marten ; also, by casting and throwing her into a certain hole, of the depth of two feet, and width of two feet, and of the length of six feet, and by casting quantities of earth, gravel, and clay, upon the said Maria Marten, &c.

The prisoner listened with the greatest attention to the reading of the Indictment, occasionally inclining his body forward, and turning his ear towards the Court ; and as the Jury were sworn, he took a small eye-glass from his waistcoat-pocket, and looked steadily at several of the gentlemen He was also indicted upon the verdict of the Coroner's Inquest. When required, in the usual form, to plead, he replied, in a firm voice, to each Indictment, " Not Guilty, my Lord.'

A plan of the barn was put on the table of the Court, and at a quarter past ten o'clock Mr. Andrews stated the case to the Jury. After several preliminary observations on the importance of the case, in which the learned Counsel said he should carefully abstain from any remark which might tend to raise unnecessary prejudice against the prisoner, he proceeded to observe, that he felt it to be his duty to lay the facts of it briefly before the Jury, in order that they might obtain a general view of it, and so be able, as the different circumstances were deposed to, to judge what was the importance and the bearing of each. The prisoner at the bar was the son of respectable parents, living at Polstead, in that county. His father had been dead for some time. Whilst living, he was a farmer, and held a farm of very considerable extent in the parish of Polstead. From the time of his father's death to the period of the transaction into which they were then assembled to inquire, his mother, first with the assistance of his elder brother, and afterwards with the assistance of the prisoner himself, was also a farmer. Maria Marten, the young woman with whose death the prisoner at the bar stood charged, was the daughter of parents in a humbler sphere of life, residing in the same parish. The prisoner at the bar and Maria Marten had, from living together in the same parish, been personally known to each other for some time, but were not intimately acquainted until a year before the 18th of May, 1827. At that period an intimacy of a very close nature took place between them, and an illegitimate child was the fruit of it. She was not delivered of this child at her father's house; but she returned to it about six weeks before the 18th of May, with an infant child, of which the prisoner owned himself to be the father. The child was always a weakly child, and died, as he believed, within a fortnight after the return of Maria Marten to her family. During this period of their acquaintance, Corder, on more occasions than one, was heard to say to her, that the parish thought of having her taken up for another bastard child of which she had been delivered; and, after her delivery of a child to him, he was heard to make to her the same declaration. They were likewise heard quarrelling more than once, and especially regarding a 5l. note, which was mentioned between them. On one occasion Maria Marten said to the prisoner at the bar, "If I go to gaol, you shall go too." It was right that he should also state to the Jury, that during this period of their acquaintance, Corder said, repeatedly, that it was his intention to make her his wife. On the Sunday before the 18th of May, which fell upon a Friday, Maria Marten (Corder having first been to her father's cottage), went to his mother's house. It was there agreed that they should go the next day to Ipswich to get married. They did not, however, go as they had agreed. They then arranged that they should go on the next Thursday; but that arrangement was not carried into effect. On Friday, the 18th of May, about the middle of the day, Corder went to the house of Maria Marten's father. At that time she was up stairs with her mother. He desired her to make herself ready and go along with him. She said that she could not go then. He replied, "You have been disappointed several times, and you must go now." Other conversation, as he was informed, also passed between them on that occasion. It was agreed that she should put her clothes into a bag, and that Corder should take them to a place called the Red Barn, which was on a farm belonging to his mother. It was further agreed, that, to escape observation, she should put on, at her father's house, a male dress; that she should change it at the Barn for a female dress; and that she should go from thence to Ipswich to be married. He should prove to them, if he was rightly instructed, that she put into a large bag several articles of female dress, which it was not necessary for him to enumerate. She also put into it a small basket, and into that small basket she put a smaller black velvet bag, commonly called a reticule. He would prove to them, that after this arrangement Corder was absent from the house of Maria Marten's mother about a quarter of an hour. When he returned, Maria Marten had put on her male attire, which consisted of a coat, waistcoat, and a pair of breeches. She had on, also, part of her own female dress, namely, a flannel petticoat and a pair of stays, into which she put a jean busk. She had, also, a comb in her hair, two earrings in her ears, and two smaller combs in her hair. The prisoner and Maria Marten left the house at the same time, going out, however, at different doors, but both taking the direction of the Red Barn. He ought, also, to state, that she had a green handkerchief tied about her neck. From that period, none of her friends have seen anything of her, nor have had any accounts respecting her, save those which had been given by the prisoner at the bar, and which would shortly be placed in evidence before them. He ought to have stated, that before they went away, and whilst they were talking of the manner in which she was dressed, Corder said to her that Baalham, the constable, had shown him a letter by which he was authorized to take her up for having had a bastard child. That constable would be called before them, and he would tell them that he never had any such letter as the prisoner represented, and that he had never made any such communication as the prisoner alleged. It so happened, that on the day on which they left old Marten's cottage to go to the Red Barn, a younger brother to the deceased Maria Marten, who was working near the Red Barn, saw the prisoner pass at a short distance from him to his (Corder's) mother's house with a pickaxe upon his shoulder. He must now inform them, that the next time the mo-ther—or he should rather say the mother-in-law—of Maria Marten saw the prisoner, was at his mother's house. Nothing material passed between them on that occasion. On the Sunday following, he came to her house and said that he had not yet married her daughter, though he had taken her away for that purpose, for it was necessary that the licence should go up to London. He added, however, that he had left her daughter at Yarmouth, under the protection of one of his female relations. On a subsequent day in the same week she had another interview with the prisoner, and she then told him that her son had seen him on the Friday previously near the Red Barn with a pickaxe on his shoulder. He replied, " It could not be me that he saw; it must have been Acres, who was employed that day in stubbing trees near the barn." Acres would be called before them, and would tell them that he was not so employed at that time, nor at any time thereabouts. From this period to the discovery of the transaction, Corder saw the father and the mother of Maria Marten very frequently. Corder was absent from Polstead for some time ; and on his return he gave accounts of Maria Marten's living with some friends of his at Yarmouth of the name of Roland. When they inquired about her health, he said that she was very well: and when asked why she did not write, he said, sometimes that she was too busy, and at other times that she had a sore on the back of her hand, which gathered, and disabled her from moving her fingers, and consequently from writing. In the interval between the 18th of May and harvest time, Corder had several conversations with other individuals respecting Maria Marten : and to these persons he gave a different account of her from that which he had given to her father and mother. He told one person that she had gone by the steam-packet to France, and another person that she was living at no great distance from them. He had a very particular conversation on the subject with a woman of the name of Stowe, to the particulars of which she would be called to speak. He told her, that Maria Marten did not live at any great distance from them. In the course of conversation, she asked whether Maria Marten was likely to have any more children. He said, " No, she is not. Maria Marten will have no more children.' Mrs. Stowe immediately said, " Why not? she is still a very young woman." He replied, " No; believe me, she will have no more; she 'as had her number." Mrs. Stowe then asked him, " Is she far from .ience ?" He answered, " No, she is not far from us : I can go to her whenever I like, and I know that when I am not with her, nobody else is." There was a trifling circumstance which was, perhaps, connected with the transaction of the 18th of May, and which he would briefly state to them. From this woman of the name of Stowe, the prisoner, about that time, borrowed a spade. She could not tell the precise period at which he borrowed it; but there were circumstances which led her to believe that it was about the middle of May. She had been shortly before delivered of a child; and it was in the interval between her getting out of bed and being churched, that he borrowed the spade. They would hear her examined, and would draw their own inferences from her testimony. The learned Counsel said that he had now come, in the course of his detail, to that part of the transaction which happened in September last. Corder was then engaged in directing the workmen to get in the harvest. For some time before the 18th of May the barn had been empty, except so far as the floor was covered with the old litter. When the wheat was cut, Corder gave directions that the corn should be laid in the upper bay of the barn. He was present when the first and second loads were taken in, and superintended the operation. The keys of the barn were always kept in his mother's house, and the barn was, besides, not easy of entrance, as it was surrounded by a sort of outhouses, and was only approached by a gate that was seven feet high.

After the corn had been got into the Barn, Corder left Polstead. He was driven, on that occasion, to Colchester, by a man of the name of Bright. To that person he gave a different account of Maria Marten from that which he had given to any other person, for he said that he had not seen her since the May preceding. Before he left Polstead, on that occasion, he saw her father, and he told him that he (Corder) should have the pleasure of seeing his daughter soon. He likewise told him that he had bought a new suit of clothes, in which he intended to be married to her. About the 19th or the 20th of October, old Marten received a letter from the prisoner, bearing the London post-mark. In that letter the prisoner said that he had made Maria his wife. He likewise expressed his surprise that the old man had not answered the letter which Maria had sent him upon her marriage, informing him, that when they were married, Mr. Roland had acted as a father, and Miss Roland as bride's-maid. He desired that the old man would answer his letter immediately, and told him to address his reply to him, under certain initials, at some place in the city. The father answered the letter, and told him that no such .etter as he described had ever been received. Corder then wrote back, that he had made inquiry at the Post-office respecting the loss of it, that no traces of any such letter could be found in the books of the Post-office at London, and that he attributed the loss of it to its having had to cross the sea, Maria having been in the Isle of Wight at the time when it was written. In November last, the prisoner met a gentleman of the name of Matthews, in London, with whom he had a correspondence, which he intended to place before them. Corder then said to that gentleman, that he had not married Maria Marten, because his family affairs were not quite settled; but he added, that he was then living with her in the Isle of Wight. Some time further elapsed without the parents of Maria Marten hearing from her; and, in consequence, they became anxious and suspicious about her fate. Their suspicions increased every day, and at last assumed a definite shape. They were directed at last to the Red Barn. The father of Maria Marten became anxious to examine it. Accordingly, in the April of the present year, he went to the Barn, and searched it. The corn was then thrashed out, but the old litter still remained in it. They searched two or three places in it, and, at length, in the upper bay, they found a place where the ground did not appear so firm and consistent as it was in other parts of the Barn. In consequence, the ground was opened, and within a foot and a half of the surface they found the body of a female. The body had on parts of a female dress: there were the remains of a jean pair of stays, of a shift, and of a flannel petticoat. Under the body was a handkerchief, and on the neck and around it was a green silk handkerchief. The body and clothes were inspected attentively by the father, the mother, and the sister of Maria Marten. They would describe to the Jury the different marks which Maria had on her person. They would also tell them the natural marks that were found upon the body in the Barn. Maria Marten had a large excrescence, or wen, about the middle of her neck;—so, too, had the female whose body was discovered in the Barn. Maria Marten had lost two of her front teeth;—so had the female whose body was found in the Barn. The features of the body were not altogether decomposed, and the Jury would hear what the witnesses had to say on that point. They would describe to the Jury the different parts of Maria Marten's dress, and particularly with respect to her stays and to her neck-handkerchief. Maria Marten had, when living, a pain in her side, and was labouring under asphixia. The surgeons who had examined the body discovered in the Barn, would tell them that they found considerable signs of inflammation in one of the sides of that body. He ought here to inform the Jury, that the body discovered in the Barn remained in the ground until the surgeon had inspected it. The surgeon who inspected it would tell them that he found a pistol-ball in the face,—a wound in the neck, and given by a sharp instrument,—a wound in the face, given by a similar instrument,—and a third wound of the same kind, between the fifth and sixth ribs, which had penetrated the heart. The first surgeon who examined the body, took the green silk handkerchief off the neck, and would inform them, that it must have pressed so tight upon the neck as to have produced death by strangulation.

In consequence of this discovery, suspicion immediately attached to the prisoner at the bar. Information of the murder was sent immediately to London. An intelligent police-officer was employed to apprehend the prisoner; and, in consequence of his exertions, the prisoner was apprehended at a house in Ealing. The officer, on first seeing the prisoner, told him that he had come to apprehend him upon a very serious charge

—indeed, for nothing less than the murder of Maria Marten. He aske the prisoner if he knew such a woman. The prisoner said that he did not. The officer then asked him this question—" Did you never know Maria Marten?" The prisoner replied, " No, never." The prisoner then said, " You must be mistaken in the person you are come to apprehend." The officer said, " No, I am not mistaken as to the person; your name is Corder, I believe?" The prisoner said it was. The officer then said again to him, " Did you never know Maria Marten?" and the prisoner again said, " Never." The officer then said, " I have asked you the question twice, and I shall only ask you a third time; " Did you never know Maria Marten?" and a third time the reply was, " Never." The officer then apprehended him. At the time of apprehending the prisoner, the officer searched the house in which he was living, and in one of the rooms he found a small black velvet bag; there was something peculiar in the bag, for it was lined with old silk, and had a broad selvage round the rim. That bag Mrs. Marten, as he was instructed, would identify as the bag of Maria Marten. In that bag were found a brace of pistols. After the officer had returned to Polstead, and had seen the shape of the wounds inflicted by the sharp instrument, he recollected that he had seen in the house a sword belonging to the prisoner. He went to Ealing and procured it; that sword would be produced that day for their examination. It had been compared with the size of the wound in the stays, and in the body discovered in the Barn, and they would hear what the witnesses said upon that point. He would prove that some days before the 18th of May, the prisoner had gone to a cutler, and had given him orders to make the sword sharp. His instructions were obeyed. The sword was ground; the prisoner took it away; and he would prove that it was seen in his possession before he left Polstead. These were the main facts of the case which he had to submit to their consideration. The observations upon them would come more properly from the learned Judge who had to try the cause, than from himself; and he should therefore abstain from entering into any analysis of them There was, however, one observation which he thought he might make,— nay, which he felt himself bound in justice to the prisoner to make to them. A case like the present always excited much curiosity, and gave rise to many reports. Now, such reports had no connexion whatever with the solemn investigation on which they were then impannelled to decide. He, was therefore sure, that if they had heard such reports, they would discharge them from their minds, and would come to a decision on this subject upon the evidence alone. Their duty to the public, to the prisoner, and to themselves, required, that in the solemn verdict which they would soon be called upon to give, they should be guided solely by the legitimate influence of the evidence tendered to their consideration. The facts which he was instructed to offer in evidence, sifted as they would be by an acute cross-examination, and commented on as they would be by the learned Judge, would, he trusted in God, lead them to a right decision. If, in the exercise of their judgment, they should be of opinion either that the prisoner was innocent of the charge laid against him in the indictment, or that he was not clearly and distinctly proved to be guilty of it, they would do their duty by acquitting him; but if they should be of opinion that the prisoner was the person who murdered Maria Marten, they could discharge their duty to God and to their country in no other way than by returning a verdict of Guilty, without any regard to the consequences which might flow from it.

The first witness called was *Ann Marten*, the wife of Thomas Marten, who deposed, that she lived at Polstead, and her husband's daughter was Maria Marten. She had known the prisoner (who lived in their neighbourhood) for 17 years. He was acquainted with Maria intimately, and used to come frequently to their cottage for more than a twelvemonth before the 18th of May, last year. Maria became pregnant in the course of that intercourse, at Sudbury. It was about seven weeks before May, 1827, that she returned to her father's house, accompanied by an infant child, who died about a fortnight afterwards. Corder still continued to come to the house, and admitted that he was the father of this infant. He used to converse often with Maria, and when the child was buried, he said he had carried it to Sudbury for that purpose. She remembered his more than once talking about a five pound note, and Maria used to say he had taken away her bread and her child's. Maria had had a child previously, which was kept by the witness. Mr. Corder told Maria that the parish officers were going to take her up for having bastard children. Recollected the Sunday before Friday, the 18th of May. On that evening (Sunday) prisoner came to the cottage, where he stopped half an hour or three-quarters, and then went out with Maria; they both saying they were going to Ipswich early on the Monday morning, after sleeping at his mother's house. She returned between three and four o'clock the same morning, and Corder came again on that day, and said that they should go to Ipswich on the Wednesday night. They did not, however, go at that time, in consequence of Stoke fair, but fixed Thursday night for the journey, when again there was a disappointment, as he said his brother James was hourly expected to die. On the Friday (the day laid in the indictment), about 11 or 12 o'clock, Corder came, and went up stairs to witness and Maria. To the latter he said, "I am come, Maria—make haste—I am going." She replied, "How can I go at this time of the day, without any body seeing me?" He said, "Never mind, we have been disappointed a good many times, and we will be disappointed no more." After they had this conversation, she asked him, "How am I to go?" He replied, "You can go to the Red Barn, and wait till I go to you there in the course of the evening." Maria said, "How am I to order my things?" He replied, he would take the things, carry them up to the Barn, and come back to walk with her; adding, that none of his workmen were in the fields or at the Barn, and he was sure the course was quite clear. Maria's things, consisting of a reticule, wicker basket, a velvet one, two pair of black silk stockings, a silk gown of the same colour, a cambric skirt, and other articles of dress, were put into a brown holland bag, which Corder carried away in his hand. She (Maria) then dressed herself in a brown coat, striped waistcoat, and blue trousers, wearing underneath, her female petticoat, white stays, green and red handkerchief, a silk one, and an Irish linen chemise, which the deceased had herself made.

Witness had laced on the stays for Maria on that morning, and knew the marks upon it (which she described) as well as those on the shoes which she wore. He assigned as the reason for going on that day to Ipswich, that John Baalham, the constable, came to him on that morning to the stable, saying he had got a letter from Mr. Whitmore, of London, which enclosed a warrant to take Maria and prosecute her, for her bastard children. Witness said, "Oh, William! if you had but married Maria before this child was born, as I wished, all this would have been settled." "Well," said he, "I am going to Ipswich to marry her to-morrow morning." Witness said, "William, what will you do if that can't be done?" He replied, "Don't make yourself uneasy, she shall be my lawful wife before I return, or I will get her a place till she can." Maria then went away about half-past twelve o'clock, Corder first desiring witness to look out to the garden, lest somebody should see them going off. They departed at different doors, Maria in man's dress, and with a hat of prisoner's. She wore a large comb in her hair, and a smaller one, having also earrings. They proceeded together in the direction of the Red Barn, and she saw neither of them again on that day, nor indeed ever saw Maria since. William Corder, when he went away, carried a gun in his hand, which he said was charged. Maria had, besides, a green cotton umbrella, with a bone crook handle and a button. On the following Sunday morning, at nine o'clock, witness next spoke to the prisoner at her own house. She said, "William, what have you done with Maria?" He answered, "I have left her at Ipswich, where I have got her a comfortable place, to go down with Miss Roland to the waterside." On asking him how she was to do for clothes, he said Miss Roland had plenty for her, and would not let him provide any for Maria. He also said he had got a licence, but it must go to London to be signed, and he could not be married under a month or six weeks. He further mentioned, that he had changed a check for 20*l.*, and given her the money. On as ing him where she dressed, he said she had put her things on in the Barn, and that ae afterwards put the male attire into the seat of the coach in which they travelled. Witness had a son named George, and she told Corder that George had mentioned he (prisoner) had not left the Barn as soon as he promised. This he denied, saying he had left it within three quarters of an hour after he parted from her house. "No," said witness, "you did not, for George saw you later going down the adjoining field with a pickaxe." "No, no," replied he, "that was not me, but Tom Acres, who had been planting trees on the hill." She was in the habit of seeing Corder repeatedly up to the month of September, sometimes two or three times in the day, and he invariably said Maria was well, and living comfortably at Yarmouth with Miss Roland. He used to leave Polstead some times for a day or two, when he was in the habit of saying he had been with Maria, who continued very well, and that at Michaelmas he meant to take her home to his mother's farm. No letter had ever come from Maria, and when she often spoke to Corder about her not writing, he replied, she could not, because she had got a bad hand.

When he left Polstead he came to take leave, saying he was going to the waterside for his health, and would call at Yarmouth to take Maria with him, and be married immediately. She never saw him after till his arrest, nor had she seen the dead body; but all the articles of dress were shown to her [which the witness subsequently identified as being those worn by the deceased on the day she had last seen her]. Maria had always a cough, had a wen on her neck, and had lost a tooth from the upper as well as from the lower jaw. Witness attended Corder's brother's funeral soon after the 18th of May, where she saw the prisoner with Maria's umbrella. After the funeral she talked to him about the umbrella, which he denied to have been hers, though he said it was like it, but Deborah Franks's, and he was going to send it back to her. He on one occasion said, that Maria had lent him hers at Ipswich, where she had come over with Miss Roland, to save him from being dripping wet. He had shown the witness a gold ring, which was, he said, to be for Maria's wedding, and also a brace of pistols which he once brought to the house.

Cross-examined by Mr. *Brodrick*.—Witness was the mother of three children Maria was her step-daughter, and had an own brother and sister. She was anxious for Maria's marriage to Corder, although Maria said nothing about it. She was gone two months at her last lying-in, and then returned in Corder's gig with the prisoner. The infant died in her arms, and Corder and Maria took it away to be buried; where she did not know, but was told it was at Sudbury. Maria used to dress a little fine, and her sister, as well as witness and her father, often quarrelled with her about it, which made her mostly very dull. There was no secret about their going to the Barn. Corder used openly to snap the pistol close to the fire. She has seen him bring ham for Maria. He used to give her money as the weekly allowance for the child; and Maria had a quarterly stipend of 5*l.* from Mr. Matthews, by whom she had a child, and another by a third party. She had never heard from any body but the prisoner, that Maria was exposed to danger by the constables, for having had these children; and this fear kept her in doors. When she went away on the 18th, she was crying and low spirited. Corder often came to the house with a gun. She had been examined before the Coroner. Prisoner called repeatedly to see Maria, and said that as long as he had a shilling, she should have it. They seemed always to be very fond of each other. She repeated the manner in which Corder and Maria left the house together for the last time, as it has already been given in her examination in chief.

During the examination of this witness, the prisoner put on his spectacles, took out a red morocco pocket-book, in which he commenced writing, and looked stedfastly at her. She appeared a decently-dressed country woman, but never returned the prisoner's glance, or took her eyes from the direction of the Counsel who examined her. About two o'clock he ate and drank with much seeming appetite.

Thomas Marten, the father of the deceased, deposed, that he lived at Polstead, and was a mole-catcher. Maria was, in May, 1827, about 26 years of age. The last day he saw her was on the 17th of May. He went out too early on the morning of the 18th to see her. He knew Corder to have been acquainted with her for a year and a half before that time. It was on the 19th of May he found out his daughter's having gone away with him; and on the following Sunday he said he had taken

Maria to Ipswich, but was obliged to go to London about the marriage licence. This witness then corroborated the evidence of the preceding witness, respecting Corder's declarations of the name and kind of place he had provided for his daughter, and his subsequent statements that he was in the habit of hearing from her, and she was quite well, except the sore hand; and also his assurance, on taking leave, that he was going to meet Maria and marry her at the water-side. The witness proceeded to state, he had afterwards received two letters, which he gave to a gentleman who had examined him, and had since searched the Red Barn at Polstead. It was on the 19th of last April.

Here the witness referred to the model of the Barn in Court, and pointed out and explained all its local bearings.

On lifting up the straw from the Barn-floor, he saw some great stones lying in the middle of the bay, and an appearance of the earth having been disturbed. On that spot he poked down the handle of the rake, and turned something up which was black. On getting further assistance, they discoverd, a little under the ground, a small round sharp iron, about a foot long, like a hay-spike, and then they came to the body, and near the head found the handkerchief tied round her neck, apparently very tight. The body was lying down, though not stretched out. The legs were drawn up, and the head bent down into the earth. He quitted the Barn for half an hour, and returned, with another person, to make a further examination. They let the body alone until the Coroner and the surgeon came, when they cleared the earth entirely from the body, and raised it up from the floor. On examining it in the light, the mouth looked like Maria's, who had a wen on her neck, and been ailing a year or two with a cough. Underneath the body was found a shawl; there were, besides, earrings, part of a pair of stays, of a chemise, and two combs in the hair.

Cross-examined.—A man named Pryke accompanied witness in this examination of the Barn, and discovery of the body. They put the rake several times into the ground before they found it. The body was not removed until the Coroner came. After the Inquest, the Attorney for the prosecution examined the witnesses upon oath, in a public-house called the Cock. The prisoner, the jury, or a magistrate, were absent at this time.

Ann Marten (sister of the deceased) deposed, that she was at home on the 18th of May, when Maria went away with William Corder, the circumstances of which she described in nearly the same words as her mother had previously done, particularizing each article of her dress. Since that time she had frequently seen the prisoner, who always said Maria was living with Miss Roland, the sister of an old school-fellow of his, and that he was preparing to marry her. Witness had seen the dead body, when the Coroner and jury were present. She saw it laid upon a door, and was positive it was her sister Maria's. She knew it by the things that were on it, also by her teeth, her mouth, and her features generally.

The witness here particularly identified the clothes as belonging to her deceased sister, as well as the earrings which were in the ears, and the combs, &c.

Cross-examined.—Her sister left home on the 18th of May in very low spirits, but she never heard her say she was anxious to be married to Wm. Corder. Witness and Maria sometimes quarrelled, and there used to be words between her and her step-mother.

George Marten (brother of the preceding witness), a boy about eleven or twelve years of age, deposed, after a few interrogatories to ascertain his competency to take an oath, which he answered satisfactorily, that he saw his sister on the day she last left the house, with Corder, who carried a gun in his hand, which he said was loaded, and therefore cautioned witness not to meddle with it. He never saw his sister after that day, but he saw Corder on the same day, between three and four o'clock, come from the Barn alone, with a pickaxe, and proceed homewards through the fields. He was positive as to his person.

He was not cross-examined.

Phœbe Stowe deposed, that she lived at Polstead, and knew Wm. Corder. Her house was about thirty rods from the Red Barn, to which it was the nearest cottage. She remembered Corder calling about one o'clock one day in May last year, when he said, " Mrs. Stowe, has not your husband got an old spade to lend me?" She lent him one, and he only said a few words, saying he was in such a hurry, he could not then stop and talk to her. The spade was afterwards returned; but she could not say by whom. On a subsequent occasion Corder again called, when she asked him where was Maria Marten's child. He said it was dead and buried. He also said the would have no more children. Witness said, " Why not ? she is a young woman yet." He replied, " Never mind, Maria Marten will never have any more children." " What do you go by ?" added witness. " Oh," said he, " she has had several, but I'll be d——d if she shall have any more." Witness continued, " If you are married, why don't you live with her ?" " Oh, no," was his reply, " for I can go to her any day in the year, just when I like." " Perhaps you are rather jealous," said I, " and when you are not with her, you think somebody else is." " Oh, no;" said he, " when I am not with her, I am sure nobody else is."

Cross-examined.—Mr. Corder managed the farm for his mother, and her husband worked for him. She knew nothing of who brought the spade back, nor did she tell her husband of her having lent one. When she was first examined before the Coroner's jury she did not tell all this. She was also sworn, and gave evidence before the attorney for the prosecution.

Rachael Buck deposed, that she knew Wm. Corder, whom she saw about last August, when he came to her farm, and said Maria Marten would not be her mistress, as she had gone to France by the steam packet.

William Marten (first cousin of the deceased) deposed, that he knew Wm. Corder, with whom he had conversed about Maria Marten, in the harvest of last year. On asking him where she was, and if at Sudbury, he replied, " No; but I can see her every day I please." He then gave witness a pint of harvest beer, and desired him not to speak about Maria, lest the people within should hear what was said.

Francis Stowe deposed, that he was last year working at harvest under Wm. Corder, who acted for his mother. Knew the Red Barn, where the first corn of that year was put. Witness assisted in placing it there: the first part was put immediately over where the body was found. He remembered Corder's coming to him in the fields, saying, " I will give you a pound note to cut my throat." He was smiling at the time, and witness took it to be a joke.

William Downes deposed, that he had been for many years a labourer on Mrs. Corder's farm, which was managed by the prisoner, whom he assisted in filling the Red Barn last harvest in the right-hand bay, by William Corder's orders.

Cross-examined.—Knew the prisoner for seventeen or eighteen years; he was a very good-natured young man to witness, and he never saw him out of temper. Within two years, a great number of his family had been cut off by death.

William Pryke deposed, that he drove the prisoner, on the 8th of September, to Colchester, and talked with him about the business of the farm. Maria Marten's name was mentioned, and he said he had not seen her since May, but spoke very highly of her. When Marten searched the Barn, witness assisted him; he had a rake in his hand, and co-operated to clear away the earth, where they found the body doubled up and lying on the right side.

Cross-examined.—Prisoner was ill when he drove him over to Colchester; he spoke highly to him of the poor girl, Maria Marten. He had the care of the Barn after the body was found. but he never was examined before the Coroner.

Mr. *Brodrick.*—It is very extraordinary that a witness so important as this should not have been examined before the Coroner, who, by the way, it ought to be mentioned, refused to allow the attendance of the prisoner during the Inquest, so that the man is put to the bar for the first time to hear the evidence against him.

The *Lord Chief Baron.*—Is it not very unusual for the prisoner not to be admitted on such occasions?

Mr. *Brodrick.*—Very unusual, indeed, my Lord; and it is likewise very unusual for a Coroner who sat on such a cause, afterwards, as an attorney, to conduct the prosecution against the same prisoner. Most unusual, too, it is, that the Coroner, while acting as such attorney, should himself, in a private room, without the prisoner's having any notice of it, examine the witnesses on oath, and collect their evidence, no magistrate being present.

The witness's cross-examination was resumed, when he said, that the attorney for the prosecution had examined him on oath at the Cock. Witness further said, that William Corder was always a kind-hearted young man.

Mr. *Brodrick.*—Pray had you not got a person preaching about this murder in the very Barn itself?

The *Lord Chief Baron.*—What! what d'ye mean by preaching? Is it a sermon?

Mr. *Brodrick.*—Yes, my Lord; and to a congregation of several thousand persons, specially brought together, after regular notice in the parish, to hear this man described as the murderer of this unfortunate girl.

The *Lord Chief Baron.*—You don't mean a clergyman of the Church of England?

Mr. *Brodrick.*—No, my Lord; I understand he was a Dissenter.

Witness, on being asked the name of this preacher, said that he believed it was Young.

Mr. *Brodrick.*—This was not all, my Lord; for in the very neighbourhood, and indeed in all parts of the county, there have been puppet-shows representing the same catastrophe.

Mr. *Andrews* rose to explain the conduct of the Coroner.

Mr. *Brodrick* objected to his learned friend being heard, unless he produced the Coroner as a witness. To that he could have no objection.

The *Lord Chief Baron.*—But I have; for the matter has nothing to do with this trial, and we've enough to do without it. It's an imputation upon the Coroner, perhaps, but we are not now trying his character.

Mr. *Andrews* then explained, that it had been arranged by the Coroner, when Mr. Humphries first attended as the prisoner's solicitor, that though Corder was not to be present at the Inquest, the depositions were afterwards to be read over to him, which was done. He believed that the practice was, that the prisoner should be absent upon such occasions.

Mr. *Prendergast* said, that the practice was directly the contrary, and so were the words of Lord Coke.

Mr. *Wm. Chaplin* was next examined. He produced two letters, which he received from Thomas Marten.

Whilst Marten was sent for to prove that those letters were the same which he received by post,

Mr. *Brodrick* asked him whether he was not the churchwarden of Polstead, and the prosecutor in this cause?

Witness replied, " I am."

Mr. *Brodrick.*—Did you hear the parson preach in the Barn?

Witness.—No, certainly not; but I heard of the occurrence.

Mr. *Brodrick.*—And you never interfered to prevent it?

Witness.—I did not.

Mr. *Brodrick.*—Are there not exhibitions going round the neighbourhood, representing Corder as the murderer?

Witness.—I have heard so.

Mr. *Brodrick.*—And you've not interfered to prevent them? Is there not a camera obscura near this very Hall at this moment, exhibiting him as the murderer?

Witness.—There is a camera obscura, I believe, about the streets, but I don't know its nature.

The letters, after being identified by Marten as Corder's hand-writing, and as those which he received, were then read.

" *London, Bull Inn, Leadenhall-street, Thursday, Oct.* 18.

" THOMAS MARTEN,

" I am just arrived at London upon business respecting our family affairs, and am writing to you before I take the least refreshment, because I shall be in time for this night's post, as my stay in town will be very short,—anxious to return again to her who is now my wife, and with whom I shall be one of the happiest of men. I should had her with me, but it was her wish to stay at our lodgings at Newport, in the Isle of Wight, which she described to you in her letter; and we feel astonished that you have not yet answered it, thinking illness must have been the cause. In that she gave you a full description of our marriage, and that Mr. Roland was Daddy, and Miss bride's-maid. Likewise told you they came with us as far as London, where we continued together very comfortable for three days, when we parted with the greatest regret. Maria and myself went on to the Isle of Wight, and they both returned home. I told Maria I should write to you directly I reached London, who is very anxious to hear from you, fearing some strange reason is the cause of your not writing. She requested that you would enclose Mr. Peter's letters in one of your own, should he write to you, that we may know better how to act. She is now mine, and I should wish to study her comfort as well as my own. Let us know all respecting Mr. Peter, and if you can possibly write by return of post, and direct for W. M. C. t the above inn. Maria wished me to give to Nancy a kiss for her little boy, hoping every possible care is taken of him; and tell your wife to let Nancy have any of Maria's clothes she thinks proper, for she say she have got so many, they will only spoil, and make use of any she like herself. In her letter she said a great deal respecting little Henry, who she feel anxious to hear about, and will take him to herself as soon as we can get a farm whereby we can gain a livelihood, which I shall do the first I can meet with worth notice; for living without some business is very expensive. Still, provisions are very reasonable on the Isle of Wight, I think cheaper than any part of England. Thank God! we are both well, hoping this will find all you the same. We have both been a great deal on the water, and have had some good sea-sicknesses, which I consider have been very useful to us both. My cough I have lost entirely, which is a great consolation. In real truth, I feel better than I ever did before in my life, only in this short time. Maria told you in her letter how ill I was for two days at Portsmouth, which is seven miles over the water to the Isle of Wight, making altogether 139 miles from Polstead. I would say more, but time will not permit. Therefore, Maria unites with me for your welfare; and may every blessing attend you! Mind you direct for W. M. C. at the Bull Inn, Leadenhall-street, London. Write to-morrow if you can: if not, write soon enough for Saturday's post, that I may get it on Sunday morning, when I shall return to Maria directly I receive it. Enclose Mr. Peter's letters, and let us know whether he has acknowledged little Henry. You must try and read my scribble but I fear you will never make it out.—I remain your well-wisher, W. C."

" I think you had better burn all letters, after taking all directions, that nobody may form the least idea of our residence. Adieu.

" For Thomas Marten, Polstead, near Stoke by Nayland, Suffolk.

" With speed."

" THOMAS MARTEN, *London, May* 23, 1827.

" I received your letter this morning, which reached London yesterday, but letters are not delivered out here on a Sunday: that I discovered on making inquiry yesterday. However, I could not get through my business before this afternoon, and I am going to Portsmouth by this night's coach. I have this day been to the General Post Office, making inquiry about the letter Maria wrote you on the 30th of September, which you say never came to your hands. The clerk of the Office traced the books back to the day it was wrote, and he said, a letter, directed as I told him to you, never came through their Office, which I think is very strange. However, I am determined to find out how it was lost, if possible, but I must think coming over the water to Portsmouth, which I will inquire about to-morrow, when I hope to find out the mystery. It is, I think, very odd that letters should be lost in this strange way. Was it not for the discovery of our residence, I would certainly indict the Post-office, but I cannot do that without making our appearance at a court-martial, which would be very unpleasant to us both. You wish for us to come to Polstead, which we should be very happy to do, but you are not aware of the danger. You may depend, if ever we fall into Mr. P--'s hands, the consequence would prove fatal; therefore, should he write to you, or should he come to Polstead, you must tell him you have not the least knowledge of us, but you think we are gone into some foreign part. I think, if you don't hear from him before long, you had better write and tell him you cannot support the child without some assistance, for we are gone you know not where. If you tell him you hear from us, he will force you to say where we was, therefore I think it will be best not to acknowledge any thing at all. I enclose 1*l.*, and you shall hear from us again in a short time. This will not reach you before Wednesday morning, as I am too late for this night's post. You said your wife did not like to take any of Maria's clothes; she said in her last letter, that her old clothes was at their service—I mean your wife and Nancy; but she shall write again as soon as possible. I must now bid you adieu. The coach will start in about ten minutes. I have been so much employed all this day, that I could not write before. Believe me to be your well-wisher for your future welfare,

" For Thomas Marten, Polstead, near Colchester. W. M. C."

" (Post paid.)"

Peter Matthews, Esq.—I generally reside in London. I have relations in the neighbourhood of Polstead. I know the prisoner, and I knew Maria Marten. I had known Maria for some length of time before last year. I had last seen her, I believe, on the 31st of August, 1826. In July last year, I was at Polstead. I saw Corder there twice, and once again on the morning of my leaving Polstead. I had a conversation with him respecting a note I had lost. It was a 5*l*. Bank of England note. I put a variety of questions first of all respecting a note and a letter He said he knew nothing of them. I told him it was a letter of the 3d of January, 1827, in which I told him a 5*l*. note was enclosed. I have a letter I received from the prisoner in August. [Letter produced.] I believe this to be his hand-writing.

Wm. Gardner recalled.—[Letter shown to him.]—I believe this to be the prisoner's hand-writing. [Letter read.]

                                                              "*August* 1, 1827.

"Sir,—After a long, restless, and wretched night of miserable reflections, I have at last endeavoured to collect my weary spirits, in order to fulfil your request ——."

When the letter had been read thus far, Mr. Brodrick interposed, and submitted that it did not relate to the subject-matter of this inquiry; to which the Chief Baron assented, and the letter was put by.

Mr. *Matthews* recalled.—I received this letter from the prisoner. [Letter read.]

                                         "*Sunday Afternoon, August* 26, 1827.

"Sir,—In reply to your generous letter, which reached me yesterday, I beg to inform you that I was indeed innocent of Maria Marten's residence, at the time you requested me to forward the letter I took from Bramford, and will candidly confess that Maria has been with a distant female relation of mine since the month of May. About five weeks ago, they both went into Norfolk to visit some of my friends. On Friday week I received a letter from my kindred, who informed me that Maria was somewhat indisposed, and that they were then in a village called Herlingby, near Yarmouth. I returned an answer by the next post, and enclosed your letter for Maria, which I found reached her perfectly safe, as I took the Yarmouth coach last Wednesday, from Ipswich Lamb-fair, and went to Herlingby, when I was sorry to hear that Maria's indisposition was occasioned by a sore gathering on the back of her hand, which caused her great pain, and which prevented her from writing to you, as her fingers are at present immoveable. Knowing you would be anxious to hear from her, I particularly wished her to write the moment she found herself able, which she promised very faithfully to do. I gave her a particular account of our dialogue at Polstead Hall, not forgetting the remarkable kindness I experienced from you, which I shall ever most gratefully acknowledge; and likewise return you my most grateful thanks for your kindness, in respect to your enterprise on my account, when in London. I remain, Sir, your most obedient, and very humble Servant,

                                                              W. CORDER.

P. S. I have already enclosed your letter for Maria, in one of my own, which I shall post with this immediately, and beg permission to add, that I have fully determined to make Maria my bride directly I can settle our family affairs, which will be in about a month or six weeks' time. Till that time, Maria wishes to continue with my kindred. In concluding, if I can at any time render you any service whatsoever, I shall be most happy to oblige, as I am truly sensible of your generosity.

"For Peter Matthews, Binfield, near Wokingham, Berkshire."

Mr. *Matthews'* examination continued.—Was Maria Marten in any way concerned with the five pound note?

Mr. Brodrick interposed, and the Chief Baron thought it was rather straining the case, and the subject was dropped.

On the 31st of July, last year, the prisoner stated to me, that Maria Marten was living somewhere in the neighbourhood of Yarmouth. Her name was then chiefly connected with the five pound note. I left Polstead on the 9th of August last; Corder on that morning told me, he had received a letter from me to Maria Marten. He said he could not tell how to forward it by post. He did not know what direction to put upon it. I told him I was afraid he was deceiving me and I must insist upon his forwarding it. He replied, he would endeavour to do so; but repeated that he could not tell exactly where she was, but he believed it was in the neighbourhood of Yarmouth. On the 19th of November following, I met him accidentally near Somerset House. I asked if he had forwarded a letter of mine written to Maria Marten, and forwarded to him in one on the 2d of September. He said he had. I told him I was surprised at not receiving any letter, or any answer at all from the young woman. He told me either that he had written an answer to me, or that he thought he had written an answer. I said, the only letter I had received from him, was that of the 26th of August (the letter just read). I asked the prisoner where Maria Marten then was? He said, he had left her in the Isle of Wight. I told him that her father had written to me once or twice respecting her, and that he was uneasy, not knowing where she was. I inquired of him if he was married to her? He said, "No;" he had not yet settled his family affairs. He had before assigned that as a reason for not having married her. I can state positively that this was on the 19th of November last.

James Lea.—I am a police officer of Lambeth-street. On the 22d of last April, I went to Grove-house, Ealing, about 10 o'clock in the morning. As I entered, he came into the hall, out of the parlour. I told him I had a little business with him Prisoner said, "Walk into the drawing-room," and we went in. I then told him I was as officer from London, and was come to apprehend him on a very serious charge, and he must consider himself my prisoner. He replied, "Very well." I told him the charge was respecting a young woman of the name of Maria Marten, whom he had formerly kept company with. I said, she had been missing for a length of time, and strong suspicions were attached to him. I continued, "I believe you know such a person? It was a young woman you kept company with in Suffolk." He said no; he did not know such a person. I asked him, "Did you never know such a person?" He said, No; I must have made a mistake; he was not the person I wanted. I said, "No: I have not made a mistake—your name is Corder;" and I am certain he was the person. I told him to recollect himself; I had asked him twice if he knew such a person, and I would ask him a third time. He still said, No, he did not; he never knew such a person. I then proceeded to search his person, and took from his pocket a bunch of keys. I then took him to the Red Lion at Brentford. On our way thither, I said, the body of the young woman had been found in his Red Barn. He made no remark then. We proceeded some distance, and he asked me, "When was the young woman found?" I told him, "On Saturday morning last." He made no further reply. I then left him at the Red Lion, and returned to his house. When I entered, Mrs. Corder showed me up stairs into a dressing-room. I opened two writing-desks with two of the keys he had given to me.

Mr. *Brodrick* objected that the mere circumstance of the prisoner having given the witness a bunch of keys, which opened some drawers, did not warrant the reception of evidence as to any property found in the house.

Mr. *Andrews* replied he would obviate the difficulty.

Examination continued.—I had some conversation with the prisoner respecting some pistols I had found in the house. As we were coming to Bury gaol, he said (to the best of my recollection) that he would make me a present of them.

The pistols, in a black velvet bag, were then produced, but immediately put by.

I don't recollect that any thing had previously passed about the pistols. He told me he had bought them when he was ten years of age, at Ipswich. This was when I was bringing him to Bury gaol, at Polstead. I had then been examined before the Coroner, and my deposition was reduced to writing. I took the prisoner to hear the depositions read over to him, and mine was amongst the number. I found, in the dressing-room at the house at Ealing, a pair of pistols. They were hanging in a black bag on a nail.

Mr. *Andrews* again called for the production of the pistols.

Mr. *Brodrick* objected, that it did not appear that the pistols were the prisoner's, or found in his house; for *non constat* that the house was the house of the prisoner, there being other persons.

By the *Judge*.—They were in my room all the time the prisoner was there.

The *Chief Baron*.—I think I should be straining the point very far. I rejected this evidence.

The pistols were then produced.

Examination resumed.—On the 30th of April, I found a sword there, which I had previously taken from the nail on which it hung when I was formerly at the house

Robert Offord.—I am a cutler, residing at Hadleigh, in this county. Last year the prisoner called at my house : this was in the latter part of March, or beginning of April, 1827. He brought a small sword, and said, " Mr. Offord, I have brought a small sword, which I wish to have ground as sharp as a carving-knife, for the use of a carving-knife." He wished to have it done, and he would call for it that night. He said he had got a cousin about marrying in about a fortnight. I think I should know it again.

Lea was then recalled, and produced the sword found in the house in which he had taken the prisoner. It was in a trunk in the dressing-room.

Offord recalled.—Identified the sword as the one he had sharpened for Corder.

It was about two feet in length, crescent-shaped, and perfectly bright.

Offord's examination continued.—I ground it up quite sharp. It took a good deal of labour to sharpen it up bright. The prisoner took it home the same evening.

Cross-examined.—I will not swear that this was not before Christmas 1826. I don't keep a job-book, and speak only from recollection. I was working by candle-light; and so I do at Christmas time.

Re-examined.—There are two or three stains which are now on the front and the side, which were not on it when I delivered it to the prisoner. There are two or three scratches on it. There is a spot or two on it at the back, and some elsewhere near the point. I can't say if they were on it when I gave it back to Corder.

George Gardner (looks at the sword).—I have seen one like this in Mrs. Corder's house.

Cross-examined.—There was an alarm that Mrs. Corder's house was about to be robbed, in the spring of 1827. I sat up all night, and this was in the house. There had been robberies in the place about the time, and the people armed for their protection.

John Baalham.—I am the constable of Polstead. I knew the prisoner and Maria Marten. I never had a warrant to apprehend her. I never told the prisoner that I had a warrant to apprehend her, or that I had a letter from Mr. Whitmore to apprehend her. The clothes which were on the body where given to me at the Inquest I have had them ever since.

Cross-examined.—I had heard it reported in the place, that Maria Marten would be taken up for having bastard children. I have known prisoner all his life, and never knew him out of temper.

Henry Harcourt.—I am a gun-maker at Sudbury, and know the prisoner. In February, 1827, he came and brought me a pair of pistols to be repaired. I don't know if these (those which Lea produced) be they. They were percussion pistols, and so are these. Percussion pistols have been invented about seven or eight years.

Cross-examined.—The prisoner and a young woman took them away. I did not know her. They called for them on the 5th of March.

Thomas Acres.—I lived some time at Polstead. I recollect Stoke fair in 1827. I know the Red Barn at Polstead, and the thistley lay there. I never went over that field with a pickaxe on my shoulder.

Cross-examined.—I don't know what I was doing at the time of Stoke fair. I don't know that I worked with a pickaxe at all that year. I wore a velveteen jacket, and so did the prisoner.

John Lawton.—I am a surgeon. I was present when the Coroner's jury went to view the body found in the Red Barn on the 20th of April. It had not been disturbed, except that the earth had been removed from the top of it. It lay in the hole in the Barn in which it had been buried. It was in the right hand bay of the Barn. It was, in parts, much decomposed—parts more than others. From my examination of the body, I should have said it had been in the ground nine or ten months or more, had I known nothing of it. The stays, flannel petticoat, shift, a handkerchief round the neck, stockings and garters, and high shoes, with portions of a Leghorn bonnet trimmed with black. [Produces a silk handkerchief.] This was found underneath her hips. This is the handkerchief I took off the neck.

The rest of the articles he mentioned, the witness produced; they were nearly indistinguishable as to material or form of article.

There was part of the sleeve of a blue coat, and the body was in part of a sack. The right hand was on the right breast. She was quite crowded down close together. It was a female body, a full-grown young woman. I examined the face. It was in a very bad state, but there was an appearance of blood about it, particularly on the right side of it. I found the green striped handkerchief round her neck. It was tied in the usual way, but drawn extremely tight, so as to form a complete groove round the neck It was apparently done for the purpose, as if it had been pulled so by some person. It was sufficiently tight, that I should say, it would have killed ary one. It would have produced strangulation. The hand might pass between the interior and exterior folds of the handkerchief. There was in the neck an appearance of a stab, about an inch and a half in length; it was perpendicular. It extended deep into the neck. I cannot say what parts particularly were injured by it, the body was so putrid. There was a wen on the neck, about the middle of the neck, in front. There was the appearance of an injury having been done to the right eye, and the right side of the face. It appeared as if something had passed into the eye, deep into the orbit, injuring the bone and the nose. I think it was done in two ways; by something passing in at the left cheek, and then out at the right orbit; and there was a stab also It appeared as if a ball had passed through the left cheek, removing the two last grinders. The brain was in such a state that it was impossible to make any thing out of it. I don't think a ball so passing through would, of itself, cause death; but with the strangulation, and the stab in the neck, would have been sufficient, with the ball, to produce death. The bone dividing the nostrils was quite broken, and driven quite out of its place, apparently by the ball which had passed through. I opened the chest, but did not discover any myself. There was an adhesion of the lungs to the membrane which lines the ribs on the right side. This would, in life, cause inflammation; and she would have complained of cough with pain in the side. I f and two small pieces of bone in the throat, which might have fallen through during the progress of decomposition. They were parts of the interior of the nose, as I should think. The left hand was separated from the body; it had the appearance of a skeleton hand, and would have been produced by decomposition. I should think that the injuries, without the handkerchief, would not have caused death; possibly they might from inflammation. I have since seen the heart and the ribs. I have myself a portion of the head. The ribs and the heart were brought by Mr. Nairn, a surgeon, to my house. I then saw where something had penetrated between the fifth and sixth ribs, and there was a stab in the heart which corresponded with the opening in the ribs. It appeared to have been done with a sharp instrument. That injury would have been sufficient alone to produce death. I found a corresponding mark on the shift; the opening in the shift corresponded in size with that of the ribs. I saw no mark on the stays; they were too much decomposed to have seen the opening on them if there had formerly been one.

have looked at the sword which has been produced, which appears to fit the wound through the ribs and the opening in the shift. I penetrated two or three inches. It passed down the wound to that extent. I found one part of the wound wide, and the other narrow, so as to correspond with the sword. The ribs were in a very tolerable state of preservation. It appeared as if the wound in the heart had been made by an instrument like this sword. I fitted it also into a wound in the spheroidal sinus. It penetrated into it about an inch. I have examined the wound in the head with a bullet.

On inquiry it turned out that no bullet had been found in the barn; but the one spoken of was found in the black reticule containing the wig.

The bullet fitted the hole. I think the ball was first fired before the stab. I saw some blood on the shift, the stays, the handkerchief round the neck, the lawn handkerchief, and the silk handkerchief, and apparently on the bonnet. I don't recollect any part of a shawl. I took off the garters; they were made of narrow white tape. In taking hold of one of the shoes, the foot came off. The lower and upper jaw had each a tooth out; but cannot say on which side; the one on the right, I think, had been out a long time. I am able to distinguish between the cavity of a tooth extracted while living, and that of one falling out by decay. I have the head here. (Jaw produced.) This is the jaw, and there are now two teeth gone: the one on the left, I think, has fallen out since death; the other has been out much longer.

Cross-examined.—I am thirty, in October. I have practised twelve months for myself. I was six years with Mudd, of Gedding. I have never seen a body dissected which had been buried nine or ten months. I did not perceive the stab in the ribs, or the pistol-bullet in the Barn,—this was because I could not then clean the bones sufficiently to examine so minutely. There was flesh on the face, but greatly decomposed. In a wound made during life the edges gape open: one made after death, gapes very little. I opened the chest and the abdomen in the Barn; when I opened the chest, I made myself one wound in the heart. I am positive this was not the wound I have spoken of. The one I made was in the right ventricle, upper part of

it, the other was just at the apex of the heart between the right and left ventricle.
I saw no injury other than I have spoken of. none made by a spade. The weight
of the body might have tightened the handkerchief round the neck in that way, if it
had been raised up by the handkerchief after death. I took the shirt from the body,
but saw no mark in the shift at that time. I did not look for it till I had discovered
the wound in the heart. The ribs, when brought to me, had the skin on. I should
have made the observations I did, with respect to the body, if it had been taken from
a grave in the churchyard. My judgment is formed from my own observations
unmixed with what I have heard since. I can speak with certainty that the ball
came out at the eye, from the manner in which the bones are driven; the bones are
very much shattered. At the Barn, I did not with certainty know whether this had
been done by a pistol-bullet, or was the effect of decomposition.

Re-examined.—I have seen the dissection of dead bodies for fifteen years. I could
distinguish between a wound inflicted on digging up the body, and one given many
months before. I believe that none of the wounds that I saw were done at the
digging up of the body. I did not very particularly examine the hips when the body
was taken up. The groove round the neck, produced by the handkerchief, could
not have been produced by the lifting up of the body by the external fold of the hand
kerchief at the discovery of the body. It might have been produced by the lifting it
up in that manner just as the person was dying. From the appearance, this must have
been occasioned at the period of the death of the person. After cleaning the bones
I could see the injury done to them better than could befo   I have no doubt it
was done by a bullet at some time or other.

Mr. *Andrews* then proposed to call another medical witness, in order
to corroborate the testimony of the preceding one.

The *Lord Chief Baron* asked the learned Counsel, whether, after
the fatigue which they had all undergone during the day, he would proceed any further that night. He should conceive that the witness whom
the learned gentleman had called would not be the only witness whom he
would have occasion to call in support of his case.

Mr. *Andrews* replied, that he certainly had other medical witnesses to
call in confirmation of his case, and not only medical witnesses, but such
others as were necessary to identify the different articles found on the
body discovered in the Barn, as articles of dress belonging to Maria
Marten.

The *Lord Chief Baron* said, that as that was the case, he thought
the hour had now arrived at which it would be expedient to adjourn
the Court. It was quite evident the case could not finish that night.
There were several witnesses, it appeared, to be examined on the part
of the prosecution; and after that there was, if he was rightly informed
(but of that he knew nothing), a defence of considerable length to be
delivered by the prisoner. After that it would be his duty to charge
the Jury; and, to say nothing of other inconveniences to public
justice, he must observe, that at the end of that time, he himself should
scarcely be in a condition to make those remarks on the evidence which
would naturally be expected from him. In a civil case, he might perhaps have been inclined to have proceeded with the trial to-night; but
in a case of such solemn importance to the prisoner at the bar, and of
such great importance to the public in general, he could not presume
to enter upon an analysis of the evidence, when they must all of them
be so extremely fatigued. Under these circumstances he thought
that they must adjourn till the following morning.

It was of course determined that this adjournment should take place.
The crier then proceeded to swear in the different officers of the High
Sheriff, each of whom had to remain during the night in attendance
upon a juror, to prevent all communication (except among themselves)
on the subject of the trial, when one of these officers refused to wait

all night upon anybody. The crier immediately asked him whether he was not a hired officer of the High Sheriff, and whether he was not acting under his authority. The man, not at the moment aware of the force of his answer, did not hesitate to reply in the affirmative; whereupon the crier informed him he had no choice;—he must take the oath, or else submit to such fine as the Court, when informed of his conduct, might think proper to impose upon him. The officer instantly submitted, and was sworn.

The prisoner, who had during the early part of the day maintained an air of indifference to his awful situation, there being generally a smile playing upon his features, although his eye had a heavy fixedness, occasionally convulsed with a sudden movement, betraying, with a character not to be mistaken, the emotion under which he laboured during the delivery of particular passages in the evidence, seemed to have lost a considerable part of his confidence towards the close of the day. Much of this alteration may, perhaps, be attributable to the fatigue incident to his situation. The fact of the alteration was, however, too apparent to escape observation. His attention was intensely directed towards the surgeon during the whole of his examination.

The adjournment took place at half-past 6 o'clock in the evening.

The anxiety of the crowd outside during the day was almost unexampled. There were few ladies within the Court, the risk of the tremendous rush being perilous enough for the other sex, but the external stone basement of the windows, particularly that behind the Judge, was filled by ladies, whose curiosity throughout the day was not damped by the heavy showers of a thunder-storm which fell in rapid succession, and pattered upon their umbrellas with a sound which once or twice interrupted the business of the Court. Several of the windows were broken by the pressure of the throng.

Corder was carried to Court between the Governor of the prison and a single attendant, in a sort of taxed-cart, out of which the prisoner jumped with great alacrity. There were some hisses from the crowd, but he was in a moment removed from their presence. It was remarked in the Court during the day, that he constantly used a small penknife, which he took from his waistcoat pocket, to mend his pencil while taking notes.

Second Day, Friday, August 8th, 1828.

The arrangements of this morning, for the admission of the public, were very well managed, and the active interposition of the Governor of the prison (Mr. Orridge) had the best effect in keeping the officers of the High Sheriff in their proper places, and preserving the avenues of the Court from the pressure of that vast assemblage which yesterday poured in when the doors were opened, with a force so tremendous as to risk the limbs of those who were not sufficiently athletic for active personal resistance. We understand that the Lord Chief Baron, who was himself carried off his legs in endeavouring to pass from his carriage to the door of the Shire-hall, has disavowed having given any such directions as were imputed to him yesterday, and which necessarily led to a scene of confusion and uproar exceeding anything hitherto observed in trials of this nature. At all events, every reasonable accommodation was this day afforded the public; and the consequence was, a befitting regularity in conducting the proceedings of the Court, and the presence of a number of ladies, whose curiosity (yesterday disappointed) was this day gratified by hearing the close of the trial.

At a quarter before nine o'clock, Corder was put to the bar. He was dressed the same as yesterday. On inquiry, it is understood his age is not 40, but about 30 or 32. He rose early in the prison, and was, during the whole of the morning, before he was brought to Court, engaged in introducing some alterations in his written defence, which were suggested to him late last night by his Counsel. His manner was collected, his complexion fresh, and he looked around him at times with seeming cheerfulness. He was not, however, so entirely at his ease as he appeared to be early on the previous day; his head was not so erect, and he repeatedly heaved deep sighs. Immediately on being put to the bar, he put on his spectacles, folded his arms, and displayed an oscillating and swinging motion of his body, while he leaned his back against the pillar of the dock. He hung down his head frequently during the examination of the witnesses.

During the re-examination of Mr. Lawton, the surgeon, this morning, who produced the skull of the deceased, which was handed from the Counsel to the Jury, and exhibited so as to be observable in its fractured condition to the whole Court, the prisoner, who had just taken off his spectacles, replaced them, and beheld attentively this painful spectacle; he inclined his body forward so as to command a full view of the skull; but, as if the effort to sustain this attitude, and evince this expression, had become too great for his nerves, he suddenly flung his back against the pillar, hastily drew off his spectacles, and evidently laboured under the strongest emotion. In a few minutes, however, he rallied, replaced his glasses, took out his pocket-book, and quickly wrote a memorandum to his leading Counsel (Mr. Brodrick), who at once wrote a reply, which the prisoner read with close attention, and on the signification of a movement from the learned Counsel, tore it into the smallest fragments. His solicitor, at the same time, went to the front of the dock, and had a long consultation with him.

At nine o'clock precisely, the Lord Chief Baron took his seat, and hoped the Jury had been as comfortably situated last night as was practicable.

The Jury replied in the affirmative, and after their names were called over, the examination of witnesses was resumed.

John Charles Nairn, examined by Mr. Andrews.—I have been a surgeon upwards of a year, and in the profession upwards of twelve years. On the 19th of last May, I attended with Mr. Chaplin at Polstead: Baalham, the constable, was present. He disinterred a body in my presence. I examined the cavities of the chest of the body so disinterred.

Mr. *Brodrick* wished the identity of the body to be proved before the witness was examined respecting it.

Baalham was then called.—I am parish clerk of Polstead, and screwed down the body found in the Red Barn into the coffin. The same coffin was afterwards disinterred by witness, and contained the same body.

Cross-examined.—I was not present when the body was buried, but am sure it was the same body.

Mr. *Nairn* recalled.—I found the internal parts of the chest in perfect preservation; so much so, that the slightest injury penetrating into it might have been observed. The heart was lying divested of its developing membrane. I discovered a large wound in the back part of the right ventricle. I could not tell if it appeared to be a recent wound. I formed an opinion on it on my first examination, but I subsequently examined it, and I then formed an opinion that it was a recent wound. I detached the heart from its connexion with the blood-vessels. I next examined the external surface of the ribs, and in the space between the fifth and sixth ribs I discovered a wound, about three-quarters of an inch broad. My opinion was, that it was a wound of long duration, and not a recent one. I again examined the heart when I returned home, and discovered a slight wound, about two inches from the apex, corresponding with the external wound between the ribs. It appeared to have been inflicted by some sharp instrument. [Lea, the officer, produced the sword.] This sword is the most likely instrument to have inflicted such a wound. Supposing this wound to have been inflicted upon a living body, it would, in my opinion, most certainly have produced death. I have since inspected the head of the disinterred body. I have applied this sword to the wound between the ribs, and it corresponds with the wound to the extent of two or three inches. There are, on the sword, some marks of discolouration, about the extent of two or three inches. I examined the wound in the heart, having this sword with me; it might certainly have been made by this sword. On examining the head, I traced the progress of a ball entering into the interior and back part of the upper left jaw, and proceeding to the internal angle of the right eye. From the size of the opening, I should conclude it to have been a small pistol ball. This wound might have caused death, but the person might have survived it. I also found a fissure, opening into the sphenoidal sinus, corresponding with the vertebræ. It was an opening produced by some sharp-pointed instrument; any sharp-pointed instrument would have produced it. It extended about a quarter of an inch into the sphenoidal sinus. I am not aware of any other wound on the head. The wound in the sphenoidal sinus might have occasioned death. The sword corresponds with it.

Cross-examined by Mr. *Brodrick*.—This was on the 19th of May, about a month after the finding of the body in the Barn. The disinterment of the body, exposure to the air, and lying on the ground, in another month, would not have caused, in such a body, much additional decomposition. I found the heart divested of the pericardium. Looki g merely at the heart, and knowing nothing of the circumstances I have heard since, I should say that the wound in the right ventricle of the heart was a recent one. I should have been of opinion, independent of anything but the inspection of the heart itself, that one was a recent, and the other a more ancient one, because the smaller wound of the two had gaping edges. From the nature of the wound, I should judge that it had not been inflicted when the pericardium was removed. The apex of the living heart touches the ribs. There are cartilages connecting the ribs with the sternum, and with each other. The bones of the head were not in a state of the least decomposition. The only parts which were out of their places were those where the wounds had been inflicted by the bullet. I first saw the head after the exhumation of the body. It was shown to me by Mr. Lawton, and I don't know, of my own knowledge, that it was the head of the body found in the barn. A knife would have inflicted the wound on the heart.

Re-examined.—The wound was broader at that part of the ribs adjoining the sternum.

Mr. *Lawton*, the surgeon, recalled.—The head I showed to Mr. Nairn, was that belonging to the body found in the Red Barn. I assisted in removing the body from its grave in the Barn, and took off the head myself. I gave it to Baalham the same afternoon; a day or two afterwards he returned it. It was the same head as the one I took from the body.

Baalham recalled.—The head which Mr. Lawton delivered to me was the same which I returned to him.

Henry Robert Chaplin, examined by Mr. Kelly.—I have been practising as a surgeon for four years. I saw the disinterred body in company with Mr. Nairn I found the chest in good preservation. There was a wound in the right ventricle, which was first discovered. That wound appeared to be a recently inflicted wound. I afterwards found another wound on the heart, but whether of recent infliction or not, I cannot tell from its appearance. I found a transverse wound situate between the fifth and sixth ribs, which appeared to have been inflicted by a weapon which had a broad back and a sharp edge. I did not see the sword fitted with it. The wound in the heart appeared to be a continuation of that between the ribs. The wound in the heart might have been inflicted in stripping the pericardium from the heart; but if the wound be a continuation of that between the ribs, it could not have been inflicted in stripping the pericardium from the heart. This is deemed a mortal wound; but whether it would have produced death or not, I do not know. I inspected the head in the possession and presence of Mr Lawton. A bullet appeared to have traversed it. I cannot say if it entered by the orbit, or made its exit from it. .t could not have been produced by decomposition. I should think it would not have been a mortal wound with certainty. There was also a thrust in the eye, which was inflicted by a sharp instrument with a broad back, and might have been the same which inflicted that on the heart.

Cross-examined.—The wound on the sphenoidal sinus might have been inflicted by a sharp-pointed instrument. It was about the eighth part of an inch. If the wound in the heart had been inflicted on a living subject, it would have occasioned a great effusion of blood, unless syncope instantly took place. From the shock given to the system, there might have been no effusion of blood. It is impossible to say whether the bullet made its entry into, or its exit from, the eye.

Mr. *Lawton* re-called, produced the head; and with the sword and the head explained to the Jury the nature of the wound on the sphenoidal sinus, and the reasons for supposing it to have been inflicted by the sword. It appeared that the sword entered by the sphenoidal sinus, traversed the mouth at the back part of the nose, and made its exit by the right eye. The sword, being applied to the supposed course of the instrument, was found to agree with the conjectured progress of the sword causing the wound. Being applied to the other eye, it was found to be impracticable to trace any opening from thence into the spenoidal sinus.

Mr. *Lawton* re-examined.—There is a tooth out on each side of the upper jaw, and one out of the lower jaw. One of the upper jaw teeth had apparently dropped out; the other, and the lower tooth, must, from their cavities, have been out for a length of time.

Mr. *Matthews* recalled.—Maria Marten had an enlargement on the centre front, which had the appearance of a wen.

Mrs. *Marten*, the mother, recalled. (Looks at the articles of dress found on the body taken from the Red Barn.)—These are Maria's combs. I saw her with them on her head on the 18th of last May twelve months. These are the earrings she had in her ears at the same time: they are both of them hers. This is the handkerchief (a silk one) she had round her neck the same day: this, also (the green one), was one she had on at the same time; this was next her throat, and the silk one over it. This is a piece of a Leghorn hat: she had on a Leghorn hat when I saw her last, trimmed with black ribbon like this, the edges of which are the same. These are the shoes she had on. This is the ashen busk in her stays. This is part of a pair of stays. This is the sleeve of a chemise, the make of which is the same as that she had on the 18th of May, 1827, when she went to the Red Barn.

This witness was so overpowered, either by her feelings, by the effluvia of the rags, or by the heat of the Court, that she was with difficulty preserved from fainting by the restoratives given her at the close of her examination.

Lea, the officer, produced the velvet bag.

The *Chief Baron*.—I don't think it is sufficiently traced to come from any place proved to belong to the prisoner.

Mr. *Andrews*.—The prisoner was apprehended in the house in which his sword was, and in which was a desk, which opened by a key he himself gave to the officer; and in the same room was found this bag

The *Chief Baron*.—I think you had better not press it.

Ann Marten, the sister of Maria, recalled.—This green handkerchief is the same that my sister went away with. This silk handkerchief she also had on at the same time. These are the same shoes. This is part of the Leghorn bonnet, trimmed with black ribbon. This is a piece of the bonnet she had in the bag when she went out; she had a man's hat on her head. These are like the combs she had in her hair at the same time. She had on a pair of earrings; and these are such ones as my sister went away with in her ears.

Mr. *Andrews* stated to the Court, that there was found in the desk, opened with the key given by the prisoner to Lea, letters directed to Corder, and also a passport for France for Corder.

The *Chief Baron* thought it safer not to receive evidence of this, especially as, in a case of this nature, all doubtful points ought, from the importance of the trial to the prisoner, to be decided in his favour

The prisoner here bowed his gratitude to his Lordship.

Marten, the father, recalled.—The soil in the Barn is a dryish, little gravelly, and stony soil.

Mrs. *Marten*, recalled, proved that her daughter wore white narrow tape garters.

Mr. *Matthews* proved that Maria Marten was able to write very well.

This was the case on the part of the prosecution.

The prisoner, being called on for his defence, advanced to the front of the bar, took out some papers, and read nearly as follows, with a very tremulous voice :—

I am informed that by the law of England, the Counsel for a prisoner is not allowed to address the Jury, though the Counsel for the Crown is allowed that privilege. While I deplore, as much as any human being can, the fatal event which has caused this inquiry, let me entreat you to dismiss from your minds the publications of the public press, from the time of its first promulgation to this hour; let me entreat you, let me dissuade you, if I can, from being influenced by the horrid and disgusting details which have for months issued from the public press—a powerful engine for fixing the opinions of large classes of the community, but which is, too often, I fear, though unintentionally, the cause of affixing slander upon innocence. I have been described as a monster, who, while meditating becoming the husband of this girl, to whom I was evincing an affectionate attachment, was actually premeditating and plotting the perpetration of this horrid crime. With such misrepresentations it was natural, perhaps, to expect that an unfavourable impression should have been created against me, and the more so when the accusation went beyond the present case, and was connected with other crimes well calculated to excite prejudice against me. It is natural you should come to this trial with feelings of prejudice; but as you expect peace and serenity of mind at home, I implore you to banish from your minds all the horrible accusations which have been promulgated, and give your verdict on the evidence alone. Consider, gentlemen, that the attorney for the prosecution is also the Coroner before whom the Inquest was taken; and his conduct, in refusing my being present at the inquest, is conduct which you cannot approve. Since my committal, the Coroner has been again at Polstead,—has got up additional evidence. My solicitor pressed for a copy of the depositions, which was refused. In consequence of these unjust proceedings, I never heard one of the witnesses examined, and cannot, therefore, have come prepared as I ought to be. The Coroner, thus acting in his double capacity, was likely enough, when meditating to act as attorney for the prosecution, to have entertained impressions inconsistent with the fit discharge of his inquisitorial inquiry; and again, as attorney for the prosecution, he was liable to be diverted from the fulfilment of his duties as Coroner; so that I was, in this respect, on the threshold of inquiry, exposed to disadvantages from which I ought to have been saved. This, however, was not all: my solicitor remonstrated; he was not only refused copies of the depositions, but the attorney for the prosecution, without any notice to me, has visited Polstead, and taken examinations upon oath, of the different witnesses, and come to this trial prepared with evidence taken behind my back, and pruned down to suit the exaggerations of this case. I therefore am brought to be tried for my life, without any fair knowledge of the evidence against me. In consequence of this unjust proceeding on the part of the Coroner, how can I controvert, as I might have done were I allowed to hear the witnesses, equivocal facts and highly coloured statements, of which I am for the first time informed when brought to trial for my life? Were witnesses to be privately examined, and their evidence clandestinely obtained? It has been well observed, that truth is sometimes stronger than fiction. Never was this assertion better exemplified than in this hapless instance. In a few short months I have been deprived of all my brothers, and my father recently before that period. I have heard the evidence, and am free to say, that, unexplained, it may cause great suspicion; but you will allow me to explain it.

Proceeding, my Lord and Gentlemen, to the real facts of this case, I admit that there is evidence calculated to excite suspicion; but these facts are capable of explanation; and convinced as I am of my entire innocence, I have to entreat you to listen to my true and simple detail of the real facts of the death of this unfortunate woman. I was myself so stupified and overwhelmed with the strange and disastrous circumstance, and on that account so unhappily driven to the necessity of immediate decision, that I acted with fear instead of judgment, and I did that which any innocent man might have done under such unhappy circumstances. I concealed the appalling occurrence, and was, as is the misfortune of such errors, subsequently driven to sustain the first falsehoods by others, and to persevere in a system of delusion, which furnished the facts concealed for a long time. At first I gave a false account of the death of the unfortunate Maria. I am now resolved to disclose the truth, regardless of the consequences. To conceal her pregnancy from my mother, I took lodgings at Sudbury: she was delivered of a male child, which died in a fortnight, in the arms of Mrs. Marten, although the newspapers have so perverted that fact; and it was agreed between Mrs. Marten, Maria, and me, that the child should be buried in the fields. There was a pair of small pistols in the bedroom; Maria knew they were there. I had often showed them to her. Maria took them away from me. I had some reason to suspect she had some correspondence with a gentleman, by whom she had a child, in London. Though her conduct was not free from blemish, I at length yielded to her entreaties, and agreed to marry her: and it was arranged we should go to Ipswich, and procure a licence and marry. Whether I said there was a warrant out against her, I know not. It has been proved that we had many words, and that she was crying when she left the house. Gentlemen, this was the origin of the fatal occurrence. I gently rebuked her; we reached the Barn: while changing her dress, she flew into a passion, upbraiding me with not having so much regard for her as the gentleman before alluded to. Feeling myself in this manner so much insulted and irritated, when I was about to perform every kindness and reparation, I said, " Maria, if you go on in this way before marriage, what have I to expect after? I shall, therefore, stop when I can; I will return straight home, and you can do what you like, and act just as you think proper." I said I would not marry her. In consequence of this, I retired from her, when I immediately heard the report of a gun or pistol, and, running back, I found the unhappy girl weltering on the ground. Recovering from my stupor, I thought to have left the spot; but I endeavoured to raise her from the ground, but found her entirely lifeless. To my horror I discovered the pistol was one of my own she had privately taken from my bed-room. There she

lay, killed by one of my own pistols, and I the only being by! My
faculties were suspended. I knew not what to do. The instant the
mischief happened, I thought to have made it public; but this would
have added to the suspicion, and I then resolved to conceal her death.
I then buried her in the best way I could. I tried to conceal the fact
as well as I could, giving sometimes one reason for her absence, and
sometimes another. It may be asked, Why not prove this by witnesses? Alas! how can I? How can I offer any direct proof how she
possessed herself of my pistols, for I found the other in her reticule?
That she obtained them cannot be doubted. All I can say as to the
stabs is, that I never saw one; and I believe the only reason for the
surgeon's talking of them is, that a sword was found in my possession.
I can only account for them by supposing that the spade penetrated her
body when they searched for the body in the Barn. This I know, that
neither from me, nor from herself, did she get any stab of this description. I always treated her with kindness, and had intended to marry her.
What motive, then, can be suggested for my taking her life? I could
have easily gotten over the promise of marriage. Is it possible I could
have intended her destruction in this manner? We went, in the middle
of the day, to a place surrounded by cottages. Would this have been
the case had I intended to have murdered her? Should I have myself
furnished the strongest evidence that has been adduced against me? I
might, were I a guilty man, have suppressed the time and place of her
death; but my plain and unconcealed actions,—because they were guiltless,—supplied both. Had I intended to perpetrate so dreadful a crime,
would I have kept about me some of the articles which were known to
be Maria's? Had I sought her life, could I have acted in such a
manner? Had I, I would have chosen another time and place. Look
at my conduct since. Did I run away? No; I lived, months and
months, with my mother. I left Polstead in consequence of my family
afflictions. I went to the Isle of Wight. It is said that the passport
was obtained to enable me to leave England at any time. No; it was
to enable me to visit some friends of my wife's in Paris. Should I
have kept her property, had I anything to fear from their detection?
In December last, I advertised, in " The Times" newspaper, the sale of
my house, and gave my name and address at full length. Did this look
like concealment? You will consider any man innocent till his guilt is
fully proved. It now rests with you to restore me to society, or to an
ignominious death. To the former I feel I am entitled; against the
latter I appeal to your justice and humanity. I have nothing more to
add, but that I leave my life in your hands, aware that you will give
me the humane benefit of the law, in cases of doubt, and that your
Lordship will take a compassionate view of the melancholy situation in
which my misfortunes have placed me.

The above was the substance of the prisoner's address. It was
delivered, in many parts, in a feeble and tremulous tone of voice, and
under considerable emotion. It is clear, from the pronunciation of
particular words, that the prisoner is not a man of particular education.
He trembled a good deal, but not more than a nervous man would
manifest in a moment of excitement. He read the address from a copy-
book; and, whether from the composition not being his own, or his
being near-sighted, he stammered over several words, and infringed the
order of the sentences. He was heard with the utmost silence and

attention by the Court and the Jury, and he occasional y drew his eyes
from the book, and fixed them on the jury-box, as if to ascertain the
impression he had made.   Towards the close of his address his voice
faltered, so as, in particular passages, to be nearly inaudible.   His
address, which was delivered between 11 and 12 o'clock, occupied the
Court about 25 minutes.

WITNESSES FOR THE DEFENCE.

Wm. Goodwin.—I live in Plough-lane, Sudbury.   The prisoner, in the spring of
last year, came to take apartments at my house.   Maria Marten afterwards came
and lay in there.   They were there between two and three months.   She was
delivered of a child there.   The prisoner came once or twice a week to see her, as
well after as before her confinement.   When I saw them together, I know nothing
to the contrary of his appearing fond of her.   She went, before or after her confinement, to Mr. Harcourt's, the gunsmith, at Sudbury.   I remember their leaving my
place, at nine o'clock in the evening, in a one-horse chaise.   This was on the 16th
of April.   They took the little child with them.

Cross-examined.—I do not know Mr. Harcourt, of Ipswich.

Mary Anne Goodwin, wife of the last witness.—I knew Maria Marten, who
lodged with me in March, 1827; she was brought by the prisoner.   She was confined there, and was there better than two months.   The prisoner frequently came
to visit her; he never missed coming once a week.   He treated her always with
kindness, and they appeared very much attached to each other.   She was generally
in very bad spirits.   I heard her say she went for the pistols to the shop where they
were.

Cross-examined.—She went for them alone to Mr. Harcourt's.

Thomas Hardy.—I was in the employ of Mrs. Corder last year.   In February last
year I saw the prisoner cleaning pistols.   I saw Maria Marten on the 13th of May,
with the prisoner, walking across the yard towards the stable.   There are two stair-
cases in Mrs. Corder's house; and a person may go up to what was the prisoner's
room by one of them without Mrs. Corder's knowing anything about it.

Cross-examined.—It was nine o'clock in the evening when I saw them going to the
stable.

Lucy Balam.—I lived with Mrs. Corder eleven months, till last Old Michaelmas
day.   I have seen a pair of pistols in the prisoner's bed-room, sometimes in a box
and sometimes out of it.   The prisoner remained with his mother till about a
fortnight before I left.   He always appeared a very kind and good-natured young
man.

Edward Liveing.—I am a surgeon of Nayland, near Polstead.   I have attended
him professionally.   About this time last year I advised him to leave that part of the
country, and to go to a warm bathing-place, particularly mentioning Hastings, and
the south coast.   He was then strongly threatened with consumption.   Some time
after that, I understood he was gone.

Thirza Havers.—I have known the prisoner from his infancy.   I have always
found him to be a kind and humane man.

John Bugg.—I was the looker of Mrs. Corder's farm.   He always bore the
character of a mild and humane man.

John Pryke, (a school-fellow of the prisoner), and Mary Kersey, who had known
him from his infancy, gave him the same character.

By Mr. *Kelly.*—Are you related to the prisoner?—His cousin.

By Mr. *Brodrick.*—And has that circumstance made you more intimately
acquainted with him and his character than you would otherwise have been?—It
has, Sir.

John Boreham and John Baalham gave similar evidence.

At twenty minutes to twelve the *Lord Chief Baron* began to sum
up the case.   He informed the Jury that the prisoner at the bar was
indicted for the murder of Maria Marten, and that the law required
that the mode in which she had come to her death should be particularly
stated in the indictment.   The present indictment, therefore, contained
the charge against the prisoner in a great variety of ways.   It stated,
that the deceased had come to her death by means of the prisoner,—
first. by a discharge of fire arms,—then by wounds inflicted by a sharp

instrument,—then by strangulation,—and last of all, by being buried alive in the ground. This was done in order to have the indictment supported by evidence in whatever way the evidence might turn out; and if the Jury should be of opinion that the prisoner at the bar had caused the death of Maria Marten by one, or two, or three of the modes mentioned in the indictment, then they would have sufficient evidence to support the purposes of this indictment, and the Crown would have a right to expect that they would find the prisoner guilty upon it. Before he entered upon the details of the case, he felt it to be his duty to advert to something which had been said by the prisoner, as to the prejudices which had been raised against him both in this county and throughout the country generally. It was unfortunate, extremely unfortunate, whenever such prejudices were raised; for they placed the life of the prisoner more in jeopardy than the ordinary circumstances of the case against him. Sorry, indeed, was he to say, that, as society was constituted at present, they could not be avoided. Accounts of this transaction, it appeared, had also found their way into the newspapers. Those accounts only related to the charge at the commencement of the business: they contained an *ex parte* statement of it, without giving the prisoner an opportunity of urging anything in his defence against it; and that was certainly a mischief, and an injury to him. The Jury, however, had a more impartial task to perform: they had to decide this issue by hearing the evidence on both sides, whereas hitherto the public had heard one side only. "We have also been told," said the venerable Judge, "that drawings and placards have been dispersed, not only in the neighbourhood of this town, but also in the immediate neighbourhood of this very Hall, tending to the manifest detriment of the prisoner at the bar. Such a practice is so indecorous and so unjust, that I can with difficulty bring myself to believe that any person, even in the very lowest class, will so far degrade himself as to think of deriving gain from the exhibition of this melancholy transaction.

Another circumstance to which the prisoner has alluded in his defence, and which I trust, for the sake of religion itself, is a mistake—another circumstance, which I feel myself bound to notice, is the assertion that a minister of the Gospel, quitting the place where he usually performed divine worship, and erecting his pulpit near the very scene of this melancholy tragedy, had there endeavoured to inflame the passions and to excite the resentment of the populace against the prisoner, when he knew nothing of his having had any share in it, except from rumour; thus inflaming them against a crime which was not then known to have been committed, and exciting their resentment against an individual who was not proved to have committed it. I cannot conceive any act more contrary to the spirit and the principles of that religion of which he professes himself a minister; and if we have been rightly informed of his conduct, the man who could commit such an act deserves the most severe reprobation. I do not know who the individual is who is stated to have misconducted himself so much. I hope we are all labouring under some mistake on this point, and that this outrage upon decency has not been committed. I mention it merely to request you to tear from your bosoms every impression which may have been made in them from such a source. I call upon you to dismiss from your consideration every impression of this case which you

may have derived, either from seeing the statements in the newspapers
or the drawings and placards in the streets, or from hearing the sermon
—if I may dignify it by that name—pronounced in the place where, and
on the occasion when, this murder was discovered. It is for you to
decide entirely upon the evidence which has been adduced before you,
giving to the case for the prosecution that weight which public justice
demands that it should receive at your hands, and to the case for the
prisoner that weight which a due regard for his life and interests
equally demands from you. That is my most earnest recommendation
to you, Gentlemen of the Jury; and I trust—indeed I am certain—that
you will pay to it requisite attention. The course which has just
been taken by the prisoner, who has been very ably advised, as we all
know, renders it unnecessary for me to state much of the evidence which
we have now been engaged two days in receiving. If the defence had
taken a different turn from that which it has taken, I should have thought
it my duty to ask you, first of all, whether you were convinced that
Maria Marten had been destroyed at all, either by the prisoner at the
bar or by any one else; and then, whether you were convinced that the
body discovered in the barn was her body or not. In that case, I
should have pointed out to you how uncertain the identification of the
body was, from the state of decomposition in which it was found; and
yet I should have stated to you that there were some circumstances
tending to prove its identity with Maria Marten: as, for instance, the
excrescence or wen on the neck, and the different articles of dress which
had been spoken to as hers from their not having undergone so much
decomposition as the human substance. All these remarks, however,
are now rendered unnecessary—for the prisoner avows to us in his
defence that the body discovered in the barn is the body of Maria
Marten. I am therefore relieved from the necessity of addressing you
upon that part of the case, as it is admitted by the prisoner that the body,
the discovery of which has given rise to this trial, is the body of Maria
Marten, for whose murder he is indicted. The prisoner admits that he
buried her in the barn, and we are therefore relieved from one of the
difficulties of this case. The next part of the evidence to which I shall
call your attention is, that which regards the different accounts which
the prisoner gave, after the disappearance of Maria Marten, of the
various places at which she was living; for those accounts have some
bearing upon his defence. I might, perhaps, be relieved from the necessity of alluding to that part of the evidence altogether, but the manner
of the prisoner's avowal may, when closely considered, be of some avail
in enabling us to discover the truth of his statement, that her death was
occasioned by a voluntary act of suicide on her part. I shall not omit
reading any of the evidence which has reference to this point, unless
you, gentlemen, state to me that in your opinion it is unnecessary for me
to read it."

The learned Judge then proceeded to read the evidence of Mrs. Mar
ten. When he came to that part of it in which Mrs. Marten swore that
Corder said, "Mrs. Marten, the reason I go to Ipswich to-day is,
because John Baalham, the constable, came into the stable this morning,
and informed me that he had got a letter from Mr. Whitmore, of London, and that in that letter there was a warrant to have Maria taken up,
to be prosecuted for her bastard children;" the learned Judge observed,
that this was very important evidence, as it bore directly upon the

prisoner's defence: it showed that he was endeavouring to seduce her away from her home, by holding out to her a terror which had no existence in reality. The Jury would consider how far this was or was not evidence to contradict the statement of the prisoner. It appeared, also, from the evidence of Mrs. Marten, that Maria Marten was very low spirited on setting out for the Red Barn, and had been so for some time previously. That circumstance ought by no means to be forgotten by the Jury in considering this case. He likewise called their attention to the circumstance of Mrs. Marten's having deposed, that Corder snapped his pistols before he set out for the Red Barn, twice or thrice by the fire-side, in the presence of the whole family—a circumstance which proved, that at that time the pistols were rather in the possession of the prisoner than of Maria Marten. The learned Judge then proceeded to read and comment upon the evidence of Thomas Marten, the father, and particularly on that part of it, in which the old man said, that in seeking for the body, he put in a spike about her hip, but that the smallest end of it was about the size of the end of his little finger, and that it grew broader as it went upwards. The learned Judge, after commenting on the evidence given by the other witnesses, till he came to that of Lea, the police-officer, said he was glad to find from his testimony, that the depositions were read over to the prisoner in his presence, by the Coroner, after the Inquest; and observed, that that was a point on which he would make a few remarks before he closed his address to them. He likewise observed, that it was very extraordinary, if the statement which the prisoner had that day made were true, that he had not said a syllable about it to Lea at the time when he was apprehended; but that he had repeatedly asserted, that he never knew anything of any such person as Maria Marten, though he was then formally informed that he was accused of having murdered her.

The learned Judge again repeated that he was glad that the depositions had been read over to the prisoner by the Coroner in the Jury-room at Polstead after the Inquest, as it took away a sting of the accusation which he had made against the Coroner. On coming to the evidence of Mr. Lawton, the surgeon, he particularly called the attention of the Jury to the evidence which that gentleman had given respecting the fracture of the skull of Maria Marten by a pistol-ball, respecting the wounds in her neck, heart, and ribs, by a sharp instrument, and respecting the possibility of her having died by strangulation from the tightness of the handkerchief round her neck. They had heard it that day asserted, that this poor woman had committed suicide; but even according to the story which they had heard, it was very strange that immediately on being left alone she should use such various instruments to destroy herself; for it appeared, in the first place, that she must have fired a pistol at herself, and then, either before or after firing it, have given herself sundry stabs in very different parts of her body. It would be the duty of the Jury to consider what credit they would give to the statements made by the medical witnesses about the stabs in the neck and in the heart; and then, if they gave credit to them, to consider what inferences they ought to draw from them, as to the story which had that day been told to them by the prisoner at the bar. The Jury had heard the defence, in which the prisoner admitted the body discovered in the barn to be the body of Maria Marten, and to have been buried by himself. He admitted that the representations which

he had made to several persons of her being alive, after her disappearance from her father's cottage, were untrue; but he said that he had
found it necessary to make them in consequence of the alarm which he
necessarily felt from a catastrophe of the following nature:—He said
that, on the 18th of May, he and Maria set out from old Marten's cottage for the Red Barn, in order to go to Ipswich to get married. That
they quarrelled at that Barn. That she used very violent language to
him. That he told her that if she used such language to him before
marriage, he could not expect to be happy with her after marriage. That
he had told her that he would not marry her. That he then left her.
That hearing the report of a pistol in the Barn, he returned to it, and
that he then found her there mortally wounded. He likewise said, that
being alarmed at the extraordinary catastrophe which he saw before
him, he buried her, and in this manner he attempted to account for the
representations which he afterwards made about her being alive. Now,
it was upon the truth of his representations of to-day that they had to
decide; and he would therefore give no opinion of his own upon the
point.

The learned Judge then read the evidence given on the part of the
defence in support of the mild and humane temper of the prisoner. On
closing the evidence as to character, he observed, that he had only one
remark to make upon it; and that was, that, in opposition to direct
evidence as to facts, it was of no avail; it was only when the balance
of evidence was equal that it proved of service to the accused. He would
not trouble them with many further observations upon this case, because
he was sure that their own good sense, after the patient attention which
they had paid to the evidence, would furnish them with all the observations that were necessary. A complaint, however, had been made with
respect to the conduct of the Coroner, which it was necessary to notice.
He was of opinion, that when the depositions, taken before the Coroner,
were read over by the Coroner to the prisoner after the Inquest, the prisoner had received all the advantage to which he was entitled as a matter
of right. The object of the Coroner's Inquest was not to charge any
person with the murder; its object was to ascertain how the death had
happened. The Inquest was conducted by the Crown, as the guardian of
the lives of all the subjects of the country, and, strictly speaking, a person
accused had no right to be present at it. If a man were found guilty of
murder on the Coroner's Inquest, it would be hard if he were not allowed
to know the evidence on which he was declared to be so; but when that
evidence was communicated to him, he had no right to complain. Now
it appeared from the evidence of Lea, that in this particular case the
depositions had been read over to the prisoner Corder by the Coroner.
The prisoner had, therefore, all the information necessary for him to shape
his defence on this trial, so as to meet the evidence to be produced
against him. It was, he believed, usual at Coroners' Inquests to allow
the parties likely to be implicated by them to be present, if they desired it; but not, he repeated, as a matter of right. The real question
for their decision in this case was this,—" Are the representations made
this day by the prisoner true or false?" If the Jury should be of
opinion that they were true, then the prisoner was entitled to an ac-
quittal. His representation was, that the deceased had shot herself with
his pistols, which she had got into her possession; and the evidence
showed that they were, on one occasion, in her possession at Sudbury,

but there was no evidence to show that she had continued in separate possession of the pistols, but much to show that she had not. The prisoner wished to have it supposed that she had carried these pistols in her pocket to the Red Barn. Now, the prisoner had seen the mother and sister of Maria Marten, in the witness-box, and he might have cross-examined them upon that point. But no one question had been put to them to show that Maria Marten had those pistols previously to leaving her father's cottage. So far as they had any evidence at all respecting the pistols, they appeared to have been in the prisoner's possession, and not in hers—for he had been seen snapping them before the fire. What had struck him from the beginning of the defence to the end, as the most extraordinary feature in it, was the manner in which this alleged suicide was committed often happened that these poor girls, when disappointed in their expectations, did lay rash hands on themselves; but then the mode of their death was in general very simple. In this case, if they were to credit the evidence of the surgeons, the wounds inflicted on the body of Maria Marten were of a double description. They were, first, the wounds in the eye, and in the cheek, by a ball; and then the wounds inflicted with a sharp instrument that was broader on one side than the other, on the heart and ribs; and the wound inflicted with a similar instrument on the vertebræ of the neck behind the skull. It was extraordinary that, instead of hanging herself upon a tree, as poor girls usually did in such circumstances, she should have used two different means to kill herself—the one by shooting herself with a pistol,—which was a very unusual weapon for a woman to kill herself with, and the other by stabbing herself with a sharp instrument. The Jury must decide on the credibility of the medical witnesses, who ventured to speak as to these two distinct causes of Maria Marten's death, independently of the third mode of death by strangulation, to which one of them had spoken; and then, if they decided that the wounds had been inflicted in the manner in which the surgeons described, they must decide how far it was possible that such multifarious wounds were inflicted by herself. These were the facts of the case as proved in evidence; and he trusted in God that they would lead them to a proper decision upon it. If they had any doubt upon it, they would give the prisoner the benefit of it; but if they were satisfied that his representations were false, and that the crime of murder on Maria Marten had been committed by him, then it would be their duty, serving their country manfully, and discharging faithfully the solemn oath which they had sworn, to bring in a verdict of guilty against the prisoner, regardless of the consequences by which it might be followed.

The *Foreman of the Jury* then addressed the Court on behalf of his fellow-jurors, and said that they wished to retire, as the case required some time to be spent in deliberation upon it.

The *Lord Chief Baron* immediately ordered a bailiff to be sworn to attend them, and at twenty-five minutes to two the Jury retired.

At ten minutes past two they came back into Court, and their Foreman returned a verdict of *Guilty* against the prisoner.

At this moment, and in the short interval which elapsed between the declaration of the verdict and the declaration of the sentence of the Court, a slight confusion arose before the bar where the prisoner was standing, relative to the possession of the pistols by which the murder was committed. Lea, the officer, claimed them as his property, in consequence of a promise which he had received from the prisoner when he first apprehended him; Mr. Orridge claimed them as the property of the Sheriff, in consequence of the verdict which had just been recorded against the prisoner. Mr. Orridge remained in possession of them, as the contest was stopped by the Crier's proclaiming silence, as the Lord Chief Baron was going to pass sentence on the prisoner.

The prisoner was then asked, in the usual form, whether he had to say anything why he should not die according to law. On his saying nothing,

The *Lord Chief Baron* addressed him in the following terms:— "William Corder, it is now my painful duty to announce to you the near approach of the close of your mortal career. You have been accused of murder, which is almost the highest offence that can be found in the whole of the long catalogue of crime. You denied your guilt, and put yourself on your deliverance to the country. After a long, a patient, and an impartial trial, the country has decided against you, and most justly. You stand convicted of an aggravated breach of the great prohibition of the Almighty Creator of mankind, "Thou shalt do no murder." The law of this country, in concurrence with the law of all civilized countries, enforces this prohibition of God, by exacting from the criminal who has violated it, the forfeiture of his own life. And as this offence indicates the highest degree of cruelty to its unfortunate victim, and as it is dangerous to the peace, the order, and the security of society, justice assumes upon it her severest aspect, and allows no emotion of pity to shield the criminal from the punishment awarded to it both by the laws of God and by the laws of man. I advise you not to flatter yourself with any hopes of mercy upon earth. You sent this unfortunate woman to her account without giving her any time for preparation: she had no time to turn her eyes to the Throne of Grace for mercy and forgiveness. She had no time given her to repent of her many transgressions: she had no time to throw herself on her knees and to implore for pardon at the Eternal Throne. The same measure is not meted out to you; a small interval is allowed you for preparation. Use it well; for the scene of this world closes upon you; but another, and, I hope, a better world is opening for you. Remember the lessons of religion which you received in the early years of your childhood: consider the effects that may be produced by a sincere repentance: listen to the advice of the ministers of your religion, who will, I trust, console and advise you how best to meet the sharp ordeal which you must presently undergo. Nothing remains for me now to do, but to pass upon you the awful sentence of the law. That sentence is, that you be taken back to the prison from which you came, and that you be taken thence, on Monday next, to the place of execution, and there be hanged by the neck till you are dead, and that your body shall afterwards be dissected and anatomized, and the Lord God Almighty have mercy on your soul!"

The *Lord Chief Baron*, who was evidently much affected, then retired from the Court.

Demeanour of the Prisoner during the Summing up of the Learned Judge, and the Sentence.

To prevent breaking too much in upon the uniformity of our narrative, we have deemed it right to subjoin to the trial itself an account of his behaviour during the latter part of it.

The prisoner paid the most eager attention to the earlier part of the summing up, in which his Lordship stated the indictment, and the necessity the law has imposed, of proving, to the satisfaction of the Jury, that the death of the person has been occasioned by one of the means laid in the indictment: but when the Chief Baron told the Jury that if they were satisfied that the death arose from any one, two, or more of the wounds inflicted on the body, and that those wounds were inflicted by the prisoner, they should find him guilty, his countenance fell, and he was apparently for some time in a state of stupor. He repeatedly bowed during the time the Judge besought the Jury to forget all the rumours and reports they had heard, and not to allow themselves to be influenced by the atrocious fact, if true, of a clergyman having preached to 5000 persons in the immediate neighbourhood of the scene, a sermon, in which the prisoner was treated as the murderer. The Chief Baron's observations respecting the probable motive of the prisoner in enticing the deceased from her mother's house under the false statement that the constable had a warrant against her for a bastard child, made the strongest impression on the prisoner, whose countenance underwent several changes during the time. At one period, during the statement of the extraordinary conversation of Corder with Mrs. Stowe, as to the number of children Maria had, her having brought forth her fated number, and his observation that " she was where he could go any day or hour he pleased, and that when he was not present with her nobody else was," the prisoner appeared almost in a fainting state; a transient paleness was visible in his countenance, his eyes rolled rapidly in their sockets, he heaved very deep sighs, and laid his head on the bar against which he had been previously leaning. In a few minutes, however, he recovered his self-possession, and resumed his former position, which was, leaning against the upright post, placing both hands on the spiked boarding before him, and fixing his eyes on the ground, raising them only when the Judge made remarks on the evidence. The mention of the letters seemed to agitate him considerably, and he sighed heavily; but the feeling quickly passed away, and he seemed to be relieved greatly by the learned Judge not reading them. He was also much agitated when the evidence of Lea was read, as to his denying all knowledge of such a person as Maria Marten; and the remarks of the Chief Baron that he did not, at once, on being told that her body was found in his barn, acknowledge that he knew her, and that she had destroyed herself, and been buried there, instead of denying any knowledge of her, caused a momentary faintness and swimming of his eyes. He again recovered himself but almost immediately on the allusion to his getting the sword sharpened, he was near falling, but was upheld by the gaoler. He, however from this time, evidently grew gradually weaker and less composed. During the reading of the important evidence of the surgeons, he moved uneasily from side to side, seemingly unable to maintain his self-possession without continual change of position. He more than once drank some cold water, which was given to him by the gaoler he evidently felt that the whole of his defence was overturned by the evidence of the surgeons of the various wounds found on the person of the deceased, and large drops of perspiration started from his forehead. The next remarkable change the prisoner underwent was, to a state of stupor, which continued for some length of time,—his eyes remaining perfectly fixed and immoveable and his arms crossed. After remaining some time in this state, he again laid his left cheek on the post, and appeared to be fainting. Recovering from this syncope, he laid his head upon his hands, and seemed dreadfully agitated for some minutes; but from the beginning of the last surgeon's evidence to its conclusion, he scarcely continued a minute in any one position, perpetually shifting from side to side, his head generally lying either very much on one side, or on his breast. From first to last, however, it was observed that he never shed a tear; but this may of course be attributed to his anxious attention to the investigation. One of the witnesses called by the prisoner, Mrs. Havers, a very pretty young woman, was frequently in tears during the detail of the evidence. He seemed to think the learned Judge would dwell at length upon his defence, and prepared himself, by a vigorous effort, to attend to the remarks he expected to hear on the subject. When, however, the Chief Baron passed over his story by a bare statement of its principal points, and made not a single remark on it, but proceeded to read the evidence of his own witnesses, he relapsed into his former state of stupor and faintness, and so continued to the end of the charge. On the Jury retiring to consider of his fate, he sat down on the bar in the dock, and leant his head against the beam on which he had previously rested his back. As each of the Jurymen passed him, he cast upon them a piercing glance of the most intense interest. During the time of their absence, nothing could be more disconsolate and desponding than his appearance. On the Jury returning into Court, he once more resumed his standing position. On hearing the Foreman pronounce the fatal word "Guilty," he raised his hand slowly to his forehead, pressed it for a moment, and then dropped it most dejectedly. His head immediately afterwards fell drooping upon his bosom. During the passing of the sentence his firmness still continued in some degree, but at the close of it, he would have sunk to the ground, had he not been prevented by the compassionate attention of the Governor of the gaol. He then sobbed loudly and convulsively for some moments, and was almost carried out of Court by Mr. Orridge and one of his attendants Indeed, it was evident to all, that at this moment his faculties, both mental and bodily, were completely paralyzed. It was said, that immediately after he quitted the dock, he fainted away; but we were given to understand that this was not the case. Shortly afterwards he was seen in the lock-up near to the Court, with his head buried in his hands, which rested on his knees, and labouring under severe mental emotions After the Court was cleared, he was removed to the county gaol.

The culprit, on his removal from Court, made a great effort to rally, even after the palpable extinction of his self-possession at the breaking up of the Court; so much so, indeed, that even some of those about his person imagined his emotion had been assumed, for the purpose of exciting a sympathy from superficial observers, which even he, degraded as he was, must have known would be denied to him by every well-constituted mind. It is even said that some unfortunate females of his family had been so deluded by representations similar to the pitiful fiction of his defence, that they were even preparing for his return to that decent condition of society, which he had with such unparalleled atrocity disgraced and dishonoured by the flagrant violation of all those household duties which reflect a peculiar character upon the middle classes of society in this country. But the attempts to sustain this mere physical insensibility, evidently required a forced excitement; he jumbled himself into the cart on his return from the Court to the prison, which is half a mile distant, more like a man who wanted to escape from the public gaze, than to invite its attention by any assumption of bravado. The crowd, who in their eagerness to catch a glimpse at every character, notorious for good or bad, oppose every obstacle which impedes the gratification of this curiosity, had broken the steps of the cart, in their efforts to get a close peep at the criminal, so that when he returned to the gaol, he had either to jump to the ground, or be assisted in his descent. He preferred the former, and alighted upon his legs on the threshold of the prison, with some appearance, at least, of renewed alacrity. He had returned, however, to the gaol in a different character from that in which he had left it. All the presumptions and reservations which the humane policy of our law sometimes throw around a prisoner whose life is at stake were removed, and he had yesterday evening to re-enter the wall of his prison, for the few hours which were counted to him in this world, as a person who was no longer to be mentioned among his species, and whose annihilation was doomed by the common injunction of every civilized community. This retributive change of circumstances removed him from a convenient apartment in the front of the prison, to a cell in the rear, and exchanged a dress of fashionable attire for the common gaol apparel. The Governor of the prison led him, upon his return as a condemned criminal, into his private apartment, where he plainly, but mildly, informed the prisoner he must now exchange the whole of his apparel, because his (the Governor's) situation with reference to him had now become one of great responsibility, and he had a serious duty to discharge, which he was, however, ready to perform with every attention to the rational wants of a prisoner in his awful situation. Corder immediately exchanged his clothes for those which were supplied to him from the prison stock, having previously given to his solicitor, from his pocket, his written defence, and some other papers. His penknife the Governor took charge of, and a gentleman present remarked to Corder, that the evidence against him was too conclusive to be parried by any external appearances of evasion, and that it was due to his family and society to deliver his mind of the facts. To this provident suggestion the criminal gave no reply, and the only desire he expressed was to be allowed the society of his wife, who has been for a short time in lodgings in the town. The Governor repeated to him that he should have every consolation which his situation and the rules of the prison permitted; but that henceforth he could see nobody except in his presence, or that of one of his officers, and that his own clothes should be at his disposal in exchange for those which he was at present under the necessity of substituting for them, on the day when he was to be brought out to die. At four o'clock Corder received some dinner from the Governor's table, and a clergyman was sent for to afford him the solace (should he prove susceptible of it) of spiritual consolation.

His mother and sister were said to be in the immediate neighbourhood of the town, anxiously awaiting the result of the trial; and his wife was, as we have already said, on the spot, under the expectation, as it was publicly said, of his deliverance, to which, in pity for the feelings of others, it is no longer seasonable more particularly to allude.

When some allusion was made to the impropriety of allowing him to retain his penknife (which, however, the Governor took from him on Thursday), he said that there was no danger to be apprehended in that respect, for he had no desire to add one sin to another. This was the only tendency towards anything like confession which the prisoner disclosed on the preceding day. Two inmates of the prison, who are represented as being of serious and prudent characters, were to remain in Corder's cell until the time of his execution. A passage was made through the wall immediately adjoining the cell, to the open paddock behind the gaol for his execution.

Bury, Saturday Evening, 8 o'clock.

Corder is confined in a room on the South side of the prison, and he is rather loquacious than otherwise. Mr. O. sat with him until half past 10 o'clock on Friday night, and he was very communicative: he observed that there was some part of the evidence incorrect; he particularly alluded to the boy (George Marten) who saw him come from the Barn with the pickaxe on his shoulder. He observed that he could not see him. Mr. O., in reply, said that he could not know of it; for it might happen that a person might see him whom he could not see. He said that was true; but did not deny having the pickaxe on his shoulder. Mr. O. asked how *it* came to be in the *Barn?* He said he could not tell.

In allusion to the sword, Mr. O. inquired whether he had ever been in the Navy? He replied, that he never intended to make the sea his profession: he got the sword for another purpose. Mr. O. inquired what could induce him to say that there was a warrant against Maria for bastardy, when, under that impression, he induced her to change her attire, and accompany her to the *Red Barn?* To this he made no reply; but hung down his head. He again reverted to his Trial, and said that the evidence was incorrect, for Maria had DIED SUDDENLY. Mr. O. observed, that it was now useless for him to be talking about it, as it would only tend to agitate him, and could not be remedied, but recommended him to attend to his spiritual adviser, who, no doubt, would give him such advice as would direct him to disclose that, which would be for his benefit in his translation from this world to another. Mr. Orridge wished him good night, and left him; shortly after which, he stripped himself quite leisurely, went to bed, and was asleep before 11 o'clock. He slept most soundly until 4 o'clock, when he was awaked by one of his attendants stirring the fire. He again went to sleep, and continued so until 6 o'clock in the morning, when he was visited by the Rev. Mr. Stocking, the Chaplain, who remained with him until 8 o'clock He was very talkative with his attendants, and observed to them, " What way could it contribute to the salvation of my soul to be telling my follies to the world?" The attendant replied, that it was not necessary for him to make a long confession, but to say that justice had been done him. Corder said, " Oh, the disgrace which I bring on my family!" The following conversation occurred between him and one of his attendants:—

Attendant.—Pray Mr. Corder, is it true, that by an advertisement you were first introduced to Mrs. Corder?

Corder.—Indeed it is.

Attendant.—Had you many answers to it?

Corder.—I had forty-five; some from Ladies in their carriage.

Attendant.—Well, that surprises me.

Corder.—Surprise you; so it may, as it did myself, but I missed of a good thing.

Attendant.—How is that?

Corder.—Why then, I will tell you. In one of the answers which I received, it requested that I should be at a certain church, on an appointed day, dressed in a particular way; and, both understanding what we came about, no further introduction was necessary.

Attendant.—But how could you know, for there might be another lady dressed in the same way?

Corder.—Oh! to guard against a mistake, she desired that I should wear a black handkerchief round my neck, and have my left arm in a sling; and in case I should not observe her, she would introduce herself.

Attendant.—And did you meet her?

Corder.—No, I did not; I went, but not in time, as the service was over when I got there.

Attendant.—Then, when you did not meet her, how could you know that she was respectable?

Corder.—Because the pew-opener told me, that such a Lady was inquiring for a gentleman of my description, and she came in an elegant carriage, and was a young woman of fortune (sighing heavily).

Attendant.—Then you saw her afterwards?

Corder.—No, never; but I found out where she lived, and who she was, and would have had an interview, were it not that I was introduced to Mrs. Corder; and we never parted until we were married.

Attendant.—Was that long?

Corder.—About a week.

This is a part of the numerous conversations he held with his attendants. His spirits seem to be volatile; at one time he appears to forget his situation, and commences a conversation ill suited to it.

In conformity with his promise, Mr. Orridge, in the afternoon, introduced Mrs. Corder to her wretched husband. She arrived at the prison at ten minutes to two o'clock, and was accompanied by a Mrs. Atherstone, an old school-fellow, who has humanely been sleeping with her since she came to Bury.

Mrs. A. remained in the Governor's office, while her afflicted friend, attended by Mr. Orridge, proceeded to the heart-breaking interview. She brought with her, for her wretched partner's perusal, a religious essay—"The Companion to the Altar," the contents of which she earnestly recommended to his reflection, prior to his partaking of the holy sacrament.

On entering the cell, she threw herself, in an agony, in his arms; and, bursting into tears, exclaimed, " Well, my dear William, this trial has terminated far differently from what we all had most earnestly expected." Corder was deeply and seriously affected at the visit, and passionately expressed his gratitude for her attachment to him, " through good report and evil report," and even to a violent and ignominious death.

For a time he was deprived of utterance; and on regaining a portion of his habitual fortitude and recollection, he expressed his anxiety for her future welfare, and his fears of the contumely she would experience in life. She entreated him to let no apprehension on her account disturb his mind, or distract his attention from a reflection on spiritual affairs. She had no personal fears for the future; " For, oh!" she said, " William, there is a good and merciful God, who will protect me; and to Him I look for support." She next implored of him to dismiss from his memory all recollection of temporal concerns, and to reflect and prepare himself for the awful account he would be so soon called upon to deliver up. The interview lasted until half past two o'clock; and, as we have understood, is calculated to arouse Corder's dormant feelings (if he has any), and lead to his repentance. Mr. Orridge was present while it continued; and, at its close, he delicately intimated to the prisoner, and his ill-fated wife, that they would again be permitted to see each other on Sunday at 11 o'clock, but that they must consider it as their final interview in this life.

Mrs. Corder and Mrs. Atherstone walked both to and from the prison. The former had a care-worn look, and a most dejected appearance, but yet, considering the situation she is so unhappily placed in, preserved a greater degree of self-possession than could naturally have been expected. Her dress was plain and unassuming: over a white gown she wore a brown silk Levantine pelisse, a straw bonnet, black veil, which was drawn closely over her face, and completely concealed her countenance, and on her shoulders was thrown a blue colonial imitation Cashmere shawl, with a variegated border. Her friend, Mrs. Atherstone's, attire was equally unpretending; and while waiting in the Governor's office, she wept most bitterly. One of the most earnest of the applicants was a Mr. Moore, at whose lectures he had been formerly in the habit of attending. Mr. O. informed him of the request that had been made, actuated by the idea that perhaps he might desire the spiritual assistance of a person with whom he had been hitherto acquainted. Corder, however, expressed a repugnance to the visit, and accompanied his refusal with the observation, that he was anxious to preserve his mind undisturbed, during the remnant of his existence, and that seeing strange faces would only unhinge him, and that he was quite satisfied with the religious instruction supplied to him by the Reverend Chaplain. In every request, Mr. Orridge has consequently proved inaccessible; and did he not consult the feelings of the prisoner, an Act of Parliament that has lately passed, and which came into operation on the 27th of June, would preclude his gratifying puritanical curiosity; or, indeed, admitting any one to an interview with a criminal under sentence of death for a murderous offence, unless authorised by the order of the Sheriff or Judge. The Act is that of the 9th Geo. IV. cap. 31; and, among other things, " It is enacted, that every person, convicted of murder, shall, after judgment, be confined in some safe place, within the prison, apart from all other prisoners; and shall be fed with bread and water only, and with no other food or liquor; and, that no person but the Gaoler and his servants, or the Chaplain, shall have any access to any such convict, without the permission in writing, of the Judge, the Sheriff, or his Deputy."

The preparations for the Execution are nearly completed.

APPENDIX.

Bury, Sunday Morning, Eight o'Clock.

ABOUT eight o'clock last evening Corder's mental exhaustion overcame his physical strength, and he dropped into a calm and undisturbed sleep, which lasted till three o'clock this morning. We understand, that though he now appears greatly dismayed at the approaching close of his mortal career, he never from the first expected any other termination to this trial. On hearing that his friends, some of whom are very opulent and respectable persons, were willing to make large pecuniary sacrifices to ensure him the benefit of all the assistance which could be derived from the talent and ingenuity of the most able and experienced advocates at the Bar, he wrote a letter to them, returning them thanks for their kindness, but at the same time declaring, that the evidence which had been taken at the Inquest would appear, to all persons who were unacquainted with the real nature of the transaction, so strong against him, that it would answer no useful purpose to expend their money in his behalf. He also stated that he had made up his mind to meet with courage and fortitude the fatal destiny which had befallen many other individuals who were as innocent as himself. It appears, from the event, that he has miscalculated his own strength of nerve; for, from all the accounts that I have been able to collect, it is quite clear that the elasticity of his spirit is entirely destroyed, and that he labours under the most poignant distress of mind.

It has been stated, that the defence to which he resorted was, even in the desperate circumstances of his case, one of the most injudicious that could possibly have been attempted. After admitting the identity of the body discovered in the Barn with that of Maria Marten, the only point of difficulty was removed from the decision of the Jury. An acute analysis of the evidence might, perhaps, have enabled an ingenious man to suggest doubts as to the identity of the body, arising out of the state of decomposition at which not only the body, but also the articles of dress found upon it, had arrived. But this line of defence was probably abandoned, on account of the difficulty which the prisoner would have experienced in explaining the letters which he had written relative to the existence of Maria Marten after her disappearance from Polstead. Still, to support the indictment, it would have been necessary to show that the body found was the body of Maria Marten; and, however much appearances might on other points have been against him, it would have been impossible for any Jury to have recorded a verdict of guilty against him, until they were convinced of the identity of the body with that of the person alleged to be murdered.

Since his conviction, various questions have been put to Corder on different parts of the evidence. Mr. Orridge asked him how he got over that part of the evidence in which it was sworn that he had informed Maria Marten that Baalham, the constable, had told him that Mr. Whitmore had got a warrant to have her apprehended on account of her bastard children, when it appeared from Baalham's testimony that he had made no such statement? To this question he gave no answer, but hung back, cast a sharp and expressive look on the questioner, and assumed, as he does upon all questions which displease him, an aspect of considerable ferocity. He was asked by one of his attendants how he could muster nerve enough to stay alone with the corpse in the Barn whilst he was digging a grave for it? and his answer to this question appears very material; for it was given in the shape of another question, and was to this effect:—"How d'ye know that such was the case?" On another occasion, he was asked to confess the justice of his sentence; and his reply was curious. " The sermons," he said, " which have been put into my hands since I came into this place, have convinced me that all confession which it is necessary for me to make, is a confession to my God of the transgressions of my life: confession to man can be of no good to my soul; I do not like, and I will not make it, as it savours strongly of hypocrisy" To another person he said, "Why should I disgrace my family by confessing the follies and transgressions of my youth? they are, indeed, manifold; the

4 s

confession would hurt their feelings, and would do me no good." It is, however, expected by those who are best acquainted with him, that though he has not yet made, he still will make, a confession of his guilt before his execution, if not in detail, at least shortly in point of fact.

In the hurry of sending off the report of the trial, we forgot to mention that when Lea, the police-officer, was under examination, Corder stamped violently on the floor of the dock, and expressed considerable indignation at the testimony which he was giving. Mr. Orridge, on returning from the Court with the prisoner, asked him what part of Lea's evidence had so strongly excited his feelings. Corder replied that Lea had sworn falsely in saying that he had made him a present of the two pistols which he (Lea) had found in the reticule in his (Corder's) house. Mr. Orridge said, that perhaps, in the hurry and agitation of his feelings, he had unconsciously made such a promise. Corder replied, that it was possible he might have done so; but he did not think it probable. He has repeated this declaration since his conviction, and pledges the faith of a dying man to its correctness.

An idle story has got about this place, that Corder was at one time a Methodist parson, and had actually preached a sermon at Polstead. The circumstance has been mentioned to him, and he gave it an unqualified contradiction. He says that he did for some time attend a Methodist chapel, because a young girl whom he admired frequented it, but that he had always been too dissolute and depraved to turn his mind to religious pursuits.

You will have heard from another quarter that Mrs. Corder received in a feeling manner the distressing intelligence of her husband's conviction, and kindly endeavoured to arm him against his fate. Another anecdote places in a strong light the propriety of her moral principles. On the first interview that she had with her husband after his conviction, Mr. Orridge felt himself compelled, in consequence of a new clause inserted in Lord Lansdown's Act, to inform her that he must be present during the whole time of its continuance, lest she should furnish her husband with some means by which he might effect his own destruction. Mrs. Corder said, "If it pleased God to take him to himself before the time appointed for his execution, I should be most happy; but I would not interfere between his God and him for any consideration. I would let him meet his fate with submission, rather than afford him any means by which he might anticipate it." The meeting between them is described as having been of the most tender and affecting nature.

The fate of his aged and widowed mother is deplorable, and entitles her to the sympathy of every humane and benevolent bosom. She has within a very short period been bereft, by the ordinary course of nature, of three sons; the only son whom she has left is now to be wrenched from her by the exterminating grasp of public justice. Can any one have a greater right to refuse to be comforted?

Half-past Eleven o'clock, Sunday Morning.

The Condemned Sermon was delivered in the chapel attached to the gaol, by the Chaplain, the Rev. W. Stocking. Besides the inmates of the gaol, there were about twenty persons present. After the debtors, confined in the county gaol, had taken their seats, the different felons, who have been tried at the late Assizes, were admitted to theirs. The latter were dressed in a coat and trousers of gray frieze, striped at intervals with two bars of black, enclosing a broader stripe of yellow, which is the costume of this prison. After the Chaplain had taken his station in the pulpit, Corder was led into the barred cell reserved for culprits under sentence of death, by Mr. Orridge and one of his attendants. He wept bitterly as he came along the passage; but buried his face in his handkerchief, as if anxious to withdraw himself from the gaze of the curious. His step was anything but firm; and he had evidently lost, beyond the power of recall, a great part of that self-command which he exhibited at the commencement of the trial. As soon as he was locked in the pew appointed for him, he heaved a deep sigh, sat himself down on one of the benches, and leaned against the side of the pew: he then raised his foot on the bench before him, rested his elbow on his knee, and his face, which he covered with a white handkerchief, on his hand; and remained in that position during the greater part of the service. The Rev. Gentleman then read an excellent occasional prayer for persons in Corder's deplorable situation: he appeared much moved by it; and betrayed great agitation, when the Rev. Gentleman bade his congregation to reflect, that but for the mediating blood of Christ they might have been shut up in hell instead of in that prison. In that part of the service of the day, in which the clergyman prays that the rest of our lives may be pure and holy, Corder's emotion was excessive, owing, perhaps, to its exciting the painful reflection, that the rest of his life was already numbered. The Psalms which were selected for the occasion were the 51st and the 130th. In that part of the 51st Psalm in which the inspired writer implores God to deliver him from blood-guiltiness, Corder sighed deeply, and showed, by the uplifted motion of his hands, that he joined cordially in the prayer. These two Psalms, which are very affecting, produced no other display of feeling from the prisoner—so deep and even stupifying was the grief by which he was overwhelmed. The first lesson read was the usual lesson for the day; the second was selected with reference to the prisoner's situation, and was that part of the 15th chapter of St. Paul's First Epistle to the Corinthians, which the Church of England, from admiration of its deep and affecting sublimity, has incorporated into the burial service. The 30th verse, "Why stand we in jeopardy every hour?" affected him greatly; but I was surprised that he betrayed no feeling at that verse in which it is declared that th sting of death is sin; nor at that in which it is also declared that death is now swallowed up in victory. At the commencement of the Litany he sighed deeply, and evidently joined in heart, though not in word, with the supplication to the Trinity to have mercy upon all miserable sinners. On coming to that clause in the Litany, in which the preacher prays that God will show his pity upon all prisoners and captives, and especially on him who is now awaiting the execution of his sentence, he let his head fall against the wall with a heart-rending sigh.

At the close of the Litany, the clergyman introduced a prayer for Corder, which affected him so much that he cried audibly. In the closing paragraph of it, in which God was implored to enable so heinous a sinner to cast himself wholly on his Redeemer, and, through the merits of his passion and death, to relieve himself from the pressure of his sins, he groaned aloud, and half whispered "Amen." This prayer appeared to make a greater impression upon him than any other portion of the service of the day. He changed his position repeatedly, but never abstained from keeping his handkerchief in front of his face. It was the only time in which he joined in the responses, though many of them were most suitable to his desperate condition. Part of the Gospel of the day struck me as peculiarly appropriate to his condition; but during the reading of it, and also during the reading of a great portion of the previous part of the Communion Service, he appeared involved in a sort of stupor. To the Sermon he paid considerable attention. It was taken from the 41st verse of the 23d chapter of St. Luke, and was in these words:—"And we indeed justly; for we receive the due reward of our deeds: but this man hath not done amiss." The reverend preacher said, that these were the words of the malefactor who was crucified with Jesus, and who, in consequence of his belief in the divine character of our Saviour, received from him a promise that he should be entitled with him to the joys of Paradise. He pointed out the happy result which the words of the text had produced to the person who uttered them, and said, that he should take occasion from them to point out the state of mind which a malefactor, appointed to die, ought to strive with all his soul to attain.

The external demeanour of a person so circumstanced should be such as not to give offence to those who should watch his actions at the time of his death; for the damage he might then do was irreparable, and he never could have any opportunity to repair it by repentance. He ought to endeavour so to conduct himself at the close of his existence, as to edify and improve by his death those who could have received nothing but evil example from his life. A death on the scaffold excited great attention on the part of the spectators; and whatever was then said or done by the malefactor doomed to die, made an impression on their memories, which rendered it incumbent on him to say or do nothing which could weaken the respect due from us all to that God at whose tribunal he was going to appear. The inward demeanour of the prisoner was that, however, to which he ought to pay the greatest concern. He should endeavour to make his peace with God, and should repent of his sins with a repentance not to be repented of. As he could not expect to bring forward in his life fruits meet for repentance, it was incumbent upon him to reiterate his prayer for a change of mind, till he became certain it was accepted. He should bow with submission to the will of God, and throw off that reluctance which too often prevented individuals from owning the justice of the sentence with which God visited them. He should be sensible that nothing was more suitable to his past transgressions than the ignominious death which he was going to suffer. The ignominy of it would exist but for a short time, and the pain of it to the mortal body for only a few minutes. The dark way through which he would have to travel to eternity, should be that which troubled him with the greatest alarm. He should prepare himself, therefore, for that awful occasion, when the dead in Christ should rise again, and when the great judgment of the Lord should pronounce absolution on the godly, and condemnation on the wicked. He pointed out the distressing situation of those to whom God should say—"Depart from me, ye wicked, into everlasting fire,"—[here Corder was violently affected, and sobbed convulsively]--and asked with great enthusiasm.

what would not the wicked give for one hour at that time to make their peace with their offended Creator? Then it would be too late to implore his mercy—their eternal state would be concluded on—and the certainty that there would be no change in it would aggravate the intensity of their sufferings.—[Here Corder's emotion was truly distressing—he moved about in his seat in great mental anguish.]—It might be that there were some persons present, who, like the Pharisee, might thank God that they were not murderers, like the unfortunate man who was now doomed to die: let those who made such comparisons beware,—they were odious to God, and dangerous to themselves Let them guard against such boastings,—for they proclaimed them to be guiltier than they themselves imagined. They might have strictly adhered to all the laws of the land; but the laws of the land were not the criterion of a Christian's duty; and those who made them so, acted more cunningly than wisely for their own spiritual interests. To wish the death of an individual was often as full of guilt as to inflict it. Let those, therefore, who thought that they stood, take care lest they fell; and let them take warning from the death which was now impending over their fellow prisoner, and endeavour not to do likewise, lest a worse fate should hereafter befal them.

The close of this Sermon, of which we have given a very faint and imperfect sketch, was the close of the service for the day. Corder was led out by Mr. Orridge in almost a fainting condition. As soon as he reached his cell, he staggered to his bed, on which he flung himself, sobbing convulsively for many minutes. In passing the pew in which we were seated, he dropped his handkerchief from his face, and nothing could be more altered than the cast of his countenance since we saw him on Friday last. His cheeks had collapsed, his eyes were swollen greatly and his whole appearance was most ghastly. He looked the picture of despair.

CONDUCT, CONFESSION, AND EXECUTION OF CORDER.

Bury St. Edmund's, Monday Morning.

Mrs. Corder had an interview with her husband yesterday. It lasted from half-past twelve to two o'clock, and was, to a spectator, infinitely distressing. Mr. Orridge, who was present, and who is not unaccustomed to such scenes, was much affected by it. The particulars of it have not yet transpired; but it is understood that Corder particularly requested his wife not to marry again, or, at least, if she did, not to obtain a husband as she had obtained him, by means of an advertisement; for it was, of all modes of getting a husband, the most dangerous and imprudent. It is, perhaps, right to add, that one of the first questions which Corder asked his wife, on seeing her led into his cell by Mr. Orridge, had reference to the advertisement by which he gained her. Mr. Orridge appeared to have some doubt whether Corder had received so many answers as he said to his advertisement, and, in order to remove them, Corder asked her how many letters she had herself seen? She replied, immediately, forty-five.

On leaving her husband's cell, Mrs. Corder was quite overcome by the violence of her feelings. She fainted away several times, and was with difficulty recovered by the restoratives administered to her by Mr. Orridge, who sincerely commiserated her sufferings. She was not able to walk to the gig which was waiting to convey her to her lodgings, but was carried into it by her friend Mrs. Atherton and one of the prison attendants. Corder, on her quitting him, said that the bitterness of death was now over; and has been heard to express a wish that there was a less interval to the time of his execution. He likewise says that he found, in Mrs. Corder, one of the most tender, faithful, and affectionate of wives.

In the course of yesterday evening, Mr. Orridge addressed a paper to the prisoner, impressing upon him the duty of making a confession of his guilt, of which he said few people now entertained a doubt. The unfortunate prisoner said that he did not see any reason why he should make it. Mr. Orridge then reminded him, that in his defence he had imputed to Maria Marten the commission of suicide; and if he left the world without contradicting that statement, he would be tainting her memory with the imputation of a dreadful crime. This argument appeared to make a deep impression on his mind, especially as it was strengthened by reference to the first duty of man—"to do unto another as he would wish others to do unto him." The Rev. Mr. Sheen, the Chaplain to the High Sheriff, who saw him about half-past five o'clock, had previously addressed him also upon the same topics; and the consequence of these solicitations was, that in the course of the night he made a confession, of which we give authentic particulars.

At half-past one o'clock last night, Mr. Orridge left Corder; and soon afterwards he fell asleep, and slept to all appearance calmly till six o'clock this morning. He says, however, that his sleep was not sound, but disturbed by dreams. He acquired considerable firmness in the course of yesterday, in consequence of the spiritual consolation afforded to him, first of all by his wife, and next by the Chaplain of the gaol (the Rev. Mr. Stocking) and the Rev. Mr. Sheen. I understand that several methodist preachers applied to be admitted to him, but were refused admission.

This morning, at half-past nine o'clock, Corder was, by his own request, taken into the prison chapel to attend, for the last time, divine service. I was present at the performance of it. He entered the chapel with a firm step, and took his seat in the condemned pew, as he did yesterday. He had, however, laid aside his prison dress, and had on the same clothes which he wore in Court during the trial. His appearance was much more composed than I should have expected, after the over-whelming sorrow and dismay by which he appeared overcome yesterday. This, perhaps, may be attributable to the ghostly consolation which was administered to him by Mr. Stocking at an early hour this morning. He did not hide his countenance, as he did yesterday, in his handkerchief; nor did he shed a single tear. He exhibited a befitting and not unmanly sense of the awful situation in which he was placed. On sitting down, he betrayed his inward feelings by a tremulous motion of his foot for some time, and then rested his head on his hand, supporting his elbow upon his knee. A part of the burial service was again introduced into the service of the day; and during several parts of it, he showed by his motions that he joined in it from his inmost soul. When the gracious invitation of God for all that were heavy laden to come to him and rest upon his mercy was read, he opened his hand slowly, pressed it to his head, and heaved a deep sigh. He likewise exhi-bited some emotion at an occasional prayer which was introduced into the service, in which the text of Scripture was introduced that says, "Whoso confesseth his sins and forsaketh them, shall have mercy." He joined with great fervour in a prayer which called upon God to spare him in the agonies of death, which he was presently to endure; and to extend to him that mercy which he had not extended to his departed sister. The latter allusion affected him deeply, for he raised up his left hand, gave a convulsive shudder, and struck it with some violence on his knee. During the rest of the service, which was nearly the same as yesterday, he did not betray any extraordinary emotion. At the close of it, his pew was opened; on leaving it, he made a few steps by himself, and then tottered, and seemed as if about to fall. One of the prison attendants then gave him his arm, and led him back to his cell. At eleven o'clock, the Chaplain was admitted into his cell, and administered to him the Sacrament. The remaining particulars of the wretched man's conduct will be found detailed with great minuteness in the statement which Mr. Orridge has drawn up, and which is as follows:—

MR. ORRIDGE'S STATEMENT.

Upon William Corder's returning from the Shire-hall, after he had received sentence, I took him into my office, and explained to him that I had a melan-choly and painful duty to perform with respect to him, and that a part of that duty was to have him immediately stripped of his clothes, and have the prison clothes put on him. This was accordingly done. I then told him, I thought the sooner he could forget all earthly matters the better; and therefore, if he had any request to make, I begged he would recollect himself and do it immediately, and that I would instantly tell him if his wishes, whatever they might be, could or would be complied with. After some consideration, he said it would be a great con-solation to him if his wife could be permitted to spend the remainder of his time with him. This, I told him, was impossible, but that she would be allowed two interviews with him: he was then removed to another room. The Chaplain (Mr. Stocking) at-tended him in the evening; after the Chaplain was gone, I continued with him till half-past ten o'clock. I hinted to him that his defence, though perhaps ingenious, could not be believed, and that surely he would feel an inward satisfaction in confess-ing the truth. He then declared his defence was true, and that he had nothing to confess; indeed, he said, the confession of his faults would only tend to disgrace his family more, and could be of no use to his soul; and upon any other question put to him respecting the murder during that evening he preserved a sullen silence.

In the course of the evening he mentioned the particulars of his marriage: he stated that he left home the latter end of September; that he went to Portsmouth, the Isle of Wight, and Southampton; that he returned to London in about two months, and then advertised for a wife; that he had forty-five applications to the ad-vertisement, and that one of them was from a lady, who wrote to him to say that she should go to church in a certain dress, and sit in a particular place; and requesting him to go to church with his left arm in a black sling, a black handkerchief round his neck, and place himself in such a position that they might see each other, and then judge if a personal interview would be desirable. He said he accordingly went to the church; but by some means he had mistaken the hour of divine service, so that he never saw that lady. He said, that after he saw his present wife he never left her till they were married; that from the time of his advertising to his marriage was about a week. I observed to him that he was a most fortunate man, under those circumstances, to have met with a woman who had been so kind to him during the whole of his confinement. I then left him

My two servants told me, the next morning, that he fell asleep about eleven o'clock, and slept till after four o'clock; that he did not talk to them. During Saturday the Chaplain (Mr. Stocking) was several times with him. At other times I now and then hinted the necessity of confession. In the course of that day he said "that confession to God was all that was necessary, and that confession to man was what he called Popedom, or Popery, and he would never do it." It was hinted to him, some time in the day, that he must have had great nerve, to dig the hole during the time the body lay in his sight. His reply was, "Nobody knows that the body lay in the Barn, and in sight, whilst I dug the hole;" and would then say no more on the subject, but exclaimed, "O God! nobody will dig my grave!"

His wife saw him in my presence for nearly an hour. He expressed much anxiety about her future welfare: she entreated him to forget her, and employ his few hours yet remaining in prayer for his salvation and eternal welfare. I went to his room on Saturday evening, about eight o'clock, with an intention of sitting an hour or two with him; but he had gone to bed, and was asleep, and my men told me the next morning that he had slept until near three o'clock.

On Sunday morning Mr. Stocking was with him early, and endeavoured to lead his mind to the necessity of confession: he attended chapel, and was very much affected. About half-past twelve his wife had her last interview: they were both very much affected. In the course of that interview he exclaimed, "Well might Mr. Orridge say, that I was a most fortunate man to meet with such a woman as you are!"

He then explained to her that he had told me the way in which they had come together, and that he had forty-five applications to his advertisement: he entreated, if ever she married again, to be sure not to answer any similar advertisement, as woful experience must have convinced her how dangerous a step it was. The parting scene was most affecting; the poor woman remained in a state of stupor for some time. Corder was much affected throughout the day. Mr. Stocking had several interviews with him; and in the evening the Sheriff's Chaplain, the Rev. Mr. Sheen, attended him, for which attention he expressed himself as feeling very grateful. About nine o'clock I sent him the annexed paper:—

"CONFESSION.—Confession to the world has always been held necessary atonement, where the party has committed offences affecting the interests of society at large.

"He that covereth his sins shall not prosper, but whoso confesseth shall have mercy.

"Surely confession to God cannot be here meant, as no man can hope to hide his sins from God. 'Confess your faults one to another, and pray one for another.' (James v. 16.)

"Archbishop Tillotson says, 'In case our sins have been public and scandalous, both reason and the practice of the Christian church do require, that when men have publicly offended, they should give public satisfaction and open testimony of their repentance. The text in James is a direct command.'

"The Christian doctrine of the necessity of restitution is strong; and if you will not confess, how can you make restitution to the reputation of your victim? You have accused her of having murdered herself. If you died without denying that accusation, how do you obey the command 'to do that to another which we would have another do to us?'

"The doctrine of confession which is objectionable in a Popish point of view, is the private confession to a priest of private vices; but the duty of making acknowledgment of public crimes can have nothing to do with such objections. Even supposing it doubtful whether a man is bound, after offending society, to confess his errors to the world, there can be no doubt that he will not do any thing wrong by confessing. One course is therefore certain—the other uncertain. Can a man hesitate to seize the former?

"JOHN ORRIDGE."

I begged he would read it attentively, and that I would come to him soon. I went to his room a little before ten, and remained in earnest conversation with him till half-past eleven : I told him that during the 30 years I have held my situation, I had the satisfaction of assuring him that no man who had been executed during that time had ever dared to take the Sacrament in sullen silence about his crime, or without confession; that I well knew, from his letters that I had seen, and from other circumstances, that the line of defence he had adopted was not the dictates of his own mind, at least for a long time after his commitment; and that I was sure that he would not and dare not take the Sacrament, and remain silent, or deny being the guilty cause of the death of poor Maria Marten. He then exclaimed, " Oh, Sir, I wish I had made a confession to you before; I have often wished to have done it ; but you know, Sir, it was no use employing a legal adviser, and then not follow his advice." I told him, that up to the time of his conviction it was proper; but that being over, all earthly considerations must cease. He then exclaimed, " I am a guilty man !" I then went for a pen and ink, and began to ask him the particulars of the offence, which I told him the public had supposed him to be guilty of. He said, " Oh, spare me ! I can only mention to you the particulars of how Maria came by her death; with this the public must be satisfied; I cannot say more." I then wrote the following confession nearly in his own words. I read it to him attentively, and he signed it with a firm hand. I left him about half-past one o'clock, and my men tell me he lay very still, and appeared to sleep through the night.

On Saturday he told a respectable individual, whom I had asked to sit and read to him, that he was guilty of the forgery upon Messrs. Alexander's Bank, and that he had been assured the money was paid: there are some parts of the foregoing statement which he also mentioned to the same individual. He also expressed much horror at the thoughts of being dissected and anatomized. He also stated, after he had signed the confession, that he felt great respect for the girl, but that he had no intention to marry her at that time.

(Signed)   JOHN ORRIDGE.

CONFESSION

" Bury Gaol, August 10, 1828.
Condemned Cell, Sunday Evening, Half-past Eleven.

" I acknowledge being guilty of the death of poor Maria Marten, by shooting her with a pistol. The particulars are as follow :—When we left her father's house. we began quarrelling about the burial of the child,—she apprehending that the place wherein it was deposited would be found out. The quarrel continued for about three-quarters of an hour upon this and about other subjects. A scuffle ensued ; and during the scuffle, and at the time, I think, that she had hold of me, I took the pistol from the side pocket of my velveteen jacket, and fired. She fell, and died in an instant. I never saw even a struggle. I was overwhelmed with agitation and dismay ;—the body fell near the front doors on the floor of the Barn. A vast quantity of blood issued from the wound, and ran on to the floor, and through the crevices. Having determined to bury the body in the Barn (about two hours after she was dead), I went and borrowed the spade of Mrs. Stowe ; but, before I went there, I dragged the body from the Barn into the chaff-house, and locked up the Barn. I returned again to the Barn, and began to dig the hole ; but the spade being a bad one, and the earth firm and hard, I was obliged to go home for a pickaxe and a better spade, with which I dug the hole, and then buried the body. I think I dragged the body by the handkerchief that was tied round her neck— it was dark when I finished covering up the body. I went the next day, and washed the blood from off the Barn floor. I declare to Almighty God, I had no sharp instrument about me, and that no other wound, but the one made by the pistol, was inflicted by me. I have been guilty of great idleness, and, at times, led a dissolute life ; but I hope, though the mercy of God, to be forgiven.

' W. CORDER."

Witness to the signing by the said William Corder,

JOHN ORRIDGE.

Sunday Evening, Half-past Twelve o'clock.

Condemned Cell, Eleven o'Clock, Monday Morning, August 11, 1828.
The above confession was read over carefully to the prisoner, in our presence, who stated most solemnly that it was true—that he had nothing to add or retract from it.

W. STOCKING, Chaplain.

T. R. HOLMES, Under Sheriff.

In answer to a question from the Under Sheriff, he said, " that he thought the ball had entered the right eye." He said this in corroboration of his previous statement, that he had no sharp instrument with him in the Barn at the time he committed the murder. The Under Sheriff stated that Dr. Probart was with him at the time when the prisoner made this last confession.

He is quite convinced the ball entered the right eye.

[Mr. Orridge informed us, there were several points in Corder's statement on which he wished to have further explanation, but that in his peculiar circumstances he could not press it; especially as Corder said to him on more than one occasion, " Spare me upon that point—I have confessed all that is sufficient for public justice."]

THE EXECUTION.

From an early hour this morning, the population of the surrounding districts came pouring into Bury ; and the whole of the labouring classes in this town struck work for the day, in order that they might have an opportunity of witnessing the execution of this wretched criminal, which was appointed to take place at twelve o'clock at noon. As early as nine o'clock in the morning, upwards of 1000 persons were assembled around the scaffold, in the paddock, on the south side of the gaol ; and their numbers kept increasing till twelve o'clock, when they amounted to at least 7000 persons. Nothing could be more decent and orderly than their conduct. The majority consisted of men, but we observed a large number of females in the crowd. Two women must have been there at an extremely early hour, for they were close up to the woodwork which surrounded the fatal drop. They appeared to be of the lowest class; but many of the female spectators were of a much superior grade. Seated on a wall, which gave a commanding view of the whole scene, were several ladies, dressed in the first style of fashion. We mention this fact, because it shows the intense curiosity prevalent in this county respecting every action of Corder; for nothing else could have brought respectable females to behold a catastrophe so uncongenial with the usual kindness and benevolence of the female character. Every building in the neighbourhood was covered with occupants, and in one of the adjacent fields were several gentlemen on horseback, expecting the appearance of the prisoner.

At ten minutes before twelve o'clock Corder was brought from his own cell, which was on the second story of the prison, to a cell on the basement story. He was there pinioned by the executioner who officiates at the Old Bailey, and who was specially retained for this event. He appeared resigned to his fate, though he sighed heavily at intervals. After his arms were fastened, he would have fallen to the ground, had it not been for the support afforded to him by one of the constables. He recovered after a moment from the transient faintness which had overcome him, and kept ejaculating in an under tone, " May God forgive me ! Lord, receive my soul!" The executioner was then going to put the cap upon the prisoner's face, when Mr. Orridge interfered, and said that the time was not yet come. He was then led by his own desire around the different wards of the prison, and shook hands with the different prisoners, who were assembled at the doors entering into them. As a proof that he was at that time perfectly conscious of what he was doing, he singled out a prisoner of the name of Nunn, shook hands with him as well as his bandaged situation would allow, and said to him, " Nunn, God Almighty bless you !" In another ward he called the same blessing on two prisoners of the names, as we were informed, of Sampson. The men addressed appeared deeply affected, as, indeed, did most of the prisoners who witnessed the melancholy spectacle.

After he had gone round the entrance to the different wards of the prison, which are ranged round the Governor's house, which is built upon an octagonal base, he proceeded to the debtor's yard, where he bade farewell to three individuals who came to shake hands with him. After he had performed this duty, which Mr. Orridge was of opinion might prove beneficial to the juvenile offenders in the prison, the procession to the scaffold was formed in the usual manner by the Under Sheriff and his attendants The Rev. W. Stocking, for whose attention the prisoner expressed himself most grateful, led the way, reading the commencement of the burial service—" I am the resurrection and the life ; whosoever believeth in me shall not die, but have everlasting life." In a few minutes afterwards the procession reached the door-way which opened to the scaffold, and Corder was placed upon the floor, which, when withdrawn, was to plunge him into eternity. The prospect from the place on which he stood is of the most beautiful description. The fore-ground consists of softly-swelling hills, bounded in the distance by extensive plantations, which form a sort of amphitheatre around the prison. But the loveliness of the scenery had for him no beauty; for the moment his eyes opened upon it they were to be closed for ever. After he was placed under the fatal beam, Mr. Orridge approached him, and asked whether he wished to address the multitude. He gave some indistinct answer, which we did not hear, and Mr. Orridge immediately said to the crowd, in a loud voice, " He acknowledges the justice of his sentence, and dies in peace with all mankind." The executioner then drew the cap over his face. The officer who supported him says, that he afterwards added, when quite unable to stand, " I deserve my fate; I have offended my God: may he have mercy on my soul!" Within a minute afterwards the deadly bolt was withdrawn, and he was cut off from the number of the living. The hangman, after the corpse had fallen, performed his disgusting but necessary task, of suspending his own weight around the body of the prisoner, to accelerate his death. At the same moment, the prisoner, who appeared to be in the last agonies, clasped his hands tighter together, as if he was forming his last prayer for the mercy and forgiveness of offended Heaven. Immediately afterwards his arms, which were raised a little, fell— the muscles appeared to relax—and his hands soon sunk down as low as their pinioned condition permitted. But life was not yet extinct; about eight minutes afterwards there was a heaving of the shoulders, a slight convulsion of the frame—an indistinct groan—and then all was still, and no further motion was observed.

The body, after hanging the usual time, was cut down and conveyed in a cart to the Shire-hall. It was placed on the table in the *Nisi Prius* Court; and after the crucial incision had been performed, and the outward integuments removed, was exposed to the gaze of the public. The exact stature of this guilty victim to public justice was five feet five inches, and the medical gentleman who performed the incision informed us, that for so small a man he was an extremely muscular subject. It was to be removed to the hospital the following morning, to be dissected and anatomized according to the sentence. A cast is to be taken from the features, and the head is to undergo a critical inspection by a physician of this town, in order that an account of it may be transmitted forthwith to the Phrenological Society. A galvanic battery has also been brought from Cambridge to perform experiments upon it.

It is an extraordinary fact, and certainly not to be accounted for on any principle of reason or common sense, that the rope with which Corder was hanged has become an article of arduous competition. We have been informed that it has been sold for a guinea an inch to the various parties who bade for it. We heard, in the course of the day, that several labouring men had walked thirty miles to witness the execution: the account appears extremely probable; for on our return to London, the road was lined for several miles with persons returning from this melancholy spectacle.

The following fact will give some idea of the intense interest which this trial has created in Bury and its vicinity. Though two booksellers in the town have each published reports of the trial, and have had their shops besieged by purchasers ever since its conclusion, five hundred copies of Knight and Lacey's edition of the trial were sold this day in Bury, within a few hours after their arrival from London.

Mrs. Corder (the mother of the deceased) has been so overcome by the disgrace which the misconduct of her son has brought upon her, that she has been for some time unable to leave her bed. Neither she nor her daughter held the slightest communication with Corder after his condemnation. His wife is, we understand, in Bury seriously indisposed. Corder wrote a letter to her this morning, shortly before the execution, of which we have just been favoured with a copy:—

" My life's loved companion,—I am now a-going to the fatal scaffold, and I have a lively hope of obtaining mercy and pardon for my numerous offences. May Heavens bless and protect you through this transitory vale of misery, and which, when we meet again, may it be in the regions of everlasting bliss. Adieu, my love, for ever adieu: in less than two hours I hope to be in Heaven.—My last prayer is, that God will endue you with patience, fortitude, and resignation to his will. Rest assured his wise Providence work all things together for good. The awful sentence which has been passed upon me, and which I am now summoned to answer, I confess is just, and I die in peace with all mankind, truly grateful for the kindnesses I have received from Mr. Orridge, and the religious instruction and consolation from the Rev. Mr. Stocking, who has promised to take my last words to you."

The above was written with pencil in a blank leaf at the end of a volume of *Blair's Sermons*, which appears to have been a gift of Mrs. Corder to her husband, from the following words on another leaf at the beginning of the book·—" Mary Corder to her husband W. Corder, a birthday present, June 22, 1828."

Corder attained his 24th year on the above day.

4 T

The warrant for Corder's execution differed slightly from the form m which all former warrants for the execution of murderers were drawn up. The alteration was made in consequence of a clause in Lord Landsdown's late Act for Malicious Injury to the Person. The old form of warrant merely ordered the body to be given to surgeons to be anatomised and dissected; the present form appoints the hospital at which such dissection shall take place. In this instance, the body was given to the hospital at this town.

The execution took place on the sout side of the prison, at tw ve o'clock precisely. A gateway was cut in the wall, through which the prisoner advanced to the fatal platform, along a stage erected for that purpose. Some of his fellow prisoners, who seem to think that life is a jest, and that death is nothing but a drunken sleep, have already cut a joke upon this door-way, by giving it the nickname of "Corder's eternal way."

LETTERS

SENT BY VARIOUS LADIES,

IN ANSWER TO

CORDER'S MATRIMONIAL ADVERTISEMENT.

SIR,

The perusal of your advertisement in the Sunday Times awakened a feeling of sympathy, as I also have been the subject of the chastening hand of Providence.

I do not reply for myself, but having the pleasure of knowing a young and amiable female, in her twenty-third year, and who is highly accomplished, it occurred to me, that she might prove a companion suited to ameliorate your present sorrows, and enliven your future prospects. You request real names and address; forgive me, Sir, if under the existing circumstances I withhold both, as I think it would be an infringement of the female delicacy, to avow them in the present stage of our correspondence. If you will favour me with an interview on Waterloo Bridge, *between* the hours of *three* and *four* on the afternoon of Wednesday next, I shall be able to communicate every particular to you: that you recognize me, it is necessary to say, that I shall wear a black silk dress, red shawl, and grey muff, claret-coloured bonnet, and black veil; our conversation *must* commence by your presenting me with this note. Believe me when I add, that I am perfectly serious, and have no other motive in addressing you than promoting the happiness of two young persons.

I am, Sir,
Yours very obediently

Monday Evening,
8 o'clock.

27*th*, 1828.

On taking up the paper this morning, your advertisement was the first thing that met my eye, and on seeing the word "Matrimony" I laughing said, a gentleman wants a wife, but I suppose he is still in greater want of money, otherwise he wishes to make himself warm this cold weather by laughing at the credulity of the female sex; yet surely no man of understanding can derive pleasure by making fools of those who are *by nature weak*, and entitled to protection and pity rather than ridicule. Having said all I had to say, I fetched a deep sigh, conscious, *I suppose, of my own defects*, and again looked at the paper without intending to do it. I read your advertisement through, and was not a little surprised on finishing it; for although there may be not be one word of truth, yet certainly it wears the resemblance of sincerity. If really your situation is what you have represented it to be, allow me, although a stranger, sincerely to sympathise with you; though young I have suffered much by unhappy differences in my own family, therefore can feel for others who endure the like misery.

I repeat, if your tale is true, upon my word I pity you : if it is a fiction, I hope my sex may be revenged by your being obliged, at some future period, to pass *a month—one month*, in a *house of discord*. But if this statement is indeed sincere, I hope ere long you may be enabled to regain peace and undisturbed tranquillity—that you may soon find a lady whose disposition may accord with what yours is said to be. For myself, I want not a home; I have every necessary and comfort, though not the superfluities of life, and am far from thinking that happiness is only the attendant on riches. I am content, and strive to make others happy; the great can do no more, and I with pleasure look forward to the day which I hope will introduce me to one who may possess some of those amiable qualities which the advertisement says belong to you. Do not hold up to ridicule those foibles which are constitutional in my sex : remember perfection is unattainable. Rather pity than condemn ; and, in return, I will wish you, whoever you may be, an the happiness you can wish yourself.

And I remain, &c.

<div align="center">~~~~~~~~</div>

Nov. 30*th*, 1827.

Sir,

If you will take the trouble to walk on the south side of Northampton-square, between the hours of twelve and one on Monday next, with a white pocket-handkerchief in your hand, I shall be there, and may perhaps have an interview with you; if my affection is engaged, your happiness will be the constant study o

~~~~~~~~~

Dec. 1st, 1827.

Sir,

In perusing the Times Paper of Nov. 25th, I observed your advertisement for a partner in the marriage life, where you say any *female of respectability*, who would study for domestic comforts, and willing to confide in you, led me to suppose that fortune was not your object, which induced me to make the application, though I must say *prudence* whispers it is contrary to the rules of decorum, and I believe this is the first time I have ever deviated from her precepts. I am a female of respectability, my father has been a very *respectable* tradesman and a man of good fortune, but Providence has now placed me in a more *humble situation;* I have had a good plain education, but no accomplishments. If I have been too presumptuous in addressing one who styles himself an independent gentleman and a man of honour, I trust *this will be buried in oblivion;* but should it be thought worthy of an answer, it much oblige

Your humble Servant.

P. S. Probably you might like a description of the writer of these lines;—she is of rather short stature, slight made, not handsome, dark complexion, dark hair and eyes, and one who has not wrote out of *impertinent* curiosity, but for particular reasons dare not sign her name in this; but if she have occasion to write a second, you may rely upon it being signed, should this be answered.

Direct for ——, Post Office.   To be left till called for.

~~~~~~~~~

Sir,

Having seen your advertisement in the Sunday Times Newspaper, I beg leave to reply to it; not from any impertinent curiosity, but from a wish that what I state may meet with your approbation. I am the daughter of a respectable tradesman; he is the only one of the family in business. I have a step-mother, and there is a second family, therefore, to prevent any disagreement amongst us, I have left my father's house, and am at this time earning my own living in one of the first establishments in ———— (not as a milliner or dress maker). My friends are kind enough to say that I possess a good temper, lively disposition, and as to appearance passable, not any pretension to beauty; with regard to property, all I ever expect to be mistress of will be a small income, left me by my mother; it is sufficient to keep me independent when I shall have the misfortune to lose my father, which I hope may be many years ere that event happens. My age is the same as your own, twenty-four; your being in affluent circumstances would not induce me to become your wife, unless I found your disposition and mine could agree, and that in every sense of the word I could love, honour, and obey, with pleasure and gratitude. I think I have said all that prudence will allow. I must add, I think it rather unfair for you to expect a respectable female would like to give her real name and address in the first letter she writes; for although your advertisement reads very fair, there may be *some little trick on your side;* but I am in earnest, and you may depend upon the greatest secrecy. Should what I have said meet your approbation, direct to me, post paid.

Monday Evening, Nov. 26th, 1827.

Sir,

By accident I saw your advertisement in the Sunday Times; its seeming honour and sincerity induced me to answer it. I feel I am guilty of an impropriety in doing so without the knowledge of my friends, but a disposition like the one you seem to possess, will pardon the indiscretion when you know the situation I am placed in. My father has received an offer from one whose disposition is in every respect the opposite of my own; I cannot accept it only by sacrificing every feeling of delicacy and affection, therefore I have taken the only means that presented of preventing the sacrifice of my own happiness, or the wishes of my friends. Your disposition seems one that would ensure the happiness of those who would entrust it to your care.

My friends and family connexions are respectable; my disposition is naturally candid and affectionate, and would make it the study of my life to add to the happiness of my friends. I am very young, not yet nineteen · perhaps that would be an objection. I have not, as you wished, signed my name, but if your intentions are honourable, and you wish to hear further particulars, a letter addressed A. B. to be left at the office till called for, will meet with every attention from

Your obedient Servant.

Nov. 27, 1827.

Nov. 26*th*, 1827.

SIR,

Seeing your advertisement again renewed, I feel inclined to take one step towards introducing you to my sister, one of the most amiable and excellent of human beings. As a preparatory step, I shall be happy in the honour of seeing you on Wednesday or Thursday morning next, at my office in ———.

Yours very respectfully

SIR,

On taking up the Newspaper of yesterday, and seeing the word *Matrimony,* induced me carefully to peruse the advertisement; and from the very affable and condescending manner in which you expressed yourself, appears to convince me that you mean to act honourable, and which has induced me to possess myself of sufficient courage, which requires a female to have to address a gentleman on so delicate and important a subject. My personal attractions I shall leave you to decide upon; my age is twenty-four, and I hope I am endowed with all those endearing qualities which is so essential to render a married life happy, assuring you that a private interview with you is most anxiously wished for; and the place I purpose meeting you to-morrow at twelve o'clock—I shall be walking towards ———, distinguished by wearing a black gown, with a scarlet shawl, and black bonnet, white handkerchief in my hand. If not convenient to-morrow, will be there the same hour Wednesday.

I remain,
Your most obedient Servant.

Sunday Evening.

SIR,

In reading the Sunday Times I find your advertisement for a wife, and in answer to it I beg to say, should you mean what you therein state, I shall expect hear from you.

Yours respectfully

—— Kent.

~~~~~~~~~~

OBSERVING your advertisement in the Morning Herald, I beg leave to state, if your intentions are serious and honourable, I shall be happy of a personal interview with you at ————, which is my house and address.

I am an orphan, twenty-two years of age, have been genteelly brought up and educated, understand the domestic concerns of a house, and qualified to make any person happy and comfortable. If this should meet your approbation and wishes, you will favour me by calling to-morrow, Nov. 30th, between the hours of *four* and *five:* be punctual, because all the other *hours* of the day I am engaged in business; you shall then know all particulars concerning myself and family.

Thursday Morning, Nov. 29th, 1827.

~~~~~~~~~~

SIR,

Your advertisement in the Sunday Times for this day was pointed out to me, and being a young person of respectable connexions, but without property or a home, I have not the opportunity of obtaining a suitable companion, and these circumstances will, I trust. offer an excuse for my making this application. I am at present, and have been for some time, a teacher in a respectable school at ————; and it is with the sanction of the lady I am now with that I address you, and she will, if you think proper to notice my letter, give you any requisite information respecting me, she is unwilling that I should give you her address, as her establishment is so well known, unless you think proper to reply to this. My age is two-and-twenty. Trusting to your honour and secrecy,

I am, Sir,

Your obedient Servant.

Address, Post-office.

SIR,

In answer to an advertisement in the Sunday Times, expressing your desire of being introduced to a female of domestic habits, and a disposition to ensure happiness in the marriage state, I beg leave to state I am of a retired and domestic character, having been always under the care of an amiable and prudent mother; I have a tolerable person, perhaps some beauty, nineteen years of age, good tempered, and of an affectionate disposition. I have resided in London about three years; my family is very respectable, but owing to some change in circumstances, my circle of acquaintance is very limited, therefore I have but little chance of forming an establishment; this has induced me to enter into a detail of my own qualifications,—a thing which is repugnant to my feelings.

I feel rather averse to giving my address upon a first communication, if you answer this application, and are serious in the professions you make, I shall not withhold it.

I remain, Sir,
Your obedient humble Servant,

Direct for

⁓⁓⁓⁓⁓

November 25th, 1827.

WHEN a female breaks through the rules of etiquette, justly prescribed for her sex, as a boundary which she must not pass without sacrificing some portion of that delicacy which ought to be her chief characteristic, it must be for some very urgent reason, such as *romantic* love, or a circumstance like the present; and in answering your advertisement, I feel that I am in some degree transgressing the law alluded to, and yet the novelty and sentiments of the advertisement itself, so entirely different from the language generally made use of (and which alone induced me to answer it), almost assure me that no improper advantage will be taken of the confidence I place in the honour of the writer; however, as you request that no person will write from motives of curiosity, I trust that no feeling of that nature actuated you in giving me this opportunity;—but enough of preface.

I need not describe my person, as, should an interview take place, you can judge for yourself; and for mental accomplishments, I am as much indebted to nature and good society, as to education; but from

4 U

my retired habits and present sphere of life, I flatter myself I should
be as well calculated to make a domestic man happy, and to enjoy the
social charms of domestic life, as if I had received the first *boarding
school* education, and mixed largely in the world of fashion.   My
prospects in life were once brilliant, but when misfortune with her
gloomy train of attendants surrounded my family, the scene changed;
but 1 have still some expectations, although, from the tenor of your
advertisement, I presume fortune is but a secondary consideration; a
companion only is wanted who would sympathize in all your joys or
griefs; one who would return kindness with kindness, love for love; and
as I perfectly know my own heart as far as regards those qualities, 1
do not flatter myself when I say that such a companion would I prove,
and where confidence was shown, the fullest would be returned ·
pardon the warmth of my expressions, nor think me forward in offering
them, as I am no giddy girl, nor am I a romantic *old maid*, but a
warm hearted, affectionate girl, whose age qualifies her to pass between
the two characters, being just turned twenty-one.   Excuse my saying
more on so delicate a subject; my family are of the highest respectability. References of course will be given and required. Waiting your
answer,

I remain, Sir,

Yours, very sincerely and respectfully

<div style="text-align:center">~~~~~~~~~</div>

Sir,

   As I was perusing yesterday's Times, I inadvertently cast my eye
on your advertisement, which I am induced to answer, not from a
motive of curiosity, but for this reason,—that from the general tenor of
its contents, it so much resembles my own fate, that I cannot help
thinking that our dispositions would in some measure be congenial to
each other, and I am very sure that time must glide on much more
agreeably when passed in the society of a tender and affectionate companion.   To convince you that I am of a respectable family, I will
give you a few particulars, which I hope and trust will be kept secret.
My father was a ————; I was left an orphan under the guardian-
ship of ————, who placed me at a school to be educated for a
governess, consequently, I have moved in society perhaps not inferior
to the rank you hold, but by a deviation from rectitude, which was

occasioned by the too easily listening to the flattery of one whose vows I foolishly believed to be true, I am entirely deserted by my family, and banished from society ; nevertheless, I flatter myself that I do not altogether merit such a fate, for I do assure you, that no one could have acted more prudently than I have done since the unfortunate circumstance happened, which has very much destroyed my peace of mind, but I still hope to see better days : I am two-and-twenty years of age, but have not the least pretension to beauty—quite the contrary. I have a sweet little girl, who is my greatest comfort; she is sixteen months old, and is beginning to prattle very prettily. I have no fortune whatever, but am supporting myself by needle-work at present, until I can meet with something more to my advantage. I mention these facts, that you may not be led into any error, for I should be extremely sorry to act with any duplicity towards any one, and I leave you to consider how far your generosity will extend to appreciate my wrongs, and excuse my past misconduct. I trust that upon acquaintance you would find that I possess qualities which may in some measure over-balance, or at least mitigate, those errors which were committed through an affection which I supposed to be mutual, and at the same time honourable, but, alas ! have found it quite the reverse. I can only add, that should you wish an interview, I am ready at any time to see you, either at my own abode, which you will find very respectable, or at any place you may appoint, appropriate with the circumstance ; and should I prove finally the female of your choice, you may rest assured that nothing should be wanted on my part towards the augmentation of your happiness, and to render your house comfortable.

I am, Sir,

Your humble Servant.

Mrs. ——

———————

Dec. 3rd, 1827.

Sir,

On perusing my paper for Nov. 25th, I observed an advertisement, the object of which appeared to be the obtaining a valuable partner. Now, I am not generally disposed to view advertisements of this description in a very favourable light, but on calmly observing this I felt a sort of sympathy, which could only have been imparted by the Disposer of all events. No doubt, ere this, you will naturally conclude that I am about to introduce myself, but this I assure you is not the case; it is an object more worthy your attention—an object, who I will not hesitate to say, would render that man happy above all others on whom she may bestow her heart, as well as hand. A more sincere friend I have never met with, and many a pang would it cost me to part with her, but it grieves my very soul to see one so delicate, and possessing so much sensibility, alone in the world. I have a brother, of whom I believe Heaven could witness there is not on earth, at least in my opinion, one more calculated for a partner; his person is elegant and prospects bright, and he idolizes her; repeatedly has he addressed her on the subject, but has unfortunately been repulsed. She has often told me she esteemed him for his worth, and were it possible I could love him with that degree of warmth of which I know I am capable of loving, I would bestow on him my heart and hand, but unfortunately for his happiness I cannot love him, for I will never deceive that man who is to be my partner for life. I will marry that man, and him only, whom I could prefer to every other; that man without whom the world will become a barren waste. She has had, to my knowledge, several offers of good settlements; but she has told me, when I have spoken to her on the subject, she could not account for it, but she had never yet seen that object whom she should feel justified in exchanging her present situation with, and added, O———I have a heart possessing too much sensibility to entrust it to the care of any man I have yet seen; recollect my happiness has once been sacrificed to parental authority. Perhaps you will be a little surprised when I tell you, this paragon of perfection is a widow of twenty-three years of age; she lives alone, with a female servant, and has the ——— business conducted for her by an assistant since her husband's decease, which has been about three years. He was a very handsome man, universally respected; he adored her: she was the faithful and domestic wife. He has observed to me, although he felt convinced he had only obtained her hand, her value was above all price; he was ill above twelve months, during which time I had, in common with many others, an opportunity of witnessing her unexampled kindness to him. Although at that time only twenty, she had the discretion of sixty, and were you only one week in her company you must adore her, if you possess a heart capable of loving one who has, in my estimation, everything calculated to make the marriage state a perfect Paradise. Her disposition is beyond everything excellent. She has property, but to what amount I am not aware.

.f you have any connexions with the —— of ——, you may know the unimpeached character of the family, as they have been well known to them from their earliest infancy. If you are still disengaged, and disposed to pay an early attention to this, you will find, should you succeed, that although a stranger to you has proved your best friend, as it regards the hand-writing, although you must plainly perceive it is an assumed one, should you ever have an opportunity to show it, for I should fear her recognizing it. I would not for the wealth of the Indies incur her displeasu e. Probably you will say the distance is too far, but what is distance to obtain an article so valuable? If you feel disposed to address her on the subject, direct Mrs. ——

Yours respectfully.

If the intention of the advertiser be truly such as stated in the advertisement, a young lady, without fortune, but of the highest respectability as to friends and connexions, would, from peculiar family arrangements, be induced to accept the honourable proposals of any gentleman of good moral character; but previous to any further communication on her part, must request a line from the advertiser (should he feel favourably inclined), with real name and address.

Sir,

In reply to your advertisement in the Sunday Times, Nov. 25th instant, I must confess, on perusing, I felt rather interested on your behalf; at the same time I am surprised a gentleman possessing so many good qualities, in addition to youth and fortune, should be under the necessity of adopting a mode so public; but there is some apology to be made after the reason you give. I am a young person without parents, possessing a small income; would of course have no objection to form an alliance with a gentleman of respectability, gifted with those desirable qualifications. With respect to myself, I have been well educated in the usual mode of polite education, music, &c., and seen a great deal of domestic life, that I flatter myself, having arrived at the age of twenty-five years, I am competent to fulfil the duties of a married life. I say nothing of my personal appearance, as I propose ocular demonstration. You must excuse my giving my real name and

address, as I feel rather reluctant, at the first, to comp y with your
Jequest. If you wish for an interview, you may direct to ————
                              I am, Sir,
                                        Yours respectfully.

                    ~~~~~~~~~~~

                                        Dec. 14*th,* 1827.

    Sɪʀ,

    In re-perusing your letter, it has since struck me you might perhaps
have expected an answer, although it does not fully express it in your
letter. Having so little knowledge of the person now addressed, I
judge you will think with me it must be a person devoid of feeling *that
could say YES* under such cirsumstances, though *we might be happy*
hereafter without being better acquainted. So much promised, I think
you will attach no blame to me, that part of your letter where it states
to give up all the *gaieties* of this world, and live in solitude, I do not
exactly comprehend; as to the *gaieties,* I have never been accustomed
to them, but confess I like the society of a few select friends, and cannot
entirely give them up. If this meets your approbation regarding
solitude, you are at liberty to treat further on the subject. Answer
this, direct as before.
                              Yours, &c.

                    ~~~~~~~~~~~

                                        Dec. 30*th,* 1827.

    Sɪʀ,

    Having been obliged to be out a great deal the last two or three days,
I was fearful your answer (if conveyed in the same manner the other
two were) might have fallen into other hands, as there are more persons
living in the house. At the receipt of your last I thought it was high
time to lay the whole proceedings (from beginning to end) before my
brother, who was *exceedingly angry* I had done such a thing, but
consented, as things had gone so far, to meet you any day you might
appoint, between the hours of four and six. I sincerely trust my not
answering your letter before has not been the means of anything serious
happening, as I should have been extremely sorry to have occasioned

such proceedings. Should have answered it before, but imagined I had said all I could, with prudence, in the other.

Yours, &c.

Signed by the same person as the last letter

~~~~~~~~~~~~

A young lady, (having yesterday perused an advertisement in the paper, inserted A. Z.) whose opinion coincides with his respecting the many happy marriages which have taken place through that medium, and who flatters herself, upon further acquaintance, that she will not be found deficient in those amiable qualities so essentially requisite to render the marriage state happy.

Further particulars may be obtained from———— respecting the lady and her place of residence.

Nov. 30*th*, 1827.

~~~~~~~~~~~~

Sir,

Your advertisement in the Times paper of yesterday has met my observation, and though I feel some repugnance in answering it, yet circumstances, I trust, will justify the measure. I must now inform you that I have been genteelly educated, that my connexions are very respectable; I have a widowed mother and only one surviving brother. Misfortunes of a painful and pecuniary nature have induced me to reside for the last three years with a lady, with whom I am treated as a daughter. My education, though genteel, has been quite of a domesticated nature, and I flatter myself that my disposition will not be found unamiable to any one with whom I might be disposed to form a permanent connexion. My friends are kind enough to consider my person pleasing, and my age does not exceed your own; you will, however, excuse my giving my name and address, as my ignorance of the party with whom I am corresponding leads to a similar feeling on my own part; and until I am acquainted with your name and residence, you must excuse my withholding my own. Should you be inclined to give them, address to ————

Nov. 26*th*, 1827.

Nov. 26th, 1827.

Sir,

Having perused your advertisement in the Sunday Times, I feel myself every way qualified to answer it; myself and friends being very respectable, being brought up in a domesticated and economical line of life. I have no property, nor have I any expectations whatever. My age is twenty-six.

Should this short epistle of myself meet your approbation, please to direct ————.

P. S. I shall observe the strictest secrecy and attention.

Sir,

As I am at present resident at ————, your advertisement did not meet my notice until this morning. Feelingly alive to the general received opinion of the impropriety of answering advertisements, I will for once swerve and reply to yours. You must at present excuse my giving you my address, as this letter is unknown to any one; and should we eventually become acquainted, I should not ever wish it known, even to my own family, the way the acquaintance was formed. My family and connexions are of the highest respectability and character, mine would bear the most rigid scrutiny. In person I am considered a pretty little figure. Hair nut-brown, blue eyes, not generally considered plain, my age nearly 25. My married friends have often told me I am calculated to make an amiable man truly happy; and without vanity I think I am, as I am cheerful, domestic, of good education and disposition, and have always mixed in good society. In a letter like this egotism must be pardoned.

Should you consider this deserving of consideration, as I trust you are a man of honour, and would not sport with the feelings of a young person of respectability; if you are serious on this subject, any farther communications you may require I will readily give; if you will direct a letter to me as under, I will call there Thursday and Saturday mornings. May I request your name, and if your residence is generally in London or in the country?

Tuesday, Nov. 27th.

Nov. 26th, 1827.

Sir,

Your advertisement, which appeared in the Sunday Times, I feel inclined to answer. If you really are inclined to marry, and all is true which you state, I think I am the person : my age is twenty-two, and am happy to say possess a most amiable disposition, can play the piano-forte, and sing tolerably well; also other accomplishments, which I think not worthy of statement. I have always been brought up domesticated, and am quite able to manage, let my situation be what it may; my wish is to settle in life, provided I meet with one who I think deserves such a wife as I shall make. If your intentions are honourable, you will not blame me for requesting your name and address. First, I am sure, if you do want a wife, that you will not lose a good one because she does not give it. If you send me yours, and a few more particulars, then I shall know how better to proceed. I am a young lady, now living in the town of ———— with my mother, and in a most respectable manner, are known and respected by all in it; therefore must say I should not like to expose myself and family to ridicule: should your advertisement be only for a joke, consequently it would, therefore I must request you to direct to ————. Write by return of post if possible, I shall send my servant for the letter, therefore pay the post if you please.

P. S. I have no fortune until the death of my mother.

~~~~~~~~~

Sir,

I was rather surprised, on perusing the Sunday Times, to see an advertisement from a gentleman whose age is the same as my own; it is strange that a person who possesses a fortune, as well as youth, &c. should have recourse to so novel a mode in order to obtain a wife; nevertheless, however odd or romantic it may appear, I agree with you there are many happy marriages accrue from the plan you have adopted.

I flatter myself I have a reasonable good disposition, with natural domestic habits, which we all know is a great essential in a connubial life.

As to personal attractions, I must decline giving a description, as a personal interview will suffice. I must quote your own words (honour

4 x

and secrecy relied on); notwithstanding I feel under the necessity, in this case, of noncomplying with your request, furnishing you at present with my address, &c., but as a substitute, I propose an interview, whenever it is convenient to have a walk. I should think Finsbury Square, or any other place in the vicinity of St. Paul's, which I leave to your option. An answer will oblige, directed to ———

Left at the Post Office.

I am, Sir,
Yours, &c.

P. S. I shall expect to hear from you by return of post, if possible.

~~~~~~~~~~~

SIR,

In answer to your advertisement in the Sunday Times, I take upon myself to say that, according to your statement, you will find me in every respect a desirable companion to make a wedded life comfortable, particularly as far as concerns domestic affairs, being a ——— daughter of respectability, and at present comfortably situated, but being aware at a future period the loss of a father will greatly alter my many comforts in a home, which makes me induced to say thus far. Should I be fortunate ever to meet with an agreeable and affectionate partner, I cannot say but I should certainly avail myself of the opportunity. I also would give you to understand I shall have no fortune till after my father's decease. It appears you are not a fortune-hunter: I trust the person who is destined to be my companion for life will never have cause to regret. Should the advertiser feel disposed to answer this letter, by directing to ———.

P. S. Or by inserting a few lines in the Sunday Times will meet the eye of ———.

~~~~~~~~~~~

Dec. 1st, 1827.

A YOUNG lady who is desirous of settling in a respectable situation of life, has seen A. Z.'s advertisement, but previous to giving her name, would be glad to hear from him, stating whether he is still entirely disengaged, as the advertisement has been out some days.

The lady thinks it rather unreasonable on the part of A. Z. to expect the "real name and address," at the same time withholding his own, as he must be aware that considerations of delicacy have, or ought to have, more weight with the female than the male part of the creation. The advertiser may feel assured that this letter is not written from impertinent motives, as the writer is really desirous of giving up the state of " single blessedness;" she is under his own age, possesses some accomplishments; has moved in a genteel sphere of life, with an irreproachable reputation, and is generally considered of an amiable disposition. Having been thus explicit, the lady thinks herself entitled to ask some further particulars of A. Z., who may (if he thinks proper to continue this correspondence) address a letter to L. G.

SIR,

The young lady who addresses you having seen your advertisement in the Times of last Sunday, and considering under all circumstances that a further acquaintance may not prove unfavourable, is desirous of augmenting it; but under the impression that some imposition may have been practised, must decline at present giving her name, except by initials; suffice it to say, that she is entirely uninfluenced, and at her own disposal, and her respectability will be better known than described. If A. Z. should consider this epistle worth attending to, and will address (post paid) to ———, he may depend on further communication from

His most respectfully.

Nov. 28th.

SIR,

Having seen an advertisement in the Times paper, wherein you wish for a respectable female of domestic habits for a partner for life, myself being disengaged, and of domestic habits, and having nothing but youth to recommend me, I take this opportunity to offer myself: if you think it worthy of your notice, a line addressed to ——— will be attended to.

A YOUNG lady, aged nineteen, most respectably connected, and considered truly amiable by all who know her, would have no objection to form a matrimonial alliance, should she meet with a gentleman (possessing the qualifications of A. Z.) on whom she could place her affections : until the lady has some assurance of the honour of A. Z.'s intentions, she cannot think of subscribing her real name and address, but should he deem this worthy of notice, a letter directed to ———— Post Office, ————, will be attended to.

~~~~~~~~~

Nov. 26*th,* 1827.

Sir,

As the marriage state may very properly be termed a lottery, I have at a hazard answered your advertisement in the Times paper of yesterday : to enter into particulars now would, I should conceive, be highly unnecessary, otherwise than I am respectably situated, with a mother ; my prospects, like many others in this life, have been greatly blighted, through the loss of a parent, but every satisfaction would be given in regard to connexions, should this bring forward an interview. To describe my person would be a vanity in myself, which I have never been taught to foster.   Depending on your honour as a gentleman, I have inserted my real address.

Miss —— ——.

~~~~~~~~~

Sir,

I beg to answer your advertisement of last Sunday, but *really think it nothing but a frolic ;* I know a charming young woman of *no property,* her friends *highly respectable,* nineteen years of age, exceedingly agreeable person, has had the charge of her parents' house these three years, and brought up by a truly amiable and virtuous mother.   I can with great truth say, the young lady is not aware of my answering your advertisement.   If you think proper, you may address a line to Mrs. ————.   I hope you will act honourably with regard to the name, as the writer is a married woman.   A friend will put this in the twopenny post.

Your obedient Servant.

The young lady has never been attached to any one, nor has she ever left her friends.

SIR,

Having read your advertisement in the paper of to-day, I have taken the liberty of answering it, for if you possess the good *qualities* you therein name, I certainly think you will make a *delightful* partner, consequently I shall expect to see or hear from you on Wednesday next, the 28th instant.

Yours respectfully.

Nov. 25, 1827.

~~~~~~~~~~

<div align="right">*Monday night.*</div>

SIR,

I read your advertisement on Sunday last, and have taken the first opportunity of answering it; if you are not in too much haste in settling your affairs, I should like to hold a correspondence with you, until we know each other better, if convenient to you, for there is more disgrace attached to me in answering anything in the newspaper, and more danger of my family becoming acquainted of my so doing; and if this does not meet your approbation, please to destroy this, and let nothing of it pass your lips; and if to the contrary, it must be by letter for a short time, until I can break it out to them. Please to write whether or no, and tell me how far you disapprove, for there is room in us all to improve. I shall be looking out for a letter at the latter end of the week, and hope that I shall meet no disappointment. Please direct your letter for ————, Post-office; to be left till called for (unpaid).

<div align="right">Good night in haste.—*Entre nous.*</div>

~~~~~~~~~~

A YOUNG lady, aged eighteen years, who flatters herself that her accomplishments, temper, and disposition, are calculated to be conducive to the happiness of such a person as A. Z. describes himself, confiding in his *honour* and *secrecy*, wishes to have an interview. A few lines, stating whether four o'clock to-morrow will be convenient to A. Z. for that purpose, will oblige.

Monday morning.

A YOUNG lady of respectability, who carefully perused A. Z.'s advertisement in the Sunday Times, feels confident she could meet the wishes of the advertiser, but does not feel authorized in stating real name and address, unless the gentleman will first favour her with his, as a sense of propriety, and not curiosity, dictates the request; secrecy may be relied on: an answer directed to E. A————, shall meet with every consideration, and a speedy acknowledgment.

26th November, 1827.

~~~~~~~~~~

SIR,

Having seen an advertisement in the Sunday Times, respecting an application for a female of respectability, I flatter myself I am competent to answer your expectations. As I am candid and honourable on my part, shall expect the same with secrecy on yours. If you think well, I should like to have an answer with your real name and address, previous to an interview. I rely on your honour, and subscribe myself

Your well-wisher.

November 25, 1827.

~~~~~~~~~~

SIR,

In answer to your advertisement of yesterday, I beg to inform you, that I am quite of your opinion, that many happy marriages have ensued by the same means resorted to by you. It is my earnest wish to meet with an agreeable companion, such as you represent yourself, and such I think to be essential to those in the married state; therefore, if you have not made your choice ere this, from the many answers which no doubt you have had, I shall be happy to hear further from you.

~~~~~~~~~~

SIR,

On perusing your advertisement in the Sunday Times, it immediately struck me that a merry-hearted, as well as an agreeable, companion might be necessary to your happiness in a wife, particularly as your spirits appear to be in a state of depression; if so, you may possibly find in your humble servant the identical little companion formed to constitute your felicity.

~~~~~~~~~~

November 26, 1827.

If the gentleman who inserted an advertisement in the Sunday Times, headed Matrimony, will call at —————, and ask to see Miss —————, between the hours of twelve and three, to-day, he may have an interview, when every other particular will be most candidly stated; should the advertiser look for accomplishments or beauty, an interview will be unnecessary.

~~~~~~~~~~

Monday morning.

Sir,

Trusting to the honour and secrecy mentioned in your insertion of yesterday, I take the liberty of stating in reply, my willingness to enter into the matrimonial engagement you propose, provided, on a personal interview, we should be mutually satisfied with each other. I am now in my nineteenth year, possessed of some personal attractions, together with a mild and domestic disposition; beyond this it might probably be deemed unbecoming to enter into further detail at the moment: I shall therefore conclude by assuring you of the respectability of my family and connexions, stating, at the same time, that as I have thought proper to answer your advertisement without their knowledge, I shall feel obliged, in the event of your considering it worth notice, by your addressing your communications to myself.

I am respectfully, Sir,

Your obedient humble Servant.

P.S.—I again repeat, that I put the fullest confidence in your honour and secrecy.

~~~~~~~~~~

22d December, 1827.

Sir,

Perusing your advertisement in the Sunday Times, for a partner, I have taken the liberty of addressing you. I must agree with you,

THE RED BARN.

that it is a strange way of forming a matrimonial connexion; however, from what you mention, I think there is a prospect of happiness. I should have no objection of forming a connexion of the kind, after a further explanation,—first, the respectability of your family and connexions, to what church you belong, &c. I am about twenty-three years of age, and I have the vanity to think that my person would please most men, and my disposition without a fault. I have, however, no fortune; but my family and connexions are very respectable. I have very near connexions high in the employ of the ——————— Company; in short, I could easily give you satisfactory references; my education has been liberal, and I flatter myself I am able to conduct myself in any company. You may, before this reaches you, be engaged; I shall therefore say nothing more on the subject without I hear from you in reply: if I am to be favoured with an answer, I beg it may be without delay.

I am, Sir,

Your humble Servant.

Sir,

In reply to your advertisement in the Sunday Times, I take the liberty of informing you I am of a respectable family; my papa having seen a reverse of fortune has occasioned my mamma to enter into a boarding house at ——————, which, if it meets your approbation, will thank you to call to-morrow evening, between four and five o'clock, as it will be the most likely time of seeing me. This being unknown to my parents, you had better come as if for boarding. I have a sister at home with me, who is twenty-one—my age is twenty-two. I must beg to excuse this bad writing, as it is done in fear.

Sir,

Seeing your advertisement of the 25th instant, and wishing to know if you really are serious in your intentions, I have taken the liberty of addressing you on the subject. As you did not mention anything concerning property, I will candidly inform you, I am not in possession of any at present, but in expectation of some at a future period : you merely said you wished for a domestic partner; as such I intrude on your notice, trusting to time to discover what good qualities I possess.   I hope you will not attribute this to vanity on my side, as I assure you I am actuated by a far better motive : but at the same time, I must confess I have not sufficient confidence to give you my address, so for the present you must excuse me.   If you answer this, please to direct —————————, to be left at the Post-office till called for.

Monday morning, 12 *o'clock*.

Sir,

Having read your advertisement of the 25th, I cannot but acknowledge myself desirous of forming a connexion with a person possessing your qualifications.   As I cannot presume I am all you could wish, (yet feeling a particular interest in you), I beg you will appoint an interview, which will enable you to judge more competently than anything I could advance.   Address—————.

Should you not notice this, accept my sincere wish that you may meet with one deserving you.

P.S.   As the above is my real name and address, I fully rely on your honour.

Sunday evening.

Nov. 26th, 1827.

Sir,

I have taken the earliest opportunity of addressing you with these few lines.   According to your advertisement, as you being the age that will suit me, twenty-four, and I am eighteen, so I think that Providence as ordained that you and me shood come together, for I

4 Y

90

am not very pleaentury situated myself, and it appears that you are not. I am o very cheerful disposition, and shood study every thing for your comfort and happiness. If it will suit you, the most convenient time to se me will be at o eleven o'clock in the morning, and at three in the afternoon. If I do not see you in a day or two, I shall think that you are suited.

Till then Adieu.

HAVING taken up the Sunday Times, I see Matrimony at the head of the paper; should the advertiser be sincere and honourable, he will meet with a lady of respectability (but not of fortune), one of very domestic habits, having been brought up by a dear and tender parent. Should the gentleman approve of this epistle, the lady will in her next note give her real name and address, and by giving her a line, post paid, to ————, she will return an answer as soon as possible.

THE advertisement of a private gentleman, aged twenty-four, in the Sunday Times paper, happened to meet the eye of a young lady, just twenty-one, of the greatest respectability. The advertisement rather struck her; and should the gentleman be really in earnest, he must advertise once again in the same paper, when he will hear further particulars. But the extreme modesty of the lady will not allow her to put either name or address; the lady is at present in the country, wil shortly be in town.

N. B. The lady is not very handsome.

SIR,

Having read an advertisement in the Sunday Times, headed Matrimony, and having duly considered every particular connected with it, I am induced to answer the applieation, not as an idle person, but as one who feels somewhat qualified to render the marriage state desirable. No mention having been made with respect to personal attractions, or pecuniary circumstances, I shall decline saying anything concerning them, as the former depends entirely on taste, the other will be explained, either on an interview or a second correspondence. It is to be hoped that the gentleman's intentions are of an honourable nature, as advertisements have been put in papers similar to the one in question, merely to sport with the feelings of the female sex.

Should you think this worthy of attention, a letter addressed ——— will meet

Sir, yours, &c.

Wednesday Morning,
  Nov. 28th.

————

28th Nov. 1827.

Sir,

Having accidentally taken up the Sunday Times of the 25th inst. I was much struck with the nature of your advertisement, which certainly appears to me rather extraordinary; however, as I have no reason to doubt you are not what you represent yourself to be, I have no hesitation in reply of saying, I am one who possesses every qualification calculated to render the object of my choice happy. You will excuse, Sir, my not being explicit, but at present I consider it quite unnecessary.

Should you think these few lines worthy your notice, I shall expect you will favour me with real name and address, as well as any particular you may conceive likely to establish confidence.

I am, Sir,
Your obedient Servant.

Address —, Post Office.

————

Sir,

Having read your advertisement in the Sunday Times, I feel induced to answer it, being desirous of engaging myself to you. I suppose we must be candid in such cases. I am a third daughter of a clergyman of the Church of England, who has eight children, therefore you may imagine that I can have no fortune; my age is twenty-one. I can give the most unexceptionable reference to character, &c. I shall not be more explicit at present.   Direct to ———.

Sunday, Nov. 25th.

~~~~~~~~~~

SIR,

In answer to your advertisement, I take the liberty of thus addressing you, stating, that I am a young widow lady, with no family, and quite competent to make the marriage state happy.   Should this meet your approbation, letters to be left, post paid, at ———.

~~~~~~~~~~

SIR,

As I am not in the habit of trumpeting forth my own praises, I can say little on the subject of merits, or personal charms; but if I may give any credit to the opinions of friends, I am possessed of those requisites so essentially necessary to constitute the happiness of married state; you however, I trust, it serious, may have an opportunity, if you think proper, to judge for yourself.   If you have not made your choice I shall be happy to hear from you immediately.

~~~~~~~~~~

——— has seen the advertisement inserted by A. Z. in the Sunday Times of the 25th; she is a *widow*, and as that may be an objection, she writes to ascertain that point before she gives her name and address, or enters into particulars.   If A. Z. has any communication to make, it must be done through the Twopenny Post Office at Craig's Court, Charing Cross.

Nov. 26th, 1827.

THE END.